OF SAND AND SNOW

BRYCE O'CONNOR

Of Sand and Snow

Book Five of *The Wings of War* series

Bryce O'Connor

ISBN: 978-0-9991920-1-6

Edited by Shawn Sharrah and Caroline Hosek
Map by Bryce O'Connor
Cover Art by Andreas Zafiratos
Cover Design by Bryce O'Connor & Andreas Zafiratos
Ebook Interior Design & Formatting by Bryce O'Connor

"No," Raz snarled, taking a half-step closer to Saresh, backing the šef up to the very edge of the roof. "What we have a right to is *life*. One where hardship comes as it wills, but with every opportunity to overcome it. What sort of madness permits you to think the Moon and Her Stars will look favorably down upon you, given the path you've walked?"

The old woman shrugged. "The same madness, perhaps, that makes you believe you know what it is They seek to draw from Their faithful." Her face hardened. "If you know Their prayers, then you must be a believer, Monster. That disappoints me. I would have thought someone like you might understand that death and belief often come hand-in-hand."

Raz felt a chill, hearing those words, and he had to struggle not to look over his shoulder at where he knew Syrah undoubtedly still stood under the shade by the stairs. They rang like an echo, reminding him of something she'd once told him, when the pillars of her understandings regarding her own god had only just started to crack.

I think that I serve a god of death as much as I serve a god of life, she'd said.

He'd replied by saying that one cannot exist without the other.

Still… Saresh's interpretation was an altogether darker understanding.

"Saying they come hand-in-hand does not mean they follow the same path," Raz snarled. "You are using faith as an excuse for death, when death should be used as a reason for faith. You shame those of us who entreat Them for the strength to do what we must for the betterment of all."

"'Do what we must'?" Saresh repeated with a derisive snort, meeting his gaze evenly. "Who is using excuses now, Arro? Who is about to murder an old woman who hasn't even been given a blade to defend herself with? Who started this war with the rings? Do you *truly* think your hands are less bloody than my own? Do you *truly* think—?!"

Sching.

The gladius rang like a hand bell as it cleaved through air and flesh, flashing across Raz's body in a silvery arc to slash open the šef's throat from collar to collar. Before the crone could stagger back off the edge, though, Raz's other hand shot out, grabbing her by the rope noose still wound about her neck. Saresh coughed and hacked as he heaved her to him, crimson bubbling and streaming from her cracked lips. More spilled from the grisly wound that had cut into her windpipe, painting the steel and leather of Raz's gauntlet a gleaming red in the light of the morning Sun.

"The *amount* of blood—" Raz heard the venom in his own voice as he hissed into the dying woman's face "—matters little. It's all dependent on *whose* blood it is, and *why* it was shed." He pressed her back, tilting her over the open drop beyond the edge of the roof. "Reason weighs in all things, death and faith included. I am not innocent, but when the time comes for the Moon to lift *me* up, I trust the lives taken at my hands will weigh less than those stolen by yours."

Then, as Saresh began to convulse from shock, he let go.

The citizens of Dynec gave a final exalted cheer below as the third rope snapped taut.

BOOKS BY BRYCE O'CONNOR

The Wings of War Series

Child of the Daystar

The Warring Son

Winter's King

As Iron Falls

Of Sand and Snow

The Shattered Reigns

A Mark of Kings

For, in no particular order:

Ashley Carlino
Jim Salviski
Meredith Guinto
Cara Reindl
Mike Tosch
Mike Shone
Clark Rasmussen
Jonathan Schwandt

and everyone else who makes SPOT cowork
an absolute blast to be a part of.

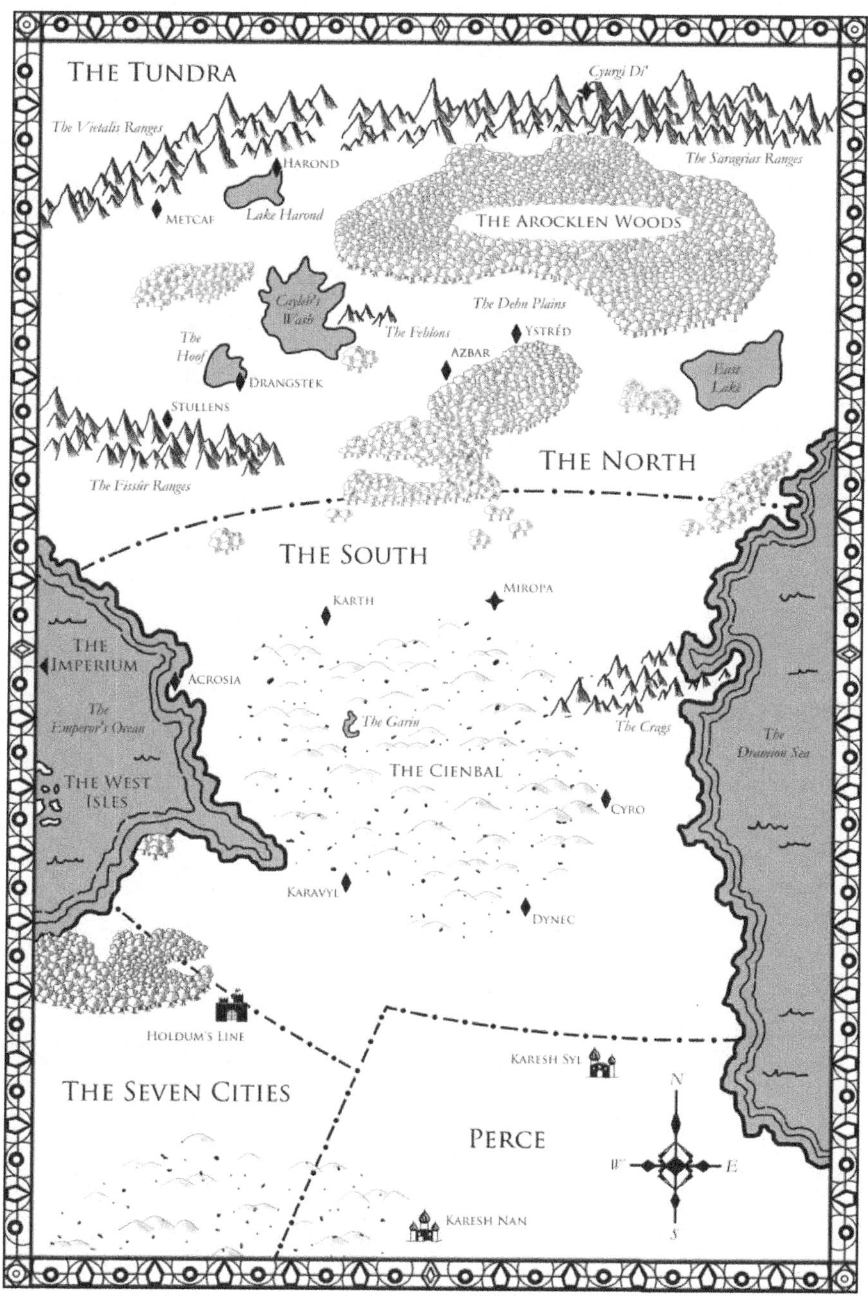
THE TUNDRA
The Vietalis Ranges
The Saragrias Ranges
HAROND
METCAF
Lake Harond
THE AROCKLEN WOODS
The Dehn Plains
The Feblons
YSTRÉD
AZBAR
The Hoof
DRANGSTEK
STULLENS
The Fissûr Ranges
THE NORTH
THE SOUTH
KARTH
MIROPA
THE IMPERIUM
ACROSIA
The Emperor's Ocean
The Garin
The Crags
The Dramion Sea
THE CIENBAL
THE WEST ISLES
CYRO
KARAVYL
DYNEC
HOLDUM'S LINE
KARESH SYL
THE SEVEN CITIES
PERCE
N
W
E
S
KARESH NAN

PART I

PROLOGUE

862 v.S.

"I do not think that I ever paused, then, to wonder if I might have been in the presence of a monster…"

Serys Benth, Karavyl šef, to Ahthys Borne of Acrosia

How quickly things change, Serys thought to herself, stepping out of the carriage as Eshed, the captain of their retinue, offered her his calloused hand in assistance. When her sandaled feet reached the swept cobblestone of the market way, she looked around, wondering what it was she was feeling. Outwardly, there was little different about the marble and granite buildings which rose on either side of her, the façade of the city itself unaffected by the darker churnings that had taken over its depths in the last year. The square behind their comfortable coach was as busy as ever, the bustle of the morning crowd doing much to drown out the cries from the infamous Cages Serys knew rose up in the center of the plaza. The dawn Sun was at her back, illuminating the street before her, and nothing appeared out of place in the glistening windows and overhanging balconies from which strands of brown and green vines hung, their resilient flowers a splash of color against the stone. The area seemed a popular quarter of residence for the wealthier middle class, likely merchants and traders who did well for themselves in the bazaar, but were yet far from the dream of an estate in the extravagant quarters to the east.

Yes, on the outside, nothing had changed.

And yet, as Serys took a step forward in order to allow her travelling companions to be helped out of the wagon in turn, she could still feel the difference in the subtle aura of the city.

It hadn't been so long since her last visit to Miropa. When word reached Karavyl that Imaneal Evony, Ergoin Sass, and the rest of their comrades had been butchered by the Monster of Karth, Serys and other representatives of the Mahsadën had rushed to the Gem of the South from each of the fringe cities, fearing what would happen if the society lost control of the largest municipality in the realm. They'd anticipated the worst, steeling themselves one and all to gather what was left of the former šef's networks and crush whatever dissent could have festered as their hand slipped from Miropa's throat. It had been surprising, therefore, to discover upon their arrival none of the expected chaos and civil unrest.

Rather, in the weeks following the death of the old masters of the Mahsadën, a new power had risen to take the reins of the city, a power Serys didn't know whether to respect, scorn, or fear.

That's what I'm feeling... she thought as she heard San Loreyn step down to the street and stretch with a groan behind her. *That's what's changed...*

She was sure of it. There was something lurking there, in the heavy presence of the buildings and alleys. Something unseen, but distinct in its attendance. There was a stillness to the Miropan streets which had been absent on any of her previous visits, a somberness to the shouting of the merchants and the rumble of their clientele. She shivered suddenly as a rare cloud passed over the Sun, wondering why the desert breeze—ordinarily so warm—gave her the impression of the winter winds she'd known as a child, living as a borderer in the thinner forests between the Northern and Southern lands.

"Carriages," San muttered, and Serys looked over her shoulder to see the Southerner using a hand to fan his thin, sweating cheeks with a disgruntled expression. "Damn things will be the death of me. Why couldn't we just ride our own horses?"

"Because a pompous trim like you wouldn't survive half-a-day in the Cienbal left to your own devices," Analla Zaren answered flatly, not even looking at the šef as she stepped from the carriage after accepting Eshed's hand with a charming smile. "I don't imagine we would have managed more than an hour's ride before you either passed out from the heat or insisted we take the long way around the desert."

San puffed out his chest indignantly, whirling on the Percian girl, his sleek brown hair seeming almost to bristle in offense.

"I tire of your insolence!" he snarled while Analla dusted her skirts off daintily, her smile turning sour in her dark features as she met the man's eye. "I should have you whipped on our return! Serys!" San turned to Serys, one hand pointing at the girl like a child wailing to his mother. "Rein in your wench!"

"Analla merely voices our shared thoughts, San," Serys told him coolly, paying him only the faintest of minds while she continued to examine the details of the buildings walling the street before them. "Give me reason to think her deductions inaccurate, and I'll order her flogged myself."

San deflated at once, his pointed finger going limp, and he seemed to shrink in on himself. In a clear attempt to change the subject, he instead turned to the nearest soldier, one of their Miropan guard that made up half their twelve-count escort.

"Is this the place?"

"Near, sir." The man indicated the cobbled lane with a leather-gloved hand, the other on the wire-bound hilt of his sword. "The road narrows ahead, so we'll be walking a short ways."

San nodded haughtily, and the soldier started forward at once, his fellows falling in at his sides. Serys, San, and Analla's own guards closed in behind them, and together the group moved to follow. They clearly didn't have far to go, but in that time Analla caught up to Serys and hooked a slender arm into hers, leaning in like they were two women gossiping about which of the men-at-arms they found most appealing.

"Do you feel that?" the girl asked softly, her ebony eyes shifting over the buildings' faces around them even as she held the façade of a simpering smile that would have fooled anyone who happened to glance at her.

Serys nodded briefly, but it was a moment before she responded, taking in the shadows of the narrow alleys they passed.

"I do," she answered softly. "And it concerns me…"

"There are rumors," Analla said, and Serys detected what might have been a note of apprehension in her attendant's voice. "About Blaeth. They say he's—"

"I'm familiar with what 'they say'," Serys cut her off gently just as the Miropan guard at their head halted before a narrow set of stairs, its worn steps leading up to the front door of an old timber structure. "Though I'm not so sure they're merely 'rumors'…"

Analla looked like she wanted to say something more at that, but bit her tongue when the soldiers parted and turned, half-bowing while the man at their head gestured to the building before them.

"This is where we leave you. Your retinue as well, I'm afraid. No one but yourselves are allowed within, along with a few handpicked sentries."

"Nonsense," San challenged the officer irritably. "We will take our soldiers with us. Do you truly expect us to—?"

"Eshed." Serys cut the other šef off, looking not at San but instead to the captain of their own retinue. "Wait here. I don't know how long we'll be."

Eshed, a weathered Southerner with a scar down one side of his neck, nodded at once, and with a quick word had the rest of his men fall in line with the Miropan guard. As San spluttered and tripped over half-formed complaints, Serys unhooked her arm from Analla and lifted her folds of her dress, starting the short climb up the stairs.

The building was a surprisingly plain thing, a lumbering structure of timber and brick that would have appeared utterly ordinary had it not been for the dozen guards and their charges gathered about its entrance. Indeed, from the corner of her eye Serys saw several passersby glancing curiously in their direction, as though wondering what such finely-dressed strangers were doing visiting a place like this.

Clever, she thought to herself, reaching up and knocking on the heavy wooden door at the head of the steps. Stepping back, she made a mental note to query after what sort of inconspicuous estates might be had for the rings once she returned home.

After a brief delay there was a *clunk* of a latch being lifted, and the door cracked open. A single grey eye peered at them through the gap, silently taking Serys, San, and Analla in for a full three seconds before the man spoke.

"Whom do you represent?"

"Karavyl," Serys replied in short.

The sentry scrutinized her one last time, and Serys was impressed by the utter indifference of his gaze. She was perhaps not as beautiful as she had been in the absolute prime of her youth some decade prior, but it was rare to find a man whose look didn't at least linger on her hazel-blue eyes, the stretch of her bust, or the slenderness of her waist. She might even have taken offense, except for the emptiness that weighed heavy in his expression. It wasn't the hollow sort of loss she'd seen in the slaves they sent to the Seven Cities, or in the Cages in the market plaza down the road. Rather, it seemed instead to be a removal of desire, an utter absence of emotion.

With a *creak* of wood, the man pulled the door open, revealing himself. He was a slender figure, garbed in grey and black fabrics that fell loosely over his body. A scarf hung limp about his neck—of the kind soldiers wore to keep the blowing sands out of their noses and mouths—and his features were plain but hard. He gave Serys the impression of a sandcat, still and patient, but ready for any opportunity to strike when the moment came.

Something tugged at her gut, and she realized it had been a long time since any man had elicited such unease in her.

"Follow me," the figure instructed them curtly, turning his back to the entrance and starting down the hall beyond the threshold. After a quick exchange of looks, the three of them did as they were told, Analla shutting the door again behind them with a creaking *thud.*

The *inside* of the building, Serys discovered, was much more along the lines of what she expected from a secret meeting place of the South's most powerful individuals. The hall was cavernous, opening into the second story with arched supports holding up walkways that encircled the high walls overhead. A thick red carpet lined the marble floor beneath their feet, muting their footsteps as they hurried to follow their silent escort, and delicate sculptures before every column complimented the frescoes that hung between and beyond the pillars. As Serys looked around, her nerves tingled again when she noticed other figures, half-hidden in the nooks and corners of the room. They, like the man leading them toward a wide granite stairway at the back of the building, were garbed in grey and black, and watched the three of them pass with the same devoid expressions. She did her best to ignore them, and was grateful when San and Analla did the same, though she heard the former offer a brief prayer to the Sun, asking that he be allowed to see the sky again.

They reached the stairs, and their guide took them up rapidly, forcing Serys to hitch her dress even higher as she trailed him. They managed one flight, then another, then finally a third which led them to the top floor of the structure. The man stopped when they made the final landing, stepping aside and allowing Serys, San, and Analla to catch up.

"They expect you within," he told them, waving at a pair of carved wooden doors opposite them. "You are the last to arrive, so I imagine they wait for you with some anticipation."

Serys almost smirked at that, wondering if this was his bland way of saying they should hurry.

Then the man was gone, making back down the stairs before any of them even had a chance to offer a word of thanks.

Serys took a breath and stepped forward. The doors were unobtrusive, mildly ornamented with spiraled carvings for flair, but there were some curiosities in the stone frame they'd been set in. Empty holes in the mortar stood out, where steel nails might once have been chiseled into the rock. What's more, the iron and wood casting of the right door looked newer compared to the left, and the hinges showed little tarnish.

This has been kicked in before, Serys realized, one brow rising unbidden in curiosity. *What sort of place have we been gathered in…?*

There was a polite, quiet cough which brought the woman to her senses. She glanced around to give Analla a small smile of thanks, then stood straight and flattened the folds of her skirts she'd wrinkled in the climb. There were voices beyond the door, she realized, a droning buzz of anxious conversation.

Gathering her wits, Serys cleared her throat, then knocked.

A scrape of a chair on stone, chased by the quick patter of feet. Another *clunk* came as the handle was lifted, and the door swung open, revealing a nervous-looking youth with long blond hair and brown eyes. Before Serys could get a word in, the young attendant stepped away quickly, revealing the room beyond as he waved them in with a wavering hand.

Serys prided herself on her nerves. She'd risen from her place on the streets of Dynec, surviving as a whore after her bastard of an uncle sold her to a passing merchant caravan following the death of her parents. She'd clawed her way up from the depths of hell over the next fifteen years, pushing her will past the rapes and abuse and violence which had been a part of her life for too long. When she set her mind to it, Serys could handle anything the world sought to throw at her.

Even she, though, felt those iron nerves strain when she stepped through the door and into the room beyond.

The chamber, while airy, was clearly not designed to board so many delegates at once. A wide, circular table took up much of the center space, around which some score of individuals were gathered, a mix of faces both familiar and new. Another twenty—the šef's aides—lined the edges of the room, most sitting in provided chairs while the unlucky remainders stood to watch the middle group with varying levels of excitement and unease. Light poured in through a set of wide, diamond-paned windows cut into the west wall, and the floor was polished stone. As she approached the last empty seat at the table, Serys noted—despite the tension of the situation—more oddities about the chamber. Here were scratches and broken chunks in the rock of the floor and walls. There were gashes and wounds in the wooden surface of the table. Even one of the windows looked newer than the others, like the iron wiring and glass had been replaced not so long ago.

Serys knew, as she took a seat in the last chair available in the center of the room—San coming to stand over her shoulder and Analla moving to join the other confidants along the wall—that there was a history to this place, and she had a nasty feeling she would be intimately acquainted with it before this meeting adjourned.

"Welcome, Serys Benth, San Loreyn," an even voice spoke up, ending the quiet. "With Karavyl's representation present, we can begin."

Among the šef gathered all about her, Serys was relieved to see she was at least passingly familiar with the majority. Acrosia, the South's wealthiest province after Miropa, had sent four delegates—half the ranks of their Mahsadën—while most of the other cities—Cyro and Dynec, as well as Karavyl—had sent pairs and trios. Only Karth had dispatched a single representative, a wiry, bored-looking borderer Serys didn't know, which hardly surprised her. Not surprising. In addition to being of greatest disrepute, Karth was the most volatile of the fringe cities, the titles of "šef" changing hands more frequently than a cheap streetwalker when those who took on the roles were either forced out or vanished mysteriously every other year or so. *This* character was of an even lower standard than what she'd come to typically expect from Karth, and Serys grimaced distastefully at the man as he gave her an oily smile from behind lank strands of surprisingly dark hair for a Southerner.

Her attention, fortunately, was quickly diverted away, drawn to the figure who had greeted her.

Sitting slightly separated from the others around the table, Adrion Blaeth took her in with eyes the color of rain-splattered slate. His gaze was inscrutable, his expression lingering in a partial smile that always made it hard for Serys to tell if the man was pleased to see her, or if he was wondering what the most entertaining way to separate her head from her shoulders might be. He was a handsome youth, likely not having yet seen thirty summers, with bleached-blond hair bound in a tail at the nape of his neck and a matching blond goatee trimmed to perfection. He wore a cut tunic of red and gold, the complementary clothes making him satisfyingly pleasing to the eye when he was seated.

If he stood up, though, Serys knew the man would take up the black wooden cane, capped with gold details, which rested against the right side of his chair, betraying the missing leg that rumors said he had lost to some desert beast in his youth.

On Blaeth's other side hovered a figure that made the presence of Miropa's only šef all the more intriguing. A woman of average height and slim proportions lingered by his left arm, one hand resting suggestively on the Miropan's shoulder. She was a Northerner, her skin tanned several shades lighter than most anyone else's in the room, and her blue eyes cut like diamonds as they met Serys'. An odd scar swept across her face in an X-shape pattern, originating from a circle about her right eye, a pattern Serys assumed likely to be a ceremonial label, maybe even some sort of brand. She wore a simple vestment of dark silks that came just short of being transparent. If Serys had not been studying the woman herself, she was sure she could have caught any number of the men gathered about the table eyeing the suggestion of cleavage and the sensual curve of lithe legs and a narrow waist beneath the cloth. She'd seen the woman before, as it was, at the announcement that Blaeth had single-handedly brought the torn remnants of the Miropan Mahsadën to heel. At that time, the stranger had been a simpering figure, doting over the new šef from her place at his right hand as he'd taken the seat which had once been Imaneal Evony's. Serys had thought little of her, then.

Now, though, bearing witness to the woman's confident smile as she stood over her master, Serys felt that pull again, the troublesome sensation she'd experienced upon exiting the carriage outside, telling her something deeper and darker was wrong in this city than the issue they'd gathered to discuss.

"Apologies for our delay," Serys finally responded to Blaeth with a penitent bob of her head in the man's direction. "Our retinue had not anticipated the traffic of the morning markets. I hope you haven't waited long."

Blaeth shrugged in an uninterested fashion, reclining in his chair to lounge against its back and arms. "It's of little import. What matters is that you all arrived safely, and in time to address the problem at hand."

"The Monster."

It was Elon Marst who braved saying the name first, and all eyes turned to him. One of the šef of Dynec, the southernmost of the fringe cities, the old borderer was generally known for keeping a level head and an even temper, particularly in business negotiations. Serys had had several prior dealings with him—Karavyl being closest in proximity to Dynec, apart from Cyro—and was therefore taken aback when she found Marst sitting rigidly in his chair, fists clenched on the table before him. The two šef over his shoulders—a man and woman pair of West Islers she did not know, though it looked like they could have been siblings—seemed equally tense.

"Indeed," Blaeth said with a curt nod toward Marst, giving no indication that he'd taken note of the man's obvious stress. "Raz i'Syul Arro. I'm sure, at this point, you're all aware of the happenings in Perce."

A chill fell over the room, though not a single voice spoke up. Of course they'd all heard. Word had been quick in arriving, at first carried as gossip and hearsay by travelers and merchant caravans, then officially by birds from the few surviving Mahsadën agents who'd been stationed in the city-states nation to the far southeast.

Finally, when refugees comprising of the former nobility of Karesh Syl had started to turn up at the gates of Dynec and Karavyl, there'd been no further denying of the truth.

Perce had fallen.

"I'm pleased to see I don't need to catch anyone up on the situation." Blaeth's dark grey eyes moved across the šef one after the other, gauging their reactions. "As you were summoned immediately following all this, though, I have graver news that may surprise most of you." As he said this, his gaze lingered on Elon Marst, like he was sizing up the Dynec delegation. "As of three weeks ago, Arro swung his army north. For most of the past month, he has been marching back up through Perce."

For almost a full five seconds, absolute silence held firm over the chamber. Most gawked at Blaeth, as though not comprehending his words, while others—including Serys—turned back to Elon Marst, suddenly understanding the man's apparent anxiety.

Dynec. The most southern of the fringe cities. A thriving economy largely due to the trade it did with Perce, formerly being closest in proximity to what had been Karesh Syl and Karesh Nan.

All at once, a dozen voices exploded together.

"He's *WHAT*?!" the unknown šef of Karth demanded, brown eyes wide with surprise.

"Three weeks ago?!" Ysera Ma'het, a Percian woman with a patch over one eye, called out from where the delegates of Cyro sat and stood. "How near is he to our borders?!"

"How many at his disposal?" Ahthys Borne—an aging former general of the Imperium who now worked as the šef in charge of Acrosia's land and sea forces—spoke up firmly. "What sort of men does the Monster command?"

As more began to shout out their questions and denials, Blaeth raised a hand for silence. Serys, who'd held her tongue, witnessed in amazement as the room stilled quickly. The fact that Blaeth had sway over all of Miropa alone, without the checks and balances of multiple ringleaders that had sustained the Mahsadën so well over most of the last decade, already bothered her.

Now, seeing the šef of the *other* cities bend too easily to even his silent command, Serys felt that unease bloom into something far more alarming.

"I will answer all your questions, given the opportunity," Blaeth said calmly, his gaze turning to Ahthys Borne, who'd taken to his feet among the other Acrosian representatives. "First, as to your concerns, Borne: Arro has an estimated fifty thousand under his control, including fifteen hundred cavalry."

"Fifty?" the former general hissed in disbelief. "*Fifty* thousand? Impossible."

"Oh, on the contrary," Blaeth answered with a solemn shake of his head. "*Very* possible. The army comprises vastly of freedmen from the Percian states of Karesh Syl and Karesh Nan. He took the first overnight, apparently, and the latter fell to an original force of thirty thousand, swelling as a result."

"Slaves," Borne murmured, sounding like he was turning this information over in his head. "That's a silver lining, at least... Soldiers require training. Discipline."

"They're receiving it," Amthel Oren, another of Dynec's šef, snarled in response to this. "Maltus Ameen oversees the security of our city, and has been sending us word via rider and bird as we traveled. The troops are being trained on the march by Arro himself, as well as several hundred former soldiers that happen to be among their number. It's slowed their progress, but they will have crossed into the South by now, and are still advancing toward Dynec even as we speak."

"Does the Monster intend to strike at the fringe cities?" the other representative of Cyro—a Southern woman Serys didn't know—asked in disbelief.

"No," a cool, pleasant voice came in answer. "He intends to strike at *us*."

Everyone turned toward Blaeth, though it wasn't the man who'd spoken. The response had come instead from the woman still standing over his shoulder, her smile easy and unwavering despite twenty of the South's most powerful—and often cruel—staring her down.

Serys—like many of the others, she was sure—felt a seething anger rise up at the disrespect of this stranger's sudden intrusion, but she bit back her words. For one thing she trusted the less-restrained among them to raise a voice for her, but something else stilled her tongue just as well. In general Serys had a talent for gauging people, men and women alike. It came from more than a decade of serving the needs of the former, then years of molding the latter into tools for the pleasure houses she ran in Karavyl. For this reason Serys was loathe to admit that she was starting to fear she'd pegged the woman wrong, the first time she had met her. Then, Serys had assumed her to be some passing plaything of Blaeth's, likely to be discarded before the next Moon saw Her full.

Now, however, as the stranger stood without so much as blinking while several of the šef of the Southern Mahsadën went stiff with fury, Serys knew there was more in this woman than she'd initially seen…

"It isn't your place to interrupt us!" Tyala Gerst spat in Lazura's direction from where she stood behind Ahthys Borne. "This is not a conversation for *subordinates*!" She jerked a hand at the wall of the room where the other confidants lingered, most of whom were still looking nervously on. "Go stand with the others, before Blaeth has you dragged out by your—"

"Lazura speaks with my permission, as she does with my authority," Blaeth cut the Acrosian delegate off smoothly. "Not only that, but she is singularly more familiar with Arro's recent activities than any other soul in this room."

Gerst spluttered to a halting silence, gaping at the young man. Before she or anyone else could contradict him, though, he continued.

"For the better part of the last year, Lazura has been tasked with tracking the atherian. A specialized unit of men she trained herself tailed him from the North all the way to Karesh Syl in Perce, with orders to kill at first opportunity."

Gerst regained some of her composure at that, sneering at the woman—Lazura—all-too-clearly unimpressed. "Perhaps you would have done better to assign such a mission to someone more adept for the task, given that the Monster still breathes."

"There are many outside this room who call him 'the Dragon' now," Lazura answered sweetly. "And as for my adeptness… I sent a twenty-man group after Arro, all uniquely prepared for their task. In no more than two exchanges, every one of them died by his hand." Her smile sharpened. "You encountered what remained of their comrades on your way up here. The ones I didn't trust were yet ready to go after your 'Monster'."

The quiet that fell this time was broken up by the buzz of whispers between the šef, and Serys heard San praying again over her shoulder. She, like him, undoubtedly couldn't help but recall the dead, cold eyes of the guide who'd led them up the stairs. She hadn't seen so much as the hint of a blade or any other weapon on his person, and yet she didn't find it hard to think the man could have ended her, San's, and Analla's lives before any of them might even have drawn breath to scream.

Gerst, apparently, was having a similar consideration, because the tanned cheeks of her face were abruptly a good deal paler as she watched Lazura with an altogether different sort of expression.

"Lazura and I shared a master," Blaeth said, narrowing his eyes on the Acrosian woman, though he clearly spoke to the room. "For those of you unfortunate enough not to know who Ergoin Sass was, I suggest you see to educating yourselves before picking a fight with her again."

There were more murmurs of surprise at that, everyone recalling the šef who'd been in charge of the assassins of Miropa—at one point even the Monster himself—before his death at Arro's hand.

Blaeth, however, didn't let them dwell on the realization long.

"*For the moment*," he said, his sharp tone saying very clearly that he was ready to carry on with their conversation, "I would ask you all to humor my understanding of the situation: Raz i'Syul Arro is more dangerous than any of us have ever given him credit for, and we've been foolish enough to allow him to raise an army that has not only ravaged an economic ally, but now threatens our very borders."

There was the thunderous scraping of a chair taking flight as Elon Marst heaved himself to his feet.

"Dynec will be under assault within a fortnight!" he exclaimed, his voice tense with anger and fear. "I would call for assistance from the other cities! We do not have the capability to defend ourselves alone."

There was a ringing silence at his words, which might have lingered as many of the other šef watched him impassively were it not for Blaeth's punctuated response.

"No. Scattered aid for a single municipality will not help us now. Dynec is already lost."

Marst's weathered face blanched at these words, and he gaped at Blaeth for several seconds, like he couldn't believe what he had just heard. Behind him, Amthel Oren and a woman Serys knew to be called Hestya Veste shared a similar expression.

Then, all three grimaced in unanimous fury.

"'*Lost*?'" Marst repeated, outraged, slamming both hands down on the table and leaning over it in the Miropan šef's direction, as though intending to throw himself over its surface and throttle the younger man. "Nothing is 'lost'! Dynec has ten thousand soldiers under its command, including twenty-five hundred mounted cavalry. Our walls were built high and wide when Perce was still a wild nation that sent raids across the border. Our economy is as solid as Miropa's, and we spent *months* providing heads for the slavers at a reduced cost *at your behest*, Blaeth! Who are you to say Dynec is 'lost'?"

"Your walls mean nothing to Arro," Blaeth answered evenly. "Not with a mere ten thousand to see to them whilst still defending your gates. He will surround you, cutting you off from the outside world. The best you can hope for is a siege in which your šef shall be starved out like animals in a cage, and I doubt very much the Monster might allow for such a drawn-out exchange."

"Our forces need only hold out until assistance arrives," Oren insisted angrily. His grey eyes moved then to Serys', and she held them without blinking. "Karavyl's army matches ours, and Cyro—" he looked next to Ysera Ma'het and her partner "—have at least six thousand at their disposal. If our men can keep Arro at bay for even a week—!"

"Then you doom the rest of us," San Loreyn cut in bluntly from behind Serys. At once all eyes fell on him, and Serys, for her part, did not disagree.

San was a fool and a coward in so many countless ways, but only Ahthys Borne—and perhaps Adrion Blaeth, it would seem—had a better mind for strategy and numbers among the šef.

Fortunately, the room's attention was not kept on their corner of the table for very long.

"The representative from Karavyl is correct." It was the woman—Lazura—who spoke this time, looking to the šef of Dynec. "Your desperation is faulted by basic math, amongst other things. Even if your hosts *combined* were indeed offered the opportunity to meet Arro's army on an open field, you would hardly number half his forces. Since your ten thousand will be pinned down in your own walls, it makes it all the more unfeasible. What's *more*—" her voice rose as Oren opened his mouth to protest "—you make a critical error in assuming Dynec is worth saving. You, old man." Her blue eyes, still twinkling over her smile, fixed on Elon Marst. "You believe your economy is as stable as that of *our* city?" She squeezed Blaeth's shoulder indicatively, waiting for an answer.

Marst took the chance at once.

"I do," he snarled. "We do not, perhaps, have the breadth of Miropa's trade, but we are strong in our own right."

"You *were* strong, Marst."

As all heads turned toward her, Serys almost bit her tongue in annoyance at her inability to keep the words buried. She'd promised herself to see where the cards fell—especially since Blaeth and his strange companion appeared to have a much better grasp on the situation than the šef of Dynec—but Oren's assumption that Karavyl would come to their aid had pushed her over the edge.

No going back now, though.

"You *were* strong," she said again, meeting Marst's angry gaze steadily when he and the other two delegates turned on her. "Your economic success was heavily dependent on trade with Perce, a partner that—for all intents and purposes—no longer exists. I imagine you could strike some sparse deals with the *kuja*, but the tribes of the savannah have nothing to offer in the way of valuables, and they don't buy slaves." Serys' jaw tensed in annoyance. "I refuse to believe that any of you can be fool enough to think the razing of the Tashes' seats will not have a devastating blow on your financial and commercial powers, much less *all* of you. Which implies you would demand that Karavyl and Cyro—" she waved a hand at the pair of Cyroan šef to her left without looking away from Marst "—come to your aid at great risk to our own homes, with little to be gained for our involvement." She let the hand fall to the table again before delivering the killing blow. "Karavyl will not offer its support. In addition, I recommend all of Dynec's assets, particularly its standing army, be repurposed, or at least repositioned outside the city before Arro has a chance to seize it."

Immediately following this last statement, everyone began shouting at once. Marst, Oren, and Veste were by far the loudest, outright screaming in her direction as the others called out their support or dismissal of Serys' recommendation. Serys herself, on the other hand, wasn't watching any of them. Instead, her eyes had been pulled across the table, and she watched with mixed suspicion and curiosity as Lazura bent down to whisper in Adrion Blaeth's ear. For a moment Serys could have *sworn* she had seen the man flinch when the woman leaned down beside him, but whatever the expression had been was gone as quickly as it appeared, and Blaeth just nodded like he were accepting some sage advice. For several seconds longer the pair did nothing, turning to the room again, and Serys barely had time to notice the woman's pale finger tapping on his shoulder, like she was counting…

Then Blaeth raised a hand, hesitated a brief moment, and brought it down in a flat palm on the table.

CRACK!

There was a flash of white which left Serys half-blind, followed by a dull blast that rocked against her body, shivering through her lungs, jaw, and skull. It wasn't so strong as to knock her out of her chair, but it stole her breath away as she blinked, and she heard San curse behind her when he was forced back a step under the pressure.

When her vision cleared, Serys found herself staring—along with every other person in the room—at Adrion Blaeth.

Or rather, what was left of the table before him.

From where Blaeth's fist still rested on the polished surface, streaking lines of ashen black had suddenly appeared in the wood, smoking and smoldering. They ripped outward from his hand like chiseled lightning, and here and there white flames flickered and faded in the charred crevices. Even as they all gaped, an entire section of the table to Serys' left groaned and fell away, nearly crushing Ysera Ma'het's foot as the woman cursed in the Sun's name and leapt from her seat to be clear of it.

Before anyone could get a word in, Blaeth spoke.

"You have heard rumors, I am sure," he said slowly, drawing his hand back to reveal a scorched blast mark where it had been resting on the wood. "Perhaps some of you from different lands are familiar with this sort of power. Regardless, take it in. Put to rest your curiosities as to how I have come to hold the reins of Miropa against all challengers who have risen to claim them."

The room held its silence, most too stunned to say anything, still staring at the smoldering table with open disbelief.

"Eighteen months ago, I stood in this very room," Adrion pressed on, looking around at them all. "There, along that wall." He raised a finger, pointing to a space at the edge of the chamber not far from where Analla waited with the other confidants. "Despite our number, despite the fact that he came alone to face us, and despite this power that was growing in me even then, Raz i'Syul Arro was unstoppable once he broke through those doors." He indicated to the room's entrance, and Serys recalled the empty holes where old nails had been torn from the mortar. "The šef numbered nine in all, most capable killers, not the least of which was Ergoin Sass himself. In addition, there were more than a dozen of us attendants."

He frowned, eyes shifting to the window Serys had thought looked newer than the rest. "It couldn't have taken him more than a few minutes, despite all that. Before we knew what to do, our blood was mixed with that of the guards he'd butchered on the way up the stairs, men whose heads he brought us as a gift. He cut us down like we were nothing, cleaving through all and anyone that got in his path. There was no stopping him, not a thing any single person could have done, nor any ten of us together. It was panic and chaos and death. Looking back, I can't even think straight enough to wonder if it wasn't Arro in the room with us, but rather a reaping wraith sent by the Moon and Her Stars ."

"Here?" Ahthys Borne breathed in disbelief, finally tearing his eyes from the ruined table to look around at the chamber. "It happened *here*, in this place?"

Blaeth nodded, leaning back in his chair again and tapping a wooden arm with one finger. "This is the very seat Imaneal Evony occupied before he was fool enough to try and reason with the beast. He died over there—" he gestured to a nearby corner, where a pair of seconds leapt out of the way to reveal a sizable chunk chipped out of the stone wall "—where Arro ran him through last of all."

He looked around again, meeting each of their gazes before settling on the Dynec delegation.

"I second the motion by Karavyl," he announced loudly, his tone changing as though nothing out of the ordinary had happened. "We should accept the loss of Dynec, and move to collect our hosts. It may give the Monster a foothold in the South, but neither I nor Lazura believe he will hole himself up for long in any one place. His goal is to eradicate our society at a scale he did not achieve when he slaughtered the former šef of Miropa." Blaeth's eyes narrowed again, watching Marst carefully while the old man's fists shook by his sides. "To put it bluntly, Marst, I would not leave the decision in your hands if I could help it. I have already mobilized Miropa's garrison, but Arro will reach your city much sooner than my forces, even if we marched directly across the Cienbal. This must be your decision, but I urge you to consider carefully. If you face his army head on, you will not only lose, but you will deny the fringe cities the troops and supplies Dynec could have provided. Between Miropa, Acrosia, Karth, Karavyl, and Cyro, we number enough to match the Arro's forces with some advantage, but I will no longer allow the Mahsadën to underestimate that creature." He gave the man a sad, almost-understanding smile. "Give us your ten thousand. Concede the city. When this battle is done, we can address the opportunity to rebuild and ensure Dynec thrives even basent Perce to support it."

Liar, Serys thought, though she was more impressed than anything. Blaeth spoke with eloquent confidence, delivering threat and reward in the same breath without even batting an eye. There was, of course, no advantage to Dynec's presence among the fringe cities if Karesh Syl and Karesh Nan were not rebuilt in the next handful of years. At best the municipality would become another Karth, a shithole with no strategic value, useful only as a haven for the thugs and vagrants of low ambition who the Mahsadën had no interest in bringing into the fold.

Not to mention the fact that the current šef would lose all semblance of power the moment their army and resources were absorbed by the other cities…

Unfortunately, Marst and his companions had clearly come to the same conclusion.

"We will not be conned into bowing to some *snake* and his whore." The old man spat on the table in Blaeth and Lazura's directions, then turned and shoved his chair aside to step away from the table, Oren and Vest right behind him. "I don't care what kind of sorcery you wield, Blaeth. Dynec will not allow itself to be swallowed so easily."

"Marst, wait!" Ahthys Borne tried to call after the delegation as they began moving for the door, their confidants falling in at their back. "Your forces could be key in this fight! Don't just—!"

"Sun curse your fight!" Marst bellowed without looking back, giving the room a rude gesture over his shoulder that Serys would never have thought the man capable of before today. "I will see to it we hire every *sarydâ* in the South if we have to! Dynec will stand firm, with or *without* your help!"

And then the delegation was gone, ripping the door open and stepping through, vanishing down the stairs beyond.

"Unfortunate," Blaeth sighed, cutting through the quiet that followed Dynec's abrupt exit. All gazes turned to him, and Serys couldn't stop herself from reeling again when she saw the devastation of the table, embers yet smoldering in the places the lighting crossed itself over the wood. "But it could hardly be helped. Regrettably, Marst will find mercenaries in short supply when he goes looking."

Several people blinked at that, and it was the slight change in Lazura's smile—the woman's hand still on the man's left shoulder as she stood beside him—that gave it away for Serys.

"You anticipated this," she said harshly, frowning at the pair of them. "You knew Dynec wouldn't care to play your game. How many *sarydâ* have you already contracted?"

"This is no *game*, Benth," Blaeth told her calmly. "But yes, it seemed the most plausible outcome. Miropa has officially employed five thousand mercenaries, and we are in negotiation with several other groups that amount to another three. I'm loathe to trust sellswords over trained soldiers, and it won't completely make up for the loss of Dynec's army, but the *sarydâ* will still give us the advantage over the Monster's forces when the time comes."

"'When the time comes…?'" the yet-unnamed šef from Karth repeated uneasily, like he didn't want to dwell on what that implied.

"Yes," Blaeth said with a nod. "Eventually, Arro is going to force our hand."

"And it will be a fight for the fringe cities as a whole," Serys breathed to herself, ensuring no one else could make out the words while the other šef leaned in, eager to hear any plan that would drag them free of the approaching tempest of fire and steel that was Raz i'Syul Arro, Monster of Karth, Scourge of the South, Dragon of the North.

Some hours later, Adrion Blaeth observed through the room's center window as the last of the delegations took their leave. He hadn't expected much from the Karavyl representatives, but Serys Benth—despite her responsibilities lying largely within the management and prosperity of her city's brothels and whorehouses—had proven herself deceptively astute when it came to plotting out the upcoming weeks. He watched her and the pair she'd come with reach the bottom of the building's steps, where a dozen guards stood waiting along the street below, then move south toward the markets as the soldiers fell in behind them.

"Your infamous 'šef' are all nothing but pompous cretins, apparently."

The feminine voice sent a shiver down Adrion's back, but he'd long learned to control that fear. He didn't turn away from the glass, even though

Lazura's words made his shoulder tingle where her hand had rested for a majority of the morning.

His fingers still ached from when she'd forced her magic through his arm in her theatrical display.

"Some, admittedly," he said with a nod, watching Serys Benth vanish beyond the lip of the window frame. "But not all. Most of them were quick enough to come together. We have assurances from Karavyl, Cyro, and Acrosia, and I have no doubt Karth will fall in line after Arro crushes Dynec."

The woman gave an unconvinced grunt, and Blaeth finally decided to turn around.

Lazura sat at the edge of the table, a finger absently playing with the carred corner of one of the cracks her power had formed in the wood as she studied him. Even now, a year after she'd forcibly taken his reins and made him her little puppet in these political games, Adrion felt a twinge of what could only be lust as he took her in. She was a beautiful creature. Whatever god it was who'd created her, be it the Sun or the 'Lifegiver' she sometimes cursed by, they'd done a masterful job in her making. She was petite, slender but not overly thin, and small enough in stature to appear delicate, though Adrion would never have been fool to say so out loud. Her features were porcelain in quality, blue eyes the color of dark water against the light skin of her face, and her hair—after years spent in the Southern climates—was more white than blonde. The only thing that marred the perfection, in fact, was the scar whose tale Adrion had never managed to parse out. It bisected her countenance in a cross pattern stemming from a ring about her right eye, forming perfectly even, distinctly diagonal lines that cut across her cheeks, forehead, and nose in perpendicular directions. Despite himself, Adrion was ever unable to find the markings ugly, but they held a sinister quality for him now they'd never possessed when Lazura had been feigning her doting role as caretaker to the Grandmother.

Adrion felt a lump swell in his throat as he thought of what had become of the old woman, the last surviving tie he had to his former life apart from Raz himself. Hate lifted its ugly head in his gut, studying Lazura's face, but he fought it back down again.

There are some fights one cannot win, he quoted to himself, recalling something his uncle, Jarden, had once taught him.

Swallowing his pride, he steeled himself.

"It was foolish of you to reveal your magic to them," he told her, doing his best to keep his voice strong as he took a step forward, leaning into the cane nestled under his left arm in the place of the leg missing from just above the knee. "You should have kept that as a trump card, for when the right time came."

Lazura made a face, sneering at him like his words were the chirpings of some distasteful insect. "No," she said, her sweet voice ill-matching the grimace. "It was time to give them a taste. You may be as capable a substitute as I could have hoped for, Adrion, but don't fool yourself into thinking you are anything more than that. Enjoy your position, while you can."

Adrion's free hand clenched into an unbidden fist at his side. "I came to terms with my position long ago," he lied, refusing to look away from her. "It doesn't change the fact that the longer we kept that hidden, the more impact it would have had under more suitable circumstances."

Lazura waved the comment off like she was bored of the conversation. "You know better than anyone that display was barely a fraction of what I'm capable of. I didn't want to risk blowing your arm off, given the weak image you *already* present." She gave him a sadistic grin, looking down at the cloth of his left pant leg, pinned back over the stub of the missing limb. "Providing them with an example of what 'you' are capable of will either plant the seed of subservience when the time comes for them to bend the knee, or spur them into action against us while they think you are still within reach. Whatever option is fine, and if any of them choose to take the latter route, I might enjoy thinning the herd a little."

Adrion grit his teeth at that. He understood the necessary evils of the world, had come to terms with the wickedness that lingered in the hearts of all men. Ergoin Sass had showed him the abhorrent realities of life, taught him how to make the hard decisions that allowed one to thrive in a place like the South. Adrion knew he had grown into a cruel man as a result, but he owed no regrets to the path he'd followed. His choices were for the betterment of the city as much as for himself. The weak and poor that leeched at the working classes made themselves useful as slaves, and crime was under the control of the Mahsadën, keeping it from raging rampant. A realistic order held firm in Miropa, balancing the needs and desires of the people who turned a blind eye on the society's authority over the city with the chaos and corruption that were unavoidable byproducts of any thriving metropolis. Adrion believed with all his heart that men like him—men like Ergoin Sass and Imaneal Evony—were key in raising Miropa into 'the Gem' it had become. They might not be 'good', per se, but they were essential.

Lazura, on the other hand, was something else altogether.

Blood excited her. She took pleasure in her sport, enjoyed pulling the strings of Adrion and the lesser agents of the city's Mahsadën to increasingly terrifying results. There was no tempering her, of late. There had been a time when he'd been able to reason with the woman, guiding her away from action that might have proven disastrous for them both in the end, but as she grew closer to her goal of dominance, Lazura had become increasingly harder to reel in. Ever since she'd regained her magic the woman had been drunk on her own power, but of late the insatiable gleam in her gaze was sharper, more dangerous. She was growing steadily more blind to the risks of her decisions, but as her strength grew—both personally and politically—so too, it seemed, did her sense of invulnerability.

Even with Raz marching right at us, she still has her eye on the šef, Adrion thought with an anxious swallow, watching the woman absently play with a loose strand of bleached hair.

Not for the first time, he found himself wondering who he would root for if the titans ever came to a head…

Adrion frowned at that, forcing the consideration from his mind. Lazura might be the demon before him now, but his cousin had long since earned a far greater form of ire.

"What now, then?" he finally asked, deciding it was time to change the subject.

In response, Lazura smiled. It was her typical, coquettish display which most found innocent and endearing, but Adrion had long learned to read the subtleties of it. There was a hunger there, though fortunately not one directed at *him*.

"Mah'sed!" Lazura called over her shoulder, and at once a figure stepped through the door into the otherwise empty room, the dark layers of his clothing rippling gently to settle around his lithe frame. For a moment, Adrion had a flashback of another such man appearing seemingly out of thin air, and he swallowed the twist in his gut.

Whether fortunately or unfortunately, they hadn't received word from Na'zeem Ashur in some months, meaning the assassin had undoubtedly fallen to Raz and his companions a long time ago.

This man, like his predecessor, said nothing as Lazura waved him in, approaching as might a loyal dog told to heel by its master. When he stood beside her, Lazura opened her mouth to say something, then stopped with a bemused look.

"Adrion," she called teasingly, glancing around at him. "What were their names?"

Adrion would have rolled his eyes if the question hadn't made his stomach wrench even further. He didn't have to ask who she meant.

"Elon Marst, Amthel Oren, and Hestya Veste," he said without looking into Mah'sed's dead gaze, making sure to keep his voice steady. "You'll find their confidants searching for representatives of the larger mercenary groups, likely in the taverns and guild halls around the market. They'll be trying to gather aid for Dynec as quickly as possible. Tail them, and they'll lead you back to the šef themselves."

The man nodded at once, bowing briefly to Lazura before making for the door again. He didn't carry himself with the same deadly confidence Na'zeem once had, but that hardly endeared him to Adrion in any greater amount. When the assassin was finally gone, Lazura glanced around.

"Oh, don't look so *glum*," she said with a titter that set the hairs on the back of Adrion's neck on end. "If they'd agreed to our terms, then they would still have some value. As is, they'll just try to sow discord among the other cities."

Adrion nodded absently, not really seeing her. Indeed, his thoughts were elsewhere, wondering silently how much longer it would be before *he* was suddenly the one who lost all value.

And so it begins, a tired sort of voice mumbled in the back of his mind, and he turned to look up this time, through the diamond panes of the window to the streak of cloudless blue sky that ceilinged the alley outside.

I

"It is in dreams that we find ourselves closest to the gods. There we are gifted the briefest chance to touch Their world, a place of infinites and impossibilities. Wonders we can only imagine, after having untethered ourselves from our mortal understandings, become reality. Beauty which occasionally leaves the waking wanting for nothing more than another moment in its presence paints itself across our thoughts.

The trouble, of course, lies in the price we sometimes pay for these ventures. In addition to the miraculous, after all, it is a fool who does not consider that the home of the gods should not also be that of the demons and devils of lesser—but crueler—power..."

— The Grandmother

There had been a time, in Abir Fahaji's youth, when he recalled being unencumbered by the dreams. It was a period in years long past, a short breath of freedom memory allowed him to revisit, before he grew from boy to man and the sight began dominating his nights. Of late, the visions had been less frequent. He didn't know if the Twins had begun to take pity on him in his old age, or perhaps if it was merely owed to the loss of faculties that were a natural part of the passage of time. More likely, Abir couldn't help but think that the recent reprieve was due to the thrum of activity that surrounded him in the war camp, the buzz of busyness that rose up at all hours of the day and well after the setting of the Sun around the little tent he shared with Karan, near the northern head of the march. He was, after all, still accustomed to huddling down in the cramped coolness of a locked room, surrounded by half-a-hundred other slaves, not a one among them brave enough to so much as whimper out in cold and hunger for fear of bringing the guards of Karesh Syl down on their heads.

The shouts of men and women, the growled calls of the atherian, even the sound of steel ringing against steel in the distance as some of the Dragon's officers put their brigades through evening drills... It all served as a soothing lullaby to Abir, reminding him that he was, in fact, still free.

And yet there were still those nights where the dreams simply refused to be kept at bay.

This time Abir found himself wandering along the shores of a lake he did not know. All about him, men and women and children were moving through rings of covered and hard-topped wagons, smiling and laughing as they set about making their camps and building their cooking fires. Most had grey eyes, and their long hair was dreaded about their shoulders, bleached by extended exposure to the Sun that blazed, alone and omnipotent, in the sky to the east. They wore simple traveler's clothes, loose and comfortable so as to fend off the oppressive desert heat, and what skin wasn't covered in silk and thin fabrics was bronzed a golden tan. Abir didn't know where he'd been taken in the stupors of sleep, but the energy in the air offered him some hints by which to make an educated guess. The happiness and joy of the families, all of them settling in for what looked like an extended stay along the borders of the lake, felt like the sort of merriment that only existed in a time long past.

Ignoring all, Abir kept walking, guided through the running groups of little ones and their working parents, the cheer and gaiety of the rings like music to his ears as something pulled him onward.

For several minutes he walked, the sand beneath his bare feet shifting pleasantly, the flat sheen of the water's surface to his right only occasionally shifting and rippling as a hot breeze whisked down from the high dunes that surrounded the place on all sides. Here and there pockets of narrow palm trees rose along the edges of the shore, their tops bent as they grew too tall for their own weight, their broad green leaves swaying in the wind. It was toward such a grove that Abir found himself moving, a large grouping of trees tucked into the nook of the southern crescent of the lake. As he approached, the festive sounds of the families began to die away, fading with every step he took even as he continued to move through the running and shouting and laughing people. By the time he was free of them, stepping beyond the larger collective of wagons and carts, the dream had gone all-but-silent around Abir, leaving nothing but the sound of the water lapping ever-so-gently up and down the incline of the shore as he kept walking.

Approaching the palms, he felt the stone of fear settle in his gut as he took in the scene nestled between the shore and the edge of the trees.

The caravan must once have been a grand thing, Abir thought. Nine wagons in all, the circle they'd once formed would have left a spacious expanse between the carts, with ample room to accommodate whatever families had once comprised its residents. Stepping toward it, for a half-a-moment Abir caught a flicker of something, a distortion, like an echo from some distant place or past. The wagons standing tall, a pen of perhaps a score of horses looped along its west edge, and a glimpse of dozens of men, women, and children crowded around a massive, multi-colored fire in the very center of the ring.

Then the echo was gone, leaving nothing but the truth for Abir to take in.

What little remained of the timber and iron that had once made up most of the wagons was blackened and smoking, and here and there fire still clung to the wood or ate at the shifting canvas cloth that roofed some of the carts. Not a few among them were overturned, flipped onto their sides as their wheels spun uselessly in the silence that still clung to the scene. To Abir's left, the horses—which had been a moment ago proudly strutting about—lay dead, scattered and still in their wide pen, fallen into the bloody sand with throats cut open in jagged wounds. Seeing this, Abir began to shake, fearing now what he would find if he kept on, praying to the Moon that She would stop him, that She would keep him from approaching.

His feet, though, kept on of their own accord.

He passed between the nearest pair of smoldering wagons into the emptiness of the ring. No bodies lay broken around him, as he'd been afraid of, but the smell of burning hair and flesh told Abir not to look too closely into the charred husks of the carts. The sand sifting through his bare toes was streaked with red, churned up and filthy by what must have been near a hundred sets of scrambling feet, booted and bare alike. Here and there bloody swords and axes and other such weapons had fallen or been abandoned, their wet blades glistening in the Sun. The still silence rang eerily, like death breathing across the remnants of a battlefield.

Without pause Abir continued to move through the circle. He still felt the pull, still felt the need to press forward, approaching the place he knew he was meant to end his dream. Across the ring, a single wagon still stood intact, apparently untouched by the fires that had consumed the others. It was—as the rest might once have been—a plain thing, lacking ornamentation or flamboyance. A simple bench ridged its leading wall, where a driver might have sat, and its surfaces had been layered with pelts and tanned skins, likely to keep away the dust and sand as the wagons made their treks across the dunes. Stepping over the singed form of a child's straw doll, Abir neared the wagon cautiously, his skin prickling with every inch he got closer.

Still, in spite of his trepidation, his hands moved without thought once he reached it, pulling aside the hide hangings that formed a door in the wagon's side before taking the frame of the floor and entrance to heave himself up into the covered space.

As Abir stood tall in the little room formed by the cart's hard top, he knew at once that he was in the right place. There was a resonance within the wagon, a mystical sort of power that flexed its will all about him. Over his head, a myriad crystalline shards of gleaming stone hung off bits of cord and copper wire from the ribbed ceiling, reflecting and refracting the limited light that slipped through seams of the plank-and-hide walls. Shelves lined either side of the space, themselves heavy with an unnerving array of objects and oddities. Animal skulls. Dried, gnarled plants. Vials of what looked like earth and alcohol and a dozen other solutions and materials he didn't recognize. To his right, a makeshift bed of the oddest proportions took up much of the room, a narrow cot with an additional section added to one side, forming an L-shaped corner. Leather and cloth straps hung loose over the ruffled sheets, like someone had been held firm upon it not so long ago.

And there, in the very center of the remaining space, a woman sat waiting for him, cross-legged on the floor on the far side of a low, flat table, her face turned up in his direction.

Abir shivered when he took in the figure, for her *figure* was truly all he had to take in. She reminded him, in a way, of the White Witch, the Dragon's companion and confidant. Both women exuded a sort of quiet power—though Syrah Brahnt's had recently been in frequent flux—and this woman had her face covered, much like the Priestess had been keeping hers since the army's crossing out of Perce and into the Southern realms two weeks prior.

Whereas Brahnt's face was covered out of necessity, though, *this* woman's shawl was more of a death mask. The fabric was rough and dirty, hanging over her features and clinging to every dip of her cheeks, mouth, and eyes until she seemed more dead than alive. It was longer as well, falling about her torso until it covered her entirely, not unlike a funeral gown.

All in all, Abir's only impression—while he moved to sit down unbidden on the other side of the table—was that he was in the company of a corpse.

Then, though, the woman spoke, and at once he recognized her calm, warm voice.

"The time approaches, Abir Fahaji," the woman said gently, though her mouth didn't move beneath the cloth. "But it has not come yet. You must tell them so."

Abir nodded slowly. In some distant part of his mind, he knew that he should ask who it was he was supposed to tell and why, but he had long since learned not to question the mysteries of his sight. Instead, he smiled. "Your grandson does well," he said quietly. "He grieved for you, when I told him you had passed."

"He will see me again," she said with a brief dip of her head, her face still not so much as flinching beneath the shawl. "But not yet. And not like this. You must tell them. The time approaches."

"I will," he said, not voicing his apprehensions.

The waver in his words, though, seemed to give his concerns away, because there was a mirthless chuckle from beneath the cloth.

"You fear you will not find them," the woman said, stating the fact. "Do not. I've little doubt that will be the case. Their ranks grow restless, impatient. They wish for their prince to rise *now*, but it is not time. Tell them they must wait a little longer."

Abir swallowed nervously, but nodded once more. "How will I convince them? How will I show them that what I say is true? I am a mad man, to most. Even those I call my friends often do not know if my tellings are fortune or folly."

"Tell them that she who is blind sees all," the woman said. "Tell them those beneath the mountains watch and wait."

Abir frowned. "Will they understand it? Will they know what I mean?"

The figure inclined her head, clearly confident her words would carry the message she intended.

"What if they don't?"

The question slipped out of Abir before he could stop himself. It was one thing to bow to the mystery of powers beyond his comprehension, but another entirely to lean against a man's own fears. Abir was happy. For the first time in fifty years—since he'd been thrown into chains for delivering a prophecy to the leaders of Karesh Nan that the Tash of the age hadn't appreciated—he was happy. But he was worried, too. He was afraid. The Dragon held him in high enough regard, but the common soldiers—and even some of the army's generals—whispered about him, the kindest of them calling him senile or touched, the cruelest claiming his sight was an affliction, an unnatural thing. He was not so easily convinced his words would ring true.

"They *must* believe."

The figure's words were not cold, but they were hard. Abir watched, apprehension crawling up his spine, as one of the woman's hands reached up, pulling at the cloth about her face. It began to slide off, slowly dragged away in the grasp of her skeletal fingers.

"They *must*," the woman repeated, and as the fabric slipped inch by inch over her head, her voice changed. Second by second it grew rough, as though her throat was becoming parched, or her lungs were falling to work. "She waits for you, to the north of the great sands. She will bide her time, will seek the right moment to bring all her strength to bear. She is the larger darkness holding the strings that make the shadows dance, and she *cannot* be underestimated." The edge of the cloth neared the crest of her scalp and shoulders. "What must you tell them, Abir Fahaji?"

"That the time approaches, but it is not now," Abir said at once, something very much like terror lancing through his chest as he watched, unable to look away. "That she who is blind sees all. That they beneath the mountains watch, and… and…"

The cloth fell away, then, tumbling free from the woman's body, and for a moment Abir could only stare in horror at the wasted figure, taking in what had been done to the corpse.

Then he screamed.

He screamed, his body frozen in place, his eyes fixated as though by some cruel magic. Even as the woman stood, the dream shifting around her, he screamed. Even as she moved around the table toward him, he screamed. His voice broke as he shrieked in fear, sensation returning to him as the vision began to fall apart around them. The cart shimmered and vanished, the wood floor beneath him becoming reed matting. She reached him just as he began to rise from the depths of the sight, her dead hands grabbing him by the shoulders as she leaned in, her terrible leer inches away.

"She who devoured me waits for you," the vision rasped into his face. "Sand and snow cannot meet flame unprepared! They must believe! Repeat the words!"

She began to fade, then, falling away like dust in the wind. Still, though, Abir could feel her skeletal grip about his arms, and in the desperate hope to be free of her he did as she commanded, howling as loudly as he could.

"SHE WATCHES! SHE WHO IS BLIND SEES ALL! IT IS NOT TIME! IT IS NOT TIME! THEM BENEATH THE MOUNTAINS WAIT! IT IS NOT TIME!"

And with that, the horrid image of the ravaged figure drifted to nothingness before his eyes, tumbling away, her nightmarish features replaced by a shocked face of very different proportions. The sensation of her hands around the wasted muscles of his shoulders, too, changed. The sharp boniness of the grasp was replaced by a stronger grip, claws digging into his skin as they held him firm. His mind reeled to catch up to the failing dream, and Abir began to tremble as his eyes took in his strange surroundings.

He was no longer in his cloth hammock, where he'd fallen asleep to the crackle of the flames in the center of his and Karan's shared tent. Instead, he was in a much larger enclosure, with a broader fire illuminating the angled leather and cloth ceiling, the smoke carried upwards and away through a large hole in the top of the space. In the light-cast shadows all around him, no less than a dozen figures were staring at him, some half-sitting up from the reeds where they looked to have been sleeping, others already on their feet. The fear the vision had instilled in Abir lingered as he took in their serpentine features, reptilian eyes gleaming in the light, clawed hands and thick tails reflected in bouncing shapes against the walls of the tent beyond them.

For some reason, however, his terror seemed to reflect right back at him in those eyes, every shade of gold wide and gaping at him with frightened awe.

"Old man. Look at me."

Abir's shivering redoubling as the accented words whispered in a hot breath across his cheek and neck. Slowly he looked around, staring into the face of the atherian who had hold of him. He recognized her at once, though this did nothing to stop him from tensing instinctively as he took in her maw of yellowed teeth, so close to his own face.

For a moment, he almost gave a shrill laugh, recalling how the ghastly specter had so casually cast aside his fear that he would not find those his words were meant for.

Sure enough, the aging female's clawed fingers tightened about his arms as she spoke, her voice almost imploring in its desperation.

"Old man," Za'len hissed again. "'Them beneath the mountains.' Tell us! Tell us what it is you know of the Under Caves!"

II

"It is a simple thing to preach peace. I could stand here before you all and tell you—as though it is the answer to every trouble in the world—that fighting is ever the fool's choice. The truth, of course, is much more complicated. There is a time for peace. Any sane man who has seen war, has shed the blood of another, will tell you that. There is *a time for peace.*

But that man will tell you also, and likely just as absolutely, that there is a time for the lifting of sword and steel."

— Jarden Arro, to the children of the Arro clan, c. 850 v.S.

When the war finally reached them, it came as a plume of dust and sand against the night.

From his place atop the highest dune Marsus' scouts had been able to find in the area, Raz i'Syul Arro watched the riders approach with narrowed eyes, following the trail that blotted out a patch of Her Stars along the western horizon. He wore a heavy pelt cloak over his armor, partially to ward off the chill of the desert evening, and partially to prevent the steel from gleaming and giving their position away in the light of the Moon that hung, bright and cool, in the sky before him. The claws of his left hand, encased in their metal gauntlet, drummed impatiently against the blade of the sagaris—a war-axe with an arched spike to counterbalance its narrow head—hanging at his hip. His right, clad in the same armor, was wrapped about the bleached wood shaft of Ahna, resting in her habitual place over his shoulder. Her twin blades, elegantly curved like antlers, were covered in an old rucksack, and he kept her heavy bottom point low to keep it, too, from catching Her light.

At his left, Syrah Brahnt's gaze followed his own, though Raz doubted she could make out much given the riders were still winding their way through the sands some mile or two away. All the same, the woman waited with him quietly, the ghostly complexion of her face—diagonally bisected by the black cloth that covered her ruined right eye—making her seem a specter from within the layers of dark silks which hung over her white hair and slender frame.

On Raz's other side, Karan Brightneck—Syrah's companion, and one of Marsus' keenest eyes—watched along with them in equal silence, crouching low at the edge of the dune ridge. The young atherian had finished her report several minutes prior, supplying Raz with the facts he'd needed. Two hundred and fifty men, all mounted, bearing no city colors but clearly dressed for battle. The timing and approach of their assault was clever enough, he had to admit. With the brightness of the Moon in their eyes, most sentries would be night-blind to the riders until they could make out the muffled sound of hooves against the sand.

Unfortunately for this attacking force, it seemed the fringe cities had underestimated the atherian outriders Raz's generals kept scattered for five miles in every direction about the army at all times.

Beside him, Syrah gave a faint "oh…" as her human eye finally made out the cloud of approaching dust. Judging the timing to be right, Raz lifted his hand from his belt and pointed two fingers to his left, then his right. At once he heard quiet orders being given behind him, quickly followed by the crunching of dozens upon dozens of boots and clawed feet against the sandy hill at their backs. He saw Syrah and Karan glance back together, but Raz's eyes stayed fixated on the westward horizon, considering the landscape.

He'd thought they would have to reposition to intercept the soldiers, but Karan and the other scouts had done well in selecting this place. Barring the riders choosing abruptly to take a different path—which seemed unlikely—the horses would pass along the valley below within the next few minutes,. Raz knew what their intention was, and to needlessly waste time shifting course at the last minute would be more foolish than useful.

As though reading his mind, Karan finally spoke from where she was still crouched at his left.

"Are they mad?" she whispered, more to herself than either Raz or Syrah. "Not even three hundred, and they're charging right at fifty thousand?"

"They're not intending to wage any sort of all-out battle," Raz told her quietly, still following the trail of sand as it continued to near. "Two hundred and fifty horses are too valuable to sacrifice, and the Mahsadën are hardly so careless."

He left it at that, wanting Karan to figure out the rest.

It didn't take long.

"A shock troop." She gave an understanding nod. "In and out, with minimal casualties."

"And maximum chaos," Raz affirmed, hiding a hard grin. The female was always quick on the uptake. "Akelo and Arnus would tell you it's a good tactic against a larger force. If they'd succeeded in taking us by surprise, it would have left the generals and I with few options to our advantage. If we ignored them, they would strike again from a different direction—twice as carefully, this time—and whittle down morale even if the toll on our numbers was negligible. If we chased them, it would allow the fringe cities more time to prepare and gather their forces to rebuff us, not to mention strain our supplies unnecessarily."

"We could have sent a contingent after them?" Karan offered, her clawed fingers playing with the leather cuirass about her torso. Even these months since the fall of Karesh Syl, she and many of the other former slaves were still unaccustomed to wearing anything other than the dirty tunics Raz and Syrah had found them in. "Hunt them down with only as many as needed for the task?"

"Which is what they probably hope so most of all," Raz said with a shake of his head. "To catch them, we would have to send out our own cavalry, at a ratio of at least two-to-one to guarantee a victory. Best-case scenario: we lose a good part of our mounted troops for what is likely to be days, which is a blow no matter how large the army might be.

"… And worst-case?" Karan asked after a moment, frowning up at him.

"Worst-case," Syrah spoke up for the first time, answering for Raz without looking around, "they have a larger force waiting somewhere in the dunes. A thousand foot soldiers, maybe twice that. Our riders fall into a trap, and not only do we lose five hundred men, but the horses as well."

Raz nodded in agreement, leaving Karan to ponder these deductions as he looked to Syrah.

"Ready?" he asked her.

The woman glanced at him, and gave him a small, regretful smile. It hurt him, that smile. It hurt him because he knew where Syrah's mind was taking her. Even in the limited glow of the Moon and Her Stars he could make out the rose-shade of her left eye, and the light of life that gleamed there. It was dimmer now than when they'd first met, nearly ten years prior. In the last few weeks it had regained a little of its shine as Syrah had found purpose again, treating the injured among the army and tending to the health of the half-starved slaves that made up much of their ranks, but it was still a sunken light. It was still a guttering shadow of the brightness he loved and missed. For the hundredth time in as many days, Raz vowed silently to himself that he would see that warmth return again, even if he had to pull the Sun Himself out of the sky to do so.

Then Syrah nodded, indicating she was prepared for her role in what came next, bringing Raz back to the task at hand.

He allowed himself another couple of seconds to take her in, then a few more, before finally managing to turn away.

"Karan," he said, resting his free hand between the young atherian's ears affectionately as he stepped passed her, "keep an eye on things here."

Karan nodded at once, standing up at last, one hand already on the hilt of the longsword at her hip. Over the last few months she'd been working hard with him to master the weapon, along with the long-dagger strapped to her forearm, and Raz was confident he was leaving Syrah in good company. Satisfied with the preparations, he eyed the incline of the dune before them.

Then he leapt from the ridge, landing along the loose slope of the hill and masterfully riding the slipping sands down toward the base of the valley below.

Captain Bahrek Lest of the Dynec guard was feeling more and more confident with every passing minute. For the last two hours, as dusk came and slipped beyond the end of the world, he and his men had been riding at an even pace eastward, careful to stay low between the dunes and keep the Moon at their back. At first Bahrek had been almost rigid with nerves in his saddle, trepidation consuming him despite the fact that this assault was *his* idea, and he had even volunteered to lead it personally. Maltus Ameen, the šef in charge of Dynec's standing army, had accepted the proposal readily, and granted him command of five contingents of fifty soldiers each. It had been an honor and an opportunity, and Bahrek leapt at the chance of his own making.

Then, over the course of the next two days, he'd gone from brimming with pride at the chance to prove himself to feeling sick every time he thought about the folly of his idea.

Now, however, as the glow of Raz i'Syul Arro's camp grew broader with every passing minute, Bahrek felt the strength of the men behind him, felt the power of their horses in the soft thundering of hooves against sand. They had done well staying in the valleys and dips of the sand plains, but all the same Bahrek had feared they would be spotted before they could get near enough the Monster's army to strike. As they closed the final mile, though, no cries of alarm or warning horns sounded out, and Bahrek felt the thrill of anticipation surge through his limbs. They were going to make it. Even if the sentries nearest the camp caught sight of them, it was too late to prepare a proper defense. They might lose a few, but the damage they would cause would be a hundredfold if they could escape without issue.

Silently, Bahrek reached over his shoulder to unsheathe the curved scimitar that was the standard blade of any Dynec soldier. The order was a silent one, predetermined before they'd even ridden out from the city that morning, and he heard the *hiss* of steel over the hoofbeats as the officers behind him drew their own blades, followed in a wave by the soldiers that trailed them.

Not long, Bahrek thought to himself as he led the way around a bend between the sands, grey eyes on the glow of the thousands of campfires that burned against the night sky. *Not long, now.*

He felt the exhilaration course through his limbs, and the man forced himself to calm, taking a deep breath of the cold air whipping past his face. He had to keep a level head. This was not some rogue troupe of bandits or *sarydâ* who had earned the ire of the šef, like the groups he'd hunted down a hundred times before. No. Raz i'Syul Arro, the infamous Monster of Karth, was an altogether different sort of beast to prod, and Bahrek needed to remember that. In all of three months the city-states of Perce to the south had fallen to Arro and his army of slaves. From there, word spread fast that the Monster had turned northward, his eyes very clearly set on the fringe cities that surrounded the Cienbal desert. Within a handful of weeks, notices came that the atherian's forces had crossed the border into the sand plains of the South.

Bahrek grit his teeth at the thought, leading his men around a bend in the valley and picturing the lizard-kind at the head of his rundown army. If Arro believed Dynec and the other Southern cities would fall as easily as Karesh Syl and Karesh Nan, then he was far more a fool than the stories allowed for. The captain half-hoped the atherian would show himself tonight. If Bahrek's assault happened to be the one that rode the Monster down, there would be no end to the rewards Maltus Ameen and the other šef would place upon his head. Maybe he would even be called to Miropa, to be praised by Adrion Blaeth himself…

"*Captain*!"

The hissed alert chilled Bahrek to the bone, dragging him from his momentary lapse of concentration. He whirled in his saddle, intent on weeding out whichever idiot had been fool enough to speak out loud, but of the four lesser officers at his back, not a one was looking at him. Every one of their faces, pale in the ghostly light of the Moon, was fixed ahead of them, and it took a moment for Bahrek to recognize the echoed shock etched into their features, hidden by the dark. He turned forward once more, fearing what he would find, and the sight had him choking.

There, not two hundred and fifty feet ahead, a single figure stood as little more than an indistinct black outline in the night, calmly waiting for them along the very path they were following. The details of the person were hidden in the shadows of the dunes that rose up on either side of Bahrek and his riders, but the hulking bearing of their form was enough to set the captain's heart to hammering horribly in his chest. All at once the thrill and excitement that had been building up drained away, replaced by nothing short of panic.

"TRAMPLE HIM!" Bahrek bellowed over the pounding of the horses, forgoing his own silence and bringing his scimitar to bear even as he felt his palm along the hilt begin to sweat.

There was a roar of assent from the soldiers behind him, and Bahrek spurred his horse forward faster, barreling toward the figure. Two-hundred feet to go. He could make out the shape of some massive, staffed weapon slung over the stranger's shoulder. One-hundred and fifty. The outline of a thick, dark tail snaked along the pale sand about the figure's feet. One hundred left. Steel gleamed in the evening light, shining from beneath a heavy fur cloak. Only fifty feet now. The cloak shifted, and the silhouette of the beast seemed suddenly to broaden inexplicably, as though the shadows all around him had formed a wall at his back.

No, Bahrek thought with a lancing fear that pierced his heart, *not a wall…*

Wings.

WOOOSH!

All at once the darkness of the night was banished in a roar of heat and brilliant light. Bahrek's mount screamed and pulled up short, nearly sending the man toppling over its neck as a veritable *barricade* of white flames erupted from nothing not fifteen feet in front of him. Sand and dust were kicked up as the horse's hooves fought the give of the loose ground, and behind him Bahrek heard the shouts and curses of the other men mixing with the shrill, terrified neighing of their own animals. His head spun, and he battled his confusion as the charge dissolved into chaos within seconds.

"HOLD!" he howled as he tried to piece together what was happening. "HOLD! IT'S A TRAP! FORM UP! FORM—!"

Zip! Thud!

Before he could finish the order, one of his officers shrieked in pain, tumbling from his horse and clutching at his stomach. Bahrek had just enough time to make out the fletched shaft buried above the soldier's hip when the sound of a dozen more arrows whistled over the snap and crackle of the fire, and he cursed as he threw himself out of his saddle. A projectile that must have been meant for him *crunched* into the sand not far away, and he heard more shouts of panic and agony rising from among his soldiers.

"Captain!" someone was shouting. "The ridges! They're up on the ridges!"

Bahrek turned his eyes skyward, still careful to stay tucked behind the thick body of his horse as more arrows screamed through the air. Sure enough, well-illuminated up and to his left, he could make out what looked like dozens of dark-skinned men in mismatched armor looming over them, bows *twanging* with each release, raining silent death down into the soldiers of Dynec. They fired with amazing accuracy, their arrows streaking down to *thunk* into Bahrek's unit one after the other while they scrambled to dismount.

"CEASE FIRE!"

The command rang like an eruption over the cacophony of the massacre. With alarming abruptness, the thrum of the bows ended, and the screaming horses seemed to quiet, struck dumb by the fierceness of the order. Unable to help himself, Bahrek turned his head in the direction the voice had come, followed swiftly by his surrounding officers and every soldier near them. Before their eyes the white flames that had cut off the charge flickered, then parted like a gate opening from some fiery underworld.

Even though Bahrek knew what it was that was going to step through, the foreknowledge did nothing to quell his horror when the figure appeared, black against the brilliance of the magic as it collapsed once more behind him.

Raz i'Syul Arro was, without exception, the most formidable presence to which Bahrek had ever born witness. The soldier had seen his fair share of atherian in his time—Dynec being a frequent hub for slave traders and head-hunters on their way to or from Perce or the Seven Cities—but *never* in his life had he encountered a lizard-kind that would have held a candle to the Monster of Karth. Arro stood an easy seven feet tall, his lithe form built for speed and power, the dark scales of his arms and legs mostly hidden by metal armor or leather wraps taut with roped muscle. His hands were gloved in steel-clawed gauntlets, and he held his massive, twin-headed spear—"Ahna", Bahrek recalled her name as he took the weapon in—easily at his side, like she weighed nothing more than a walking staff. On his hip was looped a strange-looking, long-handled axe, along with a dagger, and the hilt of a sword protruded over his right shoulder. His wings, extended some six or seven feet on either side of him from beneath a fur mantle that trailed behind him as he walked, were blood-red and spidered with dark veins in the light.

They shared their color with his spined ears, as well as the crest of leathery skin that rose like a bladed sail along the back of his neck and head.

If all that wasn't enough to bring the world to a standstill, though, the Monster's eyes could have managed it all on their own.

Their gold was of a brighter shade than most Bahrek had seen in his time, but there was something sharper and cooler about that gaze that he couldn't place at first, something almost alien. Arro's vertically slit black pupils took in the chaos of the writhing horses and gaping soldiers impassively, and only when they settled on *him*, still at the head of the surviving force, did the captain see the stillness in them, the steely edge that was not quite hunger, but something more than base cruelty.

They were the eyes of a killer, a demon who Bahrek suddenly grasped had likely delivered more souls to the Moon in his time than all the present soldiers would ever have managed combined.

"You."

Bahrek blinked, then felt his stomach flip when he realized that not only was the Monster still staring right at him, but the beast had also lifted a metal-clawed finger of his free hand to point in his direction.

"I'm assuming you're in command?" Arro asked him, dropping his hand and starting to move toward Bahrek. As he did, the nearest horses whinnied shrilly and began to shy away, shuffling back to put as much distance between themselves and the atherian as possible. Bahrek couldn't blame them. Though he had the support of his archers on the dune ridges overhead, the Monster himself was moving alone within reach of more than two hundred of Dynec's finest. It might have seemed mad, but Arro stepped forward with such confidence, Bahrek wasn't even sure he could muster up the courage to raise the scimitar he suddenly remembered he was still holding. The atherian didn't seem the least bit bothered by the dozens of blades which partially encircled him, gleaming in the light of the white fire, his eyes not leaving the captain for so much as a moment.

"Well?" the Monster snapped when he stood not five feet away.

The sharpness of the demand brought Bahrek to his senses. Keeping one hand on the flank of his horse to shield his left side from the bowmen above, he brought his sword up defensively. "Aye, I am!" he shouted back, proud of the bravado he managed to inject in his voice and praying to the Sun the men closest to him wouldn't notice his knees shaking. "Are you going to offer us terms, Monster? You won't convince us to betray our city!"

At that, Arro's golden eyes narrowed dangerously, and the tip of Bahrek's scimitar began to tremble as his quivering reached his hands.

"Convince you?" the atherian asked, finally looking away again to sweep his gaze once more over the faces of the other soldiers. "Here? When you're surrounded by your men? Of course I couldn't." His eyes fell once more on Bahrek. "As for your question…"

Had the captain blinked, he would have missed the movement. Quick as the flickering of the shadows around their trapped cohort, Raz i'Syul Arro closed the gap between them. Instead of the atherian bearing down with his spear, though, Bahrek felt the leather and steel edge of a gauntleted hand collide with the bone beneath his ear as Arro dealt him a chopping blow that sent his vision spinning immediately into darkness.

The last words he made out were the Monster's, dull and resigned, muttered mostly to himself.

"The time for negotiations is long past, I think."

And then all Bahrek heard were the screams of men and the sounds of rending flesh and shearing steel before his mind gave in to the darkness of unconsciousness.

Raz ripped into the surviving soldiers without a moment's hesitation, lancing forward and cleaving Ahna in a diagonal upwards blow through the gut and chest of two who were standing too close to each other nearby. Even as they fell he was moving again, dashing sideways and using the rearing forms of the panicking horses as cover while the dviassegai lashed back and forth. Ordinarily, Raz would never had launched himself into an offensive against such staggering odds. As it was, he was sure he would get an earful from Syrah later. He wasn't worried, though. He had faith in his generals, watching and waiting atop the dunes above.

Sure enough, as he knocked a blade free of one unfortunate soldier's hand and twisted to skewer the poor man through the throat with Ahna's bottom tip, Raz made out a familiar, gravelly voice booming out over the renewed battle.

"CHARGE!"

Leaping backwards as two more soldiers threw themselves at him, Raz disengaged from the fight just long enough to look up. Akelo Aseni's *kuja* bowmen—the dark-skinned Percian plainsmen who'd hunted the wild savannahs of Perce before being thrown into chains by the cities—had disappeared from the ridges. In their places, a thousand armored fighters were barreling down into the valley from either side, running or sliding along the smooth sand as they howled defiantly. Together they formed a myriad wash of every race of mankind: Southern, Northern, Percian, West Isler, and men and women from every other corner of the world. Interspersed among them, some hundred atherian, male and female alike, roared as they leapt into the fray. The group bore a mismatched array of armor, most with pieces of white-and-gold or black-and-red leather that had once been the uniform of the soldiers of Karesh Syl and Karesh Nan respectively, and their weaponry was equally as scattered. Some fought with swords and shields, others with hammers or axes or shortspears. Among the lizard-kind, not a few among them didn't bother with steel of any sort, ripping into the Dynec soldiers with tooth and claw and tail. Overseeing them all, one last archer stood still atop the crest of the eastern dune, clad in his own full set of white-and-gold dyed leathers, firing off arrows with such splendid precision it might have seemed inhuman to anyone who had not witnessed it before. Despite his advanced years, Akelo Aseni stood tall and strong as the last of the army poured down the hill around him, his broad shoulders straining against his armor as he drew his bow back time and time again. Even as he fired into the melee below, the old Percian shouted out encouragements to the men, spurring them forward.

Unable to keep himself from chuckling grimly, Raz dove back into the fight.

It was a short, brutal battle, lasting no more than five minutes in its extent. A few times Raz saw Dynec soldiers scrambling up the incline of the hills in an attempt to escape the slaughter of the ambush, but those that chose the east slope never made it halfway up before tumbling toward the valley floor again with an arrow between the eyes. Those that attempted the west hill were often blasted down again in flashes of magic, while the ones that actually made it to the top tended to fall back down already dead.

Raz made a mental note to compliment Karan on her improving skills.

He moved around the battlefield of his own fashion, engaging pairs, trios, and even the occasional foursomes as the opportunities presented themselves. Before long Raz had lost himself to the rhythm of the violence, burying his conscious mind deep and allowing body and instinct to take over the dance of blood. Eventually Ahna became too unwieldy to use in proximity to his own men as they drowned the Dynec riders in overwhelming numbers, and so he left her skewered through the ribs of one soldier as he ducked and rolled under the horizontal blow of another, regaining his feet with the sagaris drawn in one hand and his straight-edged gladius bare in the other. The paired weapons went about their work at once, cutting a precise pattern through the swath of fighters as efficiently as a physician might wield a scalpel. The axe hooked and redirected blows while the sword took advantage of the forced opening to do its grisly work. Before long, Raz was surrounded by bodies and pockets of fighting. Some of the soldiers threw down their armaments in surrender, but most shouted out Dynec's name as they fought to reach him, thinking perhaps to cleave the head of the army from its shoulders. He respected their bravery, in his own way. From the depths of the battle fog, Raz prayed to the Moon that she would carry their souls quickly into Her Stars even as he cut them down one after the other after the other. The sagaris whipped out, dragging a sword down before flashing up again to split the wielder's skull in two from the jaw up. The gladius hummed and splattered blood as it carved matching gashes into the throats of two men who'd approached in a staggered formation from the same side. Raz's clawed feet did their own work, ripping through leather, cloth, and flesh alike with savage kicks, and what men didn't die of their wounds fell silent as his tail lashed out to break necks and cave chests in with matching *crunches* of shattering bone.

Eventually, only a straggling few of the two hundred and fifty proud soldiers of the fringe city remained, and before long even this handful fell or tossed down their blades. As Raz retracted his gladius from where he'd buried it into the eye of a woman who'd tried to run him through from behind, he straightened to the resounding cheers of victory rising up from the fighters under his command, many of them thrusting their weapons into the air in celebration.

"Gather the horses!" Akelo's voice shouted out from nearby, and Raz turned to find the old man approaching him through the crowd to his right, bow still in one hand. "See to the wounded and the survivors! Those with serious injuries should be seen by the Witch, but deal mercy where you must!"

At once the victorious cheering subdued, replaced with shouts of "Aye, sir!" Raz gave the Percian a crooked smiled as the humans and atherian all around them began moving together, transitioning with almost-professional swiftness into triage groups.

"I'd vote that went smooth enough," he said once Akelo came to stand before him, the man's dark eyes taking in the dozen or so bodies scattered about Raz's feet. "About as good an outcome as one could expect, at least."

The Percian nodded, then lifted his gaze to scan the contingent now dutifully going about their tasks. Everywhere the horses were being calmed, and cries of the injured and dying were shifting as they were heaved up and rushed eastward, back toward the camp.

"An easy victory," Akelo answered finally, frowning as an atherian barreled past, holding a human girl of about fifteen or sixteen summers in his thick arms while being careful not to jostle the broken spearhead buried in her shoulder. "Nothing to be too proud of before we get the casualty toll."

"It's a start, though," Raz said with a shrug, moving aside as a pair of Dynec soldiers were led past at swordpoint, hands raised in concession. "It's been too long since we took Karesh Nan. An early victory will raise morale for the battles to come."

"Things don't look too bad from above either."

The voice, soothing even in its uneasiness, had an instant effect on Raz. His body loosened, and the residual tension he hadn't known had been lingering in his limbs faded away. Together he and Akelo turned to see Syrah picking her way toward them through the carnage, Karan right behind her, the female's blades drawn and bloody while she scanned the bodies of the dead for any sign of latent trouble. Raz couldn't help but feel a little relieved as the woman came to stand on his other side, opposite Akelo, her face twisted in distaste at the scene before them.

"Could you give an estimate?" he asked her, and Syrah's brow crinkled as she considered the request. She held firm to the wall of arcane fire some thirty feet up the pass from them, willing it on to illuminate the work of the army, but with her back to it and her black silk hood up over her head, the darkness fell heavily against the bags under her eyes. She hadn't been sleeping well, these last months. New nightmares plagued her every night, complementing the old ones that had been terrifying enough on their own. Only when he held her to him until the Sun came up did she ever find some measure of peaceful slumber, but their duties within the camp infrequently allowed for that, and on those nights it was *Raz* who didn't often sleep well.

Once more he hurt, looking at the toll the past was taking on the present.

"Ten, maybe fifteen dead?" Syrah guessed, her good eye following the shivering form of a West Isler being hurried eastward on a shield by two other men. "I'll get you a full report by morning."

"Afternoon will be fine," he told her gently, sliding his sagaris into the loop on his belt and wiping his hands clean of blood on his cloak before brushing her hood carefully off her head. Her white skin came alive, then, brighter in the open air. "Try to get some sleep tonight, when you can."

Syrah turned her face up to him, and the gratitude in her smile was buried under a resigned—almost amused—doubt that wrinkled around her rose-colored eye.

"Something tells me not to hold out much hope for that," she grumbled with half a laugh.

At that very moment, there was a shout from up the path.

"Witch! Someone get the Witch! We need help here!"

Syrah's face tensed, and she reached out to take Raz's hand briefly, giving it a quick squeeze through his gauntlet.

"Duty calls," she said in a hurry, and Raz nodded and let her go. The woman exchanged a look with Karan, then the pair of them took off in a rush, running toward the shout.

"I won't get used to it anytime soon," Akelo muttered in something like annoyance.

Raz, not following, cast an eye at him sidelong.

"'Witch'," the Percian quoted in clarification, frowning and tilting his head into the mass of soldiers, where more shouts for Syrah's assistance were rising from about the battlefield.

"Ah." Raz shrugged, though he nodded in understanding. "So long as it's at her request, there's not much I'm willing to do about it. I think it's an attempt to come to terms with things…"

Akelo snorted, unstringing his bow before pulling his spiked leather helm off with one hand. The older man's black hair was peppered with grey and white, but the hollowness of his cheeks and the emptiness in his eyes Raz had seen when they'd first met—when the Percian had been a slave in the oar-galley of a pirate ship—were long gone.

"Even if that's true, there must be a better way to go about it," Akelo mumbled, tucking his helmet under one arm while he continued to gaze in the direction Syrah and Karan had disappeared into the masses. Eventually, he gave Raz a questioning look. "She still hasn't picked up her staff, has she?"

Raz shook his head sadly. "Nor any of her old things."

Akelo sighed, reaching up to rub his temples with thumb and forefinger. "Well, I suppose we all have our demons to fight," he grumbled, turning away and starting back toward the flames that were finally fading with Syrah's distance. "And some are more pressing than others, for the time being."

Raz grunted in ascension, moving to follow the man the short walk back up the path.

"Have we heard word if there were any other attacks?" he asked as they moved. It had been a concern since dusk, when the first scouts had reported sighting of the riders. Where there was one assault force, there might be more.

Akelo shook his head. "None. I'm assuming Dynec didn't want to spread itself *too* thin, given our proximity."

"Good." Raz gave up a relieved huff, stepping away briefly to wrench Ahna out of the corpse he'd left her in. "Though we could have used the extra horses."

"With the numbers we've gained tonight, it will bring our cavalry up to almost eighteen hundred strong, assuming we can find decent riders," Akelo said while Raz wiped the dviassegai's blades clean on the dead soldier's uniform. "You know what they say regarding being particular about gifted horses, I'm sure."

"Eighteen hundred," Raz repeated thoughtfully, ignoring the joke and catching up to the old man in a few quick strides, Ahna back over his shoulder. "More would be better. We can count on the Mahsadën having a greater number, at the very least. Word is Karavyl trades for horses with the Seven Cities on a regular basis."

"And if Dynec was willing to risk losing two hundred and fifty in an attempt to distract us, their numbers might not be anything to sneeze at either," Akelo added with a nod.

"Well," Raz started as the two of them came to a final stop five yards from the edge of the shrinking white flames, looking down at their feet, "as for that, there's only one way to find out, isn't there?"

Akelo, for his part, only grunted in agreement, then stuck a foot out to flip the unconscious commander—still sprawled face-first in the sand where Raz had dropped him—onto his back.

"You're about to have a very, very long night, friend," the Percian muttered, sounding almost sympathetic.

III

"There are two tools one needs to make any man sing: an open hand, and a closed fist."

— Ergoin Sass

Syrah Brahnt finished her letter with a signed flourish, then dropped the quill into the inkwell on the corner of her small desk, letting out a groan of relief.

"Done?" Karan Brightneck asked from where she sat on a reed matting to Syrah's right, looking up from the book she'd been studiously perusing. They didn't have the parchment to spare for Syrah to teach the young atherian how to write just yet, but Karan had taken to reading with a gusto that made her proud seeing her friend now. The well-worn book, *The Art of Sword & Shield,* looked frighteningly fragile in the female's long, clawed fingers, and the old pages were tinged amber in the reflection of the yellow scales that formed an upside-down arrowhead along the underside of her reptilian neck.

"Yes," Syrah answered with a slow nod, reaching out to wave a hand over the letter she'd just completed. There was a flash of white, and the ink—which had been gleaming fresh and wet in the light of the open tent flap behind her—dried instantly. This done, Syrah freed the sheet from the paired candlesticks that had been holding it flat, then rolled the parchment into a tight scroll. "Can you see this off today?" she asked, holding the letter to her companion as Karan put the book down and pushed herself to her feet. "The sooner we get a response the better."

The atherian took the scroll with an uneasy look. Most humans would have found the expression strange, the shifting of the female's reptilian features too alien to understand, but after nearly a year spent with Raz—first in Cyurgi' Di, the great Citadel of the Laorin faith, then traversing world and Dramion Sea—Syrah was as familiar with atherian emotion as she was with her own.

"I'll try," Karan said, though she didn't seem hopeful as she tucked the letter into her belt. "We were short on birds last I heard, though. With Dynec so close, most of them are out with the other scouts, making sure we aren't flanked before we reach the city."

Syrah shrugged in resignation, easing herself to rest against the chair. "Whenever you can is fine, then. We certainly have more pressing problems to worry about, for the moment."

That was true enough, to say the least. As she'd feared, Syrah hadn't gotten so much as a wink of sleep the night before, having spent most of the evening assisting in prepping the counter-ambush and waiting for Dynec's assault with Raz and the other generals. After that, what hours before morning had remained to her were spent tending to the injured and dying until morning. She cursed her fatigue, drawing a touch of magic from her reserves into her body. Instantly she felt refreshed, the weight behind her eyes subsiding, but she knew she couldn't hold off sleep forever. Magic could only do so much to fend off what the body couldn't handle unaided.

"Just a little longer," she muttered to herself, standing up and stretching before looking around.

Apart from her portable desk tucked against the north wall of the circular tent, there was very little to the space that would have made it seem like the quarters of the commander of an army fifty thousand strong, not to mention one of his generals' as well. Raz's and her bedrolls were tucked side-by-side in the center of the tent, and Ahna rested against the nearest of the wooden struts that held up the worn and weathered cloth canvas, her blades covered once more in a burlap sack. Syrah's steel staff was there, too, leaned up beside the dviassegai, but she ignored it. Raz insisted the weapon be kept on hand in case of attack, and Syrah had relented to the logic of his words mostly to avoid an argument.

It had been two months now, though, since she'd handled that patterned steel…

Two months, Syrah thought to herself, blinking when a cloud shifted over the sun outside, momentarily dimming the light of the day pouring in from the open tent flap. *Has it really been so long?*

It seemed the weeks had passed at a crawl even as they tore by in a blur. The nights were longest—those Syrah spent apart from Raz due to their diverging responsibilities in the camp the hardest to get through—but the days had often been fleeting, for which she was grateful. After the slaying of its Tash and the surrender of its army, Karesh Syl had been claimed by Raz and the newly freed slaves in a matter of hours. The weeks of march after that had been tense with anticipation and fear, but Karesh Nan had proven no match for the wrath of the "Dragon of the North," especially when uprisings started to flare up *within* the city walls as the enslaved heard that Raz i'Syul Arro himself had come to break their chains. A week later they'd been on the move again, but even in the month since Syrah had kept busy, tending to the needs of men and women who'd often never known what it was to have a full stomach, much less how one properly hefted a shield or wielded a sword. Raz, his generals, and all their lesser officers pushed the army hard even while they pressed a score of miles north every day, and training injuries were common, though less and less frequent with each passing week.

Now, with less than two days before they reached the walls of Dynec, the first of the desert fringe cities, Syrah knew she'd well done her part in raising the army Raz would need to rid the world of its greatest cruelties.

"Syrah? Ya' in here?"

There was the soft *crunch* of sand outside the tent, and Syrah turned in time for another shadow to pass over the space as a figure ducked under the threshold. She'd recognized the Southern drawl at once, and she gave the man a quick smile as he stood straight and shook dust out of his clothes.

"Marsus," she said by way of greeting. "How can I help you?"

Marsus Byrn returned a toothy grin, though he looked somewhat strained as he nodded to Karan over Syrah's shoulder. Among the galley slaves Raz had freed from pirates when they'd *first* reached Perce nearly four months prior, the Southerner had been with them for as long as Akelo Aseni. An original member of the Dragon's first pitiful corps, Marsus was one of several of that group to which Raz had given the title of "general" in the week following the fall of Karesh Syl. In most cases, the statuses were for show, necessary in establishing a hierarchy within their forces as their numbers swelled from a mere score of men to thirty thousand almost overnight when the city was overrun. The generals, largely having been no more than slaves themselves for a large portion of their lives, offered their council when asked, but were largely satisfied with the broader role they played: as men Raz trusted implicitly to carry out his orders without fault. Of those that had risen in the ranks, only a few took independent action. Akelo, obviously, was one such example.

Another was Marsus Byrn, who'd been born and raised in the nearby city of Karavyl, and whose knowledge of the southern sand plains had proven invaluable more than once.

"Karan, I need ya' at the south end of the march," Marsus told the atherian, tossing a thumb over his shoulder to indicate none-too-gently that she was dismissed. "Couple of the injured last night were s'pose to scout our trail today, and yer on the reserve list."

It was Karan's turn to grumble dejectedly, but not before she gave Syrah a questioning look. Per Raz's direct order the young atherian had special privileges in the camp, and if Syrah wanted her to stay there was nothing Marsus—even as the commanding general of the army's human *and* atherian scouting parties—would or could do to stop it.

Syrah, though, nodded to indicate that she was fine.

The Southerner knew well her fears, and she trusted him to keep out of arm's reach so long as he could help it.

"I'll find you as soon as I get back," Karan promised, patting Syrah's arm affectionately with a clawed hand as she made her way for the tent flap. "And I'll see what I can do about finding a bird for your letter."

Syrah gave her a word of thanks, watching the atherian leave.

"Ya' got a good girl there," Marsus said after the female was gone, scratching at his beard. "Damn fine scout, too."

"No thanks to her commander, of course," Syrah said with a strained smile, crossing her arms over her chest. She might trust Marsus, even despite his weathered, rugged appearance, but it was still hard to be alone with any man that wasn't Raz.

The general's grey eyes fell briefly to her arms, and for a moment she saw sadness there, lingering in his gaze. She appreciated it, just as she appreciated the fact that Marsus—along with Akelo and every one of the survivors of the assault on the Tash palace in Karesh Syl—abjectly refused to call her "Witch" no matter how often she insisted.

It was heartening to know there were those who would stand by her, regardless of how much she thought she deserved it or not.

"Mind yer manners, woman," Marsus chuckled, the somberness fleeing his face as his grin returned. "Puttin' me in charge of our runners was the smartest thing yer man's done since he threw together this lil' band of his."

Syrah laughed, glad to have something to smile honestly about with Karan gone. "I'll tell you what." She raised an eyebrow in a mock threat. "You finally spit out what it is you came to see me about, and I *won't* tell Raz you think of his army as a 'little band'."

Marsus raised his hands in a playful show of terror. "Fair enough, fair enough," he snorted. Then his face grew serious. "It's actually him who's sent for ya'. I'm just the messenger. Yer needed in the general's pavilion."

Syrah's stomach sunk at that, and her unease must have shown because Marsus looked pained as he spoke next.

"He told me to tell ya' you don't have to come," he stated quickly. "We can send fer one of the healers you've been trainin' to—"

"No." Syrah cut him off, turning and moving to retrieve a length of thin grey silk from where it hung across the back of the chair before the desk. "It's fine. No sense in pretending I wasn't expecting it. Thought I'd be called sooner, honestly."

"Woulda' been preferable," Marsus grumbled, stepping respectfully away from the tent entrance as Syrah approached again, winding the silk about her neck and face. "Things are takin' longer than expected, unfortunately."

Syrah said nothing at that, stopping before the threshold just long enough to finish wrapping the fabric about her head, ensuring not even a sliver of skin was exposed, before pulling the black hood of her silk tunic over her braided hair and stepping out into the heat of the morning.

Even in the middle of the cooler season—the period of eight to ten months between the blistering desert summers—the sun's gaze was nothing short of maddening as it hung suspended in the heavens to the east. It wasn't the first time Syrah had visited the South, of course. Nearly a decade prior she'd taken a pilgrimage to the fringe city of Karth with her then-Priest-Mentor, Talo Brahnt, as well as Jofrey al'Sen and his acolyte, Rehn Hartlet. In all the time since she'd thought she'd never forgotten the misery of the heat, the wickedness of the sun in the day and the vicious cold of the nights after the moon's ascent. To her great chagrin, however, in the week since they'd crossed the border from the more mild climates of Perce into the sand plains, Syrah was rediscovering her wretchedness on a whole new level. She *hated* this place. She hated the blistering light that forced her to cover every inch of her pallid skin to keep it from blistering, down to the dark silks drawn over her face to shield her sensitive eye from the glare. She hated the oppressive dryness of the air, the peeling and cracking of her lips and the knuckles of her fingers, and the fact that they generally had to stop for a full day at every rare watering hole they found just to fill and refresh the army's barrels and pouches. She hated the utter lack of life, unable to remove herself from the depressing stillness of the land, even though she knew it was only a façade for the hidden depths and vigor of the desert.

"Lifegiver's arse," she grunted, shading her hidden face and peeking up at the sky above. "How do you *live* in a place like this?"

"Honestly?" Marsus asked with a chuckle, stepping around her and starting north through the tents that surrounded them on all sides. "After seein' a bit more of the world, I think it's 'cause we ain't got no sense that there's anythin' better out there."

As appropriate an answer as can be given, I guess, Syrah thought as she stepped in beside the Southerner, looking around.

Born and raised in the great forests and mountains of the North, it had taken a long time for Syrah to get accustomed to waking up every morning in a world where the air wasn't cool and the land wasn't a rich conglomeration of verdant greenery or snow-capped cliffs. At first it had been the vast expanse of the Dramion Sea, which she'd sailed for two months with Raz and other friends the Lifegiver had cruelly reclaimed not so long ago. After that, it had been the marshes and grasslands of Perce, awesome in their own right, extending as unbroken plains of gold and green until the world appeared as nothing more than a flat disc occasionally interrupted by herds of wild beast and massive, solitary trees. Their stays in Karesh Syl and Karesh Nan had been brief and precarious, but even then there'd been beauty in the fragile and breathtaking architecture of the cities, the clean marble and metal buildings so far removed from the rugged timber and stone of Northern designs or the plain mudbrick of the South's municipalities. There had existed something to take in wherever they went, and Syrah had never really felt much in the fashion of homesickness or nostalgia.

Now, though, it often seemed that was *all* she felt…

Rising up on either side of them, like waves of orange and red frozen in time, the dunes of the desert plains felt as solid and unforgiving as the bars of an iron cage, looming over her in a way that made her feel like the land was merely waiting for a moment to devour her whole. The wind—particularly fierce today—was tolerable down in the valleys between the hills, but overhead the sand streaked from the ridges in whipping plumes, tumbling down on their heads in an intermittent rain of dust and grit. Ahead of her, Syrah watched Marsus pull up the edge of the thin scarf he had wrapped around his neck, covering his nose and mouth as they moved.

How she *hated* this place.

They walked for about five minutes, exchanging small talk while they navigated the camp with habitual ease. The layout was structured and familiar despite the fact that the army often moved as much as twenty miles a day even across the sand, packing and unpacking almost every morning and evening. Syrah knew things got a little more chaotic as one moved south along the marching line, but here at the head of the host the tents generally belonged to the generals or their immediate subordinates, so a patterned routine had rapidly developed. The men Raz had raised as minor officers within their forces were generally former soldiers of one land or another—usually prisoners of war turned slaves and sold to Perce for a profit before being freed by 'the Dragon'—and as a result discipline had quickly found its way into the ranks of their otherwise untrained fighters. The order made negotiating what might have been a chaotic encampment much easier, so it wasn't too long before Syrah felt the ground steepen beneath her feet, and she and Marsus began to climb.

The general's pavilion—a sprawling, single-chambered marque that had apparently once belonged to the Tash of Karesh Nan himself—had been painstakingly staked out along the sweeping crest of a dune at the northern tip of the army. As they struggled up the shifting sand, both Syrah and Marsus cursed their unsteady footing and the strengthening wind, oftentimes using their hands to steady themselves. The Southerner managed the top of the hill first, and turned to see how Syrah was managing, though he didn't extend an arm in offered support.

He knew better, and she was grateful for it.

With a huff and a grunt, Syrah found her feet, standing up and grabbing hold of the edges of her hood as it rippled over her head and face, threatening to fall away,

"Inside!" Marsus yelled over the wind, indicating the heavy flap that led into the massive, beating tent. Syrah nodded, indicating that she would follow, and the Southerner hurried forward, shielding his eyes from the blowing sand with an arm as he did. For once she was thankful for her silk wraps protecting her from the worst of the elements. As Marsus made to pull open the entrance, Syrah took advantage to look over her shoulder, into the desert's abuse.

Unbidden, much of her tension and increasingly foul mood fell away when she took in the scene that sprawled southward before her, the hidden view that would never have been revealed to her from the valley floor below.

In snaking columns that followed the paths in the dips of the desert, the Dragon's army cut dark circuits against the sand, like black rivers branching out from a central pool below. Men and women of every land mixed with male and female atherian as they maneuvered around each other in the narrow passes through the tents, armed and armored as they went about their duties. Some carried food and supplies this way and that, while others had bundles of spears, arrows, and various other weaponry tucked under their arms or over shoulders. To the west, through a gap in the landscape, Syrah made out a contingent of soldiers going about their daily drills with sword and shield along the flattest areas they'd been able to find, the shouting of the officers leading the training lost to the distance and wind. To the east, smoke curled from among the dunes, whisked away into the sky from the cooking fires that would be going strong as the morning meals were rationed and prep began for the midday lunch they would ordinarily have had on the move.

And there, above all of it, cut from cloth of every shape, color, and size, the Dragon's banners hung proud.

From where she sat, Syrah thought she could see some fifty standards, if not more, staked out indiscriminately wherever limited space had allowed. Most were sewn from the white and gold cloth that had once flown opulently within the palace and over the ramparts of Karesh Syl, but there were others, pieced together out of whatever spare fabric could be sacrificed by the proud soldiers of the army. Some were well-crafted and carefully maintained, while others were weather-beaten and starting to fade after weeks under the harsh glare of the sun. Many were large, as tall and broad as a man, but still more were small, sometimes mere foot-by-foot cloths raised over individual tents. Regardless of their make, though, all depicted the same symbol:

The beautiful, bare form of a woman, her breasts hidden beneath waving hair, with dragon's wings extending from her back.

The sight of the Sylgid—the water spirit that was said to dwell in the rivers and lakes of the Northern mountains—always pulled at Syrah's heart. Heavy memories weighed down on her, but at the same time she felt the very swell of pride that had had so many flock to these banners as the Tashes of Perce fell. It seemed an apt comparison for much of the past months, when she considered it.

The dignity of triumph, after all, so often suppressed the consideration of how much victory could cost…

For a few seconds longer Syrah allowed herself to gaze out over the camp, one hand still holding onto her hood as her silks billowed around her. The banners bounced and fluttered below, making the winged Sylgid sway, and the Priestess couldn't help but give a small smile, reminded of how it wasn't so long ago that she had danced and drunk and laughed with friends now lost.

Then, gathering herself, she turned on her heel and headed for the tent, making for the entrance Marsus was holding open for her, the wind buffeting her along all the while.

IV

The inside of the general's pavilion was usually as bland and unassuming as any of the other tents that comprised the army's quarters. Weighed down by enough food and water to last them their hard march toward the Cienbal desert, it wasn't like they'd had much room to spare for ornamentations and comforts. Most nights, when the higher officers gathered to make their reports, the center of the massive space was taken up by a large, collapsible table Raz had had put together before they'd left the remnants of Karesh Syl. Everyone would gather around to review their collective progress for the day, as well as update all present on any problems that had incurred over the course of the usually-six-to-eight-hour march. Injury summaries, repairs, any fights and disagreements in the ranks—the unavoidable and all-too-frequent result of a long, arduous journey that tested the patience of fifty thousand souls. Such meetings were an active affair, sometimes almost cheerful, with pleasantries exchanged when appropriate, and spirits often high as they successfully pressed constantly northward.

What awaited Syrah within on *this* day, on the other hand, could not have been further removed from anything remotely pleasant.

Light penetrated the space through fist-sized holes in the ceiling, cutting down in shifting pillars against the dust that lingered heavy in the air. It illuminated some dozen people in somber glows, all standing silently along the outskirts of the tent, their backs to the cloth as the wind beat at the walls behind them. Most of the generals were present, Syrah saw at a glance, nodding quickly to a few who looked her way when she stepped in, pulling her hood off as she did. There were several lesser officers as well, generally standing near their superiors, and as Syrah unbound the length of silks from her face she found the lumbering outline she was looking for, waiting not ten feet away to her right, closer to the center of the room than a majority of the rest.

Raz stood side-by-side with Akelo, both men not having looked around as she and Marsus had entered. Even turned away from her Syrah could tell the atherian was in no winning mood. His arms were crossed over his bare chest, and his broad shoulders were tense to the point where the massive wings he had tucked to his back flexed and flickered testily every few seconds. He wore no armor this morning—though his gladius was hung in its usual place and the sagaris was looped off his hip—but he looked dangerously forbidding all the same. Even his neck-crest, usually only raised when he needed to make a point, stood half-erect, like the hackles of a threatened wolf, and his frown was so pronounced Syrah saw the white of fangs gleaming in the dim light.

Then again, as she moved toward him, Syrah supposed it wasn't hard to guess what had fouled the atherian's temper.

There, at the very center of the space, a man sat shivering and breathing hard, his hands and ankles tightly lashed to the simple wooden chair that was his prison. His pants were torn and dirty, but the rest of his body was exposed, his clothes likely having been pulled off or cut away in the early hours of the morning. The tan skin of his arms glistened with sweat as the limbs strained against the bindings, and the hair of his chest was matted with blood that flowed in watery trails down his stomach. He was breathing heavily, wheezing in pain and fatigue, and his head hung limply forward, long hair tumbling, damp and loose, about his ears.

A few feet from the prisoner, one more familiar figure stood silently, bloodied fists at his sides, blue eyes on the beaten man. Hur was another of Raz's most trusted, a mute Northerner who'd been born to the wild clans of the Saragrias Ranges, the mountains in which Syrah herself was raised. By the standards of his kind he was perhaps only slightly above average in height and breadth, but compared to the more slender persons waiting along the edges of the tent, Hur seemed almost half-a-giant. At six-and-a-half feet tall, only Raz stood taller than the mountain man, and both had learned to put his intimidating presence to good use. Among the generals, only Hur commanded no actual troops—his lack of a tongue would have made giving orders something of an ordeal, after all—but he'd proven himself an essential part of the army's stability as the man in charge of disciplinary action and security within the ranks of their former slaves. Raised among the violent customs of his people, the Northerner didn't blink twice at shedding blood when needed, but Syrah had also come to know him as a man of surprising intelligence and careful thought. Though she'd never seen him in action, she'd heard that Hur's brand of judgment was feared, but not unfair, and that his interventions rarely came to blows.

When they did, though, no one who'd ever gone toe-to-toe with the tribesman had ever stood a chance.

Syrah realized, now, that she was seeing why.

"Tell me you at least *tried* to reason with him?" she asked quietly, coming to stand beside Raz as Marsus slipped off to an empty place along the east wall of the pavilion.

Raz and Akelo—both having apparently been deep in thought while they glared at the bound man—twitched together at the sound of her voice. They looked around as one, and though his arms didn't uncross, Syrah felt her heart warm as she saw some of the tension leave Raz's body, thinking she might have even heard a sigh of relief from the atherian.

Just as his presence always did so much to stave away the darkness that had pressed so heavily on her mind of late, Raz had always told her the day was brighter when she was by his side.

"We did *more* than try," he answered in an annoyed grunt, looking back around at where Hur stood over the prisoner. "Akelo spent *three hours* with him, trying to get him to talk. I didn't choose to resort to this—" he gestured at the bloody scene with a distasteful curl of his lip "—until the Sun started to rise. After that..." He shrugged, letting the point hang while Akelo nodded in agreement on his other side.

"After that, he began talking fast enough," Syrah mumbled, finishing the sentence. "Yes... I can imagine why... Hur." The big Northerner looked around at her expectantly as she called his name. "Lift his face for me, please."

Hur did as she said, not even glancing at Raz for confirmation first. Stepping forward, he took a fistful of the man's matted hair and pulled his head back, raising it so that the prisoner's features were visible to the room. Syrah flinched, grimacing at the sight, but forced herself to move toward the man, taking in the damage critically.

"Dislocated jaw, contusions to both eyes, lacerations to cheeks and forehead," she grumbled, already pulling off the thin leather gloves that had shielded her hands from the sun outside. "A broken nose, too, by looks of it, and I would be shocked if he hasn't swallowed a few teeth." She raised an eyebrow at Hur. "You don't pull your punches, do you?"

In response, the mute smirked humorlessly and offered her a shrug, which Syrah might have found amusing were it not for the situation. Turning her attention back on the prisoner, she stepped around him to bend down before his face, where he could see her through his swollen lids. His eyes were so bloodshot the grey of his irises looked almost black, but his bleary gaze met hers all the same.

"I am Syrah Brahnt," she said flatly. "You may know me by a different name by now, but I trust you've heard of me?"

There was a moment's pause as the man's eyes widened ever so slightly, panic seeping into his battered face. He began to shiver, and finally nodded, the motion little more than a shaking twitch of his head.

"Good," Syrah said shortly, reaching out to free his face from some of the hair that was sticking to his bloody, sweating forehead. "Then you'll know I have the ability to ease your pain, just as I can make it much, *much* worse. Do you understand that?"

The prisoner's trembling intensified.

"I... I do," he managed to get out in an uneven breath, and Syrah felt a sickening sense of satisfaction at the response.

It was all a ploy, of course, a corrupt game she and some of the others contrived after the fall of Karesh Syl. Word of what had happened in the Tash's courtroom spread quickly with the fleeing remnants of the palace guard she and Raz had chased away, and it hadn't been hard to take advantage of the rumors that seemed to grow more twisted and sinister with every passing day. By the time they'd taken the walls of Karesh Nan, it was rare that more than a word from her was needed to get any man talking, even if Syrah never acted on her threats.

Raz, though, hated to drag her into the muck when it could be avoided. As was the case here, he'd only called for her when the work was largely done.

She loved him for that, as much as she hated herself for having brought "the Witch" into reality when grief and horror had proven too great a burden to bear…

"Good," Syrah told the prisoner, drawing her hand back from his face. "Then we'll start with your name. After that, you will tell me everything you told these officers here." She indicated the generals and their seconds, still standing about them. "Trust that I will know what is truth and what is not." She said these last words coldly, making the lie as sharp a threat as a dagger at the man's throat.

"Bah… Bahrek Lest," the prisoner wheezed through bloody lips, and Hur finally let go of his hair, letting the man hold his head up of his own accord. "I am… a captain… a captain in the Dynec guard."

"Excellent start," Syrah told him, straightening up and moving over to the mountain man, motioning for him to hold his hands out for her, palms down. Hur did as he was told, and she began weaving her healing spells into his torn and bloody knuckles—careful not to touch him—as Bahrek Lest told his story for the second time.

Dynec, it transpired, was in greater distress than they could have hoped for. The šef of the other fringe cities had abandoned it to its fate, and no significant reinforcements had been raised from the *sarydâ*, the desert mercenaries that fought for virtually anyone who had the coin to pay them. Several representatives of Dynec's Mahsadën had already been found dead under suspicious circumstances shortly after a gathering they'd attended in the great city of Miropa, across the Cienbal, and the assault the night before—which Lest had apparently led before falling to Raz not even a minute into the ambush—had been an effort to slow the Dragon's army down. The way the captain told it, the attack was intended as a last-ditch bid to give the remaining šef and the wealthier residents of the city time to flee, most heading for the cities of Cyro and Karavyl, each a week to the north and west respectively if one skirted the edge of the desert. In total, Dynec had no more than ten thousand active troops, but men had been deserting ever since they'd heard the Mahsadën of the other cities had refused to lend their support. Lest gave them everything he could about Dynec itself—from the size of the walls to the lay of the land to which of the three city gates he thought was the most defensively vulnerable—as well as the names of the trio of šef that remained within: Maltus Ameen, Kanela Saresh, and Zeres Thorne.

It was Raz that Syrah watched, as these names were listed out. The atherian's golden eyes burned into the prisoner while he spoke, though Syrah knew well where the Dragon's fury was actually directed. Lest, along with the score of others who'd surrendered to them the night before, were little more than pawns acting on the orders of those who moved them. She had little love for the likes of the captain and his riders, given what she'd heard of the corruption that plagued the South's cities of late. But Syrah—like Raz—knew that if they were to win this war, it would only be by striking at the top, at the very highest echelons of the Mahsadën. The soldiers, while still reviled, could be forgiven.

For the likes of the šef, though, there could be no such clemency.

■■

After Syrah had treated Bahrek Lest to the extent of her abilities, several of Hur's seconds were summoned to take him away. Once the prisoner had been dragged off—the wind outside buffeting those nearest the entrance every time the flap was pulled open—the generals gathered in earnest.

"This is good news!" Erom—a border from the same ship as Akelo, Marsus, and Hur—said with gusto, his hands resting absently on the handles of the daggers he always kept slung at his low back. "Dynec's defenses are weak! Taking the city will be easier than anticipated!"

"I'm not so sure," Arnus—an aging, wiry man who'd once been a legionnaire in the armies of the Imperium across the Emperor's Ocean to the west—replied with a slow shake of his head. "In the short term Dynec may indeed fall without much trouble, but the fact that the Mahsadën would so easily sacrifice one of their cities troubles me…"

"Me as well." Akelo frowned from Raz's other side, his dark eyes on the blood about their feet, splattering the reed matting where Lest had been tied to his chair. "I don't imagine it's the society's plan to simply tuck themselves away in their individual holes and hope for the best. We know each city alone has no chance against a force our size. They will be gathering their numbers, preparing to meet us on a field where they have the advantage."

"Agreed." Raz himself nodded from beside Syrah. "Time, too, is in their favor here. With their connections, the longer this war rages, the greater their amassed strength. We cannot expect the same influx of conscripts from the fringe cities as we did from Karesh Syl and Karesh Nan. In Perce, slaves with families and obligations were a rarity. Here, it is the opposite. Poverty is rampant, but the slum-dwellers are technically a free people. They will not be so quick to join us, particularly when they realize we are giving them an opportunity to take control of the cities back from the upper classes that have had one boot on their necks for generations."

"Then we must act quickly," a hissing voice spoke up from Syrah's other side. "First to Dynec, then north to Cyro. The atherian of the Crags will help us, should they hear we have flattened the two cities of man responsible for the largest portion of their enslavement."

Syrah turned to look at the figure who had spoken. Of all the generals, Zal'en was simultaneously the most sensible *and* oddest addition to their ranks. An aging atherian female, she stood with two other males of her kind flanking her, clawed hands on the hilt of their swords, vertically-slit eyes watching the rest of the table's occupants nervously. Raz had brought her into the fold not long after the fall of Karesh Nan, when the atherian had clamored for representation among the army's highest ranks. When asked whom they would choose as a leader, Zal'en had been brought forth as the most popular choice by far, and Syrah could understand why. Aside from being quick with a blade, the old female was cunning, and intimately familiar with the Common Tongue some among her people were still struggling to master. She'd been a slave for a relatively brief period—just over five years—and so hadn't yet completely lost that spark of life that many of their soldiers were only just starting to rediscover. She got along well enough with the humans of the army—even the Percian that a large portion of the lizard-kind mistrusted instinctively—and frequently assisted Hur in dolling out discipline withing the more-tribal groupings of her people when necessary.

And yet, despite all this, Syrah had never been able to bring herself to like Zal'en.

Most likely because the female very distinctly did not like *her*.

This had been clear from the moment the old atherian had ascended to the rank of general. Even when she had accompanied Raz and Akelo to deliver the promotion, Syrah had felt the coolness Zal'en emanated toward her. At first it hadn't made much sense to her, but frequently since that day—and she imagined long before that—Syrah had caught the female's eyes on her, the female's expression not hateful, but something more like disapproving. She'd noted the atherian glaring at her from across rooms and through crowds of training soldiers. She found Zal'en watching often whenever the generals met, and even once as they'd marched, Syrah with Raz and Akelo at the head atop Nymara—her beige mare—the female amid the ranks with the others of her kind.

That had been when it clicked for Syrah. At the time she'd been leaning toward Raz in her saddle to discuss what had looked like a sandstorm on the horizon. From afar, it might have seemed liked an intimate moment, which it could just as well have been.

It was her closeness to Raz, to the Dragon of the North and his army, that appeared to have earned Syrah the old female's displeasure.

After her epiphany, it had taken several days of talking herself down before Syrah was able to stand in the same room as Zal'en without fuming. In that time, she'd noticed others among the lizard-kind, too, who tended to watch her with cold eyes. It seemed always to be the older ones, those Zal'en held the most sway with, and Syrah couldn't help but wonder what sort of poison the female was whispering into their spined ears. In the year she and Raz had spent together there'd always been odd looks and strange questions—even some clear disapproval among the more hardline of the Laorin of Cyurgi 'Di—but as cruel and hateful as humans could be, none among those they'd encountered ever said a word in protest to their strange partnership. Though Zal'en and her atherian stayed just as quiet, they made no other attempt to hide their disgruntlement, and experiencing such palpable disapproval felt so odd now. Syrah hadn't even thought twice about it, had even *considered* that she and Raz might be alarming to the atherian in a way they hadn't been to the men and women who'd accompanied them in the last months. For a time she'd assumed it was merely prejudice, a wrought distaste brought on by the simple fact that she was human and Raz was the furthest thing from.

Of late, though… Of late, Syrah had been getting the impression that there was something more behind the silent glares of the lizard-kind. While she knew of no other pairs of human and atherian within the ranks of the army, friendships were abound between the two species, and no one seemed to blink twice at *those* relationships. Not even Zal'en and her older followers. It seemed too deliberate, this distinct disapproval, too targeted. Recently Syrah's suspicions had rankled her so much, she had asked Karan to see what she could find out.

Unfortunately, she and the young female's bond was common knowledge throughout the army, and they'd found Karan's questions largely dodged, ignored, or shut down entirely.

Which, of course, had done nothing to quell Syrah's misgivings…

"Ain't no guarantee the atherian would want anything to do with us," Marsus Byrn was saying to Zal'en with a frown. "Much less lend us support. Even with yer lot by our side, that don't change the fact that there'd be thirty-five thousand humans pressing on the edge of their lands. As happy as I'm sure they'd be if Cyro where to fall, we can't assume that'd make 'em open their arms to us. We might be more threat than friend."

"Precisely," Odene—a young Percian who was yet another Raz had freed at sea—said with a frown from beside his fellow former *kuja*, Kalin. "Worse still: if the atherian refuse to allow us near the mountains, the army will be in a bind. East is the Dramion, and west is the Cienbal. We've no ships, much less enough to haul fifty thousand of us. If they do not let us at least round the tip of the Crags—which means more than a week's march through the true desert already—our only other option would be doubling back south again. I would think pressing west from Dynec might be best. Karavyl isn't even a fortnight across the plains, and Acrosia perhaps three from there. If we take the coast…"

"Then we eliminate the Mahsadën's only access to the sea," Akelo finished for him, but his voice was grave, and Syrah turned to see him shaking his head. "A good plan in theory, but I don't know if it will be that easy. Dynec has lost value to the South as a whole with the fall of Perce. Karavyl, however, is more independent. I believe it has a thriving silk trade—" he looked to Marsus for confirmation, and the Southerner nodded "—and is the closest hub for shipping slaves to the Seven Cities, which has now become the fringe cities' greatest economic ally after the death of the Tashes. I doubt the Mahsadën would allow us to cut into their profits so deeply, let alone push further north to Acrosia."

"They are highly likely to defend Karavyl," Raz agreed with a ponderous nod. "And if they fail there, whatever forces remain to them need only pull back to Acrosia, as you say. Both are well fortified, if memory serves—the latter especially. I'm not convinced striking so directly is the best course of action for the time being."

"The Crags also provide an advantage," Akelo offered, looking up at Raz while crossing his arms. "While the atherian *may* not let *us* approach their lands, they are certainly not going to allow the *Mahsadën* anywhere near the mountains. If we can take Cyro, whatever forces the other cities might send in retaliation will have to either press through the Cienbal or chase us south, then east, then north around and up the border of the desert."

"That doesn't resolve our own mobility, though." Cyper Edalos—a former soldier of the West Isles who acted as Akelo's right-hand in the army—looked to be choosing his words carefully, scratching at his shaven head. "Eventually we will have to move on from Cyro. If we are forced to push through the Cienbal… It could be disastrous…"

He let his point linger, and the generals were quiet for a time, considering his words. Syrah could clearly see what Cyper meant, of course. She—like most of the others around them—had never seen the desert proper, but she'd heard enough of the place to cringe at the possible hardships such a trek might bring them. Thinking of the tales Raz had shared with her, Syrah felt her palms start to sweat, and her heart sank. A sun that devoured anything fool enough to move beneath the cloudless skies of the day. Nights that grew so cold water could freeze, straining pouches and cracking barrels. Scorpions the size of a small man, venomous snakes and insects, and the infamous sandcats of the South…

No, she thought, *the Cienbal should be our last option, if ever…*

"Speakers for the Dragon."

The voice that broke the silence was a strange one, and everyone blinked and looked around. One of the males behind Zal'en had spoken up tentatively, his words rough and drawn out, golden eyes flicking to Raz's uneasily as he continued.

"Many from the Crags, we have. Many who wish to see homes again. Speakers, they could be. Spread truth, not lies."

There was a grumbling of deliberation at this suggestion, before Raz himself eventually spoke.

"Not a bad idea," he muttered thoughtfully, clawed fingers tapping at the muscle of his crossed arms while he considered the suggestion. "Emissaries could go a long way in smoothing things over. Even if we could just get permission to approach the foot of the mountains…"

"Only so much words can do," Marsus insisted, taking half a step forward from his place in the ring, obviously intent on making sure his reasoning was heard. "Men've been poachin' the atherian for longer than anyone cares to remember. The *only* reason they ain't been butchered by the lizard-kind outright is cause they always hunt in small groups. I'm tellin' you, bankin' on 'em is a bad idea…"

"Do not speak for *our* kind," Zal'en snapped at the Southerner. Then she indicated the male over her shoulder, looking to Raz. "Urlen's thought is good. Many of your warriors were born into their chains, but hundreds of us were taken from our homes. *I* would go, if needed."

For several seconds Raz met the old female's gaze evenly, and the generals knew better than to interrupt his private deliberation. Eventually, he looked away, turning to Syrah.

"What do you think?" he asked her quietly.

"I think they're both right." Syrah looked first to Zal'en and the male who had spoken—Urlen, apparently—then at Marsus. "There's no harm in sending emissaries if the time comes, but we can't make a decision *now* banking on the Crags' assistance. These 'tribes' have little to gain from us, particularly if Dynec and Cyro both break. From what I've put together, other fringe cities primarily deal in men. Once the threat to their kind is essentially eliminated, why would the atherian risk more to assist us?"

"Our people are not so cruel as yours, Witch," Zal'en said calmly, and Syrah wondered if she was the only one who heard the undertone of distaste in the female's voice. "The Queen protects her own. Those of us who are already claws of the Dragon will not abandon him, and *she* will not abandon *us*."

Syrah had to hide a frown at that. Over the last months she'd heard much about this "Queen" who supposedly lived within the cavernous depths of the South's eastern mountains. Even Karan had heard of her, but the way the young female told the stories, they seemed more fables than facts. Then again, Karan was among those born into her former irons, separated from her parents and sold at a young age a dozen times over before ending in the labor services of Karesh Syl. To her, the idea of some grand monarch ever-seeking the freedom of her people might have been too good to be true, or at most a tale weaved together to keep hope alive where nothing else could.

Among many of the other atherian, though, the stories were more conflicted. Of those who'd lived as free creatures before the slavers of the South fell upon them, half had never heard of this "Queen" until they'd arrived in Perce. The others, though, swore by her existence, even though none of them—not even Zal'en—could say that they had ever laid eyes on her.

All and all, whenever they discussed it, Syrah and Raz could never managed to conclude whether the Queen was a well-hidden, well-protected secret among the atherian, or if she was merely an ideal, twisted from the desires and dreams of hard lives and the constant threats from the outside world.

"If your Queen exists in truth, then I am sure she will seek to aid you as best she can," Syrah said to Zal'en and her companions as kindly as she could. "But we *cannot* assume that. Dynec is before us. We must prepare for this fight before we can think of the next. At that time, we will have decisions to make, but those choices must be made *without* the promise of reinforcements that may or may not come."

Despite her calm tone, all three of the lizard-kind bristled, Zal'en even letting out a low hiss of frustration. At her side, Raz uncrossed his arms and laid a heavy hand on her shoulder pointedly.

"True enough," he said, and when Syrah turned around she saw that his eyes were on the bloody chair that stood empty in the center of the ring they had formed. "There is enough to concern ourselves with before we can look too far into the future. Marsus—" the Southerner glanced around from Raz's other side "—how long before we reach Dynec?"

"Marching at pace, scouts say not two days," Marsus answered, chewing on his lip as he thought. "We could reach the city 'afore sundown tomorrow, if we push an additional hour tonight to make up the mornin's delay."

Raz nodded, his attention shifting across the generals as he gave his orders. "Cyper. Arnus." The West-Isler and old Imperialist, the only among those present who had seen anything like true war before their shackles, looked up expectantly. "Akelo will be leading the main line tomorrow. You will act as his secondary commanders. For now, ensure all contingents are properly armed and equipped. Delegate our supplies as needed. Hur—" he looked to the big Northerner "—go with them, in case there are any problems."

Hur, Cyper, and Arnus nodded together before making for the entrance, leaving Raz to turn and face across the circle. "Kalin. Odene. You'll be with me. Find me a hundred of your most skilled bowmen. I will need them at their best, come tomorrow."

If either of the former *kuja* found this order odd, they didn't say so as they bowed briefly and traced the others' steps toward the door.

"Erom," Raz looked to the borderer, who straightened excitedly. "You'll be part of my group too, along with any you've had your eye on who you think might share your… uh… talents. We won't need many. A score would do. Make sure they can climb."

Erom grinned, perhaps more wickedly than Syrah would have thought necessary, then was gone in a flash.

Then only she, Raz, Akelo, and Zal'en and her subordinates remained.

"I have not dismissed your recommendations," Raz told the old female, offering her his full attention now. "I swear to take them under advisement once Dynec falls, but for now we need to come together. I need a force of five hundred from your ranks. The fastest and most agile you have."

For a moment, Syrah thought Zal'en was going to dare refuse. She certainly looked irritated enough, clearly not happy that the conversation had not gone her way, and she stared Raz down for a long second, the dark amber of her eyes meeting the bright sunrise of his.

Then, though, she gave a resigned face.

"I'm assuming we will know your plan sooner than later?" she asked, motioning for the two males behind her to carry out the orders.

"You will," Raz assured her, watching the males head for the pavilion entrance. "It's only an idea. I shall make my decision once I have a sense of the troops you all manage to provide me with."

Zal'en nodded grimly, at that. "I will ensure they are the strongest warriors among us."

Raz thanked her, and the female turned away, heading outside as Urlen held open the flap for her.

When she was gone, Syrah let go a sigh that came out more as a groan of relief than she intended.

There was a heavy chuckle, and Akelo stepped around Raz to close the circle between the three of them. "She certainly is a presence, that one. Good. Her kind have been in chains too long. They need strength at their head."

"I thought that's what they had *him* for," Syrah said sarcastically, rolling her eyes at Raz, who hadn't let go of her shoulder yet.

Raz, though, didn't seem in the mood to joke. His gaze was back on the chair, distant as he thought. "I am far away from them, in my own way," he mumbled, like he'd only been half-listening. "I don't even speak the language half as well as you, despite Karan working with us all this time. Their culture, too, is as strange to me as it is to anyone. To them, I think I must seem more bred of man than atherian. Zal'en is a more appropriate go-between."

"Doesn't mean I have to like her," Syrah muttered with a grimace.

Akelo chuckled again. "No, it doesn't, though that seems to go both ways. But for now," he turned his dark eyes on Raz, "are you at least going to tell *us* what your planning?"

For a second, Raz didn't look away from the bloody stains where Bahrek Lest had suffered Hur's fists. He appeared to be considering the angles, taking in everything the captain had said, turning it over and over again in his head.

Finally, he looked up, his expression hard.

"You're going to put on a show that'll make the šef wet themselves," he told the old man grimly. "And I'm going to stab them in the back while their eyes are on the stage."

V

"It is the grossest of misconceptions to assume that numbers are all that matter in war. While it is true that the strength of one's forces can certainly play a significant role in the outcome of any battle, the larger consideration of the gathered other variables that play upon a battlefield must *be of greater concern. It is not the man with the heavier sword, after all, who the Twins are most likely to grace with victory.*

It is, rather, he who knows best how to wield his blade..."

— *The Art of Sword & Shield*, by Kelo ev'Ret

Maltus Ameen had never thought of himself as a coward. He would certainly never have suffered anyone insinuating as much, at the very least. Maltus had risen as many of the šef did in the underground worlds of the Mahsadën, by clawing his way up through threat, promise, and exacted violence in equal measure. At nearly sixty summers old, he'd weathered the hardships of the world, pushing himself up through the ranks of Dynec's guard even as he'd used his growing influence to weave his dealings into the illicit slave and ragroot trades that thrived within the city's walls. He'd carved a bloody path on his way to the top, had stood his ground a hundred times against those who'd attempted to steal his place at the society's table, often seen them gutted with his own two hands. He'd laughed that morning as the other šef—Kanela Saresh and Zeres Thorne—had been scrambling to gather their worldly possessions, intent on fleeing Dynec with the time they prayed Bahrek Lest's assault had bought them. *He* was no coward, Maltus told the pair, scorning them both. Even if they would flee, *he* would stand up to the scaly bastard, so long as he did so with sword in hand.

Now, though—and for the first time in his life—Maltus Ameen was forced to consider that perhaps the cowards of the world were the ones who had the right of it...

Night had fallen on the second day after Captain Lest's departure with no sign of the man returning, nor the two hundred and fifty mounted horsemen he'd left the city with. Maltus had long since written them off already, but all the same he hadn't been able to stop himself from keeping one eye on the horizon during his inspections of the ramparts, looking for any hint of riders returning triumphant from their campaign against the Monster's disjointed forces. For nearly three days, though, the waving line of dunes, rippling in the heat of the Sun above, had stayed quiet. Not a hint of life stirred over the desert planes except for the circling of hawks and vultures overhead, and the occasional scuttling shape of a dune scorpion vanishing into the dust. The day had started to wane, the temperatures beginning to cool as the Sun dipped westward, sinking little by little below the edge of the sands. Wondering how many more dusks he would yet see, Maltus had taken up a place over Dynec's western gate, watching the fading light as night reached out over the world. All around him gathered soldiers had mimicked his study of the day's end, perhaps dwelling on the same realization as he.

Then, though, the Sun had refused to set.

As though answering some silent prayer that their final hours would linger on forever, the line of orange and yellow that spoke to the last hints of the evening suddenly stopped shrinking. For a while it lingered, flickering and wavering, like the Sun was fighting the Moon for dominance in the sky.

Then, though, the light began to brighten, and Maltus realized with a thrill of fear what he was seeing.

Torches. Thousand on thousands of torches, spreading out to coat the darkened sands like a sea of scattered fire.

That was when he'd bolted for the brass alarm bell hanging from its pole nearby, ringing it frantically.

"ARMS!" he had bellowed as the clear sound sang over the stillness of the city behind him. "HERE THEY COME! TO ARMS!"

Instantly the soldiers who'd been gathered all about Maltus sprang to life, as many scrambling to gather their weapons and shields as there were already leaning over the parapets, gaping in disbelief at the approaching horde. Even Maltus—between shouting orders to ensure the gate below was barricaded and calling for reinforcements from the city's northern and eastern entries—had trouble keeping his eyes off the horizon. With horrified fascination he watched the flood of dotted light continue to spread, engulfing the outline of the dunes in the dark. Maltus had seen armies in his time. In the early days of the Mahsadën, after the nomadic trading caravans had fallen apart, he'd held Dynec's forces firm against the desert bandits who'd come pouring out of the Cienbal looking for other ways to survive. He'd thought he'd experienced power in its rawest form, then, as thousands rushed around him when he'd called for the charge and hundreds died at his command.

Now, though… Now Maltus was forced to wonder if he'd ever held even an ounce of the strength he'd imagined…

Fifty thousand men. Almost six times the number of the city's defenders, after Lest had taken his men and nearly five hundred deserters were found to have fled in the latest nights. Maltus suspected the torches were a ploy, the Monster's army itself scattered wide in the dark to provide the illusion of this colossal vastness, but all the same he couldn't stop an icy hand from clawing at his throat when he stared out over the western plains. More arrived with every passing moment, sprouting from the horizon. They never ended, appearing by the hundreds as the flames at the foremost of the march rapidly closed the miles between them. Minutes ticked by, turning into hours in which Maltus shouted commands he could hardly remember. The reinforcements arrived from the other gates. Archers took their positions along the walls. Soldiers ran by carrying bags of heavy stones and lead buckets of pitch to be boiled over waiting fires. There were shouts as minor officers attended their details. Before the battle even started, the air smelled of iron and smoke and oil. Maltus didn't know when he started to make out the sound of tens of thousands stepping in unison, but all of a sudden it was all one could hear. Squinting over the crenellations, he realized he could distinguish shapes in the night, now, outlines that glinted of metal and leather and sleek, dark scales.

They were perhaps a quarter mile from the walls when the sound of a horn thrummed out from the army's midst. The lights shivered and stilled, expectedly just out of range of the short bows of Dynec's archers. Swallowing his nerves, Maltus studied the front line carefully, looking for signs of the infamous Monster of Karth. There was a chance the beast would want to parley, would demand terms in exchange for the city's surrender. Maltus was prepared to tell him where he could shove his terms, but even in the glow of the torches he couldn't make out much in the distance of the night. At the center of the line, the outline of a trio of mounted figures reigned over the front of the march, but all three looked distinctly human. They were broad of shoulder, like men who had worked and labored for much of their lives, and Maltus thought the man in their middle might have been Percian, judging by what looked like dark skin against the bleached leather of his armor.

Of Raz i'Syul Arro, there was no sign.

Before Maltus could wonder at the Monster's absence, though, the center figure raised his sword toward the city, and there was a second horn blast.

Immediately, it was followed by a thunderous command that rang clear over the night.

"FORWARD!"

With a roar of fifty thousand voices howling in unison, the bloom of flames before them suddenly swelled forward, barreling toward Dynec at a full charge.

VI

"Sun's mercy!" Maltus cursed, the rush taking him completely by surprise. Ripping his sword from its sheath at his hip, he bellowed over the roar of the coming army. "ARCHERS! DRAW!"

At once he was answered by the reverberating sound of a thousand bows being pulled to their extent along the wall on either side of him. He forced himself to wait, forced himself to pause and inhale a steadying breath as the flood of fire and flickering shadows rushed toward Dynec with all the power of a hundred avalanches.

Then, at last, the leading figures were in range.

"FIRE!"

Arrows shrieked through the air, ripping across the shrinking expanse. They arched up, then down, raining into the approaching storm of men and atherian. Screams of pain and horror rose up through the night, and a scattering of torches tumbled from hands to wink out in the sand. Maltus shouted again, and once more arrows were drawn and loosed to plummet down into the Monster's ranks. Over the sound of the wounded and dying, though, Maltus made out the distinct *thunk thunk thunk* of a different impact, one that didn't settle well with him.

Shields? he wondered in confusion, even as he called for yet another volley.

As death rained down again, their attackers got close enough for him to see that he was right.

For every one man holding a torch, there were perhaps ten others charging right along at their side, heavy wooden shields raised high to protect themselves from the falling arrows. Maltus felt a chill as he took them in, because the tactic made no practical sense. Shields might allow a vastly greater number of soldiers to reach the walls, but to *breach* them the men would need ladders, or at least weighted grappling lines. As he made out more and more of the assaulting forces, though, Maltus saw no such devices.

"What are they playing at?!" he snarled to himself.

At that moment there was a *whiz* of cracking air, and an arrow streaked by not two feet to his right, returned to him from below. He ducked for cover, edging along the ramparts in a crouch as he continued to shout commands.

"ARCHERS, FIRE AT WILL! PREPARE THE STONES AND PITCH! BE ON THE LOOKOUT FOR WAR MACHINES!"

It was the only thing that made sense to him. The Monster was throwing the entire weight of his army against them, but for all that strength he didn't seem intent on overrunning the walls with numbers just yet. Leading with shields meant Arro desired as many of his troops to survive for as long as possible, even if it meant sacrificing the advantage of the rush. He wanted a central force gathered at the gate, one that couldn't be easily rebuffed.

A battering ram? Maltus wondered, braving a peek between the crenellations before ducking back down again as another projectile took a passing soldier through the neck nearby. *Siege towers?*

Either option was plausible, though the latter seemed more likely. Maltus hadn't seen so much as a hint of such a device, but that didn't mean it wasn't present, disguised in some cleverly designed shadows of the torchlight. If the Monster's army could get a tower up to the wall, Dynec was done for. They might be able to hold off the onslaught for a brief period, but ultimately they would lose to the sheer mass of bodies that would come pouring over the ramparts. Eventually Maltus and his men would have to cede the outer defenses, and the moment that happened the battle was forfeit.

"The gates! They're attacking the gates!"

The shout came as a dull knock of confusion against Maltus' fears. Without a second thought he leapt up, risking leaning over the rampart in full to see what was going on. For a moment he wondered if the rushing army had somehow disguised a ram in its charge, but what greeted him instead was a mountain of shields, overlapping and interlocked, illuminated in the torchlight that surrounded them. Perhaps fifty in all at their center, the Monster's attackers had turtled themselves right up against the gate, and from within their makeshift shell came the thudding *cracks* of steel sinking into wood.

AXES?

Maltus couldn't believe it. The soldiers below seemed to be taking *axes* to the heavy timber. He almost laughed aloud as he shrank back behind the safety of the crenellations again, his mind awhirl. It hit him then that this grand enemy had no strategy, no battle tact. Any veteran worth his salt knew that attacking the doors to a city directly was foolish to the extent of the word. Dynec's gates were a foot thick and reinforced with iron cross-framings, and that was nothing compared to the two or three feet of hardwood that made up the entries of Acrosia or Miropa. They were built to withstand the beating of a fully-manned battering ram for as long as possible, as well as any attempts to burn them to the ground. Taking small arms to them was absolute madness.

They don't know better, Maltus realized. *No one has taught them better…*

All of a sudden, the šef felt the smallest glimmer of hope.

"ARCHERS!" he bellowed, leaping up and making for the closest bag of stones he could find. "FOCUS FIRE ON ENEMY BOWMEN! NO WASTED ARROWS ON THE SHIELDED UNITS! PITCH AND STONE THROWERS, TO ME!"

The commands jumped out along the wall as officers repeated them to their cohorts. As Maltus sheathed his sword in favor of heaving up the heaviest rock he could wrap his hands around, others joined him in hurried groups, carrying their own stones or buckets of boiling tar.

"OVER THE EDGE!" he shouted at once, hurrying to the parapet again. "TAKE DOWN THE SHIELD WALL!"

As soon as he reached the ledge, Maltus leaned out between the crenellations again, taking careful aim. He wasn't as strong a man as he'd been in his youth, but gravity did most of the work for him when he heaved his rock downward. It connected almost exactly where he'd eyed, catching the very lip of a shield near the center of the shell, and the defense buckled with a *crack*. Maltus had just enough time to make out a startled, pale face, blue eyes wide in surprise.

Then a stone thrown by one of the other soldiers caught the exposed man in the head, caving his skull in with an ugly, wet sound of crushed bone and flesh.

More projectiles fell, many bouncing harmlessly off the shields, but others punching holes in the defense one after the other. The pitch came soon after, hurled into the throng, and there were wails of agony as the boiling liquid rained down molten hell to trickle and drip through the gaps of the interlocking shell.

"MORE!" Maltus howled, already hurrying back for another projectile. "BREAK THEM! BREAK THEM!"

It was not so simple, though. Just as Arro seemed to have planned, his soldiers had formed something like an endless pool of bodies around the gate, shields held high. Enemy archers shot with surprising accuracy from deliberate spaces opened in the turtled defense, but the real trouble came in the fact that as soon as Maltus or his defenders downed one man, another pressed forward to stand in his place. It was a tiresome cycle, but the šef forced himself to be patient, to acknowledge that the fight was to Dynec's advantage. The Monster's men might manage to continue taking their axes to the gates, but it would be a long time before they chopped themselves so much as a single hole through the wood. Even then, Maltus would be sure to have spearman ready to take the opportunity, set to thrust steel into the heart of the army that had so foolishly packed itself right up to the city walls.

We will crush them, Maltus swore to himself, heaving yet another projectile into the shields. *Little by little, we will crush the Monster and his horde, and send them scurrying back into the sands.*

His moment of triumph came earlier than he anticipated.

For nearly half-an-hour the battle raged like this. The shield bearers below adapted quickly to the tactics of the city's defenders, tightening their overhead blockade, but all the same the falling stones and tar did their slow, steady work. Maltus knew he had lost men, picked off by the bowmen below, but he was sure the Monster's casualties were five times his own at least. He could see the soldiers below moving awkwardly over the bodies of their dead and injured, some even slipping and falling as the sand beneath their feet grew viscous with hot pitch and spilled blood. Little by little Maltus' small flame of hope bloomed. He considered what would happen if this disorderly horde, this army of rabble with no training and no leadership, lost a thousand before they had a chance to break the gates, or five thousand, or *ten* thousand. His units had the advantage, and they were trained, hardened soldiers. They would last the night through and all of the next day, if need be. They could eat away at the Monster's numbers, crush their spirits even if they couldn't crush the army as a whole.

Maybe—just maybe—there's a way to win this fight, Maltus allowed himself to hope.

And then, as though in answer to the plan that was rapidly forming in his head, he heard the horn ring out again.

Like the breaking of a dam Arro's men pulled away from the wall in a rush, pulling back in a single massive wave of soldiers and shields. They left the gate behind, timber scarred and splintered from where what might have been a half-dozen axes had bitten into it, as well as the bodies of the dead, scattered where they'd fallen to stone and tar and bow. Almost at once the city's defenders erupted in a victorious cheer, archers taking shots at the backs of the fleeing army while the other men whooped in triumph and hurled insults after the Monster's horde. Instinctively Maltus joined them, dropping the chunk of rubble he'd been carrying in favor of drawing his sword again and thrusting it in the air while adding his voice to the crowd. As the cheering swelled and lingered, though, his eyes followed the retreating form of the army. His gut itched, telling him that something wasn't quite right. While he watched, the torches of Arro's ranks began to wink out, one by one, allowing the horde to be swallowed again by the dark.

Do they realize their fear tactics didn't work? he wondered, lowering his sword and approaching the wall. *Will they try a surprise assault, now?*

His mind ran in a blur, trying to deduce what the Monster would attempt next. Numbers were still significantly on the atherian's side, but surely the brave defenders of Dynec had put at least a *dent* in the force's morale. If they could keep this up, if they could chip away at the army's spirit little by little, even till morning, they might just—

"C-Commander!"

Maltus blinked and looked over his shoulder, but the nearby archer who'd interrupted his thoughts was not looking at him. Rather, the man was staring south, along the wall, where Maltus suddenly realized the jubilation of their victory had guttered and died away. Wondering what was wrong, Maltus turned and stepped around the soldier to follow his gaze.

It only took him a moment to make out the figure, bruised and beaten, staggering toward them as quickly as he could along the ramparts.

The footman was young, likely not even twenty, but he cast about with such wild eyes as he moved that he reminded Maltus of old warriors who'd seen far too much of battle. His uniform was torn and bloody, and while he held onto his longsword with a death grip in his right hand, his left arm was limp at his side. He was shouting something, looking desperately around, and it took a moment for Maltus to realize it was *his* name the boy was calling.

"AMEEN!" the soldier was screaming shrilly, his voice cracking as he continued to stagger along. "COMMANDER AMEEN!"

"Here, lad!" Maltus hollered, hastening forward to meet the bloody figure. "Here!"

The soldier finally caught sight of him, but relief was the last thing that crossed his face. If anything, his features grew more desperate, and he stumbled to his knees just as Maltus reached him.

"What happened?!" Maltus demanded at once, hurrying to kneel before the boy, sword still in hand as he studied the soldier's beaten body. There was a gash over his heart that could only have been caused by a blade, and his left arm was distinctly broken. "Who did this?!"

"H-he came," the footman choked in answer. "He came, a-and the gate… He took the gate!"

Maltus frowned, then glanced around at the other soldiers, trying to deduce if any of them knew what the boy was talking about. Judging by their bewildered faces, they didn't, and Maltus himself was sure he hadn't ordered an assault into the plains. How else, though, would this soldier have ended up in such a condition? Was this the work of one of his officers overstepping? Perhaps seeking to gain a name for himself when it became clear the Monster's army was breaking?

"The gate holds, lad," Maltus said firmly, standing up again. "Their forces have been pushed back. How in the Sun's name did you—?"

"Not the west gate!" the soldier howled, cutting him off. "Not the west!"

Abruptly, Maltus understood, and ice washed up his spine like the dragging blade of a rusty knife as he staggered back a step.

"The east!" the boy continued, voice now liquid terror. "The Monster came from the east!"

VII

"Any idiot can run about waving a longsword. It's a dullard's weapon, a primitive evolution of a time when we huddled about open fires and fought by seeing who could swing their club at each other the hardest. Finesse—if you are looking for it—must be found in the smaller arms. Man, of course, scorns daggers, scoffs at knives and any blade smaller than your arm. He calls them the tools of a coward, wielded only by those afraid to meet steel head on.

I say man is a fool. I say he turns his nose up at anything which he does not care to understand, or put the effort in to master. With a longsword, one need only swing it in the enemy's general direction and hope for the best. Any fight dissolves into a pattern of hacking and cleaving and cutting until a single figure is left standing in a mess of blood and flesh, not infrequently including his own. It is appalling. With a knife, one needs only strike one time.

All that is required is timing, precision, and the knowledge of where exactly it is you need to bury your blade..."

— Ergoin Sass, to Lazura

Raz's claws dug into the chipping mortar between the mudstone that made up the east wall of the city. He was careful to stay tight to the surface of the bricks as he made his way up, foot by foot, quiet as the night breeze that occasionally pulled at the fur mantle cast about his shoulders. He wore none of his usual armor, stealth being paramount to the task at hand, and the only weapon he carried was the gladius strapped across his back. Raz couldn't help but be reminded, as he found another handhold, of a vastly different time, one in which he'd spent any night in two stealing across the roofs and eaves of Miropa, stalking whatever prey the Mahsadën put before him like a bloodhound following an offered scent.

Smirking at the irony of the memory, Raz heaved himself up another foot, then glanced around to see how the others were faring.

Scattered along the wall on either side of him, a score of shadows clung deftly to the brick, some almost matching his pace. With the Moon waning to the west, they were wreathed in darkness, and even *he* had some trouble making out the furthest of their forms. Most, like Erom—who was some five feet below and ten feet to the right—were human, slight figures whose slim fingers deftly found every seam and swell in and between the stones. A few, on the other hand, were atherian, bigger and longer than their counterparts, but no less agile as they clawed their way upward. As a group they moved silently, not so much as hinting at their presence even when hands slipped and feet had trouble finding their places.

Raz would have to remember to commend Erom on his selection, once this fight was done.

After leaving Akelo, Cyper, and Arnus in command of the main charge on the west gate, Raz had led his smaller unit of six hundred wide east, taking advantage of the day's end to approach the wall through the dunes as darkness descended over the world. They'd been infinitely careful in their approach, moving slowly so as not to stir up a dust cloud by which they might be spotted. When they were near enough, lookouts had set up to keep tabs on the city, waiting for the right moment.

As they'd hoped, a quarter hour after the Sun's last light faded beyond Dynec's low outline, a commotion had risen up around the city's furthest gate. Soon after, a large portion of the sentries and guards planted along its ramparts were called away, heading for the opposite end of the walls.

That was when they'd made their move, Raz, Erom, and their handful of others slinking through the shadows cast by the dunes, all but invisible in the dark, leaving the five hundred atherian Zal'en had delivered to him to wait in the hills, huddled for warmth with the *kuja* bowmen who'd accompanied them.

After another fifteen seconds or so, the top of the wall was within Raz's reach. He paused, swinging himself laterally so that he could wait beneath the nook of the nearest jutting crenellation. Short of them sticking their head out and looking straight down, he was invisible to the remaining sentries he could hear moving along the ramparts. It took another minute or so, but eventually the others were in position as well, motioning one after the other that they were ready. When Erom gave Raz a nod, signaling his side was set, Raz turned and reached up to get a good grip on the very lip of the ramparts. Swinging over to hang there for a moment by one hand, he freed his gladius slowly with the other, muffling the sound of drawing steel as best he could. He waited another few seconds, listening attentively as booted feet clicked over stone.

When the moment was right, Raz gave a quick prayer to the Moon and Her Stars that he would get to see Syrah again, then deftly heaved himself up between the crenellations.

As he'd anticipated, the paired sentries had just moved past him, stepping in practiced unison southward, to his left. As he made out the faint sounds of the others following his lead, Raz dropped down to the ramparts and darted forward, clawed feet *clacking* quietly over the mudbrick. He closed the six-foot gap with every ounce of speed he could muster without giving himself away, and the soldier on the left gave a muffled shout of surprise as Raz's hand clapped him about the mouth.

The gladius lanced forward as Raz gave the man's head a jerking twist, the steel running his partner through the back of the throat as bone wrenched and snapped.

In all of two heartbeats, both sentries fell quietly to the ground, dead before they could even think to cry out a warning.

The rest of his men, too, had had little trouble. As Raz had hoped, Dynec was truly desperate for every man it could throw into the fight he could just hear raging in the distance. Only a handful of other pairs had met them along the wall, and not a one had managed to raise a shout as the others fell on them, their ends coming quick at the edges of daggers, swords, and strong, clawed hands. All the same, as the last of the slain sentries was eased to the ground, Raz signaled for everyone to stay quiet and hold their positions. Their silence echoed their understanding, and so Raz crouched low to inch nearer the edge of the rampart, peering over it carefully.

As was typical of city entrances, a small square encircled the inner gate, narrowing rapidly into a street that led toward the heart of Dynec. In the space some thirty feet below, huddled around several wide iron braziers that burned heartily to stave off the night chill, some half-a-hundred guards lingered, most with their hands held to the flames.

Raz was almost jealous of them, flexing his fingers to keep them from stiffening up as he shifted back from the ledge, joining Erom and several of the others who'd already gathered around the borderer.

"Fifty at most," he whispered to the group, pulling his furs tighter around his shoulders when the wind picked up briefly. "Whoever is in charge of the fight might be desperate, but they're not stupid. If we'd split our main offensive, they'd have just about enough men to hold the wall until reinforcements arrived."

"What do we do, then?" Erom asked quietly. "That's more than twice our number. With you here we might with the element of surprise, but not without a lot of us dead by the end of it."

Despite his words, his voice was calm. Raz could see the fear in the man's eyes—in *all* their eyes—but he could also see their conviction. They were ready to follow his command, whatever it was. If he told them to fight to the death, they would die for him and the freedom he'd won for them and so many others.

With an odd swell of pride, Raz thought again that he would *definitely* have to commend Erom for his selection later.

"No need for that," he assured the group with a shake of his head, and he could have chuckled at the relief that played over many of the men's faces. "I've got a better idea…"

He detailed the simple plan out quickly, the others nodding along as he did. Once he'd finished, Erom passed along his secondary commands, readying them all for the quick action they would need to take when the opportunity presented itself.

"Ready?" Raz asked his general, and the borderer nodded. He pulled a small torch from his belt, as well as some tinder and flint, holding the former out to one of the soldiers to hold for him.

"Now?" he asked.

"Now," Raz answered.

Then he was moving, hurrying along the top of the wall northward as quickly as he could manage stooped, gladius still bare in one hand. Behind him, he heard the quiet *whoosh* of flame catching in oil and wood, then the sound of fire tumbling through the air like beating wings. Finally, there was a dull *thump* as the lone torch landed in the sand beyond the gate.

The signal was sent.

Raz didn't have to run far before the opportunity he was looking for presented itself. Dynec, like many of the other lesser fringe cities he remembered from his youth, kept a low profile against the desert winds that had been known to topple buildings when they were of a mind to. A few structures in the distance were taller, maybe four or five stories of marble or stone, but the rest were squat, ugly things made of wood and brick, barely ever higher than the defenses that shielded them from assault and the elements alike. A narrow street ran alongside the base of the wall below to Raz's left, a common practice designed to allow reinforcements to move easily around the circumference of the city in times of war, creating a space that was just broad enough to make him take pause. For about thirty seconds he kept moving, straightening once he was sure he was out of sight of the enemy soldiers gathered before the gate, eyes on the buildings whisking past him.

There.

The moment he saw his chance, Raz took it. Strong legs turned him in an instant, powering across what little space the ramparts offered him to build up speed. Without hesitating he launched himself into the air, aiming for the roof of a single-story home twenty feet below. His momentum closed the distance well enough, gravity dragging him down toward the flat-topped brick roof.

When he was a second from landing, Raz extended his wings to their limit, cutting his speed off with a jerk that strained at the muscles of his back.

Landing a little harder than he'd intended, Raz was forced to change his impetus into a forward roll, coming up straight again just in time to vault over the low edge of the roof. He hit the dusty cobbled street below lightly, frightening a stray cat that yowled and made to bolt at once, but he was moving again before the animal even had the opportunity to bolt. Running full-tilt now he took an alley west, then another. He guessed he was in the laborer's district, not far from the slums he knew claimed much of the northern third of Dynec. The buildings here weren't as fashionable or ornate as the haughty structures at the center of the city, but they were sturdy and well-built, indicative of the good lives the residents of the quarter strove to earn themselves through hard work. This was a place of earnest effort and happiness found in success. At this early hour, not long after sundown, the streets should have been well-lit and jovial, busy with families spending time together and youths taking in what entertainment they could within the confines of their class.

It was sad, therefore, to witness the barren nature of the scene, the emptiness of the shops and the shuttered windows behind which he occasionally spied a terrified eye peeking out. He wondered what those few that caught a glimpse of him must have thought, seeing his form tear past in the dark.

After all, Dragon or not, *he* was the one who'd brought war to the doorsteps of their homes…

Breaking out of the side-streets onto a broader fairway, Raz turned south, still hurrying. The Moon was hidden from him over the roofs of the buildings across the road, but Her Stars gleamed and glinted overhead as he ran, a hundred thousand eyes watching him, following his path like the witnesses of fate. He offered up no prayer, this time, his mind focused wholly on the task at hand as he found street he judged to be right, taking one last turn.

Having completed his loop, Raz drove himself forward at even greater speed, making for the glow of firelight and the dark shapes of the figures lingering about it, their backs outlined against the inside of the east gate.

VIII

Raz hurtled into the men before any of them had so much as noticed his headlong charge, plunging into their midst with a roar that cracked the cold of the night like fracturing ice. Screams and shouts of alarm rang up around him as his gladius shrieked left and right, joining the tearing claws of his free hand. Instantly the scene was in chaos, and by the time swords started to be drawn, four men already lay dead at Raz's feet. Satisfied that he had their attention, he didn't press further into the chaos, instead moving laterally as he ducked under a horizontal blow, his tail sweeping the legs out from under two of the soldiers even as he dealt a spinning kick that sent another careening backwards into the closest brazier, toppling it. Fire and smoke joined the mayhem, and there were yells of "To me! To me!" as the officers within the contingent tried to gather order.

Their calls, though, were drowned out by other howls.

"MONSTER!" several voices screamed as Raz sunk his fist into one guard's gut, sidestepping and spinning to cleave the man's head from his shoulders when doubled over. "IT'S THE MONSTER!"

"THE DRAGON!" others shouted, stumbling away from him as Raz split a skull open with the pommel of his gladius before bringing the blade around to run it through another man's heart. "THE DRAGON'S COME!"

There were other shouts, too, mixed in with the titles. A few called him Scourge, others throwing insults at him as they charged forward. Some shouted for reinforcements, while still more demanded where he had come from, or how he had gotten into the city. Ignoring all, Raz stayed focused on his fight, willingly backpedaling as the men finally gathered themselves and started to press him. Soon he was forced to shift from his offensive rush to total defense, plucking a curved saber from its owner's grasp and throwing the man back into his comrades before putting both the gladius and the borrowed sword to work. He had drawn the blood he needed to, had earned himself their rage and fear. They came at him as one, training taking over while they continued to call for support to be fetched. Carefully he allowed himself to be pressed backwards, grunting when he took a few shallow wounds in the process. A jab to the shoulder. A gash across his bare ribs. Ignoring the pain, he retreated foot by foot, step by step, funneling the men into the narrower street that led deeper in. They forced him with surprising aggression, and before Raz knew it he was already halfway back up the road, nearing the main fairway with every passing second. His speed and size allowed him to do a decent job of keeping them from surrounding him with the walls and shopfronts not more than seven or eight feet to either side of him, but as soon as he hit the wider space of the larger street he knew he was going to be in trouble. He'd counted ten dead and another half-dozen wounded, but he wasn't fool enough to believe he could survive long if the rest of the unit managed to encircle him, particularly without Ahna or his armor. He would have to bolt, making a break for one of the smaller alleys before they pressed him into the open. He didn't know how long they'd been fighting, how long he'd stolen their attention. A minute? Two? Was it long enough? Had he served his purpose?

His answer came a second later, with the unmistakable *zip* and *thud* of an arrow sinking through armor and flesh.

"BEHIND US!" someone at the rear of the group shouted as another could be heard collapsing and screaming. "THE GATE! THEY'VE OPENED THE DAMN GA—!"

More arrows ripped through the air in a rain of iron, and the man's cry was silenced. Instantly following this, there was a gathered roar of a hundred different war cries rising from serpentine throats, and Raz darted back, retreating from the fight just long enough to glance over the heads of his opponents. The first thing he saw was the dark mass of lizard-kind barreling into the back of the soldiers that had been pressing him. Behind them, the *kuja* bowmen were already hurrying up the steps to the ramparts, weapons in hand, led by Kalin and Odene.

And below them, grinning grimly with one foot on the massive timber strut that had undoubtedly barred shut the eastern gate, Erom stood to the side with the rest of the group they'd led over the wall, the score of them flanking the wide-open entry to the city.

Like a charm, Raz snorted to himself.

Then he plunged back into the fray, gladius and stolen sword ripping into the last of the soldiers, pinned now between the Dragon of the North and his horde.

It was a brief battle, after that. Less than twenty of Dynec's men remained standing after the hundred *kuja* had advanced the atherian's charge with their volley of arrows. From there, it wasn't more than a minute before the wave of lizard-kind tore through the soldiers like paper, ripping into their ranks with swords and teeth and claws. Many stood, bravely facing their deaths, but a few chose to run, abandoning their weapons as they made to flee.

Of these, all met just as unforgiving an end on the edge of Raz's blades.

And then, finally, the fight was over. The last of the soldiers fell, his dying scream kept terribly short as his throat was shredded in the maw of a tall female. Before the body had so much as hit the ground Raz was moving forward and shouting orders, the lizard-kind splitting for him as he hurried over and between the corpses, making for the gate.

"Atherian, hold the roads!" he commanded, reaching the open square and moving carefully around the spilled embers of several upturned braziers. "Blockade every way in and out of the square! Kalin! Odene!" He peered up into the ramparts, where the generals were each in command of some fifty bowmen, lining either side of the top of the gate. "I want half your archers supporting the atherian, with the rest sent north and south along the walls. There's a good chance Dynec's soldiers will realize we've breached the city before Akelo reaches us. Slow them down at all costs."

At once the two *kuja* turned to give quick orders, splitting their groups accordingly. Raz, meanwhile, reached Erom, who still stood by the wide-open doors.

"Drag that thing into the sands," he told the borderer, indicating the timber beam on the cobblestone between them with a bloody sword. "On the off chance we get pressed back, I don't want them being able to bar the gates again."

Erom nodded, whistling to catch his soldiers' attentions, gesturing at the strut and motioning for it to be tossed out into the desert.

"Went off without a hitch, I'd say," the general said once the climbers had heaved the thing up onto their shoulders and hurried away with it. "You're a terror when need be, you know that?"

"I may have heard it somewhere before, yes," Raz muttered in sarcastic reply, stepping closer to the nearest still-burning brazier for warmth. "Did we lose anyone?"

"One from our group. There were a few stragglers who didn't take your bait. A couple even managed to get away before we could stop them. Looks like the lizard-kind may have taken some casualties, though…"

Raz looked around, back up the main street. Indeed, the atherian were busy clearing the road of corpses, and of the lifeless forms they were carrying off in pairs, a couple were distinctly not those of Dynec's soldiers. Raz felt the weight of the sight pull at him, but he shoved it aside roughly.

War was going to claim its toll no matter what precautions he took. When taken in its most base form, his duty as commander was merely to negotiate how low he could bargain that price.

May You see them up into Your Stars, he prayed briefly to the Moon he couldn't see.

Then his eyes met Erom's again.

"When Akelo gets here, I want you to take control of the cavalry," he said. "The horses won't be any good in the city anyway, and there's something I need you to do."

"Oh?" Erom raised a curious eyebrow at him. "And what's that?"

Raz, in reply, bared his fangs into the firelight.

"You're going to make sure none of the snakes escape their nest."

It was the army of Dynec, unfortunately, who reached them first, the time to cut across the city obviously shorter than the loop Akelo and his troops were undoubtedly taking through the dunes. Their arrival was heralded almost a minute ahead of time by hurried shouts and shrill orders, as well as the disjointed sounds of hundreds on hundreds of booted feet hammering the stone in a disorganized rush. In the frontline of their blockade on the main street, Raz smiled grimly as he heard all this, taking pleasure in the panic his little ploy was causing.

Then the soldiers appeared in a surge of bodies, and he was almost impressed with the desperation with which they charged headlong down the road.

Raz showed his respect by roaring and meeting them—along with the hundred atherian at his back—blades leading the way.

The battle that followed was long and bloody. Though they were heavily outnumbered, the narrow space allowed the atherian to maintain the line without being overwhelmed, forcing the Dynec soldiers to face them on even footing, like two armies funneled into a canyon. Everywhere swords flashed, claws ripped out, spears punched forward, and teeth gnashed. Raz tempered his battle-lust as men and lizard-kind both fought and died around him, forcing himself to stay with the line and not hammer his way into the Dynec forces, as the animal inside desired. It raised its head, snarling in excitement at the chaos of the battle, but he beat it back as harshly as he beat back the footmen before him.

"HOLD!" he bellowed over the screams and clashing of steel and the iron smell of blood. "HOLD!"

A minute turned into two, then five, then ten. Dozens fell on either side, while others still collapsed with terrible wounds and had to be carried away by their comrades so that another could take their place. Raz was proud of his atherian, in that moment. Not only of their bravery and sheer willpower to stand against the overwhelming odds of the enemy, but the discipline and training they had clearly put so much effort into cultivating. No longer were they the disjointed throng of former slaves, thin and ragged and scared. No longer were they the broken souls without hope or desire or joy. The males and females around him—like the men and women at their backs firing off arrow after arrow over their heads—had found reason to fight in this purpose he and Syrah and his generals had offered them. The conviction, the promise of their freedom and that of others, held them firm, and did much to keep the soldiers of the city from gaining so much as a foot in the fight.

Raz himself did the rest.

His gladius and the stolen scimitar sheered through armor and muscle and bone in a shriek of cutting steel. In practiced patterns the blades parried and deflected swords and spears and long-handled hammers, taking advantage of every opening to snake forward and cleave into chests and arms and necks and faces. He would have preferred his sagaris to the borrowed blade—or better yet, Ahna herself—but all the same he fought with such ferocity, fed by the drive of his men, that he carved something of a hole for himself in the small battlefield, felling anyone that came within reach. Men started to fight the press, attempting to backpedal and even flee as the throng behind them shoved ever forward. When they caught sight of his bloodied form, crimson wings extended and golden eyes bright in the relative darkness of the evening, they lost their courage, fighting their own in an attempt to stay away. Raz took satisfaction in their faintheartedness, and showed no mercy as the battle raged. How many he cut down, he didn't know. How many fell at his sides, he didn't know. He had fended off the beast, kept at bay the *true* monster that lurked within him, but all the same his body took over, his arms moving independently and of their own accord, working the swords as deftly as a master painter works his brushes.

By the time he heard the sound of the horn behind them, Raz had slashed his art in savage strokes through enough men to color the world red.

"SHIELDS TO THE FRONT!" the familiar, gravelly voice boomed. "SPEARS BEHIND! FORWARD!"

The commands, rising up over the violent sounds of battle that rang out over the buildings from every direction around them, were followed by a swell of rising voices. Raz could feel the atherian behind him split and start to pull back, but his own legs refused to follow. He kept on his dance, kept on his endless drive of steel and death while the faces of the soldiers before him blanched and began to recede. He trailed their retreat, cutting them down one after the other, step by step. One died, then another, then another. Five more, he killed, before new shapes hammered past him from behind. Even then he didn't stop, shearing the head off a pike and running its owner through the eye with his scimitar. The figures closed in around him, and he saw shields being hefted, forming a wall on either side of him. Still, he fought, felling two more who made a last desperate attempt at taking him together, redirecting their blades before running them both through with mirrored thrusts of his swords.

Finally, as he jerked the weapons free from the twitching corpses, the sound of his name brought him to his sense.

"RAZ!"

The battle-fog cracked and shattered. The veil lifted, and sound returned in detail to him, like he'd just broken the surface after too long underwater. The air smelled of death and sweat and smoke. Before him, closing the space he'd taken up as they advanced, the shieldbearers Akelo had initially led against the far side of the city formed up, swords in their free hands. Crowding in behind them while the army pressed forward, men and women and atherian with long spears were setting their weapons, completing a spiked wall that was pushing steadily up the street. For several seconds Raz stood, feeling the coolness of the evening again as it bit into the wetness of the blood spattering and streaking his scales.

"Raz!"

The call came from closer now, and he turned with a jerk to face it.

From his place atop the grey-brown charger he'd claimed from the stable of the Tash of Karesh Nan, Akelo towered over the mass of the army as it poured into the city, splitting around him to support the atherian fighters who had so bravely held the gate. On either side of him, Cyper and Arnus sat atop their own horses, shouting further orders to guide the troops in one direction or the other. The Percian's eyes, though, were on Raz, fiery beneath in his spiked steel helm as they reflected the light of the braziers around the little square. He didn't call out a third time, but the steadiness of his gaze said everything.

Enough, they told him. *You've done enough.*

Raz knew he was right. Looking around, he couldn't help but stare sadly at the scattered corpses of the atherian who'd fallen at his side, who had fought and died for him. They lay where they'd been cut down, dark forms splashed with colored scales between the legs of their comrades who were careful to step over them whenever possible. He tried to count the dead, tried to guess how many they'd lost, here and in the other streets and alleys.

That was when Raz, too, decided it was enough. Exhaustion seeped into his arms and limbs, and he half-staggered in Akelo and the generals' direction, his soldiers shifting around him to let him through, the stolen scimitar clattering with a *ping* of metal to the bloody stones of the street.

IX

"The ongoings of war are multitudinous and many-faceted. With eyes blind to the complexities that form the natural cogs of any standing army, it is easiest to see only the soldiers, only those standing firm in the front lines. There are more, however, and the tasks of the hands behind the scenes of any great battle are as intrinsically important to the machinery of rank and file as the men and women wielding the actual blades…"

— *Ahthys Borne, Acrosian* šef

"Compress! I need a compress!"

"Put her here! Hurry!"

"We can't save the hand! Take it or he'll lose the arm!"

Syrah tuned out the thrum of her surroundings, the moaning and keening calls from the wounded meshing with the shouts of her trainees while they rushed about their work. She focused everything on the task before her, her hands threading over the twitching chest of the wheezing soldier she was kneeling beside. Golden light wound its way like strings between her fingers and his exposed skin, soft lightning coursing back and forth about the deep puncture wound between his ribs. Closing her good eye, Syrah allowed the magic to take over, let the power be all that whispered in her ears. She dove deep, seeking and searching, weaving the spell into bone and flesh.

There.

The hole, mercifully, was small, the blade which had caught the soldier in the overlap of his armor having just nicked his lung. Magic could only do so much, but concentrating with all her might Syrah willed the tissue back together, feeling her arms start to shake as she did. It wouldn't hold on its own, so she clotted blood about the hole, content with simply patching it until the man's body could work its own miracle.

Finally, after several more minutes, Syrah was satisfied, pulling her mind back before opening her eye again. With a measure of relief she saw some color had returned to the patient's face, and he was breathing easier despite his sweating and groans of pain.

"*Done,*" she told the young atherian who'd been waiting by her side, speaking roughly in the female's native tongue. "*Take him to recovery tents. Hurry back. All help here, we need.*"

Though her sentences were broken, the lizard-kind nodded at once, getting to her feet and rushing off to find someone to help her carry the wounded man. Syrah followed suit, standing up and taking a breath to steady herself before turning around.

The general's pavilion was—to put it mildly—a chaotic scene. One of dozens of tents they'd commandeered for the post-battle triage, it was set up between the dunes as close to the city as they'd dared. Though word had only just arrived a half-hour earlier that Dynec had fallen—its surviving soldiers having surrendered not long after Akelo led their army through the west gate Raz had successfully claimed—already the wounded and dying were pouring in, some limping back on their own, others hanging between comrades' shoulders, and still more being carried in on shields that dripped with blood which steamed and froze in the coolness of the night air. Within fifteen minutes every square foot of the reed matting along the pavilion floor was taken up, leaving nothing but the narrowest gaps between the injured for Syrah and her helpers to move through. The howls of pain and gurgled moans of the dying swallowed up the back-and-forth shouting of the caretakers, and for every man they sent to the makeshift recovery wards further south, two more were brought in. It was an endless cycle, but one Syrah was sadly getting to know well. First Karesh Syl, then Karesh Nan.

And now Dynec, Syrah thought to herself, stepping gingerly into the crowd, looking for her next patient. *The first of too many fights in this hellish land…*

Before the start of their war, Syrah had never been anything more than mildly competent at healing. Combat had always been her strong suit, a mastery of offensive and defensive spells which had allowed her to fight back to back with even the likes of Raz on more than one occasion. If she was honest with herself, Syrah thought she'd ever been a little disdainful of the Priests and Priestesses who specialized in the mending arts, men and women who so often stayed behind in the warmth of the temples while so many of their comrades travelled the harsh lands of the North, struggling for a better world.

But Syrah wasn't fighting again anytime soon. The idea of wading back into war—while more tolerable than it had been even a month prior—still brought to mind too many memories of a room littered with the smoking shapes of slain men. With that understanding, she'd rapidly developed a new appreciation for the craft, and her spellwork was improving to match that respect.

Carro could have done better, though, she thought sadly as she knelt down before an atherian male who was shivering and clutching at a massive gash in the bicep of his left arm, watching his life drip through his clawed fingers.

How long she worked into the night, after that, Syrah didn't know. She saved more than she lost, but those that were beyond her reach were often the hardest to turn away from. An old Percian with half of a spear snapped off in his gut. A female whose skull had been partially crushed by a falling stone. A Southerner so badly burned, Syrah couldn't fathom how he'd survived as long as he did. She struggled to make her choices, doing all she could to see that the dying were comfortable while seeking to save those who had not yet slipped within reach of the Lifegiver. Her trainees moved about her, following her instructions and seeking her advice. Others came, as the night wore on, soldiers who'd weathered the fight unharmed or hadn't seen any action at all. Officers and even a few of the other generals, some seeking out men who'd fought particularly well, some just looking to see what help they could offer. These she gave orders to quickly, as efficiently as she could, not allowing herself to be drowned in the chaos. She didn't notice the red that stained her hands, didn't notice the sounds of suffering slowly fading as many passed on and more were patched up and carried out to make space for the less wounded. She worked her magic in silence when she could, shouting for assistance when she had to. In some deep corner of her mind she was relieved that she was, for once, without fear, but it made her almost as ill to realize *this* was how far the world had to fall before her trepidations faded away. She could touch the men without qualm, but only so long as they were practically dying before her eyes. She did not freeze up as strangers brushed or bumped past her, but only because her focus was so absolutely on her magics. She held that focus firm, held that determination tight. She worked her spells without rest, ignoring the fatigue which built up in her head and arms and chest.

It was hours past midnight, in fact, when a clawed hand took her gently by the arm, making her start.

She'd been leaning over the body of a young borderer who'd taken a wound to the abdomen. The injury hadn't seemed too involved, at first, but as she'd worked Syrah realized the extent of the damage was far greater than she'd anticipated. She had poured her magic into the soldier desperately, striving to bind the aortic artery pierced along the man's spine even as she fought to stitch together the intestines that had been sliced apart. She'd given it everything she had, her mind diving so deep she had lost track of anything else around her as need and fatigue dragged her down.

As the scaled touch brought her back, though, Syrah realized that the man was still, his face slack. The flesh she had been working on was growing stiff and cold, the warmth of life leaving him as his spirit was lifted away.

"He's gone, Syrah," Karan was saying gently from behind her. "Leave him. You need to rest."

Syrah wanted to protest, wanted to pull her arm from the female's grasp as she looked into the soldier's distant eyes, but she couldn't muster the energy to. All the same, while she allowed herself to be helped to her feet, she resisted when Karan made to guide her from the tent.

"No," she mumbled with a dazed shake of her head. "The others… I need to see to the others…"

"You need to see to yourself first," Karan said quietly, not letting go. "That's why they called for me. They're worried about you."

Syrah blinked, then, and looked around blearily. The atherian was looking at her with sad understanding, but it was what was beyond Karan that struck more deeply. The pavilion was quieter than she recalled, now. Much quieter. The worst of the wounded had been seen and sorted out, or were being attended to in the other tents. The patients that remained were either those too fragile to move, or bore minor injuries which required only passing attention. Scattered among them, some carrying bandages and clothes and suturing materials, the dozens of Syrah's trainees were still.

All of them, men, women, and atherian alike, were watching her in concern, the distress in their eyes all-too evident.

Syrah couldn't help but smile at the sight, a little of the darkness that the night had clouded her heart with lifting.

"I'm fine," she said weakly, trying and failing again to free herself from Karan's hand. "I just need to refresh myself, and I'll be—"

She staggered, and it was only the atherian's grasp that kept her from collapsing onto the sleeping forms of several nearby patients. She'd attempted to draw a little magic into herself, attempted to replenish her energies with a spell, as she had periodically throughout the night.

The result this time, though, was her vision swimming and almost going black.

"You're *not* fine," Karan grunted, wrapping a clawed hand about Syrah's waist and drawing an arm around her scaled neck. "You're at your limit. I know it, and they know it, too."

She indicated the trainees with a jerk of her head. While some had returned to their tasks, those who still watched the pair of them nodded together, their faces blatantly anxious.

It took longer than Syrah would have liked before she could respond, struggling enough as she was to keep at bay the stars dancing before her eyes.

"I just need a moment," she breathed when she could at last support herself on her own two legs again. "Just a break. Maybe close my eyes for a—"

"He needs to see you."

Karan said the words quietly, loud enough for only Syrah to hear, but they shut her up at once.

"He didn't say so, but I got the feeling," Karan continued. "They say we lost many, holding down the east gate for the main army. I think this was a hard one for him…"

Concern welled up inside Syrah's chest, and she felt her cheeks tighten. Her tiredness faded ever so slightly, but all the same she leaned into her friend, allowing herself to be supported.

"Maybe I'll go rest after all, then," she said.

Beside her, Karan chuckled sadly, then took a careful step through the scattered rows of patients, guiding them toward the pavilion entrance.

"Is he alright?"

Syrah hadn't meant to ask the question, but—between her fatigue and anxiety—she found her self-control quickly crumbling. Beneath her, Nymara bobbed along complacently, shaking her head and snorting at the sand as though disappointed by the lack of grass in this arid land.

Karan looked around at her from the saddle of her tan gelding. She'd been smart enough to bring the horses when she'd come to fetch her, for which Syrah was grateful. The hospice tents had been set up in relatively close proximity to Dynec out of necessity, but the camp was several miles further south, where the generals had decided together the city's scouts would have been hard-pressed to find it. They'd been traveling for some five minutes already, shivering against the cold of the night despite the crowd of soldiers, mounts, and carts carrying the injured that followed the same trail they were tracing between the dunes.

"He's fine," the atherian said with a nod, guiding her horse around a pair of Percian men, one supporting the other as his comrade limped along on a bandaged leg. "A little banged up, but he's certainly seen worse."

Syrah nodded, but was unsurprised to discover that the female's assurances did little to make her feel any better.

Raz's physical wellbeing wasn't so much what she had been asking about, after all…

"The Dragon" he might be, but Syrah was finding that she resented that title more and more as time went on. "Monster" had been easy to loathe, and "Scourge" equally so. Those were titles Raz had been given out of hate and fear, names he'd been called by the very men and women they were fighting so viciously against now. "Dragon", on the other hand, had always seemed a distinction, a nod of respect to his strength and will. It described the image the world needed of him, a noble beast of wind and fire, invincible and untouchable in his own way. "The Dragon" was insurmountable, immovable, an unwavering bastion that was more myth than man.

Yes, Syrah was starting to hate that title…

Raz i'Syul Arro *was* a man, after all—or at least as close as he could come. He hurt and bled, struggled and failed. She'd seen it, had witnessed his fights and his losses and his suffering. There was value in Raz being seen as an unrivaled pillar around which the weak and enslaved could throng, but there was so much more to the atherian than his inspired words and his skill with a blade.

There was so much more to him than the blood he spilled and the war he led.

"And I thought slavery could be cruel…"

Syrah blinked, drawn away from her dark thoughts. Karan had brought her animal right up to Nymara's side as the path widened, and the female was now watching a wagon full of bandaged and bloody men rumble southward by them at a quick pace. Some of the soldiers were sitting up along the sides of the cart, wrapped in blankets, while several others were laid out on the cart bed, side-by-side beneath heavy furs.

"Those are some of the lucky ones," Syrah told her, and she frowned as the faces of those she'd lost that night swam across her mind. "If they're being sent to rest in the camp, they'll live to see another day. A lot of others won't have that chance."

Karan said nothing, following in behind the wagon as it outpaced them.

"You didn't see this, in the days after we took Karesh Nan?" Syrah asked her.

Karan shrugged, pulling her gelding a little further across the trail, her blades *clacking* against his sides as he ambled on. "I did, but I think it seemed less real to me at the time—or less *surreal*, rather. Bleeding and dying at the hands of the Tash and their men…" Her reptilian features contorted as she dredged up what were clearly unpleasant memories. "There was nothing strange about that, somehow, nothing out of the ordinary. Here, though…"

She trailed off, the wagon pulling away around a bend in the dunes.

"Strangers killing strangers," Syrah said with a sigh. "Yes… It's as bizarre and horrible a phenomenon as you'll ever find in this world, I think. My Priest-Mentor would have told you that 'war is the only evil remaining when all other cruelties have run their course'. It's a vile thing."

"But you still support it?" Karan asked cautiously, treading lightly around the subject.

For several seconds, Syrah didn't answer. Images flickered across her vision, brighter and more wretched than the visages of those she'd been unable to save. She saw burned husks of men, charred corpses in their white and gold leather armor. She saw a shattered room, fire clinging to the banners overhead and the carpet beneath her companions' boots. She smelled the smoke and flame, heard the sizzle and pop of blistering flesh.

Then, though, the image faded, and she saw a different chamber, far smaller than the first. Little more than a rectangular box, the space was cramped from wall to wall with the thin, haggard forms who'd taken her and Raz in with wide eyes which had been so vividly devoid of anything but hunger or confusion or panic. She recalled the rancid smells of unwashed bodies and waste, the creaking of the irons as the figures had shifted in fear at the sight of the pair of them. She recalled the aged men and women and atherian, children who were rarely their own chained up right alongside them, some of whom couldn't have been more than ten or eleven summers of age.

"Yes," Syrah answered finally, taking a deep breath of cool night air in an effort to push away the memories of that room and the horrors of Karesh Syl it had revealed to her. "I have to, I think. When the only choices before you lead to sin, it comes down to simply what manner of sin you can live with."

"And you can live with this?" Karan asked softly as they passed yet another group, a man and a woman carefully guiding a female atherian who was keening softly, her entire face wrapped in reddened bandages.

"Compared to the alternative?" Syrah asked in response, her good eye falling on the scars of pale flesh that ringed the blinded lizard-kind's wrists and ankles. "Yes. I can live with this…"

She didn't finish her thought, though, didn't voice that there was another whose guilt she was more concerned about…

They were quiet, after that, managing the rest of the way south without speaking, listening to the night wind blowing across the desert overhead. The moon was bright when it managed to show itself, but even when the hills swallowed that brighter light the stars formed a scattered belt overhead, twinkling and shining as a few sparse clouds drifted lazily along the heavens. They turned the sand a somber shade of faint blue around them, and despite her fatigue Syrah couldn't help but wonder sadly why the beauty of this harsh land could be found only in the darkness.

The two of them reached the camp some five minutes after that, the mass of tents that made up the officers' and generals' quarters at the north end of the march blooming like a lake from between the dunes. At the edge of the grounds, Karan caught the attention of a passing sentry with a whistle—Raz had taught her how to make the sound, and she took advantage of it whenever she could—waving the Percian over as she and Syrah came to a halt. Dismounting, the female handed Nymara and the gelding over to the man, giving him instructions to have them penned for the night. Though Karan likely held no actual rank above his own, the soldier nodded at once, bowing briefly to Syrah before starting east, animals in tow.

When he was gone, Karan silently offered her arm, and Syrah took it gratefully.

They made their way south through the tents at an even pace, Syrah allowing herself to be guided while she let her mind wander, Karan careful to slow her usually longer stride so they could walk side by side. Every now and then the female would glance around at her, but Syrah barely noticed. Her thoughts were distant, dragging her so far away that she hardly managed to nod to Kalin and Odene when they crossed paths, and she didn't so much as blink at some of the older atherian glaring at her as they passed. For a few minutes they navigated the camp, Karan pulling her gently this way and that, sometimes even out of the way when needed, or else telling her to mind her step when the sand gave beneath their feet. Finally, though, they reached Syrah and Raz's tent, and Karan gave her hand a squeeze, calling her back from her musings.

Syrah lifted her head just in time to squint at the sudden light as the tent's entrance was pushed open, and a man stepped out from within.

"Erom," she called when the figure started to turn south, about to head deeper into camp. At once the man stopped, looking over his shoulder to grin in an exhausted sort of manner at the pair of them.

"Was surprised you weren't with him," the borderer said to Syrah, waiting for the two to approach. Oddly enough, he gave her a once over, looking her up and down, eyebrow raising as though in surprise. "I guess you've been busy, too, though…"

"Do you have news?" Karan asked him, disengaging herself from Syrah's grasp gently.

The general nodded, his expression hardening into a bitter sort of triumph. "Aye," he said shortly. "Came to tell him we caught the bastards."

The words reached Syrah as a thrilled shock.

"The šef?" she demanded, taking a step forward. "We got them? That quickly?!"

"That quickly," Erom confirmed, crossing his arms, the pommels of his mismatched daggers gleaming in the starlight behind his hips. "Raz read them like a book. He had me take control of our cavalry as soon as Akelo joined us at the west gate. We caught two of them—Kanela Saresh and Zeres Thorne—hauling it west with enough gold and silver to start a tidy little life in Karavyl, if they'd made it. Had to run them down. Cyper's troops cornered the third one—Ameen. Tough old bastard, apparently. Cyper says *he* put up a hell of a fight, at least."

Syrah frowned. "Only three?" she asked. "So Bahrek's information was true…?"

"Seems that way," Erom replied with an almost-disappointed shrug. "Akelo and Hur have already had a talk with Zeres Thorne, I'm told. Cyper told me he started singing before anyone could get near him. Seems they sent three to Miropa to convene with the other cities, and they… uh… didn't come back."

"And Miropa left Dynec to its fate," Syrah muttered, finishing for him. "I imagine they didn't have much use for loose ends, and doubtlessly bitter ones at that…"

Erom nodded. "Less work for us in the end." He started to turn away from them, making to wave farewell. "Which I'm grateful for, given this night. If you'll excuse me, I think I'll try for a few hours of sleep before—"

"Wait," Syrah said, dropping her voice to barely a whisper, though she doubted it would help. "Please."

Erom stopped short at once.

"The east gate…" she continued slowly. "They're saying… I saw so many coming through the tents…. Was it… Was it as bad as it seems?"

At once, the borderer's face fell, and Syrah's heart with it.

"Yes," he said simply. "We lost about two hundred of the six we brought with us. The large majority of them from among the lizard-kind. Raz's plan saved us hundreds—maybe thousands—overall, but it was costly for those who took part."

"Two hundred," Syrah repeated in disbelief. A full third of their estimated casualties, based on the night's count. It was staggering to imagine, and she forced the weight of those thoughts away in favor of a different worry.

"And he was in the middle of it, I'm assuming?"

She was aware it was a foolish question, and asked for childish reasons. Syrah herself had made the decision not to fight anymore, but she knew she would never bring herself to ask the same thing of Raz…

"If anything, he's half the reason we held on so well." Erom's tone was understanding. "Without your man, we would have lost a lot more than just two hundred, I think."

Syrah nodded, not meeting the general's eye. His words, oddly enough, made her feel a little better.

"Thank you," she said quietly. "I'm sorry to have kept you. Please get some rest while you can."

Erom gave her a quick bow, but hesitated as he straightened. Though she wasn't looking at him, Syrah knew he was watching her carefully, the same way the others watched her when they worried.

"Goodnight, general," Karan said, not unkindly, but firmly.

Syrah almost smiled. The young female knew her well indeed.

Erom recognized the polite dismissal for what it was, bowing a second time before turning on his heel and vanishing into the winding path between the tents. When he'd gone, Syrah looked around.

"You too," she told Karan with an appreciative smile. "Go tend to Abir. I heard he's been wandering off more often recently."

Karan groaned in frustration, as though reminded of something unfortunate. "He managed to find himself in *Zal'en's* tent a few nights ago. Of all places... I was surprised they brought him back in one piece."

Syrah chuckled tiredly. "I'll see if I can find you some spare rope in the morning. Maybe you can tie him to the bed or something."

Karan cracked her own smile at that. When she looked at Syrah, though, the smile fell away, and her expression fell into lines of concern.

"You'll be alright?".

Syrah nodded steadily.

"Of course," she lied through her teeth, then bid the female a good night before turning and pulling aside the tent flap.

X

Syrah found Raz laying on his back across their shared bedrolls, wings splayed out on either side of him. He had an arm over his eyes, like he wanted to block out the warm glow of the candles someone had lit about the floor of the space, and in the faint light she could see that one of her trainees had already seen to his wounds. A heavy swath of cotton compresses was bound about his left shoulder, and bandages layered him in a half-dozen other places. Forearms. Bare chest. Stomach. Legs. Even his tail hadn't escaped unharmed. None of the injuries appeared to have been life-threatening, but all the same Syrah felt her cheeks tighten again, taking him in as she approached.

Blood is only a fraction of the cost, though, isn't it? she thought, kneeling down beside the atherian.

As the bedroll shifted beneath him, Raz stirred.

"How many?"

Syrah had known better than to assume he'd been asleep, but still his sad words took her by surprise, shivering in the quiet of the tent. For a few seconds she watched his hidden face, unsure of whether or not she should answer the question.

"How many, Syrah?" he asked again.

Clenching her fists in her lap, Syrah tried to keep herself from shaking.

"Just under six hundred total at last count." She spoke as gently as she could, and yet the reality of her answer was still harsh against her ears. "But that was over an hour before I left. It will be higher, now."

Raz nodded slightly, face still hidden beneath his arm. "And higher still by morning, not to mention the days that follow…"

"It would have been worse, if you hadn't been able to take the east gate. Much worse. Erom says so, too."

Raz was silent, apparently taking no solace in that fact.

"Raz," Syrah pressed him soothingly, "this is war. This is the fight *we* picked. We knew there would be a cost. We knew this would be the result. All you can do is battle to keep that price as low as possible, to make sure as many of our soldiers survive to see the next day."

To her surprise, Raz gave a dry laugh.

"I thought the same thing. Just before we took the wall. Still… It doesn't make it any easier in the aftermath, does it?"

Syrah had no words to answer that. Instead, she reached out and took his free hand from where it had been laying by his side. She drew it into her lap with both of her own, feeling some of the darkness fade as his clawed fingers flexed gently about hers, returning the pressure she was giving him. They stayed like that, for a time, neither speaking. Syrah's fatigue was forgotten for the moment, and she had a nasty feeling Raz wasn't going to see much sleep that night no matter how hard the fight had been.

"Erom says we caught the šef?" she finally prodded, attempting to remind the atherian that the night *had* ended in victory, even if it didn't outright seem so.

Sure enough, Raz smirked. It was the same sort of bitter grin the general himself had made outside the tent. "We did, largely thanks to him. He rode down two of them as they were fleeing west."

"And Cyper's men cornered the last, yes," Syrah said with a nod, flipping the atherian's hand over so that she could stroke the line of his wrist and palm gently, watching the candles flicker about them while she did. "He told me that, too."

She paused, steeling herself for the question.

"What are you going to do with them?"

Raz's fingers tensed in hers, but he was quiet. After a long few seconds consideration, he sighed in resignation, drawing his arm from his face. They had been together now for long enough that her heart didn't dance around her chest whenever she met his eyes, but all the same, as his gaze found her face Syrah allowed herself to be lost in the sunset gold for a moment.

Raz, though—who had looked like he was about to give her an answer she wouldn't like—suddenly sat up with a growl of surprise.

"Syrah!" he hissed, snatching her hands up in both of his. "By the Sun… I *thought* I smelled…"

He trailed off, mouth agape as he looked her up and down, and Syrah glanced down at herself, wondering what was wrong.

"Oh," she heard herself gasp under her breath.

Whether it was because she'd been too tired to notice, or merely accustomed to the sight of it after the chaos of the hospice wards, Syrah hadn't considered the blood. It clung to the folds of her silks, black against the dark fabric, a solid wash about her abdomen and breasts with streaks or splatters along her thighs and even her shoulders. Her hands were almost worse, though, dyed mostly red and flaking over her knuckles, the underside of her nails shaded by hardened crimson. She wondered, as her fingers began to shake, what her face looked like. For a second, her shock turned to anger, not understanding why no one had said anything, why Karan and Erom hadn't spoken a word.

Then, though, Raz was on his feet, bolting out of the tent, and Syrah thought she understood.

"You and you," she heard him snarl to whatever soldiers had been unfortunate enough to be passing by as he exited. "I need a basin of water and clean clothes. *Now*."

At once there was a pair of startled "Yessirs!" followed by what sounded like a bundle of armor or weapons being dropped to the ground, and through a descending numbness Syrah made out muffled footsteps running off at full-tilt. Raz reappeared, and the candlelight danced as he approached her again.

"Come on," he told her softly, offering a hand to her. "Let's get you out of those clothes."

All Syrah could do was nod unsteadily, allowing him to help her slowly to her feet. She could tell she wasn't totally present, could tell that some part of the self-hate which had been festering within her for the last months was fighting to draw her away, excited by the sight of the blood. She thought, too, that Raz was equally aware of her descending mental state, because he kept talking to her quietly as he gently drew her to him, his soft words an anchor to which her mind clung. She herself said nothing, her eye still on the red that caked her chest and midriff. Gradually Raz turned her around, still talking while his clawed fingers slowly unwound the silk shawl that had been wound around her neck, then pulling her hood down from over her head. Still she stayed quiet, holding onto his voice as far less pleasant things attempted to creep their way into her thoughts. Even when his hands moved to pull her robes up, helping to lead them over her shoulders and head, she couldn't speak. Even when she stood, shivering from more than the cold in nothing but her small-clothes, her back to him, she had no words. All she could hear was his voice, and all she could see was the blood that blackened the pale skin of her fingers, congealing beneath her nails.

Then, though, she felt Raz wrap his strong arms around her, pulling her into his bare chest.

Syrah gave a racking gasp, somewhere between a gasp of grief and a sigh of relief. There was nothing between them now, her skin naked against his scales, but not even for a moment did she feel the panic well up, the terror build. On the contrary, it was as though his contact, cool against her back, was its own gravity, dragging all of the nightmares itching at the vestiges of her conscience away and into itself. She gasped again, the inhalation sharp against her lungs, turning her face into the crook of his elbow while she brought her hands to the breadths of his muscled arms that were wound about her chest, pressing herself into his grasp. In response she felt him lower his head to hers, resting his snout into the crown of her hair. For almost a minute they stood there in silence, neither so much as noticing the chill of the night air, taking everything they needed from each other.

Then came the sound of footsteps outside, and Raz broke away from her, moving to the entrance again as the soldiers called for him in uncertain voices.

He returned shortly—backing carefully through the tent flap again—with a large wooden basin in his hands and a pile of clean linens over one shoulder. Water sloshed over the bowl's sides as he came to stand by her once more, spilling across his fingers and the reeds beneath their feet, but he paid it no mind. He knelt, depositing the basin carefully to one side before pulling the cloths from his shoulder and dropping them to the floor on his other.

Then, reaching up, he pulled Syrah down too, having her sit across from him, and guiding her hand to the water.

"You might want it a little warmer," he murmured as her fingers dipped into the icy coolness. "I won't have you catching a chill on top of everything else."

Still hearing him from a distant place, Syrah only nodded, instinctively willing her magic outward, numbly relieved when the darkness didn't swallow her again. When the water was a pleasant temperature, Raz pulled her hand away, reaching across himself to take one of the towels from the pile and dampening it.

Then, with intimate care, he began to wipe away the dried blood, starting with the hand he held and brushing about and between her fingers with a tenderness Syrah was pretty sure only she had ever seen.

Raz kept his silence while he worked, apparently sensing that she didn't require his voice to tether her anymore. Some subconscious part of her reached out to heat the tent, too, as she watched him, the cold of the night fading little by little while she absently wove a simple ward of warmth about them. More of her thoughts were given to studying Raz himself, though, taking him in as he brushed at her skin, washing away the grim reminders of the evening's difficulties. She took in his reptilian face, her eye lingering on the trio of faint scars that split his lip, where he'd told her he'd once weathered a blow from a sandcat in his youth. She studied the sunset colors of his webbed ears, the orange and red and yellow matching the shades of his frayed wings, now tucked against his back. She followed the angles of his body down, noting the nicks and dents and missing scales that told the story of his violent life, both before and after they'd come to be together. His bandages covered some of the tale, but all the same she could see the puncture mark below his ribs where he'd taken a crossbow bolt to the side. She could see the narrow crossing lines that were memories of the Azbar Arena, then wider ones where Gûlraht Baoill's axe had done its work in their duel. She saw the pale spot in his left bicep, where a wound he'd won saving her from an assassin's knife the summer before had nearly spelled the end of him.

And she saw the twin rings of bare flesh, worn of any scales by the irons that had once encompassed them, which formed bands about his wrists. They were echoes of her own marks, the pinkish-red scars she'd earned in her own trials.

Seeing them, Syrah felt the last bits of her conscience fall back into place, and she took a deep breath as the warmth of the cloth met the coolness of Raz's touch about her arms.

"Better?" Raz asked without looking up from his work.

Syrah nodded. "Yes," she breathed, not making to draw her hand from his while he worked the rag beneath her fingernails, carefully scraping them clean. "Much."

Raz gave her palm a small smile, then flipped it over and grunted in satisfaction. Tossing the cloth aside, he reached for a fresh one, dipping it into the still-hot water before looking up.

"Close your eyes," he told her softly.

Syrah did so, and didn't even flinch as he pulled the dark wraps—the length of opaque fabric that hid her ruined right eye from view—up and off her head. It had been over a year since Kareth Grahst had carved his marks into her visage, leaving her half-blind and missing most of an ear, but Raz was still the only one she'd had the strength to show the ugliness to. He never winced, never so much as blinked at the scars. At first, of course he had reacted, but not with disgust or pity. Rather, he'd always responded with nothing less than seething rage when he looked upon her face, his hate for those who'd done such a thing to her palpable in the very aura of his presence.

Although she would never admit it, she loved him for that, too.

Slowly Raz wiped at Syrah's brow, then moved to her cheeks and throat. She could feel the hot moisture of the water running in rivulets down her chest and between her breasts. She didn't open her eyes as he cleaned her, allowing his hands to shift over her shoulder and neck as needed, his touch leaving her tingling. She understood some of the odd looks their friends and acquaintances had given the pair of them over the last year. There were certainly questions to be asked, concerns and curiosities to be raised ranging from everything from desire to base anatomy. Theirs was a strange relationship in more than one way, Syrah knew. She'd enjoyed the affections of a fair few in her twenty-seven years, after all—not all of them necessarily male—and understood the reservations some might have regarding certain… activities…

With Raz, though… With Raz, the desires were different. With Raz, the need came simply in the form of an ache in her chest when she wasn't by his side. It was simpler, in some ways, to the wants of the flesh she remembered once experiencing, but it was also deeper, stronger and more tangible. With others, it had been their touch in only certain places that had left her breathless and quivering.

With Raz, all she needed was his fingers against her cheeks, as they were now, for her to feel everything there was to feel.

"Syrah."

Syrah opened her eyes, blinking a few times as her sensitive vision adjusted to the candlelight once more. Raz had finished, it seemed, because the cloth he'd been using was now on the ground atop the others. She felt herself pale, seeing the reddish tinge of it, wondering how many times she must have absently wiped sweat from her face while she'd gone about her grisly work that evening.

"Syrah, look at me."

She looked up from the bloody fabric. Raz was watching her carefully, vertically-slit pupils scrutinizing her. For a moment she felt as though she were being measured, like the atherian was attempting to test her strength, to trial her resolve.

When he spoke again, she understood why.

"You know they have to die, don't you?"

Though the ward held around them, keeping the cold at bay, Syrah felt a chill run up her back that settled painfully in her chest, wrapping itself cruelly about her heart. She met his gaze calmly, hoping the brief moment of panic and sadness didn't play itself too obviously across her scarred features. It felt as if her soul itself was being pulled in two directions, the old spirit that still resided within her—the presence of a Priestess of Laor who had fought so viciously against the taking of life—battling with her newer, harder, sadder self. On the one hand, instilled instincts and beliefs stormed, as they had stormed when she and Karan had watched the ambush and butchery of the Dynec riders a few nights before, witnessing the soldiers fall by the dozens without raising a hand to stop it.

And, like that time, Syrah's understandings of what the world *really* was, what man was *truly* capable of, won out over old beliefs.

"I know," she said, working hard to keep her voice steady as the words formed a lump in her throat. She dropped her gaze, looking again at the scaleless rings about Raz's hands, thinking again of that room in Karesh Syl, those overcrowded quarters packed wall-to-wall with hungry, terrified souls. "I understand. There are some acts which are unforgivable, some evils that…" She grit her teeth as she fought to say what she knew to be true. "Some evils that need to be dealt with in the harshest possible terms."

"That's only half the reason," Raz told her, reaching out to take her chin carefully in his hands, lifting her face to meet her eyes again. "You aren't wrong, but I need you to comprehend that the Mahsadën is a *cancer*. It's an affliction of the flesh, eating away at what little remains of the South's heart. If we leave šef be, even if we punish them by other means, the sickness will return one day. We could exile them, we could incarcerate them… It wouldn't matter. So long as they breathe, their subordinates know hope."

"But you can kill them, and there's still no guarantee," Syrah murmured, cursing herself as the pain in her breast won out for a moment, loosening her tongue. "Miropa survived, after you purged it of the Mahsadën. It rose again. What's to say anything will be different here, if you take their heads? What's to stop someone else from rising in their stead?"

"Miropa could only have survived with the support of the other cities," Raz told her evenly, still holding her by the chin, his eyes soft on hers. "The moment Evony and Sass and the rest fell, the vestiges of their rings reached out to the others across the South. There can't be any other reason. Without their unity, there was no one left with enough influence or power to gather what remained of the city's society."

Syrah's mouth was tight as her mind instinctively scrambled for a reason to argue, a reason to deny Raz's explanation. Before she could come up with anything, though, he kept on.

"It's not just these three that I'm going to kill, Syrah," he told her steadily, like he needed her to understand. "After this, it's the leaders of Karavyl, or Cyro. Then whatever city comes next, and the next, until they decide it's time to take us head-on. The Mahsadën will not die so long as there is even one head left to rise. They *all* have to meet their ends, down to the last. They *all* have to fall. If they don't—if even one slips through our hands—then the rings have a chance to survive." His lips pulled back, revealing the razored edges of his white fangs. "I can't allow that. I'm sorry, Syrah. I *can't*."

It was the pain in his face, the sadness behind the anger, that brought Syrah back under control of her own will. She forced the old voice of instilled instinct back, locking it up within the cage she'd made of her heart. At the same time she reached up and took his hand in both of hers again, sighing as she pulled it down into her lap.

"I know," she said in barely a whisper. "I know. I'm sorry. I know it's not easy for you as is. I didn't want… I didn't mean to make it any more difficult."

Unbidden, Syrah felt herself start to tremble, a knot tightening in her throat. She clung to Raz's fingers—probably harder than was comfortable—fighting back the shaking breath that pressed against her chest, trying to get out.

Just as she thought she was going to lose the fight, Raz pulled her into himself once again, bringing her onto her knees so that she fell into his arms.

"Don't come tomorrow," he told her, almost pleadingly. "I'm glad you understand, but that doesn't mean you have to witness it. Stay here. I'll have Karan keep you company and—"

"No."

For the first time all evening, Syrah heard the strength in her own voice. Though she didn't try to push herself off him, she shook her head against the scales of his chest, any threat of tears drying as soon as she heard his words.

"Syrah, there's no need," he insisted, pressing her to him. "Don't force yourself. You don't owe anyone—"

"I owe *myself*," she said, her words muffled as she shifted her face to speak into the crook of his arm. "I owe *myself*, Raz. I don't know anything, anymore. I don't know if I can count myself a believer in the Lifegiver, much less one of His Priestesses. I don't know if I have the right to carry His light anymore. This path I've taken… I can't see where it goes, or even completely how I got here."

At last she managed to gather the courage to lift her face, looking up at him again. "But I'm on it. I'm here, following this bloody road with you. And if I'm going to do that, I can't lose myself to it. I *won't* lose myself to it. If I'm to take part in the end of a man, I will look him in the eye as he dies. I will pray for him, and hope he finds a greater purpose should Laor allow him to return to the cycle of life."

She reached up with one hand, cupping Raz's cheek, feeling the fluid softness of his skin beneath her fingertips. She gave him a sad smile, hoping her resolve shined through the pain. "I'll be by your side until this madness ends. I don't want you to—no, I won't *let you*—walk this path alone."

It was her turn to pull his face down, pressing herself up from where she'd been sitting on her heels so that she could bring her lips gently to the smooth, unscarred space between his eyes.

The coolness of his skin was hot against her mouth.

"It's my war, too, now."

XI

"There is value to be had in cruelty. One may pray that it is not often, but live a life like ours long enough, and you will doubtlessly find occasion where brutality is the only means to a necessary end..."

— Alyssa Rhen, Doctore of the Azbar Arena

The heat of the day curled over Dynec's skyline, twisting the ugly buildings to weave and swirl against the horizon. For a time Raz looked on contemptuously, studying the squat structures with disdain and disappointment, wondering if the city had always been so unpleasant. He recalled it differently from the times he'd visited in his youth. Then, Dynec had been a place of small wonders and subtle miracles, a haven of red brick and cracked, Sun-bleached wood in the endless harshness of the desert that was all he'd ever really known. He and the Arros would lead their caravan through the west or north gate of the city depending on their route, often coming east laden with Karavyl's famous silks. They would settle somewhere near the slum line, and enjoy their days traveling back and forth to the market quarters. Then, Dynec had been a city of life to Raz, a place that—while perhaps not as grand or breathtaking as the greater municipalities of Miropa or Acrosia—had held its own charm, its own culture. He wondered if those memories were nothing more than the wistful recollections from a time he'd been too young to see the corruption of the world, or if Dynec itself had truly slipped so far into the pit the Mahsadën had dragged it into.

He decided—looking down from the horizon to the awe-inspiring sight that was the city's central plaza below—that he would hold onto the latter of those hopes.

It offered the place a chance for redemption.

Unsurprisingly, the tallest building among those that encircled the square had belonged to one of the šef, a man by the name of Elon Marst. It was a four-story structure of black and white granite, its ledges accented with hammered bronze in a way that reminded Raz of the ornate details of the inner city of Karesh Syl, where the nobles and the Tash's favorites had resided. The building—the top three floors of which had served as Marst's private home, with the bottom housing offices for several of the šef's apparently numerous business ventures—had the same sharp grandeur about it, that same presence of power coupled with frivolity. It was a handsome structure, obviously designed with the need for it to stand out among the simpler buildings around it, and Raz wondered with a snort what Elon Marst would have thought if he could see the use it was being put to now.

Given that the man was very likely little more than a corpse for the rats to feed on in some sewer in Miropa, though, Raz wasn't too concerned.

There were the sounds of struggling and cursing from behind him, and he turned away from the edge of the flat roof where he'd been standing on his own. Under a raised veranda, an open-air stairway led down to the halls of the fourth floor. As he watched, a number of figures came into view, apparently battling madly to make it up the stairs. The trio at their front—an aged, well-built soldier in scarred leather armor, a younger man in a torn, fine tunic, and an old woman in a skirt stained by dust and dirt—looked to be putting up quite the fight despite the fact that they were being led by all of Raz's generals and a half-dozen assisting hands to boot. They strained against the ropes that bound their wrists before them, muffled yells dull through the cloth gags knotted between their teeth. Raz couldn't blame them. This was their death march, after all. Maltus Ameen, Zeres Thorne, and Kanela Saresh.

These were their last minutes of life, and they knew it.

All the same… he only held so much pity to spare for those who'd built their lives upon the backs and blood of others.

In four quick steps he was at the top of the stairs, reaching out to take Ameen and Thorne both by the collars of their clothes, one in each hand. With a jerk he drew them to him, pulling them from the grasps of Hur, Kalin, Odene, and Marsus so that they struggled inches from his bared fangs.

"Enough of this," he snarled in their faces. "Try to die with some dignity, if nothing else."

In his left hand, Ameen only fought harder, his cheeks flushed and slicked with sweat, his gag damp as he attempted to scream what sounded like all manner of profanity through the cloth. Raz begrudgingly allowed the older man a measure of respect. Even as his own end loomed, the šef seemed more concerned with making sure his enemies knew just what he thought of them than he was with death itself.

Meanwhile, to Raz's left, Thorne paled, going half-limp, and Raz wrinkled his snout as the sour stench of urine rose from the man's britches.

So much for dignity.

He shoved the younger šef back into Hur's waiting hands, dragging Ameen across the roof himself. The others followed close behind, Thorne's will to fight gone and Saresh's apparently subdued, and when they reached the very edge of the building Raz heard Marsus and Erom whistle together.

"By the Sun," Odene added in his Percian accent, gaping out over the scene below them, and Raz grunted in agreement.

At first light, Akelo had sent fifty riders into the city bearing the army's winged Sylgid standard, each accompanied by a half-dozen mounted guards. They'd spent the morning spreading the word throughout Dynec, announcing the fall of the Mahsadën, and the public event that would mark that final end. Raz had expected a turnout, of course. Panic and fear would entice the upper classes to attend, and curiosity and concern would bring the middle and working families. The beggars and slum runners, though, the detritus of the city who'd been target and prey of the slave rings for too many years, he hadn't been sure about. He didn't know if the poor would be able to bring themselves to witness the deaths of the last of those who had so willfully trodden upon their lives. He'd feared that the masses wouldn't have allowed themselves to hope, wouldn't have allowed themselves to believe that maybe, just maybe, the era of their misery was coming to a close.

Now, though, Raz realized how much of a fool he'd been, forgetting just how resilient hope could very well be…

They wouldn't have had a prayer trying to guess how many had packed themselves in and about the square below. Thousands, Raz knew. Tens of thousands even. They undulated below like an ocean of tanned skin and dyed, colored silks. Social rank still held sway, the ostentatious sashes and turbans of the upper class distinct in a measly section along the east side of the plaza, but their number was little more than a faint splash of red and green and blue against the living current of the others. Plain shirts and pants of the city laborers. Bleached hair of those that spent their days toiling under the Sun. Bared arms of the men and women too poor to afford proper clothes. *These* were the soul Dynec, their collective mass spilling out into every road, street, and alley with a view of Raz atop Elon Marst's former home. *These* were the lifeblood of the place, and they had come in droves to cling to the chance that things might be changing. There were children, too, shifting between the adults' legs or else lifted up to sit on their parents' shoulders so they could see. Many moved in tight-knit groups, their thin rags or dark, naked bodies marking them as orphans who'd only survived be creating their own families. Raz felt a pang when he saw these youthful faces, his sharp eyes picking them out of the crowd.

This was something they, too, needed to see. This was a lesson they, too, needed to learn.

While the cruel and clever would surely rise, just as surely would they eventually fall.

"They'll not soon forget this."

Raz's attention was pulled away from the gathered citizens of Dynec as Akelo appeared beside him. The Percian had changed out of his usual armors for once, electing instead a simple tunic of bleached cloth and woven pants, though his sword still hung at his belt. His expression, looking down at the crowd, was somber but set. He had the look of a man who understood the distastefulness of what they were there to do as intimately as he understood its necessity.

"That's the hope," Raz agreed, turning back to the plaza while the other generals and their soldiers forced the trio of šef to their knees along the edge of the roof to his right. Beside each of them, a coil of noosed rope had already been staked into the mortared stone. "Butchering the Miropan Mahsadën behind closed doors was a mistake. I won't make it twice."

"Aye," Akelo agreed, watching Hur move to each of the three šef in turn, dropping and tightening the loops around their necks one after the other. Only Maltus Ameen still struggled now, the other two seeming to have given in to their fate. "Rumors and stories have their own power. It'll take time, but word will spread to the other cities. Might shake the rest of the society, at the very least."

"I doubt it," Raz said, hearing Hur deal Ameen a quick blow to subdue him. "This, though," he gestured with a hand downward at the shifting mass of people. "*This* we might be able to achieve. The Mahsadën aren't taking us lightly, this time. It'll take more than butchering their sacrificial lambs to put a dent in their resolve. But if we can rouse the citizens of the other cities… That will prove troublesome for them."

As the Percian's brow rose in understanding, Hur made a voiceless sound of confirmation, and Raz finally took his attention from the square. The preparations were complete. The three šef were kneeling at the edge of the flat roof, staggered several feet from each other as they faced outward. They displayed, in their final moments, the various natures of man when confronted with his end. Ameen, closest to Raz and Akelo, was doubled over from the punch Hur had dealt him, but he still fought to stand against the press of the Northerner's and Odene's holds, which were firmly keeping him down. Thorne, in the middle, stayed the coward, shoulders slumped and head hanging, looking like a discarded, broken doll. Saresh, on the end, was the most composed of the three, her wizened visage turned skyward, eyes closed while she took in the Sun's light. Her lips moved around the cloth between her teeth, and Raz barely made out the muffled pattern of a familiar devotion. The sound of it, that same prayer that was among those his mother and father had taught him as a child, made him tense in anger. He glared at the back of the old woman's head, wanting nothing more than to grab her by her wispy grey hair and snarl in her face that she halt her hypocritical petition.

He forced himself to calm, at least just a little. Just enough to turn away from the šef, searching the roof behind him.

He found her standing under the shade of the veranda, lingering along the top of the steps that led down into the building below.

Syrah's face was once again masked in the thin black silks of her wraps and hood. As a hot wind blew across the city, the dark layers of her robes shifted and danced around her, giving her the look of some cruel denizen of the Moon come to drag the souls of the evil to whatever punishment awaited them in death. Though he couldn't make out her features, Raz knew that she, too, was watching him, their eyes meeting even if hers were hidden. He wanted to call her over, then, wanted her hand in his while he went through the unpleasant duty that he was about to shoulder. He wanted to feel her touch even through the thin leather of her gloves, to draw hope and strength from it.

He did nothing of the sort, of course. He was not so cruel. Syrah had come, had made herself available to him—*for* him—despite the conflict of conscience he knew she was struggling with. Raz was grateful for that, more than words could tell her, and he took all he could from the brief nod she offered him after a moment, a small gesture of encouragement and understanding.

Do what you must, that nod said.

With a sinking heart, Raz silently acknowledged that it was time, and he spun to face the end of the roof before he risked losing his nerve.

"PEOPLE OF DYNEC!" he boomed out over the heavy thrum of the thousands below. "HEAR ME NOW!"

Quiet descended so quickly, so absolutely, it was unnerving. The silence had an edge to it, a buzz that felt half-excited, half-terrified.

"I will not bore you with empty words and introductions!" Raz continued more evenly, allowing his voice to ring out over the buildings. "You know my name, as surely as you know what it is I am here to do, what I am here to accomplish! You know your city has rotted beneath your very feet! You know this place has grown rank with corruption and greed! Most of you have played no part in this, of course, but *all* of you have been affected! But for a spare few among your number, you have struggled these past years to live, to see to your families and yourselves! You have fought hard to wring what you can from what little you've been allowed, and you know that that battle has only grown hard with every passing season!" Raz paused, letting his words to sink in.

Then he smiled a harsh grin.

"Today, that *ends*!"

With two steps he stood over Maltus Ameen, motioning that Hur and Odene step away. As they did, Raz himself took the man by the back collar of his armor and jerked him back, keeping him firmly on his knees but making sure his face was visible to all below.

"Maltus Ameen!" Raz shouted out. "The man responsible for the cruelties you've known at the hands of the very soldiers who are meant to protect and serve you! The man with his fingers in the trade of slaves and the spread of ragroot through your slums! You've come to fear him as an absolute power in your city, never to be crossed or challenged!" Raz shook the šef for emphasis. "Shall we see what he has to say, in his final moments?"

Not waiting for the answer, Raz slipped a steel claw of his free hand under the edge of the gag, splitting the cloth with a quick flick.

"BASTARDS!" Maltus Ameen roared the moment he'd spit out the thing. "GET YOUR HANDS OFF ME, YOU FUCKING LIZARD! GIVE ME A SWORD AND I'LL GUT YOU AND YOUR FUCKING WHORE WOMAN! I'LL SKIN YOU ALIVE AND USE YOUR HIDE AS A—!"

Letting go of his collar, Raz put a clawed foot between the man's shoulders and gave him a quick, solid shove.

Ameen's hateful words ended in a howled yell of surprise and terror, almost immediately followed by the *crack* of the staked roped snapping taut at the same time as the šef's neck broke. Raz didn't bother looking over the edge as the crowd below roared in shock and general approval, already moving to Thorne a few feet further along the roof. He knew the effect, knew the impact this act would carry.

He had hung the Tash of Karesh Nan and his Hands off the ramparts of their palace in the same manner.

"Zeres Thorne!" Raz shouted, this time taking a handful of the quivering man's long blond hair and jerking his head back to reveal his pale, tear-stained face. The throng below stilled at once. "Though few of you have seen him, many of you have felt his work and weavings in the lightness your purses and sparseness of your food stores! He is the man responsible for the taxes and fees on your services and labor which have run so many of you out of house and home! He is the man behind the tariffs on goods and imports which have made it nigh-impossible for you to sell your wares anywhere but in the crowded markets of Dynec alone! Though one to work behind the scenes, it could be argued that *he*—" Raz hauled Thorne up by his hair, the man screaming in pain as he struggled to find his feet "—is most largely responsible for the hardships and difficulties so many of you have long suffered!" He pulled the šef up another inch, bringing him onto his tiptoes and drawing out another garbled yell. "What say you, oh master of dukes and crowns? Have you any words for these people you've so readily thieved from?"

He reached up, cleaving off the man's gag as he'd done Ameen's.

"M-MERCY!" Thorne howled the instant his mouth was free, eyes screwed shut against the pain, trousers still soaked from when he'd pissed himself. "MERCY, M-MONSTER! I'VE WRONGED! I KNOW IT! I'M SORRY! I-I'VE A FAMILY! A WIFE AND SONS! P-PLEASE! MERCY! MER—"

Raz shoved him forward, and the crowd roared again, the šef not even having time to draw breath to scream before he plummeted down, the rope catching with another *crack*.

"We *all* have families, do we not?" Raz shouted out, spreading both arms as though to accept the excited shouts of the thousands in the plaza below. "We *all* have those we care and cared for! There will be no quarter for the Mahsadën, who have built their homes on the ruins of others' lives!" He dropped his arms, and the noise from below fell once again. "There will be no mercy for those who have so willingly taken without thought or concern!"

Once the square was silent again, Raz motioned to the last of the šef. Saresh still knelt at the edge of the roof, face ever lifted to the heavens, eyes still closed. She seemed to have finished her prayers, and Raz suspected she was now merely playing the passive captive, taking the opportunity to listen to every word he said.

"Kanela Saresh!" he said loudly, approaching her. "The bloody mistress of Dynec, I'm told! It's likely none of you here have ever crossed paths were her or any of her subordinates, because those that have generally don't live to tell the tale! Murderers and thieves don't tend to care for witnesses, after all, and there are some who've sworn to me she's been playing at her web of violence since before the Mahsadën even came to power! Contracts! Bounties! The acquisition of objects and people of value or interest! She is master of them all! Old, she may be, but do not be fooled! Her age means only that she has had a long, *long* time to hone her craft!" He stopped when he stood over Saresh, looking down at the woman's upturned face. "She's taken many and much from you, often without your being aware of it! She trades in lives as easily as she trades in silver and gold, and yet she sees fit to pray to the Sun and Moon as her own death looms!" He reached over his shoulder, drawing his gladius from its sheath. "Up you come, hag! Why don't you tell us what sort of deliverance you hope the Twins will bring you on this day?"

Saresh opened her eyes, their light grey meeting Raz's amber gold. She appeared to study him for a moment, taking him in as though he were some oddity she was considering collecting for auction. Finally, she sighed through her gag, and struggled to stand. Kalin, hovering nearby, made to help her, but Raz held him back with a wave of his sword.

"No," he said curtly so that only those on the rooftop with them could hear. "I would wager she's done nothing in her miserable life to deserve your assistance, or anyone else's."

That seemed to amuse the old woman, because she gave a muted chuckle before finally managing to find her feet. Reaching up, Raz wrenched the gag out of her mouth to let it settle about her neck.

"'By the Sun's grace, I grow,'" he quoted the prayer she'd been muttering, making sure to keep his tone even as the anger flared up again. "'By the Moon's, I sleep. It is in Their light that the world is, and it is by Their light that I shall live.'" He narrowed his eyes. "I'm surprised you have the gall to appeal to Them, in this moment."

To his pleasure, Saresh looked taken aback.

She recovered quickly. "No less surprised than I am that you have the stones to criticize an old woman for her faith," she retorted, staring at him impassively. "We all have the right to believe, and to seek comfort in the Twins when needed."

"No," Raz snarled, taking a half-step closer to her, backing her up to the very edge of the roof. "What we have a right to is *life*. One where hardship comes as it wills, but with every opportunity to overcome it. What sort of madness permits you to think the Moon and Her Stars will look favorably down upon you, given the path you've walked?"

Saresh shrugged. "The same madness, perhaps, that makes you believe you know what it is They seek to draw from Their faithful." Her face hardened. "If you know Their prayers, then you must be a believer, Monster. That disappoints me. I would have thought someone like you might understand that death and belief often come hand-in-hand."

Raz felt a chill, hearing those words, and he had to struggle not to look over his shoulder at where he knew Syrah undoubtedly still stood under the shade by the stairs. They rang like an echo, reminding him of something she'd once told him, when the pillars of her understandings regarding her own god had only just started to crack.

I think that I serve a god of death as much as I serve a god of life, she'd said.

He'd replied by saying that one cannot exist without the other.

Still… Saresh's interpretation was an altogether darker understanding.

"Saying they come hand-in-hand does not mean they follow the same path," Raz snarled. "You are using faith as an excuse for death, when death should be used as a reason for faith. You shame those of us who entreat Them for the strength to do what we must for the betterment of all."

"'Do what we must'?" Saresh repeated with a derisive snort, meeting his gaze evenly. "Who is using excuses now, Arro? Who is about to murder an old woman who hasn't even been given a blade to defend herself with? Who started this war with the rings? Do you *truly* think your hands are less bloody than my own? Do you *truly* think—?!"

Sching.

The gladius rang like a hand bell as it cleaved through air and flesh, flashing across Raz's body in a silvery arc to slash open the šef's throat from collar to collar. Before the old woman could fall or stagger back off the edge, though, Raz's other hand shot out, grabbing her by the rope noose still wound about her neck. Saresh coughed and hacked as he heaved her to him, crimson bubbling and streaming from her cracked lips. More spilled from the grisly wound that had cut into her windpipe, painting the steel and leather of Raz's gauntlet a gleaming red in the light of the morning Sun.

"The *amount* of blood—" Raz heard the venom in his own voice as he hissed into the dying woman's face "—matters little. It's all dependent on *whose* blood it is, and *why* it was shed." He pressed her back, tilting her over the open drop beyond the edge of the roof. "Reason weighs in all things, death and faith included. I am not innocent, but when the time comes for the Moon to lift *me* up, I trust the lives taken at my hands will weigh less than those stolen by yours."

Then, as Saresh began to convulse from shock, he let go.

The citizens of Dynec gave a final exalted cheer below as the third rope snapped taut.

XII

"It is fortunate that the world is capable of learning. Where would we be as a culture—as a people—were we not able to take in the mistakes and faults of our forefathers, to mold ourselves according to such conveniently provided lessons? Looking back, is it not painfully laughable to consider a time where the atherian were a people beneath us, traded across borders like beasts of only slightly greater value than horses or oxen or elephants? Where would the path of man have taken him, had we not learned from the darkness of our own history…?"

Commonalities of Ancient & Modern Society, author unknown

It was as though Uhsula of the Other Worlds had been living in a cave all her life, only for a small part of the wall to fall away and reveal the light of the Daystar to her for the first time. She was sleeping when it happened, of course—she often felt as though all she *did* was sleep, these days—but as the feeling bloomed in her chest she rose to consciousness, waking to the familiar blackness of her blindness. Despite the dark, however, that sensation, that feeling that a new light had dawned on her world, remained. She felt warmer, like a flame had been lit which sought to seep life back into the cold ache that ever-clung to her old bones.

It had begun, and Uhsula couldn't help but chuckle wearily at the thought.

"*Uhsula?*"

It took a moment for the old female to get her bearings, but when she did she realized that someone was sitting at the side of her stone bed, holding her wizened fingers loosely. The touch was gentle and familiar, and Uhsula had to hold back another laugh while she made to sit up. At once several additional sets of clawed hands took her by the arms and shoulders, helping her. They faded away again once she'd been assisted to perch stiffly at the edge of the slab, feet finding the cool, earthy stone of the room floor.

The one in her grasp, though, stayed.

"*Water,*" Uhsula croaked over her shoulder, in the direction she knew at least one of her acolytes was waiting. At once there was a hurried patter of feet toward the back corner of the chamber. While this happened, Uhsula was already casting around the darkness pointedly. "*The rest of you, leave us.*"

There wasn't even a moment's hesitation. By the time the acolyte who'd happened to fetch her pail of water returned to her side, the others were already gone, the *clacking* of their talons fading quickly into the tunnels of the caverns. Uhsula had the last handmaid set the pail down at her side with a nod of thanks, then dismissed her as well. When she, too, had left, the old seer turned toward the last remaining body in the room with her, speaking as she blindly searched for the ladle in the pail.

"*Hana*," she said with a soft smile, her worn fingers trembling and fumbling with the handle when they found it, "*as much as it warms my old heart to find you at my side when I wake, you must stop this. You are a Queen, not a child.*"

Shas-hana Rhan, Queen of the Under Caves, didn't give her any sort of answer, instead drawing her hand from Uhsula's and standing up. Though it had been many years since she'd been able to see her, Uhsula recalled in her mind's eye the bright, youthful figure of the younger female, the sheen of her eyes and the energy of her smile. The Queen's dark scales were unblemished, lacking the colored and patterned markings nearly all other atherian had, a trait long carried through the generations of her line. Uhsula felt the ladle being pulled gently from her grasp, then the sloshing of water as it was drawn from the pail.

"*Drink*," Hana said quietly, her voice heavy and tired, and the old seer felt the filled ladle being brought to her lips. "*You can reprimand me after.*"

Uhsula did as she was told, allowing the Queen to help her down one, then two, then three mouthfuls of cool water. As she sated her thirst, Uhsula couldn't help but feel some of the flame of her dreams fade under the weight of Hana's words, damped by the worry there. She thought—not for the first time in recent months—that her memory of the female was likely far gone from the person who stood before her now. The last decades had been hard for the lizard-kind. The men of the cities had grown steadily bolder, stealing away more and more of their kin from the lands around the mountain ranges that were their homeland. Fear ran high, and while food could be found among the cliffs in the form of small prey and ridge goats, fewer and fewer every year were willing to brave the descent into the sand plains where larger quarry like the great scorpions and desert lions were more plentiful. Likely the Queen who stood before her, helping her drink because her own hands were too frail to so much as hold a ladle now, was far thinner and more ragged than the memory Uhsula held of her.

It made what she had to say all the more important.

"*The walls are crumbling*," she said into the quiet, just when Hana was making to draw from the pail once more. "*Light is beginning to show through the stone.*"

Before her, she felt the Queen still.

"*What do you mean?*" Hana asked eventually, dropping the ladle into the water with a dull splash. "*Have you seen something?*"

Uhsula smiled, hearing the excitement only barely hidden in the younger female's voice. As hard as life was, as much as the world might place upon the Queen's shoulders, there was always one subject that could revitalize her.

Especially now.

"*One of the pillars of man has fallen*," Uhsula said with a nod, reaching out to feel for Hana's hands, taking them in her own. "*To the south. One of the cities has been claimed.*"

Hana hissed in surprise, and Uhsula had to hide a wince when the Queen's clawed fingers tightened instinctively around hers.

"*Is it him?*" Hana asked hurriedly, not bothering to hide her enthusiasm now. "*If it's to the south, it* must *be him, yes?*"

"*I imagine so,*" Uhsula agreed gently, returning the pressure. "*And the others, too. Their presence has grown clearer, in these last weeks. He has not returned alone.*"

"*The others…*" the Queen repeated, sounding like she couldn't believe it. "*To think that some would return to us, after all these years…*"

"*Your hatchling is proving himself a greater leader than either of us could have anticipated,*" Uhsula said. "*There are thousands with him, Hana.* Thousands. *I imagine many have never even seen the lands from which their sires were stolen.*"

"*He's done it, then,*" Hana managed to choke out, starting to sound relieved. "*He's done it. He's saved—*"

"*No.*"

Uhsula cut her off sharply, tightening her grip about the Queen's hands again. She felt the female jerk in surprise, but Uhsula continued before Hana could protest.

"*No, Hana. This path has not yet run its course. The walls have only cracked. We have come so far—*he *has come so far—but there is still much to be done. The cities of man will not all allow themselves to be swallowed up so easily. They will fight back, eventually. They will thrash and kick and lash out until there is not a breath left among their corpses. Now is not the time to celebrate. If anything, now is the time in which all our hopes and prayers will be put to the test.*"

In her grasp, she could feel the Queen's hands trembling.

"*What should we do, then?*" Hana asked. "*What can we do? Launch our own attack? There is the city to the south, the place they call 'Cyro'. Perhaps if we were to take—*"

"No," Uhsula said again, sharper this time. "*We* must not. *Not yet. We've neither the number nor the means, and even if we did there would be no controlling our people. Butchery and slaughter will not lend themselves to our freedom, in the end.*"

Hana stilled at her words, calming.

"*Yes,*" she said after a moment, forcing herself to breath evenly. "*Yes… Of course. Patience. We've waited so long already. Time we still have. Time we can still sacrifice.*"

"*A little longer,*" Uhsula assured her. "*Not much, I promise, but a little longer.*"

She felt Hana nod slowly.

Then something else rose up in the Queen, something harder and more regal than the person who'd just been helping the old seer to drink.

"*Can I believe that it is time, at least, to start gathering the tribes?*" she asked evenly. "*Should I order Sassyl Gal to spread the word of my summons?*"

Uhsula smiled one last time up into the darkness that hid Hana's face from her eyes, feeling the warmth within her swell with pride.

"*You can,*" she said. Then she bowed her head reverently. "*At the very least, we should be prepared to answer your child's call when it comes, my Queen.*"

XIII

"Anger has its place in many things. Do not count war among them."

— Tarruk Baoill, to his son, Gûlraht

Akelo Aseni was well aware that he was one of the steadier voices of reason within the ranks of the army's generals. Most of the others served their purposes, but keeping a level head was not always among their strong points. Odene and Kalin often unconsciously favored their *kuja* comrades when it came to making decisions, leading to strain between the other factions of the army. Hur was deceptively collected for all his imposing bulk, but his lack of a voice made his opinions difficult to convey with ease. Arnus and Cyper were loyal soldiers, but had difficulty separating themselves from the hard years they'd spent as oar slaves aboard the *Moalas*. Marsus Byrn was the most temperamental of the group, quick to anger and hard to calm since they'd arrived in his homeland, and Erom deferred all his decisions to either Raz or Akelo. As for the atherian—Zal'en—none of them had yet brought themselves to trust the female completely just yet. Raz himself was even-tempered when it came to his allies, but even *he* admitted he had trouble controlling the more vicious side of his nature when confronting his enemies.

For these reasons, when anyone was truly in need of impartial wisdom, Akelo had always felt honored that it was either he or Syrah Brahnt that they turned to.

In this moment, however, the old Percian was so irritated he wanted nothing more than to take the clay pitcher of water by his elbow and attempt to smash it and its contents over the canvas of the generals' pavilion that rippled relentlessly around them.

"I'm telling you, *west* is our best strategy." Arnus was arguing heatedly across the table with Marsus Byrn. "If we strike quickly, we can take Karavyl, effectively cutting off the Mahsadën's trade with the Seven Cities."

"And puttin' ourselves in a position to be pinched from the north *and* south," Marsus countered. "Karavyl has a standin' force of over ten thousand, and Acrosia has nearly fifteen. If they form an alliance with the Cities, we could be stuck siegin' Karavyl while reinforcements arrive from above *and* below."

"There's no indication the Mahsadën have managed that," Erom said flatly from the far end, leaning into the table with crossed arms to present his argument. "The Seven Cities are a martial land. It would take a lot to convince them to move their armies for the benefit of another nation."

"But that's banking on an assumed possibility," Cyper cut in, scratching at his stubbled cheek with a gloved hand. "It seems to me there is a small advantage to pressing west right now, countered by a *much larger* risk. On the other hand, moving east to take Cyro deals a blow to the enemy with little likelihood of any surprises—particularly unexpected reinforcements—and Zal'en has assured us the atherian of the Crags will lend us their support."

On his right, Zal'en bobbed her serpentine head in agreement, though she didn't speak. Her cheek was bound in gauze where she'd been grazed by an arrow during the battle two days prior, and one of the males standing behind her—Urlen, Akelo recalled—had one arm in a sling. Most of them, in fact, sported new wounds and scars, Akelo included. He looked around, studying the wrappings and bindings and sutures that marked the fight they'd weathered. He would have thought, perhaps, that such injuries might serve as a reminder of their common goal, as well as the sacrifices they were making to reach it.

Instead, he grumbled to himself, eyeing the pitcher again in temptation, *we've been stuck in this blasted tent for two hours, arguing ourselves in a circle.*

To be fair, a majority of their discussion had initially revolved around what to do with Dynec now that the city had fallen, and—while they hadn't been easy decisions to come to—most of those particular issues had been resolved. No matter what the army's next move was, a garrison of three thousand well-armed human soldiers would be left behind under the command of some of the lesser officers Raz, Syrah, and Akelo would soon be selecting. They would serve as a peace-keeping force, training new soldiers while monitoring the remains of the former guard, all of whom had been stripped of their weapons, armor, and ranks following their defeat. If Dynec managed to find its feet in the next few months, the garrison would rejoin the main force when they could.

"Assuming we make a decision by then," Akelo muttered to himself, earning a curious glance from Raz on his right.

He had feared, when they'd convened prior to the battle for Dynec, that this would come to pass. They had crossed the South's border nearly two weeks prior now with little that anyone could call a plan, mostly deliberately. After Dynec, they'd all suspected their war would be one of response, reacting to the Mahsadën's movements and actions.

Unfortunately, with Dynec proving nothing more than an empty sacrifice, offering no hint as to the society's retaliatory plans, it meant they were now squabbling over what their next move would be.

Personally, Akelo saw the advantage to both options, as well as the disadvantages. On the one side, taking Karavyl *would* prove a much more crippling blow to the Mahsadën than claiming Dynec. However, aside from the chance of the Seven Cities becoming involved and flanking them from the south, there was the greater issue that the collective šef of the fringe cities were *much* less likely to stand by and let their last stronghold south of the Cienbal be taken without a fight. Dynec had essentially lost all its value with the fall of Perc.

Karavyl would be a much more trying battle, with many more casualties on both sides.

On the other hand, pushing east and north to Cyro would put them at less of a disadvantage, but with lesser risk came *far* lesser potential for reward. Cyro's size and defenses were comparable to Dynec's, and the city had similarly lost value after the razings of Karesh Syn and Karesh Nan. Marsus and Raz had told them all that Cyro was largely considered the hub of the South's atherian head trade, but without access to the Tashes' buyers the trek west to the Seven Cities would be much, *much* harder for slavers to manage. If anything, Akelo suspected Cyro would be left to die just as Dynec had been, or more likely stripped of its valuable forces and left undefended for them to claim without a fight.

Still, there are some temptations… Akelo considered, glancing across the table at where Zal'en sat between Cyper and Odene, reevaluating his options for the hundredth time.

Unsurprisingly, Raz seemed to be on a similar train of thought.

"As I've said, while I'm aware of the value of Karavyl as a target, the risk does not favor us," the atherian spoke up loudly, cutting over what mumbling and minor bickering was still being exchanged. "What Erom says holds true: the Seven Cities are unlikely to move their forces far from the border of their lands if it means no more than assisting the South. However, Karavyl is almost as key to them as it is to the Mahsadën, and it isn't more than a fortnight's march from Holdum's Line. If we threaten it, we threaten the economic benefit of the Seven Cities. *If* they were inclined to get involved, we would be creating a perfect storm for that temptation. Our army would be in relatively short proximity to the border, and it would be a chance for the Cities to not only protect their own interests, but also curry major favor with the rings."

To Akelo's left, Arnus grimaced, clearly not convinced. "We could send representatives south, ahead of the main force," he suggested. "Assure the Cities we will see to it trade continues, should we overcome the—"

"No."

Several people at once cut the old soldier off. Akelo and Raz were among them, as well as Syrah on the atherian's other side. Some of the generals had similarly echoed the objection, but most firm between them was Zal'en's harsh snap.

"Seek a truce with such a land, Imperialist," she hissed in Arnus' direction, "and you will find yourself *absent* the aid of the atherian, now and forever. Perce was the greatest perpetrator of our enslavement, but they were not the only ones. The Seven Cities trades in flesh as readily as the Tashes did."

"Seconded," Cyper followed up this announcement, glaring at Arnus, his shaved head gleaming in the light of the Sun that peeked through the ventilation holes in the top of the tent. "I spent two years chained to the wall of a mine outside of Holdum's Line before being sold to pirate villages of Perce. I won't stand for any sort of truce with that place."

"Calm down, all of you. Please."

Syrah's words were gentle, but firm. At once, just as when Raz had spoken, everyone fell silent, turning toward her. Even Zal'en faced her, though Akelo felt a twinge of dark amusement at the irritation he made out in the old female's features.

"Arnus, your suggestion is tactically valid," the woman said, giving the Imperialist a nod of recognition. "Were circumstances different, I'm sure it would be worth more consideration. *However—*" she pressed on poignantly, cutting off several of the others as they started to raise their voices in outrage "—I think I speak for all of us, yourself included, when I say that establishing any sort of alliance with a realm like the Seven Cities would be a betrayal of the goal we have set out for. For that reason, despite my and Raz's welcoming of *all* possible options in this scenario, I can say with confidence that negotiations with the Chancellors is not a path we can follow at this time."

Tactfully done, Akelo thought with a private chuckle, watching Syrah, who sat with her silk hood about her shoulders. Criticism led and followed by praise. Despite the darkness that lingered so heavily over her in the last weeks, she never did fail to impress.

"Agreed," Raz rumbled after a moment's quiet. "In any other situation, Arnus' suggestion would be an excellent one. We would all do well to consider *all* the angles of this decision, not just those directly before us."

"Then we owe it to Zal'en to revisit her assurances," Akelo said, finally deciding it was time to speak up. "I admit that taking Cyro alone would be as far from a major blow to the Mahsadën as possible at the moment, but there are other aspects to consider. If our ultimate goal is the felling of Miropa—as well as the šef that we know are gathered there—then pressing west would require either crossing the Cienbal after taking Karavyl, or pressing further around the desert, sieging Acrosia, then Karth."

There was a grumbling of assent at this, and even Arnus looked troubled at the prospect.

"Best case scenario, Miropa leaves each of the cities to fend for themselves," Akelo kept on. "Both Karavyl and Acrosia are better defended than Dynec, and after weeks of march and consecutive battles, I doubt even Karth would be as easy to take as we would like to think. The šef will turn the fight into a battle of attrition until Miropa, at which point they will have the upper hand in position and morale, not to mention possibly even numbers."

"That's the *best* case scenario?" Marsus muttered morbidly.

"It is." Akelo nodded. "*And* the least likely. As we've said, I very much doubt the Mahsadën is willing to lose Karavyl so easily, much less Acrosia, their only port and access point to the West Isles and the Imperium. It is vastly more probable that Miropa will march to defend one or the other. Even if we have a numbers' edge, we could end up in an incredibly disadvantageous position. Taking Acrosia would leave us with Karth and its Miropan support to the north, the Emperor's Ocean to the west, the Cienbal to the east, and the potential threat of the Seven Cities to the south."

No one said anything this time, and for good reason. Finally, Akelo felt the pieces falling together, and he pressed on.

"Cyro itself possess no true benefit, yes, but—leaving aside the atherian for the moment—the positional advantage is much greater. Even if we are forced to march far *around* the Crags into the desert, it wouldn't take more than four or five weeks to reach Miropa. Additionally, we would have the Cienbal to our south, open sand plains to our east, and the Northern border half-a-month north of us. That leaves us not only with little risk of being flanked by the Mahsadën—not to mention the Seven Cities—but also with escape routes should the worst befall us."

"A direct assault on Miropa?" Kalin asked tentatively. "Isn't that too bold, before we whittle down the šef?"

"No, it's not."

It was Raz who spoke. He was leaning over his chair, watching Akelo thoughtfully.

"As much as it makes sense in theory to weaken the rings before we make for the main force directly, I think we may be underestimating how much of a double-edged sword that course of action can be." He turned to Syrah. "What was the final count, this morning?"

Syrah's face fell. "Eight hundred sixty-two confirmed dead," she answered sadly. "Thrice that many injured, a quarter of which won't be able to fight again. Additionally, another fifty or so are missing and presumed deceased."

"So more than fifteen hundred lost in this small battle," Raz summarized, turning back to the group, "and unlike in Karesh Nan, we will not have any overwhelming influx of new volunteers."

"We've had some," Cyper chimed in. "About five hundred so far, apparently."

"Good," Raz said with a nod in the West Isler's direction. "Assuming they're largely from the slum quarters, though, they have a long way to go before they're fighting fit. More importantly: we cannot forget that we will be leaving a garrison here, to ensure Dynec does not fall to ruin and chaos after we depart."

Another three thousand to be deducted. Akelo added the numbers up quickly. In all, the toll on their forces amounted to more around four thousand, counting the additional five hundred recruits that would likely require weeks of provisions and training before they'd be able to lift a sword properly.

The others too, seemed to be grasping the issue.

"By the Sun," Erom grumbled, leaning back in his chair to stare up at the shifting canvas of the pavilion ceiling as he crossed his arms over his chest. "If that's what each city takes…"

"It would be larger," Syrah cut in. "Karth might be comparable, but even if we are generous and assume Karavyl will be the same as well, Acrosia would not be. By the time we reach Miropa, we should estimate that we will lose an additional fifteen thousand at the very *least.*"

Her words had a chilling effect, as though the woman had used her magic to cool the very air of the space around them. All gaped at her, dumbfounded.

"Fif-fifteen?" Marsus choked out finally. "That would leave us with—"

"Barely thirty thousand," Raz finished for him. "And as Syrah says, that's being generous. Granted, we can assume the Mahsadën will weaken comparatively, but it doesn't change the other facts already brought up." He gave Akelo a sidelong look. "Assuming Miropa maintains its own army, this war would come down to a siege by our weakened, exhausted forces on the most well-defended city in the South, which would be garrisoned with fresh troops. Not exactly an ideal situation."

Akelo frowned grimly. "To put it mildly." He sighed, closing his eyes for a moment to think.

When he opened them again, he looked to Raz. "If you give the order, I will follow you west," he told the atherian. "However… it's not the option I would recommend."

"East?" Raz asked him, as though confirming.

"East," Akelo said with a nod before turning his attention across the table, meeting the waiting figure's golden eyes. "Partially because—as you said—we owe it to ourselves to assess *all* angles of this decision."

Zal'en couldn't help but feel her stomach tighten with uncertainty as Akelo Aseni's dark gaze fell on her, quickly followed by each of the other seated generals'. Around and above them, the pavilion's canvas walls beat in the desert wind that hadn't let up in the last week, shivering over the cloth and casting the light from the holes in the ceiling across the ground and table around and before her. She took comfort in that dance, allowing it to remind her that the Daystar was ever present, watching over her.

In the same moment, she remembered that the old man, the seer who often kept company with the Dragon and his consort, had told her that there were others, too, who watched from afar.

This, finally, was her chance to fulfill her greatest duty…

"The Queen will welcome us," she asserted—perhaps more eagerly than was prudent—leaning forward in her chair. "*All* of us."

There was muttering from several of the others, Marsus Byrn in particular, but Arro silenced them all with a glower. When everyone was respectfully quiet again, he turned toward her.

"Continue."

Zal'en didn't have to be told twice.

"The Queen *will* accept us," she said again, even more insistent this time. "Dynec's fall will already have released a great burden from the atherian of the Crags. If we can take Cyro as well, there would be no reason they could refuse us."

Not that they would regardless, she thought privately, allowing her gaze to drift to the Dragon briefly.

"I'm well aware of your concerns," she continued. "I know you find it troubling that none of our people can tell you we have seen the Queen with our own eyes. I cannot say I blame you for your hesitation, but you *must* believe us. The atherian of the mountains are not greatly numerous. They are not so technologically advanced as the world of man, nor have they ever managed to establish relations with humans that extend anywhere beyond basic trading, which ended when the nomadic caravans ceased their travels across the desert some years ago."

She met the Arro's eyes, now. His story was well known, even among the lizard-kind. "Keep this in mind when I tell you that the Queen has great reason for keeping herself hidden, away from the sight of the fringe cities. If the slavers discovered her existence, can you imagine the harm that might cause our people? If hunters were to raid the Under Caves, or the Mahsadën took it to mind to cut a potential enemy down before we became a threat, the atherian would be left with *nothing*. No leadership. No path. No hope. The Queen's line has secluded themselves beneath the Crags every generation, and with good reason."

"The 'Under Caves'?" Odene repeated, not understanding.

"A network of passages and caverns within the mountains," Zal'en explained quickly, not looking at the Percian. "Your 'Crags', as you call them."

The Dragon watched her carefully, processing her words. Around the table, the others were whispering again, and—though Marsus Byrn continued to look perpetually unconvinced—several of the rest seemed less reserved following her explanation.

"Assuming your story is true," Arro finally spoke up, leaning forward, "I can't say it lends itself to this 'Queen' offering us her assistance. If her family has been so keen on keeping themselves shielded from the eyes of man for so long, why would she make herself known now? Why would she open herself up to that risk?"

Zal'en had just opened her mouth to speak when an excited voice rose from over her shoulder.

"Has been waiting, she has!" Urlen practically shouted. "For the winged one to—!"

Crash!

Zal'en's chair toppled backwards as she stood up violently, the seat crunching down into the reed matting and sand. She whirled, fixing the younger male with so hard a look he shut up at once, stepping away and ducking his head meekly.

"'Waiting'?" Cyper Edalos followed this up with suspiciously. "What do you mean 'waiting'?"

"Urlen has spoken out of turn," Zal'en growled, not looking away from the male despite the fact that he didn't seem to be able to meet her eye. "I would ask you all to ignore his impertinence."

"Not likely," Syrah Brahnt answered coolly from behind her. "Not after a reaction like that. Explain yourself, if you please."

Zal'en whirled, barely stopping herself from snapping a response back in atherian. Thinking better of it, she elected instead merely to glare at the woman, who met her gaze evenly.

This one… she thought, not for the first time. *How he deemed a* human *fit to wear on his arm…?*

Unsurprisingly, Brahnt didn't back down. If nothing else, she was willful, and Zal'en had to grant her some begrudging respect for her stubbornness.

"Ah'han," she said over her shoulder, finally looking away from the Northerner, "my chair, if you would."

The second male, waiting beside Urlen, moved to pick up the fallen seat at once, standing it upright. When he'd done so, Zal'en eased herself back down, electing to cast around the table as a whole, seeking more sympathetic faces.

At the same time, she did some quick thinking.

"There is a story, among our kind," she said with a sigh that was only half-acted, resigning herself to offering up a version of the truth. "It was common enough among the atherian of the Crags, but after I was taken I found it shared even more enthusiastically within the filed lines of the enslaved. I've attempted to quell it, in my own way, seeing as it is not likely to do us any good in the long run."

"And what is this story?" Syrah pressed her with a frown.

"A simple enough tale," Zal'en shrugged, leaning back. "A child's fable if anything, telling of a great one among our race who would break the bonds of iron and lead his people to freedom. *Do not—*" she raised her voice as several of the others looked around at Arro in surprise "—read into it more than you must. It is an age-old retelling that has been around for more generations than I've seen years, ever since man first started his subjugation of our people."

There was a disquiet grumbling at this.

"I've not heard of any such story…" the Dragon spoke up, sounding almost confused. "I'd have thought Karan would have mentioned it…"

Luckily, Zal'en had foreseen this particular problem. "Karan Brightneck has a good head on her shoulders, despite her age. I've no doubt she wishes to avoid giving you the impression that she is still a child. Those among us who cling to such superstitions—" she looked around at Urlen, gracing him another warning look she hoped the rest would assume was a stare of disapproval "—aren't much more than that, after all."

"Still…" Erom said disquietly. "'The winged one'…"

He let his words trail, trusting the others would follow his train of thought. For a moment Zal'en was worried she would be pushed harder, and she cursed both Urlen *and* herself. She *wanted* to tell them the truth, *wanted* to explain to them of the Queen's greater plan, the series of events it was said she'd put in motion so many years ago. Zal'en—as Urlen apparently had been—was *itching* to shout out at the top of her lungs that the heir to the obsidian crown was there—*there!*—sitting not ten feet down the table from her. As she had every day for the last several months, though, Zal'en restrained herself. For the longest time she'd done so only as a mean to observe Raz i'Syul Arro, the male who bore the titles of both "Monster" and "Dragon". She had shouldered the leadership of the atherian from within the army itself, using that influence to study him from afar. It hadn't taken very long for her to get a sense of the winged male, to understand the greatness and potential he bore, even *if* he kept some distasteful company. By the time they'd left Perce behind for the more familiar sands of the South, Zal'en had been prepared to present Arro with the truth, to tell him of his greater purpose and the rumored prophecy which had set him on his path two decades prior.

Then, though, the man they called "Abir" had stumbled into her tent, and Zal'en had realized she was only the most inconsequential of beings to be watching the events of Raz i'Syul Arro's life unfold with interest. She couldn't begin to guess to the reason *why* the Twins had set upon her the task of staying silent. Perhaps there was still value in the Dragon not knowing of his heritage. Perhaps the Sun and Moon still wished to test him, to evaluate his worth.

Regardless, whatever the motive, Zal'en had no interest in crossing the gods just yet…

"As Zal'en says, don't look too hard into it."

Zal'en's jaw almost dropped in surprise at the words. Slowly, she turned, facing the person who'd spoken, utterly dumbfounded by this most-unlikely ally.

Syrah Brahnt was watching her again, but this time her gaze was softer, laden with some sort of quiet understanding.

"Each of us here knows what it is to lose all," the woman said, looking away to cast her one eye around the table, "to have everything stripped from us and then some. It is hard for me to admit, but my own trials were brief in comparison to the suffering all of you have been through respectively." Her right hand settled absently on the Dragon's forearm by her side. "Despite this, I recall too-distinctly the need I felt in my chains, the desire to be free by any means, to accept whatever hand might be offered."

Brahnt's jaw spasmed at some cruel memory, and for the first time Zal'en felt a pang of sympathy for the woman. She'd never outright heard the story of how the Northerner had earned the scars about her wrists—much less lost her eye—but rumors were never a hard thing to come by a place as large as the Dragon's camp.

It seemed common knowledge that the woman had suffered horrors that atherian females were, at the very least, largely spared even as slaves…

"I'm sure you have all experienced similar thoughts, at one point or another," Brahnt was continuing. "It's only natural. In a people such as the atherian, who have their own community even within the chained, such a tale shouldn't surprise us. Zal'en is asking us to base our decision off of greater merits, and I think we should respect that." Her eye, then, surprisingly, shifted over Zal'en's head. "*Urlen.*" Her atherian was rough, but understandable. "*This 'Queen'? You believe in, yes?*"

Behind Zal'en, Urlen started, taken aback by being addressed directly by the Dragon's own right hand, and it took him a moment to respond.

"*Yes,*" he answered firmly, making his conviction clear. "*I swear by the Daystar that Zal'en speaks true.*"

Brahnt nodded, then looked to the second male. "*Ah'han, your name is?*" she asked, and Zal'en looked around in time to see Ah'han nod nervously. "*The same, you would say?*"

Ah'han took an even longer time in responding, gaze jumping anxiously between Syrah Brahnt and Zal'en, who nodded encouragingly. With that approval, the male took a breath, then spoke.

"*I do. And were you to have me bring the rest of our kind here, many would say the same.*"

"*Many?*" Brahnt asked carefully. "*Not all?*"

Zal'en felt that knot in her stomach twist again, but Ah'han proved himself prepared for such a question.

"*Those of us who were taken from the Crags do not make up the entirety of our number,*" he answered quickly, speaking easier now. "*Some suffered such a cruelty, but were too young at the time to remember our homeland. Many others have been born into their chains. Your companion is an example,*" he nodded to Brahnt indicatively. "*Karan Brightneck has never seen the great cliffs of our mountains, or felt the hot wind of the true desert on her skin. Were you to ask her if she believes in our Queen, she would only be able to tell you of hopes and rumors.*" His eyes flicked briefly to Zal'en's then, almost questioningly. "*Perhaps this is another reason she has not shared such pointless stories with you? All she has ever known is the pain of the whip and the weight of rusting irons. Perhaps the hope of a savior was too much for her to cling to, even as a child.*"

"Syrah," the Dragon cut in then, just as Brahnt opened her mouth to respond. "Most of us here do not speak the tongue as well as you."

To Zal'en's slight amusement, the woman flushed in embarrassment, immediately turning to the table to apologize. Quickly she translated her questions and Urlen's and Ah'han's answers, and Zal'en had to admit to herself that the Northerner had grasped the discussion accurately. When Brahnt was done, the generals sat silent, most of them watching Ah'han with expressions ranging from dubious suspicion to keen interest.

"It seems your Queen is more than just a tale of the masses, at the very least." Cyper Edalos was the first to speak, giving the trio of atherian a brief nod of assent. "I can't say I'm really convinced, but if the idea serves even as little as an advantage to morale after our losses at the east gate…"

"It changes *nothin'*," Marsus Byrn retorted, looking around at the West Isler. "Raz is right. Even *if* there is some high-an'-mighty female sittin' around some dark 'Under Caves', *why* would she show herself now? Ain't no reason, I'm sayin'!"

"No," Zal'en answered before anyone else could raise their voice in response. "There *is* reason. Or rather, you can *give* her reason."

As one, all eyes turned to her.

"Explain," Raz said slowly, though he seemed to be hiding what might have been half-a-smile as he spoke. "Convince us to march on Cyro, Zal'en, and then on to seek audience with your 'Queen'."

Zal'en, for one, chose to grin at Marsus Bryn, who could only frown in answer.

"I will put it in the simplest of terms, so as to be comprehended by the simplest of minds," she said, momentarily allowing herself some spiteful enjoyment at the twitch of anger in Bryn's temple at the words. "Our kind have been the prey of men and women like those that make up your Mahsadën for more years than every one of us here have together. In all that time, there has been little opportunity to react, little opportunity to defend ourselves. The clans of our mountains are too few, too widespread, and the slaves have always struck with planned unpredictability and practiced speed." Her gaze, finally, shifted back to the burning golden eyes of Raz i'Syul Arro. "Put bluntly: by marching east, we would be the first to ever give the Queen a chance to *fight back*…"

XIV

"The most essential and impressive aspect of the Mahsadën at its peak was the fact that the society managed the impossible: a balance of power—however tenuous—divided in theoretical equality among many hands in every city of the South. In retrospect—and given the sorts of individuals involved in said society—it is not a far leap to deduce that such a precarious equilibrium was bound to slip off its axis given nothing more than time. Truth be told, that the Mahsadën held power for the decade it did is a feat so incredible, it has not been replicated in the centuries which have passed since the fall of the slave rings.

Still, it is a bizarre thing to consider that the rise of the most powerful šef in the most influential of the fringe cities would be not *the indication of the society's growth, but rather that of the start of its rapid demise..."*

— *As Death Rose from the Ashes*, by Kohly Grofh

Wham!

"DAMMIT, BLAETH!" Ysera Ma'het erupted from her place by the column she had just slammed her fist against in fury. "Dynec was one thing, you bastard! It was unavoidable! But NOT CYRO TOO!"

From his place above the room, seated in his stone chair at the center of the raised dais, Adrion watched the Percian woman rage with what he hoped was an impassive expression. At his right, Lazura was leaning from her own seat over to his, one hand playing teasingly with his bleached hair, putting on a show for the šef that were gathered below them.

For Adrion's part, her touch made him feel ill, and he knew it for the warning that it was.

They were meeting in the audience hall today, the chamber which had once been what amounted essentially to the throne room of Imaneal Evony himself. Narrow, spiraled pillars—like the one Ma'het had just struck—supported the high ceiling in a web of decorative ribs that lined the vaulting and ventilation holes. The walls on either side of them were largely absent, consisting of nothing more than arched windows whose blue-green curtains fluttered in the warm breeze of the early afternoon. The floor tiles of the hall—as well as the steps of the dais and the very chairs Adrion and Lazura sat in—were carved of polished marble, white except for the discolored veins of grey and black that slipped like blood through the stone.

Blood, Adrion thought absently, not looking away from Ma'het's hateful gaze. *I wonder how much blood has been ordered to be let, from the comforts of this room...*

If Ma'het and her partner—a tall, graceful Southern woman named Vyela Ehrem—didn't see reason, it would be a lot more by day's end.

"Arro is making an unexpected move," Adrion told the šef firmly. "One we did not anticipate. We assumed—" he let his grey eyes shift to the spot where Serys Beth and San Loreyn were standing expectantly "—that he would press for Karavyl after seizing control of Dynec. Both Miropa and Acrosia—" he waved a hand toward the foursome of Ahthys Borne, Tyala Gerst, Sol Fe'ren, and Mysera Morste stood "—have already been making preparations to march support troops south. Cyro is on the other side of the desert. Until now we assumed the Monster's goal would be to weaken our individual parts before striking here, at the heart." He frowned. "Clearly we were mistaken."

"MISTAKEN?" Ma'het screeched indignantly. "You were MISTAKEN? Are you a fool, or merely mad?" She stormed toward the dais, ignoring Ehrem's pleas and attempts to hold her back. "I should rip your silver tongue from your—"

It happened before Adrion had a chance to brace himself. Fortunately, the magic itself distracted the rest of the šef from the spasm of pain that ripped through his body as Lazura poured her power into him through the back of his neck. From the base of his chair, fire bloomed, exploding outward in a liquid geyser of flames. It spilled over the marble, flowing down the stairs like burning water, and Ma'het screamed as she stumbled back, kicking at the abruptly-smoking hem of her silk skirt. Lazura only held onto the power briefly before releasing it, allowing the flames to shiver and vanish in a spreading dance of ivory sparks.

When it was gone, nothing remained to hint at the fire that had enveloped the dais except for Ma'het's continued curses and *thuds* of her heel on stone as she kept stomping at the smoldering fabric around her ankles.

"Looks like your body can take more than I thought," Adrion heard Lazura mumble delightfully into his ear, sending a chill down his spine.

All the same, she'd given him a job, and he had no choice but to see it carried out.

"The situation is regrettable," he conceded with an apologetic nod toward Ma'het and Ehrem, "but it is hardly hopeless. Arro's goal is not to *raze* our cities, but rather to extract our *influence* from them. To that end, Lazura's spies report that Dynec stands largely undamaged. The last of its former šef were publicly executed, and the army has been stripped of arms and privilege, but the Monster appears intent on minimizing the impact of his presence on the citizens themselves. When he marches east, he is even leaving a garrison of some unknown number to keep the peace within the walls." He cocked his head at Ma'het. "If anything, abandoning Cyro for the time being will secure your ability to return to it, once this farce of a war is over."

"You told Marst the same thing, just before you had your bitch woman slit his throat!" the one-eyed Cyroan spat, glaring at Lazura as she spoke. She'd finally—with some assistance from Ehrem—snuffed out the embers from her skirt. "I will not be placated with honeyed words, Blaeth!"

"Elon Marst and the rest of Dynec's representatives were set upon in his rooms by thieves who'd seen them throwing their crowns around the market streets," Lazura answered, her tone cruelly teasing. "A random act of violence. My men caught the perpetrators within the day, as you well know, and they confessed shortly after."

"Confessed, my arse!" the Percian woman seethed, jerking her arm from Ehrem's grasp and braving a step forward again despite herself. "Dynec served no purpose to you, so you saw the challengers murdered! How much of a fool would I have to be to believe you wouldn't do the *exact same thing* the moment I leave this chamber?"

"Should you leave this chamber without coming to terms with us," Adrion said coldly, "then I can certainly not attest to your safety. *If* Lazura is guilty of the crimes you accuse her of, then the šef of the Dynec were disposed of not for their lack of purpose, but rather for the liability they posed by not joining forces with the rest of us. *Additionally*—!" he cut across Ma'het's attempt to get an angry word in "—you make the greater mistake of assuming Cyro has lost all value, as Dynec had. This is not the case, even remotely."

That finally shut the woman up, and Adrion thought he caught a glimpse of an approving smirk from Lazura out of the corner of his eye.

"The fall of Perce will take a heavy toll on our economic abilities in the coming years," Adrion kept on. "I won't deny that Cyro will be among those most greatly affected, either. However… Dynec built itself up almost exclusively on the trade routes it developed with Karesh Syl and Karesh Nan. With their end came the end of the city's own self-established purpose. Cyro will suffer the loss of Perce as well, but you have other advantages Marst and his comrades did not. The Seven Cities still hold a demand for atherian slaves, a demand which—with Dynec's end—only *you* are in any realistic position to supply. More importantly," he glanced around the hall, intending to study the reactions to his next words, "once we dispose of the Monster and his followers, I think it will be high time that we consider opening our own cities to the trade."

At once there was a sharp increase in murmurs and whispers from about the room, each group of representatives putting their heads together to quietly discuss this new suggestion. Even Vyres Eh'ben, Karth's only delegate, sidled over to the Acrosian group to join the conversation.

"You wish to open our walls to slavery?" Serys Benth of Karavyl asked after almost half-a-minute of these quiet exchanges, sounding intrigued.

"I wish to discuss it, at the very least." Adrion nodded. "Our head trade is an open secret. It is high time we took advantage of it outside of merely lining our pockets."

Or at least Lazura thinks so, he thought bitterly, not looking around at the woman as she continued playing with his hair in her sickeningly doting fashion. Personally, the idea didn't sit well with him. It wasn't that he was opposed to it, but rather that the timing seemed precarious.

All the same, he could hardly voice *that* particular opinion out loud, given his circumstances…

"The masses wouldn't take kindly to that." Ahthys Borne of Acrosia spoke like he'd been reading Adrion's mind, though he didn't sound too invested in the words. "At worst we would be following up this war with wide-spread revolt. Even should we defeat Arro handedly, we've already shown many of our cards. We are weakened, right now, in the eyes of the people. If we force them to swallow open slavery… It could go poorly."

Exactly, Adrion thought, almost nodding in agreement.

Lazura's fingers, though, tightened about the base of his neck, and he sighed internally.

"It is exactly *because* of this war that the time is ideal," he said firmly, shaking his head at Ahthys. "Yes, we are seen to be pressed right now, but when we crush the Monster and his army, we will send the message that no force, no matter how great and no matter how well-led, can stand against us. At that point, we will be seen as stronger than ever before."

Or more vulnerable than ever before, he thought privately, but kept on.

"Our coffers have profited from the work of our slavers, but our cities themselves have never benefited." Adrion waved a hand at Mah'et and Ehrem, who still stood at the base of the steps and hadn't spoken a word since he'd made the suggestion. "Cyro would thrive, if their atherian could be sold to their neighbors. We ourselves would gain much as well, if merely by emptying the slums and putting the beggars and ragroot addicts to work, rather than letting them leech us of our resources. Many of you had the opportunity to see Karesh Syl in its prime, before the fall of the Tash. Do you recall the city? Do you recall the discipline of it, the power and beauty? There was no poverty for its citizens, because those who would have dragged them down were given food and shelter and purpose in their binds."

And it fell because of that folly, in the end.

Once more, the others put their heads together in conversation. Adrion's gaze met Mah'et's, and with a twinge of guilt he saw the excitement starting to burn in the Percian's single dark eye. "Do you understand, now?" he asked her. "*Cyro is no Dynec.* It will suffer the loss of Perce, yes, but it may well rise to even greater heights in the very near future. For that, though, *you* must survive, and *we* must survive." He indicated the rest of the room. "Marst's refusal to gather his forces with our own was his undoing, and it took a heavy toll on our ability to launch a counter-offensive." He frowned at her. "Arro will have to push around the Crags, but it seems he will eventually come straight for Miropa, and all of us gathered here. We will need to make our stand before then, or risk losing the greatest part of our power and wealth to him and his army."

Adrion leaned forward in his chair, braving to separate himself from Lazura's cool touch.

"See reason," he implored the women, Mah'et and Ehrem both. "I have already sent birds recalling our troops from Karavyl and Acrosia, and Eh'ben has assured us Karth will join the march as well. Cyro *will* weather this test. Give the order to gather your army here. Join us, and when this madness is done you will have the chance to return to your city with far greater power than ever before."

He hadn't noticed the others going quiet, while he addressed the Cyroan representatives. When he was done, though, he saw that each of the other šef were watching them carefully, anticipating the women's decision with bated breath.

After what seemed a small eternity, Ma'het and Ehrem glanced at one another, like they were confirming each other's resolve.

Then, at last, they gave their answer.

XV

"Of all the disappointments mankind has left me with, one among them makes me ache to this day to consider it. Cyro… That is where I was finally able to separate the šef of the Mahsadën from the larger breadth of humanity. The decisions they made… The sacrifices they elected were appropriate…

Thinking of them as beings possessing even a hint of a soul became impossible, after that…"

— The White Witch

"What in Laor's name…?" Syrah muttered, pulling Nymara to a halt at Raz's left. Beside her, Karan kept her usual place, Akelo joining them as they all gaped northward. Beneath Raz, Gale—the massive, jet-black stallion gifted to him by the Laorin the winter before—shuffled nervously from side to side. Ahna bounced under his leg, and the trio of other animals huffed and whinnied in a frightened sort of way.

He couldn't blame either Syrah or the beasts their disquiet, taking in the scene before them as the sounds of the moving army at their back rumbled along over the gusting of the desert wind.

Shit, was all he could think, and Akelo's muttered curse from his right echoed the feeling.

They'd spent almost a week in Dynec before taking their leave of the city, carefully setting up the garrison's chain of command to ensure everything ran smoothly without Raz or any of his generals present. Nobody had been pleased with the delay—least of all Raz himself—but with the alternative being leaving Dynec to riot and burn in their absence, none had been able to offer up a better alternative.

Unfortunately, things had only gotten worse from there.

They'd been on the march for nearly two weeks now, their progress slowed by a series of sandstorms which bogged them down for a couple days at a time as they'd had to dig out the wheels of their provision and weapons carts. As close to the desert as they were skirting, the west flank of the army had also suffered a number of animal attacks, generally sandcats and dune scorpions that caught some sentry or another by surprise after dark. They'd lost two men to the beasts—unfortunate in and of itself—but with the attacks happening at night, each time the entirety of their host generally awoke to the sounds of commotion and screams of the injured or dying. The following days' marches were always sluggish, detracting from their pace, and by the time Zal'en told him they would be within sight of Cyro within the hour, Raz was itching for an excuse to punch someone's teeth in.

Most unfortunately—looking out over the plains from where he, Syrah, Akelo, and Karan all sat atop their mounts—Raz got the distinct impression he was going to have to set aside his frustration for some time yet.

"Akelo," he snapped, "have Cyper make an eastward loop with the advance cavalry! Tell them to be on the lookout for sentries! Karan—" as Akelo yelled his understanding and whirled his horse around back down the dune, the young female turned her attention to Raz "—find Marsus. I want *every* scout not presently in the field grouped in units of twenty and sent in. Have them report to Syrah within the hour. Areas of conflict, estimated numbers of involved, and a mapping of the city's major roads. I want it all!"

Karan yelled an "Aye!" and told Syrah quickly that she would find her later before she, too, disappeared back toward the main army.

"What is this?" Syrah asked when the atherian was gone. "Raz, what…?"

"They left it," Raz growled in answer, a building, seething rage compelling him to grip Gale's reins so tightly that his steel claws bit into the leather palms of his gauntlets. "They gathered their strength and fucking *left* it."

Beside him, apparently dumbstruck by his summations, Syrah could only stare.

Cyro was in flames. Karan had been the first to see the smoke, bringing it to his attention from some miles back, and it was a half-hour later before Raz had been able to point it out to Syrah and Akelo. As they'd gotten nearer, he'd felt worry build up in his throat, fearing the worst. It had been Akelo, even before they'd left Dynec, who'd brought up the possibility. Despite this, Raz couldn't quite bring himself to believe that even the Mahsadën would abandon any city *entirely*, that the society would withdraw their soldiers to the last man, down to the common city guard.

From his place overlooking the metropolis, though, Raz could only assume that was *exactly* what they had done.

The gate facing them—the South gate—was thrown wide open, like whoever had last entered or exited the city hadn't been bothered to close it behind them. Despite the harsh light of the full day, fire could be seen rising over the eastern districts, belching black smoke so thickly into the sky it managed to dim the Sun above. From their distance Raz couldn't make out much, but listening hard he could just barely distinguish the sounds and shouts of fighting from within Cyro's walls.

Given that fires still raged, the only silver lining he could convince himself of was that the city had been abandoned not too long ago.

"Syrah, you and your trainees will be needed soon," he said suddenly, turning to the woman. "Commandeer the general's pavilion again, and whatever other shelter you might need. The moment Marsus' scouts deliver their report, send me a messenger spell. Can you do that?"

"What are you doing to do?" Syrah asked him, ignoring his question and blanching as Nymara hoofed at the sand, nickering in fear when a shift in the wind doused them in the smell of smoke and iron.

Raz reached out, squeezing her thigh. "Don't worry about me. I'll be fine. The messenger spell. Can you do it?"

Syrah hesitated, then nodded.

Letting go of her leg, Arro kicked Gale into a gallop, leading him carefully down the dune face, toward the flatter plains that encircled the city. As he did, he made out the shouts and *thumping* of hundreds on hundreds of other riders not far behind.

Raz pulled Gale left, making for the western side of Cyro's circular wall. It was five minutes before he was approaching shortbow range, at which point he turned the stallion to follow the ramparts around, goading the horse into full speed. The white silk hood that had been over his head fell away as the air whipped around him, and Raz kept one eye on the crenellations while he rode, searching for any signs of lookouts or archers.

Nothing. Not a soul. Not so much as a hint of a person, soldier or otherwise.

After ten minutes, a mass of figures appeared around the bend of the wall, just as Raz had anticipated. At once he pulled Gale up short, stopping the horse almost directly before Cyro's north gate—which, unlike the south's, looked to be shut and barred—and raising a hand to indicate a halt. Soon after, Cyper drew his dappled gelding up beside the black stallion, looking utterly unsurprised to see Raz.

The fifteen hundred riders behind him came to a steady stop just short of them.

"Anything?" Raz asked the West Isler hurriedly.

"Nothing," Cyper said with a shake of his shaved head. "A few even volunteered to ride along the wall, looking to bait anyone who might be waiting for us to approach. What is this, Raz?"

"Greed and idiocy," Raz snarled in answer. "The Mahsadën knew we were coming, and Cyro wasn't worth marching to defend. Instead of another defeat like Dynec, they decided to condense their forces." He pointed north, where the outline of grey and red mountains could just be seen on the horizon. "They'll have made for Miropa, or we would have encountered them on the way here."

"They just left it?!" Cyper demanded in utter disbelief. "How could they just—?!"

"We can curse them later," Raz told him quickly. "The west gate was also barred. What about the east?"

"Opened wide, like the south's," the man answered at once, already turning his horse around. "Are we entering?"

"We are," Raz growled, kicking Gale into another gallop, barreling around the bulk of the cavalry as the minor officers shouted to follow him and Cyper, "before the whole damn city rips itself apart."

By the time they reached the east gate, Raz had already given his orders. Without pause they barreled into Cyro, hooves *clacking* against the cobblestone of the inner roads. All about them buildings were on fire, the structures burning so fiercely that the heat felt like a physical blow to the face. Looking around, Raz was unsurprised to see timber and stone and iron gildings in the homes that hadn't collapsed yet, rising above them to loom several stories over the street. Had it not been for the ash and debris and charred ruins that fell across their path, he knew the quarter would have been spotless, the roads tended to and well-kept, the alleys and side-streets clear and clean.

The quarters or the upper classes, where the wealthy and powerful had dwelled in comfort and safety, protected from the resentment of the poor and hungry by the city guards.

Now, though, that protection was gone.

Without any additional commands, the cavalry streaming in behind Raz and Cyper broke and separated, the men leading their horses in groups of one hundred down every major road they came across. As they moved they passed pockets of people in various states of dress and activity, some bedecked in silks and satins that were burned or bloody or dusty, others in the bare garbs of slum dwellers and beggars, hefting clubs and knives and torches while they howled and jeered in triumph. Whenever they crossed one of these latter groups, Raz would indicate them with two fingers even as they thundered by. Without looking back, he knew that a half-dozen of his would split off each time, making for the rioters with blades drawn.

He had ordered killing be avoided unless absolutely necessary, but he wasn't about to lose his soldiers to the chaos the Mahsadën had left in their absence.

Raz and Cyper pressed their mounts further into the city. One minute passed, then two, then three. He could feel Gale's powerful legs working beneath him, Ahna still bouncing along beneath his knee. He guessed he had some fifty men left of the hundred they'd started with, and he began to worry that they would be short on strength by the time they found the place he was looking for. He was listening hard, straining to hear over the horses and the fire. Cyper rode alongside him, silent as they moved, knowing it wasn't the moment for interruption.

Finally, Raz made out the greater swell of shouting and cheering, rising over the cacophony of the burning quarter not far to the north.

"There!" he shouted, pulling Gale up a right-side split in the road that led upward at a shallow angle. The West Isler followed his lead, shouting back over his shoulder for the others to draw steel. Behind him, Raz made out the answering slither of swords being pulled from scabbards, and he offered up a prayer that the soldiers wouldn't be forced to put those weapons to use on this day.

They rode for another thirty seconds, the street slowly wrapping around as it continued to climb. Eventually the space between the buildings widened ahead, and Raz pushed Gale even harder. A heavy chunk of brick and mortar wall had fallen across the path ahead, flames still licking at the rubble while the ruined building from which it had crumbled spat sparks and smoke into the heavens. Raz aimed for the lowest portion of the obstacle, a section of stone and smoldering timber barely three feet high. Without so much as pausing Gale took the barrier at full speed, clearing it with ease and thundering on into the open space of the quarter's main square as Raz heard Cyper and the others managed the jump right behind him.

The area was not as large as the main plaza where Raz had held the šef's executions in Dynec, but it was spacious enough. A portion of its center was taken up by a rectangular pool that might once have been a clear bath for children to wade across and adults to rest their feet in during the hot summer days, but its water was now murky and reddened with blood. Four corpses, three men and a woman, floated face down in the pool, the latter with a dagger still sticking out of her back. Even as Raz watched, there was a scream, and a second woman fell backwards into the water. She clutched at her throat as she sank, thrashing all the while, trying to stem the great slash that had been cleaved into one side of her neck

The gathering that had killed her only jeered and yelled in triumph, watching the blood spilling out in a cloud of crimson around her convulsing form.

There were perhaps five hundred crowded around the pool, some turned inward to watch the butchery, others busy with their own entertainments along the outskirts of the plaza. For several seconds, Raz could do little more than gape at the destruction and horrors being perpetrated around him. To the east, a group was stoning a foursome of men dressed in brightly-colored garments, hurling chunks of rubble and rock from the falling buildings around them. Nearby, a pair of bodies hung by their necks from the archway of what once had been some regal home, swinging and swaying against the silhouette of the now-burning building as the crowd surrounding them struck at the bodies with clubs or what must have been stolen swords and knives. To the west, perhaps a score of well-dressed children and youths were huddled together, crying and sobbing as the rioters screamed and taunted them. Just as he caught sight of this group, Raz saw one man step forward and snatch at one girl who was hugging two smaller boys to her as they knelt on the ground. The figure caught her by the hair, dragging her onto her feet, and the girl—perhaps fourteen or fifteen—screamed in pain and fear as she was torn away from what could only have been her brothers. With a howl of delight the man drew a knife from his belt and slashed at her, slicing through her buttoned shirt, drawing blood even as he exposed her to the crowd. The girl screamed again, louder now, but her captor only laughed, teasing the blade down until it rested in the band of her cloth pants.

That was when the world shifted for Raz. The fire and the smoke and cries of the terrified all faded away. The colors of the days vanished, the grins and laughs of the slum dwellers as they took their revenge on the wealthy twisting and shifting.

In an instant all was red and black, and the Monster of Karth replaced the Dragon of the North in a storm of fiery fury.

With a bellowed roar that shivered over the plaza, making every head that hadn't noticed his arrival already turn toward him, Raz drove Gale forward, into the crowd. Most were fortunate to leap out of his way, shouting in surprise as he barreled through them, but some moved too slow, bouncing and spinning off the stallion's sides and flanks. He didn't feel himself draw Ahna from her loops off the side of the saddle, didn't sense her weight as he brought the dviassegai up. All he saw, in that moment, was a sea of bodies parting before him in panic, and the shocked look of the man whose face his gaze was transfixed upon. In four short seconds Gale had hammered his way through the throng. The would-be rapist had just enough time to drop the knife and girl, bringing his hands above his head in a futile attempt to shield himself from the immanent blow.

Then Raz was on him, and Ahna struck like steel lightning, cutting through the man's lifted wrists before catching him in the crook of the neck, splitting him in two as Gale rode through, leaving a trail of blood in their wake.

"ENOUGH!"

Raz's howled command reverberated over the screams and yells of the crowd, sundering the madness of the riot. Instantly every voice in the vicinity of the plaza faltered, the Southerners grey eyes wide in shock and disbelief as they took in Raz i'Syul Arro, Monster of Karth, Scourge of the South, Dragon of the North.

Raz, for his part, fought back the animal within as he brought Gale around, Ahna still in one hand, her blades now wet and red.

"DROP YOUR WEAPONS, *NOW!*" he thundered, kicking the stallion fearlessly into the throng, who parted for him like he was death itself. "ANY CAUGHT WITH A BLADE WILL BE PUT DOWN! DROP THEM! *NOW!*"

Whether it was his mere presence, the dangerous promise he could hear in his own voice, or the half-a-hundred armed—and clearly *trained*—men spreading out throughout the crowd on horseback around him, Raz didn't know. Whatever the case, steel began to fall like rain, the rioters pulling back even further from him. Raz took the opportunity to look around, checking to see what had become of the girl he had saved. Cyper himself had dismounted beside her, and looked to be consoling her as he checked her injury.

The sight of the wound, shallow but long between breasts she only barely managed to cover up, sent another shiver of anger up Raz's spine.

"What is this?!" he snapped around at the throng, forcing himself to speak in a more even tone as he pulled Gale to a halt in the center of the space the masses had made for him. "What sort of *insanity* has possessed you all?! Do you know what you are doing?! *Do you*?!"

There was a fearful pause.

"Revenge!" a voice finally yelled from somewhere to Raz's right.

"Gettin' even!" another slurred from behind him.

There was a rumbling of assent from the rioters, and Raz could feel the tension building unpleasantly again.

"'Even'?!" he demanded, glaring around at them. He was all-too aware of the fact, of course, that the men and women around him outnumbered his little party at least two-to-one, but the animal had already taken him far beyond the limits of rationality. "By stoning people in the streets?! By hanging parents in broad daylight so that their children can watch them die?! Are you mad?!"

"Ain't *you* the mad one, Monster?!" a closer voice shouted in angry reply, and Raz turned to find one man braving a step forward out of the crowd. In one hand he still held onto a longsword that was far too fine for the rags that hung around his narrow frame. His teeth were stained and pitted, a blatant indication of the abuse of ragroot, but his yellowish eyes were wide and angry. "Ain't you s'pose to be helpin' us?! S'pose to be leadin' *us*?! That lot—" he pointed his sword in the direction of the pool, where the five corpses where little more than dark silhouettes in a bath of blood "—only got what was comin' to 'em! They's been in the pocket of the Mahsadën since the start!" The slum dweller took another approaching step. "For once, *we* got the power! *We* got the numbers! Ain't nothin' they can do, but you tellin' us *we're* the mad ones for takin' back everything they stole from us?! Where's 'the Dragon'?! Where's the scaly tha's s'pose to be bringin' us all out from under the boot of the šef and the stuck-up trims like those—" he jabbed the sword in toward the pool again "—who been helpin' em take from our mouths for as long as—?!"

Thump.

The man choked on his words as Raz threw a leg off of Gale's saddle and slid to the cobblestone ground. With Ahna still in one hand, he approached the figure, wings flickering outward, neck-crest up and taut over his head in anger. His armor gleamed in the sunlight, and his taloned feet *clacked* wickedly beneath him against the stone.

As he moved, he spoke.

"*I* have power," Raz snarled. "*I* have numbers. Forty-five *thousand* soldiers sit outside the gates of this city, awaiting *my* orders. Would you like it if I did what you have done here, hmm? Would you like it if I drove my army into the heart of all this butchery, and had them treat you as you have treated these people?" He waved his free hand back, toward the children Cyper was now standing guard over, along with a half-dozen others still mounted atop their steeds.

The slum dweller blanched, stumbling as he stepped back, away from Raz, who was still approaching. Still, he had some backbone in him, because even as the sword in his hand began to shake, he found it in him to snap back.

"You ain't got reason to! You ain't got cause. *We* got cause. We done spent long enough under the thumb of these people!"

"So you kill them?!" Raz demanded in a hiss. "You massacre and humiliate them as their children watch?! Is *that* your response?!"

The man swallowed, but set his face, bringing the sword up with both hands before him. "Aye!" he shouted back, his voice tight with fear. "Blood for blood! You know it's right! You know how it's done! They took from you, and you took from them! You should be on *our* side, stealin' back what was—!"

Crack!

Though he was hard tempted to, Raz did not kill the man. Instead, he lanced forward the last few feet, Ahna leading the way in a horizontal arc that caught the base of the rioter's blade, sending it *pinging* across the plaza stones. As the slummer gasped in surprise, Raz caught him by the nape of his worn clothes, gathering the moth-eaten fabric up in the steel claws of his left hand.

Then, he lifted the man clear off his feet, heaving him from the ground with one arm, and brought his face up to within inches of his own.

"Ever so much as *think* of accusing me of something like this again," he said, lifting Ahna to indicate the burning buildings, swinging corpses, and the crying children around them, "and I will take my time separating your head from your shoulders inch by *fucking* inch. I understand *revenge*. I understand tearing down the thing that has taken from you. But you…" The man's watery eyes blinked in fear, and his panicked breaths reeked of the sweet stench of ragroot. "All you have done is strike only at what you *can*, rather than what you *should*. Perhaps these people aren't as innocent as they might think, and perhaps a few of them are even deserving of this cruelty. But certainly not all. Not even *most*."

Raz held the man up for a moment longer, feeling him kick and listening to him struggle in his hand. Then he dropped him, letting the slum dweller tumble into a confused pile to the ground at his feet.

"All of you here have been wronged in some way or another!" Raz bellowed over the crowd around him. "I will not deny that. It is the reason you will be allowed to return to your homes without repercussion! I intend to deliver you all from the society that is *truly* responsible for your hardships, but there will be no tolerance of *any* who choose to strike out at those who have no means of defending themselves." Carefully, he met the eyes of several among the rioters who still looked dissatisfied. "Any who are displeased with this are free to step forward. You can arm yourself with whatever weapon you wish."

He hefted Ahna up into both hands, intent on getting his point across.

"But I hope you're ready to die for this so-called 'revenge'."

XVI

The main throng of the rioters dispersed peacefully enough after that, leaving a scattering of bloody swords and knives and makeshift clubs behind as they were escorted out of the quarter by forty of Raz and Cyper's cavalry and two groups of a hundred others that arrived on the scene shortly thereafter. Ten of their men stayed in the plaza, most guarding the children while four of them took it upon themselves to fish the corpses from the pool, drag the bodies of the stoned men out of sight, and cut down the pair who'd been hung before their home.

As this pair were eased from their place of execution, Raz heard the girl who had been attacked wail in renewed anguish, mirroring the cries of the boys who still clung to her after one of the riders had given her his mantle to cover herself up with.

Not even Raz managed to bring himself to turn and face them. He feared what he would see in the eyes of those children, feared the echo of an old pain he knew he would find in their faces.

Instead, he threw himself into ensuring no other such loss was suffered that day.

Raz and Cyper rode alone only briefly before meeting up with another of the scattered cavalry units, in the process of dispersing a smaller group of some two hundred rioters who'd been throwing stones and torches through the windows of the buildings along one particularly well-groomed street. The slum dwellers had apparently been putting up some resistance, but as soon as Raz arrived, towering over all atop Gale while he roared for them to return to their homes, their courage fled them. From there, he and Cyper split up, taking fifty riders each, leading them north and south respectively.

By the time Syrah's spell found him, Raz was pretty sure he'd chased another thousand from the quarter, some going quietly, others scattering only at the point of Ahna's blades.

"Master Arro!" one of the officers under his command—a young Imperialist whose name he didn't know—called out to him. Raz, who'd ridden some dozen meters ahead, threatening a particularly rowdy group with the dviaseggai to ensure they wouldn't take his warning lightly, looked around to find the soldier pointing east, to Raz's left. Following the gesture, Raz saw the light approaching, an ethereal orb, indistinct in the heat of the day and the dance of the fires that still rose over them. Pulling Gale about, he heeled the stallion towards the spell, which had already been dancing toward him through the debris. Within a couple of seconds he made out the thing at the center of the magic, a ribbon that twisted gently through the air as it neared, like silk pulled through water. It reached him momentarily, settling down upon the waiting palm of his free hand, where it immediately faded from the world, vanishing in a faint rain of ivory dust.

Raz did not hear Syrah's voice, nor anyone else's. It was not how the casting worked, as he had learned some time ago. Rather, the information conveyed was subtler, like the emotions and needs of the woman herself had been carried in the magic. Oddly enough, Raz knew then just how close he and Syrah had become over the last year. He'd been privy to such a spell once before, and in that moment he had felt little more than an urgency and a pull to be somewhere else.

With Syrah's magic, he understood the patterns in the conveyed emotions much more clearly, like the language of the spell had been one with which he was already familiar.

"Was that from the Witch, sir?" the officer asked nervously, guiding his tan mare around the ruins of a fallen column as he approached.

Raz had to force himself not to bristle, reminding himself silently that what Syrah allowed herself to be called was not his choice to make.

"It was," he said after a moment, dropping his open hand while the last of the light vanished, leaving only the fire and smoke and the heat of the Sun above again. "Fortunately the destruction has been largely concentrated in this quarter, and the fighting seems to be dying down. There were apparently some scattered incidents of looting in the market districts, but nothing of any significant import. Marsus and his scouts managed them without trouble."

"Any casualties on our side?" the man asked, looking around at the ravaged buildings that rose above them.

"She didn't say, but I doubt it." Raz brought Gale about, motioning for the others to join them. "Remember that these are not inherently evil people we are dealing with, despite how it might seem. They've simply been driven to the edge of a very dark place, and see the absence of the Mahsadën as a chance to fight their way away from that fall, if even just a little bit." He nodded towards the officers' wrists, where the familiar scars of iron manacles marked him, as they marked almost every soldier of the army. "We were all there, at some point. They are lost, but I don't think they're so far gone as to strike out at the hand they know is reaching out to help them."

The officer frowned, glancing down at his markings, but said nothing more.

They spent the rest of the day settling the lingering disputes and skirmishes that plagued Cyro's eastern quarters, meeting up with several other groups along the way. When Raz's forces numbered some four hundred and fifty, he dispatched a dozen riders back to the main army with instructions for Akelo and Syrah, calling them to lead ten thousand into the city proper, half of which were to be sent to him, the other half to be used in setting up a command center wherever they deemed most appropriate. Two hours later, when the Sun began dipping low towards the western horizon, light failing with the lengthening of the shadows, the supporting troops arrived in a dull drum of marching feet. The moment he met them, Raz gave orders for the protection of the quarter's citizens and dousing of the fires where possible. As Odene—who led the foot soldiers—offered his acknowledgement of the commands, Raz dismissed the remainder of his cavalry, praising their day's actions and acknowledging their fatigue and efforts.

When they had gone, heading for the eastern gate and the main ranks south of the city, Raz turned Gale in the opposite direction, leading the horse west, deeper into Cyro.

It was a few minutes before he passed out of the upper quarters, leaving the ruins of the homes and shops of the wealthy behind in favor of the more modest structures that made up the middle class and market districts. He was relieved to find that Syrah had been correct in her summation of the damage done to the area, noting nothing more than a few broken windows and doors that looked to have been kicked in. Even more encouraging, dozens of patrols of six- and ten-men units were already making their rounds of the district, settling what few troubles still lingered and saluting him as he rode by. All around, Raz also made out the residents of the districts cautiously peering from their homes, peeking through cracked shutters to gape at him and the men and women of his army—whom it must have seemed had appeared like magic—as they reigned in the chaos which had overcome the city. Raz was careful to take any opportunity he could to nod or wave to the citizens, acknowledging them and their curiosity, and hopefully appeasing some portion of any lingering fear.

Apart from the sudden occupation of Cyro, after all, there remained the fact that a number of atherian were among those patrolling the streets, keeping the peace and ensuring the safety of the citizens as a whole.

It didn't take long for Raz to find the command center, getting directions from a few officers he stopped to speak to along the way. As it turned out, Akelo and Syrah had elected to set up not far from the south gate they'd come through, commandeering a large public bathhouse in a plaza just east of the main fairway as one entered the city. Once he reached the place, Raz was glad to see that the general's pavilion and a number of other tents had been set up around the building as well. Syrah's trainees passed in and out of the entrances, some helping to support wounded citizens and soldiers, others shouting for supplies or assistance, or working on triaging the injured that were still arriving. Dismounting among the rush of coming and going patrols, Raz tossed Ahna over one shoulder and handed Gale's reins off to a waiting soldier. He gave the stallion a farewell pat, assuring him in a quiet voice that he would visit later when the animal brought his big head around to nose at Raz's arm, then made a line for the bathhouse. As Raz passed the pavilion, he heard Syrah's strong voice giving orders through the cloth, and he had to force himself not to stop and check on her.

She had her hands full, and he needed to assess their situation as soon as possible.

The bathhouse was a large, angular building with stone walls and a surprisingly steep roof. More officers moved in and out of the closest entrance, some carrying notes and orders for their comrades in the field, others hurrying off while pulling on helmets and shouting for horses. Raz couldn't help but chuckle darkly as he entered, stepping through the wide archway that led in, nodding briefly to the guards posted to either side of the entrance.

The last time we were in a place like this, it didn't end so well, did it, sis? he asked silently of Ahna.

Unsurprisingly, the dviassegai had no response, and Raz was left to reminisce on the memory of fire and falling all on his own.

The bathing chamber, it turned out, had been a single shared-sex space that took up a vast majority of the building's interior. The rectangular bathing pool in the center of the room had been drained, but Raz could still taste the humidity in the air as he moved around it, careful not to bump into any of the bodies rushing about the space in the limited light of some dozen torches staked into the walls. He was relieved to find the sense of panic and worry he'd anticipated to be largely absent, meaning the situation around the city must have been settling, and he managed to snag a passing soldier by the arm, asking her where Akelo and the others were. She pointed him toward the far end of the chamber, where he saw the table that usually sat in the pavilion had been set up in the empty bath.

Thanking the woman, Raz dropped into the pool—almost slipping on the slick tile surface that hadn't quite yet fully dried—and made for the huddle of dark figures grouped around one end of the table.

"The eastern quarters must be our top priority." He heard Akelo's gravelly voice first, seeing the man's familiar silhouette pointing to one side of what looked like a map set out before him. "Reports say Raz and the cavalry dispersed most of the slum dwellers, but we still need to worry about stragglers. As for the fires, there's not much we can do about them but try to keep the flames from spreading."

"Good," Zal'en muttered, sounding grimly pleased. "Those of greatest wealth in Cyro gained their fortune by buying and selling the atherian like cattle. Let their homes burn. Perhaps a measure of time without the comforts to which they are accustomed will open their eyes to the cruelties and evils they have perpetrated."

"I don't disagree," Raz spoke up finally, reaching the table. "Some punishment might go a long way. We just need to ensure it remains only *some* punishment."

The group as a whole turned at his voice. Akelo, Kalin, Marsus, and Hur all looked relieved to see him, and Zal'en inclined her head respectfully when he stepped into the space at the top of the table Akelo and Marsus made for him.

"Where are the others?" he asked, leaning Ahna against the wood at his hip before starting to undo the bucklings of his steel gauntlets.

"Erom led a small group into the slums about half-an-hour ago," Akelo told him, gesturing to a number of painted wooden markers scattered across the map before them. "The same men you took Dynec with. He intends to find out if there are any more major plans to attempt another attack on the other quarters. Odene and Cyper are both still in the eastern districts, managing the troops we sent you as support. I left Arnus in command of the main army, just outside the wall, and Syrah is obviously seeing to the wounded."

"Good." Raz's gaze shifted from one token to the other as the old Percian spoke, pulling the gauntlets off and setting them by Ahna. "And we're coordinating the patrols?"

"Aye," Marsus confirmed from his right. "Scouts did a fair job of familiarizin' with the roads. I've had one placed in every unit. Got us this, too." He gestured to the map. "Shouldn't be any trouble with gettin' lost, at the very least."

Raz nodded, pleased with the progress. "In that case, it's as Akelo says: the eastern quarters are our first concern for the time being. Have Arnus cycle in fresh troops at midnight, and I want priority on evacuating the women and children from the areas in danger, followed by the men."

"Where do we put them all?" Kalin asked from the right, and Hur grunted to indicate he had the same question.

In response, Raz tapped a claw along the southeast portion of the quarter. "This area was largely untouched, probably because it's the furthest from the slums to the west. The residents here will be kindly opening up their homes to those in need."

"They won't like that," Marsus chuckled.

"They won't have a choice," Raz growled, narrowing his eyes at the section of the map he was pointing to. "What the rioters have been up to is despicable in its own right, but not without reason. Those trims likely have the food, and most *certainly* have the space. They can either open up their doors and larders to those whom have been displaced, or I'll drag them from their beds *myself*." He looked around at Kalin, smiling wickedly. "Feel free to tell them that, when you wake them."

Kalin's grin was hard, but not unamused. "With pleasure," he said, taking the cue and stepping away from the table to make for the bathhouse doors at once.

"And the fires?" Akelo asked, tracing a finger along the more northern section of the quarter. "You think we should leave them?"

Raz nodded. "I have the troops already working on what they can, but I won't have any of our soldiers risking their lives to put out any of the greater blazes. Keep them as confined as possible. With luck they'll die out overnight, and Syrah can probably do something about any lingering flames in the morning."

"Assuming she sleeps tonight," Akelo muttered.

"The injured don't seem to be so many," Zal'en told him. "I do not believe your Mahsadën have been long absent from this place, for the fires to be burning still. Additionally…" she frowned, looking as though she were choosing her words carefully, "… a good number of those taken from their homes will not be needing treatment, in their states…"

There was a moment of silence at that, her implication settling over them all. Unbidden, an image of the girl and her brothers, she clinging to them and them to her as they sobbed, rose to the forefront of Raz's mind. For a brief second, an old wound broke open, and the memory of another girl flit across his thoughts, blue-eyed and raven-haired.

At his sides, Raz's hands formed into fists.

"Unforgivable," he growled, eyes on the map, though they looked beyond it. "Not leaving so much as a *single* soldier to keep the peace…"

"It is a new low, even for the Mahsadën," Akelo agreed through clenched teeth. "They *had* to know this would happen, meaning they were essentially willing to sacrifice the entirety of their upper-class to the chaos."

"S'only luck we weren't far behind," Marsus confirmed with a grunt. "They been gone two days, maybe three at most."

Not even that long, Raz thought, seeing again the bloody corpses in the pool of the center plaza.

After a moment, he took a deep breath, forcing himself to come back from the dark place his recollections were dragging him toward.

"If nothing else, we should simply take this as fuel for the cause," he said stiffly, working to keep his voice even while his eyes lifted to meet each of the generals'. "Children saw their parents butchered today, and many suffered atrocities of equal measure. When the time comes, I will not tolerate any sort of clemency for the šef responsible for this." He grit his teeth, feeling the anger seething in his chest. "We owe it to ourselves and every soul they've ever crushed under their boot, innocent or otherwise. I want their world to burn. Is that understood?"

As one, each of the others nodded.

"Good," Raz snarled, forcing his hands to loosen. "Then that's settled. For now, we will do what we can to rein in the mayhem here. I've a feeling we're going to be delayed more days than we'd like, but we can't simply leave a garrison and wish for the best, in this state. Things need to be brought under control before we'll be able to—" He paused, gaze shifting up the map to the empty sand plains north of the city. He was quiet for a time, and must have kept his silence for longer than he thought as he pondered his sudden idea, because Akelo coughed politely beside him.

"Raz?" the old man prodded him. "What are you thinking?"

In response, Raz frowned. He held his tongue a moment more, studying the waves of the dunes that had been added for effect on the map.

Who would bother mapping a desert, after all? he thought to himself.

Finally, he looked up, but it wasn't Akelo whose eyes he met.

"How many of the atherian do you think know the sands around here?" he asked Zal'en, who blinked, surprised to be addressed so abruptly.

"Enough," she replied after a considering pause. "Several hundred at least. Many of the older of our kind were hunters and scouts before we were taken. Myself included."

Raz nodded, looking back down at the map. This time, the others were quiet, letting him think, perhaps realizing where his mind was headed.

"Marsus," he said suddenly, "fetch Syrah. I know she'll fight you, but tell her I need her here. I can't have her exhausting herself tonight."

With nothing more than a quizzical glance at Akelo—who indicated with a prompt nod that he would do as he was told—the Southerner bowed briefly and hurried off, vanishing into the throng of soldiers and officers constantly milling about the table. As he left, Raz turned back to Zal'en.

"Pull every one of your people from duty, as well as the reserves. Their orders are to gather a five-days' worth of provisions and water, then rest until morning."

If the old female was taken aback by his command, she didn't show it. Like Marsus, she simply inclined her head in acknowledgement, then stepped back from the map, heading for the chamber doors.

"Raz, what are you planning?" Akelo pressed him again once it was only he, Hur, and Raz himself left at the table.

Raz stopped him with a raised hand. "Hur," he said, speaking to the massive Northerner. "Start rousing replacements for the patrols as they return. Zal'en will need your help exchanging fresh soldiers with the atherian she's going to be pulling out of rotation."

Hur made a sound of understanding. Before he turned away, though, the big man continued to watch Raz for a moment, an amused sort of dejection in his blue eyes.

As he left, Raz couldn't stop himself chuckling, thinking—not for the first time—that the giant was more intelligent than his muteness allowed to be conveyed.

He knows he's missing out on the fun.

"I'm killing half-a-dozen birds with one stone," Raz finally answered Akelo, indicating the middle-class districts on the map. "Our atherian are already making the city's residents nervous. Removing them from Cyro could help ease any future tension. More importantly," his clawed finger moved upward, to the plains north of the wall, "we were intending to negotiate with the lizard-kind of the Crags anyway. It might be easier to establish relations with them if we keep any human presence to an absolute minimum."

"So you're taking the atherian?" Akelo asked, sounding none-too-pleased with the idea. "By yourself?"

"And Syrah," Raz corrected. "She speaks the language better than anyone aside from the lizard-kind themselves, including *me*." He shrugged. "She's an ideal ambassador."

It was Akelo's turn to frown. "Assuming they take kindly to your relationship," he muttered, very obviously not liking what he was hearing. "This is needlessly risky, Raz, especially since we still don't know if Zal'en's 'Queen' is really anything more than a myth. If we wait a week, things will settle, and we can lead the army as a whole north and—"

"No." Raz cut the man off firmly, pulling his hand away from the inked outline of the northward dunes as his clawed fingers twitched in unbidden anger. "A week will be far too late. If I thought it possible, I'd leave tonight, even."

At first, Akelo didn't follow. "What are you—?" he started, Raz's plan clearly dawning on him.

"You think you can catch up to them," he said, turning back to the map and sounding suddenly much more interested with Raz's proposal. "You think you can chase them down."

Raz nodded. "The atherian alone can move faster for longer in the sand and heat. Syrah will take Nymara, and I'll bring Gale, too. She'll trade horses as needed. Worst comes to it, magic will help keep the animals fresh."

Akelo looked impressed, eyebrows rising while he, too, studied the dunes. "Zal'en and the rest probably know the sands as well as anyone in Cyro's army. And once the soldiers reach the Crags…"

"They'll be forced to either trek into the Cienbal, or try pushing over the mountains, just as we will eventually have to," Raz finished for him. "Assuming they've been gone no more than a day or two, that's when we'll catch them." He bared his fangs, then, glaring at the place on the table where the mountain ranges would be, if the map continued on.

"Akelo, I don't intend to let those šef reach Miropa as anything more than bones in a basket."

PART II

XVII

"While the later life of the Dragon of the North is largely well-documented and researched, I have found it difficult to identify enough trustworthy accounts to confidently put to paper one moment of particular import in the rise and story of Raz i'Syul Arro. In my own readings, I've been subjected to no less than a dozen different theorized retellings of this event, each more fanciful than the last.

What I would not give, now, to glimpse that true reunion of mother and child..."

— research notes of Jûn fi'Surr, author of *The Atherian*

The second pillar falls, Shas-hana Rhan repeated Uhsula's words to herself silently. *On this day, the world shakes.*

Hana, too, was shaking. She fought to control the trembling of her body as she leaned against the arm of her cold stone throne, thoughtlessly rolling her crown in the clawed fingers of her right hand. It was a dark, beautiful thing, a circlet of obsidian carved from a single block of the glass-like stone. It was a delicate piece, to be sure, but it had weathered the hundreds of years her line had ruled the mountains from within the bleakness of the Under Caves. She'd always thought it an apt comparison of the tenuous grasp by which her people clung to freedom.

Weak, and yet enduringly, endlessly persistent.

And now the second pillar falls, Hana thought again, lifting her eyes to look upon the seer once more, still not quite believing it.

Uhsula must have been having a good day, for it was the first time in several years that *she'd* come to Hana, rather than Hana going to her. Ordinarily the Queen was not a figure to be summoned by anyone, and there were those that thought her weak for allowing herself to be called on by the ancient female, but she cared little and less for their petty criticisms. Uhsula of the Other Worlds was old beyond reason, now more than twice the age to which most of their kind ever lived. To see so many seasons, Hana could only think was the will of the Daystar and the Night-Eye. More importantly, it had been Uhsula who'd largely raised her, tending to her in her youth like a doting grandmother when Hana's own mother, the Last-Queen, had been too taken with her duties to do so herself. As the years had passed, and her health had dwindled, it became harder and harder for the seer to make her way to the throne room, even with the help of her numerous acolytes.

And yet, now, here Uhsula stood, leaning heavily on the arms of two of the handmaids, her smile almost gleeful beneath her blind eyes, worn lips stretched so wide that it was possible to see every one of her dulled, blunted teeth.

"*You're sure*?" Hana asked for what must have been the fifth time. "*You're* sure, *Uhsula*?"

The old female bobbed her head yet again, taking a shaky step forward as she did, left leg and tail dragging uselessly behind her.

"*I* am," she hissed in excitement. "*The walls of my dreams are shattering. Light comes pouring in. There is no mistaking it. That cursed place has been brought to its knees.*"

Despite the assurances, Hana could truly hardly believe it. She leaned back into her throne with a hard *thump* as the strength left her body, the obsidian crown dangling from one upturned finger as her head hung and her shoulders shook.

Cyro. That was the name the world of man had for the city, according to Sassyl Gal's spies. It was not the largest realm of humankind had built for themselves around the desert, Hana knew, but nowhere else did the atherian cursed with such wicked fervor. Like some great, gaping mouth the place had shimmered as a stain on the distant horizon, several days to the south, swallowing up any of their kind that approached it. Slavers and soldiers spread from its darkness like an illness, claiming the young and old alike in irons and chains. In the last several years in particular, Cyro had become ravenous, a beast of endless hunger, pressing its men further and further north, occasionally even up into the mountain itself.

And now that beast was dead. Now they were free of its gluttony, free of the sadness and desperation that might have been suffered by those who would have lost children and siblings and parents to the clutches of man.

Hana closed her eyes, offering up a prayer of gratitude to the Daystar, thanking It for Its good will on this day.

Then she took a breath to clear her mind, straightened herself up to sit more regally against the back of the throne before looking around at the other figure waiting in the chamber, standing patiently opposite Uhsula, dark-golden eyes already set on hers.

Sassyl Gal was a rarity among his gender, to say the least. Male hatchings were far less frequent within their species than females to start with, and those that *were* birthed often tended to be impatient and unreliable. Sassyl, though—who was old already at around half Uhsula's age—had proven himself the opposite of such disappointments through decades of long service, first to Hana's mother, then to Hana herself. He served primarily as the court's master of spies, handling those among their kind they sent out into the world, collecting the information and relaying it back to the throne with impressive efficiency. Though the last decade had been hard, Hana had no doubt it was Sassyl's cleverness alone which had kept absolute disaster at bay, the old male adapting the patterns of their foragers and scouts with every report he received of slavers entering their borders. Had it been anyone else in charge of their way of life… Hana couldn't bear the thought.

In this moment, however, Sassyl Gal was not there to report on the movements and messages of his spies. Rather, as she looked to him, he stepped forward expectantly, giving her the answers she sought before she so much as asked the questions.

"*More arrived in the night, my Queen*," he told her, suppressing a wheezing cough. "*Some five hundred from a tribe to the east, among the higher peaks. Your summons have spread, it would seem.*"

"*You know full well the credit lies squarely on your shoulders, Sassyl*," Hanna said with a snort, tallying the math quickly. "*Another five hundred… Nearly ten thousand, now, if I'm not mistaken?*"

"*You are not.*" The old atherian bobbed his head in confirmation, briefly revealing the crest of stone-grey skin that rested along the back of his neck, the same color as the membrane of his ears. "*Although I fear we near our limit. Less and less arrive every day. I admit it is not the response I had hoped for. I estimate our able-bodied number five times that, spread out across the cliffs.*"

"*You cannot blame them*," Hana said with a sigh, though she, too, felt somewhat dejected. "*My line has hidden itself away for too long. I don't doubt many ignore the summons simply out of disbelief. The rest, out of fear.*"

Sassyl bristled angrily. "*Then they are* cowards," he snarled. "*Never before has one of your family made such a call to arms. It is their duty to respond when you—!*"

"*It is their duty to protect their families and tribes*," Hana cut the spymaster off gently, offering a shake of her head before pushing herself to her feet. "*If they've heard anything of what is happening in the world beyond these mountains, it is only what reaches them in rumors and stories. To be summoned abruptly to a war they know nothing about…*" She stepped forward, reaching up to perch the black crown in its customary place, nestling it down between her ears. "*If anything, I must commend those who* did *respond to my call. I owe them that, at the very least.*"

There was a moment of quiet, and on either side of her Hana knew Sassyl, Uhsula, and even the old seer's acolytes were likely gaping at her in surprise.

"*M-my Queen?*" Sassyl finally managed to choke out, "*You can't mean to…? Surely you don't intend to…?*"

"*Meet them?*" Hana asked him with a coy smile. "*Yes, I do. As you said yourself, we near our limit. It is time, I think.*"

Hana would have chuckled, thinking she saw some of the residual color drain from the spymaster's ears, but her own words were too heavy in her chest to manage a laugh. She was skilled enough at putting on a brave face, but the decision was not one she'd made lightly.

It had been a long time, after all, since she'd revealed herself to the eyes of the outside world.

There were many she saw regularly, within the depths of the Under Caves. Uhsula and her underlings, Sassyl, a handful of females from families almost as old as her own who fancied themselves advisors to the crown and came to whisper in her ear whenever the chance presented itself. Others, too, she'd met over the years, though these were generally brief encounters. Several large, dangerous-looking males Sassyl procured for her protection on the rare occasions he'd received reports of men attempting to press into the mountains themselves. A few scouts now and then whose reports the spymaster claimed he wanted Hana to hear for herself, though she suspected he did it more to keep word of her existence alive in the reaches beyond the

Caves. When she had been pregnant—in a time that seemed an eternity ago, now—Uhsula had called on the assistance of several shaman from the outer tribes, whose knowledge of herbs and potions and birthing had proven far more comforting than Hana had expected.

What she intended to do now, though, was largely beyond such passing meetings and introductions, and Hana was just starting to feel a little sick when Uhsula chuckled from her left.

"*It* is *time*," the seer told her with a nod as Hana looked at her. "*You have hidden away long enough, Shas-hana Rhan. It is time to walk beneath the Daystar once again, I think.*"

With every step she took, Hana was flooded by a mirage of dreams and memories from years long past. Torch in hand, Sassyl led the way before her—having been convinced to do so after much argument and grumbling—directing them through the maze of tunnels that made up the Under Caves, some natural, others carved from the earth and stone over more centuries than any of them could guess. They moved slowly, for Uhsula's sake, taking frequent rests that only drove the spymaster to greater irritation. Hana, on the other hand, didn't mind in the least. The pauses gave her the time to get her bearings, and for a while she was able to follow the path in her mind's eye. She might have ruled from the depths of the lowest caverns, but her realm was vast even buried within the mountains. As a child she'd lost herself countless times in the endlessness of the Under Caves, occasionally even ending up outside by following narrow paths through the bedrock she knew now to be escape routes in case the tunnels were ever raided. She cherished those recollections, but her reminiscing soon cost her her sense of direction as Hana suddenly realized—after walking for so long Uhsula had eventually allowed herself to be picked up and carried in the strong arms of her acolytes—she hadn't the faintest clue where they were. Instinctively she could sense that they were no longer so deep beneath the ground. The air was richer here, less humid and far warmer. The floor of the caves was drier, too, the hearty earth and slick stone of the tunnels surrounding her throne room having at some point given way to clumped dirt and dry rock. Even as she noticed this Hana realized also that they'd begun to climb in truth, and a thrill of exhilaration shivered down her arms, back, and tail as she heard something in the distance she hadn't experienced in many, many years.

The far-off sound of wind whistling against the arid cliffs of the mountain.

Not long after, Hana started to feel the breeze, and she had to remind herself that she was a Queen when she nearly gasped in anticipation at the sensation of the air dancing across her face. Still they climbed, the incline steepening while the tunnel wound back and forth half-a-hundred times. Abruptly she recalled in vivid detail the first of perhaps some four or five occasions she'd taken this path with her mother, decades prior. She remembered holding the Last-Queen's hand as they walked, listening to Shastonah Rhan explain how the winding was meant to allow the eyes to adjust, to ease the transition from the world of darkness to the one of sun and light.

That was the moment Sassyl dropped his torch and stamped the flames out into the ground, and Hana remembered most acutely—and felt once more—the breathtaking excitement that had been born with the Last-Queen's words.

Sure enough, once the fire died and the tunnel fell into momentary blackness, Hana just couldn't help but gasp in delight as her sensitive eyes adjusted to reveal a single sliver of light in the distance, a crescent glow that marked yet another bend ahead.

For ten more minutes they kept on, ever upward, the breeze growing stronger and hotter, the cave around them brightening a slightly with every turn they took. Each time Hana felt her eyes strain, but each time she smiled a little more broadly. This was the gift of the Daystar, after all, the First-Born. The thrill returned, and she had to force herself not to speed up while the acolytes kept pace behind her, still cradling Uhsula in their arms. All the same, impatience was abound in her step, and by the time they turned the final corner in the rising tunnel, Hana thought she would explode with delight.

The sight before her though, the vision of the cave's mouth some hundred yards ahead, opening up onto the outside world, drained away all the burgeoning energy, transforming it into awestruck wonder in the space of a single heartbeat.

As her eyes adjusted one final time, Hana could do little more than gape at the sky as they kept walking, basking in the cloudless blue, taking in the simple beauty of it which she realized suddenly she'd utterly forgotten. As they approached, the brightness grew uncomfortable, but all the same Hana knew she couldn't stop. She still stood in shadow, she realized. The line of the First-Born's light was ahead of her, cutting a jagged swath against the loose ground of the cave floor as cleanly as any blade. She watched it getting nearer, staring at it with fascination.

When they weren't more than twenty feet from the true light of the day, Hana gave in to her excitement, rushing forward with a laugh that would have more suitably belonged to a hatchling some thirty years younger.

She didn't hear Sassyl's surprised call for her to come back, nor the chuckle from Uhsula that drowned out the stifled giggles of one of the acolytes. Had she been more even-minded, Hana might have wondered at the sight of herself, the fabled Queen of the Under Caves bounding forward with all the patience of a child. In that moment, though, she couldn't have cared less.

Especially once she sprinted into the sun's warmth, feeling the heat of the Daystar shiver across her scaled skin like hot water, the wind of the cliff whipping into the cave around her to cast the cloth coverings bound about her waist dancing behind her.

And before her, spread out to the reaches of the horizon that seemed like the very edge of existence, the world expanded endlessly far, far below the cliffs she now stood atop.

Hana had been told stories of strange lands to the north and south of the Crags, where trees and grassy plains swallowed the earth. She'd even heard it said that many miles to the east, as the peaks rose higher and higher, a lake existed which had no true beginning or end. She'd never seen such wonders—though as a child she had desperately wanted to—but all the same could not fathom that there might be anything more beautiful than the rolling plains of the world sweeping out before her.

The sand stroked back and forth far below, rising and swelling like the ground itself had been frozen as it writhed beneath the light of the day. Little escaped the gaze of the Daystar, but as the mountains met the desert, shadows began to play among the rocks that became larger and sharper while the ranges rose skyward. It was a harsh, dry sight, but to Hana there was nothing possiby more wondrous, especially in the timelessness of the scene. It had been twenty years since she'd last stood upon these cliffs, looking out over the sands. Nothing had changed, nothing had shifted to mark the passage of the decades. At the time, of course, Hana knew she hadn't the heart to take in the desert as she did now, to devour them with her eyes as one can only do when all one largely knows is stone and darkness and the gentle glow of luminescent plants and torches.

She'd had bleaker thoughts on her mind, then, while she'd allowed the child she most cherished to be taken away from her for the mere chance at a world in which her people did not cower to the whips of man.

At the memory, a little of Hana's enthusiasm faded, bearing her thoughts back to earth. She found herself closer to the edge of the cliff than might have been prudent given the wind, and she retreated to a safe distance before turning around. The cave's mouth gaped before her—cleverly disguised in the overhangs of stone shelvings that made it difficult to find unless one already knew exactly where to look—but what caught Hana's attention were the paired males on either side of it, leaning against the stone of the wall behind them as they stared at her in equal surprise. She recognized them after a moment, taking note of their markings—white stripes along the arms of the one on the left, and a splash of scarlet across the chest of the right—remembering them to be among the group summoned to the caverns in times of danger. She didn't recall there usually being guards posted at the entrance of the Under Caves, however, and she did her best to cover her astonishment at seeing new faces already by looking to Sassyl for an explanation once the old male stepped out into the day, blinking and shading his face against the light.

As always, the spymaster was prompt in his answer.

"*Ma'zer and Zelys are here as a precaution, my Queen,*" he said with an impatient sort of huff, gesturing to the left and right respectively. "*With so many gathered nearby, it was a necessity. Had you waited for us, I would have made sure to warn you of their presence.*"

The words "my Queen" seemed to shake the younger males from their shock, because each dropped to one knee, dipping their heads in her direction.

"*Queen Shas-hana Rhan*," the one on the right—Zelys, Hana thought—managed to get out. "*It is an honor and a… a surprise.*" He lifted his head just long enough to glance at Sassyl, who only grumbled again. "*We were not expecting your arrival so soon. Had we known, we would have made better preparations for—*"

"*No need*," Hana interrupted him, adopting the regal smile and royal tone her mother had instilled in her so long ago. She waved a hand, gesturing that they stand. "*Rise, both of you. Do not blame Sassyl for a lack of warning. This was my doing. He has told me most of those who would answer my summons have already arrived. It is time I met their bravery with my own.*"

She chose her words carefully, and to good effect. As the pair pressed themselves to their feet, she could see the approving gleam in their amber eyes.

"*They will be grateful for your words, my Queen*," the other—Ma'zer—spoke up just as Uhsula and her helpers stepped out of the cave. Apparently Sassyl had chased her ahead of them. "*Those who have been here longest are starting to grow restless, I believe.*"

Hana inclined her head in understanding. She'd feared as much. It was half the reason she'd wanted to show herself now, rather than wait. Her existence was half-a-myth already to so many of her people. For them to rise to her call only to be met with nothing but assurances that her orders would come eventually did not sit well with her. She owed them proof, at the very least. Proof that she lived. Proof that she recognized their bravery.

Proof that she was seeking a freedom for them that their people had never before so much as reached for…

Again, the realization of what she was about to face made Hana's stomach twist into a knot, but she kept her smile and poise as masterfully as a Queen ought to.

"*Then we shan't keep them waiting any longer, I think*," she said, looking to Sassyl now. "*Lead the way, spymaster. Take me to my army.*"

XVIII

In the twenty minutes it took to reach the encampment, Hana thought she managed a good job of steeling herself for the coming challenge. All around her the world insisted on trying to distract her. The wind buffeted them against the cliffs. The shrieking calls of birds of prey echoed down to her from the outcroppings overhead. The loose stone shifting and slipped beneath her clawed feet as they moved. Just the same, Hana did everything she could to keep her mind at ease. This would be the first time, after all, that she addressed more than a few dozen. At her coronation, after the Last-Queen's passing nearly thirty years prior, there had been a crowd. The females of the old families, soldiers Sassyl trusted, runners who would carry news of her rise to the throne to every corner and crag of the mountains. Then, addressing them hadn't been so hard. She'd prepared herself, had mastered the grief of her mother's death and managed to stand before the packed cavern as a brave, young Queen bearing her line's lasting ambition to bring her people out from under the boot of mankind. Hana drew, now, on that last and only experience, trying to recall how she'd felt, how she'd willed herself to be strong.

Then Zelys offered her an assisting hand, pulling her up to crest a boulder that had partially blocked their path, and Hana felt all her bravery plummet away in an instant.

Never before, not even in her greatest dreams of freedom, could she have imagined the sight of ten thousand atherian warriors gathered there before her, writhing like a single living thing against the cliff face. The number was too staggering to fathom, even as she witnessed it for herself, too stunning to comprehend. Everywhere she looked it seemed the lizard-kind were going about their business, the sprawl of bodies largely divided into the various tribes who'd sent their champions in response to her summons. Females made up the vast majority of their number, of course, but Hana still saw dozens of males in every section of the camp, standing taller and broader than their counterparts. Their minimal garbs ranged with every clan. Knit plates of the long grass that could be found in the very bottom reaches of the mountains. Patched swaths of woven rodent pelts. Larger hides of bigger animals, from desert cats to goats to what might even have been horses. One group, a smaller tribe lingering along the lowest edge of the army, appeared to have donned what looked like pieces of the carapace of the great scorpions that prowled the dunes of the true desert to the west.

"*Breathe, child. They are but people.* Your *people.*"

Hana started at Uhsula's voice in her ear, turning to find that the old seer had been carefully hauled up after her and was now standing on her left, leaning into the arms of one of the acolytes. Despite her blindness her dull eyes were sweeping over the gathering before them, taking the vastness of their number in as though she could see the horde all too clearly.

Hana, too, looked back out over the tribes. As she did, she saw that their little group was being noticed. She clung to Uhsula's words while those closest to them, some fifty feet down the mountain, started to look around and point, passing word back through to those further beyond them. Like a spreading spell the dull buzz of conversation and activity began to fade, silence sweeping across the army as though carried by the wind that still rushed all around them.

Within a minute the gathered atherian were so still and so quiet, they might have blended in as ten thousand stone statues among the cliffs.

"*Now, my Queen*," Sassyl said gently. "*Let them understand the great cause for which they have been gathered.*"

Hana, in response, opened her mouth to speak.

Nothing came out.

She did not have to wonder what it was that had struck her dumb. She'd feared this moment, feared it from the instant she'd made the decision to show herself. Ten thousand of her people. Ten *thousand.* She knew her kingdom was vast, and she even understood to a degree that those gathered before her were nothing more than the smallest portion of the greater populace for which she was responsible.

All the same, the awesomeness of their presence weighed down on her, trapping her words within her chest.

Then, though, Hana met the eye of one figure, one female atherian who happened to be standing at the forefront of the army. She stood a little shorter than most of her brethren, in tattered hides that hung to her knees, a club of wood and stone limp in one hand. Meeting her gaze, what Hana saw there took her utterly aback. The female was not watching with confusion or suspicion, as Hana had feared. She wasn't even staring in surprise, as might have been understandable.

Rather, there, glowing as bright in the atherian's eyes as the First-Born hanging high above them in the empty sky, was nothing but innocent, absolute awe.

The sight made Hana's heart swell with pride. In that moment, she understood that her struggles and sacrifices had not been without value. In that moment, she understood that even as half-a-myth she commanded the respect of some, if not all. She *had* power, she saw in that female's face. She *had* the ability to lead these people.

She just had to take hold of it.

And with that thought, the words began to flow.

"*Bravest children of the Daystar!*" she called out, her voice rising above the gusting air and echoing back over the empty vastness of the cliffs. *"I am Shas-hana Rhan, Queen of the Under Caves, daughter of Last-Queen Shas-ronah Rhan!*" She spread her arms and raised her chin, taking a step forward as the light reflected off the obsidian crown atop her head, scattering reflections across the rocks before her. "*Firstly, I owe you a great debt! Despite what I imagine to be hardy reservations, despite what could only have been a mere hope, you came! You answered my call, and have gathered together with nothing more than a promise of my presence! But I* am *here, now! I* am *present! For far, far too long my line has lain in hiding in the deepest shadows of the mountains! We ruled as mere ghosts of the leaders you deserved, all for fear of the wrath of man should he discover our existence!*" She didn't have to fake the anger that spasmed through her jaw. "*No longer, though! NO LONGER*!"

She had to pause then, as the response from the gathered army took her by surprise. As her last words rebounded over the mountain face, a building sound, like a flooding river, began to creep out of the silence. Before long, it had pitched into a deafening roar of approval, the shrill war cries of the females drowning out the deeper bellowings of the fewer males.

"*Some of you suspect, perhaps, what you have been called for*!" Hana continued, raising her voice again as the cheer finally began to ebb. "*Some of you may already have heard whispers of the telling the great seer, Uhsula—*" she gestured back at the ancient female behind her "*—delivered to us at the behest of the Night-Eye, twenty summers past! For those of you who have not, though, it is high time you hear it for yourself!*"

She took a moment, breathing deeply and settling herself.

Then she began to recite, announcing the prophetic lines she'd long since committed in iron memory:

"Of one kind, and yet of another,
wings and wind bear him forth.
From chains comes his second birth
and never shall he stand for them.
Child of the Daystar, he will speak the language,
and be the speaker of his people.
To leave and then return,
bearing a woman of ice and snow on his arm."

When she was done, the quiet of the atherian held, and Hana took advantage of it to press on.

"*A child—*my *child—was given over to the world of man in the days after this telling was delivered to us*!" she said, allowing just the right amount of grief to leak out into her voice. "*I feared for him—I* still *fear for him—but the gods have seen fit to grant us glimpses of his life among the humans many times over the years! He has grown strong! He has grown fierce! With time he has become a force both feared and respected among their realms!*" She stopped for a moment, allowing her words to sink in before smiling victoriously over the crowd.

"*And now, Uhsula of the Other Worlds has spoken once again! Even as I stand here before you, that child approaches, returned to us at the Daystar's will, now forged into a champion who will lead us out of the shackles man has cast about our limbs*!"

This time Hana was quite sure she would go deaf as the army erupted into a thundering cheer of exhilaration and anticipation. The sound washed over her and her little group like a wave, made solid in its volume. She had to keep herself from pressing her hands to her ears—as one of the acolytes did behind her—and high above them shale and pebbles shivered and slipped into several momentary streams when the clamor shook them loose of their precarious positions.

"*Some of you may not believe me*!" Hana called out as soon as she thought she might be heard again. "*I do not blame you! I have been absent from your lives in a way that will pain me till the day I take my final breath! You have no reason to see the truth in my words! I have yet again only given you assurances and promises, with little to present to you as proof!*" She bowed her head apologetically. "*It shames me, in no small part, to address you empty-handed… However,*" she looked up again, fiercely this time, "*the proof is coming! To the south, the cities of man are falling! Cyro is no more!*"

At her words, the wind itself seemed to die. Not a sound was raised from the onlookers, for which she couldn't blame them. Cyro. The cursed place. The hunger that swallowed any who braved approach it.

She had been equally shocked when Uhsula had said those words.

"*I speak the truth, but I have greater news still!*" She raised her hands again, as though to embrace their number. "*That child returns! He returns, felling the pillars of man as he claws his way back to us! But he does not come back alone! Thousands of our lost are with him, and joined by the children of those who were long taken from us!*"

Again nothing broke the quiet at first. The astonishment at this announcement was palpable, visible in the eyes of every atherian Hana could see in the front line of the army. Then, from the masses, a single voice rose up, a keen, individual wale of grief mixed with relief. Hana found the female who'd cried out as she fell to her knees, most of those around her stepping away out of respect as she clung to herself. She was older, perhaps around Hana's own age, and the way she wrapped her arms about her body spoke of emotions with which Hana was all too familiar. Soon, others began to cry and call out. Dozens, scores, then hundreds. Many yelled out questions while others fell like the first female, or merely stared at the ground in disbelief.

"*It pains me greatly, but I have no further answers for you*!" Hana spoke to them all with a sad shake of her head, her words calming the fervor of the crowd again. "*I can only give you hope, as cruel as that may be, and offer a glimpse of the potential future of our people! Cyro falls, and our champion has only just begun his war! Uhsula has seen in her dreams that the time approaches when he will arrive at the foot of our mountains, a day for which we must be prepared! He will have need of our numbers! He will have need of our strength and our lives!* That *is why I have seen fit to summon you here!* That *is why you have suffered the heat of the days and the cold of the nights for me! I made a choice, twenty summers past, which was no more than a desperate swipe at the flame that might have been our freedom! As the years have slipped by, that flame has grown! Soon, it will be time to seize it, to wield it as a weapon for he who would see us be more than what we are, more than WHAT WE HAVE EVER BEEN*!"

The cheers returned at that, trembling over the ranges. Hana could even feel the boulder beneath her clawed feet vibrating.

"*DOES THAT MEAN YOU ARE WITH ME*?!" she bellowed.

The answering roar was instantaneous.

"*DOES THAT MEAN YOU WILL BEAR ARMS FOR YOUR CHAMPION*?"

Again, the response was like thunder in the clear day.

"*Then you are truly the greatest and bravest warriors of our time*!" Hana answered their approval more evenly. "*See to it that you rest, these next days, and prepare! When the time comes, we will not hesitate! When the day arrives, we will march out into the world, and end the horrors that have been committed against our kind for too—*!"

Abruptly, she stopped. A hand, trembling and weak, had clasped her about the arm, leaning heavily into her. With a mix of anger and confusion, Hana whirled on Uhsula, intending to demand what she was doing.

The look on the seer's face, though, the rage and fear layered into the grey-white of her blind eyes, choked off her question.

"*Soldiers*," Uhsula hissed, her thin fingers clenching tighter about Hana's elbow as she turned her head southward, lifting as though attempting to peer over the edge of the peaks high above them. "*Soldiers of man. In the mountains.*"

XIX

"I consider arrogance simultaneously among mankind's greatest follies and greatest strengths. That confidence—that unwavering certainty of one's actions and decisions—is not something I think I have ever experienced in my long years. I do not know if it is a difference of race, of upbringing, of experience, but regardless of the mechanism, I do not think there has been a single significant action in my life I have not questioned. Even Syrah—who I count second only to Talo in terms of humility among the great many humans I have met in my long life—falls the occasional victim—or beneficiary—of that unfathomable self-confidence. It has lent itself to a great many of her successes, in the decades we have been together.

Then again, it has just as distinctly lent itself to the vast majority of her most significant sufferings…"

— *The Dragon of the North*

Yres Ma'het did not know if he had ever been in a blacker mood. He felt like he'd been climbing for years, even if in reality he and his forces had only been among the Crags for three days now. Looking up, he *knew* the peaks were close, and it likely wouldn't even be night before they crested these infernal ranges and started the easier descent down to the northern slopes.

All the same, Yres cursed the Sun above for his torment, glancing back to see how his soldiers were fairing.

Five thousand men followed him, some no more than a few paces behind, some a half-hour further down the mountain face. They moved at a crawl, largely due to the packs and provisions each had had no choice but to carry on their persons, but Yres still managed a triumphant snort at the sight of them. Their number alone was an indication of his own small victory. When he, Thesus, and Malyn had reached the Crags with the nine thousand men-at-arms they'd brought with them from Cyro, the three šef had had a vicious disagreement over how best to manage the cliffs. Thesus and Mayn—cowards that they were—insisted on traveling east into the Cienbal, looping around the mountains. On the other hand, Yres—who hated the desert heat more than any other true-born Percian *or* Southerner he knew—had tried to convince them that struggling *over* the Crags was vastly in their best interests. Water would be easier to find once they were out of the foothills, and what little game they might come across to supplement their rations could only amount to more than what the sandcats and dune scorpions they were likely to encounter in the sands would provide. Thesus and Mayn, of course, countered that they would have great trouble bringing their carts and horses with them over the peaks, and that the atherian would undoubtedly descend on them if they led an army into lizard-kind territory.

This last argument had made Yres laugh scornfully in their faces, jeering at them for fearing the scattered tribes that rarely peeked their snouts out of their holes and caves for fear of Cyro's shackles.

In the end, the two sides had been unable to come to an agreement, and so Yres had left the others with much swearing and insults, calling on those loyal to him in the army to join in his trek over the Crags. To his delight, more than half of their forces had followed his lead, taking what supplies they needed from the wagons and pack horses before setting out into the cliffs.

Fear of the Cienbal, after all, was healthily ingrained into the hearts of any sensible desert-dweller.

Now, though—while Yres remained convinced his plan was the better one—he had to admit to himself that the going was far more tedious than he had anticipated.

The general misery of the journey could be attributed to a variety of factors. Injuries happened daily, and a dozen men had been lost here and there to falls after slipping on loose stone at inopportune times. They'd suffered none of the attacks from the larger predators Yres knew Thesus and Mayn would have to manage among the dunes, but any number of soldiers had been bitten by troublesome snakes and spiders secluded in the shadows and nooks of the rocky incline. Food was more plentiful than he had anticipated—their archers among had been downing dozens of large, goat-like creatures a day—but Yres hadn't counted on the time it took to prep and cook the animals each evening, nor on the bland toughness of their flesh. Despite the meals the mountain provided, many soldiers chose to sate themselves on the provisions of dried bread and salted meats they'd brought along, a tendency Yres hoped wouldn't come to bite them in the ass later.

Above all else, though, what truly made the climb insufferable was the Sun above, blazing endlessly and mercilessly from dawn to dusk down upon them. The breeze was cooler here, in the rising altitudes of the steeps, but the minimal drop in temperature did very little to balance out the wretchedness of the constant climb under harsh light. Yres had been a soldier his entire life, and was accustomed to hard marches across the unstable sands of the Cienbal's plains, but all the same he felt grossly unprepared for the trek. On the first day, several men collapsed from heat exhaustion before he finally conceded to the difficulty of the climb and called a long halt for all to catch their breaths. In the two since, they'd been forced to take frequent rests, even more often now that the air was growing thinner and thinner. He encouraged the men to find what shade they could, in those periods of rest, but—given that the Crags rose east to west, offering little respite from the day except in the very latest hours of the evening—the bare shadows of the outcroppings and boulders around them could only accommodate so many in any given space, and that number was always *far* less than five thousand. Even Yres couldn't help but occasionally douse himself with a handful of water from one of his leather drinking pouches, a dangerous habit given that water was harder to come by than anticipated, the few streams and sources they found often little more than bare trickles down the mountainside.

Yes. This journey was not going to be the convenient crossing Yres had imagined, ending in a smug reunion with the other šef in Miropa.

Even as he thought this, muttering angrily under his breath, Yres felt his left foot slip on a loose piece of shale, and he stumbled to one knee, his heavy pack dragging him almost straight to the ground.

With an irritated curse the šef looked over his shoulder to where Sehth Vehn, his first lieutenant, was struggling upwards not far behind, and he gave a sharp whistle to catch the older soldier's attention.

"We break here," Yres said, rolling himself onto his rear and slipping his arms from the loops of his bag even as he scooted towards a nearby sliver of shade. "If we keep going, I'm liable to blaspheme myself out of the Moon's embrace, when my time comes."

Sehth chuckled dryly at that, clearly sympathizing with his commander's mood. Finding some solid footing, he half-turned to bark several orders out over the ascending army. His words rang back a dozen more times as officers repeated them further and further down the mountain, and Yres felt a pang of annoyance as he distinctly heard his forces groan in unified relief.

"Regretting the decision?" Sehth asked, taking the last few heavy steps upward before dropping his pack, sword, and shield down beside Yres' own equipment and taking a seat at the šef's side.

"Hardly," Yres muttered in response, though his irritation was more directed at the arid stone and wind around them. "Once we make it over the peaks—" he jabbed a thumb up over his shoulder, to the top of the mountains "—it will be easier going. Still… I don't think I've ever been wanting for a horse so badly."

Sehth nodded in understanding. "Aye, I'll second that." He cast his grey eyes over the army settling below them, then around at the mountain face. "Still… I'm surprised we've had this easy a go of it…"

Yres grunted in agreement, requiring no explanation as to what the man was talking about.

The atherian had been deceptively absent throughout their ascent.

While he hadn't expected *much* resistance from the pockets of lizard-kind that lived as separate tribes among the Crags, Yres had expected *some*, at the very least. Even the slavers, with their mercenary guards, only very rarely pushed up into the mountains, and then no more than half-a-day's climb, he'd heard. Apparently the lizards were viciously protective of their territories, and it was only the quickest and most well-versed in the art of the trade who risked crossing into their lands. With five thousand at his back, Yres hadn't thought he'd see much of the scaly bastards, but the fact that not even a stray rock had been thrown, or a nighttime ambush had been executed, was bizarre to him.

For some reason, it gave him a bad feeling.

Yres, though, was not about to spit on the gift. Perhaps it was the Sun's way of blessing their crossing—or at least making up for the *infernal* heat—or perhaps the atherian simply got a sense that it wasn't the soldiers' intention to drag them from their homes on this particular march, and it was therefore better to leave them be. Whatever the reasoning, Yres was grateful for it, enough so that he could ignore the twinge of disquiet which pulled at his gut whenever he thought of how far they'd driven themselves behind what was, technically, enemy lines…

Still, there was a distinct difference between being brave and being foolish.

"Fifteen minutes," he told the lieutenant after he'd guzzled down a few mouthfuls of the uncomfortably warm liquid. "Then we're moving again. We're camping on the other side of these damn mountains tonight, even if I have to make them climb under the light of the Moon. I don't want to spend a second more stumbling through these rocks than I damn well have to."

Sehth nodded quickly, accepting the leather bag back and taking his own drink. They said little more, after that, neither man in much of a mood to talk. At the same time, both of them had to consciously force themselves not to turn around, to glance over their shoulders nervously, wondering if there were golden eyes watching them from the spaces between the boulders above them.

Had they known the truth, had they been lucky enough to catch even a brief glimpse of the lithe forms darting across the cliffs overhead, arms and chests patted down with dust that camouflaged their dark scales, Yres and Sehth would have thought twice about pressing on so insistently.

As anticipated, they made the top of the mountains as the day ended, just when the Sun began to sink behind the rising peaks that soared skyward to the west. Had Yres not been so exhausted, he might have taken a moment to appreciate the wonder of the scene stretched out before him, the soaring expanse of the sands and sky streaked in breathtaking colors as dusk fell. A few rare clouds clung steadfastly to the heavens, fading from white to orange to red while the minutes ticked by. Night came like a rising tide, slowly swallowing the failing light. Her Stars winked into being one at a time, waking to crown the Moon in Her crescent form, lingering over the northern horizon. To most, it would have been a once-in-a-lifetime sight, a view to be appreciated and pondered, with the knowledge that experiencing the day's final moments from such a vantage was not a chance that was likely to come again.

Yres, though, hardly glanced out over the sand plains, preferring instead to groan in relief as he began the steady downward climb, enjoying the coolness of the coming night.

He was not, of course, mad enough to *actually* push his men into attempting the descent in the dark. He moved carefully, easing himself perhaps half-a-mile further between the cliffs before he had Sehth call a halt again. Those soldiers who'd stayed with them over the course of the day began setting up camp as best they could, and by the time the stragglers managed to crest the ranges and start downward as well, the evening cooking fires were roaring, each surrounded by a score of bedrolls to take advantage of the warmth. The unappetizing goat meat was seared and distributed among those who would eat it, and the army settled into the familiar routine of the night, with conversation buzzing over the crack of flames, laughter and yells echoing over the cliffs to join with the faint shouted orders as the first shift of lookouts were selected and sent to their posts.

"How long do you figure it takes us to make the bottom?" Yres asked of Sehth. The pair of them were sharing a fire with a dozen of the šef's higher officers, all of whom were busy with their own discussions.

Sehth pondered the question a moment. "Took us four days to manage the climb?" he thought aloud. "Can't imagine it would take us any longer than that, but I don't think we'll be able to move as fast as we like, even with the slope in our favor now. I'd say four again, maybe three at best."

Yres ripped a mouthful of meat from his haunch, considering the lieutenant's summary. He'd been thinking the same thing, and wasn't displeased with the count. It would take Thesus and Malyn at *least* a fortnight to manage the western tip of the Crags and escape the Cienbal again. Even if they were delayed a few days, Yres' group would be the ones to reach Miropa first by a large margin. That was good, because it would give him the chance to size up the city's young mastermind for himself, and curry favor with him if he could. His sister, Ysera, had sent more than mere orders for their reinforcements in her last letter. She'd also taken the time to press in the fact that this new šef—Adrion Blaeth—was not one to be taken lightly. The Mahsadën had worked well for the last decade, balancing the rings' strengths and weaknesses by sharing power over the cities, but if the dynamic was about to change, Yres was going to make damn sure he and Ysera had firm footing in the winning side.

And—if Ysera's words were anything to go by—this "Blaeth" was most certainly going to be at the center of that victory.

"What do you make of him?" Yres asked aloud, swallowing his meat with a face. "Blaeth?"

Sehth looked around at his superior warily. "The Miropan šef?"

Yres nodded, then chomped down on the leg again.

"'Dangerous' is the first word that comes to mind," Sehth answered. "Among the men, there are rumors about him, and none of them pleasant. Apparently he has gifts…?"

He let the query hang, clearly looking for more information.

Yres obliged. Sehth had been his right-hand since well before he'd started rising through the ranks within Cyro's society. If there was a man whose opinion he valued more than his fellow šef, it was the lieutenant's.

"So Ysera claims." He frowned. "She wrote of some strange ability over fire. Calls it 'magic', but I have a hard time believing that."

Sehth shrugged. "The Laorin, in the North, are supposed to wield magic," he pointed out. "Often in the form of fire, I hear."

"Aye," Yres conceded. "But I've never seen hide nor hair of that either, and those stories are all about spells of healing and protection."

Sehth paused as someone nearby shouted an angry order, apparently dissatisfied that a sentry had wandered off somewhere. When the commotion subsided, he continued.

"Even if it's not magic, clearly there's more to the man than meets the eye. They say he's a cripple. For someone like that to bring to heel what was left of the Miropan society after what the Monster did … If he's not dangerous, then he's at the very *least* a person to be wary of."

Yres said nothing, turning over the Sehth's words. There was nothing in them he himself had not been thinking at some point or another, but all the same it was good to know he wasn't the only one with concerns. Blaeth had come into power too swiftly, too bloodlessly. Ysera had made the man's ability clear, but Yres thought it had to take more than personal power—even 'magic'—to pull a scattered Mahsadën together in a place as large as Miropa. His sister had been in a panic the previous summer when she left for the city, fearing what would happen if they lost control of the "Gem of the South". Miropa was their most strategically valuable position by a wide margin, even more so than Acrosia to the west. While the port city did good trade with the West Isle and the Imperium, the valley town merchants and foresters of the North bartered in far more valuable goods than the seafood, nuts, and exotic animals of the nations across the Emperor's Ocean. Lumber and all kinds of building stone—like marble and granite—were sparsely found in and around the Cienbal. Sandcat pelts went for a high price, but not as high as wolf skins or bear furs, which the elite of the fringe cities used as blankets and mantles to keep away the night chill. Even the glass they traded for with Azbar was of better quality than what they could make in the South, where the desert sand was too fine to crystallize properly.

And all of that—plus dozens of other wares ranging from food to weapons—only ever came through Miropa.

Therefore, when Ysera had sent word from the Gem that all was well, and that the Mahsadën held firm in the city despite the consecutive butchering of every former šef, Yres had hardly believed it.

That was the first time he had heard the name "Adrion Blaeth."

Yes, he thought to himself, *it takes more than strength to do what he did. It takes cunning, too…*

"What in the Sun's name is going on?"

Sehth's annoyed voice brought Yres back from his moody thoughts, and he glanced up from the cooking flames he'd been staring into to find the lieutenant pushing himself to his feet, eyes westward. Instinctively Yres looked around as well, but he was night-blind in the dark, the glow of other flames illuminating little more than dry rock and loose earth for fifty feet in every direction.

Still, that didn't stop him hearing the angry shouts that were building up, coming from the direction Sehth was watching.

Yres frowned in annoyance before he, too, stood up. As distasteful as it was, dealing with disputes among his men was part of his duty as commander. "Let's go," he grumbled, hefting his sheathed sword up from the ground and starting off through the seated and lounging men.

Together the pair of them wound their way through the camp, ignoring the salutes they got and declining with a brief shake of their heads the occasional invitations they were extended to join this group or that one in their eating and drinking. The shouting was getting louder, and by the time they reached the edge of their position, Yres had long identified the culprit responsible for the commotion.

"What do you mean, 'he's not there'?!" the officer in question was seething, berating a pair of men who were standing rigidly before him, looking frustrated. "He bloody well had *best be*, or I'll have him lashed for leaving his post without permission!"

"We checked the whole a' the area," the man on the left drawled, sounding as though he were having trouble keeping his tone in check. "Fa'hir ain't there. We're sure abou' it."

"Oh you're '*sure*', are you?" The officer dragged the word out, mocking the man. "What a *relief* that is. I'll tell you what. Why don't the two of you go back, and this time—!"

Yres took a firm hold of the soldier's shoulder then, cutting him off. At first the man whirled, expression livid, but all the color drained from his cheeks when he saw who it was he had come to face.

"Is there a reason, *officer*," Yres growled, twisting the title pointedly, "that you have seen fit to wake the *entirety of the damn mountain* with your racket?"

The soldier responded by moving his mouth like a fish out of water for a good few seconds before finally finding his words.

"A-apologies, sir!" he exclaimed, his voice suddenly several octaves higher than it had been only moments before. "Several of the men in my unit suffered minor injuries on the climb today. Our medicinal specialist, Fa'hir, was mistakenly put on watch duty. I sent these two—" he indicated the pair of men behind him with a jerk of his head "—to fetch him back and replace him, but they insist Fa'hir isn't at his post."

At the officer's words, Yres felt a stone manifest in his gut.

"He wasn't at his post?" Sehth repeated, looking between the two foot soldiers and sounding as though he didn't like the sound of that any more than Yres did. "You're sure of this?"

"Yessir!" the man who'd been reporting to the watch officer said with a firm nod. "Mahai and I—" he gestured to his partner "—checked twice. He ain't there."

"Where was he dispatched?" Yres asked, perhaps a little more urgently than was prudent.

None of them missed the nervousness of his question either, it seemed, because they all blinked and glanced at each other before the watch officer pointed due west, beyond the light of the campfires to his right.

"I'm sure it's nothing," he tried hesitantly. "Fa'hir has been known to doze off on duty every now and—"

"All of you, with us!" Yres snapped, ignoring the man's assurances and looking around at the closest group of soldiers, gathered about their fire some ten feet away. "You lot! On your feet! You can eat later."

While the surprised unit scrambled up and gathered their blades, Yres had Sehth find them a pair of torches. When their little party was gathered, he and the lieutenant led the group out into the darkness, firelight shimmering about their feet to cast weird shadows across the uneven ground around them.

"Whereabouts was your man supposed to be?" Sehth asked the watch officer over his shoulder.

"Not far," the soldier replied. "Sentries were ordered to take positions at two hundred feet from the camp."

Close, Yres thought. *Too close.*

They kept on about a minute. The distance wasn't far, but the earth shifted beneath their feet and the outcroppings jutted unevenly from the mountain face, forcing them to duck or heave themselves up onto the flatter topsides of the rocks.

"S'about here he was supposed ta' be," the soldier with the drawl said. "Comin' up ahead."

Yres, in response, scoured the ground before them carefully. For a moment, there was nothing, and the briefest hint of relief eased its way into his chest.

Then, though, there was a glint at the limit of the firelight, and the solace vanished as quickly as it came.

As they got nearer, he heard Sehth curse beside him.

"Did you bring torches, when you came to fetch him?" Yres asked quietly, coming to a stop over what it was that had caught the reflection of the flames.

Behind him, there was only silence. Of course, he hadn't expected a response. The answer was evident enough.

Had they brought torches, after all, there was no way the soldiers would have missed distinct drag trails that led out into the night, much less the smeared blood that clung as streaks and human hand-prints across the surface of the rocks.

Had they brought torches, after all, they would have noticed the clear prints made in the dust, clearly distinguished by the scraping lines of clawed feet against the ground.

"Yres, we should get back," Sehth said quietly. "We'll need to double our lookouts at the very least."

Yres nodded, looking over his shoulder toward the group of soldiers who'd followed them dutifully out into the night. He opened his mouth, ready to have them spread the order on their return.

Before he could say a word, however, a sound rose, a guttural, throaty growl, like the hungry warning of a starving animal.

Yres whirled back, torch raised high in one hand, his sword still held in the other. For a moment there was nothing to see, the noise rumbling out of the dark without form or origin. He took a step away from the night, then another.

And then, as though the creatures hiding just beyond the light had caught wind of his fear, a hundred gleaming eyes slipped into view, filling the black like a horizon of yellow, murderous stars.

XX

"BACK!" Yres roared, already turning on his heel. Sehth, like him, was a quick thinker, and the pair of them were several feet ahead of the others before the rest of the group realized what was happening. As their boots pounded the rocky ground, the two of them leaping over and skirting around the shelvings that got in their way, they could hear the growls from the dark multiplying and pitching, soon drowning out the gasps and grunts of the soldiers following behind them at full tilt.

Their pursuers, though, were faster, and Yres heard a *thud* and a scream just as he and Sehth made it back to the light of the camp's fires, bellowing orders as they did.

"TO ARMS! AN ATTACK! THE ATHERIAN ATTACK!"

To their credit, the trained forces of Cyro responded in a flurry of fire and steel.

Even as Yres and Sehth whirled to face the lizard-kind that trailed them, tossing their torches into the dark to draw steel, a dozen of the closest soldiers were joining them, swords already bare. Most of their little group had made it back, but out of the blackness at their backs the screams continued, echoing with the ripping and cracking sounds of rent flesh and breaking bones, and with a grimace Yres realized that the loud-mouthed watch officer was not among their number.

Then he forgot about the dying man, because the dark before them bent inward, like the shadows of the night itself had come alive.

The atherian attacked in a wave, and Yres and Sehth let the soldiers—half of which bore light shields—accept the rush. The lizard-kind were a faster and stronger people than man, but what few weapons they carried aside from their teeth and claws were little more than wood and stone clubs, and there was little armor to speak of among them. They managed to down several of the soldiers in the first collision, but even their tough scales and hide were little match for sharpened blades, and four of the atherian fell with shrill shrieks of agony before many of the others let off, backpedaling on their long legs to assess the situation more closely. By that time, though, more of the army had risen up around Yres and Sehth, and their dozen suddenly bloomed into several score, breaking off into ordered contingents as unit officers began taking control of their troops.

Unfortunately, it seemed the handful of lizard-kind before them hadn't come alone.

Shouts erupted up from the distant left, and Yres whirled in time to see more soldiers rushing downhill for the north end of the camp, answering calls for sudden reinforcements. Not long after, the sounds of battle spread to the east, then to the south, until suddenly the night was asunder with the roars of the beasts, the howled war cries of the men, and the screams of the slaughtered on both sides of the fight.

We're surrounded, Yres realized with a thrill of horrified confusion. *How…?*

He forced himself free of the momentary fear, gripping his sword tighter.

"Sehth, see to the east!" he yelled at his lieutenant. "At the very least we can't have them split us in two!"

Sehth didn't even nod before rushing off, leaving Yres with the task at hand.

"Come and get it, you scaly bastards," he muttered, steeling himself for a moment before rushing back into the fray, shouting orders as he did.

The battle was bloody and endless, the lizard-kind battering them in wave after wave after wave. Minutes passed in a blink, turning into an hour, then two. Neither side suffered many casualties, deadlocked as they were. The atherian were hesitant to press too hard against superior weapons, and Yres' own soldiers too well-trained to be duped into pushing out of the defensive ring they'd formed around the camp. Shield bearers made up the front line, the five hundred archers who had—most fortunately—lugged their bows and quivers up the mountains standing just beyond them. Despite orders not to shoot unless their aim was clear, in the dark and the twisting shadows of the firelight many of the arrows went wide, or struck as minor wounds. By the time the third hour came and went, the quivers were empty, and the bowmen traded their ranged weapons for swords, joining the ranks of soldiers that packed in behind the shields. The fighting was so confined, so deliberate, though, that they held out even long after Yres realized they were likely battling against *vastly* superior numbers. No more than one or two thousand soldiers were involved in the actual defense of their position at any one time, allowing for frequent and necessary reinforcements to keep fresh troops on the front lines—or at least as fresh as they could be after the day's climb. Sehth sent word frequently that the east was holding as well, and Yres was eventually comfortable enough with the rotation of the west-side units to check on the north and south, where everything was much the same.

It convinced him, for a time, that there just might be hope in the fight.

They were at a severe disadvantage. That was true enough. Somehow, for *some* reason, a large part of the scattered tribes of the Crags seemed to have been gathered, going against every story and report he'd ever heard of the lizard-kind's wild communities. In addition, the men of Cyro were pinned down and surrounded, fighting in the dark and heavily outnumbered.

And yet, they were holding out.

It was the atherian's fault, Yres knew. A tactical blunder. They were attacking in the night, which would have made strategic sense for small-scale ambushes and fear tactics, but pressing the soldiers with such massive numbers resulted only in a condensed battle with only a portion of either side involved in the combat at any given time. Even if the atherian had *twice* their number, it made little difference in the moment when the fight itself was watered down to equal sides. Had they been smarter, Yres would have thought they'd have done better to attack late in the day, when his army had been scattered across the mountain side as they'd climbed.

It gave him hope, a glimmer of warmth that drove his sword arm with terrifying strength and raised his voice over the chaos as he dictated the cycling of his troops.

The night crept on, after that, the siege holding out as bodies fell in what seemed to be even numbers on either side. The atherian put their speed and claws to excellent use, but every one of Yres' men had trained for years with the swords they held in their hands, and set them to equal devastation. He tried to keep an estimate of the casualties, sending runners every half-hour to get guesses from Sehth and the other officers in charge of the north and south sides of the fight. By the time midnight came and went, the toll had broken five hundred. A few hours later, and a thousand were dead.

It was becoming a war of attrition, and Yres could feel his flame guttering slightly each time he considered that they would lose such a fight.

Several times he had to pass along orders to pull back, to tighten ranks. Every time they did, they left a ring of corpses—human and atherian alike—to serve as excellent obstacles over which the beasts surrounding them were forced to clamber. Fires nearest the edge of the battle were doused to keep the circle of soldiers from burning themselves on the retreat, and their kindling was added to the flames nearer the center of the besieged camp. Light was still an issue, and as another hour passed, then two, the soldiers started to tire despite the frequent change-outs and reinforcements. Word came that their losses had reached two thousand, two-fifths of their original total, and Yres began to resign himself to the inevitable.

Still, if they were to die, he was damn well going to take down as many of the lizards with him as he could.

Yres fought like a madman, howling defiantly as his sword slashed left and right at every opportunity, only resting when his body told him he was on the absolute verge of collapse. Even then he bellowed encouragements to his cohorts, shouting lies about their eminent victory and promises he suspected he would never have a chance to fulfill, all in a simple attempt to keep their morale up. His fervor could be infectious, he knew from experience, and he witnessed it once again every time his troops cut down another of the enemy, cheering their small triumphs. This kept on, and Yres completely lost track of time, knowing nothing but the fight before him and the blood and sweat of the men around him. Not even when a runner came and told him that half their number were dead did he let up. Not even when his blade snapped in two, the greater portion of it buried into the chest of an oversized female, did he slow down. Not even when a clawed hand caught him across the face, slicing him from ear to chin in a foursome of parallel wounds, did he pause.

All he did was fight. Fight and scream and deal death whenever he had the chance.

Only when he suddenly realized the darkness was fading, when he noticed that the shadows of the night were becoming easier to see through, did Yres finally take a moment to bring himself back from the endless battle.

As he grasped this, as he registered that the masses of atherian before him were suddenly growing more and more distinct, he blinked and whirled, eyes wide with disbelief.

Light. Orange and pink and purple creeping over the peaks not far above them. Morning had come. The Sun was rising.

They had weathered the night.

A sweeping relief that Yres didn't really understand took him then, washing through his beaten and exhausted limbs. Perhaps it was simply that he hadn't wanted to die under the cloak of darkness, with the Moon and Her Stars looking on like silent judges to his execution. Perhaps it was merely the victory of having endured the death and butchery through those long hours, being able to tell himself he had done all he could. Regardless, Yres knew he had no *true* reason to hope anymore, because with the rising Sun came another realization, one much less comforting than the sight of a new day.

All around them, ringing their circle of dwindling survivors like an ocean swallowing a sinking island, the atherian swept across the mountains, some eight or nine thousand heavily outweighing Yres' remaining twenty-five hundred.

Despite himself, all the šef could do was laugh. It was a broken sort of chuckle, a defeated mind's last desperate attempt at seeing the humor in a hopeless situation as amusement-bordering-on-madness took the place of the relief that the morning had brought on. For several seconds, Yres considered turning and barreling into the nearest line of lizard-kind warriors, setting to work the replacement sword he'd pried from the stiff fingers of a fallen comrade. He might fall sooner, but at the very least he would ensure the beasts who witnessed his onslaught would have tales to tell their offspring of the human commander who'd butchered them even as he died.

But then, just as Yres took a firm hold of the blade, gathering himself for his rush into the Moon's embrace, the light strengthened over the mountaintops, casting the scene to the east in further detail.

For a moment the šef wasn't sure exactly what it was he was seeing. It was hazy, and he reached up to wipe blood from his brow in an attempt to clear his vision. This done, he again peered at the distant group, some four or five distinctly atherian silhouettes standing above the rest of the battle atop a low-hanging shelf, watching the massacre unfold. At first it seemed odd, such a small gathering withholding from the fight.

And then the light caught something, glinting off some sort of crystalline object that crested the head of one of the center figures, reflected and scattering across the surface of the stone beneath their clawed feet. Yres' eyes went wide as he realized what he was seeing.

A crown.

A king? Yres thought to himself, taking a subconscious step forward. *Or a queen, more likely*? Did the atherian even understand such concepts? Did they possess royalty, among their broods? Yres didn't think so, and he certainly had never heard so much as a rumor to suggest as much, but he was *sure* the shining thing resting between the spined ears of the shortest figure was a crown of some sort.

And with that conviction, a plan formed in Yres' mind, a single desperate chance at surviving the impossible battle they had on their hands.

Without a second to lose he grabbed several of the nearest officers, shouting orders quickly. The three men looked shocked at his suggestion, but nodded as he finished and dismissed them, sending them off to spread the word. Yres himself began pressing eastward, through the milling soldiers, dodging around the wounded and dying that took up the center of the ever-pressed ring.

It took him no more than a minute or two to find Sehth, who was overseeing his men from the back line. The lieutenant's left arm was in a makeshift sling, and he looked to have suffered a nasty bite to the shoulder, but he was otherwise alive and well. His back to him, he didn't notice Yres until they stood side-by-side.

"Lance formation!" Yres shouted into his ear, wanting to be heard over the fight. "Order a lance formation!"

Sehth blinked in surprise, clearly taken aback. "*What*?!" he demanded, eyeing the ugly wounds that cut across Yres' cheeks like he was worried the man had suffered a brain injury in the blow. "They'll crush us in the flank! Our only hope is—!"

"There's a commander!" the šef shouted back, in too much of a rush to be irritated by the lieutenant's questioning of his orders as he pointed east. "On the cliffs, there!"

Sehth followed Yres' finger, narrowing his eyes to take in the foursome of atherian who stood separated from the battle. After a moment it seemed he, too, made out what the šef had noticed, because his breath hissed inward in surprise.

Then, putting together the pieces of the plan, he bellowed the crucial order at the top of his lungs.

"LANCE FORMATION! PIERCE THROUGH! LANCE FORMATION!"

Never before, in all his long years leading the troops of Cyro, had Yres ever been so proud of his men. Though several faces blanched or looked around in confusion, the vast majority of the survivors instantly leapt to. The men on either side of them began to collapse inward, rapidly forming a massive arrowhead pointing due east. Looking around, Yres saw that the officers he'd spoken to had done a good job of spreading the word as well, because the soldiers to the west, north, and south were all falling in already, suffering the casualties that their breaking position was causing. Yres forced himself to sacrifice the thirty seconds they needed, witnessing a hundred men die even in that brief half-minute.

Then, sucking in a chestful of air, his words boomed over the fight.

"ALL FORWARD, TRIPLE-PACE!"

XXI

"To this day I know not if he came from the earth, the sky, or some middle plane in between the two, appearing out of nothing but fire and blood with death held in both hands..."

— unnamed atherian witness

For the first time in her life, Hana was regretting having heeded Sassyl Gal's advice.

As soon as Uhsula had been able to put into words the visions the gods had given her, Hana had sent scouts over the peaks, seeking the truth in the seer's foretelling. They'd returned within a day's time, reporting that indeed a large force of human soldiers were pressing into the borders of the ranges and had begun to climb, their strength numbering in the thousands. For near a day after that there had been debate among Hana, Sassyl, and the handful of chieftains who'd accompanied their tribes to answer the Queen's call. Hana had been hesitant when the old male had pressed for their warriors to wait in hiding until the soldiers crested the mountaintops, then ambush them in the night. He'd brought up valid points, including the fatigue of the men and their poorer eyesight in the dark, but she'd maintained her reservations. These were trained men-at-arms, hardened fighters and swordsmen. They were not the slavers and mercenaries who occasionally braved the lower reaches of the steeps. In addition, they were sure to bring torches and kindling with them, along with what burnable brush and dry roots could be found among the slopes. Hana suspected Sassyl was overestimating the toll the climb and lack of illumination would have on the humans. She'd wanted to wait and lead the attack down from the western cliffs in the early evening the following day, as the Daystar dipped toward the horizon. She argued that the soldiers would be scattered at the end of their climb—as her scouts had reported witnessing—and that the atherian would have the high ground as they charged, not to mention the light at their backs. In individual combat, she was confident her people had the upper hand, and would lay waste to the strewn soldiers.

Most unfortunately, however, the chieftains—who were all itching for a chance to exact payment for the blood and freedoms they'd lost over the years—had sided with Sassyl. Not wishing to give the impression that she intended to rule as a tyrant, Hana had bowed to their unanimous desires, giving the order for their forces to seek cover to the south, east, and west as the soldiers completed their ascent of the other side of the mountains.

Now, as the Daystar blessed the new day with Its light, Hana knew with every ounce of her being that being called "tyrant" would have been preferable to the carnage she was witnessing before her.

More men than atherian had fallen, at the very least, but all the same the price exacted for those victories was far, *far* greater than any ambush should ever have merited. Corpses, human and lizard-kind alike, lay in an awkward pattern of rings, marking every point where the soldiers had retreated inward in order to solidify their front lines. Flies woke with the fading chill of the night to buzz angrily through the air, and overhead the vultures and smaller scavenging birds were beginning to gather, a few even braving to descend from their constant circling to peck at the dead along the outer edges of the battlefield. Blood and other fluids darkened the sandy earth, forming crawling, narrow streams that cut cruelly down the slope face. Most sickening of all, Hana had to fight not to keep herself from covering her nose in an attempt to block the pungent fetor of death and iron that hung heavily over the scene. On her right, she knew Sassyl was struggling to do the same, his mottled snout wrinkled in distaste, while on his other side and on Hana's left the two males—Ma'zer and Zelys—looked unfortunately well-accustomed to the stench.

"*They near defeat, my Queen.*"

Hana looked around at Sassyl, frowning, the obsidian crown atop her head glittering over the ground. The male had spoken in a soft, sad voice that was nothing like his usual firmness, and it wasn't hard to tell why. His dark gold eyes were fixed on the continuing battle, skimming the bodies of the dead and lingering on the shivering and squirming forms of the injured who were being dragged away from the fight by their able-bodied tribemates.

"*Uhsula would tell you that berating yourself is of little use, Sassyl,*" Hana said, not unkindly. They had sent the seer and her acolytes back to the mouth of the cave once their plan of attack had been established, before making the day-long march west to intercept the soldiers. "*This is but our first battle. We cannot expect victory without sacrifice.*"

Sassyl made a face, something between gratitude and incredulity, but said no more. Hana was grateful for that, because she could not pretend she was not displeased with the outcome of the fight, turning to the battle once more. Indeed, the human army looked to be on its last legs, but she feared—scanning the corpse-riddled ground again as a great sadness settled over her shoulders—that their own losses would be terrible. A thousand, maybe two.

It seemed that being a master of spies did not coincidently make one a military tactician.

All the same, even as she watched, Hana witnessed the shield wall which had accepted her warriors' assault throughout the night finally break. With a swell of empathy and relief she saw the human's lines begin to collapse, the ring that had held so solidly caving at last. Abruptly, soldiers started to fall in the dozens, and in no more than half-a-minute some hundred lay dead, the atherian pressing their advantage with a roar of victory. On either side of her and Sassyl, Ma'zer and Zelys snarled triumphantly. Hana, for her part, began a prayer to the Daystar and the Night-Eye, wishing the souls of the fallen on to better lives.

Then, all at once, she stopped.

Something was off. Something was strange. The soldiers were indeed breaking formation, but their collapse was too structured, too deliberate. They should have been scattering, should have been panicking, as any army often does when it breaks. Instead the men were *shifting*, the survivors forming two massive, closing perpendicular lines that left their rear wide open. The atherian poured in from behind, and more humans fell.

Then, though, from above the dying screams and the sounds of steel sheering through air and flesh, a man's voice thundered out, howling what was obviously a single, all-encompassing command in their strange tongue. With timed *thuds* of some two thousand boots striking ground at the same time, the soldiers began to move, lancing forward as one at an astonishing pace, punching through the lizard-kind like a battering ram.

That was when Hana realized that the point of the formation, as viciously as a spear leveled at the enemy's heart, was directed right at her.

"*MY QUEEN*!" Sassyl howled, turning to take her by the arm. "*RUN*!"

But Hana *couldn't* run. She was frozen, eyes transfixed on the stampeding approach of the soldiers, her mind swallowed by a thousand thoughts. There was fear, of course, but there was also disbelief, shock, and even annoyance. She had been displeased with Sassyl, but it had been *she* who'd wished to witness the battle from so close a position. It had been *she* who'd foolishly placed herself in danger, assuming their superior numbers and advantage would keep her from harm's way.

What held her more firmlystill , though, was the horrifying thoughts of the future she could foresee if she fled.

The possibility was there, obviously, but it was not a choice she could make. She was Queen. She was the matriarch who had only just revealed herself to her people. What would they think, if their ruler turned tail the moment her life was threatened? What would become of the unified tribes who had come at her summons? At best they were like to scatter again, disillusioned of the hope she wished to bring them. At worst, they would start fighting amongst themselves, the chieftains all vying for the obsidian crown she would never be able to hold onto. With wide eyes Hana found what had to be the commander of the approaching men, at the very head of the arrow-like formation in finer leathers than the baser soldiers, one side of his face ruined by claws, his ugly grey gaze fixed upon her.

Did he anticipate this? Hana thought, half-astonished and half-impressed. *Did he plan this*?

Of course he had. As she shook her arms free of both Sassyl's and Zelys' insisting hands, she saw in that man's eyes what had been her greatest fear: the training and conviction these soldiers had had instilled into their very hearts. Despite the toll it took on their numbers, they had responded instantly to their leader's orders. Despite the dead it left in their wake, they rushed at her, seeking the one desperate opportunity they had to survive. They would cut her head from her shoulders and raise it above the fight, hoping to end the battle there. It was likely they would fail, but they had to *try*.

Hana couldn't help herself. Even given where the men hailed from, even given whatever hand they might have had in the stealing away of her people, she respected them.

She respected them utterly.

"*All of you, flee*," Hana said to the other three, taking a step forward, toward the coming blades. "*Go*."

"*My Queen*!" Zelys hissed in furious desperation, reaching for her. "*Don't be so foolish! Please! Get away from here! We will—*!"

He shut up when Hana turned to the young male, instilling every ounce of regality she could into the look she gave him. She said nothing, but did everything to convey to Zelys her conviction. For a second he stared at her, torn between the desire to protect her and the need to follow her order.

Then he let his hands fall, stepping away from her respectfully.

Hana looked from them again, facing the battlefield once more. "*Sassyl*," she said over her shoulder to the spymaster, fighting to keep her voice steady while the soldiers ever closed the gap, her warriors starting to attempt to head them off when they realized what was happening, "*my child comes. You and Uhsula… Guide him. Tell him who he is. Tell him…*" She swallowed the lump in her throat. "*Tell him I would have liked to meet him, at least one last time*."

There was the briefest moment of silence, and Hana knew the old male was struggling with his own anguished need to drag her away.

When he spoke, however, his voice tight, the understanding leaked into the pain of every word.

"*We will, my Queen. And we will tell him of the greatness of his mother*."

And then they were gone, talons scraping against the earthen shelf as the trio turned and ran to safety. Hana, who still watched the coming soldiers, took a shaking breath, forcing herself to stand tall. They were fifty feet away. Many of her warriors were screaming in rage and panic, fighting vainly to break the charge. Forty feet. She saw the human commander shout another order, and the lance split open, pressing out to allow him and a few others to rush forward, sprint up the incline toward her. Thirty feet. The desperation of the atherian gave the illusion that they were multiplying, swelling in number as they piled atop one another in a hopeless attempt to get to her. Twenty feet. Hana allowed herself a brief prayer to the Daystar for a quick death, as well as the well-being of those who'd carried her this far upon their weary shoulders.

Ten feet.

Shas-hana Rhan, Queen of the Under Caves, roared out her pride, lunging forward with claws bared as her war cry pierced the very stone of the mountains, rushing to meet the commander whose sword was drawn back to bring down on her head.

BOOM!

Seemingly out of the sky itself, something plummeted to the earth directly between her and the coming men, a dark form that impacted with a concussive blast that shook the earth and rocked outward in a *whoosh* of white flames. Hana found all her momentum cut short by the shock wave, suspending her in place for the briefest moment before she was blown backwards, screaming in anger and surprise as she tumbled head over heels, landing hard and sliding several feet over the pebble-strewn ground. She saw stars, then, and it was a second before she could shake herself of the ringing in her ears and the swimming of the dusty heavens overhead.

When she managed it, she rolled gingerly onto her stomach with a groan, pressing herself with shaking arms up to one knee before lifting her head to see what it was that had interrupted her final charge.

Her breath choked off in her throat, and a feeling of warmth and awe, unlike *anything* she had ever felt before, ripped across every inch of her scaled skin. Ivory fire engulfed the space between her and the human army, which had come to a stuttered halt. The soldiers, so composed even as death had dragged them down with teeth and claws only seconds before, were now shouting and screaming in what could only have been terror, for which she couldn't blame them.

There, in the center of the flames, seemingly untouched by their flickering tongues, a single atherian towered over the battlefield, his dark form wreathed in white, the details of his being shimmering forebodingly in the heat. He was a massive beast, an easy head taller than any other male Hana had ever met. His size, though, was the *least* imposing of his characteristics. Muscle twisted lithely beneath what black scales weren't covered in leather wraps or steel armor, and a cape of some ivory fabric that didn't quite reach his clawed feet flickered in the shifting air around him. In his left hand he held a straight sword, while in his right he hefted a grand, twin-bladed spear that Hana suspected any other of her people would have needed both arms to wield. The weapons were already reddened and wet, the blood dripping from the steel hissing and popping when it came into contact with the flames. Had she spent more than a moment taking all this in, Hana might have gasped at the bodies scattered before the male, five or six in all, cut down in the half-dozen breaths she'd spent getting her bearings. She might have wondered, confused, at the bloody face of the soldiers' commander, who lay slack in death among within the boundaries of the strange fire.

Hana, though, only had eyes for the wings that extended, brilliant and terrifying in their orange and blood-red expanse, from the atherian's back.

For the first time in the better part of her life, she sensed a weight lift from her shoulders, then. Even as she knelt, shaking in the dry dirt, she felt as though she could have moved the mountain beneath her had the gods demanded it.

Twenty years, she thought to herself, one hand reaching out unbidden toward the male, wanting to touch him from even a dozen feet away. *How you've grown…*

As though hearing her voice inside his head, the atherian half-turned, his sunset-gold eyes meeting hers. She took his face in hungrily, seeing the fierceness in his gaze balanced by a deathly stillness that might have been better suited to a desert viper. She studied him so intently, in fact, that it was a moment before Hana realized he was *talking* to her.

The words, though, were lost between them. She knew she shouldn't have been surprised but, all the same, hearing the human tongue from *his* mouth brought with it its own harsh reality. The first words they'd shared in two decades—the first words he would likely remember *ever* sharing—lost to the sacrifice she'd made so long ago. As the male turned around again, Hana felt a great sadness take hold of her, dragging her down like a weight.

Then, from her side, a gentle voice spoke in rough, unpracticed phrasing.

"*That was brave of you, he says.*"

Hana looked around sharply. Gazing down at her from where they stood at her back, a surreal amalgamation of figures seemed to have materialized out of the dust and chaos of the fight. Two of them were horses, the large, odd beasts the world of man used as pack animals and mounts. There were a pair of atherian females, each Hana's senior and junior by twenty years respectively. They were attired strangely, in cloth shorts and worn pants not unlike those the humans typically wore beneath their leather armor, and the younger of the two had somehow gotten ahold of Hana's obsidian crown, like she'd caught it after it had flown free in the blast. Hana, though, hardly even glanced at the circlet of black stone that was the all-encompassing symbol of her authority.

Her attention, rather, was fixed on the fifth and last of their number.

A woman—a *human* woman—stood between the two females, almost like she was royalty herself, and they her guard of honor. Hana could tell she was not atherian only from her form, though, because every inch of her figure was swathed in fragile fabrics that looked as thin as air, but had been dyed near-black. Her hands were covered in dark leather gloves, and beneath a wide hood her face was hidden behind loosely bound wrappings, concealing all but the faintest details of her features.

Far more shocking, however, was the fact that Hana knew it was *this* woman who had spoken. It was *this* woman—this *human* woman—who had translated her child's words for her.

Even as Hana gaped into the hooded face, the stranger knelt down beside her, and there was something that might have been a smile shadowed against the cloth.

"*That was brave of you, he says,*" the woman repeated. "*Now, though, you leave the rest to him.*"

XXII

"The effect of a distinct variable in any system of chaos—while sometimes difficult to anticipate—should never be undervalued. Stepping outside of the complexities of modern financial systems, let us take war as an example. While a battle can certainly be won with nothing but overwhelming odds, it is not implausible that the same outcome may be had by the actions or presence of a single individual..."

— *A Study of Modern Economies,* by Marret Vern

Raz tore into the surviving soldiers so violently, he might have been some great boulder dislodged from the cliffs above to crush their remaining ranks. Ahna and his gladius formed patterned arches of silver and red and purple as the bloody steel of their blades flashed in the dawn light. Soon more bodies fell to join the five or six he had butchered while they'd been blinded by Syrah's spellwork, and before long ten, then fifteen, then twenty corpses tumbled in awkward piles around him. Ordinarily Raz knew he would have had a harder time, but the once-proud army of Cyro was lightly armored and clearly exhausted. Even more unfortunately for them, many seemed to have lost all will to fight with his arrival, like his presence on the battlefield had crushed the last hope they'd had to live. They screamed as they caught sight of him, yelling out that despicable title he'd met once again after reaching the South.

"Monster! MONSTER!"

He almost pitied the fallen while his weapons shrieked and ripped and smashed through air and leather and flesh.

The burning ruins of the city were still fresh on his mind, though, and so the men tumbled one after the other, given no opportunity to surrender unless they dropped their swords and took to their knees.

It had taken Raz and his companions less time than he'd anticipated to catch up to the soldiers. It had been only a week since he and Syrah—with Karan and Zal'en at their sides—had led their fifteen thousand atherian north from Cyro, chasing after the city's former army. Taking advantage of the lizard-kind's overland speed and general need for fewer hours of sleep than their human counterparts, they'd closed the gap quickly. Even Syrah adapted well to the trek, refreshing herself, Nymara, and Gale with magic when needed, and sleeping in the saddle when spells weren't enough for the too-short nights. Every day their forward scouts informed them that the faint tracks the winds hadn't completely blown away were getting clearer, proving they were making good progress.

They had gained the most ground, though, just where Raz had anticipated: when they reached the foot of the Crags.

At the base of the mountains, it hadn't taken a long study of the old fires and scattered refuse to deduce that the army they were chasing had been delayed for some reason. Half-a-day at least, maybe more. Given that the trail diverged from there—the majority of boot prints leading up into the steeps, while a lesser number turned west toward the Cienbal—Raz could guess what had happened. The šef heading the march hadn't been able to agree on a path around the ranges, and had split their forces.

There had been little debate as to which group to follow, from there, given that the true mission of the outing had been to meet this legendary "Queen" of the Crags of whose existence Zal'en was so insistent.

Even Raz had been impressed at the pace which they set, then, nimbly managing the slopes in long trains that ran like threads through the outcroppings. Many of the atherian among the army had once called these cliffs their home, after all, and they took to the ascent with a fervor that had them leading the forces within minutes. Raz had to have officers call back not a few of the most enthusiastic several times, not wanting to scatter their forces too wide. Syrah's spellwork came in most useful then, too, because Gale and Nymara had to be more careful negotiating the loose earth and shale that sometimes slipped beneath their hooves. Still, they managed, taking the Crags far quicker than if the woman had been forced to handle them on her own.

Two nights later, a scout—who'd waited for the main group after clambering several hours ahead while the others slept—reported seeing campfires in the ranges above.

And now, at long last, they'd finally caught up.

Just in time, too, Raz thought to himself, spearing a soldier through the chest with Ahna before dragging the body back and kicking it free of the dviassegai's blades. Finding himself in a brief reprieve in the course of the fight, he stood straight, looking around.

His own troops had now joined the battle, swelling the eight or nine thousand atherian who had been butchering the already-outnumbered soldiers to more than thrice their original count. The men of Cyro were now being swept away by the sheer tide of lizard-kind, and many were howling in alarm as the claws and teeth and wooden clubs they'd been defending against were suddenly only scattered among the swords and spears and shields many of Raz's ranks favored instead. When they'd come across the battlefield, cresting the mountain peaks as the Sun's first light had made itself known over the eastern cliffs, the fighting had certainly already been going in the lizard-kind's favor, despite obvious losses. Even as he'd taken in the conflict, though, Raz had seen the shift in the arrangement of the soldiers, recognizing the break-charge for what it was. Since the men didn't look to be making for a last-ditch rush down the north side of the mountains, though, he'd quickly followed the angle of lance formation, his gaze finding the foursome of figures observing the battle from far, *far* closer than was prudent.

That was when he saw the crown, the fragile circlet of some black, glassy stone nestled atop of the head of an older female standing at the forefront of the other three.

As a man's voice rang over the raging sounds of bashing bodies and cutting steel, commanding the charge, Raz was already moving, shouting for Syrah's assistance.

Her spell and his blades had arrived not a moment too soon.

A man broke free of the embattled line around him, braving a lone charge at Raz, his defiant cry shrill with fear. Almost lazily he swept the soldier's blow aside with his gladius, bringing the blade up again to sever the man's neck half-in-two. Deciding it was time to rejoin the fray, Raz hefted Ahna and his sword up again, grunting as he leapt back into the melee, twisting and slashing and whirling in a storm of metal and lashing limbs. No orders were called out, no roars of retribution or howls of anger rose from him or his atherian. The only sounds came from the anguished yells and screams of the humans, as well as the confused cheers of the lizard-kind of the mountains. He had no commands for his troops, after all, trusting them to know the rules of this particular fight. These enemies were the soldiers who'd shielded the horrors of Cyro from the rightful wrath of atherian. They were the men who'd allowed the enslavement of their kind. They were the pawns of the Mahsadën, who'd so easily abandoned the entirety of a city to riots and fire. He granted his warriors their cold vengeance without remorse, released them to sate the hunger that he knew made the scars about their wrists and ankles itch in the night.

No quarter was to be offered, this time. No mercy was to be shown. The only ones who were favored with their lives were the spare few smart enough to throw their swords aside of their own volition.

This, after all, was a fight for the will and pride of an entire race.

For not even a half-hour longer the battle raged on. Raz himself allowed the animal to raise its head little-by-little, allowed the Monster some control. Drawing from the rage that still seethed within him—the fury that thundered through his mind each time he pictured those children who'd been herded into the quarter of that bloody plaza as their parents were butchered around them—he ripped through any and all who crossed his path. Minute by minute he gave in to the red and black, allowing the world to become nothing but violence and vengeance. He didn't bother counting how many he slew, didn't bother trying to guess at how many turned and fled before him. All he knew was the thudding of Ahna and the gladius into armor and muscle and bone, the sounds of death echoed in the wails of those his weapons caught in their steely strokes. The incline of the mountains became a wash of crimson wetness that dyed the parched ground like flowing ink. The scavenging birds who'd been gathering above now formed a storming cloud as they realized there would be more than enough meat to go around in the coming days. Bit by bit the brown leather and tanned skin of Cyro's soldiers began to thin against the gleaming scales of the atherian, their number falling away in the hopelessness of their struggle.

And then the final man fell, cut down from a half-dozen directions by thrusting blades and slashing claws, tumbling to the ground with a last exhalation of pain as life leeched out of him into the dirt.

At once the atherian of the Crags began to cheer, growling and snapping their victory at the sky. The numbers of Raz's host, to their credit, were more patient, more disciplined. As they had been taught they cast about, looking for any lingering signs of trouble, of will from the half-a-hundred soldiers who'd survived by surrender. Only when all were satisfied that the battle was well and truly over did they start to turn inward, seeking where Raz stood near the very center of the field, breathing hard, his black scales, silver armor, and white silk cloak splattered and splashed with blood.

Only then did the Dragon of the North heft Ahna up in the air, holding her over his head triumphantly in one hand, and roar their success out over the cliffs with every sliver of energy he had left.

The answering call of his host could have cracked the mountain in two, fifteen thousand unified voices drowning out the disjointed celebration of the atherian tribes so absolutely, many of them ceased their own cheering in shock.

"Urlen!" Raz shouted out once the echoing had faded off into the ranges, looking about for Zal'en's seconds. "Ah'han! To me!"

It took a minute or so for the two older males to reach him, wading their way through the aftermath of the battle as the atherian began picking clean the dead of weapons and armor, dragging away the yielded soldiers, and sifting through the fallen in search of survivors. When they managed it, he gave them a quick once-over. Urlen looked unharmed, and Ah'han had suffered only a shallow cut across the left side of his chest.

"Ensure the safety of the prisoners," he said, nodding down the incline where the men of Cyro were already being sequestered atop a jutting rock outcropping. "I will be speaking to them later. If any of the šef are still among them, bring them to me immediately."

As one the pair nodded, then made south to carry out his orders. Raz, on the other hand, flicked his blades clean and sheathed his gladius as he turned east, carefully managing his way through the carnage. Though he didn't look around, he knew heads following him with every step he took, the wild tribes watching him with mixed expressions of astonishment, awe, and suspicion.

He had no time for them, unfortunately. As it was, Raz was focused on another group.

The foursome of atherian, standing slightly to the side of where Syrah, Zal'en, and Karan waited for him, Nymara and Gale hoofing the shale nervously at their backs.

As he approached, his eyes found the older female in the midst of their number, taking her in. She'd once more donned the stone crown which Raz had briefly glimpsed had been lost as he'd intervened in her fight, and was watching him now with the same stunned expression she'd borne when he'd first spoken to her. As Raz began the short climb up toward them, though, he noticed something else about her, something he couldn't quite place.

Something about her felt… familiar…

Shaking this odd notion aside, Raz turned his attention to the other lizard-kind standing around the crowned female, the ones he'd seen try to pull her out of harm's way before fleeing at what he assumed were her orders. All were male, with two of them noticeably younger—likely around his own age—than the third. This pair Raz only briefly looked over, seeing nothing more of note than the fierce protectiveness in their countenance while they waited tensely on either side of the female. The last, on the other hand, he spent more time on. This old male had seen several times Raz's years and more. There was something sharp about him, too, something in the way he studied Raz with his dark-gold eyes, like he was sizing up everything about him in less time than should have been feasible. The atherian's gaze was not unkind, however, and Raz felt instead that the expression he sported across his mottled, serpentine features was one more of satisfaction, of confirmation of one's hopes, then anything harsher.

Managing the last shifting feet of the incline, Raz stepped up onto the uneven surface of the boulder, setting Ahna over his shoulder and closing the final gap between them as Syrah took a step toward him.

"Raz," she said with an excited smile that betrayed the calmness of her voice, "this is Shas-hana Rhan, Queen of the Under Caves beneath the mountains."

Raz stopped a respectable distance away, suspecting the image he cut was not ideal for such an important first meeting. For a moment he considered getting down on one knee before the female, who indeed exuded a nobility despite the dirtiness of the cloth wrapped around her waist and the continued expression of awe she was taking him in with. Again, Raz was struck by an inkling of familiarity.

However, deciding against implying submissiveness in unfamiliar lands before an unfamiliar people, he decided instead to dip his head and give a brief bow in what he hoped was a universal sign of esteem.

"Tell her I am Raz i'Syul Arro," he said to Syrah, not looking away from Shas-hana Rhan. "Give her my greetings, and convey that we have come seeking her assistance in a matter of great need."

Syrah did so, though Raz understood the language well enough to know that she had embellished his introduction. It took her almost half-a-minute to make the translation, and she even paused once to ask Karan for the word for "dragon" in the atherian tongue, which turned out to have no easy parallel. By the time she was done, the three males were taking him in with even greater interest.

The Queen merely continued to stare.

There were several seconds of silence. Just as things threatened to become awkward, the old male stepped forward with what might have been a polite cough—deliberately nudging Shas-hana Rhan with his elbow as he passed her—and began to speak. Raz caught a good portion of the words, but was still grateful as Syrah converted them into Common.

"He returns your greetings, Dragon of the North," she said. "His name… He says his name is Sassyl Gal, and he is the Queen's 'master of spies.' He says…" Abruptly, Syrah frowned, looking to Karan for confirmation, but the look on the young atherian's face seemed to confirm her surprise. "He says it is good to lay eyes on you again? And to see you have grown into such a fine example of a warrior?"

Raz started, surprised. "He *knows* me?!"

Syrah translated. Something like a sad smile crossed the old male's lips as she stated the question. Before he could answer, though, a clawed hand fell on his shoulder, stopping him.

The Queen seemed to have found her tongue. Her face was calmer, now, even if she still appeared unable to look away from Raz as she began to speak. Her voice, like those of all atherian, was double-toned and harsh in its own way.

And yet, the moment he heard it, something rose up in Raz, welling up like an old memory that was just, *just* out of reach…

What is this? he thought, alarmed and confused as he gaped at the Queen. He was so taken aback by the emotion, in fact, that he almost missed Syrah's translation.

"The Queen apologizes for her rudeness," the woman said breathlessly, like the moment was overwhelming for her. "They—the atherian, I think she means—have been anticipating your arrival for some time."

This managed to shake Raz from his bewilderment, and he frowned around at Syrah. "They knew we were coming?"

A pause as the woman conveyed the question, then the Queen motioned behind her, eastward, while she spoke. This time Syrah had to turn to Karan for help in truth.

"A seer, she says," the young female offered, the yellow scales beneath her jaw bobbing when she spoke. "A 'fortune-weaver'. An old female who wouldn't have weathered the fight well."

Another of the gifted? Raz thought to himself, impressed. It was good to know, somehow, that the Sun and Moon did not only favor humans like the Grandmother and Abir.

He had just opened his mouth, about to ask as to what the seer had told the Queen of their coming, when Shas-hana Rhan spoke again. A short request, requiring no translation for even Raz's unskilled ear, though Syrah obliged anyway.

"The Queen wishes to know if your warriors have their orders?" she said. "If so, she would like to find elsewhere to speak."

"They do," Raz said with a nod, glancing at Zal'en. "Your seconds are seeing to the surviving soldiers. Take command until my return, and—"

Zal'en, surprised all by cutting him short.

What's more, she did so in the atherian tongue, speaking plainly enough for him to understand without help.

"*I will be accompanying you, Arro*," she said slowly, her choice of tongues obviously deliberate. "*Forgive me. I wish to be a part of this discussion.*"

The quick refusal took Raz aback, and then annoyance flared in him instinctively. What business did Zal'en have dismissing his orders in front of the Queen herself, and in a language which all could understand? He knew that meeting the ruler of the atherian was important to the old female, but to allow that desire to undermine his authority before Shas-hana Rhan and her entourage was going a step too far, even for Zal'en. He was about to snap that he didn't recall giving her a choice, when a surprising voice came to her defense.

The spymaster, Sassyl Gal, spoke in quick, guttural tones.

"If you intend to dismiss Zal'en, the spymaster humbly requests that she be allowed to stay," Syrah said, looking dumbfounded. "He wishes her to join us, and…" Again, Syrah had to pause, her expression now perplexed. "And he thinks you will like her to be there, too."

Raz's irritation vanished in an instant, replaced with something between suspicion and curiosity. He glanced between the two aging lizard-kind, wondering briefly why the pair of them might be so insistent.

The request, however, was not one he could dismiss lightly.

"Fine," he said shortly after a moment's contemplation, narrowing his eyes at Zal'en to ensure she knew he was not pleased with the circumstances. "But if I'm not satisfied with your reasonings after this discussion, you and I will have words. Understood?"

In response, Zal'en smiled and nodded. It wasn't a smug smile, as one might expect, but rather one almost to match Sassyl Gal's: sad, and—somehow—knowing.

With her acknowledgement of his crossness clear, Raz grunted, then turned back on Shas-hana Rhan.

What was *this*? he couldn't help but demand of himself yet again, looking into her amber eyes and feeling a sense that *something* in the look she gave him was floating just beyond his grasp, just beyond his understanding.

He decided he had questions that would be answered, one way or the other, before their negotiations were through this day.

"Lead the way," he said, motioning respectfully to the Queen.

■ ■

Despite the seriousness of this fateful gathering, Raz could not help but be grateful to the atherian Queen for her choice of meeting places. She'd led them at once up the incline of the mountains again, heading the several-minute climb of the slope, back into the range's peaks. There, it wasn't long before they found a level space wide enough to accommodate them all, horses included, out of sight of—and downwind from—the carnage of the ended battle below. They all reached the level plateau together, just in time to witness the last sliver of the Sun escape the clutches of the horizon, the vestiges of the sunrise shimmering off into the bottomless blue of a true Southern day. There was a beauty here, however, that lacked in the endless expanse of dunes extending as far as the eye could see far, far below them. The air was cooler, *much* cooler, as high as they were, to the point where the wind had a bite to it that reminded Raz of his first days in the North, seemingly an eternity ago now. It allowed one to experience the wonder of the South in a way that was impossible anywhere else, where standing beneath the open sky meant baking in the cruel heat of the day.

Despite knowing that Shas-hana Rhan and her retainers were waiting for them, Raz let Karan and Zal'en take in the world on their own for a time, he and Syrah doing the same further along the rocky edge.

He was about to turn around, thinking they shouldn't keep the Queen waiting any longer, when Syrah grabbed him gently be the arm.

"Wait," she said quietly, turning him to face her and reaching around his body to grab hold of an lip of his silk cloak. "Come here."

Realizing what she was up to, Raz bent down obediently. Carefully the woman wiped his face with the white fabric, and he almost snorted as it came away red and sticky. For a while she doted over him, her gloved fingers trailing over his cheeks while she worked.

"Done," she said with a low laugh, pulling away again to look him over. "I thought it might be easier to talk if they could actually make out your face."

Raz grinned at her gratefully, then glanced down at the fistful of bloody silk she held. "Think you could do something about that to?"

In response, Syrah passed an open palm over the fabric. There was a flash, and most of the red fell away in flecks of black ash, like she'd burned the blood right out of the weave. She had him turn around again so she could work on the ugly crimson patterns he was sure decorated the rest of the mantle, then gave his lower back a pat and letting her hand linger.

"There," she said, coming around beside him and looking across the narrow plateau at where the Queen and her males waited. "The best I can do for now. Are you ready?"

"I'm not the one who has to translate," Raz snorted under his breath.

Syrah chuckled in response, then gave him an affectionate shove forward.

They approached the foursome, Karan and Zal'en falling in beside them again. Once more Raz stopped a respectful distance from the Queen, and this time his bow was a little lower.

"You have my thanks for hearing us out," he told the female slowly, giving Syrah the time she needed to turn the words. "I have to admit, I was skeptical of your existence. Zal'en was insistent, however." He gestured to the older female, standing at his left.

Once again, it was Sassyl Gal who answered, speaking through Syrah as well.

"He says he's not surprised. Those who believe in the Queen and her Under Caves generally have good reason to do so."

The spymaster's eyes lingered on Zal'en for a second after that, something that Raz didn't miss.

"We are pleased to find her proven correct," he said with a nod, shoving his curiosity onto the pile of other questions. "But even so it was not a guarantee that our first interaction would go smoothly. You'll notice our troops consist only of atherian. That was deliberate."

Sassyl Gal looked surprised at that, but it was actually one of the other males—still flanking the Queen like sentries—who spoke up, his eyes on Syrah.

"'There are more humans in your army?'" Syrah translated exactly before adding privately: "He doesn't sound pleased."

Raz had caught the tone of the lizard-kind's voice, too, and he leveled the young male with a firm stare. "Yes," he said simply. "Around twice as many as there are of the lizard-kind."

If atherian could blanch, Raz was quite sure the male would have done so, then. His partner looked equally shaken, and even Sassyl Gal blinked several times.

Shas-hana Rhan, though, spoke next, and Raz made out enough words to understand that she was addressing her entourage.

"It's to be expected, she's telling them," Syrah said. "He knows far less of us than he does of man. You cannot have thought he would have freed our kind and left the humans to the chains."

The three males looked mollified, and the Queen's next question was obviously directed elsewhere.

At Syrah, this time.

The woman looked taken aback to be addressed directly, but didn't have the opportunity to translate as she exchanged a back and forth with the Queen. It was Karan, standing on the other side of her, who stepped around and clued Raz in, as they were speaking far too fast for him to pick up.

"The Queen has complimented Syrah on her speech," the young female told him quietly. "She says she has never met a human who has mastered a single word, much less the language. Syrah has thanked her for the praise, and given credit to me—" indeed, Raz saw the woman wave behind her toward Karan at that "—and the other atherian who have assisted in her lessons."

Karan paused as the Queen nodded, taking Syrah in carefully, her warm, vertically-slit eyes occasionally shifting back to Raz.

When she spoke again, Syrah started in shock, Karan coughed in surprise, and even Zal'en let out something like a dry, knowing laugh.

"What is it?" Raz asked, missing what had happened.

Karan, though, looked sheepishly between him and Syrah, her jaw opening and closing like she was chewing on her words.

"The Queen has asked what Syrah's relationship is to 'the Dragon.'"

Zal'en spoke flatly, the disapproval in her voice only obligatorily hidden. Raz looked around at her, and this time there *was* a smug sort of smile on the old female lips as she watched Syrah standing still and silent, clearly enjoying the woman's quiet discomfort.

Raz, in turn, growled in anger, turning his attention back on the Queen, who was studying Syrah expectantly.

"*Partner*," he snarled in his best atherian, answering for her. "*Of life. No question like this again.*"

It was the Queen's turn to look surprised, glancing up at him, then back down at Syrah, her scaled brow furrowed as she spoke rapidly. Syrah delayed responding only long enough to flash a smile around at Raz through her wraps. Once more, Karan took up the translation.

"The Queen asks if you speak the tongue of her people. Syrah has told her you are working hard at it, but have not taken it up as quickly as she."

Sassyl Gal cut in then, his question short.

"The spymaster wishes to know why one of us—" Karan indicated herself and Zal'en "—is not acting as your translator. Syrah is saying that you yourself asked that she do so, in the hopes of demonstrating that for every human that would do harm to their people, there are others who would work to help them."

Sassyl looked satisfied with this answer, nodding slowly, but Raz noted the male behind Shas-hana Rhan's left shoulder continue to frown at Syrah, clearly left unimpressed by her words.

"Syrah," he interrupted without looking away from the atherian in question. "Tell them that is a promise *I* make, along with you. Tell them we left our human friends behind only as a courtesy, not for fear of conflict. The vast majority of our soldiers have grown up in each other's company, locked in rooms and cages that distinguished race as rarely as they distinguished age or gender. The Queen and her entourage—" he narrowed his eyes at the male, who braved meeting his gaze "—are welcome to ask the truth of this of any of my lizard-kind. Perhaps *that* will reassure them."

Syrah completed the translation a few seconds after Raz finished speaking. The Queen and Sassyl both nodded in understanding, and the male finally looked away, apparently unable to weather the silent battle of wills any longer. Shas-hana Rhan, who seemed to have sensed the tension between the two of them, glanced briefly from Raz to her sentry. When she looked back again, she spoke with a frown.

"The Queen will not pretend that it will be simple for many of her warriors to take these assurances at your word," Syrah said, "but she promises to do everything in her power to ease the transition."

Raz raised a brow at that. "So she'll lend us her strength? Just like that? She hasn't even heard out our request."

Syrah repeated the question in atherian. At first Raz thought he had imagined the quickly exchanged look which passed between the Queen and her spymaster.

When Sassyl Gal glanced at Zal'en, though, he knew his mind wasn't playing tricks on him.

Then Shas-hana Rhan began to speak again, her voice lower, slower, as though she were having a hard time getting the words out.

Syrah looked perplexed as she spoke for the Queen. "She says they have been aware of your intent for longer than you would believe. She says they know you plan to rid the world of man of the corruption and filth which has blackened it in these last long years. She says…" Syrah paused, very obviously confused now, looking back at Raz again questioningly. "She says it's been your purpose 'since the day you were born'?"

A chill swept down Raz's back at the words, and for a heartbeat he felt that thing—that inexplicable memory just beyond his reach—inch a little bit closer.

"Raz."

Raz blinked, looking around at Zal'en, who was taking him in quietly, almost cautiously. For a moment she said nothing more, studying his face steadily.

"Do you know how you came to be with the Arros?"

The question ripped like lightning through Raz's chest, pulling at the old wounds that scarred his soul. The story of his upbringing was common, by now, even among the former slaves of his army, and the way Zal'en asked made him understand there was more—much more—to her words than simple curiosity.

The thing moved closer, approaching now with more momentum than before.

"What do you mean?" he demanded, his tone angrier than he intended. He wasn't annoyed, per se, but he was guarded. He could feel walls coming up, walls that Syrah and so many others had worked very hard to pull down over the last two years.

"Do you know how you came to be with them?" Zal'en asked again calmly. "How you came to be with the Arros?"

Raz blinked. A murmuring voice caused him to look around, finding that Karan had approached the Queen and her retainers, and was translating quietly. Syrah, meanwhile, had moved closer to him, watching Zal'en even as she slid a hand into his, squeezing it tightly.

Apparently she, too, could sense whatever it was that was approaching.

Raz took strength in her touch, returning the pressure as he turned his attention back to Zal'en.

"They found me," he said slowly. "My father and uncle. Half-dead in the desert by—"

"By the corpses of the two slavers, yes," Zal'en finished for him softly. "Blanketed in sand, barely breathing."

The female spoke so quietly, it took a moment for Raz to register what she had said.

When he did, he felt his knees spasm, and he almost sagged into Syrah, though he never looked away from the old female.

"How…?" he started, but his mouth felt numb, just like the rest of him. "How… How do you…?"

"Know that?" Zal'en tried and failed at a smile, though some of her usual snappiness returned to her voice. "Someone had to keep the birds off of you and the scorpions away. Vultures had already picked the other bodies clean by the time the moving men arrived."

Again the lightning came, and this time Raz *did* drop half-an-inch as he jerked, Syrah taking his arm with her other hand so she could help him stand. His memory was good, but even *he* couldn't recall back further than a few years after the Arros had taken him in. Just the same, he could imagine it, could see in his mind's eye the scene, building it up from the stories his father and uncle had told him when he'd gotten old enough to hear them. Evening, after the Moon and Her Stars had claimed the night. Two men on horseback, scattering the buzzards from their feast. The corpses of the dead. Him, unconscious and half-covered in the wind-blown dust.

It wasn't hard to add a set of shining yellow eyes peering out of the darkness nearby, watching Agais and Jarden Arro toil in the sand, watching the fateful step that broke Raz's fragile wing and woke him up to a world of pain and fear.

"You were there?"

He didn't hear himself voice the question, but he knew he'd done so. Though he never looked away from Zal'en, his mind was far gone, and he didn't even register Syrah flinching in discomfort as he squeezed her hand harder than intended.

The female nodded. "I was. Myself, and two others. Our task was to observe, to witness what would come of the prophecy. We weren't to touch you, even if it meant you might die. All we could do was chase away the birds, and follow you to the caravan to make sure the men who found you didn't throw you back into chains."

"They… They didn't," Raz said, breathlessly. The briefest glimpse of an old memory flicked across his thoughts, the faint image of the warmly-lit interior of a hardtop wagon, crystals and stone and bones hanging from strings and wires from the roof. A face appeared, only for an instant, weathered but smiling, dark hair streaked with silver. "They took me in. The Grandmother… They gave me to the Grandmother, who saw to me…"

Zal'en nodded. "An elder of the family, we thought. She fussed over you like a mother, and they put you in a bed with leather and cloth bindings. That was when we decided you were safe."

"So you *left* him?" Syrah demanded, blatantly doing her best to control a deep-set fury that she was only barely managing to cover up. "You just walked away? *Why*? Why were you following him? And what in *Laor's name* do you mean, 'what would come of the prophecy'? What 'prophecy'?"

Zal'en looked about to answer, opening her mouth hesitantly to speak, but just then Karan finished her translation, and another spoke up, cutting through the conversation.

Raz recognized Sassyl Gal's voice without looking around. He might have been surprised had suspicions and understanding not been falling into place with every word Zal'en had said, answering many of Syrah's questions already. He didn't wait for Karan or the woman to translate the old male's words.

"He's saying Zal'en worked for him, isn't he?" he asked quietly.

At his side, Syrah—who'd tensed at whatever the spymaster's had said—froze completely. He saw her head turn inch-by-inch in the corner of his vision, and he knew her good eye had come to rest on Zal'en again, comprehension dawning on her, just as it had him.

"You were a spy," Syrah said. "For the court of the Queen. You were one of the ones they sent out into the world…"

Again, Zal'en nodded slowly. "We numbered more, in those years. Your Mahsadën hadn't yet taken the reins of the cities. Cyro was a plague, but it was one we were able to avoid more often than not, if we were smart. I think it was half-a-decade after the šef took control of the desert that I was caught, myself and the three other females I was with."

Raz blinked, another understanding coming clear. "You were so certain…" he grumbled, finally looking away from Zal'en to glance around at the Queen. "You *knew* she was real, even without having seen her."

"I did," the old female answered with a heavy sort of sigh, clearly relieved to have some of her secrets falling away. "I would have told you, but I didn't know if you'd have believed me. I would have told you *everything*, if I could have…"

"Everything?" Raz repeated, feeling again the rush of whatever it was that was approaching. "There's more?"

"Much more."

It was Syrah who answered, speaking for Shas-hana Rhan, who'd stepped forward as soon as Karan translated his question. The Queen was silent for a few seconds after that, her golden eyes on his, searching them, delving as though seeking something very specific, something she desired almost to the point of desperation.

When she opened her mouth, though, she spoke in a different way, the tones and projections of her intonations singsong, like she was reciting the rhythmed lines of some foreign poem or passage.

Syrah gasped as she took in what was said, taking her hand from Raz's arm to cover her mouth beneath its wraps. She was obviously unable to speak while she listened, and Karan, too, looked enraptured by the Queen's words.

It was left to Zal'en, therefore, to make Raz understand:

"Of one kind, and yet of another,
wings and wind bear him forth.
From chains comes his second birth,
and never shall he stand for them.
Child of the Daystar, he will speak the language

and be the speaker of his people.
To leave and then return,
bearing a woman of ice and snow on his arm."

After the Queen was done and Zal'en had completed her translation, there was a ringing silence that devoured even the distant shrieking of the breeze against the cliffs below. Raz and Syrah gaped at Shas-hana Rhan together, each registering different things about the prophetic telling.

"'Leave and then return'?" Raz quoted, unable to look away from the female and her obsidian crown. "What do you mean, 'leave and then return'? Where does this telling come from?"

"'A woman of ice and snow,'" Syrah hissed in disbelief in the meanwhile, clearly bewildered. "How… I don't… I don't understand…"

Since Karan still hadn't found her tongue—the young female was ogling the pair of them like they had suddenly turned into shining examples of two of Her Stars—it was left to Zal'en to turn their words for the Queen. In response, Shas-hana Rhan smiled—the saddest, most heartbroken smile Raz had ever seen. She hesitated, then—with an infinite sort of caution—began to move toward Raz and Syrah, lifting her arms as she did. At first Raz thought she was coming to him, and he instinctively took half-a-step back. In the end, however, it wasn't he who the Queen made for.

Rather, it was Syrah the older female approached, clawed hands reaching carefully for her raised hood.

As though understanding the importance of the moment, Syrah allowed the Queen to carefully pull down the black silks, revealing the plain shape of her wrapped head. Slowly, almost fondly, Shas-hana Rhan found the edge of the bindings and began to unwind them, Syrah not even so much as shivering despite the proximity of the atherian's sharp, curved claws.

When the wrappings finally fell—the dark fabric pulled free in the Queen's hand—Shas-hana Rhan stepped away to reveal Syrah's face to the trio of males who'd been standing silently where their sovereign had left them.

Though he didn't understand what they said, Raz could tell the three shared a combination of curses and prayers at the sight of her.

To Raz, there was nothing strange about Syrah's face. She was beautiful, even among humans, he had come to understand, but he doubted this had the slightest impact on Sassyl Gal and the two sentries. He suspected, rather, watching their reactions, that it was other details of Syrah's figure which drew their amazement. The paleness of her skin, almost translucent in the morning Sun. The whiteness of her hair, like strands of bleached bone which made her stand out even within the world of man. The White Witch, she had been called for so long now, by friend and foe alike.

A woman of ice and snow…

The line came to Raz again, striking as firmly as a blow to the chest. Though he hadn't really doubted the authenticity of the rhythmic telling

Zal'en had translated—seers and prophecy were far from alien concepts to him, after all—the realization that the atherian could not, in *any* way, have known of Syrah before her arrival brought with it an iron certainty. While he watched the spymaster and his underlings gape at the woman's one good eye—bright and warm as a newly bloomed rose, the other hidden by the diagonal loop of black cloth that acted as a patch—the rest of the telling rocked through Raz, driving even further the confusion of the remaining lines that had struck him so vividly.

To leave and then return...

He spoke, then, voicing the surge of realization.

"You... know me," he said unsteadily, eyes trailing from Sassyl Gal to the sentries before finally settling on the Queen standing not two feet away, who'd looked around at him as he spoke. "You *know* me..."

Syrah, at his words, shook herself free of whatever epiphanies had seized her own mind, translating in a shaking voice.

In answer, Shas-hana Rhan only smiled. It was different, this time. The sadness still clung there, chiseled into her reptilian features as though she'd borne it for far, far too long for it ever to truly fade away. It was muted, though, buried under something brighter, something more alive. Raz looked into the female's eyes, seeking whatever it was, *needing* to understand it more than he comprehended.

Finally, it came to him.

Hope. What he saw there, rising in the light behind the Queen's eyes, was hope.

"Who am I?"

The question slipped out before Raz could so much as think to hold it back. That thing, that memory or understanding that lingered just at the edge of his consciousness was so close now, so near he thought he could feel its presence brushing against the surface of his mind.

For a time the Queen said nothing, watching him, studying him as Zal'en had, like she wanted to make sure she knew every detail of his face before answering. Eventually she turned, and this time she *did* approach him. From a seemingly distant place Raz watched her, barely registering her steps, barely seeing the shaking of her claws as she slowly, lovingly brought them up. The female paused there for a brief moment, her fingers pulling away slightly like she was afraid to touch him, like she was afraid of what would happen when her skin met the cool black of his own cheeks. After a second, Shas-hana Rhan took in a small, steadying breath, and allowed herself that touch, her scales as gentle as silk against Raz's own.

Then she answered, and it pulled Raz down into himself, down into a deep, warm, bright place he had never even imagined might linger within him. That word, that *single* word, distinctly atherian and yet all-too familiar, called to him from a time he didn't know he could remember.

He heard Syrah sob from beside him, felt her hand still shaking in his as she told him what it meant. He didn't need her to, of course. Those faded fragments of recollection, which had been dancing along just out of reach, had fallen together all at once, slipping into his mind as mere shadows, but present all the same.

He understood, then, what it was that had been so familiar about the Queen now standing before them, looking up at him and cupping his cheeks carefully in both her hands. He understood the warmth that had seemed so peculiar, and yet so well known. The way she'd looked at him, the way she'd taken him in from the moment he erupted into her world in a wave of white flames.

It was the same way Grea Arro had once looked at him, so long ago, in a life long-since burned away…

It was the way only a mother could look upon their child…

XXIII

Raz was told the story of his birth, then. His *true* birth. He listened without interruption, neither releasing Syrah's hand, nor pulling away from the Queen's touch as it lingered about his face. In the silence that might have claimed control of the world itself for all he knew, Raz took in every word, seeing the events pass by as though in a dream across his vision.

His father, his mother told him, had been selected by the Last Queen—his grandmother—some years before Shas-hana took the throne. When the crown had passed to her, the need for their line to continue had grown urgent, and so the pair's coupling had been moved up. It had been brief and loveless, as such matches had often been for the females of their family, and his father had not stayed long after the Queen found herself with child. The male had moved on, as his gender often did within the mountains, and Shas-hana had heard he'd been killed by slavers not long after, choosing to die by their blades rather than live under the weight of their chains.

The news saddened Raz, in a way. He would have liked to meet his birth father, if only to have known his face…

Raz had been a lively infant from the moment after his hatching onward. Strong, quick, and clever beyond his age. None of this, however, was more impressive than the fact that he'd come into the world with *wings*. A winged male. The first in four generations, since the time of Shas-hana's grandfather, Raz's great-grandfather. It had been generally thought, before his arrival, that the line had long died out, that the last of the winged rulers had come and gone, leaving behind a time under "the Daystar"—the atherian's concept of the Sun, Raz came to realize—in which their kind had not bowed in fear to the whips of the cities like Cyro and Dynec. Raz's birth had shaken the court in many ways, the Queen's retainers split on what to make of him. To some, he'd been a sign of hope in the steady darkening of their fate with each passing year. To others, he was nothing more than an omen of impending war and destruction.

Then Uhsula of the Other Worlds, seer to the Queen of the Under Caves, had been granted a vision. She had given a telling before the court in its entirety, the very fortune Raz and Syrah had just heard. As a result, Shas-hana had come to a realization:

War and hope were not necessarily mutually exclusive.

His mother told him, her voice distinctly hoarse as Syrah continued her emotional translation, that she had made a choice in that moment. She had made a decision, one so difficult it had ripped her in two, and one she would both take pride in and endlessly regret for the next two decades of her life.

Bowing to the will of the Daystar and the Night-Eye, the Queen of the atherian had cast her only child from the safety of the Under Caves, banishing him from the borders of her mountains, and seen to it that he was handed to the slavers of the world of man.

A lump formed in Raz's throat when he heard this, a hard stone of pain and regret and—yet—understanding.

He had long since come to terms with the fact that the intent of the gods often made itself known through less than pleasant means.

From there, Raz knew the story, or could piece it together. He'd been taken—undoubtedly greedily, given his wings—from his home, stolen away by the slavers. Court spies—Zal'en among them—had tailed him in the hopes of seeing the prophetic words fulfilled. He'd attacked some of the drivers, very nearly earning himself a hard death at the hands of the Cienbal, abandoned to the wicked heat of the day and the cruel chill of the night.

That was how Agais and Jarden Arro had found him. A child of the Sun—no, the *Daystar*, Raz couldn't help but think—very nearly already within reach of the Moon and Her Stars.

As the Queen finished her story, she pulled her fingers away tentatively, and Raz saw that they were shaking. For a long time he could do nothing about that, could do nothing more than stand and stare at her, his free hand still trembling in Syrah's, his mind reeling with this new reality that had suddenly been thrust upon him.

His mother. His *true* mother…

Raz didn't know how to comprehend it, didn't know how to manage the emotions that were writhing within him. For the first time in a long, long time, the loss of the Arros suddenly felt raw, felt new, like he was only just stumbling free of the carnage and fire which had been all that was left of their caravan that fateful night within the walls of Karth. He saw the images of his parents, Agais and Grea, smiling and laughing over the face of his little sister, Ahna. Raz blinked, looking unsteadily away from the Queen, toward the eastern horizon where he knew the trio of Her Stars he had grown so familiar with would shine once more come nightfall. He ached for them. He ached for his uncle, for his aunts and his cousins. He ached for Lueski and Arrun Koyt, for Talo Brahnt and the friends he and Syrah had made and lost on the Sylgid, nearly half-a-year gone.

And yet now, standing before him, was something returned he had never even thought to hope for…

He was conflicted, Raz realized as he looked back to meet his mother's nervous eyes. He was torn. There, right there, was the being who had birthed him, who had loved him—*clearly* loved him—and cared for him for years he could not recall. And yet, at the same time, there was the being who had cast him out, who had thrown him into the cruelties of the world for what sounded like a mere *chance* at hope. She was the start of his path, a path which led to the warmth of family and the love of the woman standing by his side, but also to the madness and mayhem and bloodshed which had consumed him for so, so many years.

On the one hand, Raz wanted to drop Ahna and wrap his arms around the female, embracing her as he had often embraced Grea Arro, taken from him more than a decade gone, now. He wanted to experience the touch of a parent once again, to feel once more that unconditional affection any true mother has for her child.

On the other, Raz wanted to tear Shas-hana Rhan limb from limb, wanted to do to her what he had done to the man who had *truly* set him on the corpse-strewn road that was the last decade of his life.

By the time he'd been done with Crom Ayzenbas, the ragroot-addled ringleader had looked more like a bloody flower than anything human, petals made of flesh and skin and outwardly snapped ribs.

Raz's hands spasmed at the thought, though whether in horror or desire he couldn't tell, still meeting his mother's golden gaze.

As ever, a cool, calm voice pulled him away from the dangerous edge of the chasm buried deep within his own mind.

"Raz," Syrah said gently, her words reaching him as though from some far-off place, and he felt her hand come up to turn his face to hers. "Come back. Come back, now."

Then it was *her* eye he was staring into. *Her* smile he was lost in, in that darkness. Without her wraps, he took in her porcelain skin and the dance of her fair hair in the mountain wind. She was squinting in the brightness of the day, and wet tracts down her left cheek made him realize that she'd been crying what he hoped were tears of joy. Her pale lips, red only when compared to the coolness of her complexion, were slightly parted, revealing a bare hint of her white teeth.

He thought, in that moment, that if the Moon had ever chosen to take physical form, Her beauty would have paled in comparison to Syrah Brahnt's.

And then he was back, standing beneath the brightness of the early morning, feeling the chill touch of the stone beneath his clawed feet and hearing the whistle of the wind and the distant cawing of the carrion birds echoing across the peaks.

Raz drew a shaky breath, not looking away from Syrah even as her hand fell from his face. He took her in a moment more, allowing the vision of her to ground him, to settle him again into the world, removed from the momentary lapse he'd almost made into an old madness.

Then, squeezing her other hand in silent thanks, he turned once more to the Queen of the Under Caves. He found her looking between the pair of them, from Raz to Syrah and back again, and there was something almost like satisfaction in her tired face. Not quite happiness, but perhaps… content?

He decided that that alone was worth a point in the female's favor.

"*You are… You are 'mother'*," he said with some difficulty, the alternating sharp and deep syllables of the atherian language feeling all-too awkward on his tongue. "*This, understand I do. But time. Time, I will need…*"

Sadness returned to the Queen's smile, then, far come from the heartbroken pain it had borne only minutes ago, but still distinctly present. Her lips quivered, like the expression was a hard one to hold up, and her nod of understanding was unsteady. She'd expected such a response, Raz could tell. It hurt him to see the pain the memories of a child he did not remember being must be causing her, but he suspected just as much that Shas-hana Rhan knew she was fortunate to receive even such a neutral answer.

Had Syrah not been there, the Monster might just have reared its head to the great chagrin of all present.

As though she were thinking something similar, the Queen looked once more around to the woman, her eyes brightening slightly. She held out the black wrapping she'd freed Syrah's head from, and spoke a word of gratitude simple enough for even Raz to understand.

Syrah gave a brief bow of acknowledgement, accepting the silks and responding quietly.

Karan, fortunately, seemed to have finally found her tongue.

"Syrah tells the Queen that you are her balance, as much as she is yours," the young female got out in a hurry, coming to stand by Raz so she could hear the conversation. "She says that for every time she has brought you back from a frightening place, so you have pulled her away from her own terrors."

Raz frowned at that, and had to shake his head briefly to clear it of bad memories before he could keep listening.

"The Queen has told her that she understands, that losing one's self to instinct and emotion is not an uncommon trait among the males of our kind." Karan paused, letting Shas-hana speak for a bit before continuing. "She has asked Syrah how it is she came to be by your side. She asks how it is you came to find your 'woman of ice and snow'?"

Raz bristled, ready to interject again, but Syrah spoke before he could. Her expression was strange, like she was fondly recalling a sad memory.

"Syrah says that your shared tale is not a pleasant one, at least to begin with." Karan looked uneasy, and Raz could tell she knew where the story was going. Syrah shared everything with the female, so this was a tale with which she would already be all-too familiar. "She says that you saved her life, but paid a terrible price for the act. She claims you have saved it time and time again since, and she doubts she will ever come close to repaying you your bravery and kindness."

"She's not the one who's in debt, in this relationship," Raz said gently, loudly enough for her to hear.

He caught the quick smile the woman didn't managed to hide, despite never looking away from the Queen.

Syrah and Shas-hana Rhan spent a while talking after that, Karan or Zal'en occasionally stepping in to help manage a difficult word from one language to the other, though these occurrences were rare. Raz had Karan cease her translation, after a while, as Syrah told his story, then hers, then theirs. The tale did not often bring back fond memories, and when she started to speak of Azbar, of her old Priest-Mentor and the two children whose love had been Raz's light in the darkness of that city, he found his emotions stretched to their limit.

He allowed the rest of the story to be told without his hearing it, turning his eyes skyward and letting his mind wander to the greater gift the climbing Sun had given him that day.

His mother... His *true* mother...

A half-hour passed before Syrah brought her recounting to an end. Raz had drifted away from the conversation, drawn back into his own recollections and contemplations of the last two years, and had to be brought back via a quick poke to his elbow by Zal'en. He blinked as he returned to the present, realizing Karan was translating again.

"Syrah is telling the Queen of the situation in Cyro, and your decision to hunt down the city's former army. She repeats that the greatest portion of our forces were left behind to handle the riots, but that we will need to join with them again before we seek to challenge Miropa."

The Queen's expression shifted at these words, and she glanced between Syrah and Karan, as though unsure she had understood correctly. Zal'en was quickest to pick up on her confusion, answer her questioning look in atherian, and Raz understood enough that she was explaining that Miropa was the largest of the South's fringe cities, seated along the upper border of the desert, several weeks north and west. Shas-hana nodded slowly at this, contemplating this news for several seconds before looking around at Raz directly.

"The Queen says she understands." Syrah took over translating again now that their conversation seemed to have come to an end. "But she is concerned as to how the chieftains of the tribes will respond to this. With Dynec and Cyro gone, they may see little point in rallying to your banner, whether she commands them to or not."

"Dynec is likely done for," Raz acknowledged with a grunt, "but Cyro is hardly so, even if we razed half their standing army here." He finally let go of the woman's hand to indicate the north cliff of the plateau, below which the battlefield waited. "The šef of the city learned their lesson. They abandoned it deliberately, in order to conserve their strength. If we do not finish this fight, Cyro will eventually rise again, weakened at first, maybe, but not for long."

He gave Syrah a moment to catch up to his words before continuing. "The Mahsadën haven't been this vulnerable since their inception, and if we miss this opportunity I very much doubt there will be another chance to bring them down in our lifetime, or even our children's. If we are defeated—even if we merely abandoned the fight—the šef would only be demonstrated as impossible to challenge. We've an army almost fifty thousand strong. If we cannot face them, who can? And where would they gather a force great enough to do so?" Raz met Shas-hana's eyes evenly, careful not to appear imploring, but just as cautious to show that he meant every word of what he said. "Syrah, tell the Queen we have need of her strength, of the warriors of her people. Should they refuse us, we will continue on regardless, but should we fail in that fight—which we are very likely to—it's only a matter of time before the Mahsadën return to their old ways of slavery, or worse. A year, perhaps. Two at most. *Eventually,* they will return. The soldiers will come back to Cyro, and the slavers will take up their trade in these mountains. If the šef are not stopped now, then the chieftains need to be made to understand that they might well enjoy peace, but for only as long as it takes for the society to gather itself and gain ahold of the South once again, likely with an even crueler grip than before…"

It took several seconds for Syrah to finish the translation, and Raz could see the uneasiness building in Shas-hana's face, not to mention the uncomfortable shifting in the body language of the males behind her. When she was done, Syrah stood before the Queen, waiting patiently for a response.

It came in the form of a question.

"They took heavy losses, in the night's battle. She estimates they have eight thousand fighting-fit remaining of their original ten, though it may be less depending on the injured. *If* she can convince them, do you believe it's enough to win this war?"

Raz frowned at that. He had suspected as much, given his own quick estimation of the fight before he'd intervened, but he had to admit he'd hoped for more when they'd set out for the Crags. They'd been forced to leave troops behind in Dynec to keep the peace, and would undoubtedly have to do the same with Cyro. Eight thousand would bolster their ranks, certainly, pushing them back over the fifty-thousand- man mark, but he estimated the Mahsadën were comparably strong at the very least. Between Acrosia and Miropa alone he conservatively guessed there would be between thirty and thirty-five thousand troops. A little less than half of Cyro's nine to ten thousand would reinforce them, along with Karavyl's likely ten thousand and whatever Karth could offer to the mix. Even with fifty thousand, they were likely to be outnumbered, and there wasn't a doubt in Raz's mind that the šef were busy hiring every formed company of *sarydâ*—the desert mercenaries Raz had once mistakenly been considered a member of—they could.

In the end, it would be fifty thousand against the Mahsadën's sixty to seventy or more, odds Raz didn't like in the slightest.

Still… They had some advantages…

Raz's eyes flicked to Syrah briefly, but he otherwise kept the thought private. Aside from the greater physical strength of the atherian that would form nearly half their ranks, there was one trick left the woman was currently pursuing. Even then, though, he didn't think fifty thousand would do it. If the Mahsadën were desperate enough, and opened their coffers wide, they might just be able to gather an army half-again that size.

Even just a little more strength could have an impact…

"We brought no birds to send messages back to the city with us," Raz said to the Queen, slowly enough for Syrah to catch up to his words. "It will take several days for even our fastest runners to return to Cyro, and at least a fortnight after that before my generals will be able to settle things and make their way around the base of the mountains with the remainder of my troops. We likely have nearly three weeks, at the very least. Could you gather more of your warriors in that time? A thousand, two thousand?"

Shas-hana looked thoughtful at the suggestion, turning it over in her mind before glancing at Sassyl Gal and repeating the question. The spymaster, too, contemplated it for a moment. After a few seconds, he did something odd. He sized Raz up for perhaps the tenth time that morning, taking in his size and armor and weapons, then faced the two sentries on his left and did the same. With something like a smirk, he turned his attention back on the Queen, bobbing his head and speaking in what Raz could have sworn was an amused tone.

His suspicion only increased when the Queen, too, seemed to hide a smile even as she looked to him again, speaking slowly.

Syrah's eyebrows rose.

"We may be able to gather many thousands, she says," the woman translated. Then she, too, glanced around at Raz, clearly puzzled. "But she says that depends on you…?"

XXIV

There was something imposing about the gathered mass of the wild tribes of the Crags. In number they constituted barely a third of the massive, writhing ring of bodies that surrounded Raz, but their bloody furs, roughly hewn leathers, and crude weapons gave them a distinctly savage look when compared to the simple shorts and pants and relatively clean-cut armor and blades of his own lizard-kind soldiers. What's more, whereas his army stood silently, grouped mostly at his back—the exception being those hundreds who had already miraculously reunited with friends and family among the Queen's warriors—the tribes were anything but rigid and patient. They formed a patchwork within their groupings, the different clans shouting and cheering and jeering their own unique song. They were distinguishable in their varied garb and attire, and at each of their heads a distinct figure had stepped forward, called out by Shas-hana Rhan not a moment before.

It was these chieftains whose eyes Raz met. Four females and a single male, all dressed in the finest makeshift armor of their people, all armed with the best weapons they'd been able to pilfer from the Cyroan soldiers in the aftermath of the fight. They, in turn, were watching him, the females mostly impassively, but the male with nothing less than disdain etched into his scarred, scaled features.

Internally, Raz sighed, and took a moment to debate his own sanity.

He stood, stripped of his armor and weapons, in the very center of the massive circle formed by the twenty-three thousand gathered lizard-kind. Beneath his clawed feet the earth was loose and sticky with drying blood, the battleground having been cleared of the dead and injured, the captive Cyroans still being watched over somewhere down the northern slopes. Though he didn't look around, he knew that Syrah, Karan, and Zal'en waited with the horses among his soldiers behind him, with the Queen and her retainers not far away.

The Queen… His mother…

"One of questionable parental instincts," Raz snorted to himself, his gaze falling on the male chief, who bared yellowed fangs at him in open defiance.

He hadn't been surprised when Shas-hana Rhan had laid out her plan, though he and Syrah had exchanged a tired look at it. The strong followed the strong. Such was—and would likely always be—the rule of wild men and beings alike. First Gûlraht Baoill and his ilk, then the slaves of the pirate ships of Perce, and now the scattered atherian of the Crags. This time, fortunately, Raz was not fighting for his life, nor even for the right to rule so much as a single tribe among them. He was not of their people, not of the families that made up these groups, who lived and bred and died for generations within the traditions and cultures of each. He would not yet have been allowed Shas-hana's crown even if he'd proven himself a messenger of the Daystar itself, the Queen had told him.

Still, they had a common enemy, these disjointed tribes and his own army. If he proved himself a warrior worthy of leading, then perhaps the chieftains would bend a knee to his suggestions, if not his commands.

And so he had ended up in this situation, stripped down to cloth shorts, unarmed, and blinking away the flies that buzzed incessantly about while they searched for the corpses that had long since been dragged off.

Fortunately, the Queen was the first to speak, her voice ringing out across the cliffs.

Raz didn't understand most of what was said, but gleaned the gist of it all. He made out "slaves", "humans", "cities", and "soldiers". He caught "chains", "future", "children" and "fight". Steadily, one minute winding into two, he struggled to decipher the Queen telling the tribes the story Syrah had passed on to her, under the rise of the morning Sun. He continued to watch the chiefs, all of whom had given their attention to their sovereign while she spoke, though none looked happy to hear her words. On the contrary, most of their faces darkened, several of them turning narrowed eyes back on Raz, clearly not pleased with the tale.

The Queen finished her recounting with a request, one Raz understood only because it was he who had suggested it.

"*Will you help?*" Shas-hana Rhan asked of her people. "*Will you call upon the warriors you left behind, and seek for me the assistance of the tribes who have yet to answer the call?*"

As expected, silence was the only response she got from the chieftains, each of them now watching Raz, not a one among them sizing him up in a friendly manner.

Then the male stepped forward, leveling a soldier's straight sword at Raz, but looking around him at the Queen as he spoke. Again, Raz understood enough to get the basic message in the atherian's demand.

Why help him? Who is he? Why stop humans from killing humans?

These were fair questions, and ones that were not unexpected. The Queen had wanted to try to explain, to try to reason with the chieftains. Raz was the Dragon of the North. He was responsible for the razing of Dynec, the conquering of Cyro, and the saving of her—the Queen's—very life. She had wanted to plead with them for their support, to beseech them and try to get across that whatever peace they thought they had won would be nothing more than a fleeting reprieve to be counted in months rather than generations.

Raz had vetoed the argument.

For one thing, their little party had succeeded in making an ally of the mythical Queen of the Under Caves. It would be their greatest asset in dealing with the tribes should they agree to accompany them, and he couldn't have Shas-hana Rhan—his *mother*, he thought for the thousandth time in the last hour—weaken her position by beseeching the people who were supposed to be under her rule. There would be time to convince them, time to prove to them that darkness still lingered beyond the horizon that only today had started to brighten. There would be opportunity to demonstrate that the tribes needed to fight, needed to seize their future now, throttling that which threatened it with their own clawed hands.

For the moment, though, the first thing they needed to prove was that Raz was *strong.*

Fortunately, the Queen played by his rules, because her answer to the male chieftain's demands was short and abrupt.

"*Test him, and find out for yourself.*"

The responses from the chiefs were predictable. The four females, shrewder and more patient than their counterpart, blinked in slow surprise, assessing Raz in a whole new light now. He couldn't guess what they saw in him, whether they were seeking an opportunity to strike his influence down all at once, or worrying over why the Queen bore such confidence in him.

Fortunately for Raz, the chance to answer the latter question came in the form of the male chief laughing out loud, then lunging forward, sword still drawn, hurtling across the forty feet of open space at Raz with a roar of anger and spite. His carapace armor, stitched from the corpses of scorpions he'd undoubtedly hunted for himself, blazed black in the Sun's light as his tribe howled in support behind him.

Their excitement was short-lived.

Zathlys of the Lower Feet—so named for the seat of his people among the Crags—had lived a hard life, Raz knew. He was strong, fast, and very likely clever. He was not a weak opponent by any means, nor would any of the other chiefs or whatever champions they called forth be. For this reason, Raz dismissed the theatrics that might have impressed a human audience. Drawing out the fight would only put himself at risk, and give the onlookers cause to question his ability. As Zathlys thundered forward, charging with all the weight and fury of an angered lion, Raz let him come, eyes on the tip of the steel sword, the unfamiliar weapon shifting unsteadily in the chief's strong hands.

When the blade was about six inches away, Raz sidestepped, deftly slipping his right hand about the cross of the guard while his inside knee ripped upward and the stiff outer edge of his free palm arced toward the exposed back of the male's head. Hardened bone and thigh muscle took the chief in the gut in the same moment the chopping blow met the base of his skull.

In the fraction of a second required for the observers to think the fight had begun, it was done. Zathlys of the Lower Feet collapsed, doubled-over even in unconsciousness, in a dry puff of sandy dust. Slowly Raz turned to face the tribes again, nimbly flipping the grip of the straight sword he'd plucked from the atherian's grasp into a proper hold.

All at once, the jeering died down. Replacing it, clamored yells of what sounded like confusion and demands to know what had happened rose from the outer edges of the ring, where it must have been harder to see the fight.

Ignoring all of this, Raz's gaze fell on the foursome of female chiefs. Calmly he raised his stolen blade, leveling it at them in invitation.

They proved themselves smarter than their comrade.

Three—Cyrla of the High Peaks, Rhega han-Roth, and Valytha syl'Da—approached him together, baring their own swords and a pair of shields, while the fourth—the oldest of the group, Gyssa of the Upper Caverns—held her ground, instead making a quick gesture over her shoulder. Two males stepped forward at her silent command, tall and lithe, moving to support the advancing trio of females, each armed with matching, heavy clubs. They formed an ordered, concave line five-broad, and closed the distance to Raz quickly and efficiently. It was clear they intended to surround him, or at least press him back toward the living wall of soldiers behind him. Raz was almost relieved at the sight, thinking there might be more discipline to work with in this scattered people than he'd initially guessed. He grinned at the thought, and the smile must have caught his opponents off guard, because Cyrla and Valytha—in the center of the group—blinked in confusion and glanced at each other.

Unfortunately for them, the pair learned quickly that Raz i'Syul Arro had only ever needed the briefest of openings.

Raz ripped forward in the heartbeat the two looked away, the flat of his blade slamming into Valytha's gut, a massive kick crushing into Cyrla's raised shield and sending her flying. The remaining three responded as quickly as they could, turning inward to face him and moving to pinch Raz in from both sides, but too slow. Raz moved left, where the single male had been left without support, the stolen sword flicking once, twice, three times. The hammered steel split the handle of the atherian's club in two, then slammed into the fleshy meat of a thigh to bring the warrior to one knee with a grunt of pain before finally connecting a controlled blow to his temple. Even as the male tumbled, out cold to the ground, Raz was moving, ducking and somersaulting forward, narrowly avoiding the heavy strikes of Rhega and the last male still standing, who'd come up behind him together. He turned as he rolled, finding his feet facing the pair and lancing forward again, taking them by surprise with the reversal. Rather than pursuing him back, as the two had obviously expected, they were abruptly forced into defensive postures when his blade whistled out at them, she with her shield and sword hefted high, he with his club raised to block. Raz twisted the strike at the last moment, pivoting and sliding the blade dexterously behind the chieftain's arm and shield, half-cutting and half-ripping it free of the limb arm. Rhega yelped as her greatest defense was suddenly torn away, but the sound turned into a wheezing gasp after the pommel of Raz's sword took her in the chest, knocking the breath out of her and briefly paralyzing her lungs. Even as she stumbled back, however, the male leapt forward from Raz's right, snarling as he brought his club down with both hands, seeking to land a crushing blow on Raz's shoulder.

With a twist and a flick of one foot, Raz snagged the intact loop of the fallen shield in his talons and sent it sailing into the male's path.

The iron-bound wood took the atherian awkwardly in the ribs, not as directly as Raz had hoped, but with enough force to send him stumbling off course. Taking advantage of the momentary opening, Raz dashed forward, catching hold of the body of male's club with his free hand and driving it upward in the warrior's weak grasp. The stone head caught the atherian beneath the chin, snapping his jaw shut and jerking his head back violently.

The poor male hadn't even let go of the weapon that had knocked him unconscious before he, too, fell to the earth.

The fight, though, wasn't over. Raz heard shuffling behind him, and he turned to find Cyrla, Rhega, and Valytha all advancing on him. He knew none of his blows had been devastating, but he was still surprised to see the trio already on their feet, albeit wincing and wheezing. Again he found himself pleased by their resolve, and he withdrew several steps as they advanced, granting them the respect of taking them seriously despite their bruised flesh and battered egos. They followed him back, chasing his retreat, a hungry, dangerous light dancing in their eyes.

A moment later, Raz realized that said light was much more real than he'd thought.

WHOOSH!

White fire streaked across the ground between Raz and the chieftains, rising and billowing in a flickering wall four or five feet tall. It rippled and swayed, roaring as though displeased with the fight, and on the other side of the flames Raz saw the females yell and leap back, clearly taken by surprise.

"*That's enough.*"

The phrase was clear and loud, and sufficiently simple for Raz to understand. He looked left, in the direction from which the familiar voice had come, and had to disguise a grin.

Syrah, as always, had made herself known at exactly the right time.

The woman entered the ring in dramatic fashion, following the trailing line of fire so that the spell split and warped around her with every step. More flames engulfed her hands and forearms, dancing as she walked, so that she looked like some black jewel in a massive crown of ivory magic. She'd pulled her hood back up, but her face was still uncovered, and Raz made out gasps and hisses of confusion, curiosity, and fear from the warriors of the tribes to the right as they took in her pale features. Across the waving wall, Cyrla, Rhega, and Valytha were watching Syrah with wide eyes, half-mesmerized, half-terrified.

In a single move she had ended the fight, and proven that Raz wasn't the only one whose strength was worth respecting.

Thank the Sun for this woman… Raz thought privately, feeling a swell of pride that was only partially hampered by the sadness the sight of her dark silks always brought.

When she reached the center of the wide ring, standing between Raz and the three females, Syrah let the magics fall away. The flames blinked out of existence in a shower of white dust, almost like snow, scattering and fading across the blood-stained stone and earth until nothing remained of the spell. Raz kept a cautious eye on the chieftains, as well as the gathered warriors some fifty feet west of them, but if any wished he or Syrah additional harm, they seemed smart enough to know this was not the moment to try. They stood in stunned silence, the atherian at the back straining long necks to make out what was going on, and once again the wind and buzzing flies and calls of the nearby vultures could be heard over the quiet.

Taking advantage of the pause, Syrah began to speak.

There were several hisses of shock and awe as the atherian language rolled skillfully off her tongue. Raz couldn't follow what she was saying, but he knew that—at the very least—the tribes were listening to her, listening to this strange, breathtaking *human* woman who had appeared among their number. After a while he made out the crunch of clawed feet across loose shale, and Raz looked around to see Karan and Zal'en approaching him across the emptiness of the ring, the Queen and Sassyl Gal not far behind them.

"What's she saying?" he asked of the two females when they'd reached the spot where he stood behind Syrah while the woman continued to speak.

"She is telling them she understands their anger, and their fear," Zal'en answered first, golden eyes on the woman's back, and there was something almost like respect in her expression. "She says she knows that they have never been given any reason to trust 'her kind'." Zal'en's brow raised, then, and Raz turned to see Syrah raising an arm before her, tugging free the leather glove from her fingers and pulling the silk sleeve away from her wrists.

The old scar was clear against her ivory skin, iron grey with knotted splotches of pink and red.

"She is telling them that they are not alone in their hatred, and that the men that follow you wish only for the same thing as the tribes." Zal'en grimaced, clearly hard-pressed to keep at bay her own emotions as Syrah addressed the atherian. "She says that they want only to live their lives free. Free of chains. Free of fear."

As Raz watched, Syrah swept her bare arm back, indicating the gathered atherian soldiers behind them.

"She has said to ask those of their kind who have already stood by your side," Zal'en continued, "already stood shoulder-to-shoulder with men and women from every corner of the known world. She requests they seek out those who have been so fortunate as to reunite with their clans, to ask them what sort of men follow you, the Dragon who can so easily defeat the greatest warriors the people of the mountains have to offer."

Over Raz's shoulder, he heard Sassyl Gal mutter something that sounded impressed, and he glanced at Karan, who stood closest to the spymaster.

"He says Syrah has a silver tongue," Karan interpreted with an amused smirk. "He wants her to work for him."

Raz snorted. "Tell him he can ask, but not to get his hopes up."

He looked back at Zal'en, who was still translating as the woman continued her address.

"She has promised the tribes they will be surprised by what they hear." The older female was nodding along in a resigned sort of fashion, looking like she wanted to sigh in defeated agreement with the woman. "That there are friendships aplenty between the atherian and the humans within your ranks. So many of them spent years bound to one another in irons, spent countless days toiling under the heat of the Sun and accepting the sting of the whips together. She says it is not possible to keep from growing closer under such conditions, and that the war to rid the world of its chains has only strengthened those bonds."

At this, Syrah looked around briefly, pointing to Karan, who went rigid in clear surprise at being called out.

"Syrah is telling the tribes of their friendship, and how Karan has so often been her wall to lean on in the difficulties of the last months." Zal'en said, almost chuckling now. "She says that without her companionship, she so frequently feels that she would be lost in the darkness of our current ti—"

Zal'en choked on her translation, then, because Syrah's finger had shifted from Karan right to her. She didn't manage to get the words out, but Raz caught enough to figure out that the woman was telling the tribes of how Zal'en was among the generals of the army, that she was as essential to the successes and victories of the last half-year as she or any of the other officers who'd earned a place at the table with Raz.

It was Raz's turn to nod along.

Syrah spoke only for a short time, after that, not even long enough for Zal'en to find her voice again. Raz knew she was asking the tribes for their support, telling them that the promising future of which they were now catching a brief glimpse would only be possible with their help. Alone, neither of their armies had the strength to guarantee a victory.

Together, though, they numbered enough to challenge the Mahsadën at the very heart of the society's shadowed empire.

The pause that followed Syrah's speech was only brief, because Shashana Rhan herself stepped around Raz, then, moving to stand beside the woman. Gently, she rested a clawed hand on Syrah's shoulder, giving her a quick smile when she looked about at the Queen. Then, though, the aging female addressed her people again, requesting of them the same thing she'd done not even five minutes before.

"*Will you help? Will you summon the other tribes, and those you have left behind?*"

The first time she'd asked, only sour glares and bared teeth had answered her. On this occasion, silence hung in reply, lingering like an uncertain spell over the eight thousand atherian. It stretched on, second by second, almost uncomfortably so.

And then Gyssa of the Upper Caverns, the chieftain who'd called out her paired male champions to fight in her stead, took a step toward them.

Raz watched her approach with nervous anticipation, though he was careful to keep his face steady. The female was older, about Zal'en's age, but she walked with the confidence of one who had ruled for a long time, and with good reason. It took almost half-a-minute for her to close the gap between her tribe and their gathered party, passing the trio of other females who still stood, watching her go by, some dozen feet from Syrah and the Queen.

When Gyssa reached the pair of them, she looked Syrah up and down carefully, then let her attention wander over the woman's shoulder to Raz. She held his gaze, and Raz felt himself being analyzed yet again.

Whatever the chieftain saw must have satisfied her, however, because a moment later she eased herself down on both knees, kneeling before the Queen in an obvious sign of submission.

Zal'en interpreted for Raz in voice shaking with pride and sad joy.

"*The tribes of the Upper Caverns pledge themselves to your will, great Queen*," Gyssa said aloud, her words ringing over the quiet of the empty battlefield. "*Yours, and that of your champions.*"

At her words, Cyrla, Rhega, and Valytha, still bearing weapons in hands as they stood behind the older female, exchanged a questioning look.

Then they, too, lowered themselves to their knees.

Not long after, Raz's army was suddenly eight thousand stronger, with runners already being sent out to spread the word of the Dragon who would free the mountains forever from the whips of man.

XXV

"Being taken for a fool is, in-and-of-itself, nothing less than a distinct advantage in any circle. Let them think you the village idiot. People are so much quicker to make mistakes in your presence when they underestimate the function of your faculties… "

— private journal of Vyres Eh'ben, Karthian šef

Adrion felt his heart sink ominously, and his left arm—whose shoulder Lazura's hand had so casually been resting upon—suddenly began to prickle as the woman's grip spasmed and dug into his skin.

"What did you just say?" Lazura hissed down the dais stairs, her voice dangerously low. For once—and despite his own trepidation—Adrion couldn't blame her fury.

The pair standing below them, looking with uncertainty from Lazura to him and back again, had not come bearing good news.

Geal Hareth and Evangalyn Thesus were dirty, sweaty, and clearly exhausted. The Cyroan šef had passed through Miropa's eastern gate not a half-hour before, and Adrion—on Lazura's orders, of course—had summoned them to the marble audience chamber of his home at once. It was concerning enough that they'd reached the city more than a week later than Ysera Ma'het had said to anticipate their arrival.

It was far more alarming that the pair arrived at the head of less than *half* the reinforcements Cyro had promised to deliver.

"Yres Ma'het is missing," Geal Hareth repeated slowly, the accent of the Southern Cities thick across his words. "Likely dead. It was his intention to traverse the Crags, after we reached them, with the expectation of cutting several days off of the journey. Evangalyn and I—" he indicated the old Southern woman at his side, who hadn't even been allowed a chair to sit in "—attempted to dissuade him, but there was no doing so. He led five thousand of our number into the mountains."

"And never came back down…" Lazura finished for the man, and Adrion felt the prickling intensify to the point of pain throughout his arm.

Hareth nodded, eyes narrowed at the Northerner, taking in her paper-thin silks with something between distaste and lust. He and Thesus were the newest to join their gathering, and Adrion hadn't had time to give them the subtle warnings he'd woven into the meetings they'd had with the other šef.

He had a bad feeling as to how this audience would end…

"You sent men into the mountains, I assume?" Adrion asked, hoping to defuse a little of the tension. Hareth blinked, and the man's pale eyes fell to him from beneath bangs of wild red hair, his expression becoming inscrutable. Adrion didn't mind. He was accustomed to being assessed at a glance, given his missing left leg, but he was confident by now that the Citier would have heard enough about his "reputation" to keep a civil tongue with *him*, at the very least.

"We did," the šef answered promptly. "When we found no indication that Yres had marched ahead of us, we deployed a dozen scouts into the ranges. We waited more than five days for word from them."

"*And*?" Lazura demanded in an impatient hiss, earning herself Hareth's attention once again.

"None among them returned," the šef replied simply.

There was a cold sort of quiet after that, broken up only by the faint jingling of Ysera Ma'het's silver and gold bracelets as she fought to control the trembling of her hands from where she waited before a nearby pillar. Adrion might have pitied the one-eyed woman the loss of her brother, but his mind was busy processing the other implications this news carried with it. All around the chamber the others stood gathered in silence, taking in the Cyroan's words with similar trepidation. The scouts were one thing. Sending a dozen men into the atherian homeland had, if anything, been a waste of lives.

But five thousand trained soldiers, under the command of an accomplished officer like Yres Ma'het…

"The lizards are stirring," Ahthys Borne of Acrosia finally said, voicing the concern they had all been mulling over.

As one, a dozen of the others, including Adrion, nodded in agreement.

Not good, Adrion thought to himself. *Not good at all.*

Raz i'Syul Arro, the Monster of Karth, was problem enough for them. Word had come from loyalists in what was left of Dynec that the beast had delegated some three thousand troops in the fallen city as a garrison to keep the peace. If the same could be assumed of Cyro, then Arro's army would drop to not much more than forty thousand, counting the injured they'd left behind after the battles. That was almost *thirty* thousand less than the force this unprecedented cooperation of the šef of the fringe cities was expected to garner, including the *sarydâ* companies they'd contracted to bolster their number. All the same, Adrion had long since known that his cousin was not a creature to be underestimated, and the approaching battle made his stomach twist whenever he considered it. The Mahsadën would come out victorious, he believed, and stronger for it, but a nagging, worried voice whispered at the back of his mind that the war wouldn't be won so easily.

And now the atherian of the Crags seemed to be gathering for some reason, the scattered tribes of the mountains amassing at *least* enough to challenge Yres Ma'het and his army five thousand strong…

Do they sense weakness among the cities? Adrion wondered to himself, looking beyond Hareth as he turned this new threat over in his head. It seemed reasonable enough that the atherian could have eyes on Cyro, at the very least. Despite what many of his counterparts might think—not to mention the vast majority of Southerners as a whole—Adrion knew firsthand the lizard-kind were *not* a thoughtless people. He'd grown up bartering with them throughout the hot summer months, when the tribes would descend to greet the trading caravans who'd circled in and around the Garin, the great desert lake of the Cienbal. He had been raised alongside one of their kind, had seen Raz i'Syul Arro develop from a quick, clever child into a cunning, dangerous man. If the tribes managed to come together, managed to gather in truth…

Abruptly, Adrion wondered if summoning the entirety of Cyro's fighting force had been a wise decision. No one had any idea how many atherian lived among the Crags. It could be ten thousand, or a hundred thousand, or five hundred thousand. If the lizard-kind decided to press south, taking the undefended city while he and the other šef were busy with Arro, the Mahsadën would lose their foothold in the region and their greatest source of income when it came to trading with the Seven Cities.

One problem at a time. Adrion forced himself back to the larger issue at hand. *One problem at a time.*

"So we are five thousand short of our estimate…" he thought aloud, eyes on Geal Hareth and Evangalyn Thesus, still waiting below. "Fortunately, in the grand scheme, that doesn't make for much of a difference. We will still number more than half-again Arro's troops."

"He has his atherian, though," Serys Benth interjected from the right wall of the room where she stood between Ahamed Ehmeth and Kusu Kehsym, two of the three šef who'd arrived from Karavyl a week earlier with their promised ten thousand men. "Our eyes in Dynec say they're well-trained, too, and well-armed. Overwhelming numbers will only do so much against a stronger adversary."

Adrion conceded the woman's point with a shrug. "True, but they number less than a third of the Monster's army, last we heard. The advantage is still largely in our favor, and there are other opportunities we might seize."

"Such as?" Casius Jules, a West Isler and the newest šef to arrive from Karth, asked coolly.

"Our positioning," Ahthys Borne answered, the former general glancing quickly at Adrion for a permitting nod before continuing. "We have been in discussion as to our assault tactic for the last half-month."

"*Our* assault?" Evangalyn Thesus repeated in an angry hiss that belied her age. Once more, Lazura's hand spasmed on his shoulder, and he was forced to clench his fist to keep from screwing his face up in pain. "What is this rubbish? Miropa is the most well-defended of our cities. Forcing Arro to attack us here would be at a great advantage to our—!"

"Not so." Borne cut the women off sternly, frowning at her manner from among the other Acrosian delegates. "On the contrary, we'd be better served falling on our swords here and now than wait for Arro to reach Miropa."

"How so?" Ahamed Ehmeth asked from beside Serys Bern, watching the old general suspiciously. "I too, feel as though we would be casting aside the benefit of the city walls were we to—"

"Food."

It was Adrion who answered this time, seeking to take control of conversation again as Lazura's grip trembled in anger. Without looking around, he knew the woman was still glaring at Hareth and Thesus below them, and he wanted to avoid a firestorm that would leave everyone else—including himself—likely little more than charred bone on blackened marble.

When he was sure he had everyone's attention, he continued.

"Your arrival—along with that of the *sarydâ*—has more than quadrupled the size of my city's standing army. Supplies will last, for the time being, but even a short siege would put a strain on provisions, especially water."

"Then we commandeer food and drink from the masses," Hareth said snidely. "Enact martial law until the Monster's army breaks."

"In short: repeat a similar mistake as that made by the Tashes of Karesh Nan and Karesh Syl," Mysera Morste, another of Acrosia's šef, replied with equal contempt, looking down her nose at the Citier. "Perce fell to revolt. The uprisings practically *handed* the city-states to Arro. We might be able to requisition *some* supplies from the people, but you're a fool if you think they would tolerate much more than that. Most of Miropa is in Arro's corner, in this fight. All it would take is a single driven rebellion that we don't gain control of fast enough, and one of the gates is thrown open for the Monster." Morste sneered at the Cyroan šef. "Perhaps you should reconsider delegating military advice elsewhere, Hareth, given that you somehow managed to lose more than half your troops without even *seeing the fight*."

Adrion knew, then and there, that he had lost the chance to keep the peace.

The comment immediately set off the room, the representative from Cyro snapping back at the Acrosian, the other šef around the chamber shouting out their approvals or condemnations of the jab. Adrion would have sighed in exasperation, but Lazura didn't give him a moment to. It took him only a fraction of a second to recognize the spiking pain that lanced through his shoulder, into his chest, and down his legs.

Fire, white and broiling, boiled out from the floor about his feet and chair. It cascaded down the dais steps like lit oil, pouring across the polished marbled in a rushing wave. Gale Hareth and Evangalyn Thesus—who'd been standing closest to the stairs—yelled in terror, the Citier hauling the elder woman back with him as he lunged away from the chasing fire. Many of the other šef, too—particularly those newly-arrived in the city—did the same, retreating from the magic with looks of fear and shock plastered across their faces. The flames stopped when they'd engulfed a good third of the chamber, and Adrion had to fight with every ounce of his being not to scream in agony as Lazura held onto the spell.

"You bicker like *children*!" the woman snarled at the šef, all of whom had scurried back a dozen feet and were now gathered around each other halfway across the audience hall. "Your 'Monster' comes, closer every day, and you fight like infants who don't want to share a favorite toy! Enough! Our patience runs thin!"

And with that, finally, Lazura released the magic, allowing it to vanish in a *whoosh*, like wind blowing through a narrow hall. Unable to help himself, Adrion sagged ever so slightly as the pain vanished from his limbs. He straightened quickly, but only fast enough to catch the stares several of the šef were giving him. Ahthys Borne, Serys Benth, and a few others. Their eyes, shades of grey and black and green, moved slowly from him to Lazura, then back again.

He did not miss the suspicion that churned within those gazes, and knew the woman's charade to be steadily ripping at the seams.

Somehow, though, feeling Lazura's grip loosen slightly now that she'd abated some of her fury, Adrion got the impression that this was very much intentional…

"We will take the fight to Arro," he said, working hard to keep his voice even and steady, as though nothing out of the ordinary had happened. "Half-march eastward, around the Cienbal, ensuring we do not over-tax our troops. Mounted scouts will ride two days ahead, including into the desert. It would be suicide to press an army of that size through the sands, but I do not pretend to know what Raz i'Syul is thinking or capable of. They will at the very least have to follow Malyn and Thesus' route around the tip of the Crags, given their cavalry and supply carts." He paused briefly to acknowledge the Cyroan šef with a nod. "We will cut them off as they press for the city from there, and deploy a nuisance force to slow the Monster down. This will maintain not only our advantage of numbers, but also ensure the vast majority of our soldiers are better rested. It shouldn't make for a long fight." He found Ahthys Borne in the crowded group. "Is this acceptable?"

He knew it was, of course. It was the very strategy he and the former general had hammered out—along with the input of the others—over too many hours and too many arguments in the last weeks.

All the same, he was utterly unsurprised to see the Acrosian šef hesitate, once again glancing between Adrion and Lazura, standing by his side.

Play along a little longer, Adrion silently pleaded of the man, fearing what would happen if the woman was unmasked before she desired it. *Just a little longer.*

Fortunately, Borne had never seemed like a soldier who didn't enter a battle he wasn't sure he could win.

"It is agreeable," he confirmed with a nod, braving several steps forward to stand within the empty half-ring where the flames had burned only a minute before. "It's the most viable approach, lending itself heavily to our victory." He grinned, then, a light of excitement replacing the suspicion in his eyes as he raised a clenched fist. "We'll catch the lizard on the move, and crush him in his tracks."

Behind the Imperialist, several of the other šef finally found their courage at that, shouting out their support and smiling hungrily. Adrion, for his part, did nothing more than lean back in his stone throne, hoping he looked satisfied with the day's discussion.

In truth, all he could do was wonder what sorts of cards his beast of a cousin still had hidden up his proverbial sleeve…

XXVI

"It amuses me to this day, the fashion by which the varied people of this world chain themselves to their 'gods'. The Twins of the southern lands. The First- and Second-Born of the atherian. Even Laor, the Lifegiver, whom I myself unfortunately spent the premier years of my life fawning over with the mindless fascination of a child. Such memories strive beyond irritation for me, because it is only with age and experience that I have come to understand the truth. There are no 'powers'. There are no gods, no deities. What man and the subsequent races of this modern world have managed should not—nay, cannot*—be attributed to fictitious greater beings. What successes we as a people and individuals alike can claim should be credited to nothing more than our own capabilities.*

It is a pity society is not yet ready for such a revelation..."

anonymous former Priest of Laor, c.400 a.S

Twenty thousand. *That* was a number Raz could work with, and one he had taken in with astonishment and excitement when Sassyl Gal had delivered the final count to him that morning. Now, standing over the gathered tribes with Syrah at his side, Raz saw that the spymaster had not been mistaken. Over the last three weeks, an additional twelve thousand atherian warriors had answered the Queen's newest summons, the steady trickling of their arrival building into a rush of bodies with each passing day. Raz gaped over the host, the writhing wash of varied attires mixing with black scales and colored markings to make the arid surface of the mountains writhe. It wasn't the sheer mass of them that awed him. His own lizard-kind, camped out in the cliffs below several miles to the north already, already consisted of three-quarters their number, after all. Beyond that, almost thirty thousand men and women were waiting at the base of the cliffs for them, already having made the arduous trek around the western bend of the Crags, through the Cienbal dunes.

Rather, what really pressed at him now—so much so that he felt Syrah's arm tighten in his in answer to his trembling—was the fact that these warriors were his people.

His people.

It was an understanding that had come to him slowly, over the majority of the last month.

His people...

"*All is right, child?*" a hoarse, dry voice spoke quietly from Raz's other elbow.

Raz looked left, finding Uhsula of the Other Worlds at his side, her blind gaze cast out over the gathered atherian horde. As had been the case since he'd met the ancient female, Raz couldn't help but see an echo of a long-lost face in her grizzled features. The grey membrane of her ears against dark scales, largely rotted away with age, reminded him of streaked silver through black hair. Her weathered voice, steady despite her years, spoke of another's calm words, even and warm no matter the circumstances.

Where he saw the Grandmother most, however, was the quiet air of wisdom that hung over Uhsula, the clear, tempered sagacity of one who had seen more than their share of life, who had glimpsed the world through the eyes of the Twins themselves.

"*All is right*," Raz answered her carefully, looking out over the twenty thousand warriors once more. He'd spent much of the last three weeks working with Karan, Syrah, and his mother on his atherian. He still had a good amount of trouble with the complicated language, but he rarely needed a translator anymore. "*Impressed, is all. Pleased, as well.*"

Uhsula smiled beside him. "*It has been far too long since our people have had a chance to fight with hope in their hearts. We have been waiting for such an opportunity, even if they did not know it.*"

Raz nodded, looking sidelong at the seer. He and Syrah had met Uhsula not long after the tribes had bent the knee to their cause, after they and Shas-hana Rhan led their host east the day's march to the secret entrance of the Under Caves. Uhsula had been waiting for them, crooked and seated upon a stone beside the hidden tunnel mouth, like a hovering guardian to the realm beneath the mountain. When they'd crested the plateau, the seer had gotten to her feet with the help of a pair of younger females Raz later learned were only examples of her many acolytes, and approached him and Syrah without hesitation. That she was blind had been apparent from the moment they'd caught sight of her but—despite this—Uhsula's opaque eyes traveled between them with an almost frightening serenity, like she could see the two of them as well as any able-bodied being. The power she'd exuded—a sort of corporeal firmness of mind and will—had momentarily struck Raz and Syrah dumb as the female neared them.

Then she'd smiled, reaching out with both hands to cup their cheeks like a doting grandparent, and welcomed them home.

In the weeks that followed, they'd seen more of the seer than any of the other atherian, Shas-hana Rhan and Karan excluded. Sassyl Gal and his sentries came and went as needed, sometimes out into the gathering army, sometimes down into the caves. Zal'en made daily visits to report on the growth of the forces and conditions of the prisoners, as well as make requests for training units and disciplinary troops, all of which Raz formed and provided from the host they'd climbed the mountain with. He and Syrah themselves kept busy with their own daily routines, which generally started with maneuvers and practice, and ended with an afternoon of conversation with Raz's mother, Uhsula, and sometimes whatever new chieftains arrived with the day's reinforcement.

Miraculously, none had ever tried to challenge Raz's title as the Queen's champion. Karan reported rumors of a few initially intending to do so, only to elect otherwise after hearing the stories of how he'd single-handedly defeated Zathlys, Gyssa, and the rest the earlier tribes had initially put forward.

And now, as their time amongst the Crags started to approach a full month, the results of that obedience were bearing fruit.

"*Fight for us, they will?*" Syrah asked of Uhsula from Raz's right, still holding onto his arm with hers. "*We are sure?*"

The seer cracked a smile, her blind gaze not shifting away from the amassed army below.

"*As sure as the First-Born will rise for each new day,*" she answered evenly. "*Too long have the tribes itched to battle for their freedom. Let them loose, and you will see.*"

Syrah said nothing at that, earning a glance from Raz. It was an atypically overcast day for the South, the Sun's light cut into patterns of shadows which shifted across the mountains around them. Despite this, the woman's face was wrapped in her usual dark silks, making it hard to distinguish her expression through the fabric. All the same, Raz could read her body language well enough to see she was worried. He didn't blame her. He had his own reservations about the reliability of the tribes, at least as their ranks were now. They were wild and unruly, and while the chieftains were generally quick bend to his word or his mother's, it had been a different story with Zal'en and the officers he'd integrated into their families in an attempt to start training them in formal combat.

He pressed Syrah's arm against his side, hoping to comfort her. When she looked around at him, he met her good eye through the silks. "Give them time," he told her. "They've had their world turned upside down, in the last weeks. We both know what that's like."

She held his gaze for a few seconds, then took a deep, steadying breath. When she spoke again, looking back out over the army, her expression was more settled.

"Ready?" she asked simply.

Raz nodded, then turned around.

Behind him, some dozen yards away, a small crowd of atherian were gathered, many shifting about, checking packs and provisions and weapons one last time, some discussing amongst themselves. They were a diverse group, consisting of the highest-ranking soldiers of his own army, as well as the now-twelve chieftains and their confidants. In the center of them, Raz saw Shas-hana Rhan and Sassyl Gal standing with Zal'en and Karan, the four of them perusing a rough map of the South Syrah had traced out for them using coal on animal hide, lain out carefully on the flattest raised boulder they'd been able to find.

Making the last preparations for war.

"*You are staying, yes?*" Raz asked of Uhsula sadly, not looking around at the seer.

The female chuckled wheezily. "*Yes. Such a journey is many hundreds of times too long for my old bones to weather.*" She reached out, patting his arm fondly. "*This is the final leg of your journey, child. You have already walked much of the path upon which we set you. I am not needed, in this last challenge.*"

Raz frowned. He would have liked to argue, would have liked to tell the seer she was wrong. He had enjoyed her company these last three weeks, almost as much as he had enjoyed that of his mother's. Having Uhsula in his life had been much like having his Grandmother returned to him in a way Abir—the unstable seer they'd liberated with Karan in Perce—had never managed. He would miss her, to be certain.

But he knew just as certainly that she was right.

"*We will meet again,*" he said to the female, reaching around to squeeze her gnarled fingers. "*I swear it.*"

In response, Uhsula laughed again, nodding sagely as she kept her knowing smile. "*In this life, or the next, yes.*" She looked up at him, then around his chest at Syrah. "*Take care of him, child. See him safely to the end of your shared path.*"

"I will," Syrah answered, apparently so focused on the certainty in those words that she didn't realize she'd slipped into the Common Tongue. Uhsula, however, appeared to get the gist of her response, because her smile broadened ever so slightly.

Then, with a last squeeze of Raz's arm, she motioned for one of the handmaids who'd been standing nearby expectantly, and allowed herself to be led away.

For almost a minute after, Raz and Syrah stood in silence, arm in arm, enjoying a rare moment of peace while the others kept themselves preoccupied with their last-minute preparations.

Finally, though, Syrah reached up and touched Raz's bare shoulder with her free hand, shaking him from that temporary quiet.

"Raz," she said gently. "It's time."

It was Raz's turn to take a steadying breath, at that.

And then, in a thundering voice that shook out in an echoing boom across the ranges, he gave the practiced order in the tongue of the lizard kind.

"*PREPARE TO MARCH!*"

From her place at the edge of the outcroppings where the child she had watched over all his life had left her, Uhsula of the Other Worlds stood witness over the army's departure. For more than an hour she shut herself off from everything but the tremor of the stone beneath her feet and dull roar of more than thirty-five thousand bodies descending the treacherous slopes of the mountains. As they faded, Uhsula imagined she could see the dust billowing up in the wake of her peoples' hopes, following the heels of their Queen, the greatest warrior their kind had ever produced, and the human woman who was his anchor and his strength. Uhsula envisioned the colors of the passing atherian, the markings on their scales and the shades of their tribal attire. She thought of the cloudless blue of the sky and the bright, blinding gaze of the Daystar she could only vaguely remember, harsh even in its warmth. She looked up to where she knew the First-Born hung in the heavens, in the direction of the clearest heat, intending to pray for the long, dull lives of her charges once this war was brought to an end.

The words caught in her throat.

There, in the center of the blackness that had been her world for longer than she cared to dwell on, Uhsula saw light exactly where the Daystar might have hung. It was an odd thing to witness, alien in this, her hours of wakefulness, and yet simultaneously familiar. As she continued to stare, open-mouthed in wondrous confusion, the light spread, expanding in broken lines like lightning slowed to a crawl. She recognized it as not an extension of her own vision, but rather something beyond it. Instinctively she reached up, toward the greatest point of brilliance, and was astounded to take in a hand—*her* hand—raise before her, illuminated within the darkness as though from far away by the still growing rivulets of light.

She hadn't even a moment to take in the slack, worn scales of her own limb, though, before the black shattered.

As the walls of man had fallen in her dream, so did Uhsula's blindness crumble into nothingness before her. Like breaking glass the black spilled from her eyes, exposing the world for all its wonder in a brilliant wash of vibrant color. The reddish stone and earth of the mountains. The expansive, aquamarine depths of the sky. Even the Daystar blazed brilliantly, its shades of white beyond description as it met her astounded gaze with almost benevolent warmth. Strangely, somewhere deep in the back of her incomprehension, Uhsula registered that the vibrancy of the light did not hurt her eyes as it ought to.

This realization was buried deep, however, as a need the old seer did not know she could have borne made itself known with fervor.

Looking away from the sky, Uhsula peered down the slope of the mountain, into the curling cloud of dust that indeed hung thick over the aftermath of the thundering army. Her heart, which had swollen and lifted for the pause of a beat, fell again as her hope was dashed. She felt a pain build in her chest and throat, and something like grief began to press heavy upon her breast.

That was when the wind shifted.

Starting as a thin trickle of air, the current of the day began to stir and change. Whereas in one moment it had been an uneven, unkind thing, abruptly it grew steady and gentle, though stronger with every passing second. Before long it was blowing with a hearty, uplifting force, south and east in a diagonal sweep up the slope of the world, in a pattern none who stood to witness it could ever be able to recall happening before.

Of this, Uhsula took no notice.

All she cared about was the scattering of the dust, the whisking off of the inconsiderate cloud which had threatened to break her heart. She watched with a catching breath as it lifted—like the curtain pulling away from a stage—and it took Uhsula hardly more than a moment to find the forms she'd been seeking.

As though by some decree of the Night-Eye, they had not yet climbed so far down along the slopes as to be lost to the angle and the distance. On the flattop of a boulder, several figures stood overlooking the passing of the atherian, standing atop a jutting stone within a living river. Shas-hana Rhan was the first Uhsula noticed, slightest of the retinue, and yet most regal. At her side, the bent form she could only believe was Sassyl Gal stood as tall as age allowed him, taking in the sight beside his Queen. To their right, a stranger being sat astride a slight, dappled mare, her form swathed in black and her hood pulled up over her head. On Syrah Brahnt, Uhsula's eyes lingered, taking in what impression she could glean of the woman's back.

Then her gaze moved to the last figure, looming over all the rest.

Raz i'Syul Arro sat at ease atop a dark charger, the massive horse shuffling beneath him as the vastness of the atherian's gathered numbers passed around them. He was tall, taller than her imagination had ever allowed Uhsula to truly apprehend, his size only accentuated in the saddle. From his back a length of white silk twisted and kicked in the steady breeze. Sunlight gleamed off the twin blades of the great spear he had only been able to describe to her in the short time they'd had together, and his wings—his *wings*!—shown like blood made flesh on either side of him. For a long minute Uhsula watched the young male, allowing herself to bask in the hope his physical presence—inexplicably now to be witnessed by her own two eyes—bore with it.

"It was my last wish, too. That I might see him just one more time."

Uhsula did not start when the voice spoke to her, warm and kind from her right. It was like she'd known of the speaker's proximity all along, despite having indeed no such awareness before that very moment. Instead, Uhsula merely turned to take in her unknown companion.

A veil of white covered the figure from head to toe, but as the wind pressed the cloth to the frame of its bearer, Uhsula knew the stranger to be that of a human woman. What's more, this newcomer was facing her, and something between intrigue and unease filled Uhsula's thoughts when she took in the ghastly depths of an empty visage under the cloth.

"Worry not. Mine is not a face you need fear, Old One."

There was the voice once more, and again it came void of any harshness or cruelty, of any evil or impurity. It was—for lack of a better description—kindly, considerate and tender, as though the woman beneath the white knew well Uhsula's thoughts. Uhsula considered asking the stranger who she was, but after a moment's pondering thought better of it.

She had lived for too many years to bear patience for questions she already knew the answer to.

Instead, Uhsula considered the figure's first words, and looked back down the slope.

There Arro stood, framed against the rock and far distant sands below, head half-turned to shout either orders or encouragement into the descending troops. She took him in a long few moments more, allowing herself the time she needed to satisfy that desperate need which had consumed her from the moment she'd been given back her sight.

"*Will they make it?*" she asked of the woman at her side, hardly registering the difference in their tongues that seemed to carry no more import. "*Through all of this?*"

In answer, the stranger gave what was almost an exasperated laugh. "Only They know," she said, lifting a hand to gesture upward at the Daystar. "You would not hear me claim otherwise."

Uhsula nodded, not looking away from the child she'd only ever before been allowed to watch from an unfathomable distance. "Will we as well, eventually?"

"We will," the woman said with a nod. "Not even those above can stop the passage of time. There will be a day—not so soon, I hope—where you and I will have the opportunity to embrace them and ask them of their adventures ourselves."

These words did much to settle Uhsula's spirit, and she smiled. As she did, the winds faded, and the dusty gasp of the army's wake shifted back into place, shielding Raz i'Syul Arro from her sight for the final time.

Turning to look at her ghastly companion again, Uhsula held her smile.

"Well, then… Shall we?"

Beneath the veil, the grisly visage twitched in amusement. After a moment, the stranger held out a hand, and Uhsula was unsurprised to find the appendage drawn and desiccated, the fingers that of a corpse left too long in the heat and sun.

Even so, she took it without question, discovering the touch as kindly as the woman's voice had been against her scales.

With a sigh of one finding a long-awaited rest, Uhsula of the Other Worlds closed her eyes, allowing herself to be taken away, leaving her handmaids to cry out and rush forward as her body fell limp in the dust and dirt beneath the gaze of the Daystar.

XXVII

"I do not envy those whose minds have them traveling time in fractured leaps…"

— Carro al'Dor, the Peacekeeper

When Abir Fahaji came tearing into the tent, breathing like a three-day run horse, Akelo was bent with Cyper, Kalin, Odene, Hur, Marsus, and Erom over an updated map of the dunes north of them, which Marsus' scouts had drafted up only that morning. Arnus had been left in command of the garrison in Cyro—much to his disappointment—and for the last three weeks Akelo had been confident in his choice. The situation in the city had improved drastically in the six days they'd spent suppressing the rioters and stabilizing the chaos, but the relative peace had been tenuous at best. Having a former soldier commanding the three-thousand-man battalion they'd delegated had been the wisest option, and he'd suspected the old Imperialist was more likely to keep a level head than younger Cyper, Akelo's second choice if Arnus managed a compelling enough reason not to be left behind. The aging general had, however, clearly seen the wisdom in the selection as much as the others, because he hadn't done more than grumble under his breath as he nodded and accepted the charge.

All that being said, when the moment came for Akelo to realize he'd made one rather large miscalculation in his decision, it came with force. Any of the rest among those Raz had elevated to the position they shared might have served the purpose of overseeing Cyro's troops, after all. Perhaps to a lesser success, but surely with at least minimal effectivity.

On the other hand, they would have had *great* use of the Imperialist's years of experience when it came to dealing with the achievement—and inglorious *mess*—they soon discovered the Dragon of the North had managed in his near-month away from their ranks.

"They come! From the heavens they come!"

As one Akelo and the others looked up from their crude map to peer tiredly around at Abir. The old Percian's white hair ringed his mottled head, and his eyes were wide as he took them all in. He was pointing up, into the canvas ceiling of the tent, which seemed unnaturally still with the desert wind outside was largely dampened by the body of the Crags.

"Wha's got ahold of ya' now, ol' man?" Marsus asked with a resigned sort of sigh. Akelo couldn't fault the Southerner the tinge of impatience coloring the question. He trusted Raz's decision in keeping Abir close. He'd heard more than once the story of the former slave's small-but-crucial role in the stoking of the rebellious flames that had first consumed Karesh Syl, then eventually Perce as a whole. Still, Akelo—like the other men gathered about the table—hadn't been present to witness that portent, to see firsthand this "seer's" ability. As such, he often found his patience wanting when it came to the man's—there was unfortunately no other way to put it—*ravings.* They appeared to have grown particularly frequent since Raz and Syrah's departure, an escalation Akelo suspected had less to do with any will of the Sun and Moon than with the fact that Karan Brightneck had gone along with them. Karan, who'd been Abir's caretaker even when they'd been slaves. With her absence, Akelo rather thought he and the other generals were merely at last seeing with their own eyes the depths of madness into which man could slip.

And slip he did, all too often.

"The heavens!" Abir was crying out in a voice hovering somewhere between terror and exaltation. "The heavens! The wingless follow their prince!"

That caught everyone's attention, though said attention was only offered with a heavy dose of confusion.

"'Prince?'" Ertus could be heard repeating questioningly to Hur, standing beside him. The mute Northerner shrugged his massive shoulders in turn, silently acknowledging his own bafflement.

It had not been this particular phrasing that stoked *Akelo's* interest, on the other hand. Rather, it was the other odd choice of words, which had spilled from Abir's mouth in a much different manner from the rushing blather of his typical babbling.

As opposed to every other time the old man had made his voice heard, on this occassion there was something almost *clear* in his alarm…

"'Wingless?'" Akelo heard himself mutter.

That was when he realized where Abir was pointing. He was not—as Akelo had initially thought—indicating the sky directly above, the "heavens" he had stated about. In fact, Abir was pointing more south than straight up, his gnarled finger lifted to an angle, toward an altogether different place.

As the thrill of understanding shivered up Akelo's arms, he began to make out the shouting outside.

"What in the Sun's name…?" Akelo heard Odene start at the growing sounds of distress, but the older Percian was already moving before he made out any of the others echoing the younger *kuja*'s bewilderment. The plates of his white and gold leathers—well-worn to his shape and movements now—hardly made a sound when he rushed for the pavilion's entrance. Thrusting the heavy flap of the door aside brusquely, Akelo took two long steps out of the tent and into the camp lane outside. All around him the standard noises of the army's rest churned, the distant hammering of the armorers and smiths mixing with the far-off neighing of horses and the nearer calls of drill sergeants putting their charges through their paces.

Ignoring all this, Akelo lifted a hand to shield his eyes from the sudden glare of the Sun above, looking south and up, as Abir had been indicating. It was from the camp below this direction that the shouts were originating, growing louder with every second as more voices picked up the call. They had reason, of course, to chorus out their distress.

There, high, high above them, it appeared for all the world like the bluffs were starting to crumble in slow, tedious motion toward their gathered numbers.

"Landslide?"

Akelo looked around. Cyper was standing beside him, the slanted eyes of his parentage hidden behind both hands lifted to shield his own face. At their backs them the other generals had followed as well, Hur being the last to duck out of the tent, gently guiding along a shaking Abir, who hadn't yet dropped his pointing finger.

"They come!" the old man continued to wheeze, dark eyes wide despite the glare of the day. "They come!"

For Akelo, it was the final confirmation he needed.

"Kalin! Odene!" he barked, getting the attention of the *kuja* pair. "Find Aleem and the other cooks. We need a stock taken of our meat rations. Cyper—" he looked again to the shorter man at his side "—you and Hur see to it that the grounds to the east of camp are cleared. A quarter-mile squared, at least."

Cyper blinked and turned to face Akelo at that, looking a little thrown by this request.

"A *quarter-mile*?" he repeated. "You don't think…?"

"Aye, I do," Akelo answered, hiding a smile and bringing his attention again to the steady churn descending in a dusty crawl down the face of the mountains overhead. "That bloody Dragon of ours is coming back with a good few more mouths to feed."

It was several hours of waiting later, in the sparse patches of shade the arid land and jutting boulders of the Crag's foothills granted, that one of the lookouts they'd posted to watch for outriders gave a shout. Akelo—who'd allowed himself a few moments to shut his eyes in the relative coolness of a patch of shadowed sand he, Marsus, and Erom had managed to snag for themselves—woke abruptly at the call, scrambling to his feet with the other two to come around the edge of the outcropping they'd been lying under. Afternoon had pressed into early evening, and so the slowly dimming light of the Sun to the west was less cruel when they peered upward again. They located first the sentry in her salvaged red and black armor of Karesh Nan, standing atop the low sway of a dune some thirty feet above their heads. She was pointing even higher up, and the three generals followed her signal until they found what they were looking for. There was the mass, much closer now, and among them Akelo could just start to distinguish individual bodies in their shifting ranks, dark and colored scales gleaming in the light along with what looked to be wild, disjointed armors of materials he could only begin to guess at. Far ahead of the larger horde, a single smaller trail of dust was approaching at a much faster pace, and it didn't take long to recognize Nymara's dappled coat against the reddish-brown of the mountains.

"Come on," Akelo said over his shoulder to Marsus and Erom, already starting up the incline of the hill.

Not ten minutes later, Syrah Brahnt guided her mare free of the last inclines of the mountain proper. As they watched her head Nymara at a gallop toward them, Akelo saw Karan seated behind her, her lithe arms looped about the woman's waist. The moment they pulled up short of the three generals the female slid shakily off one side of the panting horse, landing in an unsteady lean against the mount's flank.

"Never again," she could be heard to mutter, reptilian features twisted queasily while Syrah let herself down from the mare's back with infinitely more grace. "Never again. Could have broken our necks a hundred times. Never. Ever. Again."

"Oh, buck up," Syrah told her companion with a laugh. "It wasn't half so awful as the climb, and you know it. Here." She raised a hand gloved in darkly-dyed leather, pressing three fingers to the atherian's chest. If there was a spark of magic, it was lost to the failing light of the Sun, but almost at once Karan stood straighter and breathed easier.

"Thanks," she managed to sigh out in clear relief.

Syrah nodded, then turned her attention to Akelo and the others.

"Well? How was your trek? Was the desert as bad as all that?"

Unable to help himself, Akelo cracked a smile as Marsus and Erom both snorted behind him.

"I think you'd best tell us of *your* journey, before we bore you with the tedious nature of ours," he said with a chuckle. Crossing his arms, he looked up pointedly. "It would appear you managed to procure… ah… reinforcements?"

"If you can call twenty thousand atherian 'reinforcements'," Karan muttered, apparently still feeling a little off as she reached for the mare's reins while the animal wheezed dryly at the sand, looking for grass or drink or both.

Together, the three generals gaped at her.

Marsus was the first to recover.

"Twenty *thousand*?" he repeated, like he hadn't heard correctly. "*Thousand*? Did I hear tha' right?"

"You did." It was Syrah's turn to laugh, but before expounding she looked to Karan. "Can you see Nymara watered and fed? Then go find Abir and get some rest."

"The old man might still be by the general's pavilion," Akelo offered at this, tossing a thumb over his shoulder toward the camp. "That was where we left him, last I saw. He was the one who warned us of your coming."

"I'd be impressed if I had the stomach for it right now." Karan thanked him with a nod, before looking to Syrah again. "Will you be alright on your own?"

"For the moment." Syrah inclined her head at Akelo, Marsus, and Erom. "I don't see these three hassling me anytime soon."

Indeed, out of habit, not one of the trio had moved to embrace the woman despite her long absence. They were all equally pleased to have her back among them, of course.

But each knew that some wounds never truly healed.

Answering with a squeeze of Syrah's shoulder and a silence that said she wasn't keen on opening her mouth again in the immediate future, Karan started to lead Nymara down the slope.

"What she says is true," Syrah began once the female had headed off. "In addition to our original fifteen, the Queen was able to provide us with twenty thousand additional lizard-kind pledged to our cause. Any chance you've already set aside space for them to make camp? It will be a transition enough *without* forcing the tribes to settle in among the human soldiers…"

"Being seen to as we speak," Akelo assured her, not looking down from the horde of atherian still descending steadily down on them. He'd taken to watching them again during Karan and Syrah's exchange. "To the east. Cyper and Hur have been at it for a few hours, and I sent Kalin and Odene to help after they ensured our rations will survive more than a handful of nights."

"You needn't worry too much about provisions, I think." Syrah glanced over her shoulder too, back up at the approaching horde. "Three days, we've been marching, and I don't recall seeing an atherian taking a meal that *wasn't* a fresh kill. Goats and smaller creatures higher up, and even some scorpions and sandcats in the last day. They're quite capable of feeding themselves."

"All the same, it will be wise to ensure our stocks are secure, in case the desert cannot provide." Akelo paused, registering something Syrah had mentioned a moment before. "The Queen, did you say? So she *does* exist?"

"She does, and you'll all have ample opportunity to meet her."

Behind Akelo, Erom coughed in surprise.

"She came with you?" the borderer asked, clearly taken aback by this.

"Her, and her spymaster," Syrah answered with a shrug, as though this wasn't *incredible* news. "She has her reasons, the least of which being that I don't think we'd have a prayer of keeping the varied tribes organized without her presence."

"Implying she has greater cause to join us…?" Akelo pressed her, more than a little curious.

At this, he was *sure* Syrah smiled at him—almost wickedly—through her wraps.

"*Much* greater cause," she told him mysteriously. "I'll fill you all in on everything once the others have gathered, but for now—" she looked around Akelo at Marsus "—*please* tell me I've had letters, in my absence?"

Night had fallen before the clambering horde made the foothills, at which point Syrah had explained once, twice, and then three times over the astonishing circumstances that had led to her and Raz's success in rousing the atherian to their flag. Akelo, for his part, was having trouble getting his head around it all, and kept finding himself thinking again and again that he would have to reconsider his esteem of Abir, or any other "seer" he ever had the fortune of coming across in whatever years were left to him. It all still hadn't quite settled in by the time Cyper, Hur, Kalin, and Odene rejoined them, nor when Raz himself finally arrived, leading Gale by the reins, accompanied by Zal'en and another four atherian Akelo had never seen.

It wasn't difficult to pick out which of the group was Shas-hana Rhan, as Syrah had informed them all the Queen was named. She was the slightest of them, and crowned with a delicate circlet carved from what looked like some slick black stone that gleamed in the gathered torches Akelo had had staked out in a wide ring as the light of the day failed. She stood proudly, her clawed hands clasped before her, and despite the fact he rose an inch or two taller than the female, Akelo sensed at once that this was not a character to be taken lightly.

This sensation was only accentuated by the looming presence of the three males close at Shas-hana Rhan's back.

Two were what Akelo would have thought of as "typical" specimens of their gender. Tall and hulking, they stood a pace back from their sovereign, steel longswords—obviously salvaged from the defeated Cyroan soldiers Syrah had explained they'd dealt with—held tight at their sides. The third, on the other hand, was an oddity, brought down to nearer Shas-hana's height only by the twisting of age, his webbed ears and neck crest faded to grey by the passing of long years. Of the three males, he stood closest to the Queen, hardly inches behind her right shoulder. His still-bright eyes moved with the speed of a snake to take in Akelo, an unmasked Syrah, and their gathered generals, then on to the handful of soldiers on either side of them, men and women Hur had personally picked for their disciplined air.

It would seem Sassyl Gal, spymaster of "the Under Caves", was not a character to let much slip his awareness.

There was a *crunch* of footsteps, and Akelo's attention shifted back to the center of the group. Whereas the majority had come to a slow halt—the shadow of the army sweeping some distance beyond where the atherian had stopped—Raz had continued his approach, Gale shuffling dutifully along to leave the others momentarily behind. The Dragon was grinning from ear to ear, and had Ahna thrown over one shoulder in his typical fashion.

The familiar pose eased some of Akelo's nerves.

"Akelo!" Raz rumbled in warm greeting when they were in arm's reach of each other, embracing the old Percian with the hand that held the horse's reins. "I'm surprised the others didn't have the sense to leave you as food for the sandcats while they had the chance."

"Marsus tried," Akelo got out with a smile as they broke apart, looking the atherian up and down. "Cyper saw fit to stop him. I think he was afraid to find out what would happen if *he* was the one left in charge."

Raz laughed at that, dropping Gale's reins to briefly greet the other generals. "Well we can't be surprised, with rogues like this tagging along." He clasped forearms with Cyper himself, then Hur, before moving on to the rest in similar fashion. "I suppose I should thank the Sun you lot didn't lose half our forces to the dunes, and consider myself lucky."

"I don't know about you, but *I* didn't bother counting while Karan and I were making the descent," Syrah teased him when the atherian reached her last, looping her arm into his with familiar ease. "Perhaps they did?"

Akelo snorted, taking the opportunity to bring the discussion around to the circumstances of the pair's return. "Even if we had, I doubt it would be such a heartbreaking loss, assuming what Syrah has told us is true?" He looked beyond the pair, into the darkness past the torches from where he could practically *feel* the eyes of the wild tribes he knew swept the foothills. "Twenty *thousand*, Raz?"

Raz's reptilian feature grew serious, and he nodded. Catching the eye of one of the closest sentries, he motioned the man over with the arm Syrah was holding onto, then indicated Gale with a dip of his head.

"Be a good man and see to my horse, will you?" he asked of the soldier, who saluted him in tight confirmation before taking up Gale's leathers to lead the stallion for the brightness of the camp proper, not far north of them. This done, Raz looked to the generals again.

"All of you. Follow us." He turned with Syrah as though to make back toward the atherian waiting for them on the other side of the ring of light. Before taking a step, however, Raz paused and looked around again. "And hands away from blades, if you please."

There was a light *clink* of shifting metal, and Akelo heard Erom muttering in an unsatisfied sort of way behind him.

Together the eight of them followed Raz and Syrah without a word, closing the distance to the line of the lizard-kind quickly. When they were what must have been a respectable pacing away, they stopped, and Syrah detached herself from Raz to approach Shas-hana Rhan directly. Akelo had never before been in the presence of royalty—unless one counted Ekene Okonso, Tash of Karesh Syl, who any of their number would have keenly *refused* to do—so he studied the woman's manner attentively when she bowed briefly to the Queen, exchanging some quick words in the atherian tongue and waving a hand back at them. He might have misinterpreted it, but Akelo thought the female took them in with interest, apparently asking a few questions of Syrah before she was satisfied, and nodded. With something like relief in her smile, the woman glanced around and motioned them all closer. Raz, for his part, stood to one side, allowing Syrah to handle the introductions as he looked on.

"No need to prostrate yourselves, but I would recommend a bow, at least," the woman told them, clearly confident in the fact that the atherian she was half-turned away from couldn't understand the Common Tongue. "We have to start somewhere with relations, and demonstrating some reverence to the Queen will be a good step in the right direction."

Akelo, for one, didn't hesitate. Bringing his hands to his sides, he offered as formal a bend of the hips as his aging joints would allow to Shas-hana Rhan. He heard Erom muttering once more as he stood up again but—judging by Syrah's beam of approval—the others must have followed suit at his back in spite of any initial reservations. The Queen, too, appeared to be put a little at ease by the display of respect, because she returned the gesture as a graceful dip of her head that Akelo feared would see the black circlet tumbling from between her dark-red ears. The crown stayed put, though, and Shas-hana spoke again, golden eyes not leaving them despite clearly addressing Syrah. The woman answered in turn, and Akelo made out the approximations of their names in the guttural language of the lizard-kind. Syrah was introducing them individually, he realized, noting her indicating each of their number one after the other as she spoke.

A bead of nervous sweat trailed by his ear even as he heard his own name shared last.

More words passed between the two, and still the Queen's eyes never left their gathered faces.

"She wishes to know your stories," Syrah translated, and Akelo saw her one good eye flick to Raz for a moment. "She understands you are her child's seconds, but she admits to having trouble understanding how men of the cities could come to follow an atherian…"

Her child. The thought still rocked Akelo, and he too glanced at Raz, who was still watching with no indication of interrupting.

Questions for another time, Akelo decided.

"We are not all men of the Southern cities, my… my Queen?" He looked to Syrah for affirmation that this was the best moniker, but the woman was already turning his words, so he kept on. "Some of our number are people of the desert and its surrounding lands, but more of us were dragged from homes far further away. The same can be said of the others who make up our forces."

Syrah finished her rendition, and only glanced at him with a smile that told him to keep going.

Steeling himself, Akelo did exactly that.

In his own words—or Syrah's, depending on how one looked at it—he shared how it was he and the six men at his back had come to stand by Raz i'Syul Arro's side. He told Shas-hana Rhan of the pirates of the Percian coast, of the fight for the *Sylgid*, and Raz's freeing of him and dozens of others from the belly of the *Moalas*, the ship to which many of them had been enslaved for more years than they'd bothered counting. He told her of their victory, and of the decision he and the other former slaves had been made to make after the *Moalas* had been captured and the *Red Turor*—the second of the coastal vessels—was driven off. Raz and the *Sylgid's* captain—Garht Argoan—had offered them three opportunities: be free, sail the seas, or seek a greater purpose with sword in hand.

For those who would eventually become Raz's generals, it had been a straightforward decision.

Akelo was somewhat relieved, when he was done, that neither Syrah nor the Queen appeared intent on pressing him for the longer story of the razing of Perce. Either Shas-hana had heard the tale before, or it was of little relevance to the matter at hand.

Instead, the Queen asked a single question.

"And you took part in the fall of Cyro? Of Dynec?"

Involuntarily, Akelo felt his jaw clench. He had not borne witness to the fresh madness of Cyro's devastation following its desertion by the šef as Raz and Cyper had, but he'd seen the aftermath, dealt with the repercussions. A foul taste boiled up in his mouth thinking about it, recalling the cartfuls of dead they'd been forced to bury in the desert, ears ringing with the screams of children as the corpses of parents and siblings were carried away to be swallowed by the sands.

Rigidly, hoping the Queen wouldn't derive the wrong meaning from the anger he knew was plastered across his worn features, Akelo nodded.

At this, Shas-hana Rhan smiled.

The fact that he recognized the expression for what it was told Akelo then that he had indeed come to understand the atherian to a respectable extent in the last months spent in their company. He had no trouble distinguishing the subtleties of the Queen's face, no trouble noting a lack of pleasure in her smile, but ample satisfaction. He understood, too, exactly what such emotions meant. Even before they'd come for him and his own *kuja* tribe, Akelo had heard tell of the reach of the Tashes, of the men sent into the plains to claim what slaves they could return to the cities. He had feared them for it, had feared them till the very moment they'd descended on him and his family to bind their wrists and ankles in chains. It had been so long, now, that he could not fathom the sort of relief he might have known if the city-states of Perce had fallen before he or his kin were taken, but he assumed it would have been of the greatest kind.

It was likely he would have smiled in the same way Shas-hana Rhan, Queen of a people whom Cyro and Dynec in particular had preyed on for time immemorial, was smiling now.

Abruptly, something like jealousy itched at Akelo, and he had to shove the unwanted envy aside. Much of his life's story had already been written. All he had left to do was see that the rest of it make up for those long years lost to the irons.

As Akelo watched, Shas-hana turned to Raz, standing some few feet to her side opposite Syrah. She spoke briefly, not losing her smile, and Raz's returning grin was ferocious. He responded in rough, tripping syllables anyone with a modicum of familiarity with the language could tell was butchered atherian. Akelo looked to Syrah for assistance, but the woman was preoccupied with listening.

"The Queen was complimenting Raz on the companions he seems to have surrounded himself with. He answered that he hopes she will take heart in the example he trusts you will pose over the coming weeks. He is telling her not *all* men are corrupted by the taint of greed and cruelty."

Unbeknownst to Akelo, Zal'en had made her way over to their side of the line at some point during his retelling of the capture of the *Moalas*, coming to stand slightly behind him. She nodded in greeting when he looked around at her in surprise.

"It is good to see you all well," she said quietly, glancing briefly at the other generals and offering them a rare smile. "I know the desert can be a harsh place to traverse."

"We managed," Marsus answered, dipping his head to answer her amiable reception. "Woulda' probably taken the time to see our provisions a little better stocked if we'd known *this* was comin', though." He waved a hand over the Queen and her retinue, into the dark swath of bodies that lumbered—unnaturally quiet against the faint rush of the desert's breath—in the night beyond the torches.

"We've nothing to be concerned of there," the female assured him, she too looking in the direction of the lizard-kind horde, likely seeing more of them than their human eyes could make out. "You'll not find them straining our reserves, I think."

"Syrah said as much, yes," Akelo cut in as Marsus treated the female to a dubious raise of one eyebrow. "We will trust in your shared judgment on that, for the time being. More importantly…" he bent back a little closer to Zal'en, lowering his voice so as not to risk being overheard "… I had Cyper and some of the others clear a square quarter-mile east of the camp for the Queen's tribe, but… Will that be enough?"

Zal'en frowned and—in a motion that was all-too telling to Akelo—let her attention drift again to the atherian opposite them. Following her gaze, he found himself meeting the eyes of Sassyl Gal. The old male was watching Akelo and Zal'en's discussion with something like a frown pulling at the edges of his scaled lips, but overall looked otherwise unconcerned.

Over the spymaster's shoulders, however, *both* of the other males who'd accompanied him and the Queen into the firelight were staring at the pair of them with open, unmasked distrust.

"I suppose that answers *that* question…" Akelo muttered, refusing to look away from the matched lizard-kind until one of them dropped their gaze. Glancing sidelong at Zal'en, then, he frowned himself. "Should I tell Hur to expect problems in the ranks?"

Almost dejectedly, Zal'en sighed and shook her head. "It wouldn't hurt to keep a wary eye out, but I doubt what trouble we'll see will be instigated from any of our current soldiers, given how long they've already spent in the company of my kind."

"But we *should* expect trouble, then?" Cyper asked. The shorter Isler had sidled nearer, not looking away from the Queen and Raz while they'd continued their unintelligible conversation. His ear, on the other hand, had obviously been on the closer discussion.

"The lizard-kind we took up the Crags with us have been working to set some groundwork of trust, but the voices of strangers—even other *atherian*—will only carry so much weight among the tribes, I fear." Zal'en grimaced between Akelo and Cyper, like she wanted to apologize for any future hassle her race were like to cause. "It will take time. I will do my best to keep a handle on things where I can, but these are not former slaves looking to jump on the first shadow that shows any backbone of leadership. These are communities. Tight-knit and well- formed, with their own hierarchies and chieftains. They've yet to come completely to terms with *Raz* as a leader, much less any of *you* as 'comrades-in-arms'."

"Well they been preyed on by men who look a lot like us for longer than anyone cares to think about." Marsus, too, had snuck closer to join in. "Can't exactly blame 'em, given the circumstances, can we?"

No, Akelo thought to himself, looking again to the two taller males behind Sassyl Gal and the Queen, now apparently working *not* to meet his eye. *I suppose we can't.*

"Akelo."

Akelo blinked, and looked around at Raz. The atherian was motioning him to approach with his free hand, steel claws shining in the torchlight. He realized Shas-hana Rhan, too, was watching him, and Syrah had stepped closer as well. Together the three of them formed a sort of half-circle, an inviting shallow that funneled him toward the Queen. Before he could stop himself, Akelo swallowed.

Then he moved forward, answering the call.

For several long seconds after he came to stand within reach of Shas-hana Rhan, no one spoke. Akelo might have felt awkward, in that hanging silence, except for the fact that Shas-hana Rhan was taking him in slowly, her golden eyes tracing the contours of his face from his stubbled chin to his curled, short-cropped hair. Her study of him even lingered for a moment on the hint of the *kuja* tattoos that snaked over his collar bone and just up his neck, peeking out from beneath the lip of his leathers. Not knowing exactly what he was meant to be doing—nor wanting to stare at the Queen of the atherian full in the face when he stood not two feet from her—Akelo kept his own gaze largely over her head, over the sparkling crown of black glass leveled between her ears.

It made it hard to miss the returned leers of the males, as well as the deepening of Sassyl Gal's frown, not far behind the female.

A shifting of movement, and Akelo looked down to see—with no small amount of surprise—that Shas-hana had lifted both clawed hands toward him, palms down, like she intended for him to take them. There was a rumble of protest from one of the young males at her back, but the female silenced the outrage with nothing more than half-a-turn and a low, quick hiss over her shoulder. When her guard was quiet again, she returned her attention to Akelo, having never dropped her hands.

It took him a breath to gather the courage to do as she clearly desired.

He had clasped palms with Raz before—along with the occasional atherian foot soldiers in congratulation of a fight hard-won—and found the Queen's grasp surprisingly gentle by all comparison. Her fingers were slight, slimmer even than Karan's, and her scaled skin was smooth and flawless, indicative of a life spent without labor or a sword in hand. Just the same, Shas-hana Rhan's hold of him was not lacking in its own sort of strength. Her hands were steady, still and calm, whereas he noted—with some embarrassment—that his own trembled ever so slightly from age and nerves. This unwavering quality was echoed when he finally managed to meet the female's eyes again, and Akelo found himself reassured without any real reason to do so. His fingers stopped shaking in hers and, as they did, the Queen smiled.

Then she began to speak.

"You have my child's trust, so I will gift you mine," Syrah translated at once. "It is all I can offer you and your kind, who would help us rid your lands of the evil which has plagued our own. Others' faith, you will have to earn on your own, I'm afraid." A subtle tilt of the Queen's head toward the males at her back told Akelo Zal'en had been right in her suspicions.

"I think you will manage it." Shas-hana Rhan kept on. She looked around Akelo at the other generals waiting a pace or two behind him. "I think you will *all* manage it, given time. For now, though, I hope my own trust will grant you and the others the patience you will need to see this alliance forged as strongly as we all need it to be."

The female's content expression shifted, then, returning to the cold, pleasureless grimace she'd held when she'd mentioned the fall of Dynec and Cyro.

"To war, then?" Shas-Hana Rhan, Queen of the Under Caves asked of mankind.

For once, it took no time at all for Akelo to return the smile, feeling his own rage sparked by the hard expectation in the female's gaze. Without hesitation he bowed a second time, nearly bringing his forehead to the scaled backs of the Queen's hands.

"To war," mankind answered with relish.

PART III

XXVIII

"A cracked stone shatters easier than solid ice."

— ancient Sigûrth proverb

It was only by the Sun's grace that Raz reached the site of the commotion before all hell broke loose. The runner who'd come bolting for him had had the sense to call for someone to retrieve Gale from where the stallion was penned not far from Raz and Syrah's tent, and so by the time Hur's hurried summons had been delivered the horse was already on hand. Despite being unsaddled, Gale was equally unblinking when Raz leapt atop him to take fistfuls of mane as reins before wheeling the animal around with his knees.

It was a good thing, too, because even a few seconds delay might have had Raz arriving to all-out war having broken loose in his own camp.

It took him not three seconds to get a sense of the scene as the soldiers—human and atherian alike—split for him and the charger when they came thundering into the training grounds ahead of a trailing cloud of dust. Without slowing he barreled into the wide circle which had been formed around the involved group, breaking out onto the cleared sand where the fight had gotten its start. He pressed Gale on with a kick, driving the horse between the three central figures and the scattered others on either side of the space. Trusting the animal not to wander far, Raz half-slid, half-leapt from Gale's back to land directly in the center of the trio, all of whom had scrambled back from each other to avoid the breadth of the stallion's chest slamming them apart. Zal'en had been in the middle, trying to keep the other two apart as best she could. Hur had the great-axe he'd carried since the day he'd salvaged it from the *Moalas* hefted by his side. These two, Raz ignored. Given it was their greatest responsibility to see peace upheld within the ranks of the army, their presence was hardly surprising.

Instead, Raz's attention was set wholeheartedly on the third party, a broad male he was steadily finding himself growing too familiar with.

The atherian still hadn't recovered from his stumbling retreat out of Gale's path, giving Raz ample time to assess his state. The male held a wooden training sword in one hand—standard equipment for the sparring drills that took up much of the army's drill work—but in the other he was gripping the live steel of the Cyroan longsword he'd undoubtedly claimed after the battle in the mountains, now ten days past, its empty scabbard banging against his scaled legs. Taking advantage of the moment of surprise, Raz moved in a blink, unencumbered by the lack of armor he'd been in the process of cleaning and oiling when he'd been interrupted. Darting forward in a spray of loose sand he took hold of each of his opponent's wrists, spinning and twisting him like a dance partner. Unable to stop the motion, the male found himself awkwardly pinned to Raz's chest with both arms locked across his own. He gave a roar of fury, but Raz answered by pulling away just enough to drive a knee into his lower back, then drop the lifted foot down to take out his weight-bearing leg. The atherian collapsed to his knees with a pained inhalation, his grip slackening on the wooden sword and bare blade. Feeling this, Raz adjusted his grasp to rip both weapons from the male's hands with a twist, leaving the figure to tumble unceremoniously face-first in the dirt.

All in all, the entirety of the exchange took less than four seconds.

"*Zathlys*," Raz snarled down in bad atherian at his opponent's quivering back. "*Third time this is—third.. time.—that trouble, you have caused me. Patience of mine… Running* thin."

Zathlys of the Lower Feet—chieftain of the tribes who made their lairs in the bottom steps of the Crags—gave little more than a snarling growl of frustration in response as he slammed a fist into the sand by his face, still doubled over while his body adjusted to the shock Raz had given his kidney. To his credit, the male wasn't long in recovering, staggering finally up onto one knee and snapping something impatiently at the two female clan-mates who'd hurried forward to help him up from where they'd been standing nearby. The pair scurried back again dutifully at the rebuke, the black carapace of their scorpion shell armor shining in the afternoon light.

Zathyls took a moment more, but was eventually able to stagger upward and turn on Raz. He had one hand clutching helplessly at his side, but he otherwise looked only livid that whatever exchange he'd been having with Zal'en and Hur had been interrupted. He bared his teeth and tried to stand taller, but only managed to wince before bending again to cradle his abdomen.

In the end, he resorted to snapping up at Raz, whose understanding of the language had fortunately come a long way in the last month, even if his conversational skills were yet lacking.

"*Your soldier* attacked *one of ours*," the chieftain spat venomously, looking around Raz to the group of humans behind him. "*I was only defending my kind when your hounds showed up*."

Raz frowned at this, glancing about as well. Zal'en had chosen to retreat and join Hur, who still stood watching Zathlys warily, but beyond these two a half-dozen men and women in mismatched armor hovered in a tense half-circle, shielding what looked to be a single figure. The boy was young—perhaps fourteen or fifteen—and of clear Northern blood given his hair was so bleached by the Sun it was nearly as white as Syrah's.

It was Zal'en's eyes, though, that Raz sought. "Is this true?" he asked of the female.

"I don't know," his general answered breathlessly. She'd clearly been hard-pressed to keep Zathlys and Hur from tearing into each other before Raz's appearance. "I arrived after everything happened. Hur saw it, though, I think."

Raz looked to the massive Northerner, then. "Zathlys claims one of ours attacked an atherian. Do you witness this?"

The silent giant's face twisted in outrage, his grip spasming on his greataxe as a dull, furious sound rose from his throat. Zal'en put a hand on his arm, and shook her head as he glared around at her indignantly. Still, the gesture appeared to calm the man, because after a breath or two to regain his composure he relaxed, then half-turned to the group of soldiers standing behind them. With a muted grunt and a wave of one massive hand, he motioned them to approach. The six hesitated, then did so, the others coaxing the Northern boy forward but staying tight to him all the while. He looked terrified, his one good eye staring fearfully at Zathlys, the other already swollen shut by a diagonal, even bruise that gashed him across the brow.

The mark of a training blade, Raz realized, and the wooden sword in his left hand trembled as he worked to keep his own cool.

"You." He called the soldier out brusquely, harboring no patience for anything other than the facts in that moment. "Your name."

"D-Danus, s-sir," the boy answered promptly, gaze flicking nervously from Zathlys to Raz and back again. "Danus-Danus Oron."

"What happened? In your own words. *Then—*" he snarled back at Zathyls, who had growled in protest, apparently having understood enough of the Common to make out the request "—I will hear out any accusations."

Danus swallowed, but one of the women at his side patted him on the back and whispered an encouragement. After a long pause in which the boy was clearly gathering his courage, he managed to speak.

"W-was partnered up with the new lizard-kind for drills, sir. We were going over some basic blocking and counters, but I-I hadn't realized Kazah didn't know much about properly using a sword and—"

"Kazah?" Raz interrupted, stopping him short. "Your sparring partner?"

Danus swallowed again, but nodded and continued. "Aye, sir. She seemed pretty eager—we couldn't talk much beyond exchanging names, you see—and I-I let the excitement get to me. Pushed her a little too hard, and accidently dealt her a good whack. She gave a yelp a-and…" Danus paled, his eyes drifting to Zathlys again. "I-I started to make sure she was all right, sir, I swear I did. But before I could check—"

"You were 'interrupted'," Raz finished for him with a hiss, piecing together the rest of the story as he turned slowly on Zathlys, who met his gaze coldly. "Yes… I bet you were."

For a long moment he stared the chieftain down. Then, when it was clear the male was going to show no remorse of his own will, Raz snapped into the crowd of atherian beyond him without looking away.

"*Kazah!*" he boomed. "*To me!*"

Whether of her own volition or because she was pressed forward by others who understood the tension of the situation, in the corner of his eye Raz saw a slender figure become separate from the surrounding circle. Zathlys, too, must have made her out, because he glanced in her direction, finally giving Raz leave to do the same. He looked and found a tall, young female standing nervously some ten feet to his right. Going by the spun tunic of rodent furs that hung from her narrow shoulders and hips, Raz judged that Kazah was not of Zathlys' own tribe. Rather, she was one of Gyssa of the Upper Caverns brood, a fact that irked him even more. Had he been defending his own family, Zathlys' argument might have held a little water.

As it was, Raz's already largely-absent belief in the tale was trickling away with every passing moment.

Kazah's shoulders were marked with bright streaks of orange-red scales that happened to match the color of her ears, and she had her right hand clasped to her upper left arm in a clear guard. Raz motioned her forward with a wave of his stolen training sword, and she approached uncertainly, clearly not enjoying her newfound place as the center of attention to several hundred pairs of eyes.

"*Attacked, Zathlys claims you were,*" Raz told her as gently as he could manage, regretting his poor grasp of the female's language for what felt like the thousandth time that week. "*Truth, is this? You will tell me.*"

Immediately Kazah's eyes went wide and—like Danus'—flicked to Zathlys in fear. Seeing the potential problem, Raz thrust both weapons into the sand by his side before taking the last step toward the woman.

When he took her shoulder lightly in a clawed hand, Kazah flinched, but did not pull away.

"*Safe, you are,*" Raz assured, half-squatting so that he was even looking up a little into the much shorter female's eyes. "*No fear, so long as the truth, you give me. Seen defeat at my hands before, Zathlys has. Doubt he wishes to try again.*"

Zathlys growled something in anger behind him, but Raz ignored the chieftain, satisfying himself instead with the small smile he'd managed to drag out of the female before him.

"*I-It was an accident,*" Kazah started, obviously having trouble meeting Raz's eye. To compensate, she looked around at the group of humans still standing nearby, shielded by Hur and Zal'en. "*I think Danus was pushing me a- and I just fell behind...*"

Raz nodded in understanding. "*Saying the same thing, he does. Apologized, he has. Many times.*"

Kazah's smile brightened a little, and she looked directly at Danus. "*It wasn't your fault,*" she told the man in her own tongue, shaking her head. "*I was too enthusiastic.*"

"Did you get the gist of that, boy?" Raz asked the soldier without looking around again, standing up and peering at Kazah's injured arm, trying to see between her fingers.

"A-aye, sir!" came Danus' relieved response.

"Good. Then have your friends see you to the healers' quarters. I believe Syrah is there now, so you're in luck." Not waiting for a reply, he switched tongues and spoke to Kazah again. "*My partner, Danus will see. You as well. But first, your arm. Examine it, I would like to. Ensure it is not broken.*"

"*I-it's not,*" the female stammered in assurance, but did not protest when Raz pulled her hand away carefully and took a look at the limb himself.

Indeed, he could tell at a glance there was hardly anything wrong. Not even a scale had been cracked, and—aside from a swelling welt beneath her skin that warped some of the orange stripes dipping past her shoulder—one would doubtfully have been able to tell if something was amiss. He didn't expect to find anything—atherian were a hardy species, after all—but all the same Raz poked and prodded her cautiously, noting obvious tenderness where she'd clearly been struck, but no discomfort when he put pressure at her shoulder and elbow, compressing the bone.

"Not even a bloody fracture…" he spat quietly, standing straight again. He'd intended the words for his ears only, but Hur's half-suppressed grunt of irritation and Zal'en's unsurprised sigh let him know he hadn't been successful.

Kazah, too, had heard him, though the language was obviously lost on her. "*S-sir?*" she asked uncertainly, moving to hold the arm again when he let it go.

"*Nothing*," Raz assured her quickly, patting her on the other shoulder again in a comforting fashion. "*All is well. But Syrah, you will see too.*"

Or we'd be giving everyone an excuse to think I'm playing favorites with the injured, he finished in private irritation. Looking over Kazah's head, he caught the eyes of several of her female clanmates.

"*You, you, and you.*" He pointed them out individually before gesturing them to approach. "*See Kazah to my partner, in the healers' tent. Check her over, she will want to.*"

There was an ample bobbing of heads, and the trio stepped forward to lead the female off through a gap in the encircling crowd Danus and his companions looked to have already forged.

Only after they were gone did Raz finally let a little of his anger loose.

"A *bruise*?!" he bellowed, whirling on Zathlys so sharply the smaller male started. Then Raz was advancing on him. "You nearly blind one of my men over a *fucking BRUISE?!*"

Raz was so taken in his own fury that he didn't realize he was speaking in the Common tongue.

Zathlys, though, very clearly grasped the gist of his intent.

"*I assumed the female was attacked*," he snarled defiantly, the confidence in his words somewhat undercut by the dusty step backward he took under the pressure of Raz's thunderous approach. "*I had no reason not to think that—*"

"BULLSHIT!" Raz was in front of the chieftain now, and he grabbed the male by either side of his carapace cuirass, wrenching him forward until their snouts weren't even two inches apart. "You had *every* reason to think otherwise! You have been given no reason *not* to think otherwise! You have been trained! You have been cared for! Your people have been allowed their liberties, and your chieftains have kept your individual commands! You *chose* to attack that soldier, Zathlys—*my* soldier! For the *third time*, you *chose* to make a scene, *chose* to try and drive a wedge between our two sides! Enough! *ENOUGH!*"

He roared the last word in Zathlys' face, and it was finally the chieftain's turn to look nervous. As though from thin air, Zal'en appeared at Raz's side. For a moment he thought the general would try to calm him down, but she instead merely began to translate in a cold voice lacking all sympathy for Zathlys' position.

Trusting her to get the message across for him, Raz barreled on, jerking the male in his hands for emphasis as he brought his voice down to a throaty growl. "Consider this your final warning. Should I find you causing trouble for me or my men—should I hear so much as a *whisper* of it—I will petition the Queen to have you escorted back to the Crags. You *and* your people. You will be cast out, to return in disgrace and explain to the rest of your tribe why you were the sole entities banished from our ranks before so much as *glimpsing* those who have been abusing you for generations, much less drawing their blood. I would like to see you hold your title then, Zathlys of the Lower Feet, when your family is left out of the histories and stories of how the atherian at last gained their freedom."

It took several seconds for Zal'en to catch up to Raz's threats, but as she spoke one could see Zathlys' expression steadily shift from nervous defiance to angry fear.

"*You wouldn't dare*," the chieftain hissed, still somehow managing to maintain a defiant grimace through just the barest note of doubt in his voice. "*Two thousand of my warriors have bent their knee to the Queen. You wouldn't dare turn us away.*"

Raz bared his teeth in the male's face, then shoved him away so that Zathlys stumbled back several paces. When he found his balance, Raz spoke to him in a dangerous rumble.

"Two thousand is not an unimpressive number, I admit." At his side, Zal'en continued to turn his words as quickly as she could. "Your strength would be missed, to be sure. However—" he raised a hand to wave at the crowd encircling them, almost equally split between human and atherian "—it is nothing compared to the risk you put this host at at if I allow you to widen this rift the rest of us are so desperately trying to close. Miropa has the strength of *five* cities at its back, Zathlys. *Five*. You cannot fathom the beast we are up against, and yet you consistently seek to press apart our factions." Unbidden, his clawed hands balled into fists at his sides. "We will not survive this battle as two people fighting a common enemy. We will be divided, driven apart, and slain. If I were to allow that, then the weight of that failure would fall upon me. *I* will have been the one to have willingly let a cancer like you fester among us for too long. So yes, Zathlys—" Raz let his crimson neck-crest rise in warning, simultaneously baring white fangs at the shorter male to speak through a clenched jaw "—I would *unquestionably* dare."

As he finished, he realized that Zal'en's translation had pitched in volume. She was no longer speaking to the chieftain alone, but instead addressing the entirety of the atherian that surrounded them. He noted, too, that her words—*his* words—were not lost on most of them. He saw serpentine heads bending to come together, whispering to each other, and even many nods of acknowledgement. Zathlys, too, appeared to have noticed the subtle shift of his people, because there was indecision in his posture when he glanced over his shoulder at them.

Not a one looked willing to meet his eye.

"*Clear, I have been*?" Raz asked the male once Zal'en was done, shifting back into atherian.

For a long moment, Zathlys of the Lower Feet didn't look around at him. He seemed intent on finding someone, anyone, who would back his word. Unfortunately for these ambitions, even the females who'd initially stood at his back had quietly melted into the crowd.

At last, with a resenting grind of gritting teeth, the chieftain looked back to Raz, and nodded once.

"*Fool!*"

Zal'en's outburst as she, Raz, and Hur were making their way back toward the forward camp took both men by surprise. She'd been largely quiet while the three of them had commanded and overseen the resumption of the drills, and hadn't spoken a word when Raz had finally motioned it was time for the trio to take their leave, leading them out of the training grounds with Gale plodding dutifully in tow. Only when they'd been walking a good several minutes did her anger seem to at last get ahold of her.

"*What is he* thinking?!" she continued in atherian, staring ahead of them while they made their way along the central fairway between the sleeping tents. "*What madness could possess him to press on with such* idiocy?"

"Zal'en, in Common, if you please," Raz reproached her in a low voice. "Hur does not—"

"Hur and I have been side-by-side for most of half-a-year now, dealing with every kind of issue between *both* our races," Zal'en cut in impatiently, though she did change tongues. "I daresay he would likely speak the language better than you can at this point, if he were capable of it."

Raz blinked in surprise at that, and looked around at the Northerner for confirmation. The blond man just grinned at him and shrugged innocently from Gale's other side, as though to say "I would have told you if I could." Raz stared at him for a moment, aware of something very much like envy building up in his gut.

"You'd think I'd have an advantage, given the circumstances…" he muttered to himself, unsure if he was more annoyed or amused by the thought.

"What was that?" Zal'en asked him impatiently.

"Nothing," Raz answered with a cough, taking the chance to cover up his lapse in decorum and change the subject back. "As for Zathlys… We should try not to judge him too harshly. It's fear that motivates him. As plain and simple as that."

The female, a moment ago so livid her greying ears had stood as rigid as the Queen's crown, seemed to deflate all at once. Her shoulders sagged as her head bowed with an audible sigh, and she brought up one clawed hand to rub at her golden eyes like she was overcome by some sudden exhaustion.

"I'm aware," she eventually managed, sidestepping a pair of Percian soldiers who were sharing the weight of a load of long-spears on staggered shoulders. "I'm aware it's fear, Raz. I have been where Zathlys stands, in a sense. Taken away from all he knows. Outnumbered by a people who he cannot bring himself to trust, no matter how many times he is assured he must. The difference—" the general's tone shifted a little, some of the anger seeping back into her words "—is that I was surrounded by slavers trying to convince me they were my only salvation left in the world. *His* demons are anything but."

"His demons are men and women you have spent years learning are not the enemy, and months forming your own particular bonds with. He was thrust into this place, Zal'en. It will take time for many of the tribes to grasp something as fragile as trust."

There was a snort, and Raz looked over Gale's loping shoulder to see Hur eyeing him with something like ironic amusement. Recognizing the implied statement, Raz sighed in acknowledgement.

"If you're pointing out that wasn't exactly the stance I took back in the training grounds, I'd have to argue time happens to be the commodity we have in *shortest* supply, at the moment. The other chieftains might not be thrilled with taking orders from me, but they *do* take them. On the other hand, the Queen and I have both made our attempts to get Zathlys to trust me on his own, and to no avail. We've not a week before reaching Miropa, and less days still before the šef's start causing us difficulties, if they've half-a-mind between them. We no longer have the luxury of giving him the opportunity to believe in us, and if he won't follow commands out of loyalty, then I have no other option but to ensure he follows them out of necessity."

"Some would call it 'fear'," Zal'en pointed out quietly.

"Some would." Raz conceded the point with a dip of his head, guiding Gale with a hand on his bare neck around a pile of plucked vulture carcasses, downed by the archers for the day's meals and fletching for their arrows. "Perhaps even with good cause. It's not a means by which I would have ever thought myself willing to leash any man, but if I must be a single individual's tyrant in order to keep together this machination of ours, then so be it. I will be Zathlys' tyrant, and he can belittle and revile me all he wants once I get him and his tribe back to the Crags *as a free people.*"

These last words rolled with a frustration he had been attempting to suppress, but Zal'en and Hur both appeared to share—or at the very least appreciate—his sentiment. They nodded together, and the rest of the walk was again held in silence, each of the three of them held up by their own thoughts.

When they reached the edge of the forward camp, where their tents were scattered among dozens kept by the other generals and their secondary officers, Raz dismissed the two to their regular duties with a thanks for their assistance. They went off together to leave him to his musings, and it was hardly more than a few seconds before even Hur's blond hair was lost to the rise and fall of wind-scarred canvas and milling of the soldiers.

On his own once more, Raz turned to look west again.

Hur and Zal'en had taken their leave atop the moderate rise of a low dune, granting him a view of the rest of the camp. There wasn't much to see—the sprawl of the army was at his back, after all—but it left the dance of the sand plains open to him in a way Raz wasn't often able to take in, even on the march when he rode alongside Syrah and Akelo at the head of the host. He was reminded, for a moment, of a childhood long left to ash, when he and his sister and his cousins would take advantage of the last hour or two of light after their parents had called an end to the day's trek across the South. He and the others of the Arros' youngest could often be found scrambling to the highest crests within the view of the wagon ring, then proceed to play "king-and-castle", fighting and laughing as they vied one after the other to hold sway over the ridge of the dune.

Kicking and screaming to lord over an arid swatch of empty nothingness, Raz thought to himself, smiling a little at the recollection.

It was almost amusing to consider that what he and the others were about now wasn't so far come from the roughhousing of nomadic children.

Grunting at the thought, Raz started down the incline below him, hearing Gale huff and follow along with careful *thumps* of his hooves in the sand.

Raz *had* intended to make for the healers' tents and check on the injured, but talked himself out of it without much difficulty. Syrah would be with Danus and Kazah, he knew, and as comforting as having the woman by his side could be, Raz had no desire to discuss his impression of the altercation, nor rehash the discussion he and Zal'en had just had. Making a decision, he instead pressed straight on through the last rows of tents before the open sweep of the South, passing his and Syrah's own lodgings, as well as the general's pavilion where he could hear Akelo speaking with what sounded like a group of cohort commanders.

When he was free of the noise and bustle, Raz took to Gale once more, hefting himself up onto the horse's back and clucking the beast into a trot westward before anyone had the chance to shout his name and list off any number of tasks for which he had no energy left in the moment.

Raz pressed the stallion up the low slump of one dune, then another, then a third. Cresting this last hill, he came across a lone sentry holding her watch dutifully, though the woman—a West Isler, judging by the straight black hair that fell halfway down her back— had stripped to skin from the waist up under the glare of the early-afternoon Sun. When she heard Gale's approach, the soldier took her time looking around, likely expecting yet another outrider heading out to scout the wastes under Marsus' orders.

She nearly jumped out of her boots, therefore, when Raz pulled Gale to a halt beside her, and he chuckled privately as the lookout scrambled for her leathers, piled nearby.

"At ease, you," he told the woman, lifting a hand to calm the sentry. "It's hotter than sin out here, and let's not pretend you wouldn't spot an assault for miles out in this place. You'll get no scolding from me for not wanting to broil alive."

Looking relieved, the West Isler straightened slowly, eyeing Raz and his mount with confused curiosity.

"Did…Did you need something, sir?" she asked after a few seconds of silence, her Common twisted in a harsher dialect than Cyper spoke. She was well-tanned from what was undoubtedly any number of past postings in the insufferable heat, and a sweat-stained swatch of cloth wrapped about her chest was all she apparently needed to keep her modesty. Against her bronzed skin, the pale lines of old lashings complemented the cruel scars that ringed her wrists, and one hand had come to rest automatically on the hilt of the broadsword hanging from her belt. "There isn't much to report, I'm afraid. Not even the dune scorpions are making a show of themselves, what with the tribes hunting them down like they've been."

Raz shook his head, lifting his eyes again to gaze out over the sand plains. "No, I'm not looking for anything in particular. Just fancied a bit of a ride, I think. Needed to get away."

"O-Oh," the woman stammered. "Of course."

They lapsed into quiet again, and for a minute Raz almost forgot the woman was there, lost in a mélange of worries and contemplations while he took in the windy horizon.

"Can… Can I ask a question, sir?"

Raz blinked, and looked down at the sentry. She didn't meet his eye, gazing off instead in the same direction he had been.

"You can…" he answered tentatively, unsure of what sort of query he could expect from this lone soldier.

"… Do you think we'll manage it, sir?"

Ah, Raz thought, rationalizing he should have suspected as much while he turned his attention back to the distant line of the sand and sky.

He took his time considering the question. The confrontation with Zathlys had done little to put him in any sort of wholesome mood, and dwelling on the greater threat that loomed ahead of them—far more ominous than even the potential uprising within their own camp—didn't help. Still, it was a question Raz, Syrah, Akelo, and all the others asked themselves every day when they met pre- and post-march.

Of course it would be weighing on the minds of the common soldiers as well…

"Most of my generals would insist that I am to tell you 'Certainly!' and do so with as much false bravado and confidence as I can possibly muster."

He grimaced a little. "I *should* probably tell you exactly that, honestly, but I've never been much of one for hollow hopes and niceties."

Below him, the woman nodded, and looking at her sidelong Raz noticed that she had started shaking.

She's frightened, he realized privately. Then he chided himself. *Of course she is. When the time comes, she'll probably be on the front lines of this whole mess…*

"What's your name?" he asked of the woman.

In response, the soldier jumped, very clearly not having expected such a direct enquiry into her identity.

"I-Issa, sir," she responded after a second of gathering herself, dark-brown eyes flicking once or twice in his direction.

"Well, Issa," Raz began with a sigh, "the truth is that I don't have the answer you are seeking, because I don't know. None of us do, as much as we would love nothing more than to be able to look all of you in the eyes and assert with the utmost confidence that this war is as good as won. It isn't. Miropa is as formidable an enemy as you can imagine, and we aren't even positive of the Mahsadën's total strength. What's more, our own strength is tentative, and balances on a razor's edge from sun-up to sun-down. So no, I cannot tell you with any certainty that 'we'll manage it', as much as I desire to do so."

Without looking at her, Raz saw Issa nod, and thought her shaking might have redoubled.

"However…" he continued, and the spasm of her posture in the corner of his eye told him the woman had not been expecting more. "What I *can* tell you is that I *believe* we will win this fight. For some foolish reason there are voices out there that call me by the various names the world has provided: Monster. Scourge. Dragon. They speak them as though these titles symbolize some special ability, some benediction or blessing that grants me more than what strength and will I was born with. It's all folly. I am—lacking a better metaphor—as human as the rest of you, as vulnerable to fear and uncertainty as I am to steel or rain or this *blasted* heat." He waved a clawed hand at the sky for emphasis while Gale snuffled and hooved at the sand beneath him, looking in vain for anything to graze on. "I am also as uninterested in dying as any of you. I *have* run from fights, Issa. More than one, in fact. I am not a fool, and I don't even think you can fairly call me 'brave'. If the odds are not in my favor—if I cannot enter an exchange without reasonable belief that I will come out the victor—then I am not so headstrong as to rush into a battle that might have been better off avoided. If I believed I was leading you and the tens of thousands of others under my command into likely defeat, what in the Sun's name would qualify me to stand at your head in the first place?"

Pleasantly, Raz heard the woman give something of a laugh at this, and so he kept on.

"I cannot promise victory, Issa. To any of you, or to myself. But I *can* promise I would not be so confidently pressing us all ever forward if I did not at the very least *believe* we are likely to be the vanquishers."

"There's rumors," Issa spoke up when Raz paused. "Around the campfires, at night. They say Miropa's numbers match ours twice over. Maybe even more…"

Raz snorted. "I would love to know by what magic or clairvoyance the men and women of this army are being made aware of this, given that neither I nor any of my generals have access to such valuable information. We've no spies—unlike the Mahsadën, I'm sure—and Miropa is yet too far out for the scouts to glean anything useful for us. Even if it weren't, I can assure you that such a case is so unlikely it borders on unbelievable."

This appeared to reassure the woman, because her nod was more confident as she made it. "Only bordering?" she asked, though. "So they *may* be stronger?"

"In number? It's probably. *However*—" Raz cut across the soldier's inhalation of surprise with a slightly-raised voice "—numbers are not all that matter in war, Issa. The Tashes of Perce had numbers on their side, I would remind you."

This seemed to settle the woman, and Raz almost smiled. He was enjoying himself, he realized. It had been too long, he thought, since he'd been able to reassure anyone as directly as he was now.

"I am not telling you not to be afraid, Issa. Only a buffoon feels no fear when faced with the sort of challenge we are setting ourselves against. But believe. Believe that we will rise above this, as I do."

Issa nodded yet again, taking a deep breath.

"'Numbers are not all that matter in war'," she repeated, almost to herself. Then her head turned, and Raz looked down to see her smiling up at him gratefully. "I'll remember that, for tonight's cooking fires."

"Good," Raz snorted. "And you can damn well tell them who you heard it from, too. Maybe then there won't be quite so many rumors. I've enough trouble on my hands as is *without* dealing with… with…"

Raz trailed away, suddenly distracted. As he'd shifted to face the woman, he'd turned north, and his sharp eyes had caught a flicker of something against the backdrop of the desert. It was several seconds more before he found it again. The day's shadows had only just started to appear as the Sun dipped westward, and so the dark shape was distinct when it came overtop one dune, only to disappear again. At first Raz thought it was a scorpion, because the form of it appeared too wide to be anything else, but when the thing crested the next rise he cursed, recognizing it for what it was.

"Issa, your sword!" Raz snapped, not taking his eyes off the spot where the shape had vanished down yet another incline even as he extended a hand expectantly downward.

To her credit, the soldier didn't hesitate. There was keening scream of steel as the blade at her hip was drawn. She only tried to voice a question as Raz felt the handle of the weapon pressed into his waiting fingers.

"Sir? What's—?"

"Back to the camp!" Raz cut her off, already heeling Gale forward to plunge down the dune at an angle. "Call the generals to meet! *Now*!"

If the woman voiced any argument or confusion, he didn't hear her. Gale's breath and the heavy *thud* of his hooves through loose sand took over all, and Raz drove the horse as hard as he dared across the uneven footing. Again the sway of the plains loomed overhead, and he had to keep careful focus on their orientation so as not to lose the line of flight he knew the shape had been taking. For nearly two minutes he pressed Gale on, further from the camp than was advisable for any single person, but Raz's thoughts were elsewhere while they thundered up and down the sands. Finally, once Gale's breath started to come in bellows after climbing more hills than he was accustomed to, Raz pulled the stallion up to straddle the edge of a sizable mound and waited, intent on finding the figure again.

He *heard* the thing before he saw it.

The sound of heavy, ragged gasps reached his ears, coupled with a frantic, irregular pounding of hooves, like a wild animal half-scrambling to manage the desert inclines. A few seconds later, the form crested a line not two dunes away, and Raz wheeled Gale around to intersect its path at an angle. He lost sight of it again as they dipped down into the valleys, but he was confident in the thing's path now. It would run straight and true, and keep running until released from that which drove its fear, or died from exhaustion.

Judging the approach right, Raz turned Gale southeast, in the direction they'd come, and slowed the stallion to a trot, looking over his shoulder all the while. At last the unbalanced shape he'd made out from so far away came into clear view over the ridge above and behind them, and with a chill of anticipation Raz took in the panicked horse, noting the froth about its mouth and the blood streaking its flanks.

That, and the limp, half-trampled form of its rider, dragged along for Moon-knew how far across the harsh sands of the South.

If the maddened animal noticed Raz and Gale, it made no indication of it. It merely continued to drive forward at such a frantic pace that Raz at first couldn't fathom how it hadn't already lamed itself.

The only answer, of course, was that the beast couldn't have been running long…

"Not good," he muttered to himself, pushing Gale a little faster and feeling the tilt of the incline steepen beneath them. With his knees he guided the stallion, adjusting the angle of their climb until they were parallel to the path he was sure the horse would drag its dead rider. Sure enough, the animal galloped ever closer, trailing dust to glimmer in the afternoon Sun like the wake of a ship. Timing everything carefully, Raz made sure he had a good hold of the borrowed sword in his right hand, keeping himself saddled with his legs.

Then, just when the horse pulled up alongside them, Raz lunged, taking up beast's bridle even as he slashed downward with as much precision as he could muster.

His cut was a little off, biting into the dead man's boot and shin, but it caught enough leather to do the trick. There was the slithering of straps through iron rings, and then the stirrup came lose, the corpse tumbling free to roll and bounce off into the sands. Despite the sudden absence of its rider's weight, the horse didn't immediately calm down, and Raz was promptly jerked from Gale's back by the more-frantic animal. Not unexpecting this, Raz let go of Issa's sword and took hold of the saddle head just in time to keep from falling under the weight of scrambling hooves. There was a moment of grunting and struggling to compensate for the awkward momentum of his dismount, but Raz finally got a leg over the beast's back and slide himself into place in the saddle.

"WOOOAH!" he bellowed, pulling back sharply on the leather reins he'd just managed to hold onto. "WOOOAH THERE! WOOOAH!"

It took a second for the horse to calm enough to recognize the command and the weight of a living being on its back, but when it did it didn't take long for the animal to slow itself to a halt. Exhausted as it was, the moment it came to a stop the horse half-collapsed, and Raz managed to leap and roll clear as its front knees gave in so that it fell awkwardly first to its chest, then to its side. There it lay in the dust, heaving in great, wheezing gulps of hot air.

"Shit," Raz muttered to himself once he'd found his feet again and brushed himself off, eyes on the horse's upturned flank. There, buried some three or four inches into the corded muscle just forward of its rear, a feathered arrow protruded almost perfectly perpendicular to the incline of the dune. Alone it was enough of a portent, but Raz had to be sure. Leaving the horse to recover, he half-scrambled, half-slid back down the slope, passing Gale as the stallion took his time climbing after his master.

Coming to a halt, Raz brought himself to stand over the beaten corpse of the dead rider, grimacing in sad disgust down at the man. He couldn't barely tell what gender the scout had been, much less *who* they'd been, the leathers—in Kareth Nan's colors—largely flayed from the figure's chest and back, along with the skin and flesh that had been beneath them. His torso was mostly caved in—undoubtedly from being frequently caught under the horse's panicked hooves—and his head and face were in similar disrepair. His sword was gone, ripped from its scabbard, but there was a knife in one boot that said plainly the man hadn't been taken any sort of prisoner.

The remnant of paired shafts protruding beneath his shoulder blades—broken and pulled at by the passing sand until the gleam of barbed steel shone through revealed ribs—told the rest of the story.

Raz looked up from the body to turn his eyes north-by-east, in the direction the horse had come. That the pair had been ambushed was clear, and that they hadn't come far was no less obvious.

"Shit," Raz muttered to himself again, moving to retrieve Issa's sword from where he'd dropped it before returning to Gale, taking to the saddle once again, and heeling the stallion back in the camp's direction at full tilt. It hurt, leaving the body of the scout behind and abandoning the horse to find its own way home when it recovered, but Raz had no time to allow his conscience to bear him down.

Miropa's long shadow had at last reached them…

XXIX

"There is an infuriating commonality in modern texts that would portray the Mahsadën of the Common Age in an insubstantial light. These baseless records would have us believe the rings that formed 'the society' were led by a conglomeration of brutish, violent men and women whose extreme cruelty and violence were all they needed to hold onto their power.

Nothing—nothing—*could be further from the truth, and this misconception is prevalent to the point of vexation.*

The šef were not merely the most vulgar selection of the base brigands and criminals who formed the great bulk of the slave rings which once ruled the fringe cities of the South. They were not extreme examples of nothing more than a violent pool of samples. The leaders of the Mahsadën were figures of cunning intellect and rare talent, the hardiest survivors of a constant struggle to seize at the highest point of power among very able individuals. There were no dunces in their ranks. There were no fools or buffoons, despite what modern recordings would have us believes. If anything, the šef are an example of the everyday greatness of which humanity is capable, reflected in the twisted surface of spilled blood…"

— *As Death Rose from the Ashes*, by Kohly Grofh

Despite whatever his compatriots might believe, Vyres Eh'ben of Karth was hardly an imprudent man. He had worked to maintain appearances, worked to keep up the façade of the cruel dullard who'd clambered his way up the ranks of the Karthian Mahsadën through simple brutality and luck, but the truth of the matter was that Vyres Eh'ben possessed a rare intelligence, and an even rarer instinct. He had intentions, had plans. He would *not* be one of his city's many rising and falling šef, *refused* to be one of dozens who'd come and gone, failing to thrive in the violent environment of the ramshackle metropolis. Vyres distinctly meant to survive, and—in doing so—cement his place in the new order he could see developing among the slave rings of the South.

Therefore, when three of his outriders had come to him the previous day with the news that they'd not only been spotted by one of the Monster's scouts, but subsequently tried and failed to keep the man from fleeing, Vyres had been hard-pressed not to have the idiots lashed to within an inch of their lives.

In the end, their assurances that they had seen the rider fall from his horse, only to be dragged off in Arro's direction at full-tilt, had saved their skins.

If all went as planned, less than a day's warning would offer little opportunity to prepare the Monster and his men for Vyres' purposes.

"Hold," Vyres muttered under his breath, and to either side of him he heard the command reverberate in quiet exchanges through the dark. Leaving his host to huddle low to the ground—using what heat was left in the sand to stay warm—the šef crawled up the height of the dune on all fours, using nothing more than the light of the Moon and Her Stars to judge where the slope was firm, and where it was most likely to give. In fifteen seconds he reached the ridge, and—checking to make sure the tanned hide of his fur hood was still high over his lank hair—Vyres peered out on the fire-lit sight some hundred meters south and west of them.

In the dim glow of the night, the Monster's camp blazed as brightly as a lake of fire in a sea of blue-black waves.

His was a simple task, of a fashion. The two hundred *sarydâ* at his back—hand-picked for their proclaimed guile and craftiness with the sort of work intended on this and subsequent nights—were hardly a match for the tens of thousands laid out before them, but *defeating* Raz i'Syul Arro was not among Vryes' orders. His directive was only to be a nuisance, to repeatedly chip away at the enemy's morale, and numbers where he could. It was not a flattering command—particularly for a šef of the fringe cities—but it was one given to Vyres directly by the master of Miropa themself, and therefore not a post he was about to scoff at. Although he suspected he was only one of several to have already deduced Adrion Blaeth's deception, the fact remained that the man's word was—at the very least—an echo of his puppeteer, and *she* was a person Vyres had no intention of crossing anytime soon. It had been with this thought in mind, therefore, that he'd set off into the eastern plains with his hired swords, as well as a trio of Miropa's own shadows.

Vyres felt a chill at the thought, glancing over his shoulder back down the hill. While the mass of his force as a whole was still, having moved in patient sweeps between the dunes so as to avoid kicking up dust and catching the eyes of the Monster's sentries, none among them compared to the indistinct blotches of grey that were black hands of Miropa. They lay with infinite patience, as unmoving as carved stone, and under the gaze of the Moon Vyres thought he saw the glint of eyes between the colorless clothes wrapped about their visages. Like wolves they waited, and Vyres had seen them pounce no less than four times already that night, on each occurrence downing pairs of sentries that formed the wide ring about Arro's position. On the first two of these occasions, Vyres hadn't even been aware of the shadows making their move. He'd been privately debating how best to handle the lookouts, in fact, when the three men delivered the bodies to him without so much as a word. The third and fourth times, on the other hand, he'd been careful to watch the assassins, but found himself no less astounded when they descended on the soldiers as silently as the desert wind, downing them and dragging the corpses away from the light of the camp to leave nothing but blood and scrawling trails as intimations of their passing.

No… The mistress of Miropa was not a person to be taken lightly…

Returning his attention to the camp, Vyres studied the edge of the firelight for any sign that something was amiss. He was confident the dead scout wouldn't have provided the Monster with enough information to deduce the force or intention he was up against, but Vryes was as equally sure that Arro would at the very least be on his guard for an attack. The šef had already been surprised to find the sentry line without reinforcement, and another man might have harbored false-confidence given the ease of their approach. Vyres, however, had no such misguided assertions. He'd long since come to the conclusion that Raz i'Syul Arro was very possibly the most cunning opponent he would ever be set against—likely more cunning than even Adrion Blaeth gave him credit for—and wasn't about to willingly grant the atherian any more advantages than he already possessed.

"Ah'leez," Vyres whispered over his shoulder, holding firm the slum-runner's drawl that had been his shield and disguise for so many years. "To me."

In what felt like less than five seconds, a form materialized at Vyres' elbow, the sensation of a presence all that gave the shadow's attendance away. Hard as he might, the šef couldn't make out so much as the man's breathing against the quiet of the night, nor had he heard any shifting in the sand at his approach.

"Take yer brothers and get as close to the tents as ya' can. See what ya' can figure out. We ain't unexpected, and I'd like to know what Arro has planned 'afore we move."

Without a word the presence vanished from Vyres' side, and the šef settled in to wait, sliding his arms and legs back and forth in the sand until the limbs were partially buried. He embraced the warmth that still lingered beneath the desert's surface, and kept only his eyes over the lip of the dune, trying to catch some glimpse of Ah'leez and his kin. Unsurprisingly, he saw nothing, not even the whisper of a shape between the hills, and eventually he gave up, resigning himself to patience. One minute passed into two, then five, then ten, and Vyres had counted every tent he could discern against the firelight two-and-half times over by the time the three shadows returned, sliding into position on either side and behind him.

"Nothing seems awry," a voice, empty and hollow as a dried-up well, whispered into Vyres' right ear. "A few soldiers still move about on patrol, but the rest would appear to be asleep. We heard horses deeper in the camp, but it's hardly odd the lizard would want to keep his mounts well-enclosed. They're too valuable to him."

Vyres said nothing for a long moment. He, too, had caught the movement of more sentries within the firelight, but that was anything but abnormal. What sort of army *wouldn't* post a night watch to guard for any trouble that might slip past the outer lookouts?

Did the scout's body not make it back? the šef considered silently, grey eyes trailing the ordered lines of the encampment. The beast hadn't had far to carry its rider, even dead, but there was always the possibility that it had lamed itself in the treacherous sway of the sands…?

Still, even if that was the case, wouldn't the Dragon's scoutmaster yet have reported a missing man? Was Arro so imprudent as to perhaps tally such a disappearance to the sandcats, or scorpions?

No, Vyres' gut answered him all-too firmly. *They're definitely expecting us…*

Making his decision, the šef pulled his limbs free of the sand to turn back and face his silent *sarydâ*. They still waited, persistent as the dead, and only the ten or so foremost among them crawled their way forward when Vyres waved them up the hill.

"We strike *only at the outer ring,*" he told the mercenary captains with firm deliberateness. "Stay as spread out as ya' can. Arro has some trick up his sleeve, I'm sure of it. Ready yer men to—"

"Wha'?" one of the captains drawled across him, speaking with barely-hidden contempt. "Wha's scrapping a few tents and killin' a couple sleeping lumps gonna do ta' slow the scaly down?"

"Likely keep us alive to do the same tomorrow night, and the night after that," Vyres replied with a snarl, looking the insolent man squarely in the eyes, daring him to keep up his interruptions. "Ya' want to dig deeper in, ya' damn well go right ahead. Killin' yerselves'll only give the rest of us a minute or two more to get back to the horses free and clear."

Cowed, the captain said nothing more, and Vyres met the gaze of each of the others before finally dismissing them with an impatient wave and a short word. He followed them back down the incline, then gave them a full minute to disseminate his instructions. Once each of the group leaders nodded their readiness, Vyres led the way west, around the large dune behind which they'd taken shelter, then south, making for the camp. At his back he made out the sounds of the two hundred picking themselves up and moving to follow, and he knew too that the shadows would be trailing him with their typical silence.

They didn't so much as make it within a hundred paces of the firelight.

Vyres had just drawn the weapons from his side—a sword and a curved longknife which had long served him well in the ugly alleys of Karth—when the lightning descended. At least he *assumed* it to have been lightning, at first. From the group's back a brilliant blaze of light illuminated the night, and before even the assassins could twist around to see where the flash had come from, an earsplitting *CRACK* shattered the silence of the desert night.

Vyres spun on the spot, cursing, mind whirling as he tried to make sense of how a *storm* could have materialized from thin air so close to the Cienbal. He was confused, therefore, when he found the sky largely clear, Her Stars winking mischievously at them through the faintest wisps of far-off clouds. He couldn't comprehend what had happened, couldn't understand where the light and noise had come from.

Then, not far to his left, one of the shadows lifted a drawn knife to point lower, much closer to world's surface. "There!"

Vyres gaze dropped, and it was a moment before he made out the shapes against the darkness of the heavens. A ways behind them, back in the direction they'd come, two forms stood on the tallest dune for two hundred paces. At first Vyres couldn't fathom how he or any of his command had missed the figures, but as his eyes adjusted to the distance he could see large divots in the hill beneath the two, and what looked like thin trails of sand still flowing from their odd garments and the heavy cloaks drawn about their forms.

They buried themselves! Vyres realized with a thrill of fear, recognizing the serpentine heads of the atherian and watching, in a frozen moment, as one of the lizard-kind raised some sort of wide tube skyward while the other lifted what looked like a burning twig or small torch in the same manner.

It took only an instant for Vyres to deduce what would happen next.

"No!" he roared, rushing forward and bowling into the *sarydâ*, shoving the mercenaries aside in his desperate need to get to the atherian. "Ah'leez! *Stop them*! *STOP THEM*!"

Out of the corner of his eyes Vyres saw the dark blurs of the shadows shiver through the *sarydâ* with a litheness he could only envy, but despite all their speed the šef knew the assassins would be far too late. Indeed, even as he watched, the burning tendrils in the second atherian's hand reached the top of the odd tub, and there was another *CRACK* as the night was cast alight once more in an all-consuming flash as bright as the Sun Himself.

Vyres cursed again, his vision stolen from him, and he stumbled forward only to collide with the body of one of his men, almost losing his footing in the process. Among the shouts and confusion, he barely made out the whirling sound of some blade or another being thrown, and as he blinked away the pulsing white from his eyes he heard a distant *thud* and an inhuman screech of pain as what must have been Ah'leez's weapon struck true.

Miserably, however, the flare had already been sent twice over.

By the time Vyres' vision was returned to him, he was aware of two things. First: while the body of one of the atherian had slumped to hang over the ledge of the far dune, still in death, the second was nowhere to be seen. Not even the shadows would catch the lizard-kind, Vyres knew, quick as the beasts could be in their natural environments.

Second, though, and far, far worse: behind them, coming from the direction of the camp, the shouts of men could only barely be heard over the sharper braying of horses echoing in the icy twilight.

"Sun above…" Vyres heard someone say, and he halted his mad scramble to turn and look back toward the light of the Monster's army.

There, between two hills that offered just a sliver of a view on the camp, a terrifying sight was in progress. Although they hadn't yet reached the edge of the tent lines, from between the organized ranks of plotted banners and quarters, men on horseback could be seen thundering along the lanes which cut carefully through the camp.

Unable to help himself, Vyres let out a single, mirthless laugh, the Monster's plan forming all at once.

Then his resolve hardened.

"SCATTER!" he boomed over the milling confusion of his men. "BACK TO THE HORSES! BACK TO THE MAIN FORCE! ANY WHO CAN!"

The panicking *sarydâ* didn't have to be told twice. Like a thrashing ocean breaking through a dam there was a surge of movement north and east, in the direction the group had left their mounts penned with a dozen guards for good measure. Vyres let himself be caught in the rush, pressing right along with the others until there was a split in the valleys between the dunes, at which point a good portion of them—including himself—tore off further eastward. He allowed himself a moment of self-congratulation when his group broke apart a second time not moments later at another divide. Several of the mercenary captains had scoffed when he'd explained their plan of retreat, disliking the structured chaos of it. Among the inconsistent swaying of the sand plains, though, such a withdrawal was far more likely to allow for the greatest nightly survival, given they'd intended to repeatedly—

"AUGH!"

Vyres' voice was only one of dozen as he and the men all around him cried out in collective pain and surprise as the night sky bloomed into light without sound or warning. This time the blaze did not fade, however, and the šef screamed a tirade of profanity as he stumbled to one side, trying to find the elbow of the nearest dune as he covered his eyes with his left forearm, still holding onto his knife and sword. He found the incline of the sand and fell there, his quick thinking deciding it was better to make himself small and inconsequential than to try and stumble onward, blinded over uneven ground.

He knew he'd chosen correctly the moment he felt the hoofbeats approaching through the earth.

There was the shriek of steel, then the heavy sound of sharpened metal cutting through leathers and furs, and the first of Vyres' men screamed. Feeling panic begin to build in his chest, the šef rubbed at his face and blinked furiously, alternating between praying and cursing to the Twins for the return of his sight. Little by little it came back to him—though Vyres had to squint to see anything—but by the time he could make out any of his surroundings again, the air was filled with the wails of the dying and neighing of frightened horses. He stayed huddled, forcing himself to wait as the shapes of three, then four, then five mounted cavalry became clear, churning and thundering this way and that while they rode down the fleeing men no longer shielded by the dark as whatever magic had turned the night into day lingered on. Vyres watched, patient despite his fear, as one after another the group he'd been with fled or fell to flashing blades. He waited, giving his sight as long as he could afford to recover.

When the opportunity came, therefore, he was ready.

As still as he'd been keeping, the soldiers must have had an easy time incautiously counting him among the fallen. When one of them finally pulled his mount near where Vyres' lay, the rider started to rein the animal around to make another pass. The moment the man did so, Vyres rolled to his feet and lunged, driving his long knife into his target's lower back. The soldier screamed in unexpected agony, but the sound was lost to the shrieks of the dying, and even when Vyres twisted the buried weapon and used it as a handle by which to unhorse the rider, none of the man's companions looked around in alarm. It wasn't until the horse itself realized that something was wrong, adding its keening bray to the mélange, that any of them turned, but by then Vyres had already hauled himself up into the saddle. With a cruel kick he drove the animal forward, angling along the closest edge of the valley. He flew past three of the mounted soldiers before they could wheel their beasts about, with only the last of the five having been quick enough to do so. The rush with which she'd completed the maneuver cost her a necessary advantage, however, because her strike came too high at his head, allowing Vyres to knock it upward in a twisted parry that brought his blade around to catch in the narrow space between the woman's open-faced helm and leather cuirass. There was a violent spray of blood as the impetus of his horse's charge carved her neck to the bone, and Vyres barely made out the choking wretch of a cough as he sped by.

Not looking back to see the soldier's body fall, Vyres yelled for his mount to go faster, pressing it further into the sands. He knew the others would follow, would chase him into the plains, but he had to hope they would either give up or be under orders not to stray too far from the camp. Sure enough, there was a yell, and a moment later the grinding pounding of hooves was trailing him through the winding ravines of sand.

Vyres didn't care. Vyres *couldn't* care. Surrendering wasn't an option, given his position. He had little doubt Arro would want some of the *sarydâ* captured, and Vyres knew unequivocally that his were the sort of men to sell him out as a šef of the Mahsadën if it meant so much as a *chance* at keeping their own lives. He had to survive, not only for his own purposes, but for those of the society as a whole. If nothing else, returning to Miropa alive would be a small victory in and of itself, because beyond simply recognizing the two who'd originally signaled their position as atherian, Vyres had noted other things about the lizards. Their attire, in particular, had been of interest. Rather than the pilfered leathers of Karesh Syl and Karesh Nan—well known to make up much of the uniform of the Monster's horde—both of the creatures had been dressed in ragged furs and kilts which looked to have been stitched from the wild skins of smaller beasts. Though Vyres was hardly as familiar with the slave trade as Ysera Ma'het and her companions, or their now-fallen comrades of Dynec, he was versed enough in the occupation to know what those garbs meant. Even as he fled his pursuers under the unnatural brightness of a Sun-less night, Vyres was already planning how to best present this revelation without putting himself at risk to the agony of white fire. More so than the blades he knew were bared at his back behind him, the šef's fears grew from another realization, another understanding, hovering somewhere between awe and panic as he finally reached the edge of the light and pushed his stolen horse back into the darkness of the twilight sands.

The tribes of the Crags have taken the Monster's hand…

"Now, Syrah!" Raz roared over his shoulder, not letting his eyes slip from the constellations of Her Stars that marked the path of the charge he was leading across the sand. The handle of his sagaris *clacked* against his plate-armored thigh with every churn of Gale's powerful legs beneath him, and his gladius was bare in the steel claws of his gauntleted right hand as he leaned over the stallion's dipping neck. He didn't have to turn around to know the body of his cavalry thundered in his wake, but even over the cacophony of their drive Raz barely made out Syrah shouting something from Nymara's back not two strides behind him. The plan having already been set in place beforehand, he had the sense to avert his gaze and guide Gale on as smooth a path as he could make out before the magic took hold in the sky.

Then midnight turned to day.

It was a spell Raz had only witnessed once before, aboard a storm-flung ship approaching a year ago now, and he recalled thinking the source-less light had been beautiful, then. It had illuminated the wind-ravaged waters of the Dramion from below, like a beacon rising out of the depths to cast the ocean aglow with green-gold brilliance.

Now, absent the filter of the sea, the light bloomed without obstacle, descending from the heavens like the Sun had decided to claim the night as His own all at once.

There was the scream of surprised horses—coupled with the shouts of many nearby soldiers who clearly hadn't appropriately prepared themselves for the magic—but Raz paid them little mind. He blinked against the adjustment of his sensitive eyes, striving to see through the sudden brightness. It wasn't long before he found what he was looking for, and with a twitch of his reins he adjusted Gale's run again, making for a low dune behind which dozens of fur-clad forms writhed in panicked confusion. Leaving Syrah to keep hold of her spell, Raz drove the stallion up and over the incline.

Then he and Gale were plunging straight into the heart of the would-be ambushers, gladius flashing as he roared into the half-blinded faces of the Mahsadën's men.

It was a short, brutal fight, what advantage the šef's soldiers had had in the dark stripped away by the light and the brute force of the cavalry. Not knowing what sort of numbers they were up against—but suspecting word would have reached them if any significant branch of Miropa's gathered army had pushed east to meet them—it had been decided by the generals that the *entirety* of the mounted legion would be held ready and waiting. As such, three thousand men and women on horseback now streamed out of the camp in structured ranks, pouring over the sands in disciplined companies to face what looked now to have been nothing more than a nuisance force of two, perhaps three hundred. Raz almost laughed at the pitiful attempt by the Mahsadën to cause discord in his army, but caught himself even as he carved blood and devastation through the fur-clad forms. For one thing, the men that fell to his blade now were clearly not the trained soldiers of the remaining fringe cities. They were *sarydâ*, and therefore more than likely dispensable in the eyes of the šef.

For another, his discussion with Issa—the sentry—earlier that day had clung to Raz like a leech while he and the others had prepped and planned. Between hacks of his blade down on heads and shoulders he wondered if it wouldn't take less than he'd like to crack the morale of his gathered ranks of former slaves and oppressed lizard-kind…

The scream of a horse ripped Raz from his semi-absence, and he looked around in time to see one of his cavalry lieutenants tumble to the ground as his beast was cut out from under him, losing his blade in the process. There was a collective cry of success from the surviving *sarydâ,* and several made to pounce on the prone form. The man managed to roll to one side, barely leaving a trio of swords to plunge into the sand where he'd just been, and he scrambled to get to his feet while struggling to free a spare longknife from his belt. Fear had his fingers fumbling, however, and the hilt slipped from his grasp as his attackers lunged for a second attack.

By that point, though, Gale—driven hard—had already closed the gap.

The first man fell as the sagaris—drawn from Raz's belt at last—took him in the side of the head. The axe stuck there, but Raz took advantage of the mercenary's dead weight to keep hold of the haft, using it as a handle to throw a leg over the saddle and slide sideways off the stallion's back. He landed on his feet in a spray of cool sand between the pressed lieutenant and the desert mercenaries, and before any of them could so much as blink Raz had ripped the sagaris free and barreled forward. The first three men fell in a pattern of flashing and bloody steel, tumbling to desert floor to make room for Raz to leave behind the officer he'd saved and press further into the melee. There were still some hundreds of the mercenaries left breathing in his direct vicinity, and he had no qualms with relishing in the butchery for a time, sword and axe dispensing violent devastation in either hand. Within seconds of his dismount a shout of realization could be discerned from the chaos, quickly echoed by another, then another as the names rang clear in the brightly-lit night.

"Monster!" one man cried out, flinging his daggers down and falling to his knees in surrender.

"Scourge!" several others followed this with, turning to flee, only to be cut off by the circling cavalry.

Most commonly, however, came the final scream, the last and most terrible of the titles the world had bestowed on Raz i'Syul Arro:

Dragon.

For once Raz embraced the moniker, roaring as he tore into the throng of failing *sarydâ*, giving leave for the animal in his heart to lift its head and grin in pleasure at the iron stench in the air. Sword and axe thrashed in mirrored blurs of crimson silver. His tail snaked out to crack limbs and necks, and the curved talons of his feet made clean work of fur mantles and leather to shred at the fragile flesh beneath. His wings whipped out, tossing men aside as easily as one might cast away a rag doll, and the steel fists of his gauntlets caved in skulls and chests when Raz found himself too close to easily wield his blades. Before so much as a minute had slipped by he'd carved something of a wedge into the constrained bodies of the remaining mercenaries, pressing into them as the mounted soldiers penned them in on every side.

"RAZ! BEHIND YOU!"

Only Syrah's voice could have reeled Raz back with the sharpness he returned, then. Without hesitating he whirled, bringing his weapons around just in time to parry a pair of mismatched knives thrust from opposite sides at what would have been his lower back. With a grunt he accepted and deflected the strikes, unsurprised by the speed and force of the attacks as he glared at the recognizable garbs of an enemy of sickeningly familiarity. Through dead grey eyes the two assassins met his gaze, disengaging to melt back into the turmoil, which was quickly thinning. Despite this, it wasn't more than a moment before Raz lost the shadows in the crowd, and even as he dodged the awkward slash of an injured *sarydâ*—retaliating with a merciful cross-blow that had his gladius separating the man's head from his shoulder—Raz kept his eyes peeled. He cursed himself for his foolhardiness, scanning the ongoing tumult of the closing battle and taking a careful step back, then another, recognizing his disadvantage. It had been so long since he'd had to deal with the Mahsadën's shadows. If he was honest with himself, Raz had rather hoped he'd seen the last of them in the scorched halls of the Tash of Karesh Syl.

Now, in the middle of the chaos, it would be hard to watch his own back effectively…

Crack. WHOOSH!

Even before the magic took hold, Raz saw the signs. The light of the night sky dimmed substantially, drawing the fight into partial darkness again as its caster redirected part of her focus. Next came the heat, rising with such force from the sand about Raz's feet that a thin layer of grit lifted with it.

Lastly, the fire itself finally erupted into being.

Like white lightning the spell raced across the ground, emanating from a single point directly beneath Raz and radiating outward like the earth itself were fracturing. Flames bloomed into existence to chase these lines, rising no more than a foot high in any one place, but licking at the legs of any men and horses standing in Raz's direct proximity. In an instant the nearby noises redoubled with screams of the animals and shouts of pain and confusion from the *sarydâ*, and within no more than a handful of seconds a radius of some fifteen feet had cleared around Raz, leaving him alone in the center of a hundred branching tendrils of ivory fire. At his back there came the nervous nickering of a single horse, and Raz allowed himself a glance over his shoulder to find Syrah guiding Nymara through the flames, the magic dying and rekindling beneath the mare's hooves as it passed to keep from spooking her too much.

"Can I *possibly* compliment you enough on your timing?" he growled up to the woman once she'd pulled up just behind him, turning his eyes back on the line of the battle surrounding them.

"Doubtful. I'd say a few seconds more and you would have made a fine pincushion for a good number of *very* sharp knives..."

Raz snorted. From the muffled sound of her voice, he could tell Syrah was facing away from him, watching his flank. "You saw them too, then?"

"I did. Two?"

"At least." Raz peered through the melee, the dulling of the illumination working largely in his favor. He could still see well enough in the more-limited light, and it wasn't hard to tell that the *sarydâ* were breaking, so vastly outnumbered as they were. Even as he took in the last of the skirmishes that were coming to an end, more and more blades tumbling to the ground, either rolling from hands gone limp in death or thrown voluntarily by wielders hoping to see the true Sun at least one more time.

In the back of his head, Raz could feel the seconds ticking down as he and Syrah's particular opponents steadily lost the advantage of the chaos to shield themselves.

"Careful," he growled. "Any moment now. Tell me if—"

"LEFT!" Syrah shouted, and Raz turned sharply to meet the assault. Sure enough, a lone figure in dark, loose garbs of a familiar cut was coming at them, his outline little more than a black silhouette against the white fire as he dodged the flames with meticulous care. The caution in his rush made some instinct itch at the back of Raz's neck.

Too slow, the animal whispered in his ear. *He's coming too slow.*

"Distraction!" Raz shouted as it clicked, whirling. "Syrah, take him!"

There was a prompt answering flash of white light, but Raz didn't look back to see if the woman would be able to manage on her own. He was setting himself, a guttural growl building deep in his throat.

Rushing to meet him, two more streaks of grey and black were bolting across the fire, clearly having been hoping to take advantage of Raz's and Syrah's turned backs.

Unfortunately for them, they were forced instead to meet the Dragon of the North head on.

Although the two were anything but unskilled, the exchange with the assassins was as brief as it was brutal. Unsure as he was that Syrah would be able to put her heart into the fight at his back even if her life were in danger, Raz traded away precaution for speed. Instead of accepting their attack and answering, he launched himself forward with a snarl, meeting them both when the shadows still had five feet to go. Word must have reached even

Miropa of the demise of the last group that had stalked him and Syrah, because this pair were not as stalwart as those who'd danced with Raz in the Tash's court. Though their eyes never betrayed any fear, their bodies did, each of the men flinching ever so slightly away when he barreled into range of their blades. The moment this wince cost them brought with it a heavy toll as Raz ducked low, under the delayed thrusts of the knives, gladius and sagaris snaking out and in again in twin sweeps. The sword caught one of the assassins above the knee, severing the limb cleanly, while the axe took the other in the gut with a sound not unlike a melon being crushed under the wheels of a passing cart. The first fell away, the uncanny silence of his kind finally broken as his screams of pain rent the air, while the other only managed to vomit up a bellyful of blood before Raz tore the sagaris free of his stomach.

Two more flashes in the dim light of the magically lit night, and the shadows fell as nothing but a pair more corpses among a field of dead.

"Syrah?!" Raz shouted half-in-question, half-in-fear, whirling yet again. He relaxed, the tension in his body evaporating, and with unsteady relief he had to restrain a laugh. Syrah hadn't even moved from her place atop Nymara, despite the mare shuffling and stamping uneasily beneath her. Indeed, the woman looked almost unconcerned as she held tight to the animal's reins with one hand, the other raised to keep taut the two blazing lashes of white light that extended from her gloved fist. Ten feet away, hardly inches closer than he'd made it when Raz had been forced to turn his back on the man, the assassin was kicking and writhing furiously on his side in the sand. His ankles had been bound together by one of the tethers, and his arms were equally immobilized, awkwardly pinned as they were to his sides.

"Like a damn pig," Raz snorted, flicking his blades clean but leaving them bare as he approached.

"More like a snake, the way he's squirming about," Syrah responded, giving the magics a quick tug as the man's thrashing almost got his knees under him. He promptly fell back to the sand again, face first. "How do you want to deal with him?"

The question was asked as evenly as the woman could manage, but Raz knew better, and he looked away from the shadow to take her in carefully. She refused to meet his gaze, her one good eye firmly set on her captive, but he could see the tension in her bearing all the same, the thin press of her lips echoed in the hard stiffness of her shoulders.

Though she'd never said as much aloud, Raz had the impression Syrah had bent some silent vow, just now, using combat magic so directly for the first time since Karesh Syl…

"Can you keep him down?" he asked her gently. "Just a while more?"

Syrah hesitated.

Then she nodded rigidly.

Raz breathed easier, and finally allowed himself to look around again. Although it couldn't have been more than a minute or two since the woman had cast her earthen fire—now fading slowly to leave scorched lines in the sand around them—the battle had come to a final close. As he watched, the milling of the mounted soldiers was slowing, with many already sliding from innumerable saddles to round up those who'd surrendered and deal mercy where it was needed.

Making his decision, Raz at last sheathed his blades.

"Survivors are to be brought to me!" he boomed over the lingering scrape and shuffle of horses and men. "Bury the dead! All higher officers, attend!"

His voice carried with ringing clarity into the night, and at once the movement of the troops around them redoubled again. Within a minute, a score of bloodied mercenaries had been dragged to kneel in a half-circle around Raz and Syrah, closely guarded by fifty ranked soldiers on foot with their horses lingering nearby. Many among their commands busied themselves pulling some hundred shovels from where they'd been kept strapped to saddles, while the rest began the gruesome task of gathering and piling the bodies of the fallen *sarydâ*. Without enough work to go around, a majority of the riders were given leave to return to camp, and as they departed a handful more men joined the waiting group, returning from what must have been their chase of any mercenaries who'd escaped into the night. Cyper—the regular commander of the mounted regiment—arrived among them, taking in the gathering of survivors at a glance before pulling his dappled gelding about to join Raz, Syrah, Nymara, and Gale. The black stallion had come ambling back dutifully after the fires finally dissipated from around his master, and was now plodding around to snort at the scorch lines with distinct mistrust.

"All's well?" Cyper asked, eyeing the assassin Syrah still had bound nearby while he dismounted. His seconds were already doing the same, having just dismissed the common soldiers back to a well-deserved rest.

"Well, enough," Raz answered the West Isler with a nod, glancing at the prone figure, too. The man had finally quit his thrashing—done in an impressively utter silence—and was now breathing hard on his back in the sand. "Do we know if any escaped?"

Cyper grimaced, which would have been an adequate response even if he hadn't gone on. "At least one, apparently. Quick bastard. I'm told he got the drop on one of ours. Managed to get him out of the saddle and steal the horse. Killed another as he fled. Those of the unit nearby chased him a ways, but…"

"They were told not to stray far, aye." Raz gave a sad sigh. "Unfortunate. It was hard enough knowing we were likely sentencing some of our sentries to die, tonight. I was hoping not to lose anyone else to this folly…"

"So small a force…" Syrah muttered from over and behind him. "What were they bloody well thinking, wasting lives like this?"

"That it probably *wasn't* a waste." Cyper scratched at the stubble of his shaved head as he took in the *sarydâ* who'd been spared. "It's not much more than luck that we had any sort of warning. If they'd managed to take us unawares…"

"They could have wreaked havoc," Syrah finished for him in a huff. "Yes, I suppose that's true enough. And no small thing, given how precarious things have been. But still… Are they going to keep underestimating us?"

"I think this was less underestimation, and more miscalculation," Raz grumbled, motioning for a handful of the closest officers to approach. "They sent mercenaries who likely know the desert better than foot soldiers, and the way they scattered… It was clever…" He glanced up at Syrah. "If it wasn't for your spellwork, we would have lost the vast majority to the valleys in a matter of minutes. That we would have a means on hand of giving us their direction of approach also couldn't have been something they'd be able to predict. This was to have been a nuisance force, designed to slow us down. At this point, the Mahsadën are just playing for time."

"Something we have in short supply," Cyper commented dryly, echoing Raz's own words from earlier in the day.

Syrah snorted in grim agreement. "And running shorter by the minute, if Miropa's forces number enough already that they're willing to throw bodies at us if it means buying them so much as a few hours."

Raz only nodded again. The officers he had summoned over had joined them before the kneeling mercenaries, and with a wave of his axe he motioned at the supine form of the assassin in the sand nearby. "Pin him. By the arms, preferably. I want Syrah back in the camp and tending to any wounded we might have. Make sure he's not going *anywhere* before she lets up on her spell."

As one the group hurried to do as they were told. There was a quiet scuffling as the shadow began to fight again when the soldiers took hold of his arms and legs, but still the man remained adamantly silent.

His devout loyalty was becoming more irksome than impressive.

The moment a few of the officers looked up to nod in affirmation from where they'd immobilized the man in the sand, Syrah released her spellwork. In matching lines the white tethers faded in a shimmer of dust, and the night seemed to brighten ever so slightly as she refocused her energy on the spell that still hung suspended over their heads.

"Cyper, see if we don't have a torch or two among the clean-up crew," Raz told his general. When the general had departed to address the order, Raz looked around and up at Syrah. "You can let that one go as well." He motioned to the heavens with his gladius. "Then head back to the camp and rouse your trainees. There's more for you to do there than here, I think."

And you don't need to see this, he tried to tell her with his eyes.

Syrah seemed to get the message, because the smile she granted him was tight, but grateful. With a word and a wave of one hand toward the sky, the light receded in a wink, and after several seconds Raz's eyes were able to make out the Moon and Her Stars again, free to gaze upon the butchered shells of men which had once housed the souls They'd already claimed.

"I'll see you back at the tent?" Syrah asked Raz quietly, pulling Nymara's reins firm with one hand. The other, she extended out to him, almost tentatively.

At last, Raz put away his weapons, tucking the sagaris into its loops and sheathing the gladius over his shoulder with a firm *click*.

Then he took her fingers carefully in his steel-clawed grasp.

"You will. This won't take long."

Satisfied, Syrah held his hand a brief moment before finally letting go. Her eye fell fleetingly on the immobilized figure of the assassin, and she paused, looking like she might say something.

Then, though, she pulled Nymara fully about and heeled the mare back toward the warmth of the camp proper without a word.

Raz watched her go, wanting her well away from the act he was about to perpetrate while simultaneously waiting for Cyper to fetch the promised light. After a minute in which the woman had largely vanished between the dunes, the glow of flames rose at Raz's back, and he turned to find almost a dozen torches lifted by the other present officers in a half ring over the heads of the beaten desert mercenaries.

"I've no doubt—" he started, addressing the bloodied faces of the kneeling figures while Cyper came to stand beside him once more "—that there are those among you who would happily sell your mothers if it meant an extra crown in your pockets at the end of the day." Looking back, he gestured to the men still holding down the assassin behind him, motioning to the cleared ground by his feet. As Raz kept on, the group hauled the man up to stand and started dragging him forward, keeping his arms securely pinned while he fought them silently all the way. "I'm not lacking in gold, but I've spent too much of my life already padding the purses of murderers and thieves for information."

Once the shadow was in front of him, Raz glared down into his desert-born face. The man's wrappings had fallen from his nose and mouth as he'd struggled against Syrah's bonds, revealing a weathered complexion of some thirty years.

"Put him on his knees," Raz growled, and his officers started fighting to do so at once.

"I've learned—" addressing the *sarydâ* once again, Raz had to raise his voice to carry over the scuffling that was happening before him "—that there is only one thing you bastards value more than the weight of your coin purses. I won't be offering you crowns, or valuables. I won't even be offering you your freedom. You rank hardly better than the Mahsadën in my eyes, and I doubt any of the belittled and the bereaved that make up the men and women who just brought you to kneel think otherwise."

There was a murmured insult from among the group, and Raz locked eyes with the mercenary he thought had spoken, staring him down through the man's lank, bleached hair until the fool averted his eyes. There was a long moment of silence in which Raz didn't so much as glance away from the beaten figure.

Finally, when he was sure his point had been made, Raz looked down again.

The assassin had been brought down as commanded, his back to the *sarydâ*. In the light of the torches his leer was almost venomous, his dead eyes betraying not even the slightest hint of fear. Raz wasn't surprised. He'd carved his way through a dozen such men, and the emptiness of their hearts was easily the most terrifying thing about them. He would not be able to frighten this man into submission, nor threaten or bribe him into divulging what he knew of the surviving šef or Miropa's inner workings.

That was fine. An unbreakable mind had other uses, when displayed before those who were far-less unyielding.

Easing himself down to one knee before the assassin, Raz met his grey eyes unflinchingly.

"What's your name?"

He spoke the question clearly, ensuring every nearby ear could make out his words, mercenary and soldier alike. He cared less for any particular understanding of the query itself, desiring more the comprehension that it had been made in the first place.

The answer, after all, was already a given.

Silence.

The shadow did not spit in Raz face, nor curse him or shower him with insults about his race or ideals. The man did nothing, in fact, his face registering only the briefest moment of amusement, like the interrogation was some sort of farce to be laughed at.

Even a farce can have meaning, though, Raz thought before pressing on.

"Who is your master? I doubt my cousin has the sort of strength that would have men such as you bending to his will."

The amusement vanished, replaced once more by the perfect façade of cold detachment. This in-and-of-itself wasn't without meaning, but Raz's objective had him setting aside the curiosity at once.

"You're not going to answer any of my questions, are you?" he asked flatly.

The barest hint of a smirk, the assassin's lip curling ever so slightly upward at one corner.

"Suit yourself."

And then, before the man could so much as blink in surprise, Raz took hold of either side of his head in each clawed hand and powered upward on strong, lithe legs. The steel plating of his right knee collided with a vile, crunching *squelch* of breaking bone and collapsing flesh, and Raz felt the man's face cave in beneath the blow. It was, of its own fashion, a merciful death, as quick and painless as any Raz might have delivered.

The point, however, was not yet made.

Freeing one hand from the side of the corpse's head, Raz crushed an armor-clad fist into the dead man's ruined features, feeling bone and brain give further. Retracting his hand, he struck again, then again, then again, not even grunting under the effort. Blood and flecks of skin splattered the sand around Raz's feet and the arms and faces of the officers who'd been holding the man down by his shoulders. One of the soldiers gagged, and all of them stepped away quickly in disgusted surprise.

Raz made a mental note to apologize profusely to the group after the mess was over with.

With a final blow that sent gore streaking in a feathery arc almost to the dusty knees of the closest *sarydâ*, Raz let up his savage beating of the body. Lifting his eyes to the pale, horrified faces of the mercenaries, Raz shoved the assassin backward, careful to have the dead man fall so that the gruesome remains of his head were on clear display for any and all to see.

"As I said," Raz began, golden eyes burning into the shocked group before him as he wiped blood from his face with the back of his semi-clean left hand, "I will not give you coin. I will not give you freedom. But when I ask my questions of you, you *will* answer."

He pointed down at the ravaged cadaver at his feet.

"You will answer, because the one thing I'm willing to gift you tonight—" he grinned hideously, letting his neck crest flair above his head and extending his wings slightly to either side of him to glow in the blaze of the torches "—is your lives."

XXX

"No. There is no such thing as a 'better path' within these walls, Syrah. Do not begrudge or belittle the healing arts just because you find yourself with a talent for battle. In the end, people like you and I are the reason Laor is not loved by all *in these, our lands. We are necessary, yes, but we are also a weight, a strain on the fabric of faith and trust our kind has been trying for a millennium to weave across the North. We may not kill, but we are still an embodiment of violence painted over in a comforting coat of white.*

In the end, it is the healers who bear the burden of spreading the Lifegiver's word most heavily…"

— Talo Brahnt, lecturing his adopted daughter, Syrah, 851v.S.

Given the very clear effort Raz had made to separate her from the violent aftermath of the Mahsadën's failed ambush, Syrah was more than a little concerned when he showed up in the medical tent barely a half-hour after she'd taken her leave of the battlefield. What's more, his entrance was less than subtle, and more than a few of the trainees shouted in angry alarm when the flap to the triage area was almost ripped free of its stitching as the man stormed in like a thundercloud.

"Oy!" one of Syrah's male helpers started the loudest, distracting her from where she'd been working horse-gut stitches into the thigh of a cavalry soldier who'd suffered an unlucky blow to the upper leg. "This is a medical ward, not a—*eep*!"

It was the acute pitch of the man's surprised inhalation as he must have realized who he was speaking to that piqued Syrah's curiosity enough to glance up from her work. For a moment she couldn't understand what she was looking at, partially because she hadn't expected to see Raz for several hours more at least, but more because he was such a mess that he had her cursing even as she scrambled to hand the stitching to a nearby trainee and get to her feet.

"Lifegiver's mercy! Raz?! What…? Tell me this isn't *your* blood?!"

Golden eyes blinked at her through a gore-stained face that would have had a less-hearty soul balking. Syrah, instead, rushed forward, concern welling up like a filling fountain in her chest. When she'd left him, Raz hadn't exactly been spotless—he had a habit of wading into the very middle of any fight, after all—but the man looked now like he'd *bathed* in blood. The black of his scales shined crimson in the light of the tent's twin lamps, and the steel of his armor was stained in such thick rivulets of red, it appeared practically painted to the effect.

"What?" Raz demanded, looking down at himself with some confusion. "Oh. No. At least I don't think so. It doesn't matter. You need to come with me."

Before Syrah could protest, he'd grabbed her by the hand and led her in a rush back toward the tent's entrance, where Cyper Edalos was holding open the flap for them. The West Isler's face was grave, and Syrah felt a shiver that she wasn't sure had anything to do with the coolness of the night claw across her skin when Raz pulled her outside.

"Raz!" Syrah exclaimed again when he didn't stop, leading her into the center of the narrow fairway along which the ward had been set up. "What's wrong?! Tell me what's going on!"

Her frustration must have rung clear, because the man before her flinched like he'd been lashed. He did, however, finally halt, and in the middle of the path he turned on her, not letting go of her hand.

"Syrah…" Raz began slowly. "Theoretically… Would it be possible for you to cover an *entire* space in fire?"

For a long moment, Syrah gaped at him. This was *anything* but the sort of question she'd expected, given Raz's state and Cyper's obviously bleak disposition, and it took her several seconds to catch up to her surprise before answering.

"Cover…?" she repeated, not quite sure she understood. "You mean like I did among the *sarydâ*?"

"No." It was Cyper who answered, moving around to stand by Raz and stare at her just as intently. "More thoroughly. *Entirely*."

Syrah frowned as some small understanding clicked into place. What the two of them were talking about was indeed possible, but…

Thinking it was better to show them, Syrah pointed one finger of her free hand at the ground.

"Like this?"

Before either of the two opposite her could react, Syrah allowed her will to pour over the packed sand of the path about her feet. Fire gushed from the space about her ankles to run wild over the earth, spreading in a solid sheet of white flames. To their credit, neither Raz nor Cyper shouted in surprise or fear, though both flinched as the magic waved about their legs harmlessly, licking at steel plate and leather armor alike.

"Yes…" Raz muttered thoughtfully, dropping her hand at last to take in the fire with a dour dullness in his usually bright eyes. "Exactly like that, I would say…"

Syrah, having had enough of being kept in the dark, extinguished the spell with a flick of her wrist.

"I don't know what you two are on about, but the fact that you would ask so specifically about uncontrolled magic is more than a little alarming. If you'd be so kind as to explain yourselves, *I would be most grateful*."

She injected as much sarcasm into the last of her words as possible, but the answering expressions she received were anything but satisfactory. Like a mirrored pair, Raz and Cyper both looked at her with something between alarm and incomprehension.

"Uncontrolled?" Raz echoed, sounding distinctly confused. "What do you mean, 'uncontrolled'?"

"I mean exactly that!" Syrah answered, heated now and waving both hands out to indicate the ground upon which the flames had burned only moments before. "Uncontrolled. Unrestrained. Unharnessed. It's the sort of magic an acolyte would be expected to perform. A novice, you could say."

"A… novice?" Cyper's question came like he didn't understand a single word she'd just said. "But… There's so much fire…"

"There is, but for no good reason," Syrah pressed, feeling her patience ebb by the second. Forcing herself to take a deep breath, she crossed her arms across her chest and looked at Raz squarely. "Look, if it will help, consider this: what *functional* difference is there between the magic you just saw, and the ground lightning I cast earlier tonight?"

There was a moment of silence.

"Very little," Raz finally said, speaking like something had just dawned on him.

"Essentially." Syrah nodded, feeling like she was back in the Citadel teaching a class of baffled converts. "Functionally, there is very little difference. However, in terms of energy expended…" She let the suggestions hang, guiding her odd pupils toward the right conclusion.

"The lightning uses less…?" Cyper attempted tentatively, and she rewarded him with a reluctant smile.

"Very much so. There's some skill and effort involved in the control, sure, but it's like an archer taking the time to shoot for the heart, rather than fire off a hundred arrows without really aiming, knowing one of them will eventually get the job done."

"So you're saying that someone who could cast a spell like that… They're not likely to be anything more than an *acolyte* of Laor?"

For some reason, Raz's question—low and still tinged with concern—had the hair on Syrah's arm standing on end.

"Likely…" she responded slowly, eyeing her partner with no lack of suspicion. "*Why*?"

Cyper opened his mouth to answer, but Raz held him up with a raised hand. The daggers in the look Syrah gave him then would have cowed a lesser man, but he pressed on.

"One last question, I'm sorry. Someone like that—an acolyte. How dangerous could they be?"

Syrah narrowed her eyes at him, her confusion growing by the second. "That depends… All our arcane lessons are overseen by skilled Priests to make certain students learn carefully and steadily. It can be difficult, grasping Laor's gifts. It takes anywhere from months to years to get the basics, and after that there are any number of disciplines one can focus on. By the time we're given leave to use our powers at will, we certainly have a solid enough grasp on the essentials to ensure that no one is put at unnecessary—"

"Syrah. To a layman like me. To someone lacking the ability to defend ourselves against spellwork. If an acolyte could use their gifts without restraint… How dangerous could they be?"

Syrah's confusion cooled all at once. There was that edge in Raz's voice again—not fear, per se, but something near enough to it— and it scraped at bad memories. For a moment Syrah was again kneeling in a crater of fractured marble, Lysa's ashes staining her white robes black and grey.

Then she blinked, and Raz stood before her again, his eyes bright and warm despite the blood that had dried across most of his face.

Syrah inhaled, steadying herself in the strength of his gaze.

"Extremely. You've seen how dangerous uncontrolled magic can be with your own eyes, Raz." She looked to Cyper as well. "Both of you have."

Understanding dawned on the paired men in the same moment. Cyper hissed in a breath, and Raz swore by all Her Stars. Before Syrah could yet again demand an explanation, however, it came unprompted.

"Syrah," Raz began. "There's good chance we have a very, *very* big problem."

Then he began recounting everything he and Cyper had gleaned from interrogating the *sarydâ.*

Almost at once Syrah understood Raz's appearance. Within a minute of the pair of them speaking, she realized that anyone with any reason would not have taken the time to call for water and a towel in the rush to seek her out. If what the desert mercenaries had to tell them was even *remotely* true…

"Impossible," Syrah finally managed to get out once Raz and Cyper were through with their summary, her voice barely higher than a whisper. "It's impossible. No one… No one among the Laorin…" She realized her hands were shaking, and she clenched them into fists by her side. "It's impossible," she said again, this time through gritted teeth.

Raz stepped closer to grip her shoulders gently, both of them uncaring of the blood-stained leather and steel of his gauntlets. "I thought so too, at first, but the rumors were consistent, Syrah."

"And specific," Cyper insisted darkly. "*White* fire? It's too much of a coincidence.

Syrah, for her part, only shook her head in a denying jerk, her eye seeing beyond the corded muscle of Raz's chest before her. "Impossible… Who…? How could they…?"

"If you don't know the answer to that question, then it's not likely I can provide it for you." Raz's eyes dipped into her vision again as he bent to look her in the face. "But we have to deal with it. Can you get a letter out by morning? The answers are coming faster now, aren't they?"

Syrah nodded automatically, only half-hearing his words.

"Syrah. *Syrah.*" She felt herself shaken lightly, and the jolt at last brought her back to the present. She blinked to find Raz's face so close to hers, her heart skipping a beat as she realized she was slipping to a darker place than she'd been in months, just then.

"I need to report all of this to the others," he told her quietly. "Cyper already sent a runner to gather everyone." He pulled her a little closer, as though wanting to assure her he was there, right there for her. "I need you with me. I can't explain this satisfactorily on my own…"

Syrah swallowed once, shaking herself free of the last images of half-a-hundred flame-torn corpses and the shattered remnants of Ekene Okonso's court.

She nodded, and then forced herself to return the grateful smile Raz gave her.

She insisted on a moment to reenter to the ward, leaving a few final instructions for her trainees regarding some of the more complex injuries some of the cavalry soldiers had sustained, and came outside again only after soaking a clean rag in warm water. This she handed to Raz as she left the tent again—receiving a quick word of thanks in return as he immediately began wiping at his face, neck, and hands—and allowed Cyper to take the lead so the three of them formed a tight triangle while they half-ran west through the camp, making for the head of the army. They reached the general's pavilion in record time, and Raz offered the now-blood-soaked cloth to the sands as the West Isler pulled the entrance flap open for them once more. Inside there was the murmur of a great number of voices, and as Syrah followed Raz into the tent, she was struck—not for the first time—by how crowded the interior had become.

She suspected this war of theirs would be over before she got accustomed to the newcomers among their highest ranks.

A quartet of small braziers—one in each corner of the staked leather and canvas—cast weird shadows through the gathered atherian who lined the outer ring of the tent's interior. Every chieftain was present—even Zathlys of the Lower Feet, though his expression was sour—and each had come accompanied by one or two trusted seconds, as Raz and the Queen had allowed for when the leaders of the Crag's lizard-kind started joining such meetings. A handful of others mingled among them, veterans of the march Zal'en had hand-picked for their command of both the Common and atherian tongues, who would act as translators. All in all, some thirty new additions had been added, making the once spacious area almost contrastingly crowded.

The fact that the center table, too, was busier now, didn't help.

Shas-Hana Rhan had been bequeathed the place of highest honor, just to Raz's right. Zal'en now sat at her side, ready to provide private translation for the Queen and Sassyl Gal, who stood just behind their shoulders like an ever-present shadow. Syrah had given up the place more than happily, eager to ensure any measure of goodwill in the eyes of the tribes, and Akelo had taken up the seat to her left, across from Zal'en. The others sat where they willed further down the table, and as she, Raz, and Cyper entered one after the other, Odene, Kalin, and Hur all made to stand respectfully from their chairs.

"Sit. Sit." Raz waved them back down with an impatient hand, the joints of his claws still crusted with red flakes he hadn't been able to scrub off as they'd hurried. He claimed his own seat at the head of the table, and Syrah sat at his left. "It's practically morning, so I doubt any of us have the patience for any pretense of formality."

A ghost of a smile crossed over the *kujas'* faces, but Hur's eyes only narrowed in concern. Akelo, too, beside Syrah, was taking Raz in very deliberately.

"Raz, what…?" the old man began in his gravelly voice, but was given a brief shake of the head to stop the obvious question. As Raz turned to greet Shas-hana Rhan, though—his *mother*, Syrah always had to remind herself—the Percian leaned in close.

"What in the Sun's name happened to him?" Akelo asked under his breath.

"You should have seen him *before* he cleaned up," she answered quietly, raising an eyebrow. "He looked like he'd single-handedly taken on butchering a week's worth of game for the entire bloody army."

Akelo snorted, straightening away from her again while hiding a smile, which eased a little of the tension in Syrah's chest. She hadn't shaken the shock of Raz and Cyper's news, but in the familiar company of these men—friends a year and more, now—she felt herself start to gain control of her fear.

"First, thank you all for gathering so quickly. Believe that I am *acutely* aware of the lateness of the hour, and I imagine more than a few of you were pulled from your beds."

Raz's words rang clear through the thrum of voices which had only generally quieted on their arrival, and as he spoke all other sound ceased but the murmur of the translators, who started their work at once. Across from her, Syrah watched Zal'en bend to address the Queen's ear.

"Like any one of us was sleepin'." Marsus was the first to answer the apology. "If a single soul at this table's gotten a wink since you three saddled up—" he waved nonchalantly at Raz, Syrah, and Cyper "—I'll eat my left boot."

Beyond the generals across from her, Syrah thought she saw as many nods of agreement from the tribe chieftains as she did looks of guilt exchanged once the Southerner's words had been turned for them.

Raz, despite himself, managed a smirk.

"I suppose I'll keep from berating myself too harshly, then. Now, first." He looked to Shas-hana, and inclined his head in an obvious show of respect. "I must thank the Queen and her chieftains for their assistance with handling tonight's assault. The buried lookouts performed admirably, as did the flares. I didn't know such mechanisms existed, and will be certain to have our forgers asking after them come morning."

Here, Raz paused, his eyes moving from his mother to scan the walls of the tent. When he found the individual he was looking for, he dipped his head a second time, even deeper.

"Gyssa of the Upper Caverns," he addressed the aged female who stood in a corner of the space, her rodent-spun furs layered thickly over her shoulders. "The pair who gave us the *sarydâ's* location were of your brood. Their bravery stands above all others' tonight, and it is with my regrets that I tell you that one of the two have fallen. There were assassins among the mercenaries, and it would appear they reacted faster than your tribesman could anticipate. You have my condolences."

The first atherian to fall since the Crags, Syrah thought to herself, realizing why Raz was taking the time to pay his respects to the chieftain. Gyssa, for her part, stiffened, her silhouette framed against the brazier at her back and the two large males who flanked her, the same specimens she'd summoned to challenge Raz among the mountains.

After a few seconds' quiet, though, the old female bowed her own head in thanks and acceptance.

"Assassins?" Erom spoke up once it was obvious the necessary formalities were over with. "As in—?"

"The same sort who came after Syrah and I in Karesh Syl?" Raz finished the question for him. "Yes, though I don't think we've anything more to fear for the time being. I have it on the authority of some twenty tongues that only a trio of shadows were accompanying Vyres Eh'ben and his *sarydâ*, all of which I saw handled personally."

There was a murmuring from the atherian at the mention of assassins, but Akelo kept the pause brief.

"Eh'ben? I've not heard that name…"

"None of us have." Cyper spoke up from the Percian's left. "He's a Karthian šef, likely sent to ensure order among the Mahsadën's nuisance troops. Apparently the mercenaries considered him something of a fool…"

"They sent a *šef* out here?" Akelo demanded, turning on his second in disbelief. "Are they mad? Is *he* mad? Tell me we have him!"

"No such luck," Raz sighed in answer. "He wasn't one of the survivors. We have a few of the spared *sarydâ* working to see if they can identify him among the dead, but I have a feeling he won't be there, either."

"Meaning some escaped?" Erom asked.

"At least one," Cyper answered with a nod. "Killed two of our own as he fled."

There was a moment of angry silence, but with a polite rumble of her throat, Shas-hana Rhan finally spoke up.

"*This* 'šef'." The Common word rolled awkwardly from her forked tongue, and Zal'en switched to translating for the table. "*He is among the leaders of the cities*?"

Raz in answer, shot Syrah a hopeful look, and she took it upon herself to answer for him.

"*He is,*" she confirmed fluently. "*He is one of many heads of the snake.*"

"*The* 'Mahsadën'?" Sassyl Gal tried from behind his Queen, and Syrah didn't think she did a good job of hiding how impressed she was with his pronunciation. The spymaster had taken it upon himself to learn as much of the Common Tongue as he could, and had made great leaps under Zal'en's tutelage in nothing more than the last ten-day.

"*Yes,*" she agreed again. "*But careful, must we be, to separate the cities from the sickness that festers within them. Hundreds of thousands of lives, are there, that have little and less to do with the society. I would swear on the Lifegiver a great majority of them would be rid of the slave rings if they could.*"

Sassyl Gal grunted in acknowledgement, apparently not wholly convinced, but said nothing more. Before him, the Queen looked ponderous, bright eyes on the table so that the clean-cut stone of her black crown shined at an angle in the firelight.

"The fact that a šef was among the ambush is less surprising—" Raz spoke up once Zal'en finished her translation "—when I tell you that there appears to be a new hierarchy within the Mahsadën, these days…"

There was a moment of silence that for once had nothing to do with letting Zal'en and the others catch up. Every one of the generals stared at Raz in open incomprehension, right up until he pressed on.

"Overall, most everything is as expected. The Mahsadën's forces stand now at over seventy thousand strong, including five thousand cavalry. Reinforcements continue to trickle in from Karavyl and Acrosia, as well as the *sarydâ* companies the šef have employed, but as a whole I believe they aren't likely to swell to any significantly greater strength."

"Seventy thousand…" Odene muttered from down the table. "Even if it's 'as expected', they still outnumber us by more than fifteen thousand swords…"

"A complication Syrah has taken upon herself to resolve," Raz answered with a dismissive wave of one hand. "More concerning… It would appear the šef are being made to bend the knee."

"What?" Marsus blurted out, sitting up straighter in his chair. "How? To who? What sort of person under the Sun would the bleedin' *šef* bow to? The whole *point* of the Mahsadën was equal control of shared power."

"Which works right up until someone shows up with significantly greater strength than any allyship among them," Cyper put in gravely.

"Then I ask again," Marsus insisted. "What sort of person holds more power than the people with armies dancin' under their damn fingers?!"

Syrah felt her throat tighten at the question, like the words she knew she had to say were clawing to stay huddled up against her heart.

With no small amount of difficultly, she forced them out.

"Someone who wields *actual* power, Marsus," her voice came quietly. "The kind of tangible ability which can be drawn on in raw form, rather than through whispered words and channels."

Slowly, Marsus turned to her, his grey eyes wide as he comprehended what she meant. For a long moment he gaped, the understanding quicker to come than the belief.

"Magic?!" he hissed, so low it was almost lost to the murmur of the Zal'en and the other translators.

Again, Syrah had to battle to get the answer out.

"Magic," she confirmed quietly.

Before the Southerner could push her any further, Raz came to Syrah's rescue.

"Apparently the Mahsadën have come under the thumb of an individual who wields gifts not unlike Syrah's own. To call this strange would be an understatement, given the circumstances, but especially considering who it is the mercenaries claimed this person to be." He paused, evidently suffering his own struggle with getting the words out. "If the *sarydâ* are to be believed, my own cousin—a man who calls himself 'Adrion Blaeth'—is the master of these abilities."

At once, nearly every face around the table darkened. Syrah knew Akelo and the others had been at their side for long enough now to have some understanding of what it took for Raz to speak his cousin's bastard name.

Only Shas-hana Rhan and Sassyl Gal looked less than unsettled.

"*Your cousin*?" The Queen's tone was betrayed as uncertainty that was somewhat beneath her usual display of calm regality. "*But... You told us that family...*"

She stopped short, realizing where she was going with her confusion. Raz gave his birth mother a sad, reassuring smile.

"The Arros largely perished, yes. The details of that story are ones best articulated another time, but for now... Some of us survived. Myself. My aunt Prida." His smile soured a little. "And my cousin, Mychal, who chose to abandon his name when he took up with the likes of the Mahsadën."

This explanation only had the Queen looking further bewildered, but Raz's expression must have gotten the message across that they would talk later, because she didn't say anything more.

"As I was saying," Raz kept on, finally addressing the others again, "this is perplexing, because for as long as I've known my cousin, he has shown no such power as those repeatedly described to Cyper and I tonight. Not even an inclination of the like. He's a clever man—devilishly so, I would grant—but barring some unfortunate miracle granted under the Sun's gaze, he is not the true bearer of these abilities. More likely is that he's acting as a puppet master to the actual wielder, or something of the sort."

Hur grunted loudly enough to garner their attention, then motioned with a big hand for Raz to elaborate.

"What sort of abilities?" Raz asked him, making sure he understood the question. The Northerner nodded briefly, and Raz visibly hesitated. Syrah forced herself not to look at him, watching Hur fixedly, intent on not meeting her partner's eyes and risk allowing him to see the fear return to her own.

Mercifully, Cyper got the ugly business over with quickly.

"Fire," the West Isler said firmly. "White fire. Flames that consume and destroy and often run wild with limited restraint."

Despite the voices of the atherian translators around them, the tent as a whole seemed to go cold. Even Zal'en failed to speak, her yellow eyes turning—like everyone else's at the table—to Syrah. Beside her the Queen blinked in confusion, but Syrah could not blame the older female's moment of distraction from her task.

The reason the soldiers of the army called her "Witch", after all, was long since certain to have become a story shared a hundred times over each evening's campfires…

There was a second rough sound, then, and Syrah was palpably grateful when Hur stole back some of the silent attention. He was, however, watching her—if not unkindly—and when he raised a hand this time it was to trace a symbol in the air that had her breath catch in her throat. First the familiar flat line, followed by the rough outline of a half-circle above it. It was such a known thing to her in particular, but to have it presented like this—in the middle of a Southern desert surrounded by worshipers of other gods—felt so bizarre that for a moment Syrah's mind failed to grasp what she'd seen.

The sign of new life, rebirth, and the rising sun.

The sign of Laor, the Lifegiver.

For the first time, it occurred to Syrah then that of everyone seated at that table—other than perhaps Raz—that it was probable the mute Northerner was the only individual who possessed any meaningful grasp on the creeds and laws of her faith, on her beliefs and her struggles. Hur's deities were not the same—or at least she had always *assumed* they were not, given the massive man's failure to indicate otherwise—but even a believer of the harsher Stone Gods was likely to have a better sense of Laor than the life-long followers of the Twins.

She stared at him blankly for what must have been nearly five whole seconds—mouth dry with surprise—before managing to find her voice again.

"The-The Laorin?" she asked of the Northerner, and Hur grunted his assent. "No. They would have nothing to do with this. For a member of the faith to be involved…"

Impossible, the word echoed about her mind, but this time she couldn't bring herself to say it aloud. She had trouble believing it, if she were being honest with herself. The way Raz and Cyper described what the *sarydâ* claimed to have heard in the frequent whisperings of Miropa's underground. The certainty with which it was known that the single šef of the city held sway over the Mahsadën as a whole.

It was magic. It *had* to be magic.

And it was *Laorin* magic.

Hur frowned. Then, lifting his hand, he made another sign about his right eye, a circle, followed by a rough cross-shape cutting diagonally across his face. Syrah was less taken aback, this time. If Hur knew enough of the Laorin to know the sign of the rising sun, the fact that he was aware of the Broken was hardly surprising.

"They would have been stripped of their powers," she said with a shake of her hooded head, wincing internally at the memory of the two times she'd been required to witness the violence of such a ritual, once recently, once some decades gone. "And long *before* anything like what the *sarydâ* have reported could happen. My—" Syrah nearly choked on the word, and the smell of smoke and scorched flesh filled her nose before she tried again. "The Laorin are a tight-knit people. If one of theirs had gone missing—especially one who showed any inclination of abusing their power—every temple in the North would have been put on alert. Raz and I were among the valley towns in the same period this individual seems to have taken their place within the slave rings. We would have heard if a Priest or Priestess—or even an acolyte—was suspected of having abandoned their vows."

Hur grunted and sat back in his chair, apparently having expected some like answer, but finding it unsatisfying just the same. There was quiet for a time, but steadily all eyes moved from the pair of them to Raz again. Syrah, too, turned to her partner, and found him oddly pensive, staring at Hur with slit eyes that seemed to be looking beyond the mountain man.

"Raz?" Syrah prodded him gently, reaching out to touch the still-bloody scales of his scarred upper arm.

Raz blinked, then looked around at her. His face relaxed, but he continued to look troubled.

"Sorry," he muttered loudly enough for the table to hear, bringing up one hand to scratch at the side of his head. "You two made me feel like I was going to remember something." He paused, expression twisting as he struggled to recall whatever it was that had itched at his mind, but eventually he gave up with a huff. "No good. Couldn't have been that important, I guess."

"I hope not," Syrah said back, studying his features more critically now without removing her hand. "Are you alright? Did you get hit in the head? I'm sorry, I didn't even think to check you over before—"

There was a polite cough from behind her left, and at once Syrah felt her face flush in embarrassment, realizing she'd forgotten where they were for a moment. She turned back in her seat to find Akelo eyeing her and Raz sidelong with his thick arms crossed over his chest, a glint of amusement in his dark eyes. She took the hint. Sitting back quickly, she cleared her throat as she hopelessly willed the blood to drain from her pale cheeks.

"It *is* magic," she told the gathered listeners, "and it *would* appear to be of a kind with that of Laor's gift, but aside from what I've just explained, there is another discrepancy I cannot come to terms with: if we theorize that this individual is—or was, rather—of my faith—" Syrah was relieved to find she could consciously claim that much still, at least "—then the spellwork described is all the more confusing. It is rudimentary. Unchanneled and with little direction. Based on what the *sarydâ* were apparently able to say, I've already told Raz and Cyper that I would guess the person in question to have the knowledge of an acolyte, and a fairly young one at that."

"An acolyte?" Erom asked from across the table.

"An individual who yet to earn their staff," Raz answered for Syrah. "Someone who hasn't been consecrated by the elders as a full-fledged Priest or Priestess. Their understanding and mastery of magic would be lacking, resulting in the sort of destructive power Cyper just mentioned."

"Ain't that a good thing?" Marsus drawled from beside Erom, grey eyes flicking from between Raz and Syrah. "If they're lackin' in ability, then it means they'll have a harder time controlling their… their…" The Southerner trailed off, seeing the issue come full circle. "Ah. That *is* the problem, ain't it?"

"It is," Syrah managed to get out with a stiff nod. "Those of the temples use the gifts of Laor to hunt for game in the harvest season, and spellwork is not without innate offensive ability even *when* controlled. Magic *can* kill."

And terribly so, she didn't feel the need to add as most of the faces around her darkened again.

"'Laor'… *This is the god you pray to, is it not, Syrah Brahnt?*"

Every eye turned to Shas-hana Rhan, who was watching Syrah carefully. It wasn't odd that the Queen would know this—she'd taken it upon herself to learn many things of Raz and his generals, in her short time among them—but her tone seemed to be prodding for something in particular.

Syrah nodded slowly.

"*Would you not be the best to challenge such an opponent, then?*"

The question came with no malicious intent, no aggressive intonation, but all the same it set Syrah's heart in a fluttering pattern that almost had her clutching at her breast. Shas-hana must have noticed her abrupt agitation, because her face was sad and kind as she continued.

"*I am sorry if this causes you pain, child, but I am not so fool as to claim that this is just* one *person to fear among the forces of this* 'Mahsadën'. *I have seen your power, Syrah Brahnt. You once used it to save my own life. That sort of strength, if raised against us…*" She glanced briefly at Raz, then back to Syrah. "*I do not know the entirety of your story, but I know enough to understand that you cannot kill. And yet… Is there another means by which to combat such an enemy?*"

The question lingered heavy in the air once Zal'en was done turning it for everyone else, and Syrah found herself struggling to meet Shas-hana's eyes. There was yet nothing malevolent in the Queen's gaze, nothing derisive or insulting. Her query came from a place of true concern, true uncertainty.

It made finding the words to answer with all the harder to come by.

"*Mother of mine…*" Raz began to speak in rough atherian, very clearly intent on shielding Syrah once more.

This time, though, she knew she needed to stand on her own two feet, there before the eyes of every general and chieftain in the entirety of the army. This was not a question anyone else could bear in her stead.

Whatever answer Raz had been trying to give died away as Syrah's hand fell on his nearest arm again, and he looked back at her. She shook her head and gave him a grateful smile, and he hesitated.

Then he settled back in his chair again, allowing her to lean over the table toward Shas-hana Rhan.

"*That I am so suited to such a task, I do not know, my Queen.*" She spoke in atherian as a sign of respect, trusting Zal'en to see to it the others understood her words. "*Not anymore. A warrior, I was once. Believe it or not, a time there was—not so far gone, now—when I stood by your own child's side in battle, often as his equal.*"

A snort of doubt rose up behind her, from among the atherian, but a burning glare from Raz in the direction of the noise stifled any other interruption.

"*That strength… I have lost it, I'm afraid,*" Syrah continued as though nothing had happened. "*Claim it was taken from me, I would like to, but that would only be half-true. The magics you have seen are the extent of what I can bring myself to perform. In a battle against one who would summon such terrible a force to bear without a moment's hesitation, to assume my triumph… As to whether I would come out the victor of such a fight, I cannot wager…*"

"*Which means another will have to be set to the task,*" Sassyl Gal said brusquely as soon as she was done, his eyes falling pointedly on Raz. "*In a battle in which we are already outnumbered, to allow these 'sef' to apply such a singular advantage against us is inconceivable.*"

"*Agree, I do,*" Raz acknowledged the spymaster's words with a nod even before Zal'en finished her translation. "*But other factors, we must consider as well. I will wield my own blades against this spellcaster, if required I am to do so, but only one of many hurdles to overcome, are they. Miropa draws nearer with every hour. Prepare for the larger battle, we must. And soon.*"

"*One of many, perhaps, but a creature such as which can employ the fires of the Daystar with wicked intent possesses a singular peril that our kind has no means of combating.*" Gal motioned to himself and the Queen, as though deliberately separating them from Raz. "*Perhaps your ranks are better suited to such evils, but we—*"

"*Not a man, woman, or atherian among this army is any better prepared for such an engagement, master of spies.*" It was, surprisingly, Zal'en who half-turned in her chair to address the conversation directly for the first time all evening. "*We are all at a similar disadvantage in this, and Arro is correct to say that we have the larger war to see to. Although you and the Queen are both wise to understand the danger this enemy might pose to* all *of us—*" she dipped her head carefully to them to show she meant it "*—there is yet the greater war we must still focus on.*"

Sassyl's bright eyes narrowed dangerously, and he bared blunted fangs at the female. "*Remind yourself of your place,*" he growled, something more than cool calculation flaring momentarily in his aged demeanor. "*You are an attendant of Shas-hana Rhan, here. You've no business injecting your—*"

"*A general, Zal'en is, master of spies.*" Syrah cut in, feeling a little of her usual fire return as she stared up at the male evenly from across the table. "*Of Raz i'Syul Arro's army. One of yours she was, once, and if she should so decide to return to your webs, Raz would give her leave to do so, I've no doubt. But that request, she has not made. Until then, insist I must that you extend to her the same courtesy you have so admirably shown the rest of us."*

It was hardly an exaggeration. Unlike his Queen, Sassyl Gal had always maintained a distance from the humans of Raz's inner circle, but he had nevertheless remained civil even in his withdrawal. Whereas Shas-hana Rhan had gone out of her way to at least learn the stories of the generals who still kept in company of the army, the spymaster had satisfied himself with whatever information his network had more discreetly provided. They formed two sides of a well-balanced coin—the Queen playing the willing liaison, while Gal saw to the secrets less readily shared—but he'd always been cordial no matter who addressed him, if a little cool.

If nothing else, Syrah would have that minimum level of equality extended to *all* who sat at that table.

The male stiffened slightly at being so directly reprimanded, his gaze falling sharply on Syrah. Rose met gold, and there was a brief moment of stillness that not even the translators appeared eager to interrupt.

Then, with a visible relaxation of his shoulders, Sassyl Gal bowed his head in apology, first to Syrah, then to Zal'en herself.

"*Of course,*" he said, and his tone stiff, but genuine. "*My apologies to the general. I am not of the habit to share authority with any other but the Queen.*"

At once—even without the words being turned for the others to understand—the tension in the room dissipated. Zal'en gave Syrah a surprised but appreciative look, then took it on herself to briefly summarize the missed exchange for the remainder of the table.

"You are not incorrect to fear this amendment in circumstances," Raz finally started to speak again in Common, addressing the spymaster directly once the female had finished her translation. "It is why I called us to meet, despite the hour. Still, this march can hardly be brought to heel over every new variable. We *should* address it—and we shall—but as part of the larger picture, rather than a singular problem all its own."

"Then how 'bout we revisit the discrepancy in our strengths?" Marsus asked, looking a little hesitant to bring it up. "My opinion is that Odene's just as right to be worryin'. Fifteen thousand heads' difference ain't nothin' to scoff at, even with our new… ah… reinforcements." He gave a dubious glance over their shoulders to the atherian lining the wall. Then the Southerner nodded toward Syrah. "I know you and the miss've been cookin' something up, Raz, but ain't it about time you told us about it, too?"

Raz in answer, looked to Syrah, and she considered for a moment. She'd intended to wait another day—perhaps even two or three. It wasn't that she didn't trust these hardened men who sat around them now. They—each and every one of them—had *earned* said trust tenfold over.

Who the generals in turn chose to have faith in, on the other hand, she and Raz had far less control over…

And one cannot presume to know where the Mahsadën have seeded their eyes and ears, she thought unwillingly, hating that she'd had to assume for so long that some information was best kept close.

Still… Wasn't it indeed about time to let this hope spread, at least among the inner circle?

Making her decision, she looked to Raz for affirmation. Her conviction must have been plain on her face, because he didn't hesitate in waving one hand to indicate the others in encouragement.

With a lifting heart, Syrah leaned forward over the table again, looking to Marsus in particular.

"Very well. But this is to be kept for those within this tent, and this tent alone, understood?"

There was an immediate rush of agreement from the men, and only a few seconds after came a similarly enthusiastic chorus of promising from the Queen and the chieftains along the wall. Even Zathlys of the Lower Feet nodded quickly enough, apparently as eager to hear of any hidden advantage as the rest of them.

Despite herself, Syrah managed the first real smile since taking to saddle earlier in the evening with the intent to see blood spilled.

"What if I were to tell you all—" she started, meeting every eye she could "—that we are no longer alone in this war?"

XXXI

"In the end, the most dangerous enemies are simply the ones you don't see coming..."

— Ergoin Sass

The summons came with the dawn, the loud cough outside her tent rousing Serys Benth to dancing rays of light streaming dimly through the pitched holes in the top of her palisade. It took her a moment to place herself, having been pulled from flickering dreams of Karavyl engulfed in ivory fire. Once she managed it, she groaned and rolled to prop herself onto one elbow on the thick bedroll.

"Enter," she called out in as assertive a voice as she could muster, uncaring of her nakedness beneath the heavy blankets she'd slept under to ward off the chill of the desert night.

Her body had been an instrument of trade and ascension for too many years now for Serys to view it as anything less rudimentary than a tool.

Her attendants, fortunately, were more than accustomed to this.

With a brief flash of light, Analla Zaren slipped into the tent, already dressed in a sensible white smock and sandals that clashed well with her ebony skin. The girl was as practical as she was pretty, however, and so delivered her message without embellishment, not even blinking at her mistress' exposed form.

"Arro has reached us."

As expected as the words were, they still sent a shiver of mixing emotions crawling up Serys' arms. Excitement. Anticipation.

Fear.

Abruptly wide awake, she heaved clear the folds of her blankets and shoved herself to her feet on the woven mat that made up the movable floor of her lodgings.

"When?" Serys asked while she strode toward the small wardrobe in a canvas corner, feeling her loose hair trail along her bare back and sand press through the reeds with every step.

"Sometime in the night. A sharp-eyed sentry apparently claimed to have spotted torchlight before the Sun rose, but no one else had seen it. He was almost lashed before a half-dozen outriders arrived with confirmations. They're saying you can see the dust clouds from the dune-tops, now."

Serys snorted, wrenching open the dresser and plucking a clean outfit of white pants and a blue silk shirt, simple-but-elegant in design. At once, Analla approached to help her dress.

"Make that one head of the watch, I say." She slipped into the pants and tied them tight about her slim waist, then accepted assistance in pulling on the shirt. "Where are we gathering?"

"Beyond the forward line," the Percian answered, fussing over her only a moment more by making sure the clothes were smooth about her form. "Arro is a ways away, yet, and Blaeth has summoned all to meet."

Serys said nothing to that, choosing instead to mull over her thoughts in silence while buttoning up her shirt.

Adrion Blaeth… Master of all, and yet master of none…

Grimacing at the mess the Mahsadën had found themselves in, Serys plucked her own sandals from the base of her bedroll and swept barefoot from the tent, calling for Eshed as she did.

It was ten minutes beneath the ugly heat of the Sun later that Serys, Analla, and San Loreyn were escorted to the foot of a broad sand dune at the eastern head of their encampment. San was still muttering unpleasantries as Serys told Analla to stay behind with Eshed and their retinue, and did not stop when the pair of them began the steep climb up the uneven embankment on their own.

"The lizard just *had* to pick today to smash himself against us, didn't he?" the šef muttered to no one in particular, blinked up sourly at the Sun glaring from a heaven as clear and azure as blue-tinged crystal while he dabbed lightly at the sweat along his neck with a kerchief.

Serys ignored the man. Their journey east with the army had been strenuous given the ease of their regular lives, but whereas she'd adapted quickly, San had only grown more unpleasant. It didn't help that he'd been in a foul mood since Ahamed Ehmeth and the others had joined them in Miropa some weeks prior, likely ruining what little sense of importance he'd felt at being one of only two to represent Karavyl at Blaeth's table for months. Serys herself wasn't pleased with the situation—neither Ehmend nor Kusu Keyshm, the city's most veteran šef, had thought to stay behind and tend to things at home, too eager were they to see the end of "the Monster of Karth"—but she kept her displeasure to herself.

Once Arro fell, it might just be for the better that all the other fringe cities had their strength already mustered in Miropa, after all…

A blast of hot desert wind caught them as they climbed, sending San stumbling several steps and tossing Serys' clothes and hair about her shoulders and face. Forced to turn her back against the gust before it threw sand in her eyes, she waited it out. Finally, it settled.

When she'd freed her vision, though, Serys had to work not to openly gape at the sight that extended over the expansive plains to the west, opened to her from the incline of the dune like the endless wash of an ocean seen from a cliff.

It was by no means the first time she'd taken in the vastness of the gathered army of the Mahsadën—they had been marching for two days eastward, after all—but on every occurrence the breadth of the columned lines of tents and soldiers appeared to swell. The majority of the host comprised of footmen in plain, common armor, the attire made uniform across each cohort of every city for tactical ease, but Blaeth was—if nothing else—a master of coin and silvered tongue. Aside from the steady influx of trained swords and horsemen who'd made their way from Acrosia and Karavyl, hours had been spent every afternoon for the weeks before their departure greeting and negotiating with some hundred *sarydâ* war bands. They'd come crawling from the depths of the Cienbal and beyond at the sound of clinking gold, rubbing elbows as they did with many others. Word had reached far that the šef of the Southern cities were paying a healthy wage to anyone who could prove themselves half-decent with a sword. Even from where she stood Serys made out the blond heads and reddened skin of the Northern sellwords, burned by their recent exposure to Sun's true gaze. Percian—some in haphazard armor, some in the colored leathers of Karesh Syl and Karesh Nan which had apparently escaped Raz i'Syul Arro's razing of those cities—moved together in small pockets. There were others, too. The black hair of the western races—straight or braided on the West Islers, ringed and looped on the citizens of the Imperium. A scattering of mountainous men of the Northern ranges could be found if one looked hard enough, not infrequently sharing fires and drinks with the auburn-haired, burly forms of mercenaries come from the Seven Cities. Unfortunately, of the Chancellors' formal armies there were no banners. Aleth Vohn, Chancellor of Holdum's Line, had sent an artistically- extorting missive Blaeth had read for them all, in which he'd made grand promises of assistance from him and the other rulers of the lands west of Perce.

Given, however, that "all" Vohn had asked for in exchange was the port city of Acrosia—along with the majority of the South's eastern coastline—the messengers who'd delivered this offer had been smart enough to excuse themselves on other errands before the creature who held the reins of Miropa could get her hands on them.

Serys shivered at the thought and managed to tear her eyes from the wash of shifting men and canvas below, turning to finish the ascent with San still cursing on her heels. It took them a moment more to crest the cap of the dune, but upon doing so Serys was more than a little relieved to note first that neither Blaeth nor his "woman" were in sight. Along the ridge a crowd had formed, and without a word Serys led San to join this group. As they approached, several of the figures turned to take them in, and Serys adopted her perfect courtesan's smile, willing her heart to steady.

She might be a šef of Karavyl, true, but in this company she was naught but one small cloud partaking a much greater maelstrom of power…

While she was pleased to realize they were not the last to arrive, enough of the other šef had reached the gathering point already to form their typical pockets. Ahthys Borne, Tyala Gerst, Sol Fe'ren, and Mysera Morste stood as a group closest to the hill's edge, and the Acrosian šef nodded respectfully to Serys and her companions on approach. A newcomer was among them—a woman Serys believed was called Zela Ureleus—but at least one of their number had yet to arrive. Ahthys and Serys traded a brief glance when they crossed paths, but exchanged not a word. The former Imperialist general was one among a few she knew to have figured out the dire truth of their circumstances, and they'd already stolen too many private conversations when they could on the matter.

Now, though, was certainly not the time for such a subject, and as Ahthys' gaze—sharp beneath a white turban he'd wrapped about his black hair and the lower half of his face—did not allude to anything having changed in their circumstances, Serys moved on quickly.

Not far beyond the Acrosians, Vyres Eh'ben stood in the sand with the other two šef of Karth, Avena Allehn and Casius Jules. Like Vyres, these two were of a particularly unsavory quality, and Serys gave all three a wide berth. She knew the trio's grey eyes followed her when she passed without any exchange, but she didn't care. If Vyres was any kind of example, they would all likely see themselves killed before the day was out, foul lumps that they were. *How* he'd managed to escape the Monster when every one of the rest of his expeditionary force had been slain or captured was beyond Serys, but she supposed the man couldn't be without *some* wiles, to have ascended to his position.

That, or the Moon has favored you with luck beyond your standing, Vyres, she thought, working to keep her smile intact as the wind wafted the sour reek of ragroot emanating from the Karthian delegation.

Fortunately, she was not forced to suffer the stench without distraction for too long.

"Ah, Serys. San. There you both are."

A calm, settled voice grabbed her attention, and she turned to find a man and a woman approaching them up the slight incline of the southern slope with stern expressions. Serys had to keep herself from rolling her eyes at the pair's obvious rigidity, instead bowing her head respectfully in their direction.

"Ahamed. Kusu." She dipped her head in greeting before casting about in feigned perplexion. "Is Myra not with you?"

Serys allowed herself some faint amusement at the disapproving frown the two older šef exchanged, then. Ahamed Ehmeth and Kusu Keyshm were of an older generation both, and quick to scorn Serys, San, and their newest edition—a young woman by the name of Myra Fohster, whom Serys had herself groomed into the position. Their severity was certainly not without its uses, but Serys had more often than not found it blinded them to the reality of the power balance within their own city.

Ahamed—a tall, stern borderer with short-cropped, dark hair that did not match the greying of his brows and goatee—was the first to reply.

"Myra was not in her tent when I sent someone calling this morning. Let us hope she will be along shortly."

"Found a more companionable bedroll to sleep in, no doubt," San muttered from behind Serys, and she had to clench her teeth to keep from stamping on the man's booted toes in irritation. San was hardly a fool—one did not ascend to the position they held by being a fool, after all—but oh could he come across otherwise. His griping and irritating character did a fair job of hiding his good head for tongues and strategy, but it was also the reason Serys had not yet confided in him her suspicions regarding the "master of Miropa."

Nor told him she'd had Myra Fohster and her entourage working the upper ranks of the army's officers every night since their departure.

It would be important to know where loyalties lay and what rumors had caught hold in the common army, once this ugly business with the Monster of Karth was finally brought to a close. Any small advantage she, Ahthys, and the other sharp-eyed among them could arrive by would come in the form of information, she knew.

And it astounded Serys—even to that day—what sorts of things desirous men felt comfortable divulging to a playful smile…

"So that's him, is it?"

Unlike Ahamed's firm, commanding tone, Kusu Keyshm's voice was subdued, almost soft. The Percian had been a whore herself, once, Serys knew, but she'd used the position to ultimately negotiate her way into a prosperous smuggling trade. Eventually, the woman had sunk her white teeth into nearly every business transaction Karavyl saw, including their lucrative dye and silk exports. Her eyes—nearly black in the morning Sun—were on the western horizon, and Serys found herself following the older woman's gaze automatically.

"So I'm told," she answered, more quietly than she'd intended.

Although the front line of Raz i'Syul Arro's army was only little more than a broad stroke through the rippling haze emanating across the swaying plains of the Southern sands, the dust of their passing was more prominent. It rose as a shifting column, dancing in the heat and light until one could almost perceive some great titan of the desert itself rising to favor the Monster's aims. They weren't more than a mile out, now, and Serys felt again that unbidden crawl of excitement and fear clinging at the back of her neck.

Forcing those feelings away, she looked back to the two older šef.

"Have we heard if we have a final count of their forces, yet? Analla said we had outriders come in the night?"

"Aye, but few since, and none that have managed to grasp any estimate more accurate than 'at least fifty thousand'." Ahamed grimaced as he peered out over the sands. "Apparently the beast is having his *kuja* indiscriminately shoot down anyone who gets too close."

"Likely why he decided to make his final approach in the light of the day," San muttered, for once showing off his mind for this sort of matter while shading his eyes with the hand that still held his kerchief. "He sacrifices the advantage his atherian would have had in the night, but given the size of this battle, it wouldn't have been that long maintained an edge to begin with. Unless we can get a firm count, we'll have to be careful in this fight…"

"Has it been confirmed that the lizard-kind have joined him, then?" Serys asked with her typical impertinence.

Kusu frowned beside her. "Only according to Vyres." Without looking away from the distant army she waved toward the Karthian delegates huddled in quiet discussion some feet away. "If we've had validation otherwise, I cannot say."

"We have."

As one, all four of them turned, and a majority of the other šef standing nearby looked around with them. Climbing up the southern slope, a group of four were making their steady ascent toward the top of the dune. Upon reaching it, they approached Serys and the others directly, the back three trailing a single Percian woman whose green eye-patch had been stitched to match the silks bannering out from her shoulders and crescent headpiece.

"We received word only a short while ago," Ysera Ma'het of Cyro continued, not looking around as she stopped to overlook the desert, taking in the rising pillar of dust in the distance with an unimpressed air. "Arro separated the atherian from the bulk of his own forces a half-hour ago. They're pressing south, at least twenty thousand in total."

"South?" Ahamed asked doubtfully, his eyes on the horizon to the right of the Monster's approaching horde. "Why south? I see no sign of them…"

"Likely in an attempt to take our army from two sides," Evangalyn Thesus offered sagely. With the death of Kanela Saresh of Dynec, Evangalyn was left as the eldest among the Mahsadën's surviving šef, and she was showing her age. Her flight from Cyro through and around the Cienbal had evidently done ill things for her health, because she rested much of her weight through both wizened hands on a cane of some grey-stained wood. Her eyes—a clear hazel that was rare in the Southern lands—looked to be going bad, too, because she had to squint to look west herself. "As for signs, you won't find any, Ehmeth." Lifting one finger, she indicated the horizon Ahamed had just been scrutinizing. "The lizards know the sands. They know how and where to step. In addition, they'll have spread out, keeping their disturbance of the plains to a minimum."

"Are they really so intelligent?" San snorted dismissively. "More likely they've thought better of this fight, isn't it? Probably looking to flee back to the Crags through the—YOUCH!"

There was a *whack* as the shaft of Evangalyn's cane struck the younger man across the shin, and San half-skipped, half-leapt away from the old woman, clutching at his leg as he did.

"*Imbecile*," Evangalyn hissed, lips pulling back to reveal not a few missing teeth. "It's thinking like that which will be the end of us."

"Evangalyn," Vyela Ehrem—the Southerner who'd been Ysera's constant companion since the šef's initial summoning to Miropa—interjected soothingly, putting a light hand on the elder's shoulder. "Let him be. Our colleagues have little reason to be as familiar with the atherian as we."

"They'd best learn, then," Geal Hareth muttered from Evangalyn's other side. Of every šef in attendance, Geal was the only one to be openly armed. A burly, broad-shouldered man with the flaming hair of the Seven Cities, he looked perfectly at ease with the massive, two-handed claymore strapped across his back. "And I suspect they will, too, by the time this day is done. Can't say I wasn't pleased to hear the Karthian's news, though." He jerked a chin shadowed with two day's growth toward where Vyres Eh'ben was still huddled with unpleasant companions. "We'll deal with Arro and the tribes in one go. Can't fathom how he managed to gather them all under that banner of his, but it makes our jobs easier, in the end."

"We are not here to facilitate Cyro's head trade, Hareth," Kusu Keyshm said calmly. "We are here to see that the Monster and his followers cease their infernal disruption in our affairs once and for all."

"In that train of thought—!" Serys cut in, forcibly changing the subject as the Citier opened his mouth to retort. "Are we not concerned that Arro has split his forces? All else aside, even if we assume his host matches us in number, is it not a risk for him to be separating from the atherian?"

"It is. Distinctly so."

As they'd all been talking, Ahthys Borne and his associates had moved close enough to join in on the discussion. Serys and the rest turned to find the Acrosians standing not far up the slope, to a one taking in the pillar of Arro's passing for themselves. The last of their number had joined them, Serys noted—an older man she knew only as "Ketres", dressed in loose wrappings of orange white that left one shoulder bare to the Sun—making their presence stand out on the hill. Six in total, the Acrosians were now the most numerous among their gathering, and held the strongest voice second only to Adrion Blaeth's puppeteer. It had occurred to Serys more than once that she would have to be wary of the port city's strength, once Miropa was unseated as the crowning glory of the Mahsadën.

For the foreseeable future, however, they were allies, and no voice was more valuable in the moment than Ahthys'.

"That being said, it's not without potential reward," the former Imperialist general kept on, lifting a large hand to point up at the billowing plume of dust. "If the beast's numbers *have* been split, that's abnormal trailing for some thirty or so thousand. I wouldn't be surprised if he's ordered his men to kick up as much sand in their passing as they can. He might even have his cavalry riding at the back of the line to do just that."

"Meaning what?" Ahamed asked, more curious than doubtful, now. "He's trying to mask the fact that the atherian have broken off?"

Ahthys nodded, his finger moving south to trace the path the lizard-kind were apparently taking. "Had we not been made aware, it's likely we'd have had to scramble to defend our southern flank once the atherian pressed out of the dunes. Even knowing, we'll have to be careful."

"Dividing our attention *can't* be worth the loss of strength," Evangalyn muttered from their midst.

"Hardly," Ahthys agreed, finally turning his scrutiny away from the sands to look at Ysera Ma'het. "Who was it that came by this information? Do you know?"

Ysera, in turn, scowled like that answer pained her. "One of that woman's shadows," she admitted bitterly. "It would seem she sent a handful into the sands once word got back that our scouts were being shot out of their saddles."

"Ah," Serys said aloud, finally understanding. "Meaning it's unlikely they were ever seen."

"And unlikely Arro knows that we are aware of his troop movements," Ahthys confirmed with a twitch of his turban that told Serys he was grinning beneath the cloth. "He's taken a gamble, hoping we'd be none the wiser and take him head on. The atherian would then have flanked us, and even with greater numbers we would suddenly have been at a disadvantage."

"The Monster has misplayed his hand," Kusu summarized, and even *her* stoic countenance cracked a little as she smiled ever so slightly.

"I would recommend none of you be so quick to assume that," a tired, youthful voice said from their backs.

Serys suspected, in that moment, that she couldn't have been the only one who's breath caught in icy surprise. With as much dignity as she could muster, she—along with all in her company—turned slowly to face the edge of the hill.

Turned, and took in the two figures waiting—inexplicably appearing as though out of thin air—there behind them.

Given his missing leg, how Adrion Blaeth had managed the slope without any of them noticing was a mystery. He'd had himself dressed in gold accented with black today, inversely matching the colors of the crutch tucked under his left arm. His bleached hair was pulled into a tail at the base of his neck, and his grey eyes were lifted, tracing the place where the rising pillar faded into the clouds. It was he who'd spoken—and he looked impressive enough despite his injury—but it was not Blaeth whose eyes Serys found.

Unlike her companion, Lazura's gaze was fixed firmly on the horizon, blue irises blazing over the dark veil that was the only addition she'd made to her usual attire of thin black silks. The circular scar about her right eye was hard to make out in the brightness of the morning, but the angled lines still cut across her forehead, exposed from where she'd pulled her white-blonde hair away in a back-knot kept tight by a loop of dark satin.

Serys shivered. Although the woman wasn't looking at her directly, the excited hunger that shined bright in her eyes was so visceral, they seemed almost to burn even in the shimmering heat of the day.

"You'll pardon my lack of understanding, Blaeth, but I'm afraid you'll have to clarify your meaning."

Ahthys spoke with tactful deference, not so much as hinting that anything was amiss. Serys, following his lead, made sure not to give away any hint on her end as well, turning her attention back on Blaeth, only half-feigning an acute interest in the man's statement.

"Arro will be trying to play us," the man answered, crutching forward across the uneven slope unsteadily and finally looking away from the sky to take them in. "Do not assume he has made any mistake. Do not assume he has done anything without purpose. If you begin to think you are a step ahead, then convince yourself instead that you are two behind."

Ysera Ma'het growled from beside Serys. "And do what, then? Sit on our thumbs and wait to get pinned in from two sides? Regardless of whether he meant to or not, the Monster has split his forces and weakened his position, if even briefly." She pointed behind her in the direction of the distant army. "If we move quickly, we may well just crush his main host before he has time enough to set whatever he is planning into motion!"

"Or you could play right into the lizard's hands, and then where would you be?"

The tinkering laugh that accompanied these words rang like bells in the desert breeze. Serys felt some instinct in her stomach clench, hearing beauty and cruelty alike resonate clearly in that voice, a disturbing combination that made it hard to look at the speaker.

But look Serys did, holding onto her charming smile with a calculated willpower.

"Adrion speaks the truth," Lazura crooned, stepping closer to the Miropan šef and taking his free arm in both her own to press up teasingly against him. "We will not have another opportunity to see the Arro struck down, so we cannot squander this by foolishly flailing right into his claws."

At her back, Serys felt Ahthys stiffen in anger. "'Foolishly flailing?'" he repeated indignantly under his breath.

Still, he had the sense not to speak so loud that either Blaeth or Lazura could hear him.

"Then what do you propose?" Serys herself asked, hoping to keep the discussion on track. It would do little good for a fight to break out among them when they were so close to freeing the Mahsadën of its greatest threat. "I'm assuming you're *not* telling us to sit idly?"

"And allow Arro to entrench himself?" Lazura snorted. "No." Detaching herself from Blaeth, she stepped gracefully forward. Serys and the others parted for her automatically, which might have earned a pleased smile from the Northern woman behind her veil. "I'm told the atherian of the Crags survive on little and less among the mountains. In comparison, what little life our sand plains boast must seem teeming with game to them. A stalemate would see the lizard and his brood better provisioned long-term, assuming we don't *all* run out of water first."

"So we attack?" Ysera pressed, her one eye narrowing on Lazura's back. "Speak clearly, woman. You've just done your best to ridicule those of us who would suggest the same."

If Lazura was bothered by the Percian's derisive tone, she didn't show it. She just laughed, then answered without turning around. "You suggested a *direct* assault, trying to overpower the Monster's main force with sheer numbers. Is that not *worthy* of ridicule?"

Ysera looked to be at the end of her rope, and had actually opened her mouth to retort when Ahthys Borne halted her with a raised hand, giving the woman the smallest shake of his head when she whirled on him.

It must have conveyed enough of the warning, because the Percian held her tongue.

"Given Arro has broken his army in half, Ysera's suggestion appears hardly unreasonable," the Imperialist said after a moment's pause, and—despite what he'd just done—Serys could tell the man was having trouble keeping his own tone even. "I, at the very least, am inclined to agree with her. What could the Monster have prepared by now that could overcome two-to-one odds? He's only just arrived. He'll have no traps set, no way to adapt the terrain to his advantage. He has tilted his hand. He does not know we know his assault is divided. If we strike hard and fast, without hesitation, we can overwhelm him."

"And cut off the head of the beast," San added his voice to the mix, clearly not wanting to be left out.

Before them, Lazura only shook her head, not so much as looking around. "Why do you assume he is not aware?" she asked them over her shoulder, the edges of her black veil and hair ribbon rippling as the wind picked up again.

"It was your own shadows that brought us the news, woman," Gael Hareth growled, crossing thick arms over the taut cloth of his chest. "Let us not pretend they would allow themselves to be spotted, even in broad daylight."

"You mean the shadows that Arro fought off not once, but at *least* twice in the last year?" It was Blaeth who asked, his voice frigid at their backs, and once again the šef half-turned so that they could look between him and Lazura. "The shadows he likely took on again, only nights ago? Arro does not let such information slip his mind that easily. He will have taken into account even the eyes that he cannot see."

For once, no one had any smart quip with which to respond. To claim Blaeth did not hold the strongest voice among them—rightfully or not—would have been a lie, but in this particular instance he spoke with an earnest fervor that belied even his position.

"So… he knows?" Serys asked slowly, finding her voice before the others.

"Without a doubt." Blaeth frowned through them at the distant line of the far-off army. "If anything, it's a deliberate feint. He will be expecting us to attempt and take advantage. He may withdraw his main host the moment we begin our approach, giving his atherian a window to get completely around us and strike at our rear. Or he may have something prepared we have not contemplated." He held up a finger to curb the start of Ahthys' denial. "You *cannot* dismiss the possibility, Borne. Not with a creature like this. Charging him *could* result in heavy immediate losses, or likewise put the lizard-kind at a similar positional advantage. We *cannot* play into his tricks. As soon as we do, we lose."

"You lack faith," Ketres of Acrosia muttered nastily, contrasting an otherwise serene demeanor by spitting on the ground at his feet between them.

"As much as you lack a level outlook, it would appear," the Miropan šef said, narrowing his eyes at the older man. "Shall we dupe ourselves into pretending anyone present knows Raz i'Syul Arro better than I? If that's a game you would like to play, I'll start planning my flight from the Southern lands now, if you don't mind."

The barb did its job, and Ketres—along with one or two of the others—lapsed into unintelligible grumbles, but made no more greater comment.

"Then I repeat my earlier question," Serys said poignantly, feeling her smile grow more and more forced on her tired cheeks. "What do you propose?"

"'If the head is armored, go for the limbs.'"

Lazura spoke like the phrase were a quote, but when Serys and the rest looked back at her, the woman still hadn't turned around to face them.

"Meaning?" Ahthys pressed irritably, his patience clearly starting to fray in truth.

"It was something Ergoin Sass would say." Blaeth cut in again. "A comment on one-on-one combat, but the lesson applies on a larger scale." He lifted a hand to gesture at the Monster's approaching army before repeating Lazura's earlier words. "We cannot play into Arro's claws. We cannot take him on directly, and risk opening ourselves up to whatever gambit he is about."

"'The head is armored,'" Serys echoed, thinking she could see where he and the Northerner were headed with their thought process.

"Precisely," Blaeth agreed with an almost-grateful nod in her direction. "Therefore, we must go for the limbs. Cripple the opponent. Attack the place they do not expect, and offer them little opportunity to respond."

It was Ahthys, unsurprisingly, who caught on next, and when he spoke there was a measurable degree more respect returned to his tone.

"South?" he asked, and Serys turned to see the taller man's eyes going wide through his turban as the plan fell into place.

"South."

Lazura had, at last, spun face them again. With her back to the Sun the scars about her eye were suddenly highlighted against her light skin, and her smile was now distinct behind the thin silk of her veil. Again Serys found herself having a hard time meeting the woman's gaze. She knew cruelty, of course, knew the power and press of it. She was a šef of the Mahsadën. Cruelty was as much an instrument of her arsenal as anything else.

But in Lazura's smile, something else lingered, something more profane and twisted than mere wickedness. It took a moment for Serys to place it, but when she did she felt her hands start to tingle again.

Desire, she realized.

"South," the Northern witch said again, her bloodlust tangible in the tremor of barely-restrained glee. "Double-pace, cavalry at the head. We'll carve the atherian of the Crags apart, and leave your Monster and his men flailing in the sand." Her eyes flashed, and her smile curved into something almost demonic. "Minus a limb, of course."

XXXII

"Do not assume he has made any mistake. Do not assume he has done anything without purpose. If you begin to think you are a step ahead, then convince yourself instead that you are two behind."

— Adrion Blaeth, aka. Mychal Arro

"Are they going for it?"

Raz didn't answer Akelo's question immediately. He was still squinting into the distance, one gauntleted hand shading his eyes as he stood tall in Gale's stirrups. The Sun was in their favor—blazing as bright as any day he'd ever known in the South—and with the light at their backs it wasn't hard to make out the shifting bulk of the Mahsadën's army. Like a cancer against the paler sand, seventy thousand trained and hired soldiers spread in an ugly blotch a mile to the west of them. Still, among the drifts and sway of the dunes it was more difficult to distiguish the specific movement of the troops themselves, and so only when dust started to rise along the north edge of the army—indicating a rapid press south—did Raz feel his pulse spike in excitement.

You're too clever for your own good, cousin, he thought, lowering himself to the saddle again.

"They are," Raz answered Akelo finally, not looking away from the distant movement of the šef's soldiers as the cloud of kicked-up sand began to grow. He himself had just had Cyper order the cavalry at the back of the march to cease the deliberate loops they'd been riding to raise just such a sign.

"Southward press," Karan Brightneck agreed loudly from in front of them. She was ahorse herself a ways down the hill they'd all lined up along, standing in the saddle as Raz had been. Her vantage wasn't as ideal, but he did not doubt her eyes were just as sharp. "They've taken the bait!"

All around Raz, there was a collective release of unwillingly held breaths.

"Should we inform the Queen?" Syrah asked from atop Nymara at his right. "She'll need to start pulling the tribes back soon."

Raz looked at her sidelong. The woman was in full garb today, her sensitive eye undoubtedly paying for the Sun's benevolence. Her face was hidden from him behind her veil, but he had no doubt she was gazing out across the sands, trying to make out for herself the movement of the Mahsadën's ranks.

She did not want to be there, on the front lines. Raz knew this, just as he knew that he did not want her there himself. For the past three days, though, he'd had the other generals take turns interrogating the captured *sarydâ*, dragging the mercenaries one at a time from the guarded enclosure they shared with the Cyroan soldiers who'd survived the battle in the Crags. In that time, not a single syllable of the story had changed.

For the time being, there was a danger among the enemy only Syrah would have a prayer of being able to face, even if she didn't want to...

"Do it," Raz answered her query. "I'd estimate the šef are marching at double-pace. Request that she hold to the plan and avoid any engagement if possible."

"I say again that the enemy cavalry is going to be an issue," Erom spoke from Syrah's other side once she'd motioned for one of the mounted messengers waiting behind them to approach. The borderer was absently stroking the mane of his brown mount while he frowned at the growing dust cloud in the distance. "The atherian will take heavy losses in a direct assault. If they get *around* the tribes and pin them in, it will only be worse."

"Won't happen," Marsus grunted from the left, and Raz turned to see the Southerner squinting at the horizon from his gelding's back on Akelo's far side. "Cyper'll get there first. It will be enough support to allow the Queen to pull back to safety, I say."

"Agreed," Akelo himself added with a nod, the steel spike that crowned his leather helm gleaming with the motion. "The timing will be essential, but if we assume that all are in position...?"

He leaned forward in his saddle to look around Raz in Syrah's direction, obviously seeking a confirmation.

The woman nodded at once. "Without a doubt."

Akelo smiled grimly, and from Marsus' far side Hur grunted in approval.

"Then all goes to plan, for the time being," the Percian said, anticipation leaking into his normally-steady voice. He looked then to Raz. "You really *are* mad, you know that?"

Raz only chuckled, knowing there was no other answer to give.

It had been a gamble, but with their cavalry moderately outmatched and their infantry severely so, a direct assault on the Mahsadën had been out of the question. Even with the strength of the atherian on their side, none of them had been keen on the idea of turning the engagement into one of open attrition. At the same time, he suspected that most any battlefield tactic he could throw at the rings would have been dissected, and in a heartbeat. As clever and brave as his generals were, as much bloodshed and heartbreak as he and Syrah had been through, not a one among them had been born to the roles they now took, had been brought up and trained for their positions. The *sarydâ* had informed them that there was at *least* one military tactician among the šef—an Acrosian who'd once been a general in the armies of the Imperium, apparently—and Adrion was not a mind to be taken lightly on his own. Not for the first time, Raz regretted not having Arnus with them, but he understood Akelo's decision to leave the former soldier in Cyro, where order had still been in need of establishment.

There wouldn't be much point in seeing the South freed, after all, if the fringe cities burned themselves to the ground before the war was even done…

So, with tactical intelligence thrown out of their favor, they'd been left only with less direct options. Shrewdness and sleight of hand would have to replace combat strategy, and a measure of deceit would have to off-balance the years of training his own soldiers lacked compared to the Mahsadën's numbers.

In the end, Raz had decided they would have to employ the same devices to the battle they'd applied to the capture of Dynec, and the city-states of Perce before it.

"How long do we have to hold out?" he asked of Syrah.

The veiled woman hesitated, her covered face turning northward, as though judging the distance. "An hour," she answered after a moment. "Probably less, by now."

"An hour is a long time when we're divided like this…" Erom grimaced as he said it, looking around at Raz and Syrah. "I don't mean to be contradictory, but…"

"No, you're right," Syrah said with a shrug that Raz suspected was meant to fake nonchalance. "If we'd held our approach out any longer, though, we risked not having the time to set the thing in motion."

"We can play cat-and-mouse for an hour," Raz assured them all. "Shas-hana Rhan understands we are aiming for a longer game, and Cyper and Odene's other thousand have their orders. The Mahsadën have already taken the greatest step for us. We need only allow them to continue thinking they've caught us."

There was a rumble of agreement from the generals—including another hearty grunt from Hur—and Raz allowed himself a moment, just a moment, to take in those last few seconds of relative calm beneath the Southern sky.

A weight settled on his lap, and he glanced down to see that Syrah had reached out to rest a hand on the leather wrappings of his upper thigh. She was trembling, betraying her uncertainty, and still had not turned to look at him. Her gaze was yet northward, her head facing away.

All the same, even from within the depths of her own fears she had sensed his need for a brevity of peace, and had made sure to let him know in her own way that she was still there by his side.

With a smile, Raz let go of Gale's reins with one hand for a moment to rest it atop hers, interweaving their fingers. One second. Then two.

Then Syrah pulled away, leaving Raz's grasp free to reach for Ahna, slung from the stallion's side.

"Make it look good and panicked, all of you," he muttered, wheeling his horse about to face his army, all standing at rigid attention beneath mismatched banners gilded with the winged Sylgid. Though he could only make out the faces of their closest ranks, he knew that every eye of each man, woman, and atherian among them was on him, in that moment. A living blanket of mismatched armor and stolen blades. His own shadow, magnified nearly forty thousand times, glistening with iron and steel in the Sun.

Sucking in a deep breath, he hefted the dviassegai above his head.

Then Raz roared, the sound joining the shimmering beat of the heat over the dune, and the Dragon's horde answered in kind.

With the purposeful sound of countless boots thudding against the sand, the march began.

"It's working!" San Loreyn blurted out with a whoop that did not dignify his position. Despite this, his voice was still only barely audible over the thunderous sounds of the army's march behind them. "They're scared!"

Serys turned in her saddle to see what had drawn San's excitement. After Blaeth and Lazura convinced them all of the plan, the šef had seen themselves armed and armored, then taken to horse. Now, they were leading the rapid press south, looking to catch the flanking lizard-kind off guard. Twenty in all, they formed the third line of the march, heading the footmen of the army while two ranks of some fifty cavalry rode before them as a precautionary defense. The rest of their five thousand horsemen were already far ahead, seeking to break up the atherian's assault, and hopefully do as much damage as possible before Arro's own riders likely arrived in support.

It was with this in mind, therefore, that Serys took in a new rising of sand and dust to the east, slighter now than when the Monster had been making his initial approach.

Ahthys was right, she considered, eyeing the distinctly lesser cloud that indicated Arro's forces were on the move. *The bastard was trying to trick us.*

Unbidden, her eyes fell on the backs of Adrion Blaeth and his woman, both of whom cantered just slightly ahead of the rest of them. It looked to her like the Monster was pressing his own army as fast as he could south-by-west, hopefully praying that he might be able to correct his overextension.

The Miropan šef had calculated correctly, and to a terrifying degree.

Serys tried to catch Ahthys Borne's eye then, hoping to convey a little of the doubt that had been growing heavy in the pit of her stomach. If either Blaeth or Lazura saw their plot coming, Serys had the distinct feeling the price would extend beyond more than just herself, the Acrosian, and the few other players they had in this game.

Ahthys, however, was turned away to her left, head tilted up to study the distant kick-up carefully. Although she couldn't see his face, something in the larger man's bearing made Serys uneasy. After a moment of studying him, she reined her horse back and fell out of the line to sidestep over and pull up beside him.

"What's wrong?" she asked in as subdued a tone as she could manage over the cacophony of the army at their rear.

Ahthys started and glanced around. When he saw that it was only her, he relaxed visibly.

We're all *too on edge,* Serys realized as she allowed the Acrosian a second to regain his composure.

"Nothing." The answer came, nearly inaudible. "Just… It's a little odd…"

"What is?"

The Imperialist's eyes showed the hint of a frown under his turban, and he looked back east again.

"It seems too quick," he answered after a moment. "The troop movements. The response seems too quick."

Serys, for once, didn't follow. "*Arro's* response?" she tried to clarify, barely noticing the shift in the incline when they started to climb yet another hill.

Ahthys nodded. "Even if he didn't hold *any* debate with his advisors, there should be more of a delay. Changing the set orders of that many soldiers…" He paused, then repeated himself. "It seems too quick."

Serys felt a chill prick at the back of her neck, but before she could say anything more there was a shout from one of the remaining sergeants of the cavalry, two lines ahead. She looked around in time to find themselves cresting the dune they'd been ascending. There, in the distance, a mass of mounted figures could be made out among the plains, some galloping along the ridges, while others leapt and flickered between the hills. Screams could be heard on the wind, even as far seperated as they were, and in the Sun's light Serys blinked at the glister and flash of slashing steel. At first she was confused, not comprehending why their horsemen would be fighting among themselves.

Then she saw the distinct white-and-gold leathers interspersed throughout the riders, and Ahthys' fears became all-too-abruptly her own.

Arro's cavalry had intersected theirs. Along with the pilfered colors of Karesh Syl, the red-and-black of Karesh Nan were heavy within the armors of the Monster's men. What's more, there wasn't a *single* atherian in sight. Either they'd retreated—if they'd ever been there at all—or the vanguard had been cut off before they could reach them.

Too quick, Ahthys' words rang clear in Serys mind.

Immediately, she looked to Blaeth. They'd come up short at the sergeant's alert, and she could see part of his face, now. The man was taking in the scene ahead of them with a tight expression. He did a fair job of maintaining his composure, but Serys did not miss the flash of alarm that crossed his handsome features, much less the uncertainty that pulled at the corner of his lip.

Far more concerning, however, was the sidelong glance Blaeth offered Lazura, as though wanting to assess what the *woman's* reaction would be before he made any decisions for himself.

Right then, in that moment, the urge to strike took hold of Serys so strongly, she suddenly felt the weight of the short-sword she'd strapped to her hip before taking to the saddle. It was like the fall of the Mahsadën were playing out before her very eyes, the power of the society—gathered so recklessly about a single man—being subtly handed off second by second to a sorceress who clearly had no intent of letting it go.

Serys was a poor swordswoman—her talents had always been best suited for other pastimes, after all—but Lazura and the Miropan šef were both still a little ahead of them. It wouldn't be hard to draw and strike before either of the two knew what had happened. She could go for the woman first, running her through, or at the very least crush in her skull with the weight of the blade. Blaeth would be handled by Ahthys as soon as the Acrosian saw Serys make her move, she trusted, leaping into action as any good soldier would. For a moment, she was so tempted that she actually brought her hand to rest on the rough, rope-wrapped handle at her side.

Then Lazura looked around at the šef that flanked her, and Serys' hand jerked away from the blade instinctively.

There was an instant, the briefest fraction of a second, where she thought the Northern woman's icy gaze might have caught the motion, but she blinked and found Lazura instead smiling at them all in turn. With less pretense than she'd ever put on, she addressed them as a whole.

"Those of you with any backbone, on me," she said with that voice that seemed ever to be laughing at the listener. "The rest of you, deploy the infantry, then stay here. You can keep a thousand to guard this position." Her smile slid smoothly into a sneer. "Wouldn't want your clothes getting dirty, or anything so awful."

Not a one among the šef responded, but Serys could just imagine the looks Lazura likely received from all angles. The woman made no indication of caring even the least bit, of course, and to most everyone's astonishment proceeded to wave Vyres Eh'ben toward her. Only Blaeth and the Karthians—Avena, Casius, and Vyres himself—looked unsurprised by the summoning, and once the oily man heeled his horse up beside hers, Lazura leaned in to exchange a brief word. Vyres said nothing, barely giving any outward sign that he had even heard the woman, and only when she'd wheeled away and kicked her charger into a full gallop down the slope—shouting for the remaining cavalry to attend her—did he pull his own horse around and return to his companions.

"What did she say?" Ahthys Borne demanded of the Southerner, heeling his mount forward as he made obvious preparations to follow Lazura. At his side, Tyala Gerst and Sol Fe'ren moved to join him, with Gael Hareth and his massive sword taking to the line as well from the Cyroan delegation.

Serys turned about in time to see Vyres offer the Acrosian nothing more than a smirk in answer. She was a little surprised to note neither he nor his fellows looked to be prepping to follow Lazura. Given they were all of a rougher variety of character, she thought the group might have been keen to bloody their blades a bit.

The fact that not one of their three moved to do so had her immediately on edge.

Seeing that he would receive no forthcoming explanation from the Karthian, Ahthys turned his attention to Blaeth, guiding his horse over so that he sat at an angle to the Miropan šef. Blaeth did not turn to look at him, watching the distant battle and the form of Lazura leading a hundred mounted soldiers in its direction.

With the woman gone, Ahthys spoke as directly as Serys knew he dared.

"Is this how you would see us end, Blaeth?" the Acrosian demanded in a hiss of the man. "Would you hand everything we've built over so willingly?"

There was a murmur of confusion from the others—most of whom Serys suspected hadn't caught onto the game—but she ignored them all. Her eyes were on Blaeth, and Blaeth alone.

The man, however, had spent more months than she knew perfecting his unaffected air. When he finally looked at Ahthys, his expression gave away nothing.

"You'll do as she says," the puppet of Miropan said calmly, his words firm as stone. "That is your place, now."

He spoke with such cool indifference that something like doubt flashed briefly across Ahthys' eyes, and his gaze flicked for the briefest moment to Serys. He looked away again before she could so much as shake her head in warning, and with a cough fought to regain his poise.

"Ketres, see that ours and the Miropan soldiers take the straight march at pace-and-a-half," he barked, saving face by wheeling his mount about and addressing the other šef. "Ysera and Serys—" he met the two women's eyes individually "—Cyro and Karavyl's force should swing east five hundred paces at double and pinch in. Have half your number engage the atherian if they can be found, and the rest Arro's infantry host once it arrives. By that point we'll either have the horsemen under control, or they'll be sounded to retreat and regroup with the main host. Vyres—" he looked to the Karthian and his two fellow representatives with disdain "—you'll do the same, but from the west. Have your men press through once we have a handle on the battle to rejoin the eastern line."

Serys half expected Vyres to snarl something mocking in retort, but to her continued discomfort the man only smiled and nodded.

Ahthys, it appeared, took the lack of disagreement in stride. When he'd confirmed that all had their orders, he spun his horse about once more and led Tyala, Sol, and Gael to chase the hoofprints Lazura and her escort had left in their wake.

They weren't even halfway down the dune by the time Serys and the others had called for messengers from the march head, delegating their commands as quickly as possible. Not long after, the gathered army of the Southern fringe cities was on the move, sweeping about the hill most of their masters still stood high upon, overlooking the dispatchment. With it echoed again the cacophony of boots on sand, armor against armor, and swords clattering against churning legs. The dust rose once more, and Serys was forced to squint and cover her mouth with a loose edge of her shirt to keep from coughing. One minute passed, then another. In five, the army had dispersed, leaving them at last in the comparative near-silence of only a thousand Miropan guards. For a long time they stood like that, watching their soldiers churn in a steady flood toward the skirmishing until their individual forms were lost to the whirling grit.

Strangely enough, it was Vyres who broke the quiet. He'd been picking sand out from between his teeth, and spat sidelong before speaking aloud.

"That'll do, I think."

There was a blank moment of quiet as all eyes turned to the Karthian. The man said nothing more, however, not even bothering to look away from the southern march.

Serys was about to open her mouth and demand what the man was talking about, when from her left there was a shriek of shock and agony.

She whirled, her horse nickering nervously beneath her, and in horror took in Ysera Ma'het writhing in her saddle, blood spraying from her open mouth as she tried to reach with both hands over her shoulders to claw furrows into her back. There, between her shoulder blades, the better part of a narrow sword protruded, its thin tip ripping several inches out of her chest to dye her originally green silks black and crimson. On her left, Vyela Ehrem had already tumbled out of her saddle, her mount rearing in fear above her as she thrashed her life away, clutching at the gash that had carved through one side of her neck.

Between the dying women, on the other hand, old Evangalyn Thesus looked to be clearly in no danger.

It was she, after all, who held tight to the handle of her narrow cane-sword, the hollow wooden scabbard which had hidden the blade thrown into the nearby sand.

With obvious strain, the elder gave the weapon a wrenching twist, and Ysera's screams pitched into something unbearable, her entire body going rigid. Then, all at once, she went limp, and Evangalyn let the blade go with a wheeze while the Percian, too, tumbled to the ground.

Serys, of course, saw almost none of this. She did not see Ketres of Acrosia draw two knives from the folds of his robes and alternately plunge them into the throat and chest of Mysera Morste and Zela Ureleus, who had been riding on either side of him. She did not see Avena Allehn and Casius Jules of Karth drive their steeds together, drawing blades to bring them down on the shocked forms of Ahamed Ehmeth and Kusu Kehsym. She did not see her fellow šef fall, absent their heads, to sprawl as dusty heaps of twisted limbs among the thrashing legs of their animals.

Serys, after all, was one of the only ones who managed to stay ahorse. It wasn't hard, given she was half-bent over the animal's neck, clutching with both hands at the broad blade of the sword that had taken her through the stomach. In the shock of the moment, as she hacked up bile and blood through her confusion, Serys almost forgot to look up, to stare into the eyes of her murderer.

The man, still holding tight to the sword's hilt, offered her a smile through his bleached hair.

"Sorry," San Loreyn told her simply. "Times seem to have changed."

Then he ripped the blade free and brought it around again, catching Serys such a crushing blow to the head, she didn't even feel the pain of her death before the world winked out around her.

XXXIII

"A-a ghost… A phantom in black… Blood… So much blood… Where did she come from? Where did she come from?!"

— unnamed soldier

Lazura regretted not being able to witness the fall of the greats of the Mahsadën for herself, but she trusted Vyres would see her commands through. Ergoin Sass had provided her with many lessons in her time under his care, and the very least of which had been how to sniff out a person's potential, whether they be a friend or foe. It hadn't taken long for her to make note of Vyres' charade of simplicity, just as she suspected it had been he who'd deduced her own deception first among the šef. To their credit, Serys Benth and Ahthys Borne hadn't been long in following, but their suspicions had always had to be carefully monitored. Her shadows had seen to that, of course, all while Vyres had proven himself a willing—and quite useful—tool.

In particular when it came to the bloody work of pruning the existing Mahsadën down to those who'd privately demonstrated themselves prepared to come under her rule.

Far behind her, Lazura thought she heard a wail of pain and surprise, and she smiled to herself. It was likely only a trick of her mind, or the wind echoing back the shouts and screams of the battle raging ahead of her, but she allowed herself the satisfaction of believing her schemes were coming to fruition in steady order. Bringing Evangalyn Thesus, Ketres Bayn, and San Loreyn into the fold had proven itself as simple a task as she could have set for herself. All she'd had to have her soulless messengers dangle before the šef was the promise of control over their individual cities all their own, and all three had leapt on the opportunity like beggars tossed a sack of golden crowns. They would make ideal pieces, in her plans for the South.

Manipulating greed and selfishness had, after all, been another of Sass' invaluable teachings.

"Lyb'en. Attend me."

Though she spoke the words without so much as raising her voice over the thunder of the horse hooves, the rider was by her side in no more time than it took to guide his charging mount over. Dressed in the same plain leathers and iron as the rest of the cavalry around him, Lyb'en was indistinguishable from the other soldiers, as were the dozen other of his brothers hidden among their ranks. He said not a word when he reigned his horse up by Lazura's own, his empty eyes fixed ever forward.

"How many have followed us?" she asked of him.

"Four," the shadow answered at once, not even having to look around behind them to check. "Though the distance makes it hard to be sure, I believe it is as you suspected. Three of the Acrosian party, and the Citier of the Cyroan delegation."

Lazura nodded. She'd indeed guessed as much—or at least been guided to the conclusion of who would tail them into battle with Adrion's assistance. It irked her that her perfect pawn was anything but useless, but she shoved aside the minor doubt this cast on her own capabilities in favor of the situation at hand.

"See to them during the battle," she told the man. "*Before* Arro reaches us. If the lizard manages to take any of their heads, it will only enliven his men."

Lyb'en nodded, and waited only a moment more before it was understood that he had the extent of his orders. With a subtle twitch of the reins he drew his animal to the side, and Lazura knew he would be spreading her directive to the others. Again she felt a vague thrill as she watched her plans unfold in perfect, steady order.

By the time Raz i'Syul Arro fell, nothing substantial enough would be left of the first iteration of the Mahsadën to challenge her position for years, if ever.

Which—to Lazura's bottomless relief—meant it was also approaching the moment to show her hand in full.

The smile that she hadn't been able to keep back for most of the morning broadened behind the veil she'd hung over her nose and mouth to shield her lungs from the dust. Reaching down with one hand, Lazura slipped her fingers into a subtle slit in the side of the silks that covered the pale skin of her leg. Finding the handle of right of the two narrow short-swords she'd strapped to her thighs, she slid it loose of its slender metal sheath, flipping it dexterously into a more secure hold. The weapon had been blackened from tip to grip so as to hopefully go unnoticed among the folds of her garments, and didn't so much as shine in the sunlight. Its singled-edged, broad blade was smoke-darkened, its thin leather wraps dyed to the same effect. It was an assassin's tool, hardly an ideal armament for a cavalry charge, but Lazura had every confidence in her ability to wield it effectively in whatever situation might be called for.

Sass had seen to that, personally and—often—brutally, and the harsh years she'd spent under the master killer's tutelage proved itself within moments of entering the fray.

Running at full gallop along the firmer sands in the ravines between the dunes, Lazura and her hundred reached the edge of the battle almost *too* abruptly. One second they were among the hills, squinting against the sun and wind and dust, and the next they had turned a corner in the valleys to find themselves plunging headlong into the mess of horsemen. Her own cavalry numbered too few to have any real long-term impact on the greater outcome of the fight—a hundred hardly added to the thousands she knew were engaged all around them—but on the immediate environment the change was instantaneous. With a barked command she released the ordered charge, and like scattering arrows the men about her broke apart toward whatever ongoing exchange was closest at hand. At once there were shouts as the Monster's soldiers nearest to their reinforcements realized they would soon be overwhelmed, and at the shout of what must have been the unit's officer somewhere in the chaos, nearly every one of the riders pulled their horses around to retreat.

Unfortunately for them, Lazura had always been one to prefer a turned back to a head-on exchange.

Keeping a straight gallop into the declining fight, the momentum of Lazura's horse caught up to several of the retreating soldiers before they had the chance to kick their own mounts into a proper pace. The first three died in similar fashion and in mirrored silence, each of them lifting one hand in surprise to whichever side of their necks she passed by, then both when their minds and bodies at last registered that the thick arteries there had been severed right along with their windpipes. Lazura struck so cleanly, so sharply, that her sword hardly came away wet from any blow. Even the single man among them lucky enough to have owned a helmet wasn't spared by his armor, her black blade flashing with all the precision a true expert of her profession could achieve. Razored metal found the gaps between chin and shoulder, artfully avoiding what leather or cloth padding might have otherwise saved them. One died, then another, then a third.

After those three, however, Lazura actually had to start paying attention to her craft.

Whether by luck or instinct, two among the retreating horsemen looked back in time to see her cleave into their comrades like steel through water. She saw their eyes go wide together, and almost laughed when the pair shouted at the others to go on, to leave this unexpected pursuer to them. Their companions ran by and between them with shouts of encouragement, Lazura hard on their heels. She didn't slow her horse as she closed the gap, but rather heeled the animal to go faster, faster. Her two opponents drew to meet her as one, mirrored blades at the ready in free hands, the opposites holding tight to braided reins. The bearing of their bodies and the angles of their arms read as easily as the script of a play to Lazura's knowing eyes, the scene of the exchange playing out in her mind in the moments before they met.

Then she reached them, and any onlookers could have blinked and missed the speed of death's descent.

Heaving her horse back sharply, Lazura allowed it to plant and slide the last few feet between them. In the instant that followed she took hold of her pommel and twisted right, off the saddle. With the sudden change in their opponent's impetus, the paired soldiers' slashes became mistimed, their swords cutting horizontally through empty space.

Lazura's blade, on the other hand, found its mark with terrifying precision.

Even as she rolled, she slashed out. Her black short-sword bit into the gap between the armors of the right man's hip and thigh, the momentum of her somersault cleaving almost to the bone. Landing lightly on her feet before he could so much as scream, she struck once, twice more, carving through the thick straps that held his saddle into place, as well as the flesh and ribs of the horse beneath. The animal shrieked in pain and reared, and with his seat undone the soldier slipped free of its back to slam heavily to the ground, knocking the wind from him. In choking silence he lay, having lost his sword, clutching at the great wound from which blood ran in a merciless torrent.

Lazura, though, wasn't done.

Not even waiting to see her first opponent hit the sand, she ducked and rolled between the stamping feet of her own charger, coming up again between it and the still-saddled second soldier. Despite his earlier bravery, the man appeared at a complete loss, now, his weapon not yet returned to any sort of useable position after his missed first strike, his mouth agape at what he'd just witnessed. Only his eyes reacted fast enough to catch Lazura's dark form slip into the narrow space between their two animals, and even as her blade flashed she saw his body strain in a vain attempt to respond.

Her sword, thrust upward, caught him below the ribs before he could begin to twist his own weapon down at her.

The soldier died with nothing but an *urk* of sound when her steel drove at an angle through muscle and lung, coming to rest finally, buried an inch into his heart. Lazura withdrew the blade with the same speed it had been driven, then whirled and reached up with her free hand for the pommel of her saddle again. With the grace of a dancer she swung and heaved herself back atop her horse's back once more, flicking her sword clean and taking up the reins again.

She was at full gallop once more before the corpse of her second opponent finally toppled to join his dying companion in the dust.

In the time he'd spent in the company of Raz i'Syul Arro, Cyper Edalos had had ample chance to reclaim and whet old skills. At the beginning—when "the Dragon" had first saved him and so many others from the belly of the *Moalas* along the Percian coast—Cyper had feared that his three years chained to those hellish oars had ultimately stolen everything he'd ever known about himself, every skill and talent honed, every harsh hour spent training as a soldier of the armies of the West Isles. He'd found it difficult to take up the sword offered to him in a clawed hand that day, difficult to reach up and accept the blade which had belonged to one of the very men he'd prayed to the Sun so many times over for the opportunity to kill. His own hands had been shaking, he recalled.

They did not shake now.

Left and right Cyper slashed in rapid succession, driving his horse about in frantic twists and turns that more often than not clouded his fights in a ring of thrown sand. The curved blade of his broad saber worked in perfect unison with the inertia of his lunges and wheels, the edge hewing through the light armor of the Mahsadën's cavalry with gruesome efficiency. Between howled orders that kept the men about him in line, Cyper alone dealt out death in equal measure to the losses he witnessed in the narrow scope of his vicinity.

Not for nothing, after all, was he among the lucky few to have been trained by the Dragon of the North himself.

All the same, despite his personal conquests, Cyper was aware they were losing the fight. It came as no surprise, of course. Even if the Mahsadën might not be aware of it just yet given the breadth of the clash, the horsemen who'd followed him into battle numbered only part of his regular command. What was more, there was no possibility of disengagement. Though he'd seen only a glimpse of them when he'd led the ambush, Cyper knew Shas-hana Rhan and her tribes were waiting patiently not far out of sight, idling until their moment to strike came. He would have to hold, would have to swallow the screams of his men and the *thuds* of steel-hewn corpses hitting the earth to be trampled beneath frantic hooves. Raz and Syrah would come in time with the others, he trusted. Before their losses became too many against these overwhelming odds, Raz and Syrah would arrive to pull these soldiers back from the brink and hold the line until they could set into motion the last pieces of their game.

They would come.

Despite himself, Cyper grinned through the open face of his helmet, turning aside an overhead slash to twist his saber and run another one of the šef's men through the belly.

"Sir!"

The shout was barely audible over the crash and thrum of the battle, and Cyper had to cast about as he wrenched his sword free of the dying man. Eventually he found one of his lieutenants fighting her way toward him from amid the carnage, weaving a careful path through the innumerable smaller clashes all around them. Pulling his gelding around, Cyper heeled his horse forward with a "*hyah*!", blade whirling at his side.

By the time he met up with the woman, he'd cleanly taken the head off one of the enemy, and claimed the sword arm of a second.

"Report!" he barked the moment he drew his horse up sharply before the officer. She looked somewhat the worse for wear, a good-sized gash over her right eye weeping blood to leave her half-blinded, and her left hand appeared to be having trouble holding tight to her reins. All the same, her voice was strong as she relayed her message.

"A woman!" she yelled over the fight, lifting her reddened broadsword to point north, in the direction from which she'd just come. "Cutting through us like bloody *paper*! I've never seen anything like it!"

Cyper's heart skipped a beat. "What did she look like?" he demanded, keeping one eye on their surroundings to ensure none of the closest enemies disengaged from their fights to charge them. "What was she wearing?"

The woman blinked at this question, but didn't delay in answering. "Dark clothes! All black, it looked like, with a cloth over her face!"

Gooseflesh crawled down Cyper's arms, and he couldn't help himself from looking west, in the direction Raz and Syrah were ever approaching from. Too far, he knew. Too far.

He suspected he could guess what the enemy in question was. He'd never crossed blades with them himself, but he had seen the shadows of the Mahsadën once, had borne witness to their dangerous dance. For a moment Cyper was back in the audience hall of Ekene Okonso, fighting with Akelo and the others to hold the doors of the chambers as the Tash's men attempted to break through. Despite their struggles, none among their number had been able to keep themselves from looking around every few seconds.

Watching the Dragon and White Witch war it out with the silent blades of the South had been all at once mesmerizing, exhilarating, and terrifying.

Cyper frowned, returning to the rush of the battle in a blink. He did not recall either Raz or Syrah ever mentioning the existence of women among Miropa's deadliest sect, but it seemed a minor detail. The fringe cities did not distinguish by gender in the ranks of their armies or šef, so why would they do so within their more specialized units?

Again, Cyper found himself gazing off in the main army's direction.

Too far, he thought again.

In the end, he knew there was no other decision to make. His had been designated the front line of the war, both the first blade and the first shield.

He could not allow the assassins to carve a dent into that wall—*his* wall—and provide a foothold with which the Mahsadën might gain greater purchase on the day's outcome.

"On me, lieutenant!" he growled, and without another word heeled his horse into a full gallop again, northward now. He heard the soldier pull her own mount around behind him and shout it into a run, and then they were barreling together up the shallow incline of the particularly broad dune over which the woman had originally come. Allowing her to catch up, Cyper motioned with his saber that she take the lead, which she did promptly, turning them slightly to the west. Fifteen seconds later they were over the hill and descending again into identical bloody fervor. Three times Cyper had to parry and deflect blows launched at him as they drove through the mess, forcing himself to leave the attackers to others. He made up for it by slashing out himself at any unprotected torso or lifted arm bedecked in the plain leathers of the Mahsadën's cavalry he passed, their uniform attire making it easy to pick opponents out among the fallen Percian colors and otherwise mismatched armaments of his own men and women. Even the lieutenant—wounded as she appeared—made a good show for herself, putting her uninjured sword arm to use carving not a few of the enemy through as they rode.

Pretty soon they were climbing, then descending again, and the actions repeated themselves. In the chaos Cyper took a shallow slash across the shoulder that certainly drew blood, but he shrugged the blow off in favor of keeping pace with his guide. They fought through a second time, and started cresting yet another dune. When they reached the top of this one, however, the lieutenant brought her horse up short, taking advantage of the largely absent fighting along the windswept ridge to squint out over the skirmishing below and before them. In the few seconds Cyper needed to catch up to her, the woman appeared to have spotted their target, because she was already pointing with her sword again by the time he pulled his gelding up beside her.

It was hardly difficult to make out the figure atop her horse, dressed in black so completely only a head of tightly-knotted white-blonde hair distinguished her from her garments. He'd been expecting it, but at the sight of the woman Cyper shivered yet again, observing her weave across the battlefield. Even her *weapon* was black—the single-edged short-sword looking like an extension of her right arm—but it wasn't the blade Cyper was watching. It wasn't her horsemanship, or the bodies she left to tumble from their saddles in her wake.

Rather, what had Cyper's eyes going wide was the *way* the woman killed.

While her animal barreled largely of its own accord about the battlefield, the assassin moved with such graceful guile Cyper found himself practically entranced by the elegance of her passing. She well-nigh *danced*—even ahorse—slashing out with a deliberateness that made the hacking swings of her opponents look like the desperate flounderings of children playing at swords. On the few occasions her victims saw her coming, the woman bent and twisted in the saddle so fluidly to avoid any incoming blows that her movements could have been choreographed. Once she even slid *off* her horse completely, crouching with one foot in the stirrups, the other trailing in the blood-washed sand so that she could duck under a heavy horizontal slash from a man dressed in the black-and-red of Karesh Nan.

After she'd passed safely by and seated herself again, the offending soldier dropped his sword with an agonized cry, clutching at the long laceration that had been carved almost carelessly length-wise up his thigh.

That was when Cyper realized he had just borne witness to the deaths of no less than four of his men in hardly thrice as many seconds, and had yet to do anything about it.

"Lieutenant," he told the officer beside him gravely, not looking away from the assassin while she continued to cleave her path of devastation through his ranks, "see yourself escorted back to the main host. Tell the first general you can find what you've seen here. They need to know there are shadows even among the common army."

For once, the woman did not answer immediately. There was a silence, like she was gathering herself up to say something.

Cyper hid a smile, thinking he knew what she would try to insist on.

"I won't be allowing you to throw yourself in front of the lion for my sake," he said in his strictest commander's tone. Turning to the officer, he wasn't surprised to find her looking down the hill, in the direction of the still-moving assassin. "You'll do as I instruct, *lieutenant*."

The inflection on their relative ranks was a subtle enough hint to get the point across. Immediately the soldier stiffened and turned to fix her superior with her one working eye.

A second later, her bloody sword came up to salute him.

"Yessir," she said, her voice subdued despite her new-found conviction.

She was gone not a handful of seconds later, headed east, shouting for the nearest available cavalry to close in on her flanks.

Cyper let his smile show at last. He looked back, finding the trailing path of the shadow again, watching her haphazard trail of lethality for a few seconds more. He granted himself a moment to be proud of the men and women under his command. No matter what else happened, he knew well and truly that he had had a firm hand in shaping the blade that now challenged the Mahsadën, that now cut into the irons the šef of the South had chained about the world.

Then the moment was over, and it was his turn to kick his steed into a gallop down the dune, charging in a loose spray of dust at an angle to intersect the black-clad figure's current course.

Not for nothing, after all, was Cyper Edalos among the lucky few to have been trained by the Dragon of the North himself.

Lazura was in her element. Like living death she swept through the battlefield, her short-sword as cruel and absolute as the Moon's judgment. Given that it was her first pitched battle, she'd been surprised to find the circumstances quite suitable for her specific skills. She had feared—as she'd steadily done her best to cut a way deeper into the fight—that her talents would prove themselves challenged once she got herself surrounded. To her delight, she'd discovered instead that the chaos worked heavily to her advantage, her passage going by largely unnoticed so long as she kept moving, kept giving her horse leeway to gallop as it pleased. There were too many soldiers for anyone to pay attention to any particular opponent apart from the ones with whom they were in direct conflict. Only those she cut down bothered to give her much of a second look, often one of disbelief as their bodies came to the understanding that they were very abruptly dying.

In the end—among the madness of the endless fighting—Lazura's hunt was not unlike stalking her marks in the blissfully confusing bustle of any other crowded space.

Spotting an enticing opening, Lazura tugged at the reins to shift her horse's run slightly southward. Her blade rose in a blur once, then descended. It cut first into the thick flesh of the underarm of a woman who had just lifted her own sword for an overhead strike, then bit into the side of a second of Arro's soldiers, easily finding a gap above the man's hip offered by his ill-fitting cuirass. From there Lazura moved on, unfazed by the screaming left in her wake, and in the space of five breaths had brought down yet another. Had she had a mind for anything else, Lazura might have chided herself for her inability to stop smiling, but her thoughts refused to descend from their state of elation.

It would be time, soon. She'd driven deep into the fight, deep into the enemy line. While she relished her sport, the anticipation of what was to come made her positively shiver.

Unfortunately for her, it was as Lazura bathed in that eagerness that a mounted form broke through the dust and fighting to her left, and only a fraction of a second later a broad-chested charger crashed into her broadside.

WHAM!

Luck and instinct were all that allowed Lazura to keep her head in the heartbeat that followed the collision. Her horse—by some miracle of the Lifegiver—managed to keep its footing, screaming and staggering sidelong to find its balance. A flash of steel caught the corner of her vision, and Lazura flattened herself backward over the saddle just in time for a heavy curved blade to shriek by exactly where her neck had been not an instant before, nearly taking off the tip of her nose in its passing. Recovering quickly, Lazura twisted and rolled left in the same motion, launching a blind kick in the direction the weapon had been swung from.

The jarring impact of her shin meeting a heavy bracer, the blocking arm brought up just in time to take the blow, sent more than pain shooting through Lazura's limbs.

Whoever she was fighting, they had just successfully read her movements.

Lazura unlocked her knee and let the remaining momentum of the kick carry her to the ground, where she bounced back up using the foot she still had in the stirrup. Even as she tossed her leg over the saddle again, though, her short-sword was being lifted, ready for the blow she anticipated would be coming around again. It descended on cue, but faster and from a different angle than she expected, and Lazura barely managed to adjust her grip to accommodate the weight of the strike and parry it away. In the brief fraction of a breath that she was able to repel the steel, she was at last given the opportunity to take in the man she was facing, and she almost cursed aloud.

There was nothing outwardly alarming about her opponent. A broad West Isler, he was bedecked in the stolen white-and-golds of Karesh Syl. One of his shoulders was bleeding, the wound not even significant enough to affect the man's ability to wield the heavy saber he was already bringing around at her for a third blow, the steel of the sword well-reddened. His horse looked to be a gelding, well-trained and responsive, snorting and throwing its head as its master brought down the blade.

Had it not been for the soldier's expression, Lazura might have assumed him to have been just another body among the innumerable horsemen of Arro's horde.

His eyes, however, told a different story.

The composure of the man's face as he challenged her was what had sent Lazura reeling. There was no panic, no fear there. He was resolute in his assault, focused and direct, lacking all hesitation and doubt. With deliberate conviction he swung, forcing her to parry a second time as he then recovered without pause to slash yet again. The onslaught was relentless and without mercy, and combined with their collision, Lazura was certain their clash was intentional.

She had been singled out, and by a man who was much more of a danger to her than the common rabble she'd spent the last quarter-hour slashing to lifeless ribbons.

At once Lazura tried to extricate herself from the exchange, digging heels into her horse's flanks in an attempt to barrel beyond her attacker's reach, but the man read her decision as cleanly as he'd read her kick. With nothing more than a squeeze of his knees he sent his own animal forward to shove once more against her mount's shoulder, off-balancing the beast for a second time. Lazura cursed again, but tried to react more appropriately by taking advantage of the momentary gap provided to swing about to the right and gain some distance. Before she had the opportunity, the sword came down again, cutting off her attempted escape in favor of keeping herself from being struck down by the savage overhead blow.

For nearly a half-a-minute this exchange repeated itself. Lazura would make a play for the separation and be foiled, fighting for her life all the while. Her speed and dexterity with the short-sword became her saving grace, and she slipped death some half-dozen times in the seconds she deftly bought for herself. All the while, though, the soldier kept the press on, unrelenting and seemingly untiring in his advance, his curved weapon continuing to cut down with frightening calm.

Only when he finally made her bleed did Lazura's building alarm boil over enough to have her change tactics.

The blow was skillful and quick, and had she not learned her trade under the hand of as unforgiving a teacher as Ergoin Sass, Lazura would have lost her leg, and subsequently her life. The saber cut upward at an angle, following through a parry that had sent it down below their hips. This first change of direction was expected, an obvious follow-up to the deflection if the soldier wanted to maintain his relentless press of her.

It was the second that she did not anticipate so well.

For the first time since the start of the exchange, the West Isler's face twisted away from its empty calmness, a moment of strain breaking the calculating façade of confidence. It was this shift in expression that offered Lazura the only hint at the change in the pattern, providing her with a instant in which she foresaw the hard redirection of the sword's momentum. With a cold wash of adrenaline she saw the sequence the soldier had drawn her into, the repetition of pressing blows which had pulled her into nothing short of a rhythm. Her keen eyes registered the break in the design of the fight, and immediately she knew she would not escape unharmed. The man's sword had the length and weight, and even she had no prayer of moving quickly enough to shift her left thigh out of the way of the descending slash.

Luckily, there happened to be another option.

With a quick twist of her hips and an awkward sidelong bend over the right side of the saddle, Lazura accepted the blow in full. Steel bit into black silks, but instead of cutting down through the flesh and bone after it, there was a *clang* of ringing metal, and the saber bounced away. She felt a searing pain along the front of her thigh, and knew the curved edge would still have managed to carve a good line into her leg. Even so, the result visibly surprised her opponent, because he grunted, fighting at once to return his sword to an offensive position.

At long last, however, Lazura had regained the advantage.

Pulling herself back into her saddle with a snap, she released the reins of her frantic horse to reach down and rip free her second short-sword from where it had been hidden, strapped to her left thigh. It came with some effort—the blow it had saved her from clearly having damaged the steel's thin sheath—but once it was free Lazura turned the mirrored blades on her opponent with a vengeful purpose, bringing them both around at once. Their shorter reach cost her a killing strike, but one did manage to catch a second gash into the soldier's shoulder while the other *pinged* harmlessly off the sword he'd managed to reposition just in time to deflect a slash at his face.

They traded blows thrice more like this, their horses half-locked together, the pair of them even bumping knees on more than one occasion as they struggled. Lazura's confidence returned—as did her smile with it—as she recognized that she'd regained her advantage. She was skilled enough with her blades to compensate for the animal struggling and kicking underneath her, and with his single weapon her opponent found himself rapidly hard-pressed to keep her slashes and thrusts at bay. Each exchange left him a little more bloodied, and she kept him on the defensive consistently enough that Lazura no longer had to worry about the saber coming around to run her through. She had him, she knew. So long as she bid her time and didn't allow herself to be played the fool, she had him.

When the moment came, she was ready for it.

The opening was slight—the man was well-versed in how best to use his weapon and position, after all—but when she saw it Lazura didn't hesitate to go for the kill. The soldier raised his saber a little too high, lifted it just a little too forcefully, exposing the vulnerable pit of loose cloth beneath his armored shoulder. With a laugh of hard triumph Lazura twisted and lunged, the blade in her left hand driving around like a scythe, seeking a quick end to the fight.

What she got instead was a chill of fear as the man's focused expression broke ever so slightly, one corner of his mouth twisting upward in grim success.

With such forceful speed it could only have been a planned response, the soldier thrust his torso forward in the saddle, slipping her aim and wrenching his elbow down as he did. Rather than burying her blackened steel in his side as she'd intended, Lazura instead found her left wrist trapped beneath her opponent's sword arm, pinned between the bloody leather armor of his chest and his bicep. It had been a feint, she realized with a cold thrill, a trap. She had misjudged her opponent, had foolishly failed to credit him the skill he deserved. Whoever had trained this man must have been a terrifying master, indeed, to have outwitted Ergoin Sass' meticulous tutelage.

Instinctively Lazura brought the short-sword in her right hand around, going for a slash at the West Isler's eyes. She'd barely had time to lift the weapon, though, before the man's left fist cocked back, reins still clenched between his fingers. With his own blade largely immobilized along with her arm, the soldier used the only offense remaining to him, and Lazura had no means of escaping the blow.

When his calloused knuckles caught her full in the side of the face, she felt a tooth come loose in the back of her mouth with a *crack*.

Lazura flipped backward, gracelessly somersaulting off her horse's rear. Her opponent had released her arm when he struck—obviously aiming to unsaddle her—and she hit the arid desert floor with a heavy *thud* that would have had her swallowing a lungful of sand had it not been for her veil. As it was, Lazura still gasped and coughed, chest seizing while she fought to regain the breath that had been knocked from her. Her body reacted on its own, rolling once, then twice, out of the way until she was clear of the horses' stamping hooves.

Coming up on one knee several yards from where she'd landed, Lazura spat out the tooth with a trail of crimson spittle from beneath her cloth, squinting as she did against the sun to meet her aggressor's eyes.

For his part, the West Isler smirked—largely unperturbed by the shallower wounds she h'd been able to deal him in their struggle—and finally spoke for the first time.

"It's over, assassin. I will allow you a prayer to the Twins, if you so desire it."

Lazura blinked at him, not sure she'd heard correctly. Her chest still hurt and her cheek ached, but she managed to shove herself onto both feet and stand unsteadily, one arm across her chest so a fist and the hilt it held could press against the sore bones of her ribcage. Every breath she took tasted of iron, and her attacker had pulled his horse about to face her, letting the gelding huff and hoof impatiently at the sand. Her own mount had fled with a terrified nicker once it had finally been allowed its escape, vanishing into the tumult of the fight still ongoing around them.

And yet, despite all of this, Lazura couldn't help but smile.

"You mistake me, Isler," she said with only half-a-wheeze, raising the sword in her right hand to shade her face with her arm. "Did you think me one of my own blades? Is *that* why you attacked?"

At once, the smirk fell from the soldier's features. He was a sharp one, she could tell. He said not a word more, but it was clear he had not missed her deliberate phrasing of the question.

'*My* blades', she had said.

The reaction, however, yet told Lazura that she'd deduced correctly.

"You did!" she said with a laugh, almost wincing as the action made her ribs throb. "Oh you poor man…"

Still smiling, Lazura brought her arm down and sheathed her short-sword back into its hidden scabbard with a practiced twist. With one hand free, she began to feel that earlier sense of anticipation bloom once more in her breast.

"You fought better than you know, soldier of the Monster," she crooned, not looking away from the man. "Had you let up even a little, our match would have ended far sooner. You kept me busy, and unfortunately most of my more useful tricks require a bit of concentration."

She raised her empty hand, palm up. Around them, the battle raged, but to Lazura there was nothing to the world but her and her mounted opponent. The excitement pulsed and swelled as she felt the time had finally arrived, the very instant she'd been aching for ever since she'd cut the truth from the fractured corpse of the old hag two long years ago.

"Thank you," she said in final farewell, wondering if her smile wasn't a little bit genuine for once. "You've provided me with a perfect opportunity, and sooner than I could have hoped."

The West Isler—indeed as keen of mind as he had been of body—seemed to sense the impending danger. Wasting no more words, he dug his heels in with a "*hyah*!" and sent his charger lancing forward. His sword raised, blazing silver in the sun.

Oh, too late, friend, Lazura thought with bittersweet exhilaration. *Far too late.*

Then her hand was alight with white fire, and with an almost-casual gesture in her opponent's direction, Lazura set the world aflame.

By some cruel will of the Sun, Ahthys Borne was granted the opportunity to witness the ivory inferno set alight. He'd followed the Northern bitch deep into the fray, half-hoping for a chance to strike her down, half-unwilling to leave her to claim the glory of bloodshed all to herself. Before he'd been forced from his lofty position in the Imperium's army—before he'd even been a general of his homeland in the first place—Ahthys had been a soldier, and a damn good one at that. He'd never let his skills fall by the wayside, no matter the numerous times his wives had begged him to retire his sword. He'd always kept his arm strong and his blade sharp, and his dedication to his craft had saved Ahthys' life any number of occasions even only in the decade since he'd claimed and held his position as a šef of the Acrosian Mahsadën. It was this pride, this soul of a warrior, which had pushed him to tail Lazura into battle, more than anything else. It was this pride that had had him losing Tyala Gerst, Sol Fe'ren, and Gael Hareth in the chaos. Even now he wasn't sure what had happened to the others, though his fading conscience was not so far gone as to fail at taking a good guess.

They, like him, were likely dying, if not already dead.

Through dimming eyes Ahthys looked down the slope of the dune upon which he lay on his side, barely able to blink away the breeze-blown sand. With every emotion he had left to him he took in the blazing firestorm that raged as violently as a whirlpool in the crook of the valley below, ripping and roaring over the screams of the dozen soldiers and horses of both sides who had been haplessly caught in its cruel current. A storm of white dotted only with the flickering forms of the thrashing doomed. Ahthys felt his breath catch as he watched it rage, orchestrated as though by some devilish maestro.

There, in the center of the flaming maelstrom, after all, was the woman, a single shape of black standing tall with one hand raised before her, the other holding a short, dark blade idly by her side.

Ahthys might have been mistaken, but he could have sworn he heard the sound of laughter ring over the sounds of the fire and screams, like the gleeful squeal of a child let out to play after too long kept locked away…

There was the snuffling of a nearby horse, then the *crunch* of sand behind Ahthys as someone dismounted nearby. A moment later a sensation both boilingly painful and oddly soothing lanced through his back. He gasped, then coughed up a spray of red across the ground before him, feeling his left lung rapidly filling with blood. There were the faintest sounds of footsteps, and both Lazura and her hellish summoning of flames were blocked by a set of plain leather boots.

Ahthys wheezed in several short breaths, rolling his head so that he could look up at the form who stood above him. He supposed he should have been surprised to find his killer dressed in the common garb of the Mahsadën's cavalry, but the fact was hardly jarring. Framed against the Sun, it only took a few unfocused seconds for Ahthys to make out the man's cold, dead gaze, and recognize him for what he was. In the assassin's right hand, a curved dagger shone wet in the morning light.

Ahthy's had no doubt it was the same blade which had taken him in the back as he'd been fighting, knocking him from the saddle and leaving him to crumple sidelong to the earth.

"Never even saw you coming," Ahthys mumbled, trying for what he knew to be a gruesome smile up at his murderer. "We were never going to win, were we?"

The assassin, for his part, offered nothing in reply, instead only easing himself to one knee before the šef.

"Of course we weren't," Ahthys answered himself, his fading vision finding the hint of the blazing white he could see again between the man's legs now. "Against something like that… We were never going to win…"

Still the man before him didn't respond. It was as though Ahthys wasn't speaking, as though he were nothing more than an injured, bleating animal in need of silencing. Ahthys let him believe what he wanted, not taking his own eyes from the boiling flames even when the assassin reached out to take a fistful of turban and twist his head to make vulnerable to meaty side of his thick neck. The man flipped the grip of his blade, then raised his arm in preparation for the final kill.

Only when the dagger started to fall did Ahthys make his move.

Twisting sharply, he blocked the downward stab with one arm, reaching up with the other to hook the shadow's elbow. With a grunt and another spray of blood, Ahthys broke the man's stroke, bending the arm inward and taking and pivoting his opponent's wrist in the same motion. Willing his failing body into motion with the last of his fading strength, the šef rolled with all his greater bulk, off-balancing the assassin before the man could think to react and slamming him onto his back. Ahthys allowed all his weight to fall, then, feeling his knuckles and the pommel of the blade press forcefully into his chest.

The assassin died by his own steel, the treacherous dagger driving first into his stomach, then up into the beating walls of his heart.

Gasping, Ahthys Borne brought himself blearily up, off the corpse of his killer. His arms barely moved, now, and his legs had gone completely limp. He could only sit back on his splayed heels, kneeling in the bloody sand as war raged on around him. Through the dust and horses and soldiers, however, the fire continued its savage consumption. It had shifted, condensing into a single broad lash of white fire, which Lazura was putting to more focused use. Through the slowing beat of his own ruined heart, Ahthys watched the woman slash the magic at a passing soldier in the black-and-red livery of Karesh Nan, the tether snaking out like a whip to wrap about the rider and his horse together. Instantly the pair, man and animal alike, where screaming and thrashing, and by the time the mount reared and tumbled sideways, fur, flesh, and leather were unanimously aflame.

Despite all his years, despite all the atrocities he had witnessed and wrought, Ahthys averted his eyes at the sight, preferring instead to seek the comforting coolness of sky above, drinking in the endless expanse of blue framing the brilliance of the morning light one final time.

"We were never going to win…" the last true šef of the Mahsadën repeated to himself, feeling an icy emptiness taking over his lungs as life fled him. "Not against… something like that…"

And then Ahthys Borne died, head falling to his chest, kneeling beside the corpse of his own murderer in the blood-strewn sand beneath the Southern Sun.

XXXIV

"Is there madness in that mind? I can't imagine denying it... The Grandmother, too, knew madness, and much of it. Throughout my childhood I saw not even an inkling of it, but after that night in Karth, well... She knew nothing but *madness, you could say.*

Abir, though... In Abir, there is a balance. A tenuous—and even tedious—one at times, I admit, but still: a balance. He rants. He raves. He babbles with less eloquence than the wind and rain and rivers of the world. But he also speaks, also dreams. He is allowed a window, however small and however steady, into the mysteries of time and distance, and returns to us with words molded by the Twins themselves.

I'd be mad too, I think, if my mind was so often used as an instrument of the gods..."

— the Dragon of the North

Senus Thowt was of the strangest two minds he had ever been made to suffer in his life. He was among the very few of Raz i'Syul Arro's army lotteried to stay back from the front line, one of only some one hundred and fifty tasked with seeing to the maintenance and security of the camp while the cooks, smiths, healers, and animal-hands worked furiously to prepare for what they all hoped would be the return of their victorious—or at the least *surviving*—troops. There was relief there, somewhere. A sort of frigid respite from the fear that dwelled in every soldier's heart, particularly when battle was on the horizon. Senus could not claim in good conscience that he was unhappy to have been one of the chosen to remain.

Nor, however, could he convince himself he was altogether pleased with the situation.

There was, for starters, the guilt. Senus had marched under the winged maiden of the Dragon's banner since Karesh Nan had been overthrown. One of the thousands of city slaves who'd joined Arro's cause in the days that followed, he was not without his own time spent on the front lines, not without his own scars and victories. The White Witch herself had seen to a nasty laceration Senus had taken in the thigh during the conquering of Dynec, and he knew he had a stronger arm than most, having been a laborer who'd spent fifteen years bricking the city-state's defenses under the Tash's lash. At that very moment, however, his brothers and sisters in arms were fighting and dying for a freedom unlike the world had known in its written history, while he in the meantime stood idly in the cool shade of a tent. He *wanted* to be out there under the Sun, bleeding with his brethren. He *wanted* to alleviate the weight of shame which sat as heavy in his throat as the sheathed sword hanging off his hip.

More honestly, however, Senus wanted to be free of the tedium of his current posting.

As though reading his thoughts, his sentry partner sighed in exasperation from the other side of the tent entrance, crossing clawed arms over the bare scales of his narrow chest.

"Think anyone would notice if the old man were to 'mysteriously' disappear," Kyth Longclaw asked with a humorous snort, noticing Senus eyeing him.

Senus grinned in return. "Probably. Karan Brightneck has a sharp eye and the Witch's ear, I hear."

The atherian grunted. "Aye, and therefore the Dragon's, I suppose." He drew in a strained breath, obviously trying to find some resolve. "Still, wouldn't it be nice?" He took on a jesting tone as he affected a clueless expression. "'No, sir. I've no idea what happened to him. Must have wandered off all his own. He did seem prone to it, didn't he?'"

Unable to help himself, Senus laughed out loud, cutting the sound short as he realized the volume of his voice. Instinctively he looked around, wondering if he'd perhaps disturbed their charge.

Not surprisingly, he needn't have bothered with concern.

Pacing back and forth in an uneven line across the tent he shared with Brightneck, Abir Fahaji's muttering was so incessant it provided a more continuous drone of white noise than even the limited bustle of camp activity and the wind outside. It had been an hour since the pair of them had taken their watch, and in that time Senus didn't think the old Percian had so much as noticed their presence, much less met their eyes or acknowledged them with a word of greeting. It was hard not to find it irritating, but it was his first occasion meeting the seer—whose name was hardly uncommon among the host—and Fahaji was very clearly not of his right mind. Aside from the mumbling and the endless, aimless walking, the old man almost constantly wrung his wrinkled hands about one another, and occasionally pulled nervously at the grey-white hair that ringed his otherwise bald head. The fact that he was dwelling in a world within his own thoughts was obvious, and Senus had no trouble feeling sorry for him.

Still, empathy did little to stave off boredom, nor annoyance.

"Where do you suppose he goes?" he asked of Kyth after another minute or so of grating mutterances. "In his own mind, I mean?"

"Hopefully somewhere better than this place." The atherian half-turned to reach up and pull the edge of the tent flap closest to him aside with a single clawed finger, peering outside. "Heat and hell. Even out of my chains, that's all I've found in this world."

Senus wasn't about to agree offhand with such a pessimistic view of his relatively new freedom, so he gave a non-committal shrug. "Can't imagine it is…" He kept eyeing Fahaji, studying the seer. "He seems so… frightened."

"Lots to be frightened of in your own head," Kyth offered, letting the flap loose again. "You're telling me you don't have nightmares, sometimes?"

The question was unexpected, and Senus felt a chill at the thought. He did indeed bear the curse so many of his comrades-in-arms shared, the cold sweats that chilled the bone when one woke up in the middle of the icy desert night. It wasn't uncommon for screams of tent-mates and even neighboring soldiers to wake whole pockets of the camp in the evening, but no one ever dared complain. They all understood, in their own way.

Even Raz i'Syul Arro, it was said, was kept up some nights by the twilight terrors suffered by Syrah Brahnt…

Unbidden, Senus found himself glancing down at his wrists. The scars there were largely hidden by the lip of his patchwork leather, but the edge of them could just be seen extending beyond the armor. The ugly knotting of skin was pale against his otherwise tanned complexion, and despite having been freed of his shackles for some long months, now, the sight of the marks still made his heartrate rise in anger and fear.

"The mask has fallen."

For some reason—whether it was the dark space of his own thoughts Senus had found himself in or the tone of the old man's voice as he spoke—the words stabbed like frozen knives. He looked up quickly, almost alarmed to find that Fahaji had ceased in his pacing, coming to a halt slightly off-center to the middle of the tent. His nervous fidgeting had ended as well, and his face was turned toward the flap between Senus and Kyth, dark eyes widening with what could only be described as horrified realization.

The change was so abrupt, Senus' hand fell instinctively to the pommel of his sword.

"Are you speaking to us, seer?" Kyth asked, uncrossing his arms and standing a little more at attention. Senus suspected the male had meant to sound commanding, but the surprise was apparent in his voice.

Fahaji didn't even blink at the question, making no indication that he'd so much as heard the male speak. He'd said nothing more, and was still staring at the entrance of the tent like he expected some horrible apparition to come tearing through the flap to claim him. After a moment or two more, he started walking again, more slowly this time, approaching Senus and Kyth while never actually looking at them.

"The mask has fallen," he repeated again, the words making just as little sense the second time around as they had the first. "She shows us her face, now."

"Who does?"

Senus asked before he could stop himself. Fahaji, however, took as much notice of both him and the question as he did the reed mats beneath his sandaled feet, and came to a halt a pace or two short of the tent's entrance.

"Fire," he muttered. "Blasphemous fire. The mask has fallen. It is the turn of the god of a colder world to make his play."

Apparently neither Senus nor Kyth had anything to say to that, because the pair of them stared at the old man in a shared silence. After nearly ten seconds more in which no one spoke, Fahaji turned abruptly on his heel and began his pacing again, the absent murmurings returning almost at once.

"What in the Sun's name was that all about?" Kyth grunted, looking at Senus sidelong.

Senus, for his part, could only shake his head in equivalent loss. Despite his confusion, though, the ache of the seer's words—spoken as clearly as a lucid man's—did not fade. It clung there, squeezing at his throat like some ill portent. He had the feeling, somehow, that he should have been afraid, in that moment.

Very, very afraid.

"Syrah. There."

Raz wasn't surprised he was the first to make out the signs. Karan rode a few paces ahead of them at a canter, as was her habit, but her eyes—even as sharp as his own—were less versed in what they should have been looking for. In truth Raz hadn't exactly been *seeking* the details he pointed out to Syrah, then. He'd been trying to keep his mind as best he could on the greater battle at hand, trying to focus his attention on the coming encounter and the horde of soldiers that thundered along at his back. Just the same, ever since they'd spotted the blotting of the Mahsadën's army that morning, a part of his conscience had been consistently diverted, drawn to the possibility of a more poignant conflict than this last grand clash of their war.

The flashes of white fire, distinct only against the milling mass of the darker forms of the clashing cavalries, had brought that anticipation to fruition.

"Yes. I see it."

Syrah had followed the steel claw of his raised finger, the black layers of her wrapped face turning to follow as he'd indicated. She said nothing more, even after Raz had dropped his hand, but she did not look away from the distant glimmer of flames peeking now and again over a portion of the dunes west of them as she rode. She allowed Nymara reign of her pace, trusting the dappled mare to keep cadence and direction with Gale beside her. For the first time in some months, Raz thought he felt a shift in the air about the woman, a tingle of power that had been almost familiar to him not even a year ago.

He wasn't sure whether he was pleased at the sensation of its return, or worried at the imminent meaning of its presence.

"It's magic, then?"

Akelo leaned around from Raz's left, peering too toward the distant ridging through the dust of their ride. Raz, in answer, only nodded his certainty. He was sure of it. The light was too distinct, too known to him. He could set aside the expert of Laorin combat magics at his right, and still he would have spent enough hours in the training halls of Cyurgi' Di two winters past to recognize spellwork on sight.

To his pleasant surprise, Syrah herself found her voice in time to echo his assent.

"Without a doubt." Her tone was tense, a forced calm which had him seeing through the front of her bravery, but she held it all the same. "We'll have to get closer before I can make anything else out, but it looks to be as we suspected: rudimentary partitioning. Untamed at best, but powerful for it."

"We're getting closer, then?" Raz asked her as evenly as he could, not looking away from the approaching edge of the battle they could start to discern between the dunes.

Syrah only hesitated for a heartbeat.

When her answer came, however, it came hard, harsh, and absolute.

"Yes. We are."

Raz nodded, and said nothing more. He thought he had a notion of Syrah's pain, suffering the bastardized use of her gifts displayed before her like this. The confirmation that somehow someone had claimed the Lifegiver's bounty and twisted it to such cruel use could only have been excruciating to witness, not the *least* because of the woman's sordid history with her own magics. Even ignoring the ever-present shadows of the past, there yet remained Syrah's conviction as a woman of faith and of the Laorin, as well as a strict belief in the value of life and its preservation.

If nothing else, as a child of her god, Raz could only imagine the sight of those white flames made Syrah sick to her stomach.

For the time being, however, there was little to be done about the distant magic-user. They would be contacting the mixed cavalry from the north and east, and Raz could not afford to shift the trajectory of the near forty-thousand-head army moving at double-pace behind them simply to make his and Syrah's personal hunt that much easier. They would have to hold to the line of their march for now, then fight their way to the center of the battle in their own time.

All, of course, while keeping in mind the looming threat of the Mahsadën's own ranks, themselves closing the distance from the north at a correspondingly rapid pace.

As their leading group met and climbed the slope of a hill, Raz glanced to his right, beyond Syrah, to take in the churning dust cloud that trailed the soldiers of the surviving Southern šef. Once above the valley proper, he could make out the seventy thousand spilling through the sandy hillscape, like a many-bodied serpent coiling between the rise and pitch of the land so that only a fraction of its form was visible at any one time. Seeing that their two forces were comparably close to the fight already raging between their horsemen, Raz was of half-a-mind to signal Odene and the remaining five hundred cavalry to the last part of their plan.

No, he had to caution himself as they topped the dune and started descending again. *Not yet. Not just yet.*

"Riders ahead!"

Karan's sharp voice stole Raz's attention from the dark currents of the Mahsadën's distant foot soldiers. The female had brought her mount up short on the descent, turning in her saddle to look back at them all while pointing forward. Raz did not pull Gale up, instead allowing Karan to fall in between him and Syrah while he scrutinized the crestline she'd been indicating. Sure enough, a small huddle of forms on horseback appeared momentarily through the valley heads, disappearing again a moment later around the bending and looping of the desert floor.

Still, they were visible long enough for him to clearly make out the mismatched colors of their own soldiers.

"Marsus! Hur!" Raz bellowed over his shoulder in the direction he knew the two men were following not far behind them. "Take control of the march! Hold pace! The rest of you, with me!"

The order given, he kicked Gale into a full gallop down the slope, the stallion responding with a satisfied nicker as he was at last allowed to open up his stride. Within seconds Raz led the others by several yards, headed for the gap Karan had pointed out the approaching messengers.

It wasn't more than a minute before the two groups met.

Raz brought Gale up again as soon as the cavalry riders appeared around a bend in the gorge ahead of him, resting one hand on the head of his sagaris on the off chance the encounter was a ploy of the šef's makings. Syrah, Akelo, and Karan weren't far behind, trailed only slightly by Erom and Kalin. One after another they came to a staggered stop on either side of him, settling in to wait at his side, their horses shuffling and sidestepping fretfully as they undoubtedly made out the growing sound of the nearing fight. Not long after, the eastbound horsemen pulled up before them, an injured lieutenant in their very center going so far as to bring her own animal right up to Gale and Nymara.

"Sir!" the female officer offered Raz in the briefest of formal greetings, dipping her head in his direction. Her left hand looked largely-limp about her reins, and half her face was covered in drying blood from a shallow wound above one eye. "General Edalos sent me to meet you! I have news regarding the enemy!"

She hesitated, then, clearly unsure as to if she had leave to speak, and Raz reflected with the slightest bit of amusement that perhaps they had trained their soldiers a little *too* well.

"Report, lieutenant!" Akelo barked, heeling his horse up at Raz's left and fixing the woman with a stern look. "We have no time to be standing on formalities right now. Speak!"

That was all the permission needed.

"I'm to inform you that there are assassins among the common cavalry! The only one we encountered was easily distinguishable in her dress, but the general seemed to think it important you were made aware!"

"'*Her* dress?'" Syrah repeated, and Raz was grateful he wasn't along in having found the lieutenant's words odds. "Did you say 'her'?"

"Aye, ma'am!" came the response at once, the officer clearly not thinking she'd said anything amiss, looking blankly to Syrah's empty veil. "A woman, alone. She was ripping through riders like paper, all in black, even most of her face. I believe General Edalos was intent on engaging her when I left him."

Akelo cursed beside Raz, who couldn't blame him. *If* the woman was among the Miropan shadows, Cyper would be in for a fight. The man was more than capable, but they—all of them there—knew well the capabilities of the Mahsadën's assassins.

Still… Something more didn't sit easily with Raz, and when he saw Syrah look around at him, he met her hidden gaze knowing she was thinking the same thing. Three times now they'd clashed with the shadows, and not *once* could Raz recall noting a woman among their number. It wasn't a stretch of the imagination—the fringe cities did not typically classify one's ability by gender, whether it was the brothel workers or the šef themselves—but it was strange all the same.

"Any idea what that could be about?" Raz asked of Syrah, happy to admit his own befuddlement.

The woman shook her cowled head, and he could just make out the hint of a frown through the silks covering her face. "No more than you, apparently. I don't remember a woman among their ranks any occasion we clashed, but *you* did most of the damage every time. If you didn't notice something like that…"

Raz grunted in assent, realizing she was right. He *had* been the one to cut down most of the blades in Ystred and Karesh Syl, and the ambush a few nights past could hardly be compared to either of those encounters.

He was certain. There had been no women among the assassins' numbers until now.

That aside, he considered privately, *this means we'll need to be careful.*

After a moment's consideration, Raz looked about at the others around him. "Each of you will keep your engagement to a minimum." He addressed Akelo, Erom, and Kalin in particular. "Fight only if necessary, and at a distance when possible." He pointedly indicated the bows at Akelo and Kalin's knees with a jerk of his chin. "I would have you pull a retinue from your commands as well. A dozen personal guards each."

Kalin started to object, but Syrah cut him off gently, if firmly. "This is for your own safety. You've seen what these shadows can do. Do not force us to grieve over your body when this battle is over."

Her grim words had their effect, because the young *kuja* shut his mouth to settle into a somber silence.

"Send one of our spare runners back to Odene to tell him the same," Raz continued on, looking over his generals' heads as Hur's broad outline peeked into view behind them, Marsus' not far on his tail. The army had nearly caught up to their lead. "I doubt he'll be in any immediate danger unless the Mahsadën have withheld a significant rear guard, but there's no sense in incaution." After the three men nodded together in understanding, Raz looked to Karan. "You stay with Syrah and I. We can handle whatever the šef throw at us, but it would be useful to have extra eyes watching our backs."

"Like I would let you two wander off without me regardless," the female snorted, pulling her horse around to heel her up next to Syrah and Nymara. "What sort of friend do you think I am?"

The moment of humor helped to lighten the mood just a little, and Raz smiled. "One who doesn't know how to save her own skin, apparently. Now—" he looked around again, seeing the front march of host come into full view "—someone make sure Marsus and Hur hear all this as well. I've no intention of losing *any* of you this day, Moon wills it."

Marsus took the news of the shadows' presence surprisingly well, spitting and cursing them by the Sun and Moon and All Her Stars, but accepting Raz's decrees with no complaint. Hur, if anything, grew visibly more eager, blue eyes widening with excitement behind his blond bangs. Without so much as a pause in their march, they pressed on, taking to leading as a group again, sensing the attendance of the war looming ever closer with each passing second. All the while, Raz and Syrah couldn't help but trade the infrequent glance, clearly still sharing the disquiet feeling that something more than the occurrence of assassins in the Mahsadën's common ranks was going on.

Whether for the better or worse, they weren't given long to dwell on such concerns before they reached the battle proper.

Deciding they were close enough, Raz called at last for a brief halt and set Gale to climbing the largest dune in view, Syrah, Karan, and the others following in the stallion's hoofprints behind them. Claiming the ridge, he found his assessment correct. Not two hundred meters west of them as the crow flew, the milling forms of the embattled cavalries were clear, rapidly thickening into a dense melee of struggling and twisting shapes. Steel flashed bright in the Sun's light, and the acrid scents of death and blood sat heavy on the air to mix with the keen sound of metal meeting metal, the screams of horses, and the shouts of men. Taking a few seconds to assess their position, Raz was pleased to find multiple avenues of assault through the hills, and he pointed them out to Akelo as the men came up beside him.

"You and Kalin take your contingent along the southern valleys, there." He indicated a wide path that wound off to their left. "Marsus, Hur, and Erom will attack from that straight route—" he pointed left toward a similar trail that extended almost directly before them into the fighting "—while Syrah, Karan, and I will take the north." He pointed right, between a trio of particularly steep dunes. "When the enemy cavalry start to make their retreat, collapse on us. Cyper will be doing the same, since our own riders will have to regroup southward to rejoin the main host when the Mahsadën's foot soldiers reach them." He let his hand fall, looking north and west again. The dust of the vaster army's movement was still present, but had started to melt into the rising storm of sand and dirt kicked up by the battle. "Our forces will likely meet in the middle with the retreat, as expected."

"What of the Queen and her tribes?" Akelo asked, reining in his animal as it shied at the smell of blood and iron the desert wind cast over them. "Do we still stick to the plan?"

"We do." It was Syrah who answered, and Raz looked to see her peering south, in the direction they all knew the atherian of the Crags were patiently waiting among the plains. "Shas-hana Rhan will know when the time is right."

Raz nodded in agreement.

"Are we all familiar with our parts?" he asked, casting about all of them for confirmation. Below and sweeping behind them, the army had come to one final stop, taking advantage of a brief rest as the winged Sylgid shivered on her make-shift banners over their heads. "This is our only chance, my friends. We will not be given another..."

There was a moment of silence, the desert and the war claiming all sound and sense. The stench of violence overpowered the ordinarily earthy aromas of the sands, and they stood in that steep of death, knowing they were all going to be wading headfirst into it soon enough.

Finally, and almost all at once, the generals of the Dragon of the North nodded together.

Raz met their conviction with a grim smile, meeting each of his companions' gazes in turn.

"Then attend to your commands, and we will all see one another on the other side of this mess, be it here or among Her Stars."

With nothing more than a salute in his direction—some formal, like Odene's, and some lighthearted, like Erom's—Raz watched his generals disperse. Only Akelo lingered any amount of time, turning his mount around to be sidelong with Raz, facing opposite directions.

Without a word, he offered his hand, dark eyes blazing through the openings of his steel-spike helm.

Raz answered the silent farewell by reaching out and grasping forearms with the aging man, returning the pressure Akelo gave him.

Before letting go, the Percian looked around Raz to Syrah.

"Take care of him, would you?" he said, managing a hard grin. "The Twins only know how much trouble he might get himself in without you on hand."

For the first time in what seemed like days, Syrah managed a laugh.

Finally, before any of them could say anything more, Akelo let go of Raz's arm, dug his heels in and was gone, chasing after Kalin down toward the southern ranks of their waiting soldiers.

Raz gave his men a full minute to position themselves, listening without looking away from the fighting to the west while his army arranged itself at his back. Syrah and Karan stood by his side, unspeaking, apparently content with leaving him to his thoughts, if only for the moment. Eventually he made out the settling of the front line, and he turned to his partner and her companion. He did not ask after their readiness. Karan had shifted her belt so that her knife and longsword sat more accessibly about her hips in the saddle, and was already toying at the pommel of the latter with several clawed fingers.

Syrah, meanwhile, had started once more to emanate that indistinct aura of heat and power, her dark silks hinting at an unnatural waver about her, even in the wind.

She was looking north and west again, and Raz followed her gaze briefly. He found no more hint of the firelight and flashing white of magic. The caster must have descended closer to the floor of the sand, at least temporarily. He couldn't bring himself to believe someone had seen to their opponent already.

That was a fight Raz knew would have to be left to him and the woman at his side…

Reaching down, Raz unhooked Ahna from where she hung under his right knee. Lifting her up, he tested her heft, getting accustomed to the shift in his weight in the saddle.

Then he pulled Gale around, looking down over sprawling wind of his mismatched soldiers under their patchwork banners, and thrust the dviassegai in the air over his head with one hand.

"CHARGE!"

XXXV

Raz drove Gale into the fray at a full gallop, Syrah and Karan not far behind him. At their backs he could make out the reverberating war cry of his command, charging from the dunes into the fight with swords and spears and axes raised. The horsemen of the Mahsadën had known they were coming, obviously—the movement of their tens of thousands across the sands could hardly have been less conspicuous than that of the šef's further to the North—but extricating themselves from the skirmishing had clearly been easier said than done. As Gale broke through the eastern edge of the battle, Raz found he had ample targets upon which to vent the cold fury that ever-simmered just below the surface of his conscience. Ahna's weight—combined with the stallion's power—had the dviassegai careening about him as he whirled her in one hand. The weapon's twin edges twisted and struck, claiming heads and limbs and even splitting not a few men nearly in two. At first Raz kept silent as he fought, focused on his desire to lead the wedge of his army as deep as he could into the battle, hoping to drive the Mahsadën's cavalry away quickly. The further into the carnage Gale carried him, however, the harder it became to contain that commonly-somber anger, and before long Raz found himself snarling and snapping with every strike.

By the time he was bellowing out a full roar, the sound shivering through the hilts of any man and woman in the nearby vicinity, others had begun to call out around him as well, their shouted words distinguishable even amid the battle-noise.

"Monster!"

"Scourge!"

"DRAGON!"

They were, of course, correct. Raz i'Syul Arro, the Monster of Karth, Scourge of the South, Dragon of the North, had well and truly come to be among them. Even ahorse, those soldiers of the Mahsadën foolish enough to brave a direct assault on him found themselves succinctly overpowered. Ahna struck in blinding arcs that formed a near-impenetrable buffer of bloodied, cutting steel while Raz had Gale skillfully twisting and lunging, the stallion working as nothing less than an extension of his own body. Bodies fell one after the other, cut down or slammed out of their saddles, leaving a distinct trail of dead men and panicking animals at Raz's back.

Just as disastrous for the horsemen of the šef, though, were the two that followed in his wake.

At first, Raz glanced back more than once to ensure Syrah and Karan weren't getting overwhelmed, but what he always found eventually had him trusting the pair to their training and talents. They worked in practiced unison, complementing each other's strengths and abilities. Syrah's magics were docile yet—mostly quickly summoned wards and spells of incapacitation—but with necessity had returned at least a little bit of the woman who'd once considered herself a Priestess of Laor. She did not kill, of course. She hardly even injured, preferring to debilitate her attackers or rebuff them with blasts of flickering power that wrenched riders clean off their saddles and sent mounts stumbling as they nickered in terrified confusion. Not a drop of blood was spilled, not a life claimed. From an outsider's perspective, Syrah might nearly have seemed returned to her natural self, serene and focused while she doled out her merciful punishment on those who dared to threaten her or her companions.

It might even have been true, were it not for the fact that the woman voiced not a word of protest as Karan tore through enough of the enemy for the two of them combined.

The young female was not without her own natural talent. Atherian as a species were quick and strong, outclassing man in practically every physical sense other than sheer numbers. Long months of training, however, had honed Karan's aptitude to a lethal edge, and she fought as savagely and skillfully as any pair of her opponents combined. Even with her horse shifting about below her Karan wielded her longsword deftly, parrying and riposting as frequently as she thrust and slashed. Men and women died in quick succession, falling to the blade or the occasional slash of her claws across their faces or necks. She moved about as best she could, taking advantage of the many hours spent learning to ride, but never strayed far from Syrah's flank, shielding the woman's side and back. Had he had a moment, Raz might have found the sight interesting, watching one edge of their charge litter itself with unconscious and unhorsed soldiers, the other colored crimson and left strewn with thrashing bodies.

Instead, Raz kept his focus on his own fighting.

He lost count of how many challenged him, how many he cut down. He merely kept pressing, letting himself to dip into the old abyss of instinct and battlelust, leashing the beast within him sharply, but allowing it to raise its head a little regardless. The world did not shift into shades, the madness kept blissfully at bay by discipline and Syrah's presence close at hand, but just the same, conscious thought faded ever so slightly.

And with it, all mercy and compassion fled.

Raz pulled no strikes, held back no blows. Ahna was cruel in her carving descents, cutting into man and beast alike as she saw fit to, as often leaving soldiers behind to be pinned and crushed under dying mounts as she left horses bolting with corpses flopping or falling limply from their backs. Blades flashed and were rebutted, the dviassegai snaking up and through the blows to smash aside the weapons, sometimes shattering them on impact to fling shrapneled steel into the faces of their wielders. Little more than an indistinct shape of flaring silver, Ahna would then come full circle to strike back, birthing more screams into the mayhem of the fight. The smell of iron soon overpowered all other scents, and from the shallows of his own mind Raz registered that the sheen of his gauntlets was steadily gleaming redder and redder in the Sun's light.

Caring not in the least, he only gave the beast more leave, smiling internally when Ahna began to fall with still greater viciousness.

Two minutes ticked by. The shouts and cries of "Dragon!" and "Witch!" pitched here as their own realized Raz's and Syrah's presence among them, there as soldiers of the Mahsadën fell to razored metal and sparking magic. Five minutes. Then ten. At last Raz started to reel himself in, taking note of the fact that their fighting was becoming less frequent and further spread. More and more of their own soldiers made up the mass of the movement all around them, many riding past from the north, opposite the flight of the šef's soldiers. Raz paid them no heed, knowing his horsemen had their orders, and pursued instead any and all he could through the confused trade of retreats as each side escaped from the larger amassments of their respective enemy. Another two fell to Ahna, then three, and Raz was hounding a fourth when Syrah called him back sharply.

"Raz! Remember yourself!"

Raz's conscience snapped into place, and he found himself overextending, one of the few figures in a quickly-developing no-man's-land that ran northeast by southwest. Behind him, he didn't have to look around to make out the churning thrum of thousands taking up position in the rank and file under the winged Sylgid. He could imagine the last of his surviving riders disappearing into the greater horde of his foot soldiers to regroup, vanishing behind the bristling line of long-spears and pikes that would now head the front of the much-slowed march.

It was before him, however, that Raz kept his gaze. For some fifty yards the desert was steadily freeing itself of living souls, leaving only the dead and dying to lie scattered about the blood-soaked slopes of the dunes. Men and women speckled the sands, most still, but some moving feebly while they tried to call out for help. The broken forms of horses, too, were not infrequent, fallen under slashes to their necks or lamed by the unstable ground and put to the sword at the mercy of their masters. It was like a living graveyard, the heat of the day making even the corpses dance if they were anything more than ten feet away.

But it was *across* this band of emptiness that Raz's gaze was fixed. There, lined up along the valleys and hilltops alike, the line of the Mahsadën's standing forces was making their steady approach, the movement of seventy thousand over the rise and fall of the land crafting the illusion of a swelling tide shifting over the earth.

"Her Stars…" Raz heard himself curse under his breath, unable to stop from staring at the true breadth of the enemy.

With the added number of Shas-hana Rhan's tribes, Raz knew the army of the fringe cities did not so drastically outnumber his own ranks. They had at *most* fifteen thousand head more than his total count, and likely less. Still, despite this very clear knowledge and the confirmation exposing itself before him now, the presence of the might the Mahsadën had managed to bring to bear descended on him in a way the formed lines of his own never had.

Perhaps it was the cohesive hues of the leathers, uniform outside of the obvious pockets of *sarydâ* and other mercenaries, the colors of the individual cities having been wisely cast aside in favor of a common regalia that would make the soldiers easily distinguishable to one another in the heat of a fight. Or maybe it was the ordered tenor with which the army marched, boots *thudding* in such careful unison that even so far away Raz could make out the beat of their approach.

Most likely, however, it was the cold intent with which the swords of the fringe cities paraded across the sand, the steely, solid resolve of a discipline that had been instilled by more years of training than some of the youngest among Raz's own had *lived.*

Even if they *had* been equal in number, he knew that this battle would never have been one of equal *footing.*

That exact fact, though, was the reason he and Syrah had been putting together other plans…

Pulling himself at last away from the approaching bulk of the Mahsadën's collective strength, Raz brought Gale around and encouraged him back toward the Sylgid banners. The formed line of the spearmen broke automatically to welcome him, then closed off again once he'd rejoined Syrah and Karan among the shifting mass of the army.

"It's time," he told Syrah the moment they were side by side again, Gale kicking up a dusting of sand when Raz pulled him sharply to a halt beside Nymara. "Send the word."

The woman didn't even nod in agreement, apparently already of a like mind. Lifting a gloved hand, she brought up a single finger and started to twist it in small, concentric circles, like one might disturb the water of a still lake. There was no flash such as was common among the Laorin's more aggressive combat magics. Instead, the air about Syrah's hand began to glow, brightening even in the brilliance of the day. Then the light condensed, and something like a strip of dazzling white silk was left swirling around her finger, tethered to nothing while its frayed edges shifted and twirled before Raz's eyes.

When the messenger spell was complete, Syrah sent it off with a flick, the solidified arcana streaking low to the ground between the legs and feet of the nearest soldiers, headed east and north, back in the direction they had come.

Odene had already been shown how to receive the spell, and would know what it meant regardless.

"Done," Syrah confirmed, looking again around at Raz, then beyond him to the gathered enemy army. "It shouldn't take more than a few minutes to reach him."

"Good," he answered, in turn glancing back to take in the soldiers opposite them. "We need only hold out long enough, then…"

In the time Raz had returned to their host, the šef had apparently called for a full halt, the far line having come to a stop some thirty or forty yards away. Though they were well-within the range of Akelo's *kuja* and their arrows, the Mahsadën seemed utterly uncaring of this fact. Raz could see archers among their own file, strung bow-tips rising above the heads of the forward foot soldiers, and he grit his teeth, considering not for the first time that his smaller army would likely be as outshot as they were outmatched in sword, shield, and spear.

There was nothing to be done for it. The Twins had cast their die on such matters already, and there wasn't a thing Raz could do to affect the outcome of the immediate fight at hand. Shoving his nerves aside, he decided he was better off trying to focus on problems he *could* influence, and looked around in search of a face he'd somewhat expected to have met already.

"Have either of you seen Cyper? He was to regroup with us once his cavalry made contact with the main army."

Syrah and Karan frowned together, exchanging a nervous look before joining Raz in searching their surroundings. The horsemen who'd driven past them were long gone, headed for the rear of the army where they would take a much-needed respite before preparing for a more-traditional assault on the enemy's eastern flank once the battle proper broke out. Cyper, on the other hand, was supposed to have joined them on the front line.

The fact that the West Isler was nowhere to be seen did not sit well with Raz…

Damn, he thought, turning his eyes skyward and offering a brief prayer to the Sun that he was wrong in his assumption. *Damn…*

"RAZ I'SYUL ARRO! SHOW YOURSELF, 'MONSTER OF KARTH'!"

There was a gasp from the collected retinue about Raz, Syrah, and Karan, and he couldn't blame them their astonishment. The call—ringing out in a woman's voice he didn't recognize—had cast his own blood to ice, interrupting his struggle to balance grief and hope. It wasn't the words themselves which had taken him aback. He'd been called "Monster"—and many worse things—more times in his life than he could count.

It was, rather, the sheer volume of the demand—ringing through his sensitive ears with the force of an avalanche—that had his wings and neck crest tensing in shock.

As one Raz, Syrah, and Karan's attentions snapped around, the three of them scouring the opposite line. Their collective eyes eventually settled on a place among the pike and spearmen almost directly across from them, where the soldiers of the Mahsadën were actively moving aside as though to make way for something. As he watched, Raz saw a single form emerge from the masses, striding out with head held high. They walked with deliberate, confident purpose, mounting the side of a ridge to stop ten yards into the no-man's-land.

Taking the figure in, Raz hissed in angry disbelief.

"COME OUT, 'DRAGON'!" the woman called again, her voice—despite being as smooth as a cool breeze on a hot day—reverberating harshly in the arid temperatures of the sands. She was dressed all in black silks so thin they were almost transparent, and the force of her speech had the veil that covered the bottom half of her face fluttering as though in a strong wind.

It was what was *above* that dark cloth, however, that had sent Raz's rage tingling.

"Raz, that's spellwork!" Syrah's own anger was clearly boiling over, the words trembling as she spoke. "Amplification and strengthening! She's had runes cast on her voice!"

Raz was already aware of this, of course. He'd borne witness to a similar event more than a year gone, now, when Syrah herself had demanded the tribes of the North take a knee before the severed head of Gûlraht Baoill, their fallen Kayle. It had been a gentler experience, then, he seemed to recall. No less commanding, but the spellcraft had been cleaner, her magnified words less jarring.

Uncontrolled. Raz remembered Syrah's frustrated description not a few nights before, when he had reiterated the magics described to him by the captive *sarydâ* after their failed ambush. *Wild. Unharnessed.*

The understanding settled, the recollection enough to solidify Raz's suspicions into reality.

"Is she an assassin?" Karan demanded in a hiss, yellow eyes narrowed on the figure, taking in the woman's distinctive garb. "I can see no weapons on her. And what are those scars on her face?"

"Scars?" This detail apparently took Syrah aback enough to disrupt her outrage, and she leaned forward a little over Nymara's mane in an attempt to peer more closely through her wraps. "What scars?"

"Syrah… She's Broken."

Raz let his words take their toll, not looking away from the single form of the black-clad figure opposite them, but sensing the change in Syrah's demeanor all the same. At first all he could tell was that she had gone rigid, freezing even as she continued to bend over her mare's neck. Next, as before, the atmosphere about her appeared to shudder, the magics within her responding to the horrible declaration Raz had just made.

Then—far, *far* more terrifying—the morning about their gathered numbers started to darken, and Raz felt his skin prickle as the temperature of the day steadily began to cool.

In unbridled alarm he whirled on Syrah and reached out instinctively with his free hand, Ahna still bare and bloody in the other. He grabbed her about the forearm before he could stop himself, intent on reeling her back in as she had so often for him. Instantly Raz regretted the act, snarling in bone-deep pain when a searing heat bit through the worn leather of his gauntlet to stab at the flesh of his palm and fingers. He released the woman at once, but either his contact or the sound of his agony had done the trick, because Syrah started and turned to him in distress, her good eye wide behind her silks.

With the break of her focus, the day returned to its harsh glare and broiling heat.

"Raz!" Syrah breathed mournfully, reaching out to snatch at the gauntlet he had grabbed her with. "Your hand! Show me your hand!"

"It's fine," he assured her through gritted teeth, but he let her look all the same. The woman turned his wrist up, cursing by Laor's name as she took in the damage. The leather was blackened and flaking, and the smaller scales of his palm and fingers had clearly blistered, visible through several small holes about which tiny embers still burned. Without a moment's hesitation the woman began to trace a series of complicated lines through the air over the charred equipment, and within seconds Raz felt the ache of the burns subside, watching—with ever-present astonishment—his boils calm and recede, his flesh stitching itself back together bit by bit.

While the spell did its work, Syrah's question came almost in a whisper.

"Broken… She's Broken… You're sure?"

Raz took a moment, working to find the right words with which to answer the woman. He was aware of the men and women on foot around them having retreated away from their three horses, either alarmed by Syrah's momentary display of Sun-swallowing wrath, or by Raz's cry of pain when he'd made to stop her.

Taking advantage of the room this offered them, he lowered his voice so that only Syrah and Karan nearby could hear him.

"She's branded. Like Carro was. A circle around her right eye, and lines crossing her forehead. I can't see her cheeks, but I'll wager my soul to Her Stars that they're there too…"

Syrah said nothing in response, continuing to work on his injured hand, so Karan took the opportunity to voice her own confusion.

"'Broken'?" the female echoed, obviously unsure of what to make of the label while she looked back across the open dunes at the woman, who appeared to be drawing a breath to shout out a third time. "What does that mean? Is there something wrong with her?"

"RAZ I'SYUL ARRO! COME OUT, COWARD!"

Raz paused on the pretense of allowing the amplified ring of the demand to fade from his ears. In reality, he was seeking Syrah's eye behind her silks. If she hadn't explained to *Karan* what the concept of "Breaking" meant among the Laorin, she had to have had her reasons…

And—given the specific nature of the act that exclusively qualified one for such a horrendous punishment—he thought he could guess at them…

"If *she's* the caster of the spells we've seen, then yes. There's something *very* wrong with her."

Syrah did not meet Raz's gaze when she answered Karan's question, instead letting go of his hand and looking back to the enemy, taking in the woman who was the center of their unfortunate discussion. She continued, but he didn't miss the trembling of her fingers as she took up Nymara's reins again.

"To be Broken means to have had one's magic ripped from them, Karan. If that woman is of those cast out of the Laorin, she should not—or rather she *cannot*—have the ability to manipulate her old powers. Most likely there is some fallen member of the faith among them using her as a decoy." Syrah's shoulders stiffened at the thought. "And—if that's true—I have a responsibility to see them brought to justice for betraying Laor so absolutely."

The explanation did not seem to satisfy the female atherian, but with a shake of his head Raz silently requested that she not press the issue.

"I'll go meet her," he told the two of them once he was sure Karan wasn't about to keep prodding. "If I delay any longer, it will shake the resolve of the soldiers. You two stay here, and see if Cyper shows up to—"

"No. *We* will go meet her."

Syrah's tone was frigid, so much so that Raz felt a shiver crawl up his arms as she made her statement. He thought to argue, thought to point out that risking *both* their heads on a trap—his as the leader, and hers as his de facto second-in-command—was foolhardy.

Even as he opened his mouth, however, Raz knew there was no value in trying to dissuade the woman. Syrah was staring out over the dunes at the figure in black, and the shifting aura in the space about her said clearly that she would not be refused. Beyond that, there was a weight in Raz's gut that told him there was more to this stranger than he could make out at a glance. She was familiar to him, somehow, like he'd seen her before, but only in passing. She stood, too, with a bearing that stated absolute confidence, her chin held high and her arms loose at her side despite the fact that she was essentially facing down a force of near forty thousand strong, with another twenty well-hidden among the hills west of them.

Raz couldn't quash the feeling that Syrah's insistence there was likely a second Laorin withing the Mahsadën's ranks was further than any of them would have liked from the truth…

Making his decision, Raz looked around at Karan. "Report to Marsus. See if he needs your eyes along the flanking scouts. If not, find Zal'en and the Queen. Protect Shas-hana Rhan with your life. Understood?"

Karan hesitated, looking between Syrah and Raz, then back again. Sensing the female's reluctance, Syrah managed to pull herself away from her brimming anger again to look around and offer a strained smile.

"Go. I'll be fine. The two of us will manage on our own."

Still Karan wavered, yet unwilling to be parted from her charge.

Finally, returning the same tense smile, she turned her mount about and set off west through the army lines, moving as quickly as the packed soldiers could get out of her way.

The moment she was off, Raz clucked Gale into a slow canter and called for an opening in the spearmen that walled them in. As before, the men and women split to provide a path.

This time, though, Syrah was by his side when they cantered out into the hilly swath of corpse-riddled sand, the pair of them knee-to-knee as their horses huffed and snorted at the dusty air.

They imitated the woman's own press from her line, guiding the horse ten or so yards into the no-man's-land until they, too, crested a hill to come to a halt hardly thirty feet from the woman in black. At this distance, Raz knew even Syrah would be able make out the scars that cut diagonally out from the woman's right eye, which shown as blue as the clear sky above. He realized, then, that the stranger was of heavy valley town descent, if not a full-blooded Northerner. Aside from her striking gaze, the bronze of her face was many hues too light for anyone of a significant Southern or border heritage. Her hair, too—bare to the day—was a blonde so bleached it might have matched Syrah's for its pallor. Her dress was tantalizing, to say the least, but it also offered an idea of her form and ability. Raz could tell she was lithe, the curve of toned arms, legs, and torso highlighted in shadow, and a pause in his inspection of her had him taking note of what might have been a pair of narrow scabbards strapped *inside* her garments, to the outside of either thigh.

Regardless of anything else, he had the distinct impression this was a character he wouldn't be turning his back on without great consideration…

"So it's true. The lizard carries a pet about with him on his arm. Greetings to you, Syrah Brahnt of Cyurgi' Di."

The woman's voice had returned to a normal tenor, though she still half-shouted over the gusting of the desert wind. Raz couldn't tell if it had been she who'd dispelled the magic, or some hidden other force in the time he and Syrah had been making their approach.

He decided to assume the more dangerous of the options, and tightened his grip about Ahna's haft at his side.

"How *astonishing* that you should know my name, after nearly a year of Raz and I dismantling the Mahsadën piece by piece." Syrah's sarcasm was flat when she answered, but her hands still clenched at Nymara's reins with a vice-like hold. "And how *brave* of you to hide your face. Are you so ashamed of your brand, *traitor*?"

She injected the last word with every ounce of sweet venom she could manage, and across from them the woman's eyes narrowed ever so slightly.

"Not half as ashamed as you must be of *yours*, 'White Witch'," the stranger replied coolly. Then her voice became equally honeyed. "Aren't you the foul little hypocrite, teasing a girl for caring about her countenance? One would assume you would know a thing or two about concealing scars…" The corners of her eyes rose as she finished, and Raz could just imagine a wicked grin splitting her visage behind the veil.

That was when Syrah's hand jerked up.

For one shocked instant Raz thought that the barb had made her loose her temper. Fortunately, she only reached up to take the silks of her wrappings in a fist, wrenching half of them down and off her face, exposing her colorless cheeks to the cruelties of the desert light. Hooking the rest with her thumb, she shoved them and the black hood back together, freeing her head completely

Her hair, braided to a plait in the back, shone almost blindingly in the Sun.

"My coverings bear no shame," she lied through clenched teeth. "And my face would be known up and down most every land the world over by now regardless. You hide in plain sight, as the rest of your ilk hide among their shadows. Even in the full light of day your kind is craven to the core."

To Raz's growing concern, the black-clad woman's smile appeared only to broaden. "My… 'ilk'? Is that what you think they are. Poor fools, the both of you… If only you knew…"

Raz did not allow himself to rise to the bait. He gathered enough from her words alone, and spoke sidelong to Syrah. "They're probably hers. All of them. The assassins are likely on her leash."

Syrah, her good eye squinting so as to keep from being completely blinded by the brightness of the sands, gave a tiny nod, indicating that she'd deduced the same.

"But what of 'the Monster'?" the woman opposite them continued, glacial attention falling on Raz now. "I had been told the beast could speak, and yet I've not heard him say a word. Don't tell me I'm going to be disappointed…"

"I've only ever found words squandered on the likes of the Mahsadën," Raz growled in answer, allowing his neck crest to rise slowly above his head as he stared her down. "You aren't worth my wasted breath, much less the time and energy of those souls at my back." He gestured behind himself with Ahna for emphasis, indicating the waiting horde of men, women, and atherian beneath their banners. "Additionally, you seem to have forgotten that it was *you* who called for *me*, and yet you've not shown manners enough to introduce yourself before two whose names you already have." He lifted a lip in a fanged sneer. "It makes one wonder who the real 'beast' is, does it not?"

The slight certainly did something to rub the woman the wrong way, because the smile faded a little from her eyes.

"You do not require my name, *lizard*." She tried to maintain her demure facade, but irritation edged at her voice now. "You need only listen, and act in your best interest. Your atherian overstretched, and your cavalry have suffered heavy losses as a result. You are outnumbered, and you are outclassed. This battle is lost to you, and the war with it. Meet our demands, and I will see to it that your 'army'—" she said word with distinct derision "—are granted their lives."

"As slaves, no doubt!" Syrah snapped. "As if that's any kind of 'life' worth living!"

Still holding Gale's reins, Raz brought up a hand to forestall any further protest.

"You've failed a crucial step, assassin," he stated flatly. "What evidence have you provided us that you even have the power to offer terms? Where is my dear cousin? I've not seen Adrion—or whatever he's calling himself these days—in nearly two years." He studied carefully what little of her face could be discerned, and continued. "It was my understanding that *he* has become something of the mastermind of this futile endeavor to thwart the inevitable downfall of your society you've taken on …"

His careful scrutiny paid off. There was real irritation there, now, playing across those blue eyes and linear scars.

Whatever was going on, whatever successes the rings had had in forming their defenses against Raz and his coming storm, this outlandish Northerner did not like to hear Adrion credited with any of it.

What have you gotten yourself into, cousin? Raz pondered, finding himself irritated at the twinge of concern that pulled at his gut.

"You are behind on your intelligence, Monster." The sweetness was gone from the woman's voice now, and her stare was inscrutable as she met Raz's eyes. "The Mahsadën as you know it is no more. The šef are done for." She smiled again, but there was something infinitely more savage in her expression as she raised both hands to either side, as though to indicate the emptiness around her. "Only *I* remain, along with those who were smart enough to bend the knee *before* my daggers fell."

At Raz's side, Syrah inhaled in quiet disbelief, and it was Raz's turn to grip his reins too tightly as a flurry of emotions overcame him. The šef, *gone*?! Was it so simple as that? Had the Mahsadën fallen in such a decisive stroke? His and Cyper's interrogations of the prisoners had provided no such revelation, so if it was true then the blow must have come recently. *Very* recently.

And yet here the army stood, without so much as a hint of disarray…

The power of a tyrant, Raz realized, and he took in the strange woman on the opposite ridge with new care, his conviction that she was more than she appeared redoubling.

"You find yourself in a position of great responsibility," he offered slowly, the wind mercifully dying away so that he no longer had to shout. "All that power in the palm of your hand, and you choose to pursue the Mahsadën's ideals still? I don't know whether to be impressed or revolted."

"What you are matters nothing to me!" came the snapped answer, and Raz saw the woman's fingers twitching as they fell back to her sides, like she itched to wrap them about his scaled throat. "Yield, or by the *Lifegiver* I will see every one of your cursed compatriots *burn*."

Syrah made another sound, a subtle hiss of understanding, and Raz knew that she had come to the same conclusion as he.

As though reading his thoughts, he felt the power about her—which had been pulsing angry and hot until that moment—still and solidify in the air about them. It was, to him, a silent confirmation.

Ready, she was saying.

Adjusting his grip on Ahna so that she hung a little more balanced in his hand, Raz pressed the woman in black silks. "Burn, will we? That would be unfortunate.... So be it. Give us your conditions, and then we will provide you with ours."

The coldness did not leave the ice-blue gaze, and the woman spoke in a tone of flat calm. "Cast down your weapons," she told them, her hands still flexing and clenching at her sides. "Accept your irons. Do this, and the only heads I will see claimed will be yours and your 'generals', as I've heard them called."

There was a pause as Raz and Syrah waited for more.

"Is that all?" Raz eventually asked with a snort. "How succinct." Bringing Ahna up, he threw her over one shoulder, feeling Gale hoof at the ground impatiently beneath them. "Then let me give you *our* terms: You and your standing armies will submit without conflict. You will have the *sarydâ* disperse, and your cavalry will give up its horses. Whatever šef remain are to be detained and brought before Syrah and I here." He nodded toward the dipping valley between their dune and the woman's. "We will march on Miropa, where the city will open its gates to us without opposition. After that, your soldiers and the prisoners we've already captured will be free to return to their homes, lacking only their weapons and armor." He bared his teeth across the way. "That will be a good start, with the rest to come soon enough."

There was a moment of silence, which Raz didn't regret. Any time he could waste here were seconds and minutes in their favor.

Even now, he knew, Odene would be making his way slowly around to the north, circling wide about the enemy's back...

"Oh, *is that all?*" the nameless woman finally asked, echoing his earlier words derisively. "And here I was beginning to wonder if you would demand we pull your Moon from the heavens and present Her to you as well."

Raz grinned, happy to display even more of his white fangs. "All in good time. Why rush something that will bring me such joy, after all?"

The woman smirked back at him. "I spit on your terms, Monster. What say you to mine?"

In answer, Raz leaned over Gale's side and *actually* spit, offering not a word more of reply.

She stared at him for a long few seconds, venomous gaze boring into him as though attempting to carve a hole through his chest. When she spoke, on the other hand, her tone was pleasant again.

"So be it."

And then, in a blur of motion that even Raz had trouble following, the woman dug a foot into the ground below her and kicked up, pulling a long shape from the sand. He only had time to register the flat blade of broadsword that must have been partially buried in the commotion before the weapon was in her hands, snatched deftly out of the air at slant. With a skillful twist of her wrists the Sun caught the reflection of the metal, blazing brilliant in Raz's eyes, and he grunted in surprised pain, his free hand coming up reflexively to shield his face. There was a whirling sound, like wind breaking against steel, and in that moment Raz understood the fatal mistake he had made.

Fortunately for him, Syrah had not been unprepared.

A surge of energy tingled through Raz's body, like the rapid passing of hot, rising air. There was an odd *thud* of sound, and he blinked away the lingering afterimages of the trick. Once his vision cleared, Raz looked up. Even expecting it, the sight still sent a thrill to the very tips of his wings and tail.

There, suspended as though by nothing in the air above and before him, the broadsword hung, its chipped point not six inches from the space between his eyes. The ward shimmered and flexed, accepting the momentum of the thrown blade, then rebounded and pushed it out, flinging it some ten feet back into the sands .

Raz didn't watch it fall. He was looking north, glaring at the ridge where the black-clad woman had stood only seconds before. She was gone now, of course, her passing marked by nothing more than the disturbed ground where the sword had been buried.

Beyond that point, however, the great army of the fringe cities was already coming, their gathering cry rising like the climbing shower of arrows arching in a cloud overhead as they charged.

XXXVI

"I have found there are far more untold heroes among the histories of our world than those fortunate enough not to have been forgotten by time. In the years of Raz i'Syul Arro's ascension, for example, it is easy to be so blinded by the notorious atherian's legend—and that of his better half, Syrah Brahnt—that one fails to make note of the vital men, women, and lizard-kind at his back who so viciously supported the Dragon of the North and his cause. As a mortal man, I find this failure of credit disturbing. These were great *figures, in their own time, officers of an army which over the course of no more than a year wiped away all but the faintest traces of the centuries-long infestation of slavery in the South of the past.*

If such disregard can be applied to the likes of Akelo Aseni and Zal'en of the Crags, then what hope have I—a mere historian with a passion for ancient tales—of surviving in any form beyond my own grave…"

— private journals of Jûn fi'Surr, author of *The Atherian*

"Careful, you lot! Stay away from the sightlines!"

Odene's order was firm, and the duo of riders who'd been straying a little too high up the hill to the left returned sheepishly to the ordered line that trailed behind him. The *kuja* watched them file back into place with narrowed eyes, wincing internally at the cloud of loose dust and sand their animals kicked up beneath their hooves in the unstable firmament of the dune.

They'd managed to stay unnoticed so far, and he had every intention of keeping things that way.

From the two strays, Odene's scrutiny moved to the rest of his command, or at least what portion of the hundred and seventy that made up the train at his back he could see. A narrow trek one or two horses across, the winding trail of hoofprints they left behind gave the impression of the passing of some colossal serpent. He knew that somewhere to his right—east of their own position—four seconds Cyper had chosen specially for the task were leading equal contingents with mirrored care. Odene hadn't seen or heard any hint of those other groups, however, and was therefore intent on making sure his own line wasn't the one that gave them away.

Not much longer, he assured himself silently, turning forward again to correct the straying path of his gelding. *A little more. Only a little more…*

As though in echo of this thought, there was a distant roar of noise over the dunes to their left, and several beasts nickered behind him nervously.

To the west, the battle proper had begun.

Odene grit his teeth, working to keep his focus on the task at hand. He wasn't ungrateful for the assignment Raz and Akelo had delegated to him. His role was a key one, critical to their victory this day against the poor odds of facing off with the Mahsadën. Still, just the same, it stung somewhat to know his friends and comrades were all at that moment staring down the coming crash of the šef and their soldiers, while he—there was no other word for it—*snuck* his way around the battlefield.

"Patience," he muttered to himself, aloud this time. He'd been repeating the word under his breath ever since Syrah's messenger spell had reached him and settled into his waiting palm. "Patience."

Still, he couldn't help but finger at the war-horn on his hip, provided to him for the particular purpose he and his five hundred served in this fight.

"Patience," he growled again, satisfying his eagerness by clicking his horse into a slightly faster trot, feeling the awaited moment coming quickly.

Adrion watched from a distance as the opening salvo of the battle rose in a graceful arc, the arrows blotting out a small portion of the horizon in their hundreds. They climbed, then took the curve of their apex to descend in a lethal pelting. He could no longer make out the distinct shape of Raz's army from the dune top he hadn't left since Lazura's departure, the form of the horde loosing itself in the shimmering outline of the Mahsadën's own forces.

Still, even from this distance, he heard the distant screams and cries of the archers' first victims.

"It's begun," Vyres Eh'ben said dryly, walking up to stand beside and below Adrion, who'd remained ahorse throughout the nasty business at his back. "Yer cousin's done for, Blaeth."

Adrion shrugged, but voiced no answer. If the treacherous Karthian was expecting some sort of rise out of him, he was pounding on the wrong door.

"Should I just kill ya' now, then, or would ya' rather wait for *her*?"

This time the words got Adrion's attention, and he barely stopped himself from reaching up to feel for the shape in the left breast pocket of his tunic. The šef—if that title indeed still described him—had adjusted quickly to his apathy, and not for the first time Adrion had to remind himself that the foolish airiness the greasy man usually put on was nothing more than his mask, his façade of folly. Adrion knew well that Eh'ben had been first to deduce he and Lazura's plot, as he'd subsequently been first to bow to the new mistress of the Southern rings. Despite his charade, the Karthian had made it clear that his was among the sharper minds to make up the Mahsadën's highest echelon.

Or whatever is left of it, at least, Adrion thought, looking over his shoulder finally to take in the carnage that still lingered around them.

The bodies of the dead had been left where they'd fallen, their confused, screaming horses led down the slope by Avena Allehn and Casius Jules, who seemed content enough to act as Eh'ben's seconds for the time being. With a pang of something between sympathy and disgust, Adrion found himself meeting the one unblinking eye of Serys Benth he could make out, half her pretty features already buried under the wind-blown sand where she lay face down in the dust. The ground around her body and head was stained black from the great wounds San Loreyn had carved into her stomach and temple, the same splotching of ugly darkness that pooled about the motionless forms of those others who'd been crushed under Lazura's brutal heel. By now the four who had chased the woman into the fray would have been dealt with as well, leaving only Myra Fohster of Karavyl—who'd never joined them that morning—to be hunted down by the shadows once they returned to camp.

Adrion found himself offering up a small prayer that the Moon would grant the young woman a chance to escape, if only to avoid the violent fate of her compatriots.

"Oy!"

Adrion blinked and at last looked back around to find Eh'ben glaring up at him sourly.

"Oh… My apologies, Vyres. Did you say something?"

His feigned ignorance sparked the anger he was seeking, the Karathian's face twisting in annoyance. They *both* knew Adrion had heard every growled word thrown his way, but there was no means of pointing it out that didn't involve the šef looking like an indigent ass.

Taking the dilemma in stride, the clever man chose instead to save face by repeating himself through a tight-lipped smile.

"I asked, Adrion Blaeth, if you would prefer me to kill ya' now, rather than wait for Lazura to return?"

Though he managed to hold onto his straight face, the rush of a faint chill came despite all of Adrion's willful desperation to fight back the fear.

"Oh, I wouldn't be so quick to cast me aside as useless just yet, friend." He was glad Ergoin Sass had long ago taught him to lie with confidence. "If you imagine your mistress has been seeing to every cog of this grand plan of hers without assistance, you will find yourself in a wanting position before the end of all this." He turned away, looking back to the fight. "Whatever it is that rises from the ashes of what you've just had a firm hand in burning down, I do not think you wish to see it guided merely by the whims of that woman."

"Careful, Blaeth," Eh'ben warned dangerously, and in the corner of his vision Adrion saw the man's Sun-tanned hand move the hilt of the saber at his side. "Don't be forgettin' yer place, now. Yer *real* place…"

As if I could forget, Adrion wanted to snap back, feeling his heart thud uncomfortably against the ribs of his chest, and wanting again to feel for the bundle in his breast pocket. *As if I wasn't the* most *aware of where I stand…*

It had come. The moment where he lost his armor, his one feeble defense again Lazura's ire. His place as an instrument had not been without its pains—Sun knew he would not miss the feeling of fire being channeled through his limbs and body—but it had provided him with a measure of security, a tether—thin, but impervious—upon which his life had hung.

That was gone, now. All gone. It had taken long months and more than one bloodied dagger in the night, but Lazura had spun her web of influence well. Eh'ben, along with Allehn and Jules. San Loreyn. Ketres Bayn of Acrosia. Evangalyn Thesus of Cyro. The Northern bitch had picked her pieces with deliberation and care, corrupting them to her side one after the other. Adrion had even assisted her in these recruitments, had offered his confidence and advice as she desired. He hadn't had a choice in the matter, of course. He'd been as much a prisoner as a puppet.

But still—standing there among the very men and women he'd helped elevate to their gainful positions in the coming new order—Adrion couldn't help but grimace at the fact that he was very likely a key contributor in his own demise.

He was struggling to come to terms with this idea, battling to see a way out of the trap into which he had allowed himself to be intimately entwined, when the sound of a war-horn buried the distant sound of fighting.

BOOOOOHHHHHHR!

"What in the *Sun's name*—?!" Eh'ben yelled, whirling where he stood. Adrion, too, was shaken from his dark musings, a more pressing fright suddenly pushing aside all other worries. He pulled his horse around so sharply the mare nickered in protest, but followed his directive all the same. Managing the turn, he found himself looking at the backs of Loreyn, Bayn, and Thesus on their own horses, along with Allehn and Jules standing in the bloody sand among the corpses between them.

And beyond them, streaming out and over the dunes north and east of their small party and guard, five rapidly-broadening lines of horsemen were suddenly coloring the sand with their shapes and shadows.

"Those aren't ours!" Adrion bellowed. "Eh'ben! Those are not our cavalry!"

Even at the distance they were—some half-mile off—he could tell the soldiers were not riders of the fringe cities. The šef had outfitted the entirety of the army in plain Miropan colors for exactly that reason, knowing the shambled armors of Raz and his host would stand out against uniformed leathers. From atop their dune, Adrion could make out the primary whites and blacks of the fallen Percian city-states, along with other mismatched armaments from Sun-knew-where.

"No shit!" Eh'ben snapped back, bolting for his charger, which had been staked and blinded nearby. Vaulting skillfully into the saddle, he drew his sword and shouted to his Karthian companions. "Avena! Casius! Mount! Bastard's gotten behind us!"

The two šef didn't need to be told twice, sprinting for their own animals as—down the hill—the thousand foot soldiers who'd been kept back as their personal protection spun in an ordered sequence, responding to the northern threat they'd heard but had yet to see, depressed in the valley as they were.

"They're far enough away!" Adrion yelled as Eh'ben reached out to tear the blinders of his horse. "If we make for the main line, we can outpace them!"

"*Shut up*!" Eh'ben snarled back, but he paused as the other šef turned in their saddles to look between the pair of them expectantly. He hesitated, clearly not wanting to do as Adrion said, but seeing no other smart option.

The distant cavalry was already thundering toward them, the churn of their hooves—there must have been five or six hundred of them, Adrion thought—once again kicking up a thick dust cloud into the air to blot out part of the northern horizon.

At last, Eh'ben gave in.

"Sergeant!" he bellowed down the hill, and at the rear of the thousand soldiers a man with several gold markings on his shoulders looked up expectantly. "Horsemen, chargin' our position! Five hundred at least! We're makin' for the main host! You lot're to follow at double- pace! Do not engage! They're as like to steer around ya' as they are to ride ya' down! Understood?!"

The officer in question—looking not-unduly relieved at the orders—yelled a quick "Yessir!" before turning back to his unit to start barking his own commands. By the time the soldiers about-faced again, Eh'ben had pulled his horse around once more and was kicking it into a full gallop southward, down the slope and toward the relatively safer chaos of the battle proper. The others all followed him in a staggered line, churning ruts in the loose sand as they descended into the dip between the hills.

After some ten seconds, only Adrion remained.

For a few moments more he sat upon the ridge, alone with the dead, considering his options. It was an opportunity, he had to admit. He could try to run, try to flee. The camp—still tucked to the west of the combat—would have no idea what had transpired among the Mahsadën. It might look odd—him riding through the sentry line without escort—but he would have no trouble appropriating enough provisions to at least see him the days' return to Miropa.

From there, though…

Unbidden, the image of Lazura welled up in his mind, her cursed smile echoed in the dozen shadows at her back, each twisting into the shape of a man in black and grey garbs to stare at him with cold, soulless eyes.

With a sigh, Adrion set aside the idea, instead choosing to turn and kick his horse after the fleeing šef south, toward the battle. Whatever was to come, he would have to face it head on. Absently he allowed himself at last to reach up and feel the breast of his tunic, an odd sense of terrified relief settling over him as his fingers made out the small, slim form still tucked into the inner pocket. He'd managed to prepare the blade in the rare moments of the last week he'd been free of Lazura's watchful gaze. It was a whore's dagger—designed to be easily hidden and therefore barely longer than his shortest finger—but it would do the trick. He had seen to that, applying a few of Sass' more sinister teachings to the thin steel.

Adrion's final thought as he left the ridge behind was that—if it came to the worst—he would at the very least go to Her Stars on his own terms.

Had the fallen šef of Miropa taken a few moments longer before turning his back on the coming cavalry, however, he might not have been so quick to tail the others toward the fighting. Indeed, a strange occurrence happened hardly ten seconds after he'd dipped down into the valley. From the north, a second horn-blow came, shivering through the heat, and at once the approaching forms of Raz i'Syul Arro's five-hundred riders shifted their direction. Instead of charging due south, as they had been, they began to weave haphazardly among themselves, twisting and darting so close to one another there occurred more than a few near-collisions. They still came, but their approach slowed to a crawl, their initial driven pace turning into a seemingly-confused display of erratic disarray. To any knowledgeable rider, it might have looked for all the world like the Monster's horsemen had collectively lost all sense of reason and order.

Their mad scattering, after all, appeared to do nothing more than spread the great cloud of churning dust and sand in their wake, thickening it until a hefty portion of the northern horizon as a whole was all-but invisible to even the most attentive of eyes…

XXXVII

"Raz. If yer askin' me who'd I'd rather fight of the pair of them, I'd pick Raz. At least there's a chance, there, pitiful as it might be..."

— Marsus Bern, conversing about the evening fires

Syrah—godsend that she was—did not release her ward until after the first shower of arrows fell in their deadly rain. Although he was aware that the magics still held around them—the distortion of the arcana just barely visible in the strange twisting of the morning light—Raz couldn't help but bring his armored left arm up to shield his head and shoulders when the shafts descended. Every muscle in his body tensed unwillingly, and even Gale appeared to sense his trepedation, the stallion rearing slightly between his legs.

Then the arrows were upon them, and Raz muttered a prayer to the Sun, the Moon, and All Her Star combined.

Thud! Thud! Thud-thud-thud!

Again and again the projectiles struck, and again and again Raz winced. He watched with mixed apprehension and awe as they hit the spell with the same absorbing impact as had the broadsword thrown by the Broken woman, the magics giving slightly with each consecutive strike. Five. Ten. Twenty arrows slammed into the barrier to hang suspended overhead, the scene and sky about them warping a little more every time. The ward bent, accepting the impetus of each, bowing inward until Raz feared the spell would crack under the strain.

"Syraaaah...?" he asked tentatively, not pulling his arm down as he peered up over his steel bracer, hoping he didn't sound *too* worried.

"I've got it," the woman grunted from his side, and he glanced sidelong to find her trembling with both arms raised over her head, elbows slightly bent, like she where holding up the weight of the sky.

Which—in a way—she was, he conceded.

Thud-thud-thud! Thud! Thud...! Thud...!

Eventually the peppering slowed, then came unsteadily, then stopped altogether. When she was sure the arrows had quit in their coming, Syrah muttered and strained, pressing upward with both gloved hands. In almost-eerie silence the ward finally rebounded, sending the dozens of projectiles flying tip-over-haft to scatter and *thunk* into the ground around them.

Then the magics faded away, and sounds Raz hadn't noticed had been absent returned abruptly to the world.

There were wails and screams from both sides of the no-man's-land, and he realized that Akelo must have ordered a return fire from his *kuja* and the other archers. There were distant cries for help and healers, as well as the shouts of officers trying to keep their units in line despite the losses they must all have suffered.

Above everything else, however, there was the roar of the charge.

From before and behind Raz watched and heard as the two massive forces barreled toward each other, the swordsmen and shield-bearers breaking past their spear and pikemen at full sprint. The rising pitch of their battle cries intensified with the approach, and with dull, echoed thrums, each side released a second volley of shots. With a curse Syrah expanded her ward again, but unnecessarily. Apparently a portion of the previous salvo had been deliberately aimed precisely at them.

This time the shadow of the arrows traded arcs almost directly over their heads, *thudding* down among the charging footmen on either side to the piercing shrieks of those unlucky enough to be hit.

And then, faster than Raz would have thought possible, the waves were upon them.

"Syrah! Front!" he roared the instant the leading soldiers of the fringe cities started to spill over the opposite ridge, on which the black-clad woman had stood not two minutes before. Trusting Syrah to have his back, he heeled Gale into a full run down the slope before them, Ahna leveled at his side.

Sure enough, just as the line reached him, there was a *whoosh* of magic, and a solid wall of bone-white fire erupted into being between him and the coming swords.

Immediately chaos took hold of the frontrunners, many yelping and managing to come to a skidding halt along the slope of the hill, others failing to do the same as the incline they'd been charging down betrayed them. With yells of fear some dozen stumbled or tripped in the loose sand, the momentum of their armored bodies bringing them through the flames even as they screamed. Syrah's magic—of course—worked according to the laws of Laor, doing no more than searing exposed skin and tearing at the men and woman's leather armor.

Raz, on the other hand, was limited by no such convictions.

Once again Ahna fell in blistering sweeps, swung down from Gale's impressive height while Raz pulled the stallion sharply right to run along the wall of ivory fire. Once, twice, three times the dviassegai struck, cutting here into a flaming back, there into a burned neck. As he rode, Raz was aware of the magic expanding, spreading horizontally, then curving inward. He knew Syrah would be at the center of the spell, carving them out a space even the tremendous multitude of the coming army would hesitate to cross into. Beyond the fire, Raz could see the endless flood of the soldiers descending into the valley, and he became conscious of the precariousness of their situation. Even in the confines of Syrah's rapidly-closing circle they would soon be surrounded. Ahna, in his hands, began to fall faster, Raz suddenly more intent on downing as many potential opponents than he was on going for the clean kill.

Fortunately, his concern was forestalled by the pitching roar of some thousand new voices joining the fray, bellowing out from behind.

Wrenching Ahna from the chest of one hapless soul who'd been desperately trying to bat his armor free of Syrah's clinging flames, Raz couldn't help but glance over his shoulder. There, thundering down from the crest the pair of them had just left, an equal number of soldiers in mismatched leathers were sprinting down into the valley. With a *crunch* of hundreds of armored bodies crashing into each other the two armies collided, meeting almost exactly where Raz and Syrah had been holding their ground.

After that, the morning devolved into nothing but blood and violent turmoil.

Raz thought of little as he killed from Gale's back, Ahna cutting up and down with such repeated ferocity that she more often than not left arcing trails of wet red splashing through the air. He concerned himself only with sticking close to Syrah, he and the stallion circling her and Nymara steadily, keeping at bay the constant press of the soldiers of the fringe cities. For her part, with one hand the woman held up a section of the wall directly in front of them, forcing the enemy to break and reconvene if they didn't want to chance the fires.

With the other, she rained arcane devastation into the chests, faces, and backs of those simpleminded enough to step within range of her spells.

Raz saw stuttered flashes as stunning spell after stunning spell were sent lancing into the melee. Occasionally there would be the more brilliant glow of a lash snaking out, and he would catch the screaming forms of two or three soldiers careening through the air, tethered together by the woven flames as Syrah imbued her body with enough strength to pull them clean off their feet. Now and then *more* fire would erupt into being, splitting larger groups or pooling among particularly dense companies of enemy soldiers to send them yelling and scattering.

With a strange sense of gratitude, Raz found himself silently thanking the Broken woman who'd taunted them from the dune top.

Her presence—and the fury it had wrought with it—had done more in a handful of minutes to bring back the old Syrah Brahnt than he'd managed himself to do in months of coaxing and comforting.

... Booooohhhhhhr...!

Raz's spined ears pricked up, and finding a gap in the fighting he looked north to the bright sky of the day. The sound had been distant but unmistakable, reverberating dully down on them.

The call of a war-horn.

"Odene's making his move!" Syrah shouted, lancing a series of flickering spells into the faces of a group who were attempting to press her together.

Raz's immediate concurrence came only in a loud grunt as his focus returned to the combat, Ahna swinging to claim the head of a man and woman alike, the former about to cut at his legs with a longsword, the latter unlucky enough to have been standing foolishly nearby.

"Let's hope the Queen could hear it too, then!" he finally managed to articulate more fully, kicking out to knock a Miropan soldier to the ground, stopping him just from finishing off a fallen Percian.

There was a *crack* of white light, and Raz felt the heat of a lash scream by the tight folds of his right wing. He didn't have to turn around to hear the gasped curse of someone at his back, and knew Syrah had likely just saved him a sword through the ribs.

"Let's!" the woman agreed through clenched teeth, heaving on her end of the brilliant tether to the success of a yelp and a *thud* as whoever had been behind Raz was pulled off balance. "We're a little bit *fucked* otherwise, I think!"

Raz snorted, whirling Ahna about his head to bring her down again, but he didn't disagree. He knew that he could swing the dviassegai all day, and it would matter little. He knew Syrah could weave her spells until she collapsed from exhaustion, and it would do no good. Against the odds they were facing—their forty thousand, an important arm of which comprised exhausted and wounded cavalry likely already riding eastward—would not last long on an open field against an enemy twice their size.

They would need reinforcements, and they would need them soon.

… Boooooohhhhhhr…!

The second call was a little easier to distinguish, as Raz had been half-waiting for it. Adrenaline lanced through his limbs when he heard it, knowing what it meant.

The last part of their plan was in motion. All that was left was to trust in the Twins, the Queen, and Syrah's convincing ink.

… Boooooohhhhhhr…!

Shas-hana Rhan felt her breath catch in her throat, and she looked up from the huddle consisting of Ma'zer, Zelys, and the other broad-shouldered males Sassyl Gal had delegated to the pair of them as a cautionary last line of defense. The sound of a horn, carried on the desert wind even within the dipping of the dunes they were hidden among to the west of the fighting they could discern already raging. It was the second ring of the call, the final summoning of all blades to bear.

Finally, the Queen thought to herself.

Turning to the spymaster—who stood ever at her side—she nodded once. Sassyl only bowed briefly in return, then looked in kind to Zal'en and Karan Brightneck, the latter of which had come thundering through the valleys on horseback to join them not a few minutes prior. The young one's presence was welcome, particularly given that her animal would help carry the word swiftly to the chieftains furthest from their gathering point.

With only their echoed nods of understanding, the two females vanished to spread the silent order, one galloping north—in the direction most of the tribes had taken refuge as they waited—the other dashing off to the south.

Barely a minute's patience passed before the quiet anticipation of the delay began to fracture under the building roar of twenty thousand battle-hungry atherian.

"RaaaaawwwwWWWWRRRRRRRRR!"

Judging the moment right, Shas-hana took in a single, great breath.

Then the Queen of the Under Caves bellowed out the single greatest command she might ever form:

"*CHARGE!*"

Despite his superior position and the bowmen at his side, Akelo was being hard-pressed. The portion of his command who'd first braved the descent into the closest valleys had found themselves facing off with a heavy contingent of the Mahsadën's hired *sarydâ*, and subsequently discovered their capacity ill-matched against the steel of men and women who'd long lived a life of daily death and violence. The soldiers had made their stand bravely, had held at bay the desert mercenaries to the best of their lesser training and abilities, but too quickly had they been overcome, run down by their enemies' greater experience.

Now, standing tall among the ridges where he'd been overseeing the southwest edge of the battle, Akelo was in the process of arguing with the *kuja* he'd tasked at Raz's order to see to his own protection.

"Sir, you need to *go*!" a young archer named Nahla was howling at him, dropping to one knee and sighting down her drawn bow. She released, taking a man who'd been sprinting up the hill toward them in the throat. Tugging another arrow from the quiver hanging off the back of her hips, she knocked it even as she yelled again. "*Go*!"

Akelo ignored her, just as he'd been ignoring the last minute of the rest of his protection's insistence. Instead, he drew his own string, aimed, and let the shot fly to strike what he suspected was a captain of one of the mercenary companies through the eye.

His entourage had reason to scream for his retreat, he knew. He could see the battle below breaking out of their favor, the outpouring of their own soldiers being steadily beaten back up the dune line by the *sarydâ*. Just the same, he could not find the will to turn tail, to leave these men and women to their fate alone. His horse had already been fetched and was being held nearby, snorting and kicking in fear at the smell of gore and the sounds of battle.

And yet Akelo could not bring himself to flee.

"*Sir*!" another of the *kuja* half-pleaded, half-bellowed, a straight sword in his left hand, his drawing arm incapacitated by the feathered shaft buried into his bicep. "There's no time! Please! Go!"

Still Akelo ignored them, tugging yet another arrow free of his own quiver and sighting. What must have been his tenth fell to his eye, then his eleventh. He droned out the yelling of his guard, satisfied with his place. If the Sun willed it that this was his time, let it be so. Despite all Raz had said before their last parting, his first duty was not to survive this battle.

It was to ensure victory, at any cost.

"Right! RIGHT!"

It was the Nahla who shouted, and for the first time her voice carried a note of fear that had nothing to do with Akelo's safety. He whirled and drew in the same motion, but it took him a moment to find the source of her alarm, the oddity not immediately apparent among the clamoring mess of the mismatched armor of his soldiers and the *sarydâ's*.

Still, when he found the man, Akelo felt his mouth go dry.

The figure wore the plainer leathers of the Miropan rank, but he did not wield the curved scimitar in his sword hand with the blunt discipline of a trained solder. Rather, he moved as silk might in a light wind, as unperturbed by the passing current of the fight as would a shark be in the gentle waters of Sun-warmed shallows. His blade flashed and slashed in almost lazy curves, parrying and deflecting with imperceptible effort the blows of those few fast enough to meet him steel to steel. He killed as easily as he walked, cutting a swatch through the fighting with effortless efficiency. His focus was intense, his attention flitting from one target to the other in quick succession while he climbed the hill with steady sureness.

In the brief reprieves he found, however, the man's cold, grey gaze always lifted upward, seeking Akelo's face in the crowd.

"Damn," Akelo muttered, speaking for the first time in several minutes, and releasing in the shadow's direction.

He repeated the curse when the man twisted sidelong, dodging the blurred form of the shaft, allowing it to bury itself in the chest of one of the many sellswords who were taking advantage of his carved path to clamber up the dune themselves.

Several more arrows immediately trailed Akelo's, but the assassin moved in and out of the crowd with effortless ease, forcing their shots wide if they didn't want to risk injuring any of their own. Like a rising storm he climbed higher and higher, billowing up toward them with the same inevitable presence Akelo recalled feeling in the closing maelstroms of the open ocean. They could not down him, could not even touch him. Every moment he grew closer, weaving in and out of the combat, killing all the while.

Finally, when the shadow had only twenty feet or so left to conquer, his free hand snapped out.

Akelo saw only the dim glint of darkened metal before the dagger *thudded* into Nahla's chest, burying itself to the handle in her heart. She died with nothing more than a single gasp of confused shock, going limp to tumble backward at his feet. Before Akelo could even take in her sad, still form, three of the others had closed in to take her place, shielding his front. One died immediately to a second knife, thrown with equivalent accuracy.

Then the shadow was on them, and the other two fell with barely enough breath between them to shout one last time for Akelo to flee.

Even if he'd wanted to, though, Akelo knew it was too late. He watched with grim resignation as his *kuja* were cut down before his eyes, the assassin's scimitar knocking aside the desperate thrusts of their drawn blades with the ease of a grown man batting away the feeble blows of a child. The curved sword screamed as it came around, slashing the face of one of the men before cleaving into the throat of the other.

Akelo said a silent prayer to the Moon, asking that She might look after those friends he would soon leave behind, and cast aside his bow in favor of wrenching free his own blade from its sheath at his hip.

There was no hesitation between the assassin's final kill and his leap at Akelo, not a pause in the figure's lethal intent. The blow fell, slaying the last of the trio who'd sacrificed their lives as living shields, and then the man was a blur of leather and tanned skin, launching himself into what was left of Akelo's protective ring without pause. The scimitar rose, as did Akelo's own sword to meet it, and he braced himself for the impact.

The blade never had a chance to fall.

Shtunk!

With the unpleasant sound of splitting bone and flesh, a spear appeared in the shadow's side, taking him through the ribs as he was practically in midair. The weapon was a crude thing—its haft and grip roughly shaven, its head looking to have been bound with a stone tip—but it had been thrown with such unforgiving force that the man was blown sideways, glancing off the shoulder of one of the still-encircling *kuja*. He tumbled down then to lay twitching in the sand, typically-empty eyes wide with pain and fear while both hands came up to grasp weakly at the thick spear, trying in vain to pull it out.

Before he could do so, a massive form blurred between Akelo and the others, reaching to wrench the weapon free of the man's side with one hand, and brought it down again to take the assassin through the neck.

When his prey was good and still, the shape turned to look at Akelo and his surviving bowman with fiery yellow eyes, his chitinous armor gleaming in the morning light. He took them all in, noting the wounded among them and the dead sprawled along the dune slope at their feet, riddled with skillfully aimed arrows.

Zathlys of the Lower Feet grinned, baring his curved fangs in what might have been approval, and turned to leap down the incline with a roar, bloodied spear in hand.

It was as Akelo watched the savage chieftain slam into the still-climbing wave of the *sarydâ* with vicious efficiency that he became aware of other guttural voices joining the battle. He snapped around, looking west to the dunes beyond his edge of the fighting. With a wash of relief he would later feel a little ashamed for, he took in the trampling approach of the atherian rising from the dips and edges of the plains. The fastest among them had already reached the desert mercenaries' largely-open flank, and were ripping into the sellswords with teeth and claws and clubs and blades. Almost at once the current of the combat shifted, the officers amongst the companies screaming for formation as the lizard-kind cleaved into their scattered ranks.

With a grin, Akelo sheathed his sword again, holding out an empty hand expectantly. Without a word one of his guard handed him the bow he'd just cast aside, the string and grip already strummed free of dust and grit.

"FORWARD ALL!" Akelo roared, reaching back to draw yet another arrow from his quiver, his order echoed by the bellowed cheer of the men and women of his command as they drove down the slope with renewed vigor.

XXXVIII

"The reign of Adrion Blaeth is as perplexing as it was brief. Records of that time are inconsistent, particularly *when it comes to the man himself. On the one hand, it is clear that Blaeth wielded an authority over the Mahsadën which had never before been allowed by the šef, who had to that point built and maintained the entire society on their precious balance. On the other, however, facts regarding that control are varying at best, the only consistency among them being in their unreliability. There appears to be an implication of power—of real, tangible power—but within the slave rings of the South such a suggestion could merely have been referring to the strength of the šef's backing. Even if there* were *something more visceral to Blaeth's individual capabilities, how would he have come about such gifts? It is a commonly accepted truth that the man was a child of the same prodigious family as the Dragon of the North, who himself never demonstrated any such métier, as far as the histories allow for..."*

— *Shadow's Fall,* by unknown author

Lazura did not make herself known as she slipped her way through the chaos of the fight. On foot she moved, both black blades at her side, stalking her prey with careful deliberation. Having left her horse behind, it wasn't hard to stay inconspicuous in the havoc and bedlam of the battlefield. She killed only when necessary, the weapons moving largely of their own instinctive accord, her blue eyes rarely leaving the massive form atop his impressive black charger. She'd forced herself to be patient, willed herself not to lose out to her desire to let the magics consume once again. She was free, now. She was without chains, without the bindings of the Laorin code, without the weaves of the Breaking ritual, and without even the irritating necessity for secrecy as she'd gathered her allies among the Mahsadën. She was free.

But that freedom could yet be finite, if she allowed herself to stumble now...

A man in the black-and-red of Karesh Nan charged her, shield first, sword raised and ready. Hardly glancing away from her target, Lazura sidestepped the stroke, bringing one of the short-swords up to stab down into the opening between the soldier's helmet and cuirass. He died with the "*urk!*" of his jugular and windpipe being severed together as his lung and heart were run through, but Lazura had already moved on by the time he fell to his knees.

She had interest only in one.

Closer she stalked, sometimes darting through gaps in the fighting when she could, other times cutting her way steadily through. She made no show of herself, made no theatre of her skills. When either of the two mounted figures she was approaching happened to cast their gaze in her direction, she would slip quickly back into the carnage, little more than a flitting shape among the swinging blades and crashing bodies. It took her a long time to close the distance—a full minute made out of what could have been seconds if she'd so desired it—but Lazura didn't mind. Let them tire themselves out. Let their focus fade and fix itself on the fighting at hand. Let them fall into the rhythm and sway of their skirmishing.

There was nothing half-so-appetizing to a hunter's pallet.

Two came at her this time, coincidently attacking from either side. With a casual arching roll Lazura twisted over the thrusting pike in the left man's hands. The flat of one short-sword hooked the head of the polearm and lifted it higher than intended, while in the same motion the other slashed out deftly. The left soldier let go of his longer weapon at once to clutch at an opened throat.

The second—rushing from the right with axe swung high—took the point of the pike full in the chest, running himself through as the bottom tip of the dropped polearm braced itself naturally in the sand.

Lazura moved on without so much as a backward glance.

For a little while longer she made her careful deliberation through the fighting like this, as often whispering off into the madness to vanish as slicing her way directly toward the pair. Fifty feet. She was yet unnoticed. Forty feet. She ducked to the side, dodging to crouch low between the corpses of a fallen horse and its rider. Thirty feet. She killed another foolish enough to get in her way, cutting the woman down from behind as she passed. Twenty feet.

Now, Lazura thought gleefully.

Timing everything with the current and flow of fighting all around her, she paused only long enough to sheath one black blade back along her hip.

Then—with the same grin she just hadn't been be able to rid herself of all morning—she drew power into her right hand, feeling the flames roar into easy existence. The moment the magics formed as desired, she lifted her arm, then brought it slashing down as one might crack a whip.

With the ripping sound of fire breathing itself into life, the lash of white flame snapped outward.

Snapped outward… and struck.

Amid the *pops* and *whooshing* of Syrah's own magics, Raz had only the barest opportunity to make out the incoming attack. He'd tried to stay vigilant, tried to keep the awareness of his surroundings sharp. He knew better than anyone some of the dangers that lurked within the frenzied bloodshed all around them, and was just as conscious of the reality that there were others he had too-little knowledge of. All the same, the press of the army of the fringe cities was relentless, and eventually his focus had had to shift to nothing more than keeping himself and Syrah alive among the turmoil.

It was this fact that very nearly lost him an arm.

WHOOSH!

Only the blistering sound of fire led the strike, and despite Raz's focus the animal within registered the odd notion that the spellwork didn't seem to have resonated from Syrah's direction by his right shoulder. Reflex more than anything had him whirling in the saddle, raising Ahna up in anticipation. He knew even as he turned that the weapon would provide him little defense from the assault he suspected to be coming, but instinct screamed that he had to defend himself.

Unfortunately, it ended up that not even the Dragon of the North was quick enough to outrace corrupted magics.

The lash—a brilliant, knotted mess of blazing white fire that was so far gone from the tight weaving of Syrah's tethers—failed to take him about the chest as it looked to have been intending. Instead it wrapped itself about his left arm and Ahna's haft, coiling around the steel of his bracer and the dviassegai's bleached wood handle. *Instantly* Raz roared in pain, feeling the metal about his forearm superheat on contact, but before he could shout for assistance all slack was pulled out of the arcane whip.

Then he was falling, wrenched off of Gale's back as an unnatural strength heaved from the far end of the spell.

Raz bellowed again when he slammed into the ground, crashing painfully atop Ahna and the hilt of the sagaris on his hip. Distantly he was aware of Gale screaming too, the stallion thrown into confusion by the sudden lack of weight on his back. Raz wanted to call to him, wanted to calm the animal, but all his focus was consumed by the boiling agony of his arm cooking inside its armor.

And then, just when he thought he couldn't imagine a greater pain, the sensation of heat intensified, and Raz blinked as he caught what looked like a wave of fire hurtling up the length of the lash at him. He bared his teeth in the only means he had left to defy the terrible death careening in his direction at full speed.

Shing!

There was a flash of white, more brilliant even than the spellwork of the fetter bound about his gauntlet, and something like a curved blade of guttering ivory flames cut through the air across his vision. It struck the binding line of the lash, severing it with a ringing sound not unlike the tolling of a hand bell, and almost immediately the tether looped about Ahna and his arm fell apart in a glistening shower of gold-white dust. The flames that had been charging up the spell reached the cut end and erupted in a storming conflagration some six or seven feet wide, enveloping and consuming several unfortunates from *both* sides of the fight. The soldiers screamed and thrashed, unable to do anything more than stumble out of the roiling blaze while still afire, spreading the flames to any they knocked into.

Raz saw only part of this, having heaved himself onto his knees to slash with steel claws at the leather straps that kept his left gauntlet strapped about his elbow. The bindings split easily, and with a snarl as a good slough of the scales and skin of his forearm came with it, he wrenched the armored glove off.

It smoked and *popped* with heat when it fell to the sand, part of the steel still glowing red-hot.

There was a *thud* of boots hitting the ground nearby, and in an instant Syrah was at his side. Raz became aware, then, that she'd been calling his name, but his mind was clouded with the stinging ache of the raw burn that extended nearly half-a-foot from his wrist down. He clutched at his hand with the other, teeth grinding as he fought off the pain, eyes shut tight against the threatening darkness of shock and merciful oblivion.

Then the agony receded, dulled by the warm, gentle sensation of healing magics Raz had grown all-too familiar with.

He sighed, opening his eyes and looking to Syrah, planning on thanking her. The woman's face was stricken, however, and all at once he heard what she was yelling, felt the pull of her other hand on his armored shoulder.

"RAZ! MOVE!"

He answered with the coiled speed of a snake, launching himself at Syrah and slamming her back even as he wrapped her tightly in his arms. As he tucked and rolled, the sizzling sound of new fire rent the air.

The second lash slammed down into the ground exactly where the pair of them had been a moment before.

Raz grunted against the stinging ache of sand caking the raw flesh of his open burn. Still holding Syrah tight, he bowled himself to his feet and came up standing several feet from the charred line of the missed attack. Gale and Nymara were *both* shrieking, now, kicking and rearing so aggressively that the nearest soldiers were backing away, forming a sparse circle of space around the animals.

And there, crowning a narrow lane ahead of them that she'd cut through the fighting, a now-familiar figure in black silks stood with one hand aflame, watching them with a grin cutting a shadow behind the veil that covered the lower half of her scarred face.

"*Bitch*."

Held firm to his chest as she was, Raz felt the physical press of Syrah's flaring anger, catching sight of the Broken woman together. He let go, allowing her to step free of his embrace, reaching for his gladius and the sagaris. The sword came loose easily from the sheath across his back, but his left hand refused to take the weight of the axe, and he growled in throbbing exasperation as it slipped awkwardly from his fingers into its loop on his belt again.

The sound distracted Syrah just long enough to blink and look at him. She didn't glance away from their opponent for more than a second, her reflexive concern for his well-being only barely overpowering her rage.

In that instant, though, the woman vanished.

"Where is she?!" Raz snarled, the gladius at the ready while he spun in place, claws and tail kicking up dust and grit all around him. "Syrah! Where did she go?!"

"I don't know…" Syrah's answer was tense, and she too turned on the spot, opposite him, peering with her good eye into the crowd. Her hood had been thrown back up over her head in their tumble, but she still lacked the wrappings that usually shielded her sensitive vision from the Sun's cruelty. "I don't—"

WHOOSH!

Alerted to the hidden menace now, Raz was able to respond more appropriately when he made out the sound of fire from his right. He spun and stepped clear of the lash's expected trajectory, one wing barely clearing the angle of attack before the flames slammed down into the sand with a flare of colored light. He leapt back, fearing another explosion like the one he'd just witnessed, but the line vanished in a gleaming blink.

Raz cursed, realizing he hadn't even gotten a glimpse of their attacker.

"Bloody COWARD!" he roared into the battling throng, his rage so visceral several of the closest skirmishing soldiers started in fear. "SHOW YOURSELF!"

There was the tinkling of laughter, barely audible behind him, and Raz whirled in place. Almost at once, he regretted it, because the sparking stutter of spellwork ripped through the air from behind. He managed to throw himself sideways, rolling to his feet beside Syrah, and came up to stand back to back with her in time to see the lash that had cracked down into the earth vanish yet again.

He hissed in frustration, but just as he was about to start cursing into the combat again, he felt Syrah touch his injured arm lightly from behind.

"Tell me where it's coming from next time," she said as quietly as she could manage, facing away from him. "You can make it out faster than I can."

Raz hesitated, not sure what the woman was intending. He thought he had an inkling, though, and so twitched his sore fingers in the best confirmation he could offer. Syrah seemed to understand, because her touch vanished from his skin. For a time longer they stood like that, circling slowly in place, Gale and Nymara still bucking and rearing not far away.

The crackling sound of power.

"RIGHT!" Raz roared, rolling left. Syrah responded as expected, turning and stepping between him and the incoming spell. He had thought she'd prepared some sort of ward, some barrier that would spare them the blow while giving Raz a chance to find their enemy in the chaos.

Instead, Syrah reached up and *caught* the descending lash.

Raz started to yell in reflexive fear, but the sound died in his throat as he witnessed his partner weave her own spell. The moment the wild light of the fire wrapped itself about her gloved hand, it changed, condensing and weaving into a different form. In an instant the uncontrolled rage of the white flames became a single solid line, and with the speed of an arrow the binding raced up the length of the whip. Before he could blink, the untamed tether of roaring heat and power was gone, replaced by Syrah's own focused spellwork. There was a cry of shock audible despite the mayhem, and even with her back to him Raz could just imagine Syrah smirking in success.

Then she planted her foot, drawing magic into her body with an almost-imperceptible shifting of the air around her, and heaved on the lash.

Lazura could not pretend she did not enjoy toying with the lizard and his whore. She'd been disappointed—and grudgingly somewhat impressed—when Raz i'Syul Arro had demonstrated himself cognizant enough to react to her first spell before it took him about the body. The woven flames had still gotten ahold of his arm, however, and Lazura tingled as she remembered the glee of unhorsing the Monster of Karth and watching the legend crash to the ground as he bellowed in pain.

Even if Syrah Brahnt *had* managed to stop her ending Arro's life then and there with a focused pulse of flames, the fun had only just begun for Lazura.

That is, until the moment the Priestess of Laor *caught* her lash, and began weaving her own spellwork against her.

The change in the resonance of the arcane pattern was too quick for even Lazura to respond to. She tried, attempting desperately to release her bond with the magic, but Brahnt's work was as fast as thought. In one moment Lazura was rejoicing, watching her fire loop about the hand of the woman in dark robes, thinking it a perfect opportunity to see the Priestess made absent a limb at the very least.

The next, it was *Lazura* who found her palm and fingers bound in the braided threading of Brahnt's power, and as she cried out in surprise as the treacherous lash was drawn brutally tight.

Then she was pulled off her feet, cursing as she slammed to the ground to be dragged mercilessly across the hot, bloody desert in the direction of those who would have been her prey.

Despite her shock, Lazura's mind did not betray her. Even through the grating wrench of the sand under her side the potential solution came, and she struggled to gather her focus, to consider how best to imitate what she'd just seen. She pieced the parts of the spell together desperately while the tearing grit pulled at her thin clothes and ripped her veil from her face.

Lazura was almost within the cleared circle her spells and the panicking horses had carved around Arro and Brahnt when she called on her power, channeling it into her left hand and the short-sword she'd managed to hold onto, using it as a focal point. When she slashed at the string, the keen outline of focused magic that bloomed about the smoke-darkened metal was neither as clean nor as clear as the Priestess' summoned blade had been.

Just the same, it did the trick, cutting into the magic with the shearing sound of steel ringing against glass.

Shing!

The momentum dragging Lazura across the sand cut short, and she used the last of her impetus to tuck and roll to a stand. She came up with both swords bared, her left still bright with white fire while the right had been slid free in the same motion she'd gained her feet. She was ready for the slicing strike of the lash—thinner and brighter than her own incomplete version of the spell—that came from the left, hearing it sizzle as it formed and screamed through the air. She ducked, then somersaulted sideways when Brahnt changed the angle of the magic with nothing more than a flick of a wrist to bring it low from the other direction, aiming at her legs. Lazura marked her landing, already preparing to dodge again, calculating how best to retreat back into the combat. Fear had started to creep into her judgment. It had been so long since she'd seen *true* Laorin magic, tempered with the unforgiving years of training the Priests and Priestesses of the Northern temples saw their acolytes through before they were granted their staffs. She had power, yes, but hers was a raw, brutal spellwork that had not yet been honed, not yet had been allowed the opportunity to take shape. It could overwhelm, could consume and devour in a way Laor would never have wanted his gifts to do so.

But what sort of matchup would it be against the *intended* strengths of a god?

Lazura landed with a spray of grit, body tense and ready for the coming blow. Her every sense was on absolute edge, anticipating the sound of the striking flames she knew would be descending with unforgiving persistence.

Nothing.

The absence of the attack was so jarring, Lazura actually froze, not grasping how her opponent could fail to press her when she was so clearly at a disadvantage. She looked up, seeing first Raz i'Syul Arro towering behind the Priestess, the straight edge of his famous gladius gleaming in the Sun.

Then she met Syrah Brahnt's eye, and understanding clicked.

The Priestess was gaping at her, mouth hanging open in surprise, her expression having transitioned from righteous fury to disbelief in the span of a heartbeat. The lash had settled, snapping and sparking in the sand about her feet, dangling with no more use than a limp length of rope from her right hand. For a long moment Brahnt was silent, apparently struck speechless.

When she finally spoke, the question was so quiet it was very nearly lost to the cacophony of the war still raging all around them.

"…Lazura…?" the Priestess asked, her voice tinged with the keening of pained denial.

In answer, Lazura smiled. It was a true, clear smile, open and plain now that her face had been freed of the obscuring veil.

"Hello, Syrah," she said amiably, speaking with the familiar ease of family and old friends.

Then she launched herself forward, bringing both blades up to thrust them together at Syrah Brahnt's heart.

That was when the drums began to beat.

XXXIX

"One need not dig far into the cultures of the wild tribes of the Northern ranges to understand how they have so successfully sown fear among the softer societies of the valley towns…"

— *Studying the Lifegiver*, by Carro al'Dor

Something's wrong…

Adrion knew nothing more than that, could speak to no greater awareness than this simple understanding. He'd ridden hard after Vyres Eh'ben and the rest of Lazura's pawns, coming to join them at the churning edge of the battle's rear line. They'd called for reinforcements from the army, delegating several contingent commanders to redirect their units to surround them in anticipation of Raz's clever attack riding up on their flank. It had been a long five minutes of apprehension, of officers shouting for their spearmen to take to the lead and prepare for an incoming cavalry charge.

Instead, it was their original guard of a thousand who caught up to them first, marching into the ranks at triple-pace, every one of the soldiers sweating and breathing bellows when they reached the main army at last.

That was the moment the nagging doubt became certainty.

"Something's wrong," Adrion repeated, out loud this time. Although he hadn't directed the comment to anyone in particular, Eh'ben was ahorse only a few feet away, and the Karthian's sour silence told Adrion he wasn't the only one who was worried. After a second the šef leaned over and spoke quietly to Casius Jules, who was knee-to-knee with him. At once Jules dismounted, slipping into the lines of the ranks, forcing them to split for him as he moved. Adrion watched him go until he disappeared into the shifting bodies of the soldiers, suspecting Eh'ben's intent.

He was rewarded with confirmation not a few minutes later when Jules finally returned leading the company sergeant of the guard, the very man who'd followed the orders not to engage the coming cavalry.

"Report," Eh'ben told the soldier brusquely. "I find it hard to believe Arro's horseman didn't catch up to ya', sergeant."

The officer—his dust-caked face cut with sweat lines from the rapid withdrawal—fought through his obvious fatigue to bring himself to quick attention.

"Sir," he said breathlessly. "I'm as at a loss as anyone. We made triple time because we feared the horsemen would have already reached you, and were planning to take them from the rear if at all possible." He frowned. "Obviously I was mistaken to command such a pace."

No, Adrion thought to himself, lifting his gaze to the hilltops above them, over which the screen of kicked up dust that had to be the wake of Raz's riders could be made out. *You weren't.*

Unsurprisingly, Eh'ben appeared to be of a similar mind.

"Ya' did well enough," the šef answered dismissively, and Adrion looked around in time to see the man's own eyes on the ridges. "Return to yer command, sergeant. See them rested while ya' can."

The officer saluted a second time, then turned and moved past Casius Jules to make for his soldiers again.

"Somethin' wrong?" Jules asked from his place on the ground, watching the sergeant pass him before looking again up to Eh'ben. "It's odd, ain't it? Them riders not reachin' us yet?"

Eh'ben treated the man with the sort of distasteful look a prince might grace the raised hands of a pock-marked beggar. Instead of answering, he turned to the line of other šef still waiting at his back.

"Loreyn. Bayne. Take a dozen scouts with the best eyes ya' can find. Figure out wha's going on."

Ketres Bayne of Acrosia looked less than pleased to be taking orders from the greasy man, but swallowed his pride to click his horse into motion.

San Loreyn, on the other hand, was much more vocal about his discontentment.

"Eh'ben, you can't be serious?" he whined, pale eyes lifting to the dust-choked sky. "There's got to be five hundred fucking horsemen out there! What in the Sun's name are we supposed to do with a handful of scouts?!"

Vyres Eh'ben, in reply, bared ragroot-stained teeth at the younger man.

"I said 'figure out wha's going on', not 'take on the whole fuckin' army', ya' primmed-up trim. Now go, and take the cripple with ya'." He waved an indifferent hand in Adrion's direction. "Might as well make 'imself useful while he's waitin' to die."

Loreyn stammered a few more sentences, clearly none-too-pleased with this response, but Adrion didn't wait to see the pair exchange any further words. Happy enough for an excuse to satisfy his curiosity, he pressed his horse forward with a kick, following the gap in the soldiers that had only just started to close behind Ketres Bayne.

It took the three of them a few minutes to gather the scouts according to Eh'ben's instruction, most of the outriders having been recalled to their individual units after the battle proper broke out. Once they had their assigned dozen men and women, along with a mount for each of them, Adrion followed only a little ways behind Bayne and Loreyn when they led the way north once more, back through the dunes. They did not immediately take the ridges, electing instead to pass through the valleys at a good pace, keeping a close eye on the sky. Only when they judged themselves to be about halfway between the two groups did Bayne shout for a majority of the scouts to press on while he motioned for Loreyn, Adrion, and the two remaining soldiers to climb with him. They took the next rise—a broad-based dune with a generous slope—and, after several seconds of struggling through lose sand, crested the peak. The wind returned, blasting about their faces and clothes, and it took a little bit for Adrion to blink away the tears and raise a hand to shield his eyes.

When his vision finally cleared, he stared out over the swaying of the land in speechless disbelief.

It was San Loreyn who summarized the confusion of the moment first.

"What in the Sun's *fucking* name…?"

Adrion couldn't blame the Southerner his bewilderment, just as he couldn't blame Ketres Bayne the baffled expression that shown plain on the Acrosian's aged face. He could only believe that he looked much the same, gaping out across the desert at the senseless farce taking place still some half-mile in the distance.

In the brightness of the morning, the only sign of a majority of Raz's horsemen were outlined movements through choking cloud of sand and grit they were managing to kick up in their madness. They *had* to have gone mad, too, because even Adrion had trouble fathoming what purpose could be had in the chaotic dance occurring before them. While the riders they could make out from the hills *were* approaching, it was an almost imperceptible advance. They were creeping forward—at least compared to the pace a cavalry host *could* have set—but doing nothing to break the wild sprint of their horses. Instead, they weaved and circled through each other in an endless churn, dark shapes milling about in the rising dust like layers of ants crawling over and around each other. It lacked sense, lacked all manner of purpose given the battle at hand. Some five hundred horsemen could have offered significant support to Raz's efforts, especially if they'd moved more quickly to take advantage of the rear approach they'd managed to steal for themselves.

Instead, they were wasting their time and horses on *this*…

"It's a distraction."

Adrion had been so involved in the struggle of his own confusion that Bayne's words made him start and look around. The older man was frowning at the distant madness, studying the line of the riders they could make out as they slowly moved across the uneven terrain.

"They're trying to take our attention away," he continued after a moment's consideration. "They *want* us to be watching them."

"Take our attention away from… what?" Loreyn asked doubtfully, voicing the question Adrion had wanted to pose. "They're not likely to distract any of our main host from their engagements. The battle is already too involved."

"Then they're trying to keep us busy, to keep our eyes on them rather than something else." As Bayne said it, he began to scan the horizon to the northwest and east, going so far as to stand in his saddle and cover his eyes with both hands to squint against the mounting glare of the still-rising Sun. "They'll have something coming, mark my words."

"If they'd have something coming, it wouldn't be from a direction we would be inclined to spot by *keeping an eye on their distraction.*" Loreyn said the last few words through gritted teeth, obviously feeling this conclusion should have been obvious. "We should be looking *south*, not north."

"Through the Cienbal?" Bayne asked with an air of derisive amusement, sitting down again to smirk at Loreyn bleakly. "What sort of significant support could make it through the desert?"

It was a fair question, Adrion granted, but he was only half-paying attention to the pair's bickering. He was himself peering at the horsemen, unable to escape the nagging feeling that something more was going on than a mere distraction. Raz was a beast in his own right, to be sure, but Adrion of all people wasn't about to underestimate his cousin. The Monster of Karth was more than the incarnation of savagery and bloodshed his legend so often made him out to be. He was more than brute force and razored steel.

And the trick of common misdirection just seemed far too simple for the likes of a man who had earned himself the moniker of "Dragon"...

"Arro has had atherian among his ranks since before crossing into the South, and now he's been bolstered by the tribes of the Crags." Loreyn had continued their argument without missing a beat. "If there are *more* lizard-kind to be summoned, there's no reason they wouldn't be able to manage the desert better than any force *we* could send into the sands."

"If there were more lizard-kind, he would have brought them with him," Bayne snapped in retort. "Why go through the effort of a diversion when he could have just arrived in greater strength."

"The advantage of *surprise,* dolt. Turning an apparent disadvantage to your favor is a basic tool of warfare. How by Her Stars did you get to be a šef of the Mahsadën with a mind like yours? One would think some of Ahthys Borne's knack for the subject would have *at least* rubbed off on you."

"Say that again, you pompous bastard," Ketres growled, and there was the *clink* of the man taking hold of the sword he'd used not an hour before to cut down the other leaders of his city's society.

Seeing Loreyn open his mouth to jibe back, Adrion decided he had better things to do than witness whatever childish conclusion came of their squabbling.

"I'm getting a closer look," he said without looking around at the two men, choosing instead to shift around in his saddle and point to one of the two scouts who'd accompanied them up the dune slope. "You. With me."

Then, before anyone could voice a disagreement, he clicked his horse into a trot again, heading back down into the valleys.

He didn't turn around to see whether or not the soldier he'd ordered to follow him had done so. It mattered little, given that a single blade wasn't going to value for much if they got caught by the five hundred ahead of them. More importantly, too, Adrion was keen on clarifying something odd he'd noticed about the building screen of sand and grit being kicked up by the horses. He deliberately kept his eyes on the path before him, closing another eighth of a mile or so before taking to the upward slopes again. Only when he reached the crest did he look to Raz's riders once more, studying the cloud they were very clearly and consciously whirling into being.

Instantly, he knew he was right, the momentary reprieve he'd given his eyes from the sight confirming his confusion.

The cloud was darkening.

"Magic?" he muttered to himself, not comprehending what was going on, watching the pattern of the horsemen from closer up now.

There was a snort and shuffling behind him, and Adrion turned in the saddle, surprised—and not a little bit amused, despite the peculiarity of their situation—to find not only the single scout, but all *four* of the men he'd left following his horse's hoofprints to trail him up the dune. Apparently Bayne and Loreyn had decided their tiff wasn't worth the risk of being called cowards later, because they were leading the two scouts up the climb quickly.

"Are you out of your mind, Blaeth?!" Bayne demanded furiously the moment he'd brought his charger up beside Adrion's. "If they charge, then we're done for!"

"A quarter-mile lead, with that again from here to the front lines," Adrion answered with a shrug, looking away from the Acrosian to study the cavalry again. "We're not in any danger. More importantly—" he lifted a hand to point, cutting Bayne off as the man began to formulate some undoubtedly seething reply "—do you see that?"

The question, fortunately, was enough to temper Bayne's anger at least the few seconds the man needed to look back to the rising pillar of dust. He blinked once, then twice, then frowned and returned his attention to Adrion.

"See *what*, exactly?"

"The dust is darkening."

It wasn't Adrion who answered, thankfully. Instead, San Loreyn had spoken up, and with distinct concern. He even pressed his horse between and beyond Bayne and Adrion's mounts, like the few feet of extra proximity might answer his silent questions.

"Darkening?" Bayne repeated angrily, obviously disliking the fact that he was the only one not understanding. "What do you mean?"

"There." Adrion pointed again, more deliberately this time, drawing a line to indicate the lowest layer of the rising cloud. "Just above the heads of the cavalry. Do you see it?"

The Acrosian spent another several seconds peering in the direction indicated to him, but his scowl didn't change.

"The sand is thicker lower down," he growled eventually. "What of it? How does this help us? If they're trying to distract us, then what are we doing just—"

"Riders!"

The shout came from one of the scouts at their backs, and Adrion suffered one horrible moment of terror that he'd been a fool to bring them so close to the enemy. They had a lead, yes, but a mad sprint back to the main army was not without its own dangers regardless. Cold swept through him, but he realized whirling around that the soldier in question was not pointing at Raz's cavalry, but rather down the slope ahead of them and to the right, slightly eastward. There, among the dunes, a much smaller group were approaching at full gallop, hugging the corners of every turn in the valley floors like they couldn't waste even a moment in their mad tilt.

"Our scouts," Loreyn said unnecessarily, but Adrion did not miss the note of disquiet in the šef's voice. He, too, appeared to have taken notice of the unit's hurry. Given that the distant enemy had made no indication of a sudden rush, whatever news they were bringing back with them could bode nothing good to warrant such reckless speed.

Silently Adrion, Loreyn, Bayne, and their two escorts watched the closing of the ten men. One of the group took note of them, because a hand rose to point in their direction, and the horses were suddenly being trained toward their hill. The soldiers reached the base, and did not slow as they climbed, driving their mounts so mercilessly that Adrion could hear the dry rasp of the animals' breathing before they were even halfway up the incline. The lead scout was near enough now to shout, opening his mouth as though to scream out some warning.

Whatever words he had for them, however, were lost as a deep, echoing thrum began to resonate suddenly across the otherwise still heat of the day.

BOOM. BOOM. BOOM. BOOM…

The sound took hold of Adrion so abruptly, he thought the grip of it would tear his heart from his chest. His breath caught, and he choked, whirling atop his horse to look north again, eyes wide. He was—had always been—a well-read man. He'd never had opportunity to travel the great expanses of the known world, chained as he'd been to the sands of the South first by his family and handicap, and then by his chosen profession. All the same, he was versed in the written lores of the world, knowledgeable enough to recognize that sound, recognize that resounding beat. He knew of only one source from which such a warning ever rang over the mayhem of the battlefield, and it was an understanding that terrified him to his very core.

BOOM. BOOM. BOOM. BOOM…

"What in the blazes…?!" Bayne was yelling, getting ahold of his charger, who'd been spooked by the building noise. "What is that?!"

"Drums?!" Loreyn demanded, obviously at an equal loss. "Where is it coming from?!"

Adrion might have answered, but his fear had swallowed his voice along with his courage. Instead, he could only stare wide-eyed northward, at the distant blotting of Raz's cavalry.

Raz's cavalry, who had abruptly ended their senseless dance among the dunes.

BOOM. BOOM. BOOM. BOOM…

"They've stopped!" Bayne howled, noticing as well the sudden settling of the horsemen north of them. "Damn! Retreat! Before they run us—"

And then the šef, too, fell silent. The world as a whole might have fallen into utter stillness in fact, for the five of them atop that hill. There, in the distance, the ceased milling of half-a-thousand horses had stopped feeding the great cloud they'd been throwing into the air. As the sand and dust drifted and faded, carried off by the desert wind or settling back to the ground about the riders, the stolen horizon was returned to them.

That, and a clear view of the army that seemed to have appeared out of nowhere—easily twenty thousand strong—rising up from the shelter of the dune valleys to reveal itself like a living cloak across the sands.

Boom. Boom. Boom. Boom…

"BEHIND THEM!" the words of the scouts now reached Adrion's ears, screamed as the group finally made the ridge. "BEHIND THEM! NORTHMEN!"

No, a voice in the back of Adrion's head whispered, knowing better. *Not just Northmen.*

Mountain men.

And it was true, he knew. Even so far away, there could be no mistaking the presence which had appeared beyond the distant cavalry, as though summoned into being. Over the yelling of the others and Bayne's shouts for them to get back to the army, the beat of the Kregoan war drums continued, incessant and insistent, singing out their promise of bloodshed and glory.

Somehow, for some reason Adrion could not fathom, the wild tribes of the Northern ranges had arrived on the pitch of a Southern war.

And they were marching with terrifying speed on the exposed rear of the Mahsadën's gathered forces.

BOOM. BOOM. BOOM. BOOM…

XL

"I shall not condone the acts of him, the Warring Son. I shall not offer him safe harbor, nor shall I provide him comfort from the judgment of Laor's will when his time in this world ends.

Ask me if I would extend my trust to the man, however, and I would tell you it has been firmly his since the moment I came upon him, bloody and battered and worn to the bone, carrying Syrah Brahnt up the Citadel's mountain stairs..."

— Jofrey al'Sen, High Priest of Cyurgi' Di

Had Raz not been at her back, Syrah would have died with smoke-darkened steel in her heart.

She watched—her body unwilling to move—as Lazura leapt at her, striking with such sinuous speed it might have taken Syrah's breath away had she been of any other state of mind. As it was, she was only numb, and barely even felt the clawed hand take hold of the back of her robes and wrench her backward.

SCHLANG!

The screech of metal slamming aside metal brought her back to herself, and she blinked. Lazura's face was hardly a foot from hers, what had been a too-familiar grin turning into a grimace of annoyance as the woman found her blades—one bare and one aflame—smashed downward and away from Syrah's chest. Syrah herself was being pressed back into Raz, the man in the process of wrapping his injured left arm about her protectively, his right at hip-height with gladius in hand. He'd swept the black swords down and away, and Syrah felt his body tense and coil against her back. The gladius came up again, clearly hoping to deal the killing blow.

Unfortunately, Lazura demonstrated her guile for them once more, turning the redirection of her initial attack into a forward roll that brought her by the pair of them and just clear of Raz's counterattack. There was an ugly *snick* and *hiss* of splitting flesh being cauterized as she passed, and Raz snarled in pain, his left arm pulling immediately away from Syrah. Freed, she shouted, whirling in concern, and found him stumbling back a step to press his bad hand to his side. Between his fingers she could just make out the shadows of two parallel gashes along his ribs, one open and bleeding, the other black and smoking.

And beyond him, flicking her swords clean, Lazura was coming to a stand with her back to the pair of them.

Lazura...

The name—the *memories*—returned Syrah's rage with a boiling fury. It clawed its way out of the pit to which it had been secluded for so many months, clambering forth from the darkness where she'd managed to bury it since that horrible morning in Ekene Okonso's palace. All around her the day grew cold, and yet within her chest—like a spike of white-hot iron pressing between her lungs—heat began to build until it threatened to split her in two.

Lazura.

Traitor. Blasphemer. Torturer. *Murderer.* All words that roared across Syrah's mind while she watched the cunning woman turn to face her and Raz again. The scars of the bitch's Breaking were plain in the shadows of her cheeks and forehead as the Sun rose above them, and the sight of that brand only lanced the heat in Syrah's bosom to greater extremes. She could feel the energy thrashing to escape, scraping at the limits of her body. She imagined what she could do with that magic, that power. She knew this feeling now. She contemplated if she could perhaps channel it, perhaps focus it on the one person before her who deserved the sort of death only fire could deliver.

Then, unbidden: the memory of cratered marble and burning corpses. As though she were there once more, Syrah smelled again the scent of charred meat, saw blackened, faceless skulls screaming at her in silent misery. The tattered, smoldering banners of the Tash's court hung above while soot and ash fell down upon her bent head, and Raz was kneeling at her back, embracing her as she sobbed into his arms and clutched at him.

The image—that dreaded recollection which had plagued her every nightmare since that day—choked away the heat in Syrah's chest to leave her cold and frozen and staring.

Fortunately for her, Lazura did not for once seem keen on taking advantage of this second opening offered to her. Oddly enough, she wasn't even looking in their direction, her interest in Syrah and Raz apparently distracted by something else, off to the north. She was frowning now, her gaze fixed over the heads of the fighting all around them.

At last, Syrah, too, made out the sound, a little faint in the distance.

Boom. Boom. Boom. Boom…

Warmth—of a different kind than the cruel flame of anger that had only moments ago seared within her—bloomed in a pleasant tingle across her skin. The rage of battle returned in full swing, deafening in its presence, but over all of it the Kregoan war drums could still be heard. Around them, the sounds of the fighting shifted, shouts of alarm and confusion rising from both sides of the army as those able to do so looked northward, all of them imitating Lazura's expression of surprise.

"Right on time," Syrah heard Raz grunt from behind her.

And then it was *he* who took the initiative, claiming the momentary distraction to launch by Syrah and bring the gladius to bear on their enemy.

Lazura saw the attack coming, and reacted with the speed of a snake. Even so, she only barely managed to parry Raz's first blow, so quick was the flashing cross-slash. She regained her composure fast, her focus returning to the fight at hand with snapping precision, and soon she was matching Raz's tempo as their exchange became a blur of black and silver. She made up for their unbalanced strength with magic and litheness, bolstering her limbs with pulses of spellwork which were simultaneously crude and precise. The castings were so wasteful in their expenditure that Syrah could *feel* the weak ripple of power each gave off, and yet timed so accurately with Lazura's blocks and ripostes they made up twice-over for their coarseness. It was impressive, in its own way. The woman may have been lacking in training, but one—especially a master of combat magics—could not deny that she'd adapted what power she held admirably. *How* the woman had regained her abilities, Syrah feared to discover, but for the time being it mattered little.

In the moment, all she knew was that here was a foe who needed to be stopped at any cost.

Syrah gathered herself, shaking her mind free of the lingering fear and the chill of nightmarish memories that threatened to drown her. In the background the drums of the wild tribes of the North beat over everything, but Syrah found focus in the cadence. It took her a single deep breath to sharpen herself to the battle happening before her.

When she was ready, she gathered her magic in both hands, and shouted at the top of her lungs.

"RAZ! BACK!"

Raz reacted with all the dexterity of his legend, ducking a cutting blow from one of Lazura's swords and aiming a low, spinning kick at her legs. When the women leapt to avoid the strike, he turned the momentum into a retreating roll, coming far clear of his opponent. He too, seemed to share an understanding Syrah had come to over the course of the last long minutes of combat. He might have been stronger than Lazura by magnitudes, but she matched him for speed blow-for-blow, avoiding those strikes she could not otherwise defend herself from. What was more, the woman had the advantage of spellcraft, and while he'd thus-far been able to keep her busy enough to prevent her from weaving anything more destructive than her bolstering spells, he was injured, and armed with nothing more than his sword. Their match was more even than Syrah would have liked to admit, and tediously balanced at best.

There was a better way to fight fire, after all…

Even before Raz was completely clear of her line of sight, Syrah was moving, trusting him to keep pace with her. With a prayer and a twisted shaping of her hands, no less than five stunning spells materialized in a horizontal line before her, flicking and sparking where they hovered suspended. The magic shimmered and pulsed, Syrah taking the moment she needed to stabilize the energy.

Then, with a word, she let them fly, and the White Which took on the enemy that the Dragon of the North could not.

By the time she landed, Lazura had five sparks of ivory fire lancing toward her from every angle, their trailing light leaving white afterimages in arcs through the air. To her credit the woman did not falter—not even for an instant—and kept her dancer's guile as she dodged sideways. Three zipped clean by her, striking the sand and blinking uselessly out of existence. The other two had come at her from the direction she'd moved into, but this pair splashed harmlessly against a conjured ward she brought up along the sword blades crossed over her leading shoulder, their fire guttering out in short ripples against the summoned shield.

It made no difference. Syrah had suspected the woman would snake her way through such a telling assault.

She'd just wanted Lazura busy enough to miss the sixth spell she sent in a broad, barely-visible wave behind the others.

Among the most simplistic of the Laorin combat magics, the flood of force Syrah conjured at the end of a thrusted fist expanded as it sped away from her. She could have controlled it, could have focused it on a more acute point, but she did not trust that her enemy would not be able to outmaneuver such a deliberate assault. Instead, Syrah allowed the power to unfurl, sacrificing potency for size. The moment Lazura noticed the spell, Syrah knew she had chosen correctly.

The blank shock—like a deer caught in the light of torch—was that of someone realizing they had nowhere left to run.

The blast took Lazura full on, launching her backward. Her blades went flying, the impact of the magics rippling along the edges of her black silks that had been torn when Syrah had dragged her across the desert floor. The woman yelled in outrage, tumbling through the air, but she tucked as she fell and struck the ground in a rearward roll, bouncing lithely back to her feet.

That was when Syrah's lash took her about the neck.

Lazura had clearly learned a good many things in her time spent in the South, but it was her *magic* that was most terrifying. The Broken could not wield Laor's gifts. It was a known fact, a belief upon which the entire premise of their faith's punishments were balanced and mitigated. That Lazura had found a way to regain her confiscated powers meant that she could not be underestimated.

And so it was that they began their dance.

Lazura was a quick learner, and proved to need no blade to summon a second edge of white fire, lining it along the bottom of an open hand to slash down and sever the line of magic looped about her throat. Syrah, however, had already sent another duo of stunning spells in her direction, and the woman was forced to dip and somersault sideways, coming up in time for the ground around her boots to erupt in ivory flames. She leapt back once, twice, three times as Syrah sent similar lines of fire chasing after her over the sand, until finally Lazura landed and conjured her own flames about her feet to counter Syrah's. The magic was wild, brutal in its uncontrolled channeling, and the first attempt to puncture them failed, giving Lazura a much-needed opportunity to counterattack. With a scream of frustration she drew power into both hands and brought them slashing down in Syrah's direction, sending a spewing geyser of almost-boiling ether cascading through the air. Syrah reacted in sharp instinct, summoning up a ward with the complex pattern formed with the fingers of one hand while the other manipulated a different spell at her hip. The liquified magic splashed against the shield, engulfing the barrier and completely blocking Syrah's vision as it erupted into flame. She had anticipated this, and held the ward strong, waiting for the attack she knew would be coming.

Sure enough, a disturbance of power to her right—on the side of her useless eye—had Syrah whirling in time to see Lazura come blurring around the edge of the flaming barrier, another of her unformed lashes already slashing. It was a clever move on its own. Any other person might have been blind to the attack, given Syrah's disadvantage.

But Lazura had only proven once more that she had never understood the potential of Laor's gifts as He had truly envisioned them.

Syrah did not catch the cutting line, this time. Instead—and while still holding at bay the raging fire that hung suspended on the ward above and before her—she slammed a foot into the ground, conducting the readied spell through the limb. Beneath and around her the earth pulsed, sand churning up and away as a visible ripple of pure energy exploded outward in all directions. It was similar to the invisible force that had originally disarmed the black-clad woman, but broader and stronger. The wild lash connected with the expanding magic like a rope slapping uselessly against a tidal wave, the greater spell carrying the weaker fire away without so much as shivering. Lazura had learned her lesson, however, and was not rocked this time by the blast, her feet planted and her whole body clearly reinforced against the impact. It ripped over her, tearing free the tight knotting in which she'd kept her bleached white hair, so that once it had passed she stood looking wind-worn and breathless.

But she *stood.*

Grimacing, Syrah muttered a curse, finally dropping the ward as the ether which had originally blocked her vision dissipated at last.

By the time Lazura lunged at her, she was ready with both hands already bright with ivory light.

Syrah did not know how long their exchange lasted, how many blocks and blows they traded. She had discipline and training on her side, but what edge that offered her was largely countered by the older woman's natural skill and lack of restraint. Where's Syrah's spells were clean and focused, Lazura's were brutal and untamed. Sparks of magic splashed against waves of fire. Torrents of flames were redirected by skillful barriers. The ground around the battling women—already hot under the summer sun—began to sear the soles of Syrah's feet even through her boots, and the air was a consistent, blistering wave of lashing power. They fought, neither quite able to outdo the other, spellwork flashing and cracking against one another in an endless cacophony of magic and flame. Lazura was a master of speed and dexterity, her body and movements as essential to avoiding Syrah's attacks as her aggression and shields.

In the end, however, years spent under the guiding hand of Talo Brahnt, High Priest of Cyurgi' Di and former champion of the great Arena of Azbar, won out.

Lazura did not make setting the trap easy. She was constantly moving, continually demanding every focus and reflex to answer. The pattern Syrah kept trying to form into the sand with her shifting feet was ruined once, then again as she was forced to move and adjust, foiling the spell. Eventually, however, she managed to subtly trace the last curved line to finish the simple script, oversized as it was. She tossed a ball of unfocused fire in her opponent's face, forcing Lazura to concentrate on a broad defense for the two seconds Syrah needed to pour magic into the rough lines. There was a dull flash that Lazura missed, preoccupied as she was, and the rune took hold in the earth.

Then Syrah waited.

Relentless as the enemy was, she did not have to strain her patience long.

The moment her path was clear of obstructing flames, Lazura launched herself forward, teeth bared. Magic rippled across the fingers of both hands, churning and wild, and even as she leapt she threw paired fistfuls of flame. Syrah braced herself, knowing the woman would fall for no show, no theatrics. The vulnerability would have to be real, or only Laor knew when the next opportunity to strike would come. Bringing a hand up, Syrah made sure to summon her ward a fraction of a second too late. The trailing fireball slammed harmlessly into the broadening barrier, rippling in white waves across its surface.

But only after the first, leading barely inches ahead, got past and struck Syrah full in the abdomen.

Syrah hardly had to feign a scream. Despite precautions, the heat of the spell ripped through her thin silks and licked at the sensitive skin of her stomach. She staggered back several paces, bent double under the impact and flailing at the flames that clung to her clothes, the dark fabric catching fire quickly to accentuate the display. Over her own shrieks she heard a yell of victory, and could not stop herself from looking up, praying for just enough luck to win her the day.

Laor saw fit to grant her request in excess.

Lazura made no attempt to attack from any angle this time. She lanced forward without hesitation, acting on whatever instincts had been instilled within her to strike the instant the opportunity came. Seeing her opponent aflame was enough for her, clearly, and so she charged straight on, summoning her crude spells once more to each hand. Syrah let her come, barely feeling the heat of the fire now as she watched the woman barrel toward her with murder in her blue eyes.

Then Lazura broke the invisible limit Syrah had just vacated, and the trap triggered in an eruption of sand and light and heat.

It was hardly a complex enchantment, but Talo had long since taught Syrah that excess in battle rarely ever earned one victory. Combining unassuming scripts of flash and force and fire, the explosion was potent, but largely harmless. It blasted up and outward in a brief blaze that seemed even to outdo the sun for the briefest of moments, and Syrah only just got one hand up in time to shield her good eye, the other already working to weave together a more complicated series of spells. With a thought she extinguished the flames she'd allowed Lazura to believe were consuming her alive, feeling the ragged remnants of her burned cloths hang limply about her wrists and waist. When sand began to patter down like rain, she dropped her arm to gauge her success.

The sight had her offering the Lifegiver a silent word of thanks.

Whatever talents she possessed, even Lazura had not managed to escape the radius of the blast. She appeared to have been thrown off her feet to slam down again into the small crater the spell had made of the ground, and was coughing and wheezing on her back. Her black silks were in complete tatters, her white hair a dirty mess about her head and face. She looked stunned, blue eyes blinking rapidly against the scars of her Breaking while her mind clearly fought to catch up to what had happened.

Unsurprisingly, it didn't take her long.

Syrah saw the focus click back into place, saw the woman still and tense. Lithe, scarred muscles—revealed now through her ruined garments—flexed, and almost too-quickly she was up again, looking feral in her disheveled state.

For once, she wasn't quick enough.

CRACK!

Syrah's finished spell shot out of her downturned left hand in a flash of five white lines. They punctured the searing sand beneath her feet with the sound of a tree breaking at its center, then exploded out of the ground again all around Lazura, flashing upward like snapping, coiling vipers. Before the woman could fully get her bearings the lashes were wrapping themselves about both wrists and knees, the last taking her around the neck. As she snarled in anger the magics flexed, the ones encircling her legs buckling the joints to drag her down into a kneel, those ringing her arms wrenching them to either side so that she was pulled spread-eagle. Instantly flames bloomed into life in her palms, but before she could do anything with the power Syrah was on her with a fistful of her own fire flickering not six inches from the woman's cheek. Syrah hissed into Lazura's ear, her fury pulsing in the beat and dancing of the threatening magics.

"Try it, and the scars you bear now will be as *nothing* to what little face I leave you with."

Lazura tensed, straining instinctively away against the arcane bindings. Her head turned with some difficulty to meet Syrah's cold gaze, not an ounce of fear shimmering in the ice of her irises.

She did, however, banish whatever spells she'd been in the process of crafting, the light winking out in her palms.

"You should have *burned*," the woman spat, eyes narrow behind the untidy curtain of hair she was now forced to look through. "Why didn't you *burn*?"

Syrah answered through bared teeth. She was having trouble being so close to the woman, memory and imagination making the proximity almost nauseating. "Child's play. You'd know the answer, if Eret hadn't had you Broken and banished, *murderer*."

It was a lie. Syrah had manipulated every ward she'd casted during the fight, diverting a little of their energies to her own body until she'd sufficiently shielded herself to accept the one blow she knew she would need to take. The shield had been a weak thing—tenuous and difficult to maintain over the shifting of her limbs and torso—and the heat of Lazura's fire had only been dampened enough to stave off any real damage. It had been a complicated casting, and one Syrah hadn't even been sure she would be able to pull off.

But she wasn't about to tell that to the woman before her.

"Murderer?" Lazura repeated with an air of mock fright, letting out a bark of a laugh. "Laor's name, Syrah! How could you call me such a thing? You'll break my heart!"

"*Silence*," Syrah snarled, and the flames between her fingers throbbed and grew with her fury. It was enough to make Lazura lose her smile.

"I should kill you now," Syrah kept on, feeling her hands—both of which still held firm to their respective magics—begin to shake. "To use His gifts like this... Unforgivable..."

Despite her predicament, Lazura snorted. "Then *do it*." She glared at Syrah, her taunting suddenly replaced with disdain. "*Do it*."

She held Syrah's gaze, not once looking away even with the fire shaking so near that the hair by her left ear began to curl and smoke. For a long several seconds the pair of them stayed like that, staring each other down.

Then, at last, Lazura sneered.

"Of course, you *can't*, can you? Or at least you *won't*. You and the rest of your kind... Cowards, all of you. You. Talo. Eret Ta'hir. The only 'unforgivable' thing about magic is how the Laorin have castrated it, have chained it up and left it to rot in a dungeon walled in their own *morality*." She said the last word like it carried a foul taste. "Don't preach at me, Syrah. Either kill me, or come to terms with the fact that you can't bind your 'gifts' any longer."

Again Syrah stood frozen for a long time, desire battling with desire. Lazura was right, in a way. The only thing stopping her was her own self-imposed limitation. Magic *could* kill, *could* devour and destroy and lay waste to everything and anything. It was a fact she was aware of more than anyone of her faith, an understanding she alone had to bear.

She, and the twisted, vile creature kneeling defiantly at her feet.

Syrah swallowed, the turmoil in her soul raging hot and wild. On the one hand she could force Lazura to reveal how it was she'd regained her powers. That one of the Broken had learned to recover their magics was a problem of cataclysmic proportions, given the hate those banished from the faith often bore toward the men and women who'd ripped Laor's gifts from their very core. If word got out… If Lazura's methods spread…

But no… The woman before Syrah was very clearly not one to tilt the cards she had in hand. Whatever Lazura had done, whatever abominable means she had found to repair her lost connection to the magics, they would be locked in her head for her use alone.

The head that was now straining away from Syrah's own fire, rippling white-hot between her fingers.

Do it.

Lazura's own words, spoken with the utmost confidence that she would not, echoed in Syrah's ears.

Do it.

For the first time in her life, Syrah wanted to. *Desperately* wanted to. If not even for the atrocities she'd witnessed, simply for those of decades past. Suddenly she understood something Raz had been trying to tell her for a year now, came to terms with it in a way she could never have managed before.

This was the choice… This was the decision Caro had had to make, which had seen him Broken. This was the moment where faith failed, where reality ripped apart the ideals of the Laorin.

This was the scale upon whose plates death lay only in different measures…

Do it.

Syrah had done so before, hadn't she? She had slain—if not intentionally—in the name of the greater good. Would it be so hard to do so again? Would it be so difficult to swallow her pride, and face the beastly truth that lay in the existence of the creature kneeling before her…?

And then the memory was back again, and Syrah was drowning in a ring of rubble as embers and sparks drifted lazily down upon the burned husks of the dead that surrounded her.

Unbidden, Syrah's flames guttered. The magics fluttered and dipped as cold filled her chest, then went out with a spark of light. For a fraction of a moment she met Lazura's eyes, the smile having returned to the woman's face.

"Thought so," Lazura said, sounding almost disappointed. "Too, bad, really." She cocked her head with a smirk. "Goodbye, Syrah."

And then, through the dull thrum of the fighting that Syrah had forgotten was still going on all around them, she heard her own name screamed from her back.

"SYRAH!"

She whirled just in time to see a dead-eyed figure darting toward her—blindingly fast despite the plain soldier's leathers he was dressed in—curved blade plunging in an arc down at her chest.

XLI

"They are less human than creature… They lack… existence. Whatever it is that bitch did to those men, it robbed them of the spark that provides one with life. There is no warmth, there, no sign of anything but submissive willingness. Even in their killing there is an absence of pleasure. The death they deliver, it would appear, is only merely another moment passing in the void.

It is as though they have been separated from their very soul…"

— private journals of Akelo Aseni

They came as soon as Syrah took point in the fight with the strange woman she had called "Lazura." Like shades of the recently slain they slipped out of the battle still raging all around, as though summoned by some soundless call. Gale and Nymara had finally broken away, bolting into the fray as the flash and crack of fire at last became too much for them, and so it was into a rough circle of bloodied sand and charred corpses that the three figures stepped, eerily familiar despite their matching, undyed leathers.

"Well, shit," Raz grumbled to himself, watching the assassin closing in and flexing his empty left hand only to wince when the tendons of his burned forearm protested.

With nothing but his gladius with which to defend himself, he knew this would not be an easy fight.

Especially when the trio wasted no time in rushing him all together.

The fact that Syrah's back was to them and she was preoccupied with her own opponent was not lost on Raz. He could not dance as freely about the field as he would have wanted, could not let any of the three men slip by him, even at the cost of his own life. Ordinarily he would have moved as fluidly as the shadows, putting his greater reach and strength to use in taking them down one at a time.

As it was, he had no choice but to meet them head on.

The first exchange did not end in his favor. Three blades slashed and stabbed at him from every angle. Raz managed to parry the right-most, twisting to avoid the left as he brought a leg up, looking to slam a clawed foot into the chest of the center man. The assassin dodged the kick, but his strike was foiled in the process. The attacker on the left, on the other hand, was quicker to adjust the angle of his sword, and Raz snarled as a third slash paralleled the two cuts Lazura had already carved into his side. He struck at the man, aiming to backhand him, but the assassin was gone, pulling away with his comrades as one fluid unit.

"Shit," Raz repeated, muttered under his breath this time, eyes darting to each of his enemies' soulless gazes one after the other while they regrouped. At his back he could *feel* the fight raging between the two women, the heat and power of the spellwork as tangible as the audible *cracks* and *pops*. It felt like a storm was churning behind him, summoned by Syrah and Lazura to darken the desert morning. Even the sound of the Kregoan war drums was lost to the cacophony.

And still Raz did not allow himself to be distracted.

The assassins lunged again, together once more as though nothing but thought needed to be shared between the three of them. This time Raz was better prepared, and the man on the right hissed in a rare failure of silence as he took a spray of sand in the mouth and eyes, scooped and kicked up into his face on clawed toes. Simultaneously, Raz brought the gladius around, deflecting one of the blades as he slashed out with his left hand. His fingers were half-limp from the ache of the burn, and his steel claws had been lost when he'd cast away the searing gauntlet.

Just the same, even weakened his own talons made short work of the skin and flesh of the center man's neck, momentarily exposed as he'd thrust for the kill.

With one assassin dying and another still rubbing sand from his eyes, Raz at last got to turn his full attention on the last of the trio.

They traded blows in a rapid shrieking of gleaming steel. Each of them fighting one-handed, the exchange happening in a blur of silver that might have made the average soldier dizzy to witness. Had he had Ahna—or even been able to wield his sagaris—Raz knew the fight would have been over in a flash, but as it was he was almost as matched for speed and skill as he'd been during his brief duel with Lazura.

Raz, however, had certain advantages no man could imitate.

Offering an opening in his guard, he allowed the shadow to press the advantage. The man came at him carefully, however, too well-versed in the arts of death to be so easily taken in by the trap. In answer, Raz deliberately overreacted to the calculated strike, feigning a mistaken assumption that his opponent would lunge, rolling right to leave his wounded side truly vulnerable for the space of a breath. As expected, the man read the difference, and darted forward the instant the opportunity presented itself.

His commitment cost him his life, Raz's tail—coming around with the momentum of the sacrificial twist of his body—taking the assassin full in the side and caving in his chest with a *crunch* of splintering ribs.

The fight, of course, wasn't over. Before his second victim had even hit the ground, Raz was turning, suspecting the attack. He knew he'd left one man half-blinded at the very least, but was ready nonetheless with a raised guard.

It was fortunate, because the dagger he adjusted to deflect would have otherwise taken him in the gut.

Raz cursed, glaring at the shapes of not one, but *three more* shadows who'd materialized out of the battle as he'd been engaged with their brethren. At once he was on the defensive again, twisting and dodging another slash of the knife, along with strikes from twin swords that cut down at him one after the other. Beyond this new trio, the fourth looked to have finally started to regain some of his vision, and a tingle of worry itched at Raz's neck as the assassin moved to join his comrades.

With nothing else to do for it, however, Raz fought on.

Faced against four of the Mahsadën's best, even the Dragon of the North was more than hard-pressed, poorly armed and injured as he was. Pretty soon Raz was bleeding from several near-misses, instinct and years at the sword all that kept him from any number of fatal wounds. His opponents attacked with the consistent steadiness of surgeons, angling for all the vital points he could only just defend. Twenty seconds into the fight and the leather wrapping about his thighs were dyed red from shallow stabs that had been going for the thick veins of his hips. Forty, and the straps holding the remaining armor about his left arm were sticky from a slashed collar bone. He was beaten back inch by inch, pushed to use every ounce of his speed and power to keep the attention of the four men on him. If any one of them got by, it was over.

But Raz would never have been fool enough to claim he was without limits.

It happened in a flash, and Raz knew his mistake even as he made it. With that same silent communication that so unnerved him, the assassins wheeled as one to his left, the leading two cutting at him together in parallel blows at his face and waist. He caught the wrist bearing the higher blade only barely, blocking the lower blow with his gladius. A third stab came at his open side, and he was forced to extend a wing violently, catching the would-be killer in the chest and sending him staggering back.

The choice, though, cost Raz clear sight of the fourth man, and his spined ears pricked as he made out the *crunch* of shifting sand the instant the assassin took hold of his chance.

"No!" Raz howled. Thinking fast, he pulled the arm he had ahold of down, entangling its owner with the blade he'd blocked to earn him just a few seconds. He knew he would be too late even as the two shadows grunted and fought to extricate themselves from their dangerous knot of limbs and steel, knew the one who had gotten by would be too quick. All the same he whirled, intent on lunging for the man's legs at the very least, if he could.

Fortunately, his panic turned out to be unnecessary.

Zip! *Thud*!

The sound of an arrow tore by his right ear, and a feathered shaft took the sprinting shadow through the back of the throat, sending him tumbling not paces from where Syrah and Lazura were still intently focused on one another. Raz blinked once against the flash and fire of the duel, then turned again when a guttural roar managed just to echo over the chaotic sounds of the spells.

Following on one another's heels, Akelo and Hur drove into the clearing on horseback, the first already knocking another arrow to his short-bow, the second wielding his great-axe in one massive hand. Together they bore down the remaining threesome of assassins, sending them scattering in all directions. Hur swung at the head of one, but the man ducked nimbly sideways, throwing himself into a roll to get out of the way.

"We saw the fire!" Akelo shouted in answer to Raz's inquisitive look once he'd pulled his horse up beside him with his knees. "Met up, and thought you might need a hand." He drew the arrow, sighted, and released, then cursed when the shadow he had been aiming for knocked the projectile out of the air with a timed swipe of his sword. Going for another shaft, Akelo's eyes fell on the ongoing duel still raging at the far end of the circle. "Who in the Sun's name is that?!"

Raz—welcoming the momentary reprieve—glanced over his shouldert at the two women. Syrah was in the process of carefully fending off several waves of the roaring white flame with a steadily held ward, but Lazura was unrelenting in her assault.

Forcing himself to look away again, he yelled back at Akelo while taking the opportunity to sheath his gladius over his shoulder and dart toward a familiar form closer to the center of the circle. "Not really sure!" He could hear Hur circling his horse around to his right so that all three of them were facing the regrouping shadows. "Syrah seems to know her, but aside from that your guess is as good as mine!"

Akelo frowned in answer, knocking his third arrow. Hur was breathing as heavily as his horse, and together the pair of them kicked their animals forward to flank Raz as he reached his goal.

Reaching down, he lifted Ahna up with one hand, noting with a wince of guilt the charred lines Lazura's lash had burned in the white wood of her haft.

"Sorry, sis," he muttered to the dviassegai, whipping her clean of offending grit.

Then his eyes fell on the assassins, and without a word the fight began again.

It was Raz, this time, who rushed the three men, angling to keep them from reorganizing. As expected Akelo's arrow sang from his left before he reached them, and again one of the shadows deflected the shot. Still, it gave Raz the moment he needed to pick his own target, hearing as he did the thunder of hooves that meant Hur was driving after him into the fight. The one who'd raised his sword in defense of the arrow was first to fall. He wasn't too slow to bring the weapon down to block the incoming blow, but the thin steel was nothing to Ahna's heft and half-inch-thick blades. She crushed through the man's meager obstruction without so much as a pause, shattering the metal and slamming into and through his chest with all her slashing weight, taking the better part of his left arm with her. The dviassegai must have cleaved through both lungs, because the assassin made no more than a choking gurgle of sound when he collapsed.

There was the thudding of hooves, and Raz leapt over the corpse just in time to see Hur careen by, his black-and-white charger nearly matching Gale for size. The Northerner's axe ripped downward, but again the shadows were too quick for him, darting just barely out of the way. Fortunately, one of the two dashed directly into the waiting path of Akelo's keen eye, taking a well-timed arrow straight to the chest, quickly followed by a second as he staggered in surprise.

Unfortunately, the other managed to get behind Hur's mount, and the animal's scream was horrendous as a blade slashed into the fragile tendons along the back of one muscled leg.

Hur went down at once, his horse collapsing under him as the limb failed to accept the weight of its next step. The Northerner gave a cry as he hit the ground, vanishing behind his animal as it slammed down and slid across the sand, and Raz lanced forward to intercept the assassin who'd been looking to finish the job. His first slash with Ahna shrieked over the man's head as the shadow ducked, and he was forced to bring a leg up to block the answering sword with the steel bracer of one shin.

Turning the motion into a full kick, though, his foot caught the man under the chin, snapping his neck back with such force that the *crack* of a breaking spine could still be heard over the battle sounds all around them.

"HUR?!" Raz called out, backing up slowly and eyeing the line of the fighting still encircling them on every side. Six were down, now, but he knew better than to assume that—

There was a *thunk* of steel in flesh, followed by a brief scream, and Raz whirled around, fearing the worst.

He almost laughed in relief when he found Hur on one knee, what looked like a broken left arm hanging uselessly at his side. The amusement, on the other hand, came at the expense of the man standing over him, clutching at the haft of the Northerner's axe with his one functioning hand, half of the thick double-head buried some six inches deep between his neck and collar. The assassin had clearly just arrived, and—judging by the dagger lying listlessly by his feet—had made the mistake of going for what he'd thought was the easy kill.

Unluckily for him, it would take more than a fall and a few broken bones to put down a man born of the mountain clans of the North.

Hur used the still-standing assassin to heave to his feet, pulling himself up by the handle of his axe. This done, he wrenched the weapon free with a jerk, then brought it around again to strike the dying man's head clean from his shoulders in a single blow.

Once the body had fallen to the sand, Hur turned to grin at Raz through a bloody beard, looking like he was having the time of his life.

Then Akelo's bow thrummed again, the streak of his arrow blowing by so close to the blond man's temple that a few strands of his long hair fluttered in its passing.

"They're still coming!" Akelo shouted from his place closer to the center of the clearing. "Right! *Right*!"

Raz turned, and sure enough two more shapes were making a line straight for Syrah and Lazura. He cursed and bolted for the pair, intercepting their trajectory before they got too close. Ahna sang along with the thrum of more of Akelo's arrows, and together they managed to cut the assassins down with surprising ease. In short order, however, a third form rushed him, rapidly followed by a fourth and a fifth, and Raz again felt that tingle of worry.

Then the men fell in similarly quick fashion, and the realization clicked.

"Regular soldiers!" he bellowed to his two generals, the pair of them looking to have joined to take on their own wave of enemies. "They're regular soldiers! It's a distraction!"

"And it's working!" Akelo shouted in reply, firing so quickly the string of his bow hardly had time to stop shivering between shots.

Raz didn't have a chance to answer back.

BOOM!

An explosion of heat and light, outdoing every other spell the two women had casted so far, rent the desert air. The shockwave wasn't staggering, but it caught everyone in the vicinity completely by surprise, with more than one of the incoming footmen startled by the eruption. Raz—recovering the fastest—took immediate advantage, and three of the five men who'd been rushing him died in as many breaths as Ahna sliced and struck with terrible speed.

Regrettably, Raz didn't have a moment to turn and see what had transpired behind him before the remaining two became six, joined by a further outpouring of soldiers clearly commanded by some invisible authority to rush into the fight. He was forced to give all his focus to the battle at hand, and before long the bodies were again tumbling before him like dead leaves on autumn wind.

He knew the game, of course, and even as he danced and dodged Raz kept a sharp eye out for the play he suspected the shadows had in mind. He struck and blocked and parried in blurred streaks, the common soldiers of the Mahsadën no individual match for him. Still, they pushed without hesitation, the open ring originally carved out around Raz and Syrah collapsing steadily with the absence of rippling magic.

Absence? Raz repeated to himself, realizing abruptly that the sounds of spellwork had ceased at his back. The drums, too, had ended, but he was less concerned about that fact for the time being. He wanted to turn around, to glance over his shoulder and see if an end had been brought to the fight between Syrah and Lazura, but the soldiers folding in on him gave him no such opportunity. For every one he cut down it seemed some two more were keen on taking their place. Even with Akelo firing arrows into the throng when he could, Raz was soon being hard-pressed by sheer numbers. The assassins hiding among the ranks were obviously willing to sacrifice any number to him and his generals, and Raz couldn't blame them. All it would take was a moment—a single heartbeat in which their eyes were drawn away together—and the blades would fall. That they hadn't managed to circle around through the fighting already was a miracle, but Raz would have to trust in the density of his own men on their side of the field to keep that threat at bay. He could only face what was before him, but a wall he *would be* between *these* swords and Syrah.

That was when he heard the hooves.

The beat of approaching horses started as a faint rhythm ahead of him, to the north. Quickly it grew, and within a half-minute—in which Ahna felled some four more men—the sounds had grown to a dull, constant rumble that shivered through the soft sand of the plains.

When the riders crested the caps of the dunes above them, Hur could be heard roaring with delight.

Raz cut down yet another, twisting to kick the legs out from the two soldiers beside the falling man while his tail caught a fourth in the side of her helmeted head, breaking her neck with an ugly *crack*. The rapid removal of so many immediate dangers offered him the briefest respite to glance up, over the heads of his opponents, and it only took him a second to recognize the figure leading the horsemen now pouring into their wide valley.

Odene had reached them.

And the enemy took its chance.

The animal in Raz's chest screamed as he saw his mistake. Despite his will, despite his focus, he had allowed himself to be distracted, if only for the space of a breath. For the shadows of Miropa, however, he knew that was all the soulless men had ever needed, and so it was that the assassin broke from the group among whom he'd concealed himself, lancing by Raz and his uplifted eyes. Raz snarled, lunging for the man and managing to get ahold of an arm with his free left hand. The act made his forearm throb, jarring pain up and down the limb, and Raz's clawed fingers gave, scraping limply against the hard leather armor of the assassin's disguise. Raz tried to bring Ahna around, tried to bring the figure down in time, but the man was as quick as any of his kind, bolting out of range to make a line straight for Syrah.

Syrah, who Raz realized had her back to the incoming danger, oblivious as she stood before a kneeling Lazura, who was restrained at her feet in the sand by several threaded lines of magic.

"SYRAH!" Raz bellowed, whirling Ahna about. He made out Syrah's face when she turned at the sound of her name, saw the shock painted in her pale features. He pulled his arm back, preparing to launch the dviassegai like a javelin, his entire body straining in preparation for the throw he knew would be too late.

A flash of light, familiar and yet so unexpected, cut across his vision, singing over the heads of a thousand warring soldiers to take the shadow squarely between the shoulders.

At once the man went limp, his body partially collapsing as unconsciousness took him midstride. The momentum of his rush carried him, though, and his weight crashed into Syrah's stomach and hips, slamming her back. She fell in turn into Lazura—still bound by the burning tethers—but the spells winked out as the three forms tumbled together in a useless tangle about and over one another.

Uncaring of anything else, Raz pulled Ahna back and sprinted with all speed toward the struggling figures.

He reached Syrah just in time, looping his entire left arm about her hips as she was fighting to get to her feet, carrying her with him when he leapt clear and away. There was a *thunk*, and he saw Lazura bury a dagger—the very one the shadow had been bearing down on Syrah a moment before—into the ground exactly where the pair of them had just been.

So fast, he thought to himself in disbelief, seeing the woman—her black silks now in tatters about her lithe form—tug the blade free and shove herself shakily up to stand.

"Don't let her get away! DON'T LET HER GET AWAY!"

Syrah was shrieking in his arms, light blooming along her fingertips despite the fact that he was still dragging her back. She flung two hastily conjured stunning spells one after the other in Lazura's direction, who chose to summon a ward to deflect the magic directly, clearly too unsteady on her feet to dodge. The spells splashed in visible ripples of fire against what even Raz could tell was a poorly-summoned shield, the barrier twisting Lazura's face into an ugly mess of loose hair, scars, and burning blue eyes. She was staring at them, taking them in with a predatory sort of fury that had Raz baring his teeth at the woman in answer.

Then, Lazura's attention lifted, looking beyond them. She hesitated, her hungry expression changing so rapidly into something between cold fear and hot hatred that Raz couldn't stop himself from half-turning to follow her gaze.

Odene had made it to them, having broken through to join Akelo and Hur in the closing circle. Passed the trio, the rest of the cavalry was pouring into and out of the valley, encouraging the flight of the Mahsadën's soldiers. Heavy sabers slashed down, felling bodies to tumble under churning hoofs, and all around them the šef's officers were screaming for units to regroup and retreat. Like a receding wave they were pulling north, through the valleys and back up the hills, trying desperately to get out from under the legs and swords of Odene's riders and those who had joined his charge from the east flank.

Instead of life and freedom, however, what they ran into along every ridge and path was a solid line of bare-chested men who stood a head taller and half-again as broad as the vast majority of the fleeing footmen.

Whereas Raz's forces had lacked training and experience against the soldiers of the fringe cities, the mountain men of the Saragrias and Vietalis Ranges possessed no such shortcomings. Raised from birth to wield the swords and axes and shields they brought to bear against the enemy who had so willingly flown into their grasp, the warriors of the Northern peaks fought with the clean, brutal savagery Raz recalled all-too well. Before he had a chance to so much as properly take them in, the slopes were streaming with blood, ichor running like black tar as it pooled and collected in the sand. With a collective cry that seemed as endless as it was deafening, the Stone Gods were made to have their merciless fill. Yells to gather and fight became desperate all around them, and Raz couldn't help but shiver as he imagined what a sight the wall of giants must be to the soldiers finding themselves trapped in their closing teeth. He counted no less than a half-dozen different tribes among the mountain men, noting their marks and symbols even from this distance. Their ordinarily pale skin was somewhere between Sun-burned and tanned from long days on the march, and the shedding of their regular furs to fend off the unfamiliar heat made the distinctions all the easier. There were the red-painted faces of the Amreht, each warrior's pattern unique to the individual. The Kregoan's ceremonial scars and piercings extended below their faces and necks, he discovered, and the bone necklaces of some of the Velkrin fell nearly to their waists. The more slender Gähs were represented, having clearly refused to shed their signature skulls, and even the wood and metal decorations of the Sigûrth could be made out, gleaming from where they were braided into hair and beards. Side-by-side they killed and died, holding their immovable stand, the men and women of the šef breaking against them like dry clay across Sun-baked stone.

And yet, despite the immense presence of the wild tribes, it was the only two who sat ahorse among them that drew Raz's eyes most.

The first was a massive figure, garbed in a sleeveless tunic and bearing an odd wooden staff in one hand. Though he could not see them from where he stood, Raz knew scars identical to those that had decorated Lazura's pale cheeks would be carved into the man's face and forehead, circling and marking the blue eyes of his bastard father. Beside this broad silhouette, a second, more slender, bespectacled man was standing in his stirrups, familiar in his shape despite the lack of white robes that usually adorned his narrow shoulders. One hand was about the reins of his animal, steadying himself, while the other was lifted to one side.

Between his free fingers, bright even against the empty blue of the heavens, light flickered and danced as a second stunning spell was gathered into being.

Then, though, the magic went out, and the man took to his saddle again with what might have been a disappointed expression.

"Raz…" Syrah said, going limp in his grasp, her quiet voice distraught. Raz looked around at once, fearing what he would find.

Sure enough, an empty patch of scorched sand lay bare where Lazura had stood only seconds ago, the woman having taken advantage of the chaos to slip away as quickly as a passing breeze.

Raz snarled, letting Syrah gain her feet so that he could stand tall, straining to look over the heads of the milling soldiers still swarming all around them. The cavalry were everywhere by then, however, and any prayer he might have had of glimpsing black silks or white-blonde hair amidst the bedlam was stolen away by the dust of the passing horses. He took an instinctive step forward, unsure himself of what he intended to do, but

Syrah—reaching across herself to lay her gloved fingers gently against his chest—brought him up short.

"No," she said, sounding like the word was painful against her lips. "She's gone. We won't find her in there."

Raz couldn't argue, of course. He had seen the way Lazura moved. She put the others of her kind to shame, and he was more convinced than ever that the Miropan shadows were hers to command, if not of her direct making.

"You know her?" he asked. He knew it was a blunt question, but neither of them were in a position to humor any sensitivities.

Sure enough, Syrah tensed briefly before answering.

"I *knew* her," she corrected him quietly, reaching up with her other hand to pull her hood up over her head, the cloth having fallen down in the tumble she'd taken. "Years ago.... I..." She hesitated, having trouble forming the words. "... In a sense, you could say I grew up with her..."

"You *what*?" Raz demanded, unsure if he'd heard the woman correctly. Again he saw her shoulders stiffen, and he immediately regretted his astonishment.

"Sorry," he said more gently, lifting his aching left hand to rest it carefully over the fingers she still had resting against his scales. "You don't have to explain now. You'll have to do it again soon anyway, I suspect."

Syrah nodded slowly, not looking around at him. His words had meant to be encouraging, but the near-imperceptible tremble in her form brought to mind that what was to come next wouldn't be *all* joy and celebrations.

Some truths, after all, could not be hidden away forever...

Casting around, Raz saw that the remaining men surrounding them were largely his own. Only a few soldiers of the Mahsadën who had been too slow or unable to retreat were putting up their last desperate moments of fighting, or else throwing their weapons to the ground in surrender. Satisfied that the two of them were safe for the time being, Raz guided Syrah around, pressing her gently back toward where Akelo, Hur, and Odene were waiting for them, the two *kuja* in the process of organizing the rest of the rout with shouted commands. To the east and west the sounds of war could still be made out, but even as he listened an unfamiliar horn blew across the late morning. It was rapidly echoed by another, then another, until the air vibrated with the chorus of the same deep note.

Raz could guess what that sound meant, and it brought him such satisfaction that he felt drying blood on his face stick and crack as he smiled.

"Are they sounding a full retreat?!" Akelo demanded, the spike atop his helm gleaming in the Sun as he looked skyward.

"Likely!" Odene answered enthusiastically, following the older Percian's lead and looking up the hill to their right. "We cut through their rear flank straight to you, with the main cavalry spearing through the east! They might have no choice but to regroup!"

Between them on foot, Raz realized it was time to resume the mantle of his greater responsibilities. Taking a breath, he stepped to Syrah's side, though he did not release the light grip about her shoulder he had guided her with.

"Akelo, get the word that we are *not to pursue*!" He addressed his third-in-command firmly. "The Mahsadën's highest echelons are going to be in disarray. We can afford the time it takes to reorganize our ranks and start seeing to the prisoners and wounded."

The old *kuja* looked at him curiously, but Raz answered the unasked question before he could voice it.

"Apparently the šef are all but eradicated. Someone's been doing our job for us."

"*What*?!" Akelo hissed, and Hur and Odene both whipped around to look at Raz sharply with the same astonished expression.

Raz tossed Ahna over his right shoulder, but raised the fingers gripping her handle in a halting gesture to forestall any further inquiries. "Syrah and I don't know more than that ourselves, and right now it doesn't matter. We need to see to recuperations. Odene—" he looked at the younger man pointedly "—get to Shas-hana Rhan and Zal'en. Make sure they get ahold of the tribes. We *cannot* have the atherian trying to chase the fringe cities down, and I can't imagine Zathlys and some of the others will take that order well. The Queen will need to be strict with them."

That he was not about to tolerate any potential delays seemed to get through in Raz's tone, because Akelo and Odene both did nothing more than offer the group a quick shout of confirmation before whirling their horses around and kicking them into a gallop south by east. Before the pair were even out of sight, Raz had turned his gaze on Hur, then on his broken left arm.

"Syrah, can you do anything about that?" he asked the woman still standing beside him. "I need Hur to handle the gathering of the prisoners."

As he'd suspected, a task she could focus on dragged Syrah resolutely from the bleakness of where Raz feared her thoughts were leading her. With a little start she, too, looked to the big man, then hurried over with an "oh" of realization. Taking the injured limb up gingerly, she moved her fingers up and down Hur's corded muscle, not so much as flinching at the contact even when the Northerner grunted in discomfort.

Once again, Raz had to stop himself from thanking the strange woman—"Lazura"—out loud for whatever weight she'd so-abruptly added to his months-long battle. Despite the cloud hanging over her now, some of the darkness that had so often threatened to drown Syrah since the fall of Karesh Syl appeared to have lifted, and it was with a confident eye and high head that she completed her rapid examination.

"Humerus looks to be snapped," she said aloud after a moment, her gloved fingers coming to rest lightly on a spot just above Hur's elbow, where the hint of a thick mass of purplish bruising was already starting to form. "I'll need assistance setting and splinting, then something to help the pain. Aside from that, I can't do much here." She looked up, meeting Hur's face, scrutinizing his expression like a mother watching for a lie. "You'll have to survive until we can get you back to camp. Will that be alright?"

Hur started to shrug in his typical silence, then made a sound somewhere between a yelp and a growl as the movement disagreed with the broken bone. After a moment of fighting obvious discomfort through clenched teeth, the mute man decided a plain nod was the better answer.

Syrah snorted, going back to feeling at his arm with both hands. "Fine. Play tough. See if you're not regretting it later tonight." Without looking around, she addressed Raz. "Can you help me? I won't be able to set it on my own."

"If you need two hands, I don't think I'm going to be any great use," he answered, stepping closer and flexing his left fingers. "I can't hold much of anything, at the moment."

"Shouldn't be a problem. I doubt the poor man is too keen on the idea of those claws digging into him anyway."

The voice, coming from above and behind them, had Raz and Syrah both turning so fast Hur gave another unbidden sound of complaint as the woman let go of his arm too quickly. There, having ridden up unnoticed at their backs in the rowdiness of the surrounding soldiers, two familiar figures were in the process of dismounting, their horses flanked on either side by a dozen bare-chested mountain men with bloodied weapons. Clearer now than they'd been on the hill, the pair smiled broadly at Raz and Syrah together, laugh-lines and wrinkles creasing their Sun-touched faces. The one who'd spoken stepped forward at once, clapping Raz on the shoulder, the top quarter of the solid wooden staff in his other hand carved into the faces of several kindly, pensive old men.

"Hello, lad," said Carro al'Dor, Peacekeeper of the North and former Priest of Laor, tilting his scarred face up to grin with fatherly affection at Raz through blond hair dreaded and decorated in the fashion of the Sigûrth. "It's good to see you. Now get your scaled arse out of the way so Jofrey and I can see to your man's arm, won't you?"

XLII

"Looks to me like that scaly arse is in need of his own healing," Jofrey al'Sen, High Priest of Cyurgi' Di, added with a grim chuckle. A slimmer man with a smartly kept beard, he was coming to stand beside Carro to squint at Raz's bloody figure while he cleaned the dusty glass of his spectacles with a corner of his light vest. "What in the Lifegiver's name did you do to your arm, boy?"

Unable to help himself, Raz grinned at the unlikely pair, and opened his mouth to welcome them upon the hellhole to which they'd allowed themselves to be summoned.

Before he could get the words out, though, Syrah careened by him, a blur of white hair and charred black silks, practically slamming into Carro al'Dor as she enveloped the man in as tight an embrace as Raz had ever seen her offer.

"*Ooopb*!" the Peacekeeper managed to get out through half-a-laugh, taking his hand from Raz's shoulder to rest it fondly atop Syrah's hair, her face buried in the thin cloth of his unfamiliar Southern garb. "Hello, dear. Would it be that we had met again in a different—"

The big man stopped abruptly, his bearded features falling into a clouded well of concern. Syrah had lifted her gaze from his chest to look between him and Jofrey, and the smudged lines cutting through the dust that caked her left cheek told Raz very clearly that she'd shed tears.

A moment later, he understood why.

"Lazura."

The name spilled from Syrah's lips in something between a whisper and a hiss. Every miserable emotion imaginable could be made out in that single word, from fear to hate to grief.

Carro and Jofrey, for their part, exchanged a look of confusion.

"What was that?" the High Priest asked eventually.

Syrah swallowed, and answered this time with more detail.

"Lazura, Jofrey. The woman you saw just now, the one that got away. It was *Lazura*."

In all his life, Raz wasn't sure he had seen a human face flash half-so-quick from relaxed to fierce as Jofrey's did then. In a blink the man stepped closer, gripping Syrah by both shoulders to pry her away from Carro and turn her so he could look her in the eye.

"Lazura?!" he demanded through a clenched jaw. "What?! Why?!"

"I don't know. But she's regained her gifts…"

Whereas the strange woman's name alone had clearly caused more than its measure of disquiet, *this* statement of Syrah's had an altogether more substantial effect. Both men—Jofrey *and* Carro—stilled so abruptly their presence became almost eerie, like living flesh made statuesque. They stared, eyes wide and appalled, at Syrah, as though unable to believe what they had just heard.

It was Carro who managed to speak first.

"*How*?"

The way he asked resonated with such deliberate force that for a second Raz thought he saw another man—just as tall and broad, but with a long tail of grey-brown hair rather than a mess of beaded braids—standing in the Peacekeeper's place.

Fortunately, with the shadow of Talo Brahnt came a moment of awareness.

"Is this the place to have this discussion?" Raz interrupted the three, looking beyond their shoulders at the guard of bloodied mountain men waiting patiently while the war died away all about them. "I don't know what's going on, but we are still standing in the middle of a—

"Yes, Raz. It is."

Jofrey didn't so much as look around when he answered, so intensely was he still staring into Syrah's eye. Carro, on the other hand, seemed more appreciative of Raz's confusion, because the former Priest stepped by the two to approach him.

"Is it true?" the scared man said in a low voice, meeting Raz's gaze with stony severity, the marks of his Breaking bright against his newly-tanned cheeks.

"What is? The magic?"

Carro nodded once.

Raz lifted his left hand, displaying the raw, sand-caked skin where his scales had been largely seared off most of his forearm. "You asked me how I got this?" He brought his eyes around to look at Jofrey, who granted him his attention at last. "*She* gave it to me. Lazura."

"And you saw them?" Carro pressed. "You *saw* the scars?"

Raz arched an eyebrow, a little annoyed now. "The bitch gifted me these, too." He dropped his hand to indicate the slashes at his side, one of them cauterized and already scabbed. "By *blade*. So when Syrah and I tell you we got up close and *bloody* personal, I suggest you believe us. Yes. I *saw* the scars, Carro."

Another moment of phantom silence, frighteningly still in the bustle of the ending battle. Even Hur—who yet stood with his broken arm nearby—hadn't so much as made a sound, apparently understanding that something very wrong was happening.

"Laor have mercy," Jofrey finally managed to get out, at last letting go of Syrah's shoulders and standing straight, his face slack. "Did she continue after Eret Broke her? Was she *that* desperate for power?"

"Jofrey, she butchered three of our own before she was caught." Carro's voice was flat and listless. "We *never* should have assumed stripping her of her gifts would have been enough."

"We had no other choice," Jofrey answered back, though with little enthusiasm. "Laorin law does not allow—" He seemed to catch himself, heaving a sigh that had the man looking more his sixty-something years than Raz had ever seen before. "It's irrelevant, regardless. If what you're both saying is true—" he looked from Raz to Syrah and back again "—then we have far more pressing concerns."

"Like *what?*" Raz growled, starting to feel distinctly irritated now. "There's still a war to be won. Carro—" his eyes fell on the Peacekeeper "—I don't imagine you coaxed twenty thousand men of the clans out of their mountains in order to hunt down *one woman.*"

"No, Raz, and nor did Jofrey convince the fifteen hundred Priest and Priestesses camped out two miles to the north to join your cause for that purpose. *But you need to heed us now.* Lazura is more dangerous than you know."

"She seemed plenty dangerous already," Raz couldn't help but snap back. He was ready to add more, too, but a calming hand came to rest on his upper arm.

In an instant his irritation faded to a low thrum, and he turned to find Syrah's eye lifted to his. She'd wiped the tear tracks from her bared cheek, leaving her pale skin smudged, but what drew him was the warning in her gaze, a half-pleading, half-dangerous look.

"Raz, *listen,*" she beseeched him, fingers spasming about the muscles of his arm. "There's more going on than we thought. Jofrey and Carro are hardly expressing that we change our priorities. If anything, our fight has just become that much more pressing."

Raz frowned, not sure what to make of this explanation. After a second he glared around to the two men, who confirmed this with solemn dips of their heads.

"Don't misunderstand, Raz." Carro spoke first. "We came for all the reasons Syrah inked in her letters, and we will stay for them. Your Mahsadën is a plague, and my clans have been itching for a reason to war since the fall of Gûlraht Baoill. As for the Laorin, they had a foot in this fight already, after what happened in Ystréd." He grimaced. "But Lazura… Lazura is only further cause for us to see this conflict of yours brought to a close as quickly as possible."

"If her method of regaining her gifts is anything like those she has applied in the past, then we *need* her dealt with," Jofrey kept after Carro, answering Raz's obvious continued confusion. "She *cannot* be allowed to harvest freely. If she grows too powerful, she could become impossible to—"

"*Wait,*" Raz cut in, taken aback. "What do you mean, 'harvest'? You make it sound like she's reaping her magics from somewhere. And how would she grow more powerful? Wouldn't she need tutelage for that? What Priest or Priestess in their right mind would teach a creature like—"

"Raz, Lazura was Broken and cast out of Cyurgi' Di for murdering and dismembering three acolytes while she herself was a student of the Citadel."

Raz's words choked off as Syrah spoke with flat hollowness, and he turned slowly to look at her.

"She was a few years older than I," the woman kept on, "fourteen or fifteen, and she… she killed them horribly…" Syrah swallowed, her face losing what little color her paleness allowed. "They weren't even half her age. Maybe five or six."

"Young ones rescued from the orphanages of the valley towns." Jofrey confirmed. "We think she picked them because they couldn't fight back. Age didn't matter, after all, based on what she was looking for."

"And what was that?" Raz asked, unable to stop himself from feeling like he distinctly did *not* want to know the answer.

"Life, Raz," Carro told him regardless. "That intangible spark granted to us by Laor. That which makes us beings of laughter and sadness and emotion. She claimed to have drawn it from them, somehow, pulled it into herself. It's not completely without evidence, either. When we caught her, she was… unnaturally capable. Her strength wasn't so far come—still well below that of an average Priest or Priestess—but her instructors swore to the heavens and back again she'd not possessed the abilities she fought us with *before* the murders. We subdued her, and Eret Ta'hir saw her Broken."

Understanding began to dawn on Raz, but still he looked to Syrah, seeking that final push to assure himself of the most petrifying of truths.

"The soul, Raz," Syrah told him, her voice coarse as she struggled to get the words out. "We think Lazura found a way to drain strength from the soul…"

EPILOGUE

"I call any person of faith who claims they are without their moments of doubt by one name: liar.

The gods of this world—Laor included—test us. They push and pull and press at our loyalties, at our convictions and beliefs. Typically these challenges are small, often even so minute we do not register their strain. Sometimes, on the other hand, they come in greater form, and all the more terrible for it.

Standing over the bodies of those children… Seeing what had been done to them by a mind so warped with desire as to have lost all semblance of humanity… I recall that being the only moment in my life I ever truly *failed in my belief, if for nothing more than the space of a single breath…"*

— private journals of Eret Ta'hir

"Let. Go."

The hands about Lazura's arms released her with the same speed one might drop a biting snake. While gratitude was not in her nature, she was aware that the appearance of Ly'ben and Sureth—two of the more trusted of her surviving shadows—had very possibly preserved her freedom, and perhaps her life. Syrah Brahnt's spellwork had left Lazura weak and wavering, and it would have been a challenge to escape a pursuing Raz i'Syul Arro, had she been forced to do so alone.

The assistance of her men had been timely, and would therefore be rewarded with a lack of repercussions for having dared lay their hands on her without permission.

In her chest, Lazura could feel her heart thrumming out a frantic melody. At first she thought it was nothing more than the adrenaline of the fight, the rush of the battle and the near-miss that had been her defeat. She took several deep breaths, fighting the disgust with herself as she contemplated her loss, and by whom it had been handed out. When she imagined her adversary, however, Syrah's pale face was *not* the one that flickered through her mind.

Rather, Lazura saw the outline of two riders, their features lost to the distance, but their forms distinct all the same…

Fury pulsed through every inch of her being, and she stared through a wild curtain of the white-blonde hair at the ground before her feet. It took her several breaths more to calm the rage, to still the hate which had only ever been scarcely under control in the long years since she'd gained the scars that marred her visage.

But master it she did, before finally looking up.

All around Lazura and her two escorts, the camp was being broken down with rapid, chaotic sequence. Ly'ben and Sureth had found her a mount and kept her ahorse as they'd fled with the majority of the Mahsadën's army west, and on their arrival the position had already been in the process of collecting for the retreat despite Lazura herself having given no such order. The thought scraped at her, but she shoved it away, suspecting Adrion had a hand in the withdrawal, and grudgingly admitting it was the only feasible course of action to be taken in the moment.

Carro al'Dor and Jofrey al'Sen, after all, had arrived on the battlefield to flank them with enough troops to swing the war massively in the Monster's favor.

Ly'ben and Sureth had had the forethought *not* to deliver Lazura directly onto her destination, instead having dismounted to help her down before half-carrying her much of the rest of the way through the structured confusion. Exhaustion had dulled pride until that moment, but now—with the others in sight—Lazura knew she could present no hint of weakness to the starving dogs she'd worked so hard to collar for herself.

And so it was that she dismissed the assassins at her back with a wave of one hand, listening to them vanish into the cacophony with nothing more than the faintest *crunch* of sand shifting underfoot.

Lazura reached for her gifts, seeking to draw a little bit into her exhausted limbs. She managed a very little before the start of a throbbing pain between her temples told her she was closer than was prudent to the limits of her abilities. The fight with Syrah had already pushed her to take more from her raw magic than might have been wise, and so with a groan Lazura released the power, feeling the ache dim in response. She gave herself a moment, going so far as to close her eyes to steady her still-weary body.

Then, opening them again, she lifted her head high and strode forward, putting up the façade of confidence and authority she knew she would have to hold until she recovered enough to attend to her drained strength.

It took her a little less than a minute to maneuver her way through the officers' tents in process of being hastily collapsed and dragged away. The bustle of the running and shouting soldiers provided her ample cover, and so it was without difficulty or notice by any but a few of the footmen around her that Lazura reached the half-circle of empty sand carved out of the east edge of the camp by the great pavilions that made up the šef's quarters. A handful of the marquees had already been disassembled and packed into the carts that would see them fleeing back to Miropa, but most stood still and untouched, hollow reminders of the men and women who'd once occupied them.

Men and women Lazura had seen cut down with precise intent barely an hour before…

Ignoring everything else, however, Lazura kept her eyes directed instead on the center of the cleared area, where a group of seven figures in finer tunics and armor than any other example of the army retinue were gathered in a loose circle. From the side she was approaching from, she could see Adrion's, Vyres', and Ketres Bayne's faces, along Evangalyn Thesus', San Loreyn's, Casius Jules', and Avena Allehn's backs. Unsurprisingly, it was

Adrion—seated on a barrel he'd seen provided to him—who noticed her approach first, but he offered no more reaction to her return than a subtle shift in the tension of his posture. His expression was somewhere between impassive and irritated, giving him the look of a man who had much to say, but thought better of doing so. This was as expected, of course. He was likely only part of the group out of habit and necessity, and was undoubtedly only being addressed when the need arose.

And—given what Lazura started to overhear being discussed with every step she took nearer—she doubted very much he was about to brave making himself heard.

"Vyres, I don't give a *fuck* about your overblown confidence in that bitch." San Loreyn was in a rare mood, his bleached Southern locks in disarray about his ears from what must have been a rapid retreat west. "She's meant to be our great mistress of guile and deceit?! Then how is it that we ended up *being taken from behind?!* Those fucking Northmen cut us off from almost a *quarter* of our standing army, the majority of which happen to have been *Karavyl's* forces! Now we're running, and where is *she*?! Hopefully dead at the Monster's feet, if the Sun is good to us!"

In the time it took the Southerner to finish his ranting, Vyres too had seen Lazura approaching, and the relief in his eyes was balanced only with a note of trepidation. Ketres Bayne, for his part, was far less subtle, because the moment the bald Acrosian saw her he snapped something at San Loreyn, which had the šef whirling along with Thesus, Jules, and Allehn. The last of Karavyl's delegation—Myra Fohster—had apparently still not been found—or more likely the search had been abandoned in the withdrawal—but Lazura cared little for a single loose end that would be clipped in good time.

Her eyes, instead, were on Loreyn.

She approached with a swift grace held together only by stubborn willpower, denying her legs their shaking, denying her lungs the wheeze of bruised ribs. With viperous elegance she closed the gap between herself and the taller man, crossing the last few yards of empty sand in three rapid strides. For once she did not smile, and Lazura could only imagine her face had taken on the semblance of death itself in her approach.

So be it. There was one last well of hope yet to be tapped in this war so suddenly turned against them. One last opportunity and chance on which she'd settled while Ly'ben and Sureth had seen her safely back to camp. It was not an easy solution to weather, much less a hand she wanted to take.

But it was necessary, and San Loreyn—ceaselessly insufferable insect that he was—had just made the choice significantly easier.

The man tried to take a step back from her, tried to jerk away, but even in exhaustion Lazura was twice as quick as a trim like the pompous Southerner could have ever hoped to be. As her open palm settled on his chest—light as a feather falling to earth—Lazura reached into herself again, seeking just the breath of strength she needed for the task. It was not an easy feat, but it was one she'd practiced a half-a-hundred times over the last year alone, and so even through the building ache of a mind pushed ever-closer to its limits the magic came as commanded.

Came, and lanced into Loreyn as invisible lines of hot, boiling power.

"*AAAAAAHHHHHHH!*"

The šef screamed, a keening, tortured wail that went beyond pain, beyond physical agony. It was a sound of sheer terror, a sound produced from the depths of one's conscience, the heart aware of what was happening even if the mind was not. Ignoring his deafening shriek, Lazura pressed her will deeper, feeling the magic snake its way through blood and bone, muscle and sinew. For a moment she felt herself become a part of the screaming man, her tendrils an extension of herself, seeking and finding and ensnaring the intangible light that flowed through him.

Whether it was a gift of the Lifegiver, the creation of another god, or the results of some natural phenomena Lazura had yet to wrap her head around, the Laorin had been right about one thing, at the very least: Life *did* possess a spark, *did* possess a warmth and existence. In man in particular it shone brightest, reflecting against the myriad complexities of emotion, ego, and individuality baser animals lacked. It shaped what *made* the "person", what allowed them to exist as more than a puppet of suggestion and direction.

And it was this very spark which Lazura drew from the intangible essence which formed San Loreyn's spirit, pulling it from him with almost loving care, her closing fist as steady as stone as she withdrew her hand from his chest.

With the removal of his soul, the man's screams lessened, then silenced altogether.

By the time Lazura stepped away from him, the once lofty šef of the Mahsadën was left standing slack of face and limp of limb, his grey eyes abruptly dulled and empty of anything one might have once called "life".

"Take him," she told the wind.

In answer, Ly'ben and Sureth appeared once more as though from nothingness, each taking one of Loreyn's arms to lead the man away into the bustle of the camp. He went without protest, responding to the assassins' guidance like a doll absent all will. Lazura did not watch them leave, knowing she could attend to her newest shadow anytime she liked.

Only briefly, however, would she be able to address the energy that swam and pulsed in the caging fingers of her left hand.

To the untrained eye, Lazura supposed Loreyn's soul looked very much like any other summoned spell of hers. It bloomed brilliantly against the sheen of the sun above and the glare of the sand, but whereas her flames bent and danced with only the slightest force of thought, *this* power provided an altogether different sort of struggle. It did not thrash, did not fight and bash itself against her grasp, but all the same she could feel the press of it growing steadily, like a blooming stone that refused to be contained. With practiced calm Lazura brought the energy up to herself, resting the tips of her fingers against her chest, between the sway of her breasts.

Then, clenching her jaw tight, she pressed Loreyn's soul inward, extending her own magic to encourage it through skin and bone, until the spark found itself free within the vessel of her own body.

At once a faint bit of strength returned to Lazura's limbs, and she stood tall again with a subtle breath of relief. She flexed the hand which had been holding firm to rebellious energy, then summoned a fistful of fire with a flick of her wrist. Her head no longer ached as it had, and she liked to think the flames shone with just a touch more radiance than they had before.

Inch by inch, she grew steadily stronger.

And to keep doing so, she had to ensure this war of Raz i'Syul Arro's did not end with her head on a spear.

Steadying herself in her decision, Lazura cut the flow of her magics again with a thought, watching the fires vanish in a glister of white-gold dust.

Then, without turning around, she addressed the collected masters of the fringe cities with a calm that belied the anger of witnessing her own forced hand.

"Vyres. Send a bird to Holdum's Line. Tell Chancellor Vohn I offer him *Karavyl* for the support of the Seven Cities..."

Note From the Author

[aka: The Plight of the Writer]

It's literally unbelievable that I am—once *again*—at this point, putting the finishing touches on *Of Sand and Snow*. It is such an incredible feeling to see your characters come to life, and yet the prospect of releasing them out into the world is also terrifying. Release them we must, though, and we do so with the hopes of getting them in front of as many eyes as the world will allow.

It is with this note that I move on to a more personal plea, a cry for assistance from all of you who got to the end of the book and were even just a little bit sad to have to put it down:

Please, *please*, consider rating and reviewing *Of Sand and Snow* on Amazon or any of your favorite book sites..

Many people don't know that there are thousands of books published every day, most of those in the USA alone. Over the course of a year, a quarter of a million authors will vie for a small place in the massive world of print and publishing. We fight to get even the tiniest traction, fight to climb upward one inch at a time towards the bright light of bestsellers, publishing contracts, and busy book signings.

Thing is, we need all the help we can get.

Your positive input into that world, however small you believe your voice may be, makes the climb just a little bit easier. Rating and reviewing books you enjoy gives your favorite authors a boost upward.

With that all out of the way, thank you so much for picking up *Of Sand and Snow*. If you'd like to give me feedback directly, have a question about Raz and his adventures, or just want to chat, drop me a message on Facebook, or directly at bryce@bryceoconnorbooks.com.

As ever, it has been an honor to entertain you, and I vigorously hope you continue to follow *The Wings of War* series to see what becomes of Raz i'Syul Arro.

Bryce O'Connor

https://www.patreon.com/bryceoconnor

Made in the USA
Coppell, TX
04 January 2021

47568960R00239